The
Queen's Physician

The
Queen's Physician

BY

EDGAR MAASS

NEW YORK
CHARLES SCRIBNER'S SONS

CONTENTS

*

*

"Believe me, our moral and political world, as a great metropolis used to be, is undermined by subterranean corridors, cellars and cloacae, the relationships and conditions of which are quite unknown to the inhabitants above—indeed, mean nothing to them; now, anyone who knows a little about these matters becomes far more knowledgeable when an earthquake destroys the surface, thus allowing vapors to escape from this pipe, and mysterious voices from that unsuspected conduit."

Goethe to Lavater, 22 June, 1781.

PROLOGUE

*From the Papers of
N. W. Wraxall, Esq.*

November, 1774
Rotterdam, about to sail for England

IF ANYONE HAD TOLD ME three months ago that I should wake up one morning and find myself a secret agent mixed up in international intrigue, I should have laughed him down. Or had anyone prophesied to me that I should be hopelessly in love with an unattainable lady, and that on her account, merely in the wild hope of seeing her again, I should be engaged in the most hazardous adventures, I should certainly have sent him packing as a fool. For, understand, up to three months ago I was a confirmed bachelor, ready enough to please women as they chanced along, but no more than that.

We all know that German roads are about the world's worst, surpassed in inconvenience only by those of Russia. I, personally, can bear witness to the difficulties of travel in Germany, for I have been jogging over German highways weeks and weeks on end in the most wretched conveyances imaginable. I have encountered autumn storms and cruel winter weather. There have been coachmen to put in their place and, of course, grooms to bribe. This while I have been wearing all manner of disguises, going about with my hat pulled down over my eyes, laboriously composing letters in code and in general leading a catch-as-catch-can existence. Nights I have scarcely slept at all this past three months, and this not entirely because of the armies of fleas devouring my hide in all sorts of miserable taverns and posthouses. The fact is, and I should like herewith to record it, that I have been profoundly absorbed in a new book called *The Sorrows of Werther*. It was written by a young German poet and came out, I should say, about the time of the Leipzig Fair.

Up to very recently I might have tossed such a sensitive piece of literature out the window without a second glance. But not now. The story of Werther exactly hits off my present mood and circumstances. Like my own life, it is bizarre, quite mad, in fact. Each night I drink thirstily of its effusions, and take pride and comfort in having Werther as a spiritual comrade, poetic figment though he may be. At the same time it is obvious, as anyone can see, that I could never write of my own experiences in Goethe's exquisite style. No matter. Let me talk a little about myself as best I can.

Not so long ago I celebrated my twenty-second birthday. I was just an ordinary young Englishman, comfortably off but by no means wealthy, and living without a single real tie in the world, or indeed without any paramount interest to develop into a career. Still, I had a normal desire to make something of myself. My parents had died when I was young. A couple of years at Oxford had taught me little, for I was not attracted by the pedantry of philosophical pursuits. After leaving Oxford I toyed with the idea of selling my English properties and settling in Virginia. But the unsettled situation there, the increasing unrest, indeed, throughout all our American colonies, counselled against this move.

A distant relative of mine chances to be secretary in our embassy in St. Petersburg. On his invitation I journeyed to that capital in order to acquaint myself with life at the Tsarina's court. Since England is grossly ignorant of Russian affairs, it was my aim later to write a book about this enlightened, revered and yet imperfectly understood sovereign. Eventually considering my Russian experience adequate and having collected much material of an intimate nature, I then traveled to Sweden and Denmark, that I might get to know these lands as well, the peculiarities of their governmental forms and their courts.

By this time, however, my interest in the game was beginning to flag. Homesickness had overtaken me. I longed to be back in England, home again in London, installed in my peaceful quarters on Jermyn Street. Because of this unsettled state of mind I paid scant attention to the situation at the Danish court, although an event recently occurred there which was a sensation throughout all Europe, and had repercussions in England itself. I was simply saturated with the many impressions of my long trip, and was only too glad to arrive in Hamburg at the beginning of September of this same year. From Hamburg I hoped to take passage to London. This, however, proved impossible. Like it or not I had to drive by coach through Hanover, Westphalia and the Netherlands to one of the Channel ports. The weather, fortunately, was still pleasant, and so I was not too much disconcerted by the delay.

The first night of my journey I reached the little Hanoverian city of Celle, which lies about halfway between Hamburg and the city of Hanover. I was disappointed to find that not till the morrow could I catch another post. I should very much have liked to continue on, for in Celle there was nothing to see but the one-story houses inhabited by a provincial population. I reconciled myself to this fresh delay and took what solace I could in the evening meal that the landlord—I recall his wearing an old-fashioned cap with a long peak—hospitably arranged for me. The main course was the finest brook trout I have ever tasted. The landlord uncorked a bottle of excellent Rhenish wine, which did much to lighten my spirits.

Outdoors it was already dark. The mild September moon hung among the fruit trees of the inn garden. I had little desire for bed, and so inquired of the landlord whether there was any diversion in Celle for a bird of passage. Wiping his hands on his blue apron he told me that Schroeder and his players were in town. I had already seen Schroeder in Hamburg. He was what one might call the German Garrick, and had done much to popularize Shakespeare, up to his advent practically unknown on the German stage. I decided to have another look at the troupe. The landlord told me that Schroeder often came to Celle with his wandering players. "On the command of the King of England," so he said.

This made me laugh to myself. With the best will I simply could not imagine why our plump George should bother his head about having plays performed in such an out of the way place as Celle. Moreover, it struck me as exceedingly comical, I remember, that my tasseled landlord should have so reverential an opinion of the king we had imported from the unprepossessing territory of Hanover. The landlord was only too ready to accommodate me, but I sought no further information, took my hat and cloak and made for the theater.

It was a very lovely evening. The houses dreamt in the moonlight, the clean smell of apples was in the air. I felt extraordinarily gay and prepared for interesting adventures. It had been a long time since I had kissed a pretty girl. The happy prospect of being homeward bound and within fair distance of my goal buoyed up my heart. I was free as a bird. Not a soul in the whole town knew me, and tomorrow I would be gone, in all likelihood never to return.

The performance was given in a barn furnished with rough benches for the spectators, who were packed in as tight as herrings in a tub. Just as I entered, before I had time to look around, the lights were turned down and the violins scratched out an overture. Not Shakespeare this time, but one of Holberg's comedies was being presented. Schroeder did very well in the role of a respectable *pater familias*. Then, very suddenly, something happened to me. In the oddest way imaginable, even as the audience was roaring with laughter, anxiety gripped me. I could hardly draw my breath, the heavy air inside the barn-theater nearly made me swoon. From the footlights, the actors' painted faces had inexplicably taken on a queerly threatening significance. And ordinarily I am the last person to give way to such quirks.

I had to get up and leave. Stammering apologies I forced my way through a thicket of knees and legs, trying not to see the annoyance in the white faces turned up into my own in passing. I threw a last glance at the stage. Two children, a boy and a girl, were clinging to their mother's skirts to prevent her from leaving them. With a rush I went out into the lobby.

There I mopped my brow, shook my head to clear it of vapors and was just getting my cloak about my shoulders when I became aware of a gentle weeping sound. I looked around in amazement. A few steps away from me was a young woman, her face turned to the wall. She was dressed in black silk which set off the remarkably pure white nape of her neck and her silvery blonde hair, worn combed high. Her shoulders shook convulsively with emotion; indeed, emotion ran through her in waves that cramped her back and hips. I moved closer. I wondered at the tenderness of her skin and the quiet elegance of her costume, so much were they at variance with my expectations of Celle. "Madame," I said softly, "could I be of help to you?"

Swiftly she wheeled about and faced me. Her features, though blurred by teariness, were the most enchanting I had ever seen. Her face was round, yet not overly full. The cheeks were refined by suffering, the lips rich, the eyes large, blue and at this moment stary and out of focus from grief. She tried to control herself but again pain got the upper hand. "I cannot live without my children," I heard her say thickly. "I cannot go on like this."

"Madame, were those your children?" I asked in bewilderment. "I mean the children up on the stage?"

"No," she whispered.

In my confusion once more I offered to help her, though I could see she was hardly listening to me.

"It's my fault," she said. "All my fault."

I dared not pry any more closely into the mystery of the beautiful stranger. A singular nobility radiated from her, a proud loneliness which bade me keep my proper distance. And so there we remained, she staring at me wide-eyed with sadness, I taut with solicitude. I noticed that despite the elegance of her attire, she wore no ornaments at all except a small, old-fashioned cross set with dark-red garnets.

At this point a man dashed into the lobby, a fellow of about sixty or so, carrying a stick and wearing an official's gold braid. He was red in the face from excitement. Immediately he took me by the shoulders and pushed me away from the weeping lady. "How dare you molest Madame!" he menaced. "Get back, there!" A boy of twelve, dressed in silken livery, obviously a page, had come trotting in behind the man. He now placed himself protectively between me and the lady.

"It's quite all right, Count Seckendorff," the unknown lady said. "The gentleman simply wanted to be helpful."

"My name is Wraxall," I took this opportunity to announce, and bowed to the lady.

"There's a Wraxall in the English embassy at Petersburg," said the Count, suspicion still tightening his mouth.

"That's my cousin, sir," I told him.

"What are you doing in Celle?" the Count demanded.

"I am on my way from Hamburg to England," I explained.

"And where were you before that?"

I had to smile at the man's impudence; the conversation was becoming an inquisition. However, I stayed calm and said: "Since you must know, I was in Copenhagen, sir."

"What were you doing there?" insisted the Count.

"I had an idea I might write a book on the courts of the North," I informed him. "With that in mind, though it's none of your concern, I visited the court in Copenhagen."

Now the lady was looking at me with great intensity. Gently she pushed the page aside. "Did you happen to see the King's children when you were there?" she asked tremulously.

"I saw the heir-presumptive in Christiansborg," I said. "He's a fine young fellow."

Tears sprang into the lady's eyes. "Did he look well to you?" she asked. "Was he happy, did you think?"

"Why, yes," I said in surprise. "He did look quite well, I'm sure, Madame."

"And the little girl?" she asked, pressing closer.

"She is still very small," I said. "I saw her with her nurse in the garden of Frederiksborg."

"Tell me what the little girl was doing when you saw her," the lady asked imperatively.

"Not a great deal," I stammered. "As a matter of fact she was playing—playing with a ball, as I remember."

From within the theater came a surf sound of applause. Benches scraped loudly on the floor as the audience scrambled to leave. "We must go now, Madame," the Count put in. "We shall only cause talk if we stay here."

"I must speak further with Mr. Wraxall," the lady said. She nodded at me, turned and swept away.

Count Seckendorff took me by the arm. "Naturally you will stay as she suggests," he said firmly. "However, I implore you, be very discreet."

"Discreet?" I said. "Stay here? What are you talking about! Who is this lady, if I may ask?"

"You don't know who she is?"

"I haven't the faintest idea," I said.

He bowed his head until it almost touched mine. "She is the Queen of Denmark," he whispered out of the corner of his mouth.

I was rooted to the spot. My mouth hung open like a hungry carp's. The spectators were now streaming out, pleased with the play; respectable burghers and burghers' wives with their countless children.

Seeing that we were attracting a great deal of notice, the Count motioned me to accompany him outside. There he made arrangements to see me in the morning.

Afterwards I wandered through the town, mechanically putting one foot in front of the other as if walking in my sleep. I ran into the night watchman with his lance and rattle, and he stared at me over his shoulder. Moonlight and shadow filled the narrow streets. The wide, still night beyond the walls of the town was bathed in light, the masses of copse were inky dark. It was a changed, an enchanted world.

Count Seckendorff, for whom I was waiting on tenterhooks, arrived the next forenoon at the agreed time and at once invited me to dinner and an audience at the castle. Again he cautioned discretion. "Don't mention Copenhagen at the table," he warned me. "The Queen's sister will be there, the Princess of Braunschweig, you know. Do you understand?"

Actually I did not understand at all, but I bowed in silent assent.

The dinner passed quite uneventfully. However, my state of mind was anything but tranquil. I was constantly wavering between intense happiness and unhappiness. I was desperately afraid that the Princess of Braunschweig should notice my agitation, though to all appearances she was a harmless sort, lusty, plump and red of cheek. In any case, I flushed with showers of fever, only to pale the next instant with chill. It was all I could do to get off some coherent sentences about my stay in Petersburg to satisfy the Princess' lively curiosity.

Again and again my eyes drifted to the head of the table where the Queen sat beside her sister. Again she was wearing a black dress and her blonde hair was unpowdered, contrary to the prevailing mode. The little garnet cross lay in the faint hollow where her breasts began, I could not help but notice, for she was wearing a very daring décolletage. At the beginning of the meal she smiled at me in friendly recognition. Her eyes, I saw, were the color of forget-me-nots. After this silent greeting she seemed to forget me completely. It seemed as if she were sitting in a trance, from which she awoke only momentarily when someone addressed her directly, as her sister did fairly often.

Once I caught myself staring at her in delight, and looked away in utter confusion, though I am sure she had not even noticed my boldness. If the truth be known, I was glad when the dinner was at an end and the Queen rose from her place. An elderly servant of ice-gray mien came over to me as quietly as a cat and told me in whispers that I was to follow him. He conducted me to the second story of the castle, into an octagonal room where the windows were hung with blue silk curtains filling the place with a mild blue twilight. The hangings were pulled back at only one window which gave out on a neglected formal garden, beyond which stretched the Hanoverian countryside of heath and woods. A harp stood at the open window, with a bench for the harpist.

The Queen came in immediately after me and motioned with her hand for me to sit down. She herself took the bench beside the harp, but in deference to her rank I determined to remain standing. She inquired after all the particulars of my sojourn in Copenhagen. She mentioned her children repeatedly. Unfortunately there was little I could add to what I had already told her, but this little I offered freely. She did not forget to inquire about my family and my plans, and I had a distinct feeling as we conversed that we were becoming fast friends. However, when I summoned the courage to look her straight in the face, it was terribly upsetting. Several times I stopped short in the middle of a sentence, then blundered and stammered like a fool.

The Queen's physical beauty was by no means the only quality that attracted me. She showed every sign of resignation amid a most penetrating unhappiness. An innate humanity illuminated her gaze, her features were faintly carved by sadness and loneliness. Her withdrawal was especially moving because she was so young and pretty, still at that age when other women with gifts like her own look on life with imperious confidence.

However, I saw that behind the sadness and withdrawal lurked vestiges of what must once have been a totally different personality. I could imagine her as candid and gay, utterly trusting of the future, bubbling over. A chance remark, an unconscious movement of her hands, an almost childlike and inexpressibly tender way she had of widening her eyes revealed this other, brighter person. I was reminded of how the wind, blowing a woman's garments tightly about her body, reveals the otherwise hidden curves and sweet promise of the wearer.

In other days I had often laughed coarsely to myself when I heard some smitten lover describe the object of his affection as an "angel." Now, in the Queen's presence, this epithet sprang naturally to my lips. She seemed, I swear, not to belong to the crude world of everyday. The melancholy pervading all her words and gestures, a sort of intangible element in which she lived as a bird lives in the air, seemed to me, in my heightened awareness, to emanate from the small, dark-red, simply cut garnets of the cross on her breast.

We talked for a time and then she led me to a portrait hanging on the wall. It was a very bad likeness of her son, the heir to the Danish throne. She had received it quite recently, she informed me, through the good offices of Baron Buelow. The execution was wooden, but somehow the very stiffness of the image was attractive. The boy in the portrait was seven years old, I judged. He looked out blond and pale from the canvas, his hands dangling helplessly at his sides and the much too large Order of the Dannebrog pulling at the breast of his jacket. He was unmistakably the Queen's son. The similarity, however, resided not so much in the cut of the two faces as in the expression of sadness common to both, a certain anxious reserve tightening both faces. Under the picture the Queen had written the following verse in a steep, girlish script:

> "Oh, who more than I could enjoy the sweet
> Delight of calling thee my son, whilst our hearts beat
> Together in dear unison. But from me they have torn
> Thee, and so I weep, and grieve, and mourn."

The verse, I grant, was crude enough, and yet I was as keenly moved by it as by the portrait itself. When the time came for me to leave I was desolated by the fear that I should never see the Queen again. The ice-gray servant, whose name I subsequently discovered to be Mantel, led the way. He took me to another room where Count Seckendorff was waiting. Upon his polite invitation I sank into a chair, quite exhausted by my strong feelings. I anticipated that he would have letters and advices for me to take along to England. As it proved, he proposed an altogether different commission.

"You can see, my dear sir," he said, "how unhappy the Queen is. The chronic longing for her children and the enforced isolation in this strange castle are disturbing her to the core. Her doctor fears that the slightest illness may carry her off, for the good reason that she no longer has any particular desire to live."

Gloomily I acknowledged this fact, whereupon the Count rose, opened the door and cautiously peeked up and down the corridor. The servant Mantel was standing guard outside. "Keep your eyes open, Mantel," the Count ordered, "and be sure to knock instantly if anyone comes." Then he pulled up his chair and said in a whisper: "Matters cannot continue like this, Wraxall. Something has got to be done, and done at once."

I recoiled from his intensity and could only stare at him.

"Do you believe in freedom?" he asked suddenly.

"What do you mean by that?" I countered.

"You're an educated man," he went on. "You've heard of other names besides Voltaire and Rousseau. You must be aware that our times are sliding inexorably, with ever increasing speed, into an abyss."

"My dear Count," I said, more confused than ever. "I really am unable to follow your drift."

"Come, you understand me well enough," the Count insisted,

smiling at me. "All the young people nowadays understand these things. Fools excepted, of course, and you hardly fall into that category. You simply don't believe that I, Count Seckendorff, a man nearly sixty years old, should have an idea or two himself. My good fellow, let me assure you that even at sixty not all men are cretins."

Hastily I minimized this peculiar statement with a wave of my hand, but the Count went right on in the same vein.

"Hear me out carefully," he said. "If you do not share my beliefs we can simply shake hands and bid each other goodbye as friends. But if you do share them, I have an important mission for you to perform. And this is what I have to say. The days of absolutism are numbered. The injustice of unlimited monarchy, its hostility to life itself, stink to high heaven. The old world is played out. The supporters of absolute monarchy know this very well. Therefore it is the duty of every honest man to attack them and set the new and better world in motion."

I thought this over for a time and found I had nothing cogent to say either way. But aloud I said: "That is also my conviction, Count Seckendorff."

"Very good," he said. "I wasn't mistaken in you after all. Mr. Wraxall, you can materially further constitutional government in Denmark and Norway. At the same time you can help the Queen get back her children and her crown."

"You overestimate my powers, Count Seckendorff," I told him, shaking my head. "Or are you merely making game of me, sir?"

"I am doing nothing of the sort," said the Count. He pressed me back into my chair. "I expect no superhuman accomplishments from you at all. Almost all the Danish nobility and the majority of the bourgeoisie are ranged on our side. The situation is well prepared. What we lack at the moment is a man to act as secret messenger between Celle, Copenhagen, Hamburg and London. Is that clear to you?"

I could not contain myself, I leapt to my feet. The idea, of course, was fascinating, but my strength and my experience still seemed grossly disproportionate to the needs of any such far-reaching plan. I hesitated. Yet one thing drew me irresistibly. At least I would be able to see her again.

"Does the Queen know about this?" I asked breathlessly.

"No, right now we must spare her all unnecessary worries," he told me. "But if you agree to my proposition, I'll speak with her this evening about it."

"I agree, then," I said. "You have my word." At this moment I felt enormously good and important.

Observing my mood of dedication Count Seckendorff looked at me somberly. "I must warn you," he said, "that you will be running grave risks. The country is swarming with spies in the hire of the present Danish government. Even here in Celle we are by no means safe. Not so long ago I had to get rid of an Italian musician because he was sending confidential reports to Copenhagen. The only ones you can trust absolutely are Mantel and myself. I must say, in short, that if you are found out, it means death."

"Nevertheless I still agree," I said impatiently. "I am ready for your orders, Count Seckendorff."

"Not so fast, my friend," he said. "Tomorrow morning when I've spoken with the Queen I'll consult with you."

That night I could hardly sleep for excitement. Count Seckendorff arrived early. He, too, looked as if he had not slept a wink. "It was not so easy, dealing with Madame the Queen," he told me. "She has no political ambitions whatsoever and agreed to our project only when I emphasized that by this means she would be able to see her children again. Now, this is what you have to do. Go to Hamburg and call at the Hotel Koenig von Preussen. There you will find Baron Buelow. Approach him casually. Give him this password— Struensee."

"What does that mean?" I asked.

"Later on you will understand everything," he said. "Baron Buelow, when he hears the password, will give you a rendezvous. When you meet him at the designated place, show him this. It will serve to identify you." Hereupon he took the Queen's garnet cross from his pocket and handed it over to me.

I was so overcome, holding the cross in my own hands, that I began to stutter something about eternal loyalty. The Count cut me short.

"Baron Buelow will let you know what sort of guarantees our friends expect from us," he said, watching me closely. "He will tell you how far preparations in Copenhagen have progressed. Should he give you anything in writing, read it until you have memorized the contents word for word and destroy the paper. Come to an understanding with the Baron about a place where you can meet him again in ten days or thereabouts, preferably some village in the moorland. And after Buelow has talked with you and given you whatever information he deems proper, return unobtrusively, traveling by night if you can, here to Celle. Leave your coach at Sandkrug, and assume the name of Chevalier d'Autan. The Queen thinks you look like a Frenchman. You have a Frenchman's easy manner, she says."

I blushed with joy and embarrassment.

"Each morning the castle gets a list of the strangers arriving in Celle," the Count continued. "By this means we will learn of your arrival. Then I shall send Mantel to meet you, and he will conduct you to the Queen."

An hour later I left, taking the same route back over which I had traveled two days before, moving across the sunny heath country. But in these two days a great deal had happened to me. A strange power had come into my life, and I was no longer my own master. Without any act of volition on my part my whole being had grown immeasurably greater than I had ever dreamed. I took the garnet cross out of my pocket and passionately kissed it. The sweetest, most sorrowful, most blessed feeling overcame it. Through the window of my coach the monotonous landscape of the heath rolled by, the little birches and the dark junipers of torch-like shape.

I had no trouble finding Baron Buelow in Hamburg. A servant in the Hotel Koenig von Preussen pointed him out to me readily enough. He was talking at the time to the Count and Countess Holstein, so I learned from him later on. I managed to get close to him and whisper my password without being noticed by the rest of the company. He turned white as a sheet and for a long time stared at the floor without answering me. Then he nodded and I followed him unconcernedly, as Count Seckendorff had instructed, out behind a column in the vestibule. Casually, as planned, we came together. He let his snuff box fall and both of us bent at the same time to pick it up.

"Tonight, at eleven, at the Dammtor Cemetery," he whispered, and aloud said: "Je vous remercie, Monsieur."

"Not at all," I replied in French, then in German added: "I shall see you at eleven."

Promptly at the agreed hour I was at the rendezvous. It was preternaturally still in the cemetery. The autumnal moon cast a mildly glittering light on the tombstones. The Baron drew me off into the deep shadow of a willow clump. Concealed there I showed him the garnet cross.

"I recognize it," he said. "It's the Queen's cross. And who are you?"

"I am the Queen's agent."

"I don't want to know your name, then," he said. "Not yet, at any rate. It will be better for both of us if I don't."

I concurred in this and then, as I had been told, asked: "Are they ready in Copenhagen? What guarantees do your friends want?"

"Listen to me very carefully," the Baron replied. "I have nothing written with me, for that would be too dangerous." He drew me deeper into the still clump of willows and we found seats on a flat tombstone. He proceeded to explain the situation in Copenhagen in detail. Having asked him many questions, all of which he was able to answer exactly, I realized that the revolt against the regime was far advanced. Presently he came to speak about guarantees. In this regard he asked that England, by means of a confidential letter from the King, or by some communication from our foreign secretary, Lord Suffolk, should acknowledge the sovereignty of the Queen's government, once power had been seized.

"From the Queen herself," he added, "we ask that she give Denmark and Norway a constitution and free the peasants from serfdom."

"You can rest at ease on these issues," I said as learnedly as I could. "Beyond a desire to have her children with her the Queen's only purpose in advancing her claim to the throne is to institute a liberal constitution."

"On what do you base that conclusion?" he inquired.

"I got it from Count Seckendorff," I said. "But I assure you, my dear sir, that I shall not forget to speak with the Queen personally about it."

"Very good," he said. As Seckendorff had done, he warned me to watch my step. "You are very young, Monsieur," he said. "You young gentlemen are apt to underrate the opposition. You blunder forward, and we wise old owls begin to sweat. You must not lose sight of the fact that the lives and property of many people depend entirely on your wit. You must make yourself as obscure as possible. And above all I warn you to keep an eye on the Princess of Braunschweig, the Queen's sister. We have good reason to suspect that she is an informer for the present Danish government. The House of Braunschweig wishes our cause nothing but ill."

I promised to keep a close watch on myself, although I must admit that secretly I thought his cautiousness rather overdone. In any case, a week later, after I had also consulted with young Baron Schimmelmann, one of the richest nobles, reputedly, in Denmark, I traveled back to Celle. This time I took the Lueneburg road instead of going by way of Bremen, so as not to arouse public interest by frequent comings and goings over the same route. I wore different clothing, a blue coat with silver buttons, white leather trousers and yellow top-boots. Now I not only felt like Werther, but looked more or less like him.

I arrived at Celle about midnight, that is, I arrived at Sandkrug just outside Celle, and there left my coach. The next morning I rose early and spent the whole forenoon writing a letter to the Queen in which I described developments in Denmark and the demands of Baron Buelow. Since I had heard that the Princess of Braunschweig was again at the castle, I said at the beginning of my letter:

"Madame, the contents of this letter are extremely secret and of critical import for Your Majesty's future. Furthermore, should they become other than privily known the lives and property of many others will be seriously endangered. On this account I beg Your Majesty to read this message in strict seclusion."

About one o'clock Mantel appeared and took me to the castle for dinner. The company was already assembled in the dining room. I kissed the Queen's hand, and her sister's as well. The Queen greeted me cordially.

"I'm very pleased to see you among us again, Mr. Wraxall," she said. "Count Seckendorff tells me that you have news for me from Hamburg."

The Princess of Braunschweig, who had been keeping her ear cocked, now said:

"What sort of news, pray, Caroline?"

Before the Queen could answer I thrust in my oar. "I have a letter for Madame from the English consul in Hamburg," I lied. "It concerns the French comedians, I believe, who are scheduled to play here in Celle."

"Really? How nice," the Princess said and was content.

Thereupon I handed over the letter to the Queen. She withdrew with it in her hand to a bay window, the while I did my best to hold the Princess in conversation about the newest modes. A quick side glance convinced me that the Queen had read and responded to my warning. She dropped the letter into her pocket without attempting to read further.

The dinner passed with much lively flow of talk, an exchange, however, in which the Queen herself took little part. In order to divert the Princess' attention from the Queen's preoccupied state I remember that I told the old anecdote about the Earl and Countess of Effingham, which I had heard from the Duke of Mecklenburg-Strelitz. The Earl, who is famous for his eccentricities, at the close of a dinner and in the presence of the Duke, called loudly to the Duke's wife. "Open your mouth wide, darling," he commanded, and this she did unthinkingly. Then he threw sugar plums across the width of the table into the astonished lady's maw, with such skill that they landed like balls in a net. The good Duke was amazed to observe this novel method of offering sweets. He had asked me whether this practice was customary in English society. Had it something to do with the sporting interests of my people, he had wanted to know?

The Princess laughed and the conversation was deftly turned to the endless social peculiarities flourishing in the English homeland. Meanwhile I noticed with some apprehension that the Queen had taken my letter out of her pocket again and now was reading it held in open view propped against the table edge. Her lovely face flushed and paled, and repeatedly she made her characteristic gesture of running the tip of her tongue along her lips. But the discourse was so merry, the laughter so uproarious, that no one but Count Seckendorff and myself noticed anything amiss.

After dinner I returned to Sandkrug and Count Seckendorff followed me in due course. Rubbing his hands with gratification he told me that the Queen had been astounded to learn how far our plan had progressed. He said that even now he was busy getting ready for delivery in England letters which would open the way to an audience with His Britannic Majesty.

Count Seckendorff bade me forward his respects to Baron Buelow, with whom I had arranged a second rendezvous at some lonely spot in the heath. I was to tell him that the Queen was in complete agreement with his projects and would do everything in her power to further the necessary measures of security. For my part I promised the Count that I would come back to Celle, there pick up the letters and instructions which would go with me to England.

I left on the evening of that same day and about noon on the morrow left my carriage at Zaehrendorf, a village on the moors consisting of a miserable posthouse surrounded by some thatchy peasant hovels. Baron Buelow met me there an hour later, arriving in the ordinary open post-chaise. We greeted each other like strangers, and politely passed the time of day amid the smoked hams and sausages suspended from the low beams of the posthouse common room. The only other person besides ourselves in the place was an old shepherd, who sat solitary at the table knitting stockings. Baron Buelow invited me to take a walk with him and so, leaving the inn, we soon found ourselves in completely deserted country, with the heather growing knee-high about us.

Baron Buelow embraced me in a surge of gratitude and thanked me profusely for the services I had rendered him and his friends. I now revealed my proper name and reported that the Queen had agreed to his conditions. She was ready, I informed him, to write the letters to the King which I was to take with me to England.

"Everything depends on you at this juncture, my dear Wraxall," he exclaimed enthusiastically. "You are the ambassador, so to speak, of a coming power. You may tell the Queen that the Viceroy of Norway, Count Laurvig, has become one of us. You may tell her, too, that the commanders of the Glueckstadt and Rendsburg fortresses are ready to open their gates when we give the word." Smiling, he looked to see how I was taking this piece of news, and then added: "In one respect I envy you, Wraxall. You're young and you have a great future. Some day you will have to be addressed as a lord and prime minister of England. I look forward to that distant pleasure, sir."

"I must tell you, Baron Buelow," I protested, "that it is not the prospect of advancement that is enlisting my interest in this affair."

"Well, whatever it may be that brings you on our side, my dear Wraxall," he said, "I am deeply appreciative."

"To tell the truth, what decided me," I said, "was my wish to see a very unhappy lady made happy again."

Buelow gripped my hand. "You will ease the Queen's lot immeasurably, Wraxall," he said. "Yet you can never expect to make her really happy."

"What makes you think that?" I asked.

"Wraxall, there are certain things that a human being can experience only once in a lifetime," he explained, "and these things can never be repeated. When they have come and gone, one lives on, of course. But ever to be really happy again is simply out of the question."

"I don't know what you mean!" I said.

"You don't?" he said incredulously. "Haven't you ever heard of a man called Struensee? You must know the story."

"You're quite right, I have heard the name," I said. "I've heard all sorts of rumors, I'll admit. But when I was at Oxford I didn't pay much attention to topical matters. Then when I was at Copenhagen I was so anxious to get home that I never dug into the story. In fact, I never thought of it at all."

"Well, I'll tell you about it," said the Baron. "When it was going on I wasn't in Copenhagen. But my good friend, the Countess Holstein was there, in fact, belonged to the Queen's inner circle."

And so he told his story. The afternoon hours sped by. Sometimes we sprawled on the heather, sometimes we walked about, stretching our legs, the springy heath plants muffling our steps. The Baron had not finished the tale when twilight overtook us. We went back to the inn and sat alone at the table, where somebody had lighted a candle. Over our heads hung the ubiquitous hams and sausages of Hanover.

It took the Baron until one o'clock in the morning to tell the story with all its nuances. The Baron then departed in his postchaise, retracing his earlier route.

I, in my turn, got into my carriage and tried to sleep, but sleep would not come. The people and events of the Baron's tale whirled like mad through my head. It was a moonless night, dark as a grave. I could hear the wind over the creaking of the wheels and the squealing of the springs as we ploughed over the sandy road. The wind sighed across the moors with the sound of many little bells. The vivid images of the Baron's story revolved round and round the figure of the Queen. My thoughts were focussed on her and her strange fate. The peculiar fearfulness that had overcome me in the theater here overcame me again, apparently evoked by the Baron and enhanced by my lonely ride across the moors.

Are we nothing but the playthings of dark powers, I asked myself; are we cast into this world for their casual amusement? Or are we, as we like to think, self-determined creatures. I remembered that I had the Queen's garnet cross in my pocket. Feverishly I ran my fingertips over the uneven facets of the stones. But in such a troubled mood I did not venture to kiss my talisman.

Having failed to sleep a wink during the night I arrived in Celle and put up at Sandkrug, according to orders. Towards evening Mantel arrived and told me that the following afternoon I was to present myself at the pavilion in the French garden of the castle, where the Queen would meet me.

The next forenoon it rained, but towards noontime the sun came out and the day turned out to be lovely. I went directly to the garden, and of course arrived too early. The pavilion was closed. There was nothing for me to do but wander up and down the paths. In the middle of an open lawny space strewn over with yellow autumn leaves stood a little sandstone of Amor, with the features broken off and the bow gone. Yellow asters, their withered bloom bedraggled by the rain, were all about. From adjacent fields came the rank smell of burning potato-tops.

The Queen came accompanied by an elderly lady called Frau von Ompteda, whom I had met during my last visit to the castle. The Queen wore a black cloak over her carmine-red gown. After the customary greetings she looked distastefully into the damp pavilion, decided to take off her cloak the better to enjoy the sun's warmth and expressed a wish to talk with me out in the gardens. We strolled over the lawn, then down winding paths hemmed in on either side by high beech hedges. This while I told her the news I had gathered in Zaehrendorf. The Queen was restless and abstracted. I cut my story short and suggested that she give me the orders I was to carry out in England.

"Count Seckendorff will give you the letters I have written to Lord Suffolk and Baron Lichtenstein," she said, looking directly into my eyes. "I have taken the precaution of not going into detail. The letters merely say that you have an important mission and must speak personally with my brother, the King."

There was a little pause and then, as I was about to take my leave, I remembered that I still had the Queen's garnet cross. I gave it back to her and she said casually: "Oh yes, my cross." And afterwards, out of her deeper thoughts, she went on to say to me: "Believe me, Mr. Wraxall, I really have no desire for the crown."

I looked at her questioningly.

"If I had my children with me," she said, "I would remain here in Celle for the rest of my life." She took out her handkerchief and lightly dabbed at her eyes.

We continued our walk through the autumnal shrubbery. Suddenly she stopped again and said: "I don't quite understand, Mr. Wraxall, why you are willing to run such risks on my account. Do you intend to write a book about them?"

"That can wait, Madame," I replied.

"You don't know who I am or what I am," she said. "Do you?"

"But Madame!" I objected.

"You don't really know," she said. "I have no right to take you away from your friends and perhaps ruin your life."

"The little that I can do, I do willingly, Madame," I assured her. "I voluntarily offered Count Seckendorff my services."

"No, that isn't so," she said. "Actually Count Seckendorff exploited your sympathies. I hold nothing against him because of that, because his intentions are the very best. And of course I am deeply grateful to you. You see, it's so very seldom that I ever have young people here. It's such a pleasure. You must be about the same age as myself."

"I have just turned twenty-three, Madame," I told her.

"Then we are both the same age," she told me. "Though really I'm very much older than my years, as you see."

"I should have taken Madame for younger than myself," I said.

She looked at me quickly and smiled. "How gallant you are, Mr. Wraxall," she said. "But how am I to get away from myself, can you tell me? That's the worst of it, worse really than the loss of my children. I have to carry all the past locked within me. Whom shall I talk to? Frau von Ompteda and Count Seckendorff and perhaps Mantel are always willing to hear me out when I have to talk, but their generation is not mine and they cannot really understand me. My sister? She is a good woman and in her way she loves me, but she must be loyal to her husband. Nothing would tempt me to divide them. But you, Mr. Wraxall! You come to me like manna from heaven. Without my even soliciting your aid, you become my friend and put yourself out on my behalf. Yes, I trusted you the very first evening in the theater, and if Seckendorff had not come along I believe that I should have told you everything. Don't imagine, though, that I'm always as woebegone as I sound now. Or looked then. Actually it had been a long time since I had lost control of myself. But ever since that terrible night in the theater something has been telling me, he has come at last. I can tell him everything. He will understand, he is wise and young."

"But Madame!" Joy filled my heart, though it was frightfully embarrassing to be praised thus to my face. I knew well enough that in her need she was grossly exaggerating my virtues, to say the least.

"I won't hear your objections," she said severely. "If you didn't want to share my lot, surely you wouldn't have said what you did in the theater. Why, you have done everything to make me like and respect you."

"Madame," I said, all trembling, "surely you must know my feelings."

"I do, and I value them greatly," she said. "I am still young. Yet what can I look forward to? You see? I am walled in. I am exiled, banished from free society."

"If all goes well, Madame, you will be free once more."

"Never, never again, my good friend," she said. "The walls that hem me in are not what you think. They are not real walls of stone. They are in myself. I myself am a wall, a cell. I am my own dungeon and keeper. Hidden guilt is a terrible thing, Mr. Wraxall. It corrodes and bites far more than any publicly acknowledged guilt. I am sure I shall never conquer it by myself."

I scarcely believed my ears. Such a breach of polite forms by a Queen was more than I had ever dreamed of hearing. Then she told me her version of the past.

Her story—I might almost call it her confession—revolved about the same events that Baron Buelow had painstakingly described to me. But when the Queen herself talked about the strange affair I ceased to see it from the outside, as just another dramatic historical anecdote. Coming from her own tongue the toughness of fact, the strangeness, the remoteness of what was past and done all melted away. The tale became poignant with feeling. She poured forth despair, hope, love, guilt, so bitter was her need to have someone share her travail.

Now I had come to the living, inner kernel of the events which Buelow had so dutifully and drily recounted. At last I felt the reality of the Queen's passion, wherein feeling was not subject to any mechanical necessity, but wherein the personal decisions of the principals, their private concept of responsibility and reckoning due, their own emotions dominated the scene.

And because of this personal quality the Queen's words, despite their melancholy drift, despite their terror, gave me sweet release. I felt myself lifted out of the leaden flow of time marked off by the clock's fingers, quite out of the range of life's humdrum necessitousness.

Although I was listening attentively to everything that the Queen said, at the same time I was conscious of deliberately trying to avoid asking myself certain questions which, at this heightened moment, I was unable to formulate as I should have liked. But these questions burned strongly, if not clearly, within my mind and I was sure that, once asked, they would reveal things of much deeper meaning than anything she had so far told me during our walk in the gardens of the castle. For however impassioned and personal her story, it was something more than this. As she told it I got the impression that everything had been motivated by someone else, and everything mainly borne by this other one. She seemed to want to efface herself that this other mysterious person might stand forth more boldly. My first vague image of him gradually became fixed in outline, larger, of greater consequence. As she ordered her feelings and her thoughts relating to him, I followed her lead. Her description of the man moved me very much. I thought it superlatively feminine of her that even in retrospect she should trust the man more than she trusted herself. And this was especially noteworthy since what she told me of him was of a nature hardly conducive to implicit trust.

Although she still admittedly loved the man, as the expression in her eyes and the quiver in her voice betrayed, in good measure she was also able to see him as he really had been. She did not try to conceal his faults. She pictured him neither stronger nor weaker than he had been.

But if she moved and freed me with her legend from the past, the abyss which she opened up before my eyes shattered me. I thought how, though no older than myself, she had balled together as much experience in two or three years as I might expect to accumulate in seventy. Again I was gripped by the suffocating sensation of terror I had felt on the night in the theater. The root of this fear I am yet quite powerless to fathom. I felt so upset, indeed, that I would have liked to intervene and cut her off, and this I would have done had I not realized each memory uttered was so much less burden on her heart.

The light was beginning to fail when the Queen brought her reminiscences to an end. Frau von Ompteda was walking back and forth nervously in front of the pavilion like a hen worried about her brood. All this while she had been carrying the Queen's cloak over her arm, and was manifestly relieved to throw it back over her charge's shoulders to ward off the impending night chill. Mantel had spread fruits and sweets on a table in the pavilion, but neither the Queen nor I had any appetite.

The Queen expressed a wish to see me immediately upon my return from England. I left her with Frau von Ompteda in the garden, she smiling at me through the barred gate as she slowly closed it behind her. To spare the ladies any discomfiture, I waited a few moments and then followed after them, going back eventually to Sandkrug.

The next morning I was given the letters for England. At nine I was ready and seated in my carriage. The rain was coming down very fine, and autumn, it appeared, had settled down in earnest. I was thoughtful, but calm and warm within as I sat wrapped in my cloak in a far corner of the seat, my hat pulled down over my eyes.

Endlessly the rain sifted down. The roads became sloughs through which we crawled at a snail's pace. But so absorbed was I in the pageant of the past that the Queen and Buelow had depicted for me that I paid no heed to the dreadful weather, the horrid roads and the cursing postillions, nor to the desolate taverns where we stopped to change or rest the animals.

Yesterday I arrived at last in Rotterdam. Thick fog lay over this city of canals. Since it is impossible for my ship to sail in such murk, I am making use of my idleness by putting these thoughts down on paper. This very moment I went to the window. I see that the fog is beginning to stir. There is hardly any wind, just enough to roll the fog into thick rolls which drift through the streets like clouds. Yet if I am not mistaken a roof tile is gleaming. The sun is going to break through. I believe I shall sail tonight.

BOOK ONE

A Doctor's Ambition

ON HOT SUMMER DAYS, under the white glow of midday, sometimes a puff of wind sweeps across the earth, the portent of storms to come. Suddenly the branches of the trees flatten and bend, and the tree-crowns twist and whiten. The bushes darken under the wind's press, and over meadows and fields run great waves, pulsing through the silvery green grass and the golden grain. Hens flutter about wildly in the barnyard, sheep huddle together, horses lay back their ears. The folk at work in the fields pause in their labors, wipe hot sweat from their foreheads with swollen hands, and look up into the cloudless sky. An old man, a man of much experience, an old shepherd, perhaps, who knows the weather and its moods from an acquaintance of seventy years, shakes his gray head. Not yet, he mutters, not yet, but soon.

Then all is still again, indeed, more poised and quiet than before. The trees stand motionless, their leaves seemingly veined with lead. The impact of so much heat breeds a profound tension. Unwillingly the hands in the fields bow their backs and resume their toil. But deep in their hearts, so deep they are scarcely conscious of it, lurks the consoling thought that soon the storm will come.

There are periods in history that are like the oppressive weather before a great storm. In the history of mankind, too, there come these sudden dry wind-squalls, these swift stirrings among all living things. There is the same tired hopelessness mingling with a presentiment of the end of drought and barrenness, a dumb sense that mighty storms of release are gathering just over the horizon.

Shortly after the middle of the eighteenth century, about the year 1765, such a vast tremor of foreboding coursed through the western world. In Portugal, Spain, Sweden, masses of common people collected before the white palaces of kings. The growling, ragged crowds had no clear idea why they were fusing together. They knew only that the times were bad, that something was critically wrong in the flow of their days. Within the palaces, amid the rooms hung with silken tapestries and fitted with elegantly curved and gilded furniture, the nobility were as ignorant as the crowds of impending change. As always they whispered among themselves, they smiled and coquetted. Ministers rose and fell, privy councillors and court favorites grabbed for power and had it torn from their hands. Mistresses fled,

[23]

carrying their pet toy spaniels under their arms, rustling with agitation, petticoats all entangled about their pretty legs. So they went and others came to replace them. Nothing changed. The kings became more stupid, lost and sick until in the main they were so many vicious idiots. Yet beneath the dusty level of everyday even the brittle people of the courts felt the coming storm, and consoled themselves with the thought that at least, as they said, it would never break in their day. In someone else's time, next year, next week, tomorrow. But never in their time.

Sporadically, with no apparent connection, and yet subject to the inexorable logic of fate, came these ominous buffets of wind. They gave their warning and were gone.

It was an uneasy time.

In this epoch a certain doctor lived in the small provincial city of Altona on the southern boundary of the Danish kingdom. His name was Johann Friedrich Struensee. He was a very well-made man, a tall fellow with darkly blond hair and blue eyes that took on a deeper color in moments of excitement. His forehead was high and white, his bearing graceful, his body slightly inclined to fullness, though he was only thirty years old. In contrast to the majority of doctors in his period he did not powder his hair, seldom if ever talked in Latin and did not wear the black-rimmed spectacles that were practically a hallmark of his profession.

The city of Altona, which lay, then as now, on the northern bank of the Elbe in close proximity to the thriving harbor and commercial city of Hamburg, was an ugly nest of old gable-roofed houses and dirty, angular streets, these filled with a populace notorious for its bigotry. There was more than enough sickness to go round. The newly established Doctor could hardly complain of any lack of patients. However, the financial yield of his practice was another matter. From his ministrations he made a niggardly income all out of proportion to the long hours and the strain of his nightly excursions. And unfortunately the Doctor lacked the self-sacrificing, Hippocratic spirit, a cast of mind which, in truth, is as rare among men of medicine as in any other profession. By temperament he was much more a man of pleasure than a physician. An epicure, in sum, as he often called himself with a wry, prideful smile.

In Altona there was nothing to appeal to an epicure. The climate was damp and windy throughout most of the year. The Doctor's dwelling was cramped, the rooms twilit the day through, and the stove smoky. At nights hordes of mice gnawed busily in the wainscoting, disturbing his much-needed rest. The meals prepared by his elderly servant consisted of mutton with cabbage, sowbelly with rutabagas and the like. These aliments were of powerful consistency, but desperately unpleasing to the palate, especially when repeated week in and week out, varying only with the seasons. Winter rutabagas gave way to spring carrots and white cabbage to green after the first fall frosts.

The Doctor sometimes took comfort in a bottle of Spanish wine. After his meal he would withdraw into his study with the half-filled bottle. His study was a sanctuary where his garrulous servant dared not intrude. He would throw himself into a chair, making it groan under his considerable weight, thrust out his legs and mull over the present and the future as he sipped the wine.

The first thoughts were invariably unpleasant ones, and concerned his patients. How he hated them. When they disrobed under his nose, how they stank, especially in the wintertime. How he hated all their miseries, their frostbites, their broken limbs, their sores, inflamed lungs and ailing hearts. He did not limit his hate, like any good physician, to the maladies themselves. Rather he hated the bearers of disease, the foolishly bereft faces of the suffering, their stupid and hesitant explanations, their helplessness, their timidity and the smell of pus about them, the tremblings of their fevered bodies, their aimless, fruitless groans of pain. Sitting in his study contemplating these horrors he would throw a despairing look about the room. Was it worth while coming into the world to wallow in filth and disease, to tend foul wounds, to comfort death's candidates? And never once to have enough money in one's pocket to buy a horse, not to mention a carriage?

Maddened by his frustrations he would spring out of the chair and open the closet door, revealing the man of bones he had brought along with him from Halle. It was this skeleton that kept his prying housekeeper in her place, far more effectively than any iron door. No mastiff could have kept more perfect watch over the Doctor's loneliness and maunderings. It hung in the closet as fixed as a guard in a sentry-box, grinning broadly, showing large, naked yellow teeth, the arms loosely dangling, the femurs curving in lightly at the knees, the slender ribs springing neatly about the small chest hollow. The Doctor knew the history of his skeleton intimately.

Not too long ago the man of bones had been a skilled and successful Halle thief who, caught one day in the act, had been summarily hanged. He had swung on the scaffold in wind and rain until his bones came through and began to show signs of bleaching, whereupon he had been removed to the anatomy theater of the university, there stripped of his tatters of muscle and his dry sinews by the students. With the help of wire and pins they had put him together again as a first-class skeleton.

The man of bones was not only the Doctor's tireless watchman, but his inspiration as well. Like the skeletons of the Egyptian feasts silently he preached the message that time flies and soon comes the night.

But the Doctor, good materialist that he was, drew no religious, no renunciatory conclusions from death's quiet aspect. During his youth he had been incessantly tormented with Biblical quotations, with the Lutheran catechism and Count Zinssendorf's pious writings. The Doctor's father, a preacher in the Church of St. Moritz in Halle, had drummed so many discourses on original sin into his son's head, apprised him of so many evil consequences and orthodox means of escaping them that the boy lost all taste for religion. He became exactly the opposite of what his good father had intended. As the common people say, ministers' daughters make fine whores. The Doctor illustrated the masculine counterpart of this sentiment.

Whenever the Doctor mused over his skeleton in a winy mood of resignation he always fell into the same line of reasoning. The bony old man of bones, he would think, is nothing more than an automaton, a sort of machine. At present the automaton was useless because its mainspring, the heart, had run down and was broken. At an earlier date, when the man of bones was still clothed in flesh, the mainspring had kept the machine in motion. Being in motion it committed thieveries, ate food, slept with women and performed all the usual acts which, in sum total, pass for living.

Having already formed this opinion of mankind, the Doctor, to his secret surprise, chanced to discover this same mechanical notion of the human organism in a little French book by a certain M. de la Mettrie. This public affirmation greatly strengthened his creed. Still, the Doctor thought that between an automaton and a man there was some irreduceable difference. For the machine is designed and assembled by a mechanic and obviously has no nerves. So the Doctor was unable to decide whether God was a superior mechanic, as the Deists suggested, or whether the prime mover was Nature, so-called, an uncertain something beyond comprehension. Feeling might be the intangible product of the human machine, the Doctor would think, something analogous to the chimes played by a clock. In this regard he felt it significant that sensations, like the soft playing of the clock, were most desirable when soft and harmonious.

And always, when the Doctor came to this point in his dubious nocturnal cogitations, he would sigh in regret. He would think back on the years of his youth, when, Bible in hand, he had been taught so much more consequential notions of man's nature. Endless lectures on the soul of man had been volleyed at him. In his father's harsh Lutheran sermons the soul had not been described as a fleeting breath or evanescent melody, but as a *bona fide* substance from which developed all being in its infinite variety. The body was a subordinate entity, a wicked and inconstant thing. Yet, if the body really were the faulty thing it had been supposed in his youth, if it were subject to a thousand ills and to ultimate dissolution in death, unfortunately, the Doctor had come to believe, the case for the soul was little better. That, too, was seldom completely stable and healthy. There were illnesses, too, in this category, all the more serious since they struck not at transient corporeality, but at the very eternal substance. Should God will, it appeared, the soul itself succumbed to another, and far more disastrous, species of death.

The Doctor often ruminated on his childhood anxiety about life after death. As a boy he had been unable to sleep nights so troublesome was the obsession. Unsettled imaginings of God's anger and revenge had harassed his tender years. The irreconcilable God of his father had sat beside him on the school bench whispering dreadful admonitions, addling his brains so badly that he could hardly grasp the simplest lessons. Sabaoth reached out to stay the child's hand, and the flying ball fell uncaught to the ground. Even the landscape had ominous qualities for him as a child. The rustling of the trees betokened dissolution, likewise the brook's mysterious murmurings. The last light of the setting sun symbolized the unchangeable fact of death eternal. God had surrounded the boy on all sides. It had been like being trapped, a squeaky mouse, by an omnipresent cat.

Of course there had been ways to escape the anger of the godly presence, for example, through enlightenment and grace. The boy had striven to find the path to grace, but wherever he turned, incomprehensibilities balked him. Boyish intelligence, it appeared, did not measure up to God's inscrutable ways. Leaving aside such ticklish matters as the trinity and original sin, precisely what did Christ's death mean? God's sacrifice of His own Son to redeem mankind? Was not justice overdrawn? Did it not verge on barbaric cruelty? Or could it have been that God was not so potent after all? Perhaps, in the final analysis, He had let the great tragedy unfold while He sat by with folded hands. Or were there two powers, an evil one which had made the world and a good one productive of redemption? It was hard to know.

The boy had laid these questions before his father, Manichean heresies, had he but realized, over which no end of theologians had vainly wracked their brains. The pastor had been deeply shocked. Pride and boldness, the father had said, accounted for this regrettable display of forwardness. With tears in his eyes the Doctor's father, who actually loved his child in his own austere way, had begged the boy to put aside such thoughts. Give up and believe, he had implored the distracted boy. To emphasize his warnings he had striped his son's back with twenty lashes, using a leather strap.

This parental consultation had one definite result: the boy never again trusted his father, at least when it came to the human soul and its redemption. The youthful sinner slid deeper and deeper into a pit of defection. In Halle there was no lack of conventional believers. Their conduct confirmed the youth in his backsliding. The righteous ones acted very oddly for heirs to paradise. At the altar, the boy observed, they lowered their eyes, they adopted a sadly silly expression, they pretended to be fearful of allowing the consecrated wafer to dissolve on their tongues. They nipped at the sacramental wine with an air of supreme delicacy, as if to show that such precious stuff was virtually wasted on such rude creatures as themselves. Yet once outside the church and out of reach of the clerics, they behaved quite differently. Apparently thinking they held a mortgage on salvation, they did just as they pleased. They drank themselves drunk as a tick in the inns of the town, they rolled dice, cheated each other, cursed until the very beams sagged with shock. In the fields outside the city, should opportunity offer, they made no bones about reaching under the petticoats of willing peasant girls. Indeed, they dragged them all twittering into the bushes and amused themselves as naughtily as possible. Could it be that the Bookkeeper of Book-keepers made mistakes?

The youth's rebellion against a churchly God flowered still more when he entered the medical course at the University of Halle. Here God was never mentioned at all. To explain the ways of man it was enough to discuss bones, ligaments, muscles, nerves and blood vessels. However, enough pastoral influence lingered so that young Struensee was not really attracted by the cynic tone of the students. Like all medical students since time immemorial they tried deliberately to cultivate a rough manner, the better to look death and suffering straight in the face. When the prosector was out of the room, the students hurled bits of excised organs at each other. They stuck their pipes between the cadavers' teeth, they laid their noonday sandwiches on dead and leathery chests. Death was no more a mystery than in a slaughterhouse. The prosector himself, a grizzled old fellow, had no philosophical gifts whatsoever. The Doctor never forgot how, removing a partially developed embryo from its dead mother's womb, his hands smeared with cold and rotted tissue, he had looked up and remarked with a smile: "You see, gentlemen, *inter faeces et urinas nascimur!*" From this bare fact the prosector drew no metaphysical inferences, nor did his students.

Step by step the budding physician had become hardened to life's shocks. He no longer doubted the existence of God; he simply ignored the issue altogether. The soul and its fate were not his concern. Religious preoccupations, he had come to believe, were so much weakness, a sure sign of being behind the times, like wearing armor, or the curly perukes affected by the learned.

How miserable, he would tell himself, that a man of the world

[28]

and an epicure by temperament should be stranded in such a vile hole as Altona. Here he was, a pleasure craft tied up among dull work barges.

Having energy to spare, he would spring impatiently to his feet, slam the door on his skeleton and begin to plan moves to more promising scenes. The last glass of fiery Spanish wine would invariably give him a new grip on life and new hope.

★ II ★

*D*R. STRUENSEE FELT that life owed him greater rewards than those available to a provincial sawbones. Others made no move to improve his condition. Well, then, he thought, I shall do something about it on my own account.

Over a considerable period he tried methodically to improve his knowledge of extra-medical matters. In time he felt pretty much at home in the speculative regions of political history, economics and philosophy, as well as in geography and biology. Gradually, having sat up half the night racing through every book he could lay his hands on, he acquired a moderately encyclopedic fund of knowledge. He was greatly aided by a powerful memory and a talent for quickly grasping essentials. However, though extensive enough, his knowledge inevitably lacked depth. It was not genuinely anchored within his personality, it had not been disciplined by reflection and firsthand experience, fixed by long repetition and elaboration. His learning, so to speak, was like a floating island, pleasing to look at, alluring of contour, but nothing to build on.

The Doctor himself realized that random knowledge alone guaranteed nothing. Moreover, pedantry went against his grain. And so he strove experimentally to pass along the fruits of his erudition in popularly understandable forms. For a while he nourished an ambition to be a poet. He tried his hand at a number of odes, satires, drinking and love songs, in imitation of Horace, Juvenal and Catullus. But as he himself ruefully saw, his rhymes were hopelessly inept. He consigned them to the fire, saving only a few of them in his desk drawer, where he hid them among prescriptions and patients' accounts.

Since poetry was too coy, he turned his attention to prose, and discovered that he was much more at home in this pedestrian field. Yet even here he could not hope to compete, he found, with his French and English models. Finally he landed where every scribbler who lacks sound wind must land, in the manufacture of feuilletons.

Once Dr. Struensee had found his aptitude for this pleasant and irresponsible genre—the period excelled in critical and moral sketches

—his next step was to undertake the publication of a magazine with the backing of an Altona bookseller. He was on the way to being another Dr. Johnson or Lessing, so he thought, when fate rudely intervened. The broad, dignified figure of Pastor Goeze loomed between him and home. Each Sunday this Hamburg worthy, gowned in his long robe, his many double chins embedded in stiff ruffles, thundered to a frightened congregation from the pulpit of St. Catherine's. One of these shattering Sundays the Pastor denounced an article entitled "Contributions to Spiritual and Practical Instruction," written by none other than Dr. Struensee for his little magazine.

Pastor Goeze blasted the article as an immoral, free-thinking piece of filth. He branded the author as depraved, a criminal menace to the community. Dr. Struensee, it appeared, had urged that illegitimate children be accorded the same human consideration, legal rights and education as legitimate ones, on the grounds that they were in no sense responsible for the shortcomings of their parents.

What had particularly irritated Pastor Goeze was not so much the author's manifest doubt of the validity of original sin, nor his opinion that illegitimate children should receive better treatment. It was the article's covert appeal for a more relaxed moral code, an appeal directed mainly to the female half of the community, and so doubly inclined to promote moral decline. What, the Pastor reasoned, would prevent young men and women from having the freest of relationships, if the fruit of their casual pleasure were given the same legal and spiritual status as the productions of the marriage bed? All in all Dr. Struensee's article struck the righteous Pastor as a brazen assault on the world order prescribed by God. According to this predetermined order, as the Pastor understood it, delinquency should be followed as a matter of course by punishment and public humiliation. The Pastor was well aware that among the aristocracy and at court there was no lack of bastards. There a different outlook prevailed. All the more reason, therefore, he thought, to fear that the same defects would arise in the bourgeois world. In good conscience he strove to prevent any such vile contingency, with vigorous threats of hellfire and a nasty reception on judgment day.

Pastor Goeze's intervention was a piece of bad luck for Dr. Struensee. It injured Struensee's professional standing, for one thing. Indeed, it made him liable to serious reprisal. The Danish government might easily deny him the right to practice medicine on account of his being an immoral person. With this dreadful possibility in mind he wrote several humble petitions to Minister Bernstorff in Copenhagen, hoping to ward off the worst. His father, who now held the important position of religious superintendent of Schleswig, reluctantly countersigned these anxious epistles. Some of the Doctor's friends lobbied in his behalf in influential Copenhagen society. In the end the incident passed as a storm in a teacup, when the Doctor solemnly promised never again to stray into forbidden territory.

Struensee's "Contributions to Spiritual and Practical Instruction" was abruptly proscribed. The next issue of the magazine was already in type, and the unhappy bookseller did not want to kill it and write off his losses. He tried to salvage the situation by giving the magazine a new title—*Out of the Realm of Wit and Knowledge.* But the Doctor dared not contribute further. There was a superfluity of such little magazines in any case, and in the end the publication, like so many others before and since, died a natural death from a lack of readers.

Dr. Struensee's literary flight would have had no further consequences except for the numerous aristocratic families living on their country estates in the vicinity of Hamburg and Altona. The petty landed nobles of Holstein were not rich people. Their income did not suffice to support life in Copenhagen. They depended rather precariously on income drawn from the land. Their sons served as officer-candidates and lieutenants in the Danish, Prussian and Hanoverian armies, or tried to get a footing for themselves as officials in the various states. The many daughters had the worst of it in this peculiarly provincial situation. Their chances of marriage were minimized by reason of the constant migration of the young men. A minority among them, prettier and more spirited than their sisters, wrenched themselves free, not infrequently with the aid of venturesome itinerant males, with whom they eloped, to fashion a career of sorts for themselves, or perhaps to end in the brothels of Hamburg, Paris, Copenhagen or even London. But the vast majority simply sat at home with their families. They assisted at the frequent pregnancies of their more fortunate married sisters, they took care of the younger children, managed the servants, the peasants, the cattle. At last, when they had finally become irretrievable spinsters, they withdrew to one of the many old ladies' homes for the well-born. There they spent the rest of their days in a condition of beguinage, living in two rooms where they kept busy with needlework, gossip and coffee parties.

These stay-at-home elements had a great deal of time on their hands, and since most of them were fairly well brought up, and beyond reading and writing had learned, perhaps, to speak French and a little English, to play some instrument and sketch a little, they devoted their leisure to the fine arts and literature. A predilection for Young's "Night Thoughts" was common in Holstein county society, likewise for Gellert's songs and the lays of Ossian. Even the pious Klopstock and his longwinded "Messiah" were warmly received. Others, especially a younger group, were drawn in a spirit of revolt to the French rationalists. Diderot's encyclopedist writings, Voltaire's dramas and *Candide,* and above all the widely admired Jean Jacques Rousseau passed from hand to hand until they were tattered rags, their pages tear-stained as they were loaned from castle to castle, bedchamber to bedchamber. Nor could these life-hungry sprigs of nobility have their fill of topical writings. They eagerly devoured everything from the *Hamburger Korrespondenten* to the *Courier de France.* To forget the excruciating boredoms of rustication they relived imaginatively all the happenings of the great world. They gloated over accounts of earthquakes and court balls and executions. They all but committed to memory descriptions of the hunting costume worn by the Landgraf von Hessen. And their interest was never more pleasingly tickled than when they ferreted out some intimation of free-thinking among the crabbed print.

Dr. Struensee's "Contributions to Moral and Practical Instruction" had not escaped their watchful eyes. They were naturally interested in any such topic as the care of illegitimate children, in a purely theoretical way, of course. They judged the article to be excellent, just suited to stimulate lively private conversations from which males were barred. Not only was it humanitarian and liberal; it exhaled a delightfully pleasant eroticism. Chief Clergyman Goeze's denunciation sharpened their partisanship. The inflammable tinder of their hearts promptly burst into flames of dedication when they discovered that the author was a qualified doctor, with dark-blond hair and blue eyes, a gallant block of a fellow with fine manners despite his burgher origins. In sum, Dr. Struensee took shape in their minds as a most sympathetic victim of the same niggardly spirit of reaction which kept them immured out in the country among swarms of grubby children and stupid herds of cows.

Much additional information about Dr. Struensee was spread throughout the Holstein countryside by no less a personage than Count Karl Asche von Rantzau, formerly Major-General, A.D., of the Russian service. The Count, with his iron-gray hair and his tall figure, was something of a ladies' man. In fact, too much conjugal response had originally driven him from the nest. He had wandered abroad and finally come to rest in Russia as another German officer in the guards of Catherine the Great. The Tsarina, of course, was fond of large men such as Count Rantzau.

But in this current epoch the Count had returned to his wife and child in Holstein, on the way suffering a minor, but fateful, accident. Having a jolly time for himself in Hamburg, Count Rantzau slipped the full length of the cellar stairs of the Eimbeck'schen Haus. A statue of Bacchus eating grapes was posted unwisely at the entrance. This unyielding object the Count struck head on. The accident, everyone thought, was highly symbolic.

A nearby doctor was called, a certain Dr. Struensee. With three deft stitches he sewed up the gash on his drunken patient's forehead. Not only that. The next morning Struensee appeared at the Zum Koenig von Preussen to inquire about the military gentleman's health. The patch was still stuck to Rantzau's head and he was suffering from a monumental hangover. At first the Count behaved like a caged tiger freshly caught, but soon relaxed when the Doctor got off a series of anecdotes told with a nice mixture of professional gravity, respect for his betters and common human sympathy. After a cup of coffee and several liqueur pick-me-ups the ice was definitely broken. In his snoring, guardsman's voice Rantzau accommodated with some of his own colorful adventures in foreign parts. He told how, in Rome, dressed as a priest, he had seduced a pious contessa. In Danzig he had cheated a merchant out of three hundred gulden. In his repertoire there was no end of peccadillos. Rantzau was a man who could look back on a lively, if not exactly honorable, life. As the scion of a noble house he had worked very hard at being a hellrake. He had betrayed his friends, stolen whatever he could lay his hands on and even cheated at cards.

Dr. Struensee, the minister's son, had little to offer in return for these amazing confidences. He was almost abashed by his highborn patient's tone of ribald self-amusement. Then he was inspired to mention his own altercation with Chief Clergyman Goeze.

Rantzau was quite taken by the Doctor's free-thinking habits. He praised his epicurean outlook. In the end they parted as good friends. They shook hands with a will and promised not to lose sight of each other. This protestation occurred immediately after the Count had borrowed ten reichsthalers from the Doctor, for him a formidable sum, for Rantzau a trifle, at least judging by the way he let the gold piece slide into the pocket of his gray silk vest of military cut. In actual fact, notwithstanding his resounding title and his glamorous past in the Tsarina's guards, the Count had hardly a penny to his name. Dr. Struensee's loan enabled him, indeed, to pay his bill at the Koenig von Preussen and his fare on the mail coach, into which vehicle he carelessly swung himself after pinching the chambermaid's cheeks in lieu of a tip.

And so Rantzau rumbled away through the Dammtor of Hamburg. Heralded by the merry blast of the coachman's horn he bounced on through Holstein to his family seat, the Schloss Ascheberg. The battered enfant terrible was welcomed by the women of the family with squeals and tears of joy. With him Rantzau brought something that they yearned for much more than for hats, clothes, chocolates and perfumes—news from the outer world. The kind of news that he brought with him was not meager newspaper novelties, dry advices at second and third hand, but news fresh from the lips of a man who had actually dallied with the Tsarina in Peterhof, who had snapped the Duchess of Courland's garter in place above her impassioned knee, having found his way with military ingenuity through the folds of silken petticoat barring the road to that delicious territory, who had led the Marquise of Pompadour, so he said, by the elbow into her very own boudoir, to admire Boucher's paintings on the walls. Yes, they depicted exquisite scenes, there was no other word.

Many of his intimate revelations were not really fit for ladies' ears. No matter, Count Karl Asche von Rantzau was a broad-minded, easy-going man. The pleased scream of girlish voices was often heard in the salon of the Schloss Ascheberg when the Count entertained his nieces, cousins, sisters-in-law and other assorted female friends. The dear things blushed to the roots of their hair at what they heard, but just the same they strained every nerve to hear as he doled out his reminiscences.

It was a local tradition that the young women should gather about "Uncle Rantzau." They embroidered vests and handkerchiefs for him, they sewed lacy wrist-frills onto his shirtsleeves. They plundered their fathers' wine-cellars for him, and for him they unearthed thalers secreted in a stocking in bureau drawers underneath the linen. When the Count accepted the thalers it was his custom to pass them lightly under his nose, to smell, so he declared, the faint perfume of their owners still clinging to the metal. Gold was said to have no odor, he pointed out, but that was plainly a lie. And then, with an air, he slipped them into his pocket. But the tireless sponge got more than material gifts from his coterie. They competed for his attention, they breathed their ideas on the arts, the sciences and religion into his hairy ears. He roused their feminine stubbornness, in his company they were prickled into showing off their learning. Their views, they assured him, derived from famous sources. The Count graciously let the Muses have their day. He would admit that being a simple soldier he felt ill at ease amidst so much high thinking. He was a past master at chaffing his way along, he knew how to slide from under. "My dear children," he would snore, "if that's what interests you so much, you should listen to my friend, Dr. Struensee. Why, my dears, he talks better than a book, upon my soul."

What! The inimitable uncle, then, even knew Dr. Struensee! It was a discovery of the first rank. Rantzau did not really understand why the dear children should get so excited about an obscure doctor. But recalling that his wound had been cared for gratis, that he owed Struensee ten reichsthalers, and realizing that here was an easy chance for him to shine by reflected glory, he polished up the story of how he met the Doctor in Hamburg. He praised Struensee's wit, his physique, his elegant manner. The young ladies sighed. Ah, if we could only see him, they told the Count.

"Nothing easier," said Rantzau. "Simplest matter in the world."

"Uncle Rantzau, you're joking again," the girls trilled. "We think you're mean."

"A man is as good as his word," said Rantzau, and for once in his life actually meant it.

The Count soon found an opportunity to draw Struensee into his circle. One of the Count's sisters-in-law, a young lady in her twenties, became very ill. She was suffering from the after-effects of a difficult delivery and seemed unable to get back on her feet. Her husband and relatives were worried, thinking she might have consumption. They debated whether she should be taken to Copenhagen for examination, or whether royal medical councillor Berger should be brought to her from the city. Either alternative would cost a fortune. Rantzau saw his chance and suggested Dr. Struensee. "A distinguished physician, a phenomenal comer in medicine, much superior to Berger," he announced. "He's an enlightened man, familiar with all the latest methods. And he's cheap, too. On my word, he'll not only cure her, he'll do it for practically nothing."

The issue was discussed for days in family conclave. In the end Rantzau had his way. And so, one fine morning a heavy black coach came driving up to the long, white manor house and out sprang the renowned Doctor. Struensee was in fine fettle, ready for anything. He was taken directly to the patient. Pale from months of confinement and lying virtually suffocated by pillows and covers in a tightly sealed room, the young mother was horribly upset at first by the sheer vitality of the Doctor. She blushed furiously as he marched up to the bed, hat under his arm, blond hair unpowdered. It almost seemed as if health flooded back into her cheeks at the mere sight of him.

Struensee assumed a confident medical stance beside the bed, while the uneasy relatives hovered behind. He felt the patient's pulse, he sounded her lungs, tapping the naked, ivory back. Gently he shook his head, displeased. He looked about the room. Then without a word he threw up the windows, one after the other. The early summer morning poured into the room. In came a freshet of sweet air, spiced by rose bloom and birdsong.

"*Mon dieu!*" said plump Aunt Amalie von Rantzau, who had come from the old ladies' home at Itzhoe to care for her niece. "Do you think that's the right thing to do? Draughts are terrible for sick lungs. We all know that, sir!"

"Madame has the soundest lungs in the world," retorted the Doctor. "What the lungs lack is something to breathe."

"Don't you think we ought to have Berger after all," Aunt Amalie whispered. "This man's going to be the death of her, mark my words."

"This afternoon Madame can lie out on the terrace," said

Struensee. He bent quietly over the sick woman and enfolded her fine white hand in his long, cool brown one.

"But that will spoil her complexion," groaned Aunt Rosalie, another spinster member of the family. "I know it will, I just know it."

"Madame can wear a large straw hat if the sun is too strong for her," said Struensee.

"A straw hat!" exclaimed Aunt Amalie. "How vulgar! Do you want the girl to look like a peasant's horse?"

"Even the ladies of Fontainebleau wear straw hats, I believe," said Struensee. "Is that not correct, Your Excellency?"

"You're quite right, Struensee," said Rantzau. "I've seen the Marquise herself in a straw hat, one with rose-colored ribbons."

As they were all leaving the sick room Aunt Amalie managed to get in a last word to Aunt Rosalie. "That man is no doctor," she said. "Why, he doesn't even smell like one! The way he talks you might think that getting well was just having a good time. Did you notice, Rosalie? He didn't even bleed the poor dear. We might as well brace ourselves for a funeral."

Yet curiously enough the patient did regain her health. On the terrace, between Struensee and Rantzau and surrounded by a swarm of visitors, she rediscovered normality and got a grip on it. She could not help but see how the girls fluttered about Struensee. She herself fell a little bit in love with him and experienced mild pangs of jealousy when the others made off with "her doctor" into the garden. This happened a good deal. They would coax Struensee down to the pond and get him to row them over the smooth, reedy, willow-garlanded surface, while they sang songs and coquetted. The patient tried hard to get well that she might do the same. And get well she did.

By St. John's Eve in late June she was strong enough to lean on Struensee's arm and watch the fireworks, spraying up from a float on the pond. That evening when he brought her back to the house he kissed her lightly on the neck, which, of course, was rather over-doing his medical obligations. Still, he refused to accept any fee for his efforts, since the case had been so mild. His stay at the Schloss Ascheberg had been so very pleasant, he declared, that he considered himself more than well paid.

Struensee knew something about the feminine soul. His period was a feminine one. The sickness of the times was *"ennui."* Beneath the suave surface flourished a hidden doubt of all elegance. Behind the mask lurked a sickly hatred of accepted modes, the varietism, superficiality, the elaborate playfulness, the inane pursuit of charming sensations. But this hatred was never quite able to break through the enameled surface. So long had the mask been worn that it had become almost second nature. At the same time, however, despite this secret self-disgust, these same people cherished a lingering affection for the sugary and the sentimental. In a loose sense the period was schizoid, all but split into two irreconcilable halves. The more dry and objective the intellect, the more estranged from life the sensibilities. Struensee vaguely believed that at the bottom ennui was a kind of fear, a chronic premonition that nothing less than violence could ever weld the human soul together again.

In his own person Struensee embodied the elegance and charm of his times, these attributes qualified by his intense desire to get along in the world. The will to success was in his eyes when they suddenly darkened. Ambition betrayed itself in his impatient gestures, in his plangent voice. Many other men harbored the same desire to make something big of themselves. But their quest expressed itself, unlike Struensee's, in the established forms. They practised the stereotyped, Chinese smile, the whispered tone, the exaggerated politeness. Their way was intrigue and cabal, a cat-like insinuation into the sources of power and status. Guile won them money and offices. Theirs was the soft approach, an approach that quick as lightning could turn into tigerish assault.

Women who called Struensee to their bedside felt the difference in him, the impact of a new, romantic attitude. The young physician had an indefinable something about him that, they knew instinctively, could end their ennui. How fine a passage from Rousseau or Voltaire sounded on his tongue, so much better than when they read the same thing in a pretty volume in half leather set off with gold. How full and fresh and genuine the Doctor's laughter, how superior to the soft tittering they were accustomed to hear. How exciting it was when his strong, slender hand reached out unaffectedly to enclose their own!

Small wonder, then, that after the miraculously rapid cure of the Countess Rantzau, Dr. Struensee's reputation became a byword throughout Holstein. Whenever a young lady lacked a healthy appetite, whenever a young wife coughed or awoke in the morning with a light fever, at once she would think of Struensee and secretly welcome the little indisposition making it possible to call him to the house. Dr. Struensee's hired coach presently was seen rocking here and there and in all directions over the roads of Holstein, as far away as Schleswig, even as far as Ditmarsch and Tondern, moving from one white country place and toy castle to the next. The Doctor himself sat back deep in the leather cushions and read. His name became known even among the bondsmen and peasants along the way, for his fame filtered down to the common folk by way of the mamselles and the serving girls. These lowly admirers wiped the sweat from their foreheads and bowed deeply to the tall man in black, remembering to sweep their hats from their heads. And the peasant girls, of course, waved and danced as the Doctor clattered by.

Almost all of Struensee's patients fell in love with him, giddy fifteen-year-olds and stiff spinsters in their seventies. The flowers he brought his patients—leaving flowers was one of his typical gestures—in many a castle lay carefully pressed between the leaves of *The New Héloise* or "Night Thoughts." His bravely scribbled prescriptions often found their way under a cambric pillow rather than to the apothecary.

Being a man of taste the Doctor bought himself new clothes, simple ones suited to his bourgeois station, yet made of the finest worsted. He also wore fine linen, but without lacy trim. Almost invariably he now ate his meals as a welcome guest in country manor dining rooms, and when at home frequented the Hotel Zum Koenig von Preussen. He made himself a connoisseur of wines and was able to tell his patients' husbands that the best burgundy came from Lueneburg, bordeaux of the finest bouquet from Luebeck, the driest sherry from Hamburg.

It was a delight to watch him open an oyster, pry rosy flesh from a lobster's claw, heap a mound of caviar on his round cake and sprinkle it ever so lightly with lemon juice.

Mutton was forgotten, so, too, cabbage and turnips. And in the closet his man of bones gathered dust.

* **III** *

ONE SPRING DAY the Doctor's carriage suffered a breakdown. A wheel gave way, the conveyance sagged to a standstill by the roadside. The coachman stared at the broken wheel and scratched his head, the Doctor looked idly about him. Great beeches grew along the highway, their new foliage a delicate bright green. Thrushes fluted a sweet song, hidden in the cover. Evening was drawing on.

The Doctor had an odd feeling that he knew the neighborhood, but could not place it. The beeches, the flowery meadows, the brook, the little arch of some bridge over it somehow seemed familiar to him. The coachman told Struensee that he doubted a wheelwright could be found so late in the day. The last village lay a long way behind. The best thing, he said, would be to try their luck at some country estate nearby. They would probably have some means of temporary repair.

The Doctor took his medical kit and slowly walked back along the road. He was not at all upset by the accident, though in Luetzelburg, some miles ahead, a lady patient was expecting him. He drew the cool, damp evening air into his lungs, he marched more briskly, with pleasure his eyes drank in the idyllic Holstein landscape. He had a foresense of something desirable and important.

Having gone a moderate distance the Doctor came upon a high, rather run-down yew hedge fencing off the highway at his right. Through the trees he could see the gleam of a pond, and, on a little rise, surrounded by a greensward, a round temple of love, with white columns and a pointed straw roof. Then almost at once he saw the house of the estate, and immediately took a liking to it. It was a long, two-storied structure with innumerable small-paned windows, built in an old-fashioned way. Some of the windows, he discovered, were merely simulated, painted on the walls to complete the impression of symmetry. This bit of architectural naïveté amused and pleased the Doctor. He noted that the house was badly in need of whitewash. The steep gray roof gave the house a habitable, but comical, air.

The Doctor came to a white wooden gate breaking through the yew hedge. It hung open at an angle, inviting trespass. He walked up the garden path over the flags. A sun-dial of gray stone stood in the middle of the unmown lawn, which was heavily sprinkled with yellow dandelion bloom and populous with fat thrushes in search of worms. For a moment the Doctor paused, again drew in long sweet breaths of air perfumed by the damp meadow grasses. The smell of new green things mingled with a faint brackish damp odor from the pond. Then he went directly up the path to the house, the door of which was also ajar. A delightful little shower of excitement ran down the Doctor's spine. It was something like a fairy story. Who would be the princess awaiting within, he wondered.

But the hallway showed no sign of life. Armor and lances hung on the walls, interspersed among huge stag antlers and old-fashioned hunting weapons. The Doctor hallooed, but no answer came except a hollow echo from the upper level of the house. Hesitantly the Doctor penetrated more deeply into the house and came to a large room filled with rickety furniture. On a couch a young man was lying sound asleep, resting peacefully. His composed features were both handsome and ugly in interesting combination. The mouth was nicely sculptured, the eyebrows nobly arched, the cheeks of delicate contour, but the forehead was low and the nose overly, though not altogether unattractively, long. The young man was an arresting sight and instantly, for some obscure reason, the Doctor felt a strong stirring of sympathy for him. His hose were ludicrously shabby and even the dim light could not diminish the shine at the knees. The heels of his once elegant shoes were almost worn away, one stocking hung down over the calf of his leg and his shirt, which was open at the neck, was badly frayed at the collar. Yet over a chair-back hung a brand new coat of the latest cut, contrasting grotesquely with the rest of the young man's attire.

How very curious, the Doctor thought. I wonder if I know the fellow. He debated whether he should wake him, and finally decided to steal off as quietly as he had come. But he could not hold back an impulse to tiptoe closer and get a better look at the young man on the sofa. Under Struensee's intent gaze the stranger suddenly opened his eyes, which proved to be very large and brown, as the intruder noticed despite his embarrassment. Huddling back the young man said to Struensee: "Who are you, sir?"

"I am Dr. Struensee," he replied.

"You're who?" The young man blinked and propped himself up on his elbows. "You aren't the Struensee, by any chance, who cured my dear Aunty Rantzau, are you?" He smiled with fine irony. "Are you the fellow who made me quarrel with Cousin Isabel? Or, I should say, are you the gentleman that Alvina is in love with?" The more he talked, the more confident and flippant he was. "Of course, of course," he continued, "you must be the one they're all in love with."

"If you say so," said Struensee. "All sheer nonsense, of course."

"Nonsense?" The young man was now wide awake and alert. He proved it by jumping up off the sofa entirely. "That's not the way I've heard it at all," he objected. "Such amazing luck! Every petticoat in Holstein begins to quiver when the Doctor comes along. Tell me, sir, just how do you get such happy results?"

The Doctor cleared the discomfiture from his throat. "Forgive me, sir," he said flatly. "I've just broken a wheel on my carriage and I came here to see if you have anything to offer me in way of a wheelwright."

"Well, a lucky accident for me," exclaimed the young man, ignoring Struensee's request. "I'd enjoy your company for the evening. You can teach me your trade, that is, certain parts of it. If you're of a mind, of course. I suppose your mysteries are rather sacred. Do you know who I am?"

"I have no idea," said Struensee.

"Indeed, why should you," said the young man. "In any case, I'm the crazy one." He told this quite proudly, hitching his stocking into place and stuffing his shirt-tail into the top of his pants.

"The crazy one?"

"Crazy Brandt, they call me, otherwise Enevold von Brandt. At your service, Doctor. My people are all out amusing themselves somewhere on the grounds. You know, music, dancing, girls and afterwards love in the hay. It's Sunday today, in case you haven't noticed. Surely you wouldn't want me to interrupt my peoples' day off just to fix your wagon wheel, sir!"

Struensee laughed good humoredly. "I have heard about you, Brandt," he said. "But I must admit you're even more . . . what shall I say . . ."

"You think so?" Brandt was visibly flattered. "My aunts and those cousins of mine have no originality," he explained to Struensee. "They jog along the same old paths. When the chickens hop up on the roost, they take the hint and go to bed. If you don't play faro, you know, they actually believe something's wrong with you. They're museum pieces, my dear Struensee."

"Well, I'm another who can't play faro," smiled Struensee. "So there you are."

"It's a different matter with you, Doctor," said Brandt. "When you don't play faro they excuse you on account of your learning. You had the best damned luck imaginable to come into this world a bourgeois. But I, well, I come from one of the oldest families. There are Brandts by the dozens all the way from the North Cape to the Straits of Messina. And yet I'm on my own, for my particular Brandts, my parents, I mean, departed this earth at a horribly indecent date. They scooted off and didn't leave me a single brother or sister to keep me company. And it would have taken so little effort! And so, you see, when I have enough money—which is not very often—I prey on the hospitality of my well-fixed relatives. Oh, there are hordes of them. I try to entertain them, I sing for my supper, Struensee. They've drunk so much beer and stuffed in so much ham and cabbage that it has thickened their blood. Well, I do what I can to stir it up. I'm their *maître de plaisir,* you might say. Still, it's not very polite, is it, for me to gabble on about myself. Actually I'm about the least important and certainly the unluckiest person who ever set foot on earth. *Dubiosum est,* Doctor, everything's in a fog. But don't worry about that broken wheel. My smith will tack it together for you. In the meantime consider this house your own, sir. Stay here with me overnight and let me have your company for dinner. I think we can find a fresh fish somewhere or other, and there's bread and wine, at least, to go with it. What more do two philosophers need, may I ask!"

Brandt offered his hand to the Doctor, rather timorously despite his easy language, and smiled an ingratiating smile. Struensee accepted the proferred hand and shook it heartily.

The evening meal was simple, as the host had promised, but Brandt managed to spice the fare with amusing observations in endless variety. *Bons mots* fell from his lips one after the other. Drinking the wine he slumped back at ease in his chair, his leg hanging over the arm. His carelessly barbered hair was all awry and again one of his stockings slipped down. It might have been the heavy sweet wine, or perhaps the host's vivacious manner, or his laughter, which barely concealed the melancholy and sensitiveness behind it. Or it might have been the soft light of the candles in the old silver candelabrum, the sheer comfort of the room with the spring night dreaming outside the windows. In any event, Struensee's tongue wagged with an eloquence which surprised himself.

He told young Brandt about his literary venture. How laughable it was in retrospect. He told him about his belief that man was primarily a machine which is built to enjoy and enjoy again, squeezing experience from life like juice from an orange. He talked about the future, about his fond hope of discovering a wider field of operations. And as he talked on Brandt retreated, became more taciturn and at last completely silent. He simply slumped there with his head bowed and thoughtfully stared at his guest out of deep brown eyes.

"A man must take a chance," said Struensee smoothly. "It's absurd to be afraid. Not only to be afraid of other people, but of oneself. How idiotically we struggle to make ourselves exactly like other people, even though in our lucid moments we may despise them! Why is it so many of us lack the courage to be and do what we will? It's pitiful."

"Thieves think the same," Brandt reminded him.

"Well, then, in a way I take my hat off to thieves," Struensee retorted. "Is it not stupid to endure hunger simply because the distribution of goods in our society happens to be what it is? Is not a thief a man who corrects gross inequalities. At least so far as his own person is concerned, he restores the original and natural condition of mankind. Great men, you may have noticed, are always criminals from the standpoint of the society they attempt to supplant. Caesar, Luther, Cromwell, Voltaire and Newton—were they not all renegades, in a sense? One defied the Roman republic, another the Church, another the King's party, another social orthodoxy, another scientific prejudice. So it goes. Did they not, to a man, pit themselves, their own person and will and insight against infinitely stronger established forms? And were they not great just on that account, just because they dared to live out their lives as they saw it, and think as they wanted to think?"

"One could look at it that way, I suppose," said Brandt, and poured out his guest another glass of wine.

"But it must, I insist, be looked at that way," Struensee said. "There's no point in regarding history as something done, dead and finished. One must make use of its lessons. We are not dealing here with an herbarium, or with a museum choked with curiosities. The river of time flows on, and we have to navigate with the stream, or perish beneath it. And the time has come, I believe, to move into positive action. The order in which we live, the beliefs that are groaned out from our pulpits are hopelessly out of date. Are the ideas of Montesquieu and Voltaire nothing but playthings for young ladies, who would really be a great deal better off wrestling with hot young men among the potted plants? Do you presume to imagine that our world is so good it cannot stand improvement?"

"That's right, quite right," murmured Brandt. "However . . ."

"However what?"

"All you say rather rubs me the wrong way," said Brandt. "It's too strenuous, for one thing. You look forward to the end of a world. But this world, I know perfectly well, is my own world, however much I may mock it. Nothing attracts me less than revolution, my good fellow. Revolutions are desperately vulgar affairs, and also extremely exhausting, so I've been told. Now, what I'm looking for is beauty. I'd like a change of scene once in a while, a little real pleasure. Actually, what I really would like is the position of *maître de plaisir* in Paris, or Petersburg or even in Dresden. Anywhere but this silly Holstein. Then I could honestly enjoy life. In my declining years I could relive it all again and amuse myself by writing memoirs."

Struensee laughed at this frank confession and Brandt joined in. As the hours moved along the conversation became more egoistical and disjointed, and Brandt finally brought it to a close with a last dusty bottle of wine fresh from the cellar. Long after midnight the young man lighted his guest up the stairs. They went up together tipsily, arm in arm, laughing over everything and nothing. The Doctor was given a small white room. He could hear the treetops whispering and rustling in the night wind. It was almost like the murmur of the sea. A hound belled far off on the heath. Gradually everything was still.

The Doctor slept fitfully, woke up, dozed again. In his dreams Caesar came to him, wearing a red-seamed toga, a baldheaded, severe man. Luther came to him, with a Bible and finger lifted in admonition and the devil grinning over his shoulder. Cromwell in iron armor rode a heavy brown horse over the Doctor's laboring breast. Diabolic Voltaire sat on the edge of the bed and deliberately spattered ink over the sleeper's face. Then Luther became Newton, crashed open a window and shouted his *"hypotheses non fingo"* into space. Outside the stars and all seven planets revolved, turning smoothly in their paths. A thin celestial music sounded in the ears of the sleeping Struensee, a broken, tinkling sound like that made by an old striking clock. "Enjoy your life, while the lamp glows, pick lovely roses, while the bloom blows," it seemed to be saying.

The Doctor awoke with a violent start and began to smile, thinking about Brandt where he had left off. Though he was clear-headed enough, considering the wine, the evening's argument seethed in the back of his head. At last he had freely spoken thoughts that had troubled him for years. His own words had a power over him, now they were uttered, the unfathomable magic of the spoken word, which presentiment with form and permanence, fixes fleeting moments of illumination. What hitherto had been merely possible suddenly moved from a misty limbo into noontime reality, into a foreground of decision, from which vantage newly won beliefs could be easily projected into the objective world. Fate had done the trick. Fate, Struensee told himself, had led him to this particular house, to this particular young man who was so sympathetic and ridiculous at the same time. He had loosened the Doctor's tongue, without really trying lured him into baring his inmost thoughts.

Lying in bed on his back Struensee shuddered as he listened to the mighty soughing of the old beech trees girding the estate. It seemed as if they were talking to each other in their own tree language, talking with each other and the night about past and coming things, in deep alien voices and strange accents. Not until the first streaks of dawn when the crowing of the barnyard cock dispelled all nocturnal spooks from the scene did Struensee fall into a black, dreamless sleep.

He awoke with a little start and saw by the warm flecks of sun playing on the bedcovers that the forenoon was already well along. He dressed hurriedly, washed and went downstairs, to find the house empty. He walked outside in the garden, where the birds were singing loudly. A warm wind moved like a caress over the lawn and grassy places about the house and ruffled the mirror of the pond. From the barnyard came strong peasant shouts and the laughter of a milkmaid. A feeling of great happiness was in Struensee, a profound sense of health, solidity and comfort. It seemed to him as if the birds were singing in his heart and the sun actually shining warmly throughout his inner parts. Taking long steps, smiling to himself, he strode through the garden, and sought out the belvedere. There he found Brandt.

They looked at each rather shyly at first. The heated conversation of the evening before was a barrier, now that the sun was out. Yet only for a moment. They embraced cordially.

"My good friend," said Struensee, "I've just had the most frightful dreams. I was tossing about in bed all night long. I couldn't get my own thoughts out of my head."

"I didn't sleep any too well myself," said Brandt. "I was making up all sorts of schemes in my sleep. And would you believe, I think I've found a way."

"A way?" said Struensee. "What do you mean?"

"A way for us to get somewhere, my friend," said Brandt. "I can deluge my aunts in Copenhagen with letters. I can present myself at court. I can start currying friends there and make such a nuisance of myself that they're bound to give me some sort of post to get rid of me.

Once I have my foot in the door, it will be simple enough to keep it open while you slide in. Struensee, we're perfect complements, you and I. I'll leave the serious people to you, the ones who batter their brains over the future. For my part, I'll deal with the present. How will that be?"

Struensee looked carefully at Brandt. "And money?" he asked. "How are you fixed for money?"

"Well, well," he muttered. A shadow of discouragement passed over his face. "I'd quite forgotten that point," he said. "Just like me."

Struensee laughed and Brandt ruefully laughed in chorus. Then they both composed themselves and Struensee said: "Just lately I've been doing very well. In fact, though I'm not a rich man by any means, I have more than enough to get along. I can support you in Copenhagen for a time, my dear fellow."

"But can I do it?" said Brandt, more to himself than to Struensee. "This is a very doubtful proposition, if you come right down to it."

"Nothing ventured, nothing done," Struensee reminded him.

"Sleep alone, beget no son," echoed Brandt.

"It's agreed, then," said Struensee. "We've made a partnership."

"Very well," said Brandt. "Next week I'll visit you in Altona."

"I must be getting along," said Struensee. "My patient will be very angry with me, I'm afraid."

"Let's hope she's young," said Brandt. "And not too ugly."

The two shook hands on it and walked through the spring morning to the road, where the carriage, its wheel repaired, was drawn up waiting for the Doctor.

A week later Brandt arrived in Altona, and Struensee took him to his own quarters. Brandt was delighted with the rooms, even with the man of bones.

"That fellow is a grim one, isn't he," he said appreciatively.

"He was a thief, and a very good one, they say," said Struensee.

"So good, I take it, that he ended up by being hanged," Brandt suggested.

"The cards were stacked against him, my good boy," objected Struensee. "He hadn't a ghost of a chance, if you examine the situation."

"Quite right, not a chance," said Brandt. "In short, it pays to play in tune, as I've been telling you right along."

Struensee stifled the retort on his lips, and shut the closet door in death's face. Brandt began to tell him about his plans for making a success in the capital. Opportunities were rather scarce for the reason that everyone with any power was incompetent and lazy. Just the same it was necessary to attract the attention of some highly placed personage, Brandt explained enthusiastically, and secure his protection.

To break into the circle of influence it was additionally necessary to make endless acquaintances and be invited everywhere. One had to be charming, perform small services for others. One had to be able to talk well and understand how to make oneself liked by the women. For women, Brandt expounded to Struensee, so long as they were not too plain, nor too morally inclined, were social coin, so to speak, moving freely from hand to hand. Women, then, were highly acceptable in an intermediary role, providing they were adequately frivolous, or so to outward appearance, and had a fine complexion, an interesting bosom and a graceful manner of speech.

"In the Koenig von Preussen," Brandt went on to say, "two ladies are stopping over right at this moment. One of them is a certain Frau von Gaehler—her husband is a major in the Danish army—and the other is Frau von Ahrend, whom I know slightly. We should do something about making their acquaintance. Try our hand out, you might say."

Brandt was right; the two young women from Copenhagen were bored to tears at the Koenig von Preussen. They were only too happy to have two personable young men, that is, more or less young men, do them homage. Frau von Gaehler was all but swept off her feet by Struensee.

"Yes, but Annette," her friend cooed, "the little one is very nice, too, don't you think?"

"All right, you take him," said Frau von Gaehler. "You like him, so you have him. And do please keep your hands off the dear Doctor, will you?"

"That suits me," said the other. "I do hope this business turns out to be a little adventure, don't you? Something we can dream about. That is, when our beloved husbands are snoring away the watches of the night."

The four ate together, and found the dishes and the wines splendid, especially the wines. They drank Ruedesheimer, then Beaujolais and finally Sekt. Frau von Gaehler coquettishly dipped her strawberries in the Sekt, to show the men how it was done in the capital. But the conversation was the best part of it all, the witty questions and the wittier answers, which floated like feathers all about the table. Brandt was extremely diverting. His jokes were a little strong and made the ladies gasp, but, after all, blushing and gasping were delightful in themselves. And Struensee's glance was so warm when it sought out Annette von Gaehler's dark eyes. The wines did their work. Annette let the tip of her toe play over Struensee's shinbone, telling small secrets all of its own. Casually he allowed his hand to fall on her knee and feel out the outline of her garter under the smooth silk of her dress.

It was still early in the afternoon when the last tickly glass of Sekt had disappeared down their throats. Thereafter they decided to go boating on the nearby Alster. Emerging from the inn the warm spring air was refreshing to their faces. The women could feel their own bodies under the billowing dresses. They seemed to themselves larger and more sinuous than usual, their breasts firmer, larger and more erect. They were happy, bursting with youth. The champagne bubbled in their brains and made their hearts sing, the warm sweet perfume of the blossoming lindens addled their sense exquisitely. A brilliant clarient timbre came into their voices.

Pedestrians filled the streets this merry spring afternoon, all shapes, sizes and occupations; scurrying ladies' maids, fishwives in stiff costume, solemn merchants' wives in white lace coifs, pretty strumpets in highheeled shoes. It did not escape Annette that many of these last wenches shot quick, appraising looks at Dr. Struensee as he passed them by, those instinctive looks which women give men in whom they sense the power to bestow intimate satisfactions. And Annette noted, too, that she received similar compliments from the men along the way. The dandies, lazing haughtily through the crowd, and the men of commerce, stumping along soberly in grown fustian and tricorn hat, all had an eye for her. We must be a striking couple, she thought. The world's hunger for both their persons kindled urgent wishes and longings in Annette's heart. The random lust of the passersby titillated her and heightened her half-drunken euphoria.

Once in the boat it was even better. The soft gliding through the water, the gentle rocking of the boat seemed not quite real. It reminded Annette, so she said, of Watteau's picture, the "Journey to Cythera." Sympathetically she recalled the distress of the lost and loving pairs on the canvas. The towers of the city over the steep rooftops against a soft blue sky, the splashing of the water, the heavy river smell added to the enchantment of the situation. Delightedly she watched the swans paddle by, followed by their little gray brood. She saw country houses in the distance, shining white amidst the fresh verdure of their grounds.

Nobody talked much in the boat excepting Brandt who, like a wound clock that must tick itself down, chattered on incessantly. The others hardly heard him and did not mind his buzz. The water was bluer than the sky. Struensee drove the boat with strong strokes farther and farther over the blueness. From other craft came the sound of low voices. Now and then they heard the song of a bird from the shore, or the sigh of a little wave on the sandy beach. Drifting through the spring afternoon, the boat came to the other end of the lake at Harvesthude. There they landed on a damp meadow bank, forcing their way ashore through the reeds, moored the boat and the gentlemen offered the ladies their hands for a lift up.

Beyond the wet meadows, where ancient oak trees grew, was the Harvesthude Cloister. For many years it had no longer been used as a cloister and, indeed, was not recognizable as an ecclesiastical edifice. The buildings had been turned into barns and now smelled strongly of hay and stored potatoes. In the courtyard lay a plough tipped on its side, like a child's abandoned toy. A black cat slunk lazily across the flags, found a likely place to rest, lay down and stretched. Not a soul was stirring about the place.

Struensee and Annette, who had drifted apart from the other pair, agreed that they were tired and sleepy. They went up creaky stairs into one of the barn lofts. Sweet-smelling hay was piled up high in one corner to the beams. They kicked up a cloud of hay dust and the motes danced wildly in the shafty light. Outdoors hens clucked and tame doves cooed. They lay down together in the warm hay. Annette closed her eyes and pretended to breathe gently and evenly as in sleep. Struensee bent over her and admired her white forehead. He examined the black, steeply curved eyebrows, the little beauty patch on her right cheek, the swell of her breasts. At this point Annette opened her eyes, looked into his and read his desire. She stretched out her arms, hugged him about the neck and drew him down to her.

In actual fact Annette was not so casual about love-making as appearances might have indicated. When she came to herself about an hour later, and propped herself straight up on the heels of her hands, she was more than a little shocked to discover herself so suddenly in a lover's possession. Thoughtfully she sized up the man at her side, who had really fallen asleep. The damage was done and nothing could be done to remedy it. She would continue, she told herself, with an affair of such great promise. Time, she thought, that I pay a little attention to my own needs. Up to the present her husband's career had always taken first place in her considerations. It was her burning ambition to make Major Gaehler, though he was neither much of a soldier nor much of a bureaucrat, into a general. To this end she had consistently sacrificed her own pleasure. Up to meeting Struensee, whenever she dallied with a lover, it had always been some man who might push along her husband, either with gifts of money or with political influence.

She blushed, she looked very pretty and naïve in the hay as she thought how primitively she had lain down for Struensee. In the hay, mind you, just like a peasant girl. Then she felt a trifle sick with apprehension when the thought occurred to her that concupiscence might have serious consequences. After all, she was by no means sterile. Already she had borne her husband two little girls.

There was only one way out to restore her moral equilibrium and right the wrong done her deserving husband, and that was to deceive herself into believing that she had played with Struensee only to advance her husband's career, and by corollary, of course, her children's prospects. Major Gaehler, as a matter of fact, was not jealous about his wife's physical gratifications. They had often discussed this possibility pro and con when some exploitable lover had chanced along. In fact, not so long ago a rich military contractor had been seriously considered by common consent of the married couple as third member in a *ménage à trois*.

Presently Struensee awoke and smilingly craned his neck, the better to have a look at his new beloved's profile. She looked down at him, in that comical, doubting way that young wives have when they look at their husbands upon first realizing they are not trusted with a single real thought or emotion. He drew her, protesting, down to him and kissed her lustily.

"No, no, dear," she said firmly and pried herself loose. "Not any more. We have to be serious. Please!"

"I am serious," he said. "I do believe I love you."

"Of course you do," she said. "However, we've got to be practical!"

"Practical?" he said. "What a miserable thought to have in the hay!"

"You've got to come to Copenhagen," she said.

He stiffened with annoyance and was about to contradict her when he remembered that it was for the very reason of getting to Copenhagen that he and Brandt had approached the ladies. But he still pretended not to be interested. "What would I do in Copenhagen," he complained. "I haven't the means to live a life of leisure, you know."

"What's to prevent you from finding patients in Copenhagen?" she asked.

"That takes a long time, my sweet," Struensee told her. "One doesn't build up a practice overnight."

Annette considered this objection. "Gaehler has good connections," she said, but not very enthusiastically. Then suddenly she let out a pretty shriek of joy. "I've got it," she said. "I can't imagine why it didn't come to me before."

"Well, what is it?" he asked.

"You've got to be made the King's physician-in-ordinary, my darling," she said. "Then all doors will be open to you." She was so happy about it that she damped his face all over with kisses.

"Upon my word," said Struensee, "I believe I've met an ambitious woman!"

"I am ambitious, terribly," Annette confessed. "I have to look out for my men, you see."

"Men?"

"Why, yes," she said, "for you and Gaehler. He's really a decent fellow and I'm sure you'll like him. I'm sure it won't be long before you're as fond of him as you are of me, darling."

"God forbid," said Struensee. "I certainly hope not."

"You're not jealous, dear," said Annette. "Are you?"

"Jealous?" said Struensee. "Why, no. Should I be?"

"He'll be so glad to meet you," said Annette. "How lucky I am, don't you think, to be able to call two such intelligent men my own!"

"What firmer bond of friendship than a lovely lady," said Struensee.

"Of course, that's just it," said Annette. "Idyllic, isn't it. We shall be one happy, tender family."

"Let's hope so," said Struensee. He was tiring of the game. "But what makes you think that the King needs a physician-in-ordinary? Isn't Dr. Berger good enough for him?"

Annette looked away and did not reply. The barn loft was growing dark and the oaks out in the meadows now cast long shadows of deep green on the gold-fuzzed carpet of grass.

"Come, my friend," Annette said at last. "We must leave. But you'll come and stay with me tonight, won't you, dear? Sleeping alone is such a dreary business, I think, and such a sinful waste. Don't you think so, too? Tonight I'll tell you so many things. You'll be amazed, beloved, I promise you."

Struensee reached down and hauled Annette to her feet. "Yes, you'll be astonished," she said again as she adjusted her dress, smiling quizzically into his face. "In Copenhagen there's all sorts of troubles you've never even heard of. And all they need to cure them is a good doctor. I think I've found him. I'm sure he could cure anybody. Of practically anything. Am I not a clever woman, darling?"

"You overwhelm me," said Struensee. He kissed her so ardently that her knees slacked and he had to hold her up. "You are indeed a desirable little woman," he assured her, wiping the wet of the kisses from his mouth. "We had better go before the sun sets altogether."

★ *IV* ★

IT WAS COZY that night in Annette's room in the Hotel Zum Koenig von Preussen. The candles were lighted, and the wide chairs with curved elbow rests covered with flowered silk had an air of expectancy. At her dressing table, before the gold-framed mirror, Annette was seated, arranging her dark loosened hair, polishing her finger nails, and then again dabbing her powder puff carefully on her cheeks and her shoulders.

The dressing table was covered with a number of small boxes and vials emitting manifold sweet odors which mingled with the natural perfume of her hair. She was dressed in a wide loose gown of yellow silk which fell back around her thighs, thus affording Struensee a generous look at her well-rounded knees and the smooth skin of her legs. But her mind was no longer set on love-making. Her face had an abstract, preoccupied air. She had turned her back on Struensee, who was seated in one of the chairs, but once in a while her eyes sought his in the mirror with a fleeting smile. After having listened, more courteously than delighted, to some gallant phrases and remarks which Struensee thought the occasion called for, she began to speak in an unemotional though low voice.

She spoke unconcernedly, objectively, so that Struensee was not a little disappointed and shocked. He was deeply disappointed to see that even this fair woman did not live in some imagined Cythera, in that fabulous world of tender feelings and raptures, but that she too, the sensuous delight of his heart, had a strong and unconcerned will with which to make her way through this everyday world, and that, therefore, she observed, registered and judged the feelings and facts of this world with a detached, cool, almost an historian's eye.

Struensee, the lover, the gallant, felt quite let down and suddenly deflated. But Struensee, the doctor, the ambitious man with wide projects of his own, could not help but be interested in Annette's report.

Yes, it was nearly a report, an unemotional statement of cold facts, as if delivered by some bureaucrat, that Annette unfolded for him. His eyes still rested on her broad bed from which her maid had lifted the covers for the night. Inaudibly sighing, he turned his attention from the bed with its more attractive prospects to the fate of kings and history which, as he thought, were none of his or her business, at least not at this hour, so full of promises of an entirely different kind.

But, willing in the beginning to listen to what he thought to be the hardly understandable folly of a pretty woman, he began after a while to attend with genuine interest, forgetting his own gallant covetousness. It was no mere historical interest which was aroused in him. It was his curiosity about the soul of man, his thirst for psychological insight, which made him sit up and cock his ears. And it was not the scientist alone who harkened, because for Struensee, scientist though he was, the science of psychology or even the art of healing a sick soul was by no means an end in itself, but only his natural way of furthering his own, Struensee's aims. Behind the pictures of a soul's disease, suffering and despair, behind the panorama of a nation's anguish and a people's distress, he saw his own glory rising, red and gigantic like the sun after a stormy night. He saw his own power, his own riches, his own happiness—all of which could only be realized by means of another man's sickness and his own healing hands.

In later years, it often seemed remarkable to him, and a marvellous coincidence of fate, that his life's task should have come to him in a pretty and very obliging woman's bedroom and from this woman's soft and yielding voice. He felt then that dark-haired Annette at the mirror, before her rouge pots and powder boxes, had been his Delphic priestess, vaguely reading the future, his sybilla, calling him to his supreme adventure, as those others had called the warriors and heroes of yore.

Very much later, in a very lonely spot, with much more insight than he had at this particular moment, he was inclined to sense a certain irony of fate, of which he was by no means conscious at present. But even now, as Annette's story progressed, and detail unfolded itself after detail with the inexorable logic of fate, his eyes wandered from the feminine figure in the long gown and from the lovely face in the mirror. He gazed abstractedly at the long white curtains of the open windows, which rose softly billowing in the breath of the night-wind and then fell tired and despairingly, like human hands. In his heart, yes even in his bowels, he heard, as if it came from the far wide spaces of the night, a muffled and senseless, a despairing cry. A cry for help.

It was a blond young man who touched his heart in this mysterious way. His name was Christian. Behind him, there was a whole people, dark and numerous in the night. For this young man happened to be a king, Christian VII, King of Denmark and Norway.

Christian lost his mother at an early age, when he was not quite five years old. His father, King Frederick, was a good-natured, timid man, loving peace and the arts, particularly the ballet. During his reign he was timid to a point where he frankly distrusted his own judgment. He could hardly bring himself to sign the state papers his ministers laid on his desk. He was constantly in flight from himself all during his lifetime. When forced to show himself in public, his habit was to hold a handkerchief before his face, as if to spare the world the sight of his own intolerable ordinariness and ineffectuality.

After his wife's premature death Christian's father had married again, this time the Princess Juliana von Braunschweig, a very forceful woman like so many members of the Braunschweig clan. One of Juliana's sisters had married Frederick the Great of Prussia, and this piece of luck had filled Juliana with such envy that she could not sleep at night for thinking about it. She nagged and nigged her husband to emulate his Prussian namesake, she flattered him to this end, taunted him, even wept. And in the end she broke her weakling husband's spirit. His wife even managed to poison his genuine love for music. With ferocious persistence Juliana reminded him that a true king made the acquisition of new territories his life affair, he did not fritter away his days collecting new minuets and new portraits. At last the harassed Danish King withdrew from his spouse, but too late. He could not rid his inner being of the barbs she had carefully planted there. To heighten his most unkingly lack of self-esteem, he began to carouse in the company of loose women. Yet even in these pursuits he was no success. He cut a pathetic figure when he stole away furtively to chambers where excesses within his poor scope had been arranged for him.

Denmark became governed by ministers, who functioned as if there were no king at all. Unable to tolerate this decline of royal prestige, Juliana rusticated in the provincial castle of Fredensborg. Besides the humiliations heaped on her by her husband, she had to accept a cloudy future for the son she had borne the King. Thwarting her burning desire to have her own son wear the crown was Christian, fruit of the King's first marriage. His cheeks were delicate, his wrists slender, his hair a wave of gold. Neither the father nor his stepmother showed the slightest inclination to have the boy educated for kingship. Since the heir to the throne could hardly grow up half wild, the ministers gave him over to the care of Count Reventlau.

Reventlau was a big man, but short of stature, a powerful brute with a wide, peasant face heavily marbled with little blue veins. His nature was choleric to the extreme. Fits of rage sometimes robbed him of his speech. He took his tutelary obligations very seriously, though more fitted to train a fractious horse than educate a delicate boy. Christian was mustered out of bed at six every morning. After a morning prayer and a simple breakfast he was given lessons in reading, writing and arithmetic. With two hours break at midday this process of instruction lasted until six in the evening. He was not allowed to play with boys of his own age. After he had laboriously learned how to read, for his brains were a pudding, he was given the Bible, out of which he had to memorize whole passages that he simply could not understand. If he asked about the sense of a verse, Reventlau immediately gave way to a fit of temper and bellowed so loudly that the grenadiers on watch in the castle courtyard shivered in their boots. If the boy faltered in his recitation of a psalm, Reventlau would shout at him: "You're going to become the same kind of useless pig as your father!" Or—"I can just see you squandering your time with the whores, the way your silly father does!"

Sundays, Christian was twice taken to church services. The sermons were tremendously long and stuffed with edification. Christian sat beside Reventlau in an appropriately stiff and pious posture.

If his head nodded, if he stole a sidewise glance, Reventlau would jog him briskly in the ribs. "I demand reverence in the house of God, sir," he would say, in such a loud tone that the whole congregation started in amazement. And after the services were over, it was Reventlau's custom to quiz his charge on the content and meaning of the sermon. If Christian slipped up on some particular, if he were unable to explain the nature of God's grace, Reventlau would roar: "Why, you godless wretch! You'll be damned to hellfire forever, mark my words. The sins of the fathers will be accounted for." But if Christian accurately repeated the text of the sermon, Reventlau would say contemptuously: "You gabble like a parrot, my boy." If he altered a thought, Reventlau's comment would be: "So your nine-year-old mind isn't satisfied with God's teachings. They aren't good enough for you, is that it?" If the boy thought through what he had heard, interpreting it in his own fashion, Reventlau was annoyed and suspected free-thinking.

When the boy was ten years old his outlook brightened somewhat. He was given over to the charge of a new teacher named Reverdil. The new tutor was a sober, placid Swiss, brought to the Danish court on the recommendation of the philosopher Voltaire to teach Christian foreign languages, history and philosophy. Reventlau very properly considered himself unfitted to handle these departments of learning.

Unfortunately the boy's nature was already ruined by the time Reverdil arrived on the scene. As soft and weak as his father, Christian had cracked under Reventlau's sadistic pressure. He hated learning, and only pretended interest when his nemesis Reventlau was in the offing. In vain Reverdil struggled to win over his coy pupil. In contrast to Reventlau, the Swiss seemed comical to the boy's twisted mind. What Reverdil tried to teach him also contrasted absurdly with the dogmatic nonsense which had been Reventlau's stock in trade. Christian noted the same discrepancy in the French books he was introduced to. He sensed a totally foreign outlook in the witticisms of Lesage, in La Fontaine's fables. And yet he could not free himself from Reventlau's menacing impress. It was very confusing. With a child's clear eye he observed that, when all was said and done, Reventlau was the master and Reverdil the one who bowed his neck. His intelligence could not get beyond this crude disposition. Gradually he learned how to play off one against the other, meanwhile committing himself to neither party.

About the time of Reverdil's advent he was taken to the theater for the first time, to see an Italian opera. Christian was charmed. The melodious, easy music, the skillfully painted stage settings showing improbably perfect gardens, the elegant, swishing costumes of the singers, their fine maquillage, their large shining eyes excited him wonderfully. Here was something much more desirable, he thought, than anything Reverdil, and certainly anything that Reventlau, had to offer. Here was real life, the real thing. After the performance he said to Reverdil, imitating Reventlau: "Today for once you have failed to bore His Majesty."

Christian thereafter tried as best he could to mimic the actors, their dancing gait, their toothy smiles, their involved gallantries, the epicene gestures of their manicured hands. Reverdil was rather pleased with this development—it continued through the years—since it was better than no development at all. He took pains to have his pupil instructed in the art of dancing. Reventlau, however, was incensed. He saw to it at once that the influence of the Frenchman was lessened. The young prince was now handed over to the care of Reventlau's nephew, Sperling, the Kammerjunker.

Only two years older than Christian, Sperling leaped at the chance. Precociously mature and already more than a little corrupt, he realized that such intimate connection with the heir-apparent would ensure him a lifetime advantage. In all things Sperling acceded to Christian. After a show of reluctance he even promised to initiate him into sexual matters. When they were alone in Hoersholm or Frederiksborg, Sperling promised, he would get Christian to a girl. She would teach him all about the female body and the facts of life.

And Sperling was as good as his word. The adventure was discovered by Reventlau. He was overcome by a terrible spasm of rage. Panting like a congested pug dog he chased Christian with his walking stick raised to strike. "I'll kill the monster," he roared. "I'll flay the hide from his body." Frightened out of his wits Christian raced to the section of the palace where his father had private apartments. The doors were locked and Christian hammered hard against them with his fists. "Papa, Papa, please help me!" he shrieked in utter terror. "Reventlau is going to kill me, Papa!" But the King was surrounded by some young ladies at the time and could not very well let his son in, since they had loosened their hair and removed most of their upper garments. The King himself was so drunk that he could not stand unaided. When he started to go to his son he fell from the sofa under a table and lay there. Big tears rolled down his cheeks and wetly he mumbled: "What a sad, sad world."

This event was a prime topic of conversation in Copenhagen for several weeks. One of the King's obliging young ladies had been unable to curb her tongue and spread the story. Out of pity, of course, so she said, for the King and his darling son. Some of the bourgeois element praised Reventlau's harshness, others thoughtfully shook their heads. Christian had finally escaped Reventlau by running down into the palace cellar among the cooks and scullery maids, where his body-servant, Kirchhof, was quartered. Crawling under Kirchhof's bed he had remained there shaking like a dog for some hours, until the servant finally discovered him and dragged him off screaming to Reventlau. In the meantime the old blockhead had cooled off. With infinite diplomacy Reverdil had made it clear to him that the nephew, Sperling, and not Christian, was to blame. The upshot was that both Christian and Sperling were ordered to get on their knees before Reventlau, two shattered sinners, and take solemn oath on the Bible that never again would they experiment with the girls.

Little by little Christian was introduced to Reventlau's circle of friends, so he might have a taste of society. Landed nobles and representatives of foreign powers bowed before the boy. Reventlau presented his charge as "my doll" and made an unpleasant practice of mocking him before the assembled guests. If Christian hesitated to drink wine, he would say across the table: "Come on, boy, drink up and don't act like a girl afraid of peeing her pants." Yet if he drank readily of the wine, Reventlau would say, for example, to the Russian ambassador, Filosov: "Just like his father, Your Excellency. He has all the earmarks of a drunk."

During this same critical adolescent epoch Christian had a shattering experience, the effects of which never left him so long as he lived. His study hours had been notably lengthened to prepare him for public examination. Reverdil was reinstated to teach him the philosophy of Wolff, such concepts as knowledge *a priori* and *a posteriori,* and pre-stabilized harmony. These notions haunted the very dreams of the muddled prince. They became intellectual *incubi* that all but split his soggy brain. He suddenly became a horrible bundle of nerves. His head was stuffed with weighty nonsense as impossible to digest as gravel. Then, one fateful evening when he was exhausted from twelve nerve-wracking hours over his books, he was told to dress up in his best. Why, he had no idea. Reventlau pushed his way into Christian's room without knocking. "Follow me, boy," he commanded, and that was that. Weak with foreboding the Prince tripped along after the massive Reventlau. Outside the palace a carriage was waiting, guarded by dragoons with long sabers that glittered in the lantern light. Reventlau hustled the boy into the vehicle, got in himself and sat silently beside him as they drove away.

By sheer coincidence, Sperling had told Christian the lurid story of the assassination of the Tsar Peter of Russia on Catherine's instigation. Filosov had made ominous mention of the event at the table, the boy had wondered and Sperling had explained. The bloody tale haunted Christian. Up to hearing it he had never given a thought to his own royal security. Now, sitting in the coach with Reventlau, again he pictured Peter's death, a slow and painful death by smothering and strangling. The dark, heavy coach, the cold leather upholstering, the hollow clipclop of the dragoons' horses on the paving stones, the coachmen's whisperings, Reventlau's sinister, broad countenance all spelled catastrophe for the frightened youth. He was sure he was being carried off to his death, apparently somewhere on the island of Amager. There the dragoons would be ordered to kill him and throw his corpse into the swamps. Frantically he debated whether he should fling himself at Reventlau's feet and beg for mercy, or whether he should leap out of the carriage into the night. He did neither, instead sat tight, quaking with fear, his back icy cold, his palms running sweat. Eventually the coach drew up before a large building. Strains of music came floating on the wind, mild candlelight shone obliquely on the bluish snow.

"Up, boy!" said Reventlau, and gave the Prince a handsome poke in the ribs. "We're going to a masked ball at Count Moltke's. Straighten up now, little sop."

"Why didn't you tell me where we were going?" whined the Prince. He was relieved and shaken with irritation beyond measure.

"Do I owe you explanations?" cried Reventlau. At once the veins in his temples commenced to swell. "If you had an ounce of common sense you'd realize the whole thing has been arranged for your benefit."

The Prince was taken to a podium covered with red velvet and there told to stand and say appropriate nothings to each lady as she was introduced. This ritual he performed to the best of his small ability, stammering, looking away, hopelessly gauche, especially since Reventlau had taken a post directly in back of him that he might raise his brows in contempt at each gaffee. The boy, who had fully expected to be thrown dead into a wet grave, suddenly found himself in a brilliantly lighted room amidst perfumed women showing a great deal of white breasts, with laughter and gaiety all about. It was too much to comprehend, a sickly, frightful confusion to the senses.

Some days later Christian was led off to a public examination. He was handled like a trained poodle. The consistory of examiners was made up of pastors and members of the royal ministries. Innumerable questions were fired at him, on theology, philosophy, morality and history. These he answered like an automaton. The creaking and rattling of the machine was obvious. The questions entered poor Christian's brain like so many coins in a slot, and the proper answers came out forthwith, tailor-made and meaningless. He stood before his inquisitors like a lifesize doll in immaculately cut coat and hose, silk stockings on his legs, his hair carefully waved and powdered. His face was like a mask, though occasionally an expression of fear came into the eyes whenever his glance encountered Reventlau who, for the ceremony, had assumed a beaming, fatherly expression. Whenever a question was especially difficult, Christian's extraordinary mentor would nod encouragingly.

The consistory pretended to be overwhelmed by the Prince's dumb show of learning. On the spot they recommended an honorarium of a thousand gold pieces for Reventlau and allowed the boy a three days' vacation from his studies. It had occurred to no one to ask the boy any practical questions. The ministers did not dream that it might be worth while, for example, to acquaint the future king with the nature of money, or with some manual trade. Their preference was for a king absolute, a king whose absoluteness went so far that he would sign every document put on his desk.

Christian was just sixteen years old when his father died, overcome by venery and the emptiness of life. Those around the boy noticed that he was crushed by this event and frequently wept, which of course they ascribed to grief over his father's departure. Shortly, however, they found out that Christian's melancholy had a different source. As crown-prince, and free at last from the threat of Reventlau's ferrule, Christian had hoped to lead an irresponsible existence, a sort of opera bouffe round of pleasures with giddy women and heavy-drinking young men. Christian had intended to play the favorite tenor, the darling of all the world. In the company of the indefatigable Sperling he wanted to skip from the court of One Serene Highness to another, feted, envied for his youth, his charming complexion, his elegant manner. With his father's death all this suddenly came to nothing. Death had played him a nasty trick, and so he sniveled.

At last, then, he was standing in the softly snowy winter twilight on a balcony of the Christiansborg Palace. Before him the gray towers of Copenhagen melted into gray air. Reventlau, Moltke, Bernstorff and Saint-Germain were arranged in phalanx behind him. Below the people rumbled and seethed in the square. Great crowds were still streaming in from the Fishmarket and the Exchange, out of the narrow streets of the inner city. Steady burghers with their wives and children in tow, artisans, fishermen stinking of oil, market-women, soldiers, servants and beggars formed an enormous, uneasy mass of gray humanity in the half light. "Long live Christian!" they shouted at intervals. And again: "Long live the King!"

Women wept when they saw how blond and pretty the new King looked, a young man straight out of a fairy tale, so young and nice. They could not know, looking up at him posed on the balcony, that even now he was older at heart than the oldest of them, his spirit as lifeless and cold as a dead flounder on the dock. They had no way of knowing that it was costing him a great effort of will even to raise his hand to acknowledge the mob's salute.

The regime stayed the same after Christian's accession to the throne. Even had Christian actively wanted to bring about administrative improvements, he would have been utterly helpless, for he would not have the least idea where and how to begin. In Reventlau's study were large files labeled "Norway," "Holstein" and "Schleswig." These provinces he had reserved for himself; as if they were his personal property. Revenues from Denmark were assigned to Worthey, Reventlau's brother-in-law, for this gentleman had sired twenty-four children and needed quite a bit of money to get along.

Bereft of thought and decision Christian sat before a pile of letters and documents. He was staring over them at the wall when Reventlau came in unannounced and shouted at him in his usual arrogant tone. "What's wrong with you now?" "Why don't you open your letters? And sign those orders there? Are you going to be the same lazy dog of a man your father was?"

Goaded into action by Reventlau, Christian called in Reverdil. Shaking with apprehension he asked the Swiss what he should do. Reverdil promptly broke the seal on one of the documents and read off the contents to Christian. Then he explained what was wanted and why. "Sign here, Sire, to show you've read it," he said, handing the King a quill. The King did as he was told without further comment.

"From now on you're the royal letter-opener, Reverdil," he said. He was greatly relieved. "Please do that for me, my dear Reverdil."

"I thank Your Majesty," said Reverdil. "It will be a great honor."

Christian smiled slyly. He thought signing letters a great joke.

The central question of the day was the emancipation of the serfs. Christian's father had taken some preliminary steps in this direction. But the difficulties besetting the transformation of slaves into citizens had proved insuperable. The father had soon tired of the endless haggling, preferring to sport with his women friends. The question of manumission was very complex, since merely altering the legal status of large numbers of the Danish population was only a first step. The freedmen would have to be furnished with land and money in the form of agricultural loans, small sums and small acreages individually, to be sure, but adding up to a vast subsidy for a country so heavily in debt.

Yet Reverdil had not talked with Voltaire for nothing, nor for nothing exchanged long letters with Helvetius and read deeply in the works of Rousseau. He saw a golden chance to build the state of Denmark into a polity organized to promote justice and opportunity. At the same time he realized that he was neither statesman nor diplomat. He did the best he could, that is, struggled to make clear the essentials of the situation to the languid Christian. He took the young King to inspect the royal domains in the vicinity of Copenhagen. He showed him how the serfs lived in huts, he familiarized him with their diet and life habits. He did what he could to figure out for

Christian how large an acreage of pasture would be required to feed one cow, how much vegetables and potatoes a farming family would need to maintain life, how much money the state would have to advance to purchase land, chickens and geese for the prospective freedmen.

For a time Christian was mildly responsive to Reverdil's enthusiasm, not so much perhaps because he cared for the peasants themselves, as because he imagined great fame in bringing about their manumission. He fancied himself being recorded in future history books as "Christian the Emancipator," or "Christian the Beloved." He would be praised by Voltaire, revered in all the councils of Europe. He shed tears dreaming about his future glories, he lost himself in woolly fantasies. But Reverdil was forever spoiling his swimming reveries, with his ridiculous figures, tables, prospectuses and his Frenchman's insistent skepticism. Christian would shrink and yawn as he sat at his desk and think how much pleasanter it would be to go hunting, or to have a game of battledore and shuttlecock with some pretty wench. One day he frightened Reverdil by casually announcing that he had drawn up an edict of emancipation and signed it. Reverdil begged for time to study the matter. In a few weeks the paper was forgotten and began to gather dust in a far corner of the personal files. Reverdil's dream collapsed.

During this epoch it was Frederick of Prussia who held Europe's undivided attention. The bitter recluse of Sans-souci, with his Italian greyhounds, his snuff-stained vests and his cynical smile kept Christian on the hop trying to imitate him. Christian got himself a crooked walking stick, a severe blue coat and a gold snuff-box. He, too, tried to assume a caustic tone and rode before the troops on parade, though military antics secretly bored him. He had his minister of war, Saint-Germain, brought before him for an audience. He was told to bring data on the number of Danish regiments with him, the count of squadrons and batteries, an inventory of weapons, tactical plans and all his strategic maps. Saint-Germain adroitly dragged the names of Turenne, Marlborough and Prince Eugen into the preliminary conversation. He recommended that his King read Caesar's *Gallic Wars* and Vauban on the construction of fortifications. These studies, he admitted, were onerous and made demands on one's time, but such was the military art. Christian suddenly objected. A genius, he declared, did not need to bother his head about pedantic detail. His free flights, for he was having some, might indeed suffer from too much cogitation.

"Saint-Germain," he said, rapping the floor with his Prussian stick, "my plans are made. I'm going to declare war on Prussia."

The minister of war turned pale. His jaw actually dropped and for a little while he was quite unable to speak. At last he stuttered:

"But, Your Majesty, our relations with Prussia are perfectly amicable. Why, they couldn't possibly be better!"

"How dare you tamper with the royal will!" screamed Christian, in the violent style of Reventlau. "Do you understand me? It is the royal will that we declare war on Prussia and conquer this Frederick. Who conquers him will be considered the greatest general of all time."

"Unquestionably," said the minister of war, slowly gathering his wits. "So Your Majesty would be considered, and I do not gainsay it. That is, if Your Majesty won."

"That's treason," shouted Christian. "I'll banish you to Norway, my good man."

"Me!" said Saint-Germain.

"I said you," Christian told him. "To Norway. For good."

"I am not doubting Your Majesty's military prowess," said Saint-Germain smoothly. "I merely point out that our army is very small and certainly not prepared at the moment to wage war."

"What am I paying you for?" Christian demanded. "I give you three days to bring the situation to order."

"That's utterly impossible, Your Majesty," said Saint-Germain. Again exasperation and disbelief were undermining his self-control. "If Your Majesty persists in this matter, I must tender my resignation."

Now Christian was stumped. He looked in perplexity at Saint-Germain. "I cannot accept your resignation at this time," he said finally. "But I'm convinced we must fight. Perhaps I can give the army some practice by declaring war on Russia."

Saint-Germain smote himself on the forehead with the flat of his hand. "*Sacré bleu,* fantastic!" he nearly shouted. "Does Your Majesty not understand that the Russians, who outnumber us, I should say, ten thousand to one, would devastate Copenhagen with fire bombs? They would make an alliance with the Swedes in a twinkling. Surely you must see that war on Russia would end in the conquest of Denmark. Even Your Majesty's life would not be secure!"

"I'm no coward like you, Saint-Germain," retorted Christian loftily. "Kindly remove yourself from my presence and do something about the troops. My decision is irrevocable. We must have war, I say. I won't be hindered by such old fogies as you. Get out of here, before I lose my temper."

Saint-Germain stumbled out of the room and ran to Reventlau, in such agitation that against sacred precedent he burst in without knocking. Hardly able to talk straight, he recounted Christian's remarkable proposals. Reventlau turned mulberry red. The veins in his head swelled to cords. Blowing like a sick horse he heaved himself to his feet. "I'll crack that idiot's brainpan," he assured Saint-Germain.

"I'll cut him to pieces if he dares put a finger on my army and my provinces." Bellowing incoherently he looked around for his cane, found it and dashed out of the room. With thunderous steps he strode down the marble corridor to Christian's apartments.

"What is this I hear," he said to the King without even bothering to greet him. "Why, you absurd little rat, you criminal! How dare you upset people with your damnable stupidities! How dare you fling your country about like a rag! Will you make me lash the skin off your back, you cretin!"

Cowed by this onslaught Christian slipped out of his chair and crept into a far corner of the room, put his hands before his face and burst into tears. Reventlau, his rage seething like a cauldron of brass, seized Christian's fancy Prussian stick and broke it over his knee. "Why, how dare you imagine you're a Frederick," he said, his words an avalanche. "You puppet, you couldn't make war on a milkmaid." And then a curious thing happened. Suddenly Christian began to scream at the top of his lungs drowning out his tormentor.

"I've had enough, I've had enough," he screeched. "I'm the King, not you. Do you know that I can have you exiled and put in chains, you dirty old man? Do you know I can have you thrown into Kronborg, if I please? If I want to I can have you seared with hot irons, you beast!"

Reventlau stared in disbelief. His eyes were bursting glassily from their sockets. Mechanically he took one step towards Christian, then began to sway. He toppled forward, making the parquet floor tremble as he crashed, a fallen oak. Christian cried out in horror. Like a trained monkey with one leap he was at Reventlau's side. He lifted the lolling head onto his knees, and in a paroxysm of terror watched the swollen lips turn blue, and the thick tongue protrude from the gaping mouth like the tongue of a slaughtered ox. "Reventlau, Reventlau," the boy King stammered tearfully. "Dear Reventlau, please don't die."

The unconscious man did not stir. Christian folded his hands and prayed. "God, help my friend and teacher," he whispered hoarsely. "He is all I have. Denmark needs him. What can I do without him. Where will we be without Reventlau." Servants flocked into the room, curiosity overcoming their discretion. They stared reproachfully at the King. They saw him kiss Reventlau's limp hand and weep wildly when four lackeys came forward to lug away the helpless carcase. Wringing his hands and chafing his thin wrists the King trailed after the fallen giant.

But as it happened Reventlau recovered rapidly from his stroke. The only visible result was that Christian permanently washed his hands of military projects. He found this easier than he had imagined, for someone graphically described the rigors of military life for his benefit. According to what was now fixed custom authority in Denmark continued to be invested in the ministers. The question now was not who would rule, but how. This interesting question was solved in a negative fashion by a certain Count Holck. Count Holck was a big man with a mighty barrel of chest and simple features. Behind the surface simplicity was a cunning mind. Holck was a very sly fellow indeed, ambitious and corrupt under his attitude of clumsy *joie de vivre*. Through his intervention Christian was removed entirely from the process of governance, and the ministers did as they pleased.

The King, already accustomed to Sperling's abject sycophancy, was greatly taken by Holck. At last, Christian thought, here is someone that I can like, a good horseman, a hunter who holds a musket as if it were a feather. Holck was past master at playing the good companion. He was the sort of man who could bend a thaler double between forefinger and thumb, lift the back-end of a sledge knee-high and knock a lackey unconscious with a clip on the chin, which last he often did to amuse Christian. Holck was also a powerful tippler. In the course of an evening he could make away with a whole bucket of wine. His wig might get out of place, his tongue might thicken but he took great pride in never falling under the table. He had countless shortlived affairs and not only with the court ladies. In erotic regard Holck was very democratic. Indeed, he had little sexual respect for what he described as powdered nannygoats. They had too much on their minds, he declared, to know how to please a vigorous swordsman like himself, for that was an affair requiring wholehearted concentration. It was his athletic habit to assault the women of his fancy like a bull at stud, hardly waiting for them to compose themselves for passion's play.

To Christian his friend Holck was a Hercules. A sort of rude brotherhood, a sensual affinity, held them together, though actually they were an unlikely pair. People smiled to see the small-boned, willowy Christian with his gigantic companion, who had a neck on him the size of a capstan. Steadily Holck gained ascendancy over the boy King and finally ruled him completely. With chosen companions the two would slip out nights to revel in the taverns and brothels of Copenhagen. Christian loved these incognito excursions, the free and easy conversation about the long inn tables. Great quantities of beer and wine were drunk at these tavern brawls while half-naked strumpets danced and diverted the guests with coarse mockery and humor.

In good time these royal expeditions occasioned public complaints, especially after Holck, emerging tipsy and inflamed from an inn, seized a girl passerby who happened to come from a respectable household. Holck was prevented from raping her—Christian was fascinated by the big Count at work—only by the timely intervention of the night-watchmen, who raced to the spot with pikes on guard and lanterns swinging. A regular street fight ensued. Good burghers were roused from their sleep by the shouts and thuds. They hung out the window with their nightcaps askew and mortification in their hearts. One spirited old crone emptied a chamberpot on the battlers' heads, thoroughly dousing Christian, and still not satisfied she denounced him as a "whoremaster." Not till the King was fully recognized did the night-watchmen cease their determined struggle to preserve public peace. By then the damage was done. The next Sunday the escapade became the subject of a dozen sermons, many drawing heavily on the analogy afforded by the wayward Absalom. The congregation looked at each other out of the corners of their eyes. When the time came to say the obligatory prayer for the King, this ritual was deliberately scuffed through, to underscore respectable sentiment.

Count Holck was unmoved. He cursed the Philistines who dared interfere with youth's exuberances. But he resolved in the future to curb himself, at least for a time, especially since it was becoming noticeable that Christian was not equal to so much night life. The King was pale, irritable and very shaky on the morning after. Moreover, he often exhibited much more disturbing symptoms of weakness. The King had confessed to Holck that he suffered from bad dreams.

The King's dreams were so bad, in fact, that sometimes he was afraid to go to bed. There were periods when the prospect of nocturnal horrors depressed his whole waking existence. A candle had to be kept lit at his bedside. Sperling, who slept in a room off the King's bedchamber, had standing orders to wake him should he groan or toss in his sleep. The content of these nightmares the King would divulge to nobody. But no doubt they were shockingly disturbing. Coming out of them he would foam at the mouth, and cry out in a frenzy, not knowing who or where he was. On one occasion he had a seizure during which he tried to smash his brains out on the marble of the fireplace. Afterwards he lay propped up among the pillows, trembling and pale as death, lisping incoherently.

Although Holck was by no means a student of human nature, he realized that there was a definite connection between the King's nightly visitations and his dissolute life. He introduced Christian, therefore, to a different form of entertainment, the worst possible for one mentally out of kilter. Holck had noticed that the King found a peculiar satisfaction in looking at pain and blood. If someone was injured at a hunt, if a servant was thrown from a horse and broke his leg, if a lady had a nose-bleed, Christian was beside himself with pleased interest. In view of this predilection Holck was inspired to introduce the King to the torture chambers of Copenhagen. Here he had ample opportunity to feast on human suffering. The gloomy rooms were filled with the shrieks of unfortunates subjected to the press of boot and pilliwinks and even more ingenious instruments designed to squeeze out the truth till it was white.

At these extraordinary séances Christian would sit very quietly and watchfully, his blue gaze riveted on the prisoner's twisted features. When the sufferer screamed in agony, the King would start with delight and hug himself. He had been known to remark, when the criminal's broken and bleeding body was being carried off: "Fine, fine, that was a good one!" Still, these violent distractions failed to counteract Christian's dreams. In fact, the terrors of the night grew worse under their stimulus, and there were times when they became so acute that the King shook, twisted and strained his body as if he, himself, were in the hands of some invisible torturer.

Holck decided to alter his tactics. He smiled to himself to think how stupid he was not to have thought of it before. What the young King needed was a regular mistress, a woman of his own. Of course Holck was not too keen about actually supplying this deficiency, for he was afraid of the common fate of friend rejected for lover. The temperate pleasures of friendship, he realized, could hardly compete with the charm of female conversation and the magic of an experienced female body. His choice, therefore, had to be extremely judicious. There was a certain young woman in Copenhagen who was under Holck's thumb, since he had a dossier on her shady past. She had spent a year in a Hamburg prison for robbing a drunk. This was the woman Holck picked out for his King.

The young lady was widely known as "Booted Kate"—her real name no one knew—and at the time Holck picked her up was making a fair living for herself by catering to Copenhagen young bloods. She was a dark-haired girl, slender of build, with dark and rather protuberant eyes in a long, faintly horsy face. She liked to wear a riding habit, the more easily to lift the folds of the costume to show off her slim legs, on which she wore gold-trimmed boots of calf length made of special soft leather. It was her habit of wearing these fancy boots that had got her the nickname of "Booted Kate." But she was also called "Milady," since for a short interval she had been the favorite of the English ambassador, the Marquis of Keith. Kate had proved too strenuous a lover for the elderly ambassador. Milady, as he called her, had a peculiarity that rasped his ancient nerves, namely, a sadistic turn. She was no run of the mine slut, people said. Word spread that she had noble blood and probably was the illegitimate daughter of a Holstein aristocrat. When she felt like it she was capable of showing good breeding, though her polite moods were rare. In moments of erotic excitement it was her sexual custom to strike out and claw at her lovers, then sink her teeth into their shoulders, weeping hysterically, as if to avenge her shame.

There are men who enjoy such types of women, and Christian was among them. He had scarcely set eyes on her when they became thicker than thieves. Milady rode with him on hunts, she sat beside him in his carriage and in his theater stall. She ruled him as if he were a servant, she had him tie and polish her famous boots. When he was awkward in assisting her from her horse, she would strike him smartly across the face with her crop. But these love-taps were nothing compared with the exotic practices that the pair carried on in privacy.

When Kate showed her temper, when her black eyes began to pop neurotically out of her head, when she began to rave and stamp the floor with her booted feet, an expression of fearful delight would steal over the King's narrow, pretty features. Once, on a hunting party, she refused to speak with him because he had forgotten to drink to her success, the King ran after her with tears in his eyes, begging for mercy. She had him kneel down before her, whereupon he impulsively covered her boots with kisses and flung his arms tightly about her knees, until she detached him with a cut of her riding whip across the shoulders, saying: "Come, now, that's enough, little fellow."

Milady took no interest in politics, and her financial demands were not excessive. But Denmark was so heavily in debt and taxes so high, the poor so utterly without hope and so bitterly disappointed in the new king, that Christian's affair got him in terribly bad odor. The Danish people had dreamed of the emancipation of the serfs. Instead they were fobbed off with more promises. They wanted to be rid of oligarchic rule by the ministry, they wanted to cast out the teeming nepotistic elements milking the treasury. The people had also expected that Christian might do something about abrogating the use of torture in the legal process. He did none of these things. Instead he became the disgustingly ignominious lover of a perverted whore. He would have been forgiven an ordinary royal mistress, some retiring young woman in crinoline, wearing her hair heavily powdered, tinkling prettily on the spinet amid the usual circle of sporty aristocrats, demi-mondaines, would-be poets and philosophers with an argument to peddle. But this blood-curdling, randy fishwife, this horrid virago in boots, was too much of a pill to swallow.

About this time—it was now the sweet spring of the year—the failure of the last fall's harvest inexorably began to make itself felt in the capital city of Copenhagen. Incessant rains had rotted and mildewed the sheaves as they stood in the fields. Simultaneously an epidemic broke out among the sheep in Jutland. During the winter the coast of Norway had been battered by unprecedented gales, which worked havoc with the herring catch, and inundated whole islands along the western coast. The poor of Copenhagen, who even in normal times lived pretty much from hand to mouth, no longer had even a crust to eat. One herring cost as much as formerly a turbot. Crowds of angered, bewildered people roamed the streets. Theft and murder were daily occurrences. Mothers killed their own children to relieve their sufferings.

In their seethe of discontent the people imagined they saw the retributive handiwork of God. When the stables housing the royal stud burned flat they were doubly sure that God was very, very displeased with Denmark. That Sunday Pastor Muenter preached from the pulpit of St. Peter's on a text from Ezekiel: "How ye, Woe worth the day." The church was packed, even the aisles, and more still tried to fight their way in that they might take comfort in explosive language. The wonder was, people said, that the walls did not burst. With his fist raised like a mace, Pastor Muenter turned towards Christiansborg and cried: "Woe to them, I say, who bring misery on us. Better to hang a stone about his neck and drown him in the deeps of the sea than to tolerate this corruption!" Hollow-eyed, cheeks sunken in, many shoeless and in rags, the congregation listened in an awful deadly silence. The drop of a pin would have echoed through the church after the Pastor's ultimatum. Then the choir sang: "Lord, have mercy on Thy people."

After the service men, women and children poured out of the church and raced towards the palace, gathering recruits on the way. They plundered shops, they hurled stones through the shiny windows of the fine houses in the Amaliengade and Bredegade. They massed by the thousands in the Fishmarket, roaring denunciation at the King. A delegation went to Fredensborg and there petitioned the intervention of the Queen-Dowager. The guardsmen protecting Christiansborg whispered nervously among themselves, not really knowing where their duty lay. The crowd threw filth and stones at them, knocking off their tall hats, but failed to budge them from their posts throughout the critical night.

During this uprising the King was deep inside the palace. One minute he threatened to order the troops to open fire on the people. The next he burst into tears and wept on Reventlau's breast. He threw his arms about Saint-Germain, he kissed Moltke and whined: "I'm good, I've done my very best, haven't I?" He agreed to dismiss Milady, though it was really unnecessary, for she had had the good sense to flee Copenhagen a day or two before the storm broke. Moltke eased the situation by having rations of bread and fish distributed among the poor. About midnight the crowds began to break up and filter homeward. The next morning, on Saint-Germain's command, the Zealand dragoons came to Copenhagen on the gallop and set up posts and patrols covering the key streets and squares of the city. In this way order was restored for the time being. Still, the crisis had merely relaxed and was not in the least permanently solved. The root of it, Christian's irresponsible behavior, would have to be extirpated. The privy council met in emergency session and it was decided to marry off the young King, to pin him down in marriage and so bolster the rapidly waning prestige of the royal house.

When Annette, with a senseless sigh, had finished her lengthy and matter of fact report of a king's youth and the ominous beginnings of a reign, she obviously thought that she had done too much of a good thing and was suddenly, as is the way of women, completely tired of life's seriousness and matters of state and even of her own future. She raised herself from her chair, her eyes smiling, opened her arms and cried softly, laughingly, "Enough, my darling. The night is so precious and short."

For the second time this evening, Struensee found himself rushed from one region of feeling into another unexpected one. But, though he was now anxious to know more about the king and to explore the king's fate and his possibilities in even greater detail, he took the sudden change in his mistress's intentions with good grace, after the perfect manner of his frivolously civilized time, in which matters of grave importance were broached in the vicinity of silken petticoat and God Himself in his heaven was discussed over little porcelain cups of chocolate and boxes of perfumed powder.

He lifted her hair charmingly and kissed first one ear, then the other, slowly, devotedly. She sighed: "You are so good, my friend."

"You are not bad at all yourself, my love," he laughed slyly and took her gown from her shoulders, not forgetting to touch these shoulders with lazy caressing movements of his hands.

"You should extinguish the candles first, *mon coeur*. My good Gaehler always does that," she said smilingly, reprovingly.

"But I am not your husband, love! I am your lover. Don't you know that only a bachelor, like myself, understands the true feelings of a married woman?"

"Coquin!"

"Besides, what is there to hide! The beautiful limbs of a goddess should be seen in the full light of the midday sun. So, do not be suspicious of these poor trembling candles."

"You fascinate me, darling," she said, half seriously.

"As a snake a bird?"

"No, not that way," she said, and pressed his hands against her breasts, *"vos jolies phrases caressent mon oreil et flattent mon orgueil. Elles m'emportent."*

"Would you have it different, my love?" he asked, with half hidden satisfaction.

"Oh no, never, never," she said with conviction, and kissed him fervently, "it is such a relief to have and to give, darling."

He led her toward the bed. It did not, he observed, require much guidance.

When, finally, the lights were being turned out for the night in the Hotel Zum Koenig von Preussen, Christiansborg, palace of the Danish kings in Copenhagen, about three hundred miles to the north of Hamburg, was still brilliantly lighted. A thousand windows blazed in the night. The palace was like a Christmas tree.

However, the atmosphere within the enormous building was anything but festive. Even the Palace guards, as a rule so stonily indifferent in their white uniforms and two-foot grenadiers' busbies, stood about with worried mien, industriously chewing their mustache ends. Up the great staircase, past little marble gods ornamenting the balustrades, hurried an elderly gentleman with a great deal of gold braid on his coat and a wide red ribbon of silk draped across his chest. This was the Marquis of Keith, the English ambassador. The lackey who led the way with a candlestick smirked as much as he dared. It amused him to be able to read the Marquis' evil mood. The old gentleman had been disturbed at one of his beloved champagne suppers, at eleven in the evening, just at the point when he was beginning to make a little progress with the French dancer, a feat that took some doing at his advanced age. The diplomatic corps had been summoned to emergency discussion and so there he was, puffing up the palace stairs.

Meanwhile, in another section of the palace two much younger gentlemen, Kammerjunker Sperling and Count Holck, supported between them, one holding each arm, a blond youth of seventeen or so. Firmly they dragged their charge towards the throne room, and argued as they went.

"Pull yourself together, Christian, my boy," said Count Holck, a rough even in his court costume. "They're not going to cut your throat, you know."

"You want to marry me off, that's what you all want to do," the boy moaned and stared into the Count's slabby face with tragically distended eyes. "I'm too young, I tell you. I don't want to do it. Now, let me go, both of you."

"Shut up," said Holck. "You bleat like a sheep, Christian. The little one, they say, is very nice, a sweet little pullet."

"But she's too blonde," the boy said. "Why, her hair is nearly white, her hair's so blonde."

"She looks all right in the picture they sent you," growled Holck. "Watch your tongue, will you!"

"But I like brunettes," the boy said in tearful irritation. "I don't want any blonde, I tell you."

"You like Milady, you mean," said Holck.

"Yes, I do like Milady," the boy sobbed. "Whatever will I do about her? You'll tell me, Sperling, won't you, even if Holck won't? What will I do? There's only one Milady in the whole world, Holck."

"That's no exaggeration," said Sperling.

"Of course, she is a rare bird," said Holck. "But when everything is fixed up nicely and calmed down, you can have her brought back, my dear Christian. You see?"

"When I'm married, you mean?" Christian asked. He began to wipe his eyes dry as much as the grip on his arms would allow.

"Of course, why not?" grumbled Holck.

"Yes, but what would the other one say?" said Christian. "Do you think my wife would allow it?"

"What do you care about your wife, damn it," said Holck in sheer irritation. "Christian, you talk like a dealer in fish. Are you trying to tell me that marriage is a sacrament? *Mon dieu!* Were you seriously thinking you'd have to be glued fast to one woman? Especially the one you marry! Sperling, listen to the boy. Feel the wet behind his ears, will you. No wonder the poor pet is so troubled!" Holck laughed like a bull and was echoed by Kammerjunker in a more moderate outburst. The earthquake of laughter affected Christian. He, too, squeaked with amusement, his tears now suddenly forgotten.

"By Milady's riding whip," he said showily, "I'd forgotten that I'm His Majesty the King and can do what I please. And, in case you've forgotten it, you two, have others do what I please."

"Well, that's the first sensible thing you've said this evening," Holck said. "Come on, now. Forward march. The wedding can't be delayed forever, my son."

"I know, Holck, I know," said the boy, smiling crookedly. "I have my own little idea. This blonde is going to pay through the nose for upsetting the applecart, I can tell you that."

"Don't be sure about that, Christian," said Sperling. "You may even come to like the little lady in good time."

"I may, and I may not," said Christian. "That all depends. But I'll say this much. No little English slut is going to look down her nose at me. Is she, Holck?"

"Bravo, the King speaks," said Holck drily. "If you want some private advice, my boy, let me warn you that most women are a good deal better off if their husbands give them a backhander across the mouth every so often. It sweetens their disposition, it tickles their feminine nature, so to speak. Nothing like it to sharpen their affections, Christian."

"You don't understand me, Holck," said Christian. "My blows will wound the soul."

"Fine, fine, all the better," said Holck. "After all, we Danes are not Russian peasants, are we? Now, get on ahead of me and stop talking so much. It will make a better impression."

With dancing steps Christian moved ever closer to the throne room. A frozen, silly smile was on his face. Holck and Sperling trailed behind him at a carefully maintained distance of three paces. The guards presented arms smartly when Christian, without so much as turning an eye to look, pranced by.

Reventlau and Moltke, seeing Christian come prancing non-chalantly to the throne room where they awaited him, could hardly believe their eyes, for they had nerved themselves for scenes of hysterical resistance. Instead the King bowed to his step-mother, the Queen-Dowager, who looked back at him as black as a dragon, her brows knitted together. He bowed to his brother-in-law, Prince Karl von Hessen, and waved his hand elegantly in recognition of his ministers. Then he made a pretty little speech, right out of a clear sky.

"Mesdames et messieurs," he said, "allow me to anticipate your worthy decisions. I thank you all beforehand for your devotion, and in addition may I say that I have decided to marry the beloved Princess Caroline Matilda, to whom I have been betrothed these many years. I have been considering this step for a long time, and have decided to delay no longer. I would like all my relatives, friends and trusted servants to be the first to know about it. I feel sure that I can count on your joyous approval, mesdames et messieurs."

The Queen Dowager embraced her step-son. Reventlau gaped at Count Holck, who winked at him confidentially, as if it were all his doing. A deep sigh of relief went through the room. Christian sat down and turned to the English ambassador. "My dear sir," he murmured silkily, "I feel certain that with your usual adroitness you can overcome any obstacles that may conceivably arise." Smiling to himself he pretended to think things over, with one thin finger stroking the large diamond on his other hand. He kissed the stone, slowly drew the ring from his finger and gave it to the Marquis of Keith, saying: "My dear Keith, would you have a special courier take this to my bride as a token of my enduring affection?"

★ *V* ★

STRUENSEE WAS FULL of ideas, bursting with plans. Annette's bill of particulars on conditions at the Danish court had whetted his impatience to get on with important works. Now that his mistress had returned to the capital everything seemed flat and stale in crabbed Altona. Sitting long hours in his coach, keeping vigil at his patients' bedside, he was hardly aware of what he was doing. He even became indifferent to the stenches of poverty. In spirit he was already with Annette in Copenhagen, in Christiansborg, performing miracles for the King, whose ailing personality drew him like a magnet. Medicine would be more than a mere profession; it would be a great vocation.

Half the night through he sat in his room and read in Rousseau's *Emile*. He had dug the book out of his closet to compare natural education according to Jean-Jacques' prescription with the brutalities and pedantries of the King's upbringing as visualized for him by Annette. He still sensed a call for help from afar, a cry of dire need for reason and order. He came to feel that he was ordained to bring succor not only to Christian but to the whole Danish people. The feeling of dedication unfolded within him like a flower in the sun. He did not think it strange at all that he, a relatively obscure and unimportant doctor lost in the outer reaches of Denmark should be chosen to solve the nation's problems.

He gave his friend Brandt money and sent him off to Copenhagen. Then, regularly each week, he wrote two letters, one to Brandt, another to Annette, who of course had returned home to her husband. Annette having cleverly acquainted him with Struensee's possibilities, the elderly officer fell genially in line. In Struensee he saw at least an off chance of improving his finances. Then there was Rantzau. Smiling broadly, clapping Struensee familiarly on the shoulder with a great display of bonhomie, Rantzau visited the Doctor in Altona. In no time he had let it be painlessly known that recently he had lost a considerable sum of louis d'or at faro. This, of course, was a barefaced lie. For years he had never had as much as one louis d'or to lose at gaming. Women, too, he told Struensee, were costing him a pretty, pretty penny, and his family were forever pestering him for advances. In short, he was stony broke. Struensee took the hint. He fumbled in his drawer, counted out twenty louis d'or and passed them over to the Count, who had his hand all ready. On becomingly sentimental impulse the Count embraced his dear friend, the Doctor. Already he imagined himself capitalizing on his new source of revenue. He saw himself strolling to the gaming tables, knocking like a man of means on brothel doors, becoming perhaps the King's confidant. Was he not a Rantzau born? Yes, life owed him something.

Struensee's clandestine undertaking did not interfere with his medical activity as such. It was obvious that he must settle down to business and earn more money than ever. Both his emissaries in Copenhagen had to be supported, and Rantzau, being a seasoned aristocrat, cost far more than Brandt, who cost enough. Now and then he had to send Annette a bottle of perfume, a cake of fine soap, some delicacies, just for memory's sake. Then he had to lay aside a sinking fund, against the time when he would remove to the capital. He would have to arrive freshly outfitted and prepared to make the most of any opening. And so the Doctor's heavy coach rumbled this way and that over the Holstein roads, wheels squealing and groaning from overuse. Through village streets, frightening the geese, over lonesome fields, into castle yards, up to white country homes the Doctor went his solitary way, not caring whether the sun shone or not.

Steadily his reputation as a doctor grew. Had he lived merely to accumulate money and local fame, there would have been no reason for his ever leaving Altona. Had he wanted to commit himself, he could easily have had a woman to amuse and care for him. In the isolated country estates that gave him the best of his practice there were many eligible young women who would have sacrificed a little finger to marry the Doctor. But he steered a cautious, neutral, midstream course and passed up a dozen lesser opportunities in favor of the one great one he deemed his due. There were times when he thought over the teachings of Leibniz, those arguing that elemental monads underlie reality. He liked this theory of monads. Like tiny crystals, as Struensee imagined them, they presented an infinity of surfaces, each reflecting in its specific way the remaining totality of the universe. The world was populated by a myriad of crystalline souls, some bright, some dull. And as for himself, his soul reflected the world in its unique way, a superior way.

He speculated, too, on his origins. Looking back on his forebears, he felt sure he came from fine stock. Its potentialities, he felt certain, were equal to any and better than most. Struensee's grandfather, though he hardly remembered his face, had once been a simple seaman. On one eventful voyage the grandfather's vessel, a commercial craft from Luebeck carrying a valuable cargo, was given up for lost by captain and crew. High seas whipped the ship about so furiously that the shrouds snapped and fell to the deck in a tangle. One mast split off, seams opened and let in the sea. Struensee's grandfather alone had not despaired, even in the face of what seemed to be certain death. With some small help from the crew he saved the ship after the captain and others had gone over the side in small boats to be swallowed up. When the grandfather brought the vessel limping into port at Luebeck, with cargo intact, in a burst of gratitude the merchant owners voted him a third share of profits, which they promptly advanced him over the green counting house table. Then on the spot they made him a captain. After this phenomenal success the Doctor's hardy ancestor went by a new name, "Struensee," which in the dialect means "stormy sea."

And what about the son of a man able to conquer stormy seas? He made himself a minister of the gospel, and sailed equally dangerous oceans. He made it his life work to deal with winds and tides that threatened not merely the body, but the very soul of the voyager.

As so often happens, the Doctor felt himself much closer to his grandfather than to his father. He was a true child of the world. He was strongly drawn by politics and the hurlyburly of large cities. Still, even in this sense, was not mankind like the sea, now broken in stormy tumult, now glassily tranquil? Like his grandfather he had implicit trust in his own judgment. His compass, he chose to think, was reason, the logical way of seeing and doing things. The main difference between him and his grandfather was that he had no experience in handling men. Nonetheless Struensee was confident that in time he would learn the ropes and develop sea-sense.

That winter the Doctor had something happen to him which he never forgot. Like so many men of good will, he had combated poverty and suffering largely on a theoretical basis, as if they could be thought out of existence. As for the actual poor and suffering in person, for them he had never felt anything but revulsion. Being a man of studied pleasures it chilled him to look at pallid, unhealthy faces, to hear rough speech, to see patched clothing, dirty homes and children with runny noses. His reaction was purely aesthetic. The poor offended his senses, they smeared his orderly picture of the world. When possible he avoided contact with the lower classes, and this was fairly easy, since by now he had an excellent practice among the best houses in Holstein. When duty forced him to break this rule, he got the job done as quickly as he could. He would hear reproach creeping into his tone, a reproach directed not so much towards the unfortunates themselves as to the feeling they aroused in him. This odd sensation of discomfort in the presence of indigence pricked his conscience. He was, after all, his father's son.

On this particular winter evening the Doctor was riding over a road skirting the sea, not too far from the place where he had first met Brandt. To his right stretched out a flat waste of beach covered with a litter of bleached gray stones. The wind swept in icy gusts off the Baltic, which was a chilly blue-gray except in distant reaches where, with the waning of the day, it had fused smokily with the sky. Thorny thickets grew near the beach. The wind moaned passing through the tangle and rattled the wiry twigs. Not a human being, not a habitation relieved the disconsolate landscape. The Doctor shivered in his carriage. The gray strip of shore between land and sea looked like a fragment of the original chaos which God had over-looked. Struensee longed keenly for tavern light and warmth. When, without previous warning, his carriage jolted to a stop, he was so annoyed that he opened the window to upbraid the driver, and was about to do so but stopped on seeing a little girl, far too thinly clothed for the bitter weather, looking up at him in the twilight. Over blonde hair she wore a tattered shawl. The child looked unreal staring up at him, motionless and frightened to death against a vast background of sea. Struensee gathered his wits and inquired what was wrong.

"My mother," the child said. She was hardly able to form the words so badly was she chilled. "It's my mother."

"Is your mother sick?" he asked the child. "What is it?"

"She's going to have a baby," the girl told him. "She's making a lot of noise, but the baby won't come out. It's stuck inside her."

Struensee wrapped his mantle about him, took his bag and stepped decisively from the carriage. "Let's have a look at her," he said. "How far away is it?"

"Not very far," the child assured him.

"Come, then, get under my coat," he said and held the child to him as they walked side by side. He could feel the fragile bones of her shoulders and the thin stalk of neck. I shouldn't do this, he thought to himself, for she's probably crawling with lice. But aloud he asked: "Where's your father? Why isn't he home?"

"My father went to sea last spring," the child said, "and he hasn't come back yet."

"Well, why didn't you call a midwife?" he continued.

"What's a midwife?" the child said, looking up at him.

"Very well, then," he said and held his tongue.

Proceeding over dunes and stony hollows they came to a steeply roofed cottage, lost among sandy hillocks. A powerful odor of fish was in the air despite the cold. Within, the mother lay on a pallet directly on the earthen floor, groaning, feverish and only semi-conscious. A miserable fire flickered on the hearth and a little boy, albino pale, with whitish blond hair straggling down to his shoulders, goggled at the visitor.

Struensee kneeled down and made the woman understand that he was a doctor and had come to help her. A shimmer of hope came over the worn face. "But I can't pay for a doctor," she whispered in the midst of a cramp. "No use, I can't pay."

"Never mind that right now," Struensee assured her, and turning to the little girl bade her heat a kettle of water. "Afterwards you can take care of your little brother," he told her.

"Yes, Doctor," she said eagerly and rushed to do his bidding.

Struensee examined the woman, took an instrument and used it. Only once did the woman shriek, otherwise she lay motionless and let him have his way, like an animal. An hour later he had success-fully delivered the child, a boy. Struensee cleaned and washed the infant and swaddled the umbilicus. The bands had been freshly washed, but nevertheless still smelled faintly of fish. The child had thin blond down on its head and big quiet eyes.

Suddenly the fire seemed to throw more heat and the poverty of the hut struck Struensee as not quite so terrifying. He wiped sweat from his forehead and was greatly pleased with himself. The mother slept, her face flushed with fever. Struensee washed his instruments and returned them to the case. He inspected the fishnets, the oars and rudder propped against the wall. A crucifix hung in one corner, a Bible under it on a rickety table, the most pretentious piece of furniture in the place. There were only three rough chairs. On a primitive sideboard were ranged some cups, brightly painted plates, clay pitchers, one small dish filled with meal, another with salt. Three dried fish hung from a string fastened to the rafters. Struensee carefully took in all these homely details.

"What's your name, my child?" he asked, turning to the little girl.

"Antje Maria," she said.

"And how old are you?"

"I'm thirteen, Doctor," the child said.

"You look younger than that," he said, then quickly added: "But you have very pretty yellow hair, I think."

The child flushed with pleasure and dropped her eyes. What's wrong with me, Struensee asked himself, what makes me so talkative?

"Can you take care of the baby for a few days until your mother is on her feet again?" he asked.

"Oh yes, I can," the girl said earnestly. "I took care of my brother, Klaus, when my mother was sick before."

Struensee, in ever increasing good humor, looked around the cottage for signs of food. "What will you feed the baby?" he asked.

"Warm water and meal," the girl said.

"But he'll never get fat and strong on that," he said. "You'll have to buy milk for him, my child."

"Buy?" the girl said. "We couldn't do that."

"What do you live on, then?"

"We fish," she said, "but when the fall storms come, we can't go out. Now we're waiting for the ice to come. Then we'll start in again, and fish nighttimes by torchlight."

"Well, now," said Struensee, impressed, "you are a clever little girl. But where's your father? Is he off drunk somewhere maybe? Tell me the truth."

"Oh no, no," she assured him, genuinely horrified. "He's at sea, like I told you, up near Sweden or Russia or Finland. If the winter comes early and the Finnish sea freezes over, then he'll be back by spring. When he comes we'll have a lot of money. We'll tar the seams of our boat and weave new nets. When he comes back we can buy milk, too."

She was very proud, telling the Doctor all these things. Importantly she began to rummage on the sideboard, found a jug there, poured something out of it and mixed it with hot water. She gave the drink to Struensee, who raised it to his nose to smell.

"Why, it's rum!" he said.

"It's my father's rum," the child explained. "Go ahead and drink."

He drank with pursed lips. The fiery liquid warmed his entrails. A pleasant feeling crept over him immediately from toes to fingertips.

"Thanks, many thanks, Antje Maria," he said to the child.

"No, thank you," said the girl. "Mother would have died without a doctor. And the baby wouldn't be alive either. But we can't pay you until Father comes home from sea."

"Never mind, forget that," said Struensee, beaming. "Where the poor can't pay, the rich must." He rolled his drink around in the beaker. "You've made it far too strong," he said. "You'll have none left for yourselves, Antje Maria."

"That's all right for this once, Doctor," the child said gravely. "It isn't just to drink. It's Christmas, you know."

"Christmas?" Struensee rubbed the back of his head. "Why, so it is. My God, I'd completely forgotten. Thank you, my child. Of course it is."

Then he remembered that the Baroness Buelow was expecting him in Luetzelburg. They would eat goose, crisply browned, a magnificent bird, no doubt, carefully stuffed with apples and raisins and accompanied by hot dumplings and stewed plums. Before the goose there would be a fat carp, perhaps, boiled in vinegar to a blue tint. And after the goose there would be a steaming pudding with almonds. He who found the most almonds in his puddings—and Struensee suspected that he would be the lucky one—would have to kiss all the young ladies. When the meal was over dancing would follow. There would be flirtations in the candlelight, a spicy punch to drink before a crackling fire. A stab of regret went through him thinking how little Antje Maria and her family would have in comparison to so much. Even during his boyhood in the strict pastor's home in Halle things had been far jollier than in a fisher's hut. For the first time in many years Struensee thought sentimentally about his father. He had a vision of him in a flannel house-coat with his pipe sticking out of the pocket.

He broke off his thoughts and looking about vacantly his gaze happened to fall on the family Bible, an ancient, weighty volume bound thickly in pigskin. Giving way to his swimming emotions, partly but not altogether experimenting with himself, he opened the Bible and went over to the firelight. Then he read from Luke to the children, as his father had read to him in other earlier years under like circumstances.

"And there were in the same country," he intoned, "shepherds abiding in the field, keeping watch over their flock by night. And lo, the angel of the Lord came upon them, and the glory of the Lord shone about them: and they were sore afraid. And the angels said unto them, Fear not: for, behold, I bring you good tidings of great joy, which shall be to all people. For unto you is born this day in the city of David a Saviour, which is Christ the Lord. And this shall be a sign unto you; Ye shall find the babe wrapped in swaddling clothes, lying in a manger. And suddenly there was with the angel a multitude of the heavenly host praising God, and saying, Glory to God in the highest, and on earth peace, good will toward men."

The firelight flickered over the thick, old-fashioned print. The blonde little girl and boy stood beside Struensee, breathing into his ear, looking at him closely as he read, waiting patiently until he cleared his throat. They said nothing and were still full of wonder when he clapped the book shut. Then he gave Antje Maria a gold coin from his purse, closing her fingers over it. "That's for you, little mother," he said. "Buy some milk with it, and don't forget. Now, good night, good night."

Before the little girl could thank him he had taken his bag, thrown his cloak over his arm and ducked out the door. He heard the child shout her thanks after him. The thin, high voice was echoing in his ears as he set off through the dunes. Snow had begun to fall. Striding along with strength to spare, holding his medical kit suspended from his teeth, he struggled into his cloak without bothering to halt. Overhead was a uniform ashen grayness. The Doctor was borne along by an absurd feeling of elation, a sensation so strong that at one point he made a little skip and a jump over a stony spot. In this way he swiftly maneuvered through the dunes and back to the point where his coach was standing at the roadside. The horses' heads were drooping from boredom and cold and the chilled driver in an ugly mood. Ostentatiously he slapped his arms crosswise about himself to indicate exactly how cold he was.

"Merry Christmas," Struensee greeted him and whacked him amicably on the shoulder. The driver was so taken aback that he forgot to complain. "Let's go, let's go," Struensee ordered as he climbed into the coach. "Let the horses trot. A little sweat will oil their joints. Let's get on to Luetzelburg, to have something to eat. And drink. And some women, for that matter." Laughing heartily he flung himself back into his usual corner.

Hastily the driver mounted to his perch, laid on the whip and brought the coach in motion. The horses soon worked into a fast trot. Rapidly they thrashed along through the falling snow and darkness, by snowy heath and lonely wayside cottages, rumbling over little bridges and shallow fords towards the season's pleasures at Luetzelburg.

* VI *

*I*N *FEBRUARY THE* principal streets of Altona were cleared of snow and swept clean, an event that occasioned no little amazement among the inhabitants. Bare streets in the month of February were an unheard of novelty. The City Hall was scrubbed down, the windows polished until they shone like mirrors and a long strip of red carpet laid on the main steps. Down at the harbor where seagoing folk and fishermen lived in one-story hovels just back of the wharves, a triumphal arch was erected, richly decorated with fir boughs. Between the Hanoverian coat of arms, which featured a white horse rampant, and those of Holstein, which showed a fat, grazing cow, appeared this inscription: *Vivat Regina Carolina Mathilda.* Over this device flew the Dannebrog.

The city was filled with strangers. In Struensee's house every room was crowded with friends and acquaintances of various degree. The bare bachelor's apartment smelled strongly of feminine perfumes and powders. Ladies' dressing gowns and *peignoirs* lay about the dining room, and of an evening all had to be cleared away to prepare the table for twenty guests. The housekeeper was quite distracted and wandered in confusion from one room to the other, although every evening meal, at least, was brought over from the Koenig von Preussen in Hamburg. The culinary arts of this good woman, Struensee had wisely decided, would hardly advance his social cause. In their whole lives his guests had probably not one of them ever eaten her chef d'oeuvre, sowbelly and green cabbage.

The Rantzaus were as numerous as sands of the shore, and two young ones, maidens of seventeen and eighteen respectively, were quartered in the Doctor's study. There they had scattered their baggage, which contained a vast number of combs, stockings, petticoats and more intimate articles of wear. And there they let their pet spaniels roam. On the first evening of their visit one of the busy little dogs had snuffled excitedly at the closet door. Something on the other side made him scratch like mad and emit low growls of concern. No doubt he scented a mouse, or even a rat. To satisfy their curiosity Lili and Mimi had carefully peeped inside the closet door, holding up lighted candles to the shadowy interior. There hung the man of bones, grinning eyelessly at them. In their horror they let the candles drop. Out they had fled in their nightgowns, shouting piteously for help. The whole house had rushed to their aid. Struensee had finally calmed them. It was nothing but a harmless anatomical specimen, he said. He went off with the drily clicking man of bones into the cellar. Aunt Amalie, as usual, had made a great fool of herself. "You shouldn't bury him in the cellar," she had told the Doctor. "That would be a mortal sin. Why don't you take him to the churchyard?"

The preparations which so upset the innocent city of Altona revolved about the arrival from England of King Christian's bride. She was expected daily. The nobility and court hangers-on were in Altona in hordes to make the most of a fine opportunity to present themselves to the young Queen and perhaps perform some small service for her. The catch was that the Queen did not arrive. Day after day they waited, but no sign of the newcomer from across the sea. Meanwhile everyone amused himself as much as this was possible in Altona. Struensee's hospitality was costing him a deal of money. Personally he inclined to view the whole ceremony as pretty much of a joke, though Brandt had written him from Copenhagen strongly advising him to do everything within his power to make himself known to the Queen. What can she look like, he asked himself? She must have an affected manner. Her nose will be long, her brains eider-down. His estimate of queens as a class was very low.

At last came the great day. The English man-o'-war *Medusa* warped her way at a snail's pace up the Elbe, with Christian's betrothed below decks. Salvos fired from small cannon saluted the royal passenger. A crowd had assembled amidst the long gardens and terraces flanking the river. They did not tarry long, for suddenly the February sun disappeared behind clouds and icy rain began to pour down, as if the local weather gods wished to give the foreign Queen a proper sample of their power. Quickly the disappointing news spread round that the Queen would set off by land again at once, on the King's express orders. She was to receive no one in Altona but the Marquis of Keith. The excuse for this last was that the Queen was still suffering from the effects of seasickness.

Struensee was not at all put out, rather relieved, in fact, that his home would shortly be his own again. His guests were crowded in the dining room. Each one had heard this or that, each had something a little different to report. Lili and Mimi knew for certain that the Queen was wearing a rose-colored costume richly decorated with lace, a lilac velvet jacket and a cap of the same hue. Aunt Amalie, of course, was not to be outdone, and told how the Queen's chief lady-in-waiting, Frau von Plessen, had already sent messages from Cuxhaven to Copenhagen, asking that her mistress might have a week's rest to recuperate from the voyage, but that this request had been curtly denied. To this Frau von Plessen had supposedly said with great heat: "If that selfish young fool were going to be my husband, I'd show him a thing or two, you can depend on that. He'd dance to my tune, or I'd know the reason why!" All this was probably an exaggeration on Aunt Amalie's part, for she was unable to say to whom the good lady had expressed herself with such appalling frankness. More interesting and very likely more accurate was Count Rantzau's story. Milady, he said, was once again in Copenhagen and Christian was again playing with his booted mistress, to the horror of all the ministers. It was because of Milady that they had forced Christian to have Caroline Matilda come to Copenhagen without delay, so that her curative presence might begin its work as soon as possible.

Struensee's male guests shrugged off the idea of expecting mitigation from Christian's marriage to Caroline. It was absurd, they said. What could an innocent like her offer in competition with a Milady? "But there's the charm of the ingenuous, gentlemen," Struensee commented, which made everyone titter. Lili and Mimi, for some obscure reason, found this observation very acute. They inscribed it forthwith in their diaries as a *bon mot*. Then someone brought notice that the Queen, after eating a brief lunch in City Hall, intended at once to take a coach to the capital. Struensee's guests rushed to the window just in time to see the Queen's carriage come rolling up the street. There were outriders and lackeys, and eight horses to pull the ponderous conveyance, which was set off with a gilded wooden crown attached to the roof. This most splendid carriage was followed by a dozen others of less pretentious structure, but also protected by outriders and lackeys. The coachmen had fancy galloon on their coats and huge, cockaded tricornes on their heads.

Rain was coming down in buckets, the day already darkening into a twilight. The drenched horses moved along with their heads down, the drivers shivered, hunched down in their coat collars. The procession bounced forward over the cobbles of what was optimistically called "Broad Street," a thoroughfare pitted with pot holes and so narrow a strong man could spit across it against the wind. Peering over the straining shoulders of Lili and Mimi, Struensee was moved to fancy that the procession much more resembled a funeral cortège than a bridal retinue. The weather, indeed, was good for nothing but dying. Struensee was honestly bored as he peeked with the rest into the street. Then he saw a small hand lying on the window sill of the royal coach. A diamond ring was on the ring finger of the hand. The stone was fabulously large, much too large for such a childlike hand, which seemed to be oppressed by its weight. So far as Struensee could make out in the bad light the hand lay lax and resigned on the sill. Could it be the Queen's hand, he wondered? Unquestionably, for stout Madame von Plessen would hardly have such refined appendages. Struensee was momentarily lost in thought. He became deaf to the whispering and chattering of Lili and Mimi, though they were making as much noise as a flock of starlings. He thought of Christian, whom Annette had so graphically described as a debased, uncontrolled, weak-willed adolescent. There were people, it was said, who could read meaning in hands like the gypsies. But I am not one of these soothsayers, Struensee thought. Suddenly the hand was drawn back into the coach, as quick as a flash, as if it had realized that someone was staring at it. Struensee sighed. "Looking at hands brings bad luck," he muttered to himself. "I wonder."

"Did you say something, Doctor?" Lili asked, turning her merry face up into his.

"No, no," he told her. "Nothing at all."

Caroline Matilda was glad to be back on solid earth and composed again, to be able to collect her flustered self after the strain of the sea journey, the long coach ride, the confusion of the official reception and her vague disappointment in her future husband. At this first meeting Christian, considering his quixotic makeup, had behaved quite well. Oscillating between shame and boldness, with the indispensable Holck hovering at his side, Christian had kissed her hand, made inquiries about her health and finally shown her his white poodles. To amuse her he had made them jump through rings. Then he had taken her to see his parrots and cockatoos, which were quartered in long rows in the palace conservatory among the potted trees. One of the parrot specimens spoke broken English. In a raucous monotone, with the malice peculiar to these gaudy birds, he had kept screeching: "Milady is a puss-in-boots, puss-in-boots!" The parrot had screamed his single piece over and over again, innumerable times as fast as he could get out the sounds. Really, it had not been very pleasant. But Christian had smiled and snickered behind his hand while, for some reason or other, Count Holck almost burst from the effort of restraining his laughter. It was so odd that the Queen herself laughed nervously, not really knowing why.

At the table Christian had exchanged compliments with her, responding in whispers to her own platitudes. After he had been poked in the back by Holck—Caroline Matilda caught Holck in the act, and was astonished—Christian made some observations that the bride only dimly understood. In some way they referred to her imminent status as married woman, and that made her blush and feel horribly upset.

Now, after this strange round of mummery, Caroline Matilda stood in her bedchamber in Frederiksborg, a small person with light blonde hair. She let her lady-in-waiting undo her several petticoats, and they fell, one after the other, with a soft rustle about her legs. The delicate, girlish flesh of her thighs showed between the rolled tops of her stockings and the feathery lace of her drawers. Her faintly rounded belly was bound in by smooth batiste. Her big blue eyes looked simply into space and she let out a sweet sigh of satisfaction as the maid loosened her underwaist. Breathing in deeply she made her small breasts stick out, two pink-eyed cones. A maid then brushed up her hair as she strolled slowly about the room. When the bristles caught in a tangle she winced like a child. At last, sighing sweet satisfaction, she stretched out under the bedcovers. Over her arched a canopy decorated with cherubs. She pulled the fresh, rustling batiste cover up under her chin.

But she could not sleep. She could not rid her mind of the day's confusion of impression. The bed was strange and Denmark in the spring had a strange feel. The sweet trilling of the thrushes drifted in even now through the windows. Among the images whirling through her head was one of a man's face peering out at her carriage, his face between two girl faces. As she remembered the face it had no fixed lineaments. But it was a serious, pensive countenance. She had the ridiculous notion, thinking back on it, that it was not a real face, but the incarnation of her intense homesickness.

She tried to comfort herself with thoughts of England, but could not. She could not, imaginatively, evoke the fleshy, good-humored presence of her brother, George. Her ever-solicitous mother, too, seemed hopelessly beyond reach. She felt exiled, forsaken, abandoned to indifferent fate and thought sadly how unhappy was the life of a queen. She heard the servants whispering and laughing softly in the ante-room. She listened more closely, but the women were speaking Danish and she could not make out a single word. Perhaps they were laughing at the new Queen of Denmark.

The sound of a minuet came to her from somewhere below in the palace, now strongly, now faintly. Listening to the tantalizing music the stony massiveness of the palace in which she was embedded became light and fluid. All Denmark seemed to be sinking with her into an incomparably soft and inviting sea. Presently she was fast asleep. Her full lips parted, she breathed evenly.

Christian was celebrating his impending marriage. Now that the bride was out of the way he felt his importance as a bridegroom. Holck slapped him violently on the back and cried: "Where you belong is in bed, Christian, old son, next to your little sweetmeat."

"Music, music," shouted the King. "Let's have it, you scratchers." All the ladies had to take turns dancing with him. Dizzily he staggered from one hot, grasping hand to the next. He was quite drunk, having gulped down the many glasses of champagne that Holck kept getting him. "I'm the King!" he cried out. "And I command a polonaise through the whole palace!" Christian's face was fiery pink.

"When you command, that's all there is to it, my friend," Holck said with mock truculence. "Does anybody say different?"

"Holck, you're a gem, you're a pearl," said the King. "You can read my very soul, can't you!"

"I can if you have one, my boy," Holck laughed and signaled the musicians to follow him.

They made a long, straggling procession through the corridors of Frederiksborg, up and down the staircases, through the same dim stone tunnels once traversed by Christian the Great, the one with the pointed beard like wire. Through the same echoing rooms once thronged by conquering Swedes in hip boots and feathered helmets they went. In these same rooms the Swedes had drunk themselves blind and whored until their knobby knees were weak as water. But that was all long ago. Their hoarse voices had long since been stilled. Yet intimations of a rude past hovered all through the great palace. The old walls brooded over the old days when Fredericksborg was young and the king a true king. Down below, lining the main stair-well walls, hung relics of more vital times, armor of all shapes and styles, with dangling leg and shin pieces and grated visors.

Past these iron fossils the procession went, preceded by servants bearing candelabra. Then came the fiddlers and the King's brother-in-law, Prince Karl von Hessen. Behind him was Christian, supported by Holck, then many couples bringing up the rear. Stragglers reached all the way back into the darkness of the unlighted corridors. Everyone hopped along to the jigging music, laughing, squealing and chattering wildly. The ladies' silken gowns rustled enticingly, their faces were pale as chalk under a pile of whitely powdered hair. Beauty patches were pasted to their cheeks, and looked like places where a snake had bitten and turned the flesh black. The men were gallant fellows, but almost feminine with their ornamental daggers, their prettily buckled shoes and silk stockings. At last they arrived at the door of the Queen's apartment. Prince Karl stopped short. The guests' babbling died away into a hush of curiosity.

"What's the matter up there ahead?" Christian called loudly.

"The Queen is asleep," said the Prince. "We'll be waking her."

"What of it!" said Christian. "Open the door."

"But she must be exhausted from the trip," the Prince objected.

"En avant," insisted Christian. "Let the music play."

The Prince shrugged his shoulders and opened the door. Hesitantly the procession crowded into the apartment. The maid-servants jumped up from their chairs in the ante-chamber, frightened out of their wits. Christian pushed forward through the boudoir directly into the bedroom, leaving doors open in his wake.

The Queen lay diagonally in bed, her head buried in the pillows. She awoke with a little scream of fear. Her nightcap tipped awry on her tumbled hair. Hurriedly she raised the bedclothes to cover up her exposed bosom. Her face was rather swollen with sleep and her big eyes looked almost black in the candlelight. Uncomprehending she stared at the embarrassed, yet curious, people crowding around her bed. "Who are you people?" she found the breath to say. "What do you want in here?"

"It's just me," said Christian, reeling close to the bedside. "All I want from you is a little kiss, just one. I'll let you keep count, dove." He bent down over her and his winy breath struck her nose with sickening effect. His small mouth was pursed into an odd little pimple of expectation, his eyes closed, a smirk wrinkling the corners.

The Queen ducked away. "I will not, I certainly will not," she said. She pulled back as far as the head of the bed allowed. "Get out of here," she ordered. "All of you kindly leave at once."

"I command otherwise," said Christian birdily. "I am the King."

"No, I won't," said the Queen, close to tears and looking to Prince Karl for help.

"Christian!" implored the Prince. He was panic-stricken. "Don't you think it's terribly late for this tomfoolery? Come now!"

"What do I care, what do I care about anything!" said the King. And with this he suddenly threw himself on top of the Queen, at least over her legs. "I want what's coming to me," he said vaguely. Then he looked up foolishly from his disgraceful posture and added with alcoholic gravity: "What about the law of *coram publico,* Karl, old boy? How are you people going to know whether you're getting the real article or just another little bastard? Now, be nice to me, you dear little chicken."

Caroline buried her face in her hands, and at this point, fortunately, Madame von Plessen burst into the room. In her nightclothes she was even more formidable and heavy than during the day. Her mighty chins wagged with rage, her vast bosom rose and fell. Like a rhinoceros she charged Christian, seized him by the slack of his coat and dragged him from the bed, with such vigor that he slid across the smooth floor and crashed gently against the wall. "You, you hog of a man, get out of here!" she gasped in a menacing contralto. "How dare you molest the Queen! How dare you! We'll see what England says to this, you birdikin! Don't cry, Madame, don't cry. I know how to deal with this breed. And you, Prince Karl, out of this room at once. Make way, here, make way, I say!" With wide arms she herded ladies-in-waiting, maidservants, lackeys, musicians and guests out of the apartment. The Prince and Holck dragged Christian, who kept trying to hold onto his head, along with them. Outside in the corridor he sobered up enough to say viciously: "That Plessen, that fat bag, I'll fix her. I'll banish her from the court, that's what I'll do. She can't do that to me, Holck, not by a damned sight."

"That's right," agreed Holck and yawned in the King's face.

"Holck, if the little one is so hard to get along with and is going to cry every time I want to have a bit of fun," the King said, "what's the point in being married? What are women for, if a fellow can't have a little fun with them once in a while, Holck?"

"But you've got to go about it a little more tactfully, my boy," said Holck. "There are some fortresses, you know, that can't be stormed the first try. You've got to undermine them, old fellow. See?"

"Tact?" said Christian. "What are you talking about. I'm the King, am I not?"

And the next day Madame von Plessen actually was banned from the court. Christian had insisted on it, his face green with pique and hangover.

With Madame von Plessen gone, Caroline Matilda felt terribly lonely and scared, especially after the marriage ceremony. But Christian's sister, Wilhelmina, who was married to Prince Karl, on her husband's instigation interested herself in the young Queen. Caroline Matilda turned to her new friend with an almost erotic fervor. They became inseparable, as is so often typical of newly married girl-wives. Wilhelmina was always with the Queen, at receptions, during walks, and indeed often slept in the same bed with her. She kissed the Queen at every excuse, exactly like a lover. Before going to bed she combed the Queen's hair and led her so solicitously through the gardens of Frederiksborg that Caroline called her "my cavalier."

Prince Karl was amused by this extraordinary amity, but not so Christian. When he realized that Caroline Matilda preferred his sister's company to his own, he was furious and tried to force his way between the two friends. He darkly implied a "terrible scandal" to Holck and repeatedly suggested, each time more peremptorily, that the Prince go back where he belonged in Hessia. In the end Prince Karl could not overrule the King, and so acceded to his wish. Then the Queen was alone. Now for the first time Christian attempted intimacies with her. The idea that his sister loved Caroline burned perversely in his imagination and whipped up his desire to possess the bride. He became a devoted husband and spent whole afternoons sitting on the floor beside her knees. He pretended an interest in her relatives and in her clothes. Sometimes he would stealthily enter her apartment on tiptoe and surprise her at her needlework with a kiss on the nape of the neck. Her squeaks of fright were delicious, he thought.

At last the morning came when the people of the court were able to wink and nod wisely at each other. The ladies whispered excitedly. Reventlau and Moltke bowed to each other with mock gravity. Only Count Holck was put out by the news that Christian had actually slept with his wife. Reventlau was as proud of this consummation as if he were keeper in a zoo, and Christian some surly, alien beast most difficult to serve. By afternoon all Copenhagen knew about the happening. On Sunday Pastor Muenter chose to interpret to his delighted flock the literal meaning of the Song of Songs. In contradistinction, of course, to the spiritual sense.

Copenhagen really believed for a time that Christian, the beast, was tamed. This belief became a virtual certainty in the popular mind when it was announced that the Queen was with child. Christian was now regarded as a *pater familias,* well launched on the road to being a patriarch. Sentimental folk pictured him surrounded by a dozen tots. He would be vitally concerned about their welfare and, by extension, about the welfare of his larger family, the Danish people. For in this period, of course, the state was, in a sense, the King's person greatly multiplied. The bourgeoisie, peasants and serfs all considered themselves to be distant members of the royal family.

Yet it was the Queen's pregnancy which eventually caused popular hopes to be dashed. Whether Christian was motivated by an unconscious desire to bring about the destruction of his line, as has been depicted in ancient myth, or whether it was the corrupting influence of Holck, the King gradually withdrew from his young wife as she fattened with child. He purposely avoided her company and presently left for Holstein and a round of entertainment by the provincial nobility. There were times when, fuddled by wine, he admitted that he felt he had done his duty by Denmark. The time had arrived, he said, to do some thinking about his own good for a change. Count Holck strongly seconded these opinions. Holck was again the pivot of the King's life. He sat around more like a king than the King himself, his features full, large and fair. He handed out offices and royal favor. And with Holck once more a central feature of the royal scene, Milady returned.

Milady sat in the royal box at the opera, she traveled with Christian, rode to the hounds with him and, as before, treated him like a thing, in word and deed. The folk muttered at this degraded state of affairs, Christian with a trollop while his wife was bearing him a child. In the taverns of the Fishmarket rebellious utterances were reported daily by the royal agents, likewise along the docks and throughout the whole island of Amager. In the aristocratic houses of the Kongens Nytorv and the Bredegade means were earnestly discussed of getting Christian replaced by his step-brother.

Caroline Matilda bore a son, who was named after his grandfather, Frederik. Exhausted by his bouts with Milady, nerves shattered by constant drinking, suffering from incessant nightmares and daytime delusions that bordered on full-blown paranoia, Christian took his stand in Hoersholm, a country villa belonging to the crown. Here he played games with his Negro slave and his lackeys, hide-and-go-seek and the like, until he was somewhat restored to normalcy and able to undertake new excesses with the aid of the tireless Holck. His ministers met in consultation and it was decided to send Christian off on a grand tour of the European courts. It was felt that perhaps the many new impressions and the influence of foreign princes might waken in him a now dormant sense of royal responsibility. Though he might never make a king, they reasoned, at least he might make a man of sorts.

All these events Brandt distilled into letter form for Struensee's information. To Brandt the King's behavior was a matter of paramount concern, not merely because it was so spectacular, but also because as a would-be courtier Brandt's own future depended on the keystone in the hieratic arch. If the keystone failed, the arch would fall, bringing all constituent members to the earth. Though he appreciated Brandt's position, Struensee felt in no way involved in kingly foibles, and so often threw Brandt's letters aside half-read.

Court gossip, court intrigue, the endless plotting for advantage and all the rest of the stupid farrago contrasted dramatically with the ideas simmering in Struensee. His conviction grew that it was his duty to restore justice and order in the ailing state, to supplant the feeble puppetry of the times with a new, bright reality. He was obsessed with a desire to act, to get something done, but liked to tell himself his lust for action was concerned with the promotion of justice, not with the acquisition of power. The more he came in contact with Danish fishermen, day-laborers and peasants, the more fixed became his messianic notion.

Evangelical blood throbbed in his veins, he was under the sway of an inherited compulsion to speak and be heard. Whereas Struensee's father had depended strictly on the Lutheran Bible, Christian morality and salvation through God's grace, the son depended entirely on reason and the rationalistic teachings of his century. Mankind must be redeemed not from original sin, but from the inadequacies of an outmoded social and economic order, and this through willed, planned personal effort, rather than by recourse to God's grace. Struensee, in short, was a new type of man, a revolutionary, but one able to act, the situation being what it was, only through compromise with already recognized social means and forces. Like David, he had to play the harp before destroying Saul.

Struensee's contempt for the Danish court and its swarm of parasites, however, did not extend to the youthful Queen. She is young, he told himself, she is innocent. Indeed, she is practically in the same boat as myself. Thinking this, he was touched. The fact that he was dealing with a woman who, according to all reports, was beautiful, naïve and spirited enhanced his romantic partisanship.

★ *VII* ★

*T*WO YEARS HAD passed since Brandt settled down in Copenhagen, and still Struensee was living on promises. Fairly recently Count Rantzau had succeeded in winning the favor of Saint-Germain, the minister of war. He had chanced to say to Saint-Germain: "How remarkable that such a small country should be blessed with so great a minister of war! Really, an amazing paradox!" This piece of flattery had catalytic effect and Rantzau had been reinstated as a lieutenant-general in the Danish army, the same rank he had held in the Russian service. Rantzau described his freak ascendancy in a very ironical letter to Struensee. Afterwards, no longer needing financial aid, he wrote less and less, and always more briefly.

As always Brandt sent off long letters, containing descriptions of court life heavily interlarded with protestations of eternal friendship and detail generated by a series of love affairs. His intercessions on Struensee's behalf seemed doomed to lead to no positive result.

Struensee, for his part, chafed bitterly. He saw a great future sliding slowly but surely out of his reach. He felt very definitely older and less flexible. Among many of the younger men and women he was taking on an avuncular aspect. His female patients still fell in love with him now and then, but one after the other they turned away to more concrete requitements. Even though he had done nothing to hold them it was always a heavy blow to his pride when they cooled. Like everybody else in his period he had no feeling for age, no way of coming to terms with it. Age betokened in his mind the cessation of youthful desirability, a regrettable loss of the sensual capacity to enjoy and through enjoyment keep in contact with reality. Out of fear of growing old, he began to dress with minute care. Each week he had his hair singed and curled and looked anxiously afterwards in the mirror, spying out the first gray strands.

During his long and lonely journeyings through Holstein he often had a chilling premonition that his hope of a Danish career would prove to be nothing but an idle fancy. Gripped by these cynic moods he considered all sorts of erratic alternatives. With an English merchant he talked over the possibilities of shipping out to the Orient as physician and adviser at some Indian court. For quite some time he was absolutely convinced that his future lay in India. Then he swung round to the idea that America offered him more opportunity, but this fancy did not last long. For it was obvious that in the American colonies there were no princes or courts, lacking which he could not seriously visualize any advancement for himself. He imagined that in the new world across the sea lived a population of peasants and artisans, petit-bourgeois types in gray, men of simple understanding and practicality with as little use for his *savoir-vivre* as swine for pearls. And so he let America go by the board, and turned to other parts of the map; to Spain, Portugal, Russia and the like. He wearied his head debating imagined possibilities. They lured him on, but ever escaped his grasp. Sweat gathered on his brow and his feet grew chill as he tossed and thought all the night through.

One of these hectic nights Struensee had a wonderful dream. It was not an especially complicated affair, but it left a tremendous impression. Struensee dreamed about horses playing in a summery pasture, their huge bodies arched, manes flying, splendid muscles working like pistons. The thunderous play of powerful bodies suggested the elemental, the primitively large in scale. Sportively the dream horses rubbed their long heads together and reared high on their hind legs. Their hooves flashed as they rushed across the trembling earth. High grass grew in the dream meadow, so high it tickled the horses' ribs. They dipped their muzzles into the scented green stuff, like swans dipping into water. They lashed their sides with their long tails. They were horses from some heroic time, akin to something in man's soul, something hostile to bit or curb. So strong a feeling of happiness came over Struensee in his dream that he woke up, to see the spring morning brightening his windows. Outdoors the east was gray and full of hope for a fine day. Mating birds called loudly from the hedge-rows. Struensee quickly shut his eyes that he might recapture the bright vision, but the horses had gone, lost somewhere in a summery meadow region of his deeper being. But he imagined that he could still hear the hollow thud of their hooves on the earth. With a great leap Struensee sprang out of bed, found the floor cold underfoot, dressed hastily and went out at once into the open.

It was a Sunday morning. Blue smoke spiraled thinly out of the chimney-pots of the town. The old houses leaned protectively against each other and with a hundred window-eyes seemed to be looking shyly yet trustingly into the limpid morning. At such an early hour few pedestrians were abroad, and to Struensee it seemed as if the magic of his dream had enchanted the city, as if the curious intimation of deep happiness still lurked among the trees, leafless as yet, but spangled with oily bright buds of green. The crosses in the little churchyard leaned comfortably this way and that, not caring, and on the ridge of the steep church roof, which shone silver in the slanting morning sun, two blue-gray doves balanced, with the church tower looking gravely down upon them. Bright green willows, all fuzzed with buds, drooped over the sunken grave markers and the simulated antique marble columns artistically broken off to improve the effect.

At the tavern "Zur Kugel" a globe hung from a cleverly contrived iron arm. Cool draughts smelling of stale beer slops issued from the open door and struck Struensee's nostrils in passing. The innowner was sweeping the steps with an old-fashioned besom and greeted the Doctor with a rough: "Good morning, sir!" Struensee kept on until he reached a height overlooking the Elbe.

On the slope before him were many neat little gardens marked off by green hedges or wooden palings, plots in which the provident inhabitants of Altona grew summer vegetables. Down below ran the gray Elbe, a broad band of water flowing westward towards the sea until lost in a translucent cloud of morning mist. A freshness puffed up from the river level smelling of fresh water and tar. For a long time Struensee drank his fill of the morning, happiness warming the cockles of his heart. He looked intently far off towards the west where the mighty stream debouched into the open sea. Slowly a three-master drifted downriver with the current.

Returning home hungry for breakfast, the Doctor found a letter awaiting him. It had not come by ordinary post. A special messenger had delivered it in person, his housekeeper informed him. Struensee tore open the seal and read. It was hard to believe. He had to scan the contents several times before he was convinced.

"I'm going away!" he shouted to his astonished housekeeper. He threw his arms about her shoulders, almost knocking her wind out.

Two weeks later, near Hamburg in the Ahrensburg Castle, Struensee made contact with the King's party. Christian lay abed. There, among the pillows, he decided to give the new physician an audience.

"Doctor Struensee wishes to present himself to Your Majesty," announced the chamberlain and Christian nodded assent.

Struensee bowed deeply to the King, who responded by staring at him with undisguised curiosity. Annette had correctly described Christian. He was very blond and fair of skin, his shoulders were narrow, his mouth small. The angle of the retreating forehead was emphasized by the manner in which Christian wore his hair smoothly combed back, also bringing into prominence the long, thin nose. This nose, complemented by the round, glassy eyes, gave the King a birdy look.

"I'm overjoyed, my dear Doctor," said the King. Waving his hand, he added: "This is my friend, Count Holck. And this is Baron Schimmelmann, Denmark's financial genius, you know. He sees to it that I stay within my means." Saying this he turned his stary eyes and looked pensively at the two hangers-on, who were seated near the bed. Count Holck, who sitting down looked like an Egyptian statue, could hardly be mistaken. Baron von Schimmelmann was a short, gray man of Jewish cast with keen brown eyes.

The conversation was free from the formalities Struensee had expected in dealing with an absolute monarch. Baron von Schimmelmann correctly interpreted Struensee's look of surprise. "His Majesty is traveling incognito under the name of Count von Gottorp," he explained smoothly. "He is desirous of sparing his hosts the expense of entertaining on a royal scale."

"Yes, kindly address me as Count," Christian said. "I need all the practice I can get in this Count business."

"Tell us, Doctor," Holck put in, "is there any proved means of curing dizziness, headaches and depression? And . . . well . . . unpleasant ideas? I suffer from these in the morning."

"There are several cures, so-called," said Struensee, "but only one I'll vouch for personally."

"And what is it?"

"Don't drink more than two glasses of wine the evening before."

"So?" said Holck. He pretended to be disappointed. "Why, the cure's worse than the disease."

"That I'll admit," said Struensee. "As a matter of fact, I often use homeopathic methods. Like cured by like, as they say. A small glass of wine in the morning may do the trick for you. One small glass works against many glasses, so to speak."

"Perhaps we're going to understand each other," said Holck. "Your methods attract me. And what do you do about women? Do you cure the effects of a big one by prescribing another small one?"

"Now you're leaving the field of medicine," said Struensee. "But if a patient comes to me with women troubles, I try to help him according to Aristotle's remedy. *Ne nimis.* Celibacy sours a man. It makes him fanatical and dry. On the other hand too much indulgence makes him weak and miserable. The middle way is best."

"Pastor Muenter would damn your theory as unorthodox," Holck reminded Struensee. "That is, as un-Christian."

"What do you say to that, Doctor?" said the King, ready to laugh. "Is it un-Christian?"

"Well, in our times reason has parted company with belief," said Struensee, refusing to be baited. "We don't bow our necks any more to any supposedly supernatural being. We ourselves must decide what is good and what is evil."

"Then you don't believe in God?" said Christian, the smile fading away. He rose up out of the cushions and stared blankly at the Doctor.

"God made the world, I believe," said Struensee coolly. "He gave us faculties to get along in it. But having done so much, in my opinion, He withdrew and thereafter very properly left us to our own devices."

"So you think He keeps His nose out of it?" murmured Christian. "Well, well . . ."

"Why should he not?" said Struensee, warming to a familiar subject. "Does not a watch, the mechanical product of man's handiwork, run on without the aid and supervision of the watchmaker? Is God less of a genius than a man who makes a watch? Is not the history of mankind the record of a gradual moving towards freedom of choice? Must we always have God and His surrogates do our deciding for us?"

"Freedom, you say?" said Christian. "I am the King, and even I must knuckle under. I must make concessions to my advisers, to tradition, to the institution of marriage. I'm not in the least free, Struensee, my friend, though I am a king. Though of course right at the moment I'm Count von Gottorp and things are a little bit different."

"Let's drink to freedom, gentlemen," said Holck. "How about it?"

Wine was brought in and the company drank. Presently the conversation turned to the itinerary of the trip, the courts yet to be visited, the novelties and the banquets. Like Christian, Struensee felt himself free, from the past, from his practice, from the press of worry over the future. It was early summer and traveling would be very pleasant.

The King's party continued on through Holstein, over rolling country dotted with villages of whitewashed houses with straw roofs so thick that the buildings seemed all top and no sides. They drove past innumerable well-tended garden patches, the beds geometrically measured off, the fruit trees spaced evenly in straight lines. The grain was already high and fat kine wandered about the meadows.

South of the Elbe the landscape changed. The distances between villages stretched out, the dwellings looked poorer, the gardens were smaller and carelessly tended. The roads became sandy and held back the wheels. The heaving flanks of the carriage horses ran dark with sweat. Little birches, all leaning eastward, lined the roads. Heath country billowed outward in all directions to far horizons, a dun earth dotted with broom in butter-yellow flower and clumps of juniper. Scattered among the moors were occasional sorry acres of buckwheat, sprouting meager shoots like the last hairs on an ancient's head. The smell of resinous conifers and the rough perfume of the juniper were strong in the warm midday sun.

Evenings, as the cool of night began to fall, the west wind sprang up over the wastelands. The sun sank in a great sombre glare, making a slanting half-light in which the landscape stood out in stark relief. Broad-backed hills and wide valleys like the waves of a sea transfixed suggested the prehistoric times when the country actually had been part of the ocean's bed. Deposits of salt still lay buried under the moors, some directly beneath the sparse covering of soil.

One evening after a particularly long jog the party arrived at the little town of Celle and stopped at the Castle which, together with all the heathland of Hanover, belonged to Christian's brother-in-law, the King of England. The Castle of Celle was old, dating back to the Thirty Years War. Its walls were very thick, its ceilings low. The party gathered in an octagonal room, the best the old castle offered. The walls were hung with silk tapestries and at the open windows fell long, blue drapes, these just now pulled aside because of the sultriness of the night. The curtains lifted in gentle puffs of wind, harbingers of a storm that was rumbling and growling over the dark horizon. Someone seemed to be looking through the windows, first through this one, then through that.

Had there really been a ghostly peeping-tom he would have seen nothing but four men eating about a round table, each elegantly garbed in a silk jacket, four tired, well-groomed, rather spoiled creatures to all appearances. They handled the silverware very expertly and expertly raised the thin goblets of wine to their lips.

After the meal the King's party lingered about the board. No one had any desire to rise and seek his bed. More burgundy was drunk, but instead of lightening the bibbers' hearts it made them more leaden. Holck was moved to relieve the heavy spell by broaching his favorite topic—women. Without women to talk about Holck, indeed, would have passed for a mute.

"I find it curious," he said with a malicious grin, "that we should never tire of women. It's always the same old song in the grass, when you stop and think, and the same old song, though it's a catchy tune, I grant, does get to be a bore. All the little deceptions, the caresses, the grapplings—why, a man gets to know them by heart. Why isn't there more variety in love, Doctor? Can you riddle me that one?"

"It's the economy of nature," Struensee told him. "Even Baron Schimmelmann could not be more penurious. Nature's concern is to have us reproduce, not to enjoy ourselves. On the other hand nature has given us reason, to help us survive. So the epicure uses reason to create variety in love. Of course, that's going against nature."

"Make it clearer," said Holck. "Are you talking about Plato?"

"If you like, I am," said Struensee. "He offers two kinds of love. There's the Athenian kind, that he didn't think much of. Then there is the real Platonic form, which Socrates learned from Diotima."

"As for me, I like neither," said Holck. "Athenian love turns my stomach and to my mind there's little to choose between Platonic love and impotence. Don't you know any other kinds?"

"Well, there is always the Marquis de Sade," said Struensee.

"I'd forgotten about him," said Holck. "Tell us something about the fellow, Doctor."

"I'm afraid I can't," said Struensee. "I'm a physician, not a pornographer."

Christian had been taking in the conversation with all his might. His fishy blue eyes hung on Struensee's lips. His weariness had vanished. Over-eagerly, hands trembling on the table-edge, he thrust himself into the discussion.

"I know what the Doctor means," he said with pride. "I've made love with use of reason. It's very strange. Let me tell you about it."

"But, Christian," objected Holck, "isn't it too late to begin telling stories?"

"What does time matter when we're all together," said the King. "Don't be a spoilsport, Holck. Pour yourself some wine and drink up. I know a woman . . . see how discreet I am, Holck . . . I know a woman whom I won't name by name. This woman has a beautiful white skin. And royal blood, mind you. You can see it in her manner, her very being. She goes around wearing little shoes and a white crinoline. She holds her nose up in the air. Not out of pride or because her brother is a king. It's not that at all. She's proud because she's innocent and chaste. She is really untouched, I'd bet my neck on it. She's an Artemis. She's coy, hard to get at. She doesn't belong in this world at all, Holck. Only the lace hem on her dress comes in contact with the vulgar world. Her cool eyes, her round arms, her little breasts . . . well, all the rest of her, I mean, will have nothing to do with it . . ."

"In that case," Holck interposed, "why waste your wind talking about her?"

"Never mind," said Christian. "Wait and you'll see. Now, there's something insulting about innocence, I find. It's a sort of chronic condemnation of myself and my friends. This damnable mistrust of her! And really she's hardly aware of how she looks to others. No, I say to myself, it can't go on like this. His Majesty the King looked down on in his own house? By a little girl only sixteen years old?

"I see I have to do something to remedy matters. But what can I do? Innocence won't be melted. It's diamond hard. Her eyes are so proud, not intentionally, but naturally proud. The look in her eyes makes her unimaginably attractive to me. It cuts into my feelings like a razor. And so I think to myself, wait, young lady, wait. But aloud I say, you don't seem to care for me very much, do you, my dear?

"No, she says truthfully. It makes her blush to say it. Very lovely, of course, just like a shepherdess on Meissen china. No, I don't dislike you, she says, I just don't know you very well. Or words to that effect.

"Oh, but you will know," I think to myself. A day will come! Out loud I sigh reproachfully and leave the room. She's sitting with her ladies. I drop my head to show her how badly she has hurt my feelings.

"I see that I have unsettled her. You know how children are upset by what puzzles them. She begins to look at me all the time when she thinks I'm not looking. She turns red suddenly for no reason at all. She eats less, she just nips at her wine. In the evening while the music is playing, she glances my way all the time, smiling to herself. But I keep to the other side of the room, my eyes lowered as if I were suffering. When I see that she is keeping time to the music with her toe, I bow slightly, my hand over my heart. Sad, devoted, hopeless. In short, I play the fool in great style.

"You may think this laughable, Struensee, but I'm telling you the gospel truth. The girl gradually comes to think that I'm simply mad about her, so overcome by my passion that I can't talk or think straight. She then commences to do everything that might make the next step easier for me. She smiles at me, she feeds my parrots, she holds the rings while my poodles are doing their tricks. That sort of thing. She floats at my side like a breath of lavender. She tells me about her childhood, if you can imagine it. About her mother, her brothers, her big garden, about the sheep with the silk collars around their necks. About no end of things that bore me sick. But I listen as if she were a philosopher of philosophers. Wonderful, I say, wonderful. And pretty, it must have been lovely. All that rot.

"Sometimes she lets her hand fall over mine and looks at me with her eyes rolled up. Why, gentlemen, they're as big as saucers. Imagine, this goes on for weeks. And the longer it lasts, the more the prize glitters, the more perfectly I develop my policy of harass and retreat. You see?

"Now, to cut the story short, one night I find myself in her room. She's very tender. The pullet is cooked to a turn and ready to eat. She tells me I may have her, if I like. Of course I do. Then, immediately afterwards, before I've rested my back, she begins to moralize. First she talks in parables, then more directly. All the time I'm pretending I cannot follow her argument. She regrets my nightly carousing, she says. She doesn't like me to go to dives. She doesn't think it's right for a king to sleep with wharfside whores. And so on and so on, *ad nauseam*. She ends up by laying into Milady. That beast, she says, that monster ought to be driven out of Denmark.

"All this while I am smiling vaguely at her. A candle is burning on the night-table and I can see her face. Her cheeks are all rosy with sincerity, her hair is loose. Her hair's darker at night, by the way. And all the time a little idea is snuggling in back of my head.

"Gradually I stop smiling, though I can hardly stop grinning when

I think how anyone can be so silly as to imagine that sleeping with me makes her my keeper. So I pull back on the pillows, straighten up in bed and make a very, very thoughtful face.

"What's wrong, Christian, she asks?

"I sigh. Don't you think your admonitions go a little too far, my sweet, I say to her. Aren't you just a tiny bit presuming?

"She turns pale. She looks at me incredulously. I've done my duty by you as king and man, I point out to her, so what more do you want? It doesn't give you the right to treat me like one of my poodles. Here, Christian, come, do this. Come, Christian, do that. Jump through the hoop, darling. No! Don't do that. Why, I'm a man in my own right, I tell her.

"Then you don't love me after all, she groans. Do you?

"Well, I think you're very gentle and very nice, I assured her. In fact, considering your inexperience, I find you extremely desirable. But . . . ! Then I laughed at her.

"Now she begins to act. She flings her hands up to cover her face. Very dramatic, believe me. I feel like a strumpet, she says. Oh, I'm a . . . a . . . Bag, I finished for her? That makes her jump right out of bed. You might think a scorpion had nipped her you know what, gentlemen. She wraps herself in her negligee. I shan't see her twinklers any more, you see, no, I shan't, not a one. Nor her pretty little tummy. She's terribly worked up. I hate you, she hisses, I dessssspise you! All sorts of things like that. What a rigmarole!

"At your command, my dear, I say, and get up to leave in all my royal dignity. She now gives me a punch in the kidneys with her pretty little fist. To hurry me out, of course. I nearly fell flat on my face, or pretended to, at any rate.

"I hate you, I hate you, she keeps on squeaking. Such a little bat! She tries to hold back the tears. She shakes her fist at me. I'd never have thought the doll has so much passion in her. Now I almost like her. Wasn't it odd? So much passion! Her face is all twisted and swollen with tears. Really utterly delightful. My heart begins to thump and heave like an earthquake. And when I was really making love to her I was as unmoved as if chewing tripe. I kneel at her bed. I fold my hands and beg. My dearest, I say, my lovely little one, my precious, please let me stay, please, please let me stay and play with you some more. Will you? Oh, please do let me stay and have some fun.

"At this juncture she strikes me in the face. Quite hard. Get out, she shouts, I'm no toy.

"That's what you think, I say to myself. And with that unheard remark, gentlemen, I leave the room.

"So there you have my variation on love, one that Plato didn't think of. It works and it's very refreshing. Yes, women must be kept in their proper place, gentlemen."

Struensee looked at Schimmelmann, who coolly shrugged his shoulders at the King's peculiar revelations.

"Oh, so that's how you feel," Christian laughed. "You don't think much of my compositions, do you! Especially the good Doctor. And you, Holck? Is it *et tu, Brute* with you, my dear chap?"

That night Struensee had great trouble finding sleep. Over his head he heard restless pacing footfalls until the morning grayed. Unquestionably they came from the King's quarters.

The following evening the party arrived in Hanover, where they passed the night in the enormous Schloss an der Leine, the Castle-on-the-Leine. The furniture, the candelabra and statues were all covered with dust-cloths for the King of England seldom visited his ancestral home. The odor of the past lingered in the cool halls and corridors, of past feasts, of faded perfume and the faded scent of candle fumes. But the odor had a saddening rather than pleasing effect. The huge castle was populous with the ghosts of dead kings and electors, of once vital but now completely forgotten court ladies and favorites. In this window embrasure the young Count Koenigsmarck might have kneeled at his Queen's feet. Through the long galleries, where the walls were hung with portraits by the Flemish masters, the wise Sophie Dorothea might have wandered in the company of Baron Leibniz, philosopher and savant, listening to him tell her in his careful French all about the monads. And this while, no doubt, not really following his abstractions, she might have been thinking of her niece, Elizabeth Charlotte of the Palatinate, a simple, hearty girl transplanted in the luxurious court of the Sun King.

But now they were all gone, lovers, queens, electors and philosophers alike. Only the pictures that they had looked at, the chairs they had sat on, the tables where they had eaten were still there, like empty shells on the shore from which the soft, living parts have long since disappeared.

The travelers next came to Bad Pyrmont, where fashionable ladies and gentlemen strolled about the park in their finery and drank saline waters from the warm springs. This bright gathering bowed and nodded to the passing retinue like so many puppets, for they were well aware of the real identity of Count von Gottorp. Christian experimented with a glass of the curative waters, took one mouthful and spat it out. "Wine suits my taste better than this loathsome stuff," was his comment. Many women looked hard and long at Struensee and told themselves that he was just the well-built sort of man for a night's pastime, could they get their hands on him. So unlike their own husbands, the fat, gouty husbands of Bad Pyrmont.

The king's party moved steadily westward. The moors leveled off into marshland. On all sides there were pools and streams of water, grassy dikes and wooden bridges. The soil of the region was thick and heavy. The peasant houses had a prosperous look. The windows shone with cleanliness, and on the sills, set off by snowy curtains, were potted tulips, geraniums and hyacinths. Clean brick floors were strewn with sand, the simple furniture was highly polished. This was the Netherlands, the blessed country of Holland.

Struensee was much impressed by the Dutch country folk in knee pants, knitted stockings and coats with silver buttons as large as thalers. They bore themselves with great dignity and self-assurance. When they took off their black hats to salute the royal cortège, there was no slavish submission in the gesture. The essential misery of the German territories did not carry over into the Netherlands. The Dutch cities also bespoke prosperity and a solidly established bourgeois life. The houses were large compared to the German ones familiar to Struensee, and were all made of neat red brick. The streets were straight as a die and bordered by elms, the churches were of simple, cleanly white Calvinistic inspiration.

After the Netherlands came England, a new land entirely. Struensee had never seen so much humanity as in the streets of London. Craft of bewildering variety trafficked up and down the Thames. The bowsprits of three-masters projected inward over the docks, sails hung loosely furled drying out on the yards. Many of these ships had been to the East Indies, to the Antilles, the American colonies, to Brazil and to Portugal. It was very exciting for Struensee, the landsman. About the wharves there hung a powerful scent compounded of the odors of coffee, tar, rum, carnations, dried hides and a hundred other products from strange places, an exotic and yet attractive smell which seeped through the whole city, into the counting rooms, the inns and the coffee-houses. For the Thames, though its waters stank and were yellowed by commerce, was like a great artery pumping life-blood throughout the entire country. Shipping nourished the city, made it spread out steadily in vast reaches under foggy skies, always encroaching into the quiet green fields of the English countryside. From the docks all sorts and shapes of humanity, brought thither by ship, spread out into the city, Negroes, Chinese, Malays and turbaned Hindus.

Christian and his entourage were quartered by royal command in Buckingham Palace. At this time the Palace lay on the outskirts of London, surrounded by broad gardens and lawns where fat George and his German wife and daughters liked to stroll. Struensee had a great deal of time on his hands during the English sojourn. Christian had inclined to avoid his company since the confessional evening in Celle.

Struensee made the most of his freedom by visiting the display of anatomical specimens at the Royal College of Surgeons. He wandered through Hyde Park, where the young bucks and light women met in rendezvous while children played and sheep grazed quietly on the green grass. Evenings he often went to the theater, but it was hard for him to keep track of the complications taking place behind the footlights, since his knowledge of English was very limited. He preferred to go to the coffee-houses and look over the *habitués*. They sat about tables smoking churchwarden pipes, talking incessantly and incessantly drinking cups of coffee. Then he regretted his ignorance of the language, particularly because he had to sit to one side without contributing a single idea to the melee. And his regret was never so keen as one night when, sitting just outside a circle of animated conversation, he saw an awkward giant of a man come into the room, a titan with his wig awry and his coat hanging like a sack. This man proved to be a magician of words, or so it seemed to Struensee. For at once he took charge of the talk, and was heard with the gravest attention by the rest, among whom sat a red-haired fellow with Irish features, flanked by pretty, young trollops. The Irishman said nothing, but looked volumes of amusement and appreciation, as the untidy man, bursting with conviction of his own absolute rightness, talked so long and so loudly that the whole room gradually turned in his direction, the waiters becoming rooted where they stood, napkins dangling forgotten.

In this instance it would have paid Struensee to know English, for later he learned that he had seen and heard the "Sage," the English Socrates, Dr. Samuel Johnson. Like his Athenian prototype he amused, charmed, rallied his fellows, out in the street, in tavern, coffee-house, attic and drawing room, quite indifferent to the physical situation. The great man had written *Rasselas, Prince of Abysinnia* and published the *Rambler,* copies of which Struensee hastened to purchase as souvenirs of the trip.

Struensee could sense freedom in the very air of London. He could not fathom whence it came, what made London so different from any other place he had ever known. Did it originate in the very size of the metropolis? Each day he wandered out among the crowds, laying himself open to all impressions, trying to read the mystery of the crowd's face. Did freedom come in some fashion from the ships, from the proximity of the sea and the watery highways to distant places, did it derive from the fact that London was the maritime crossways of the world? Gradually Struensee came to believe that the atmosphere of individual freedom was generated by the political attitudes of the people, especially as realized in the House of Commons. Here in England, as in Denmark, there was the glitter of pure privilege. There were dukes and lords who dwelt in arrogant, columned palaces, whose women wore precious stones, who were attended by fat priestly people. Here, as in Denmark, there was abysmal poverty, especially in quarters of the city lying along the Thames, where it was dangerous to walk at night alone and unarmed. Yet both rich and poor were but ancillary to the great mass of bourgeois, these ranging through all stations from affluence to respectable indigence. Peacefully, steadily these folk worked out their lives, going about their affairs as regularly as clockwork.

And the press, Struensee was quick to remark, was astonishingly free. What could not be uttered in the newspapers on the censor's account came out full force in pamphlet form, or dramatized on the stage, or depicted in satirical etchings and drawings. Across coffee table and shop counter the people talked much as they pleased. Unlike Danes or Germans, they did not whisper when they described the King's deficiencies, dissatisfaction in the American colonies, the fate of the Stuart clan, the strange affection of Chesterfield for his very ordinary son. Even the divinity of Christ was freely debated, a circumstance that quite took Struensee's breath away.

Yet in actual fact England's true, and subtle, nature largely escaped Struensee. The idea of freedom hovered in the very air, exactly as Montesquieu and Voltaire had said. And yet Struensee, the idealistic man of reason, did not really see that beyond politics the English were a mercantilist people, desirous of a condition of freedom everywhere in the western world in order that they might unrestrictedly pursue commerce on land and sea. Struensee contented himself with recognizing England's political climate. He told himself at once that his duty was to spread this English parliamentary concept of freedom throughout the European continent, beginning with Denmark.

In this limited respect Struensee's English stay was instructive and of definitive importance in shaping his future actions. Fate was slowly tightening a net about him. In this period it became inexorably knotted, though Struensee was no more aware of it than a man is aware of his ultimate mortality as he moves about the house and home where he is destined to breathe his last.

Baron von Schimmelmann was busy with dealings that carried him to the banks and countinghouses of the City. Count Holck stuck close by Christian, who was behaving himself under the eyes of his brother-in-law, the potent King of England. Struensee was present when Christian gave the actor Garrick a gold snuff-box decorated with his, the Danish King's, miniature. In Christian's honor Garrick had given a performance of Hamlet, which he had found exceedingly boresome. Struensee himself had not properly grasped the meaning of the tragedy, though by this time he was well enough acquainted with the English language to appreciate to some degree the baroque power and flow of Shakespearian imagery.

Before his wondering eyes Shakespeare had conjured up a maelstrom of fate, which whirled its victims about helplessly in dizzy circles, always keeping them away from the smooth, mysterious center of the turbulence. He watched Hamlet, poised in frustration until, the equilibrium of the maelstrom changing, he kills the first person to encounter his explosive release into action. How well Garrick played Hamlet, how artfully he feigned madness, how significant his clowning. How he laid on with language as if it were a whip, thrashing and striping himself and others with words. How awful his descent into a bottomless abyss of despair.

Yet Struensee only partially responded to the dramatic miracle unfolding before his eyes. He leaned forward intently in his seat next to Christian's, then drew back as he struggled to understand and failed. Hamlet's outcry against the haphazard workings of fate seemed irrational to Struensee, unworthy of a prince, somehow irresponsible. Nothing here, he saw, of Corneille's lucent causalities, of Racine's somberly methodical passions. No stately alexandrines to veil the primordial. With Racine, Phèdre could even love her step-son, Hippolyte, and not offend, so remote and dignified was the setting.

Struensee essentially failed to see that a veritable piece of the natural process was being played out for his delight and pain. As a child of the enlightenment, a disciple of the encyclopedists, he was quite out of touch with nature in the Shakespearian vision. When the soul of man was bared to the last roots and brought ruthlessly out into the light of day, it was too much for Struensee's powers of comprehension. He did not see, for example, that the freedom he so passionately adored was expressed far more clearly in the plays of Shakespeare than in Rousseau's sentimental idylls. He failed to understand that freedom has a tragic, demonic, paradoxical character, and no humanistic attitude to be put into effect through plans. Or by any stroke of the pen, as Christian had once feebly imagined in the instance of the Danish serfs.

But in spite of Struensee's lukewarm reaction to Shakespeare, at least one bit of verse from Hamlet lodged permanently in his mind. Indeed, it bored into him like a worm into an apple. "The time is out of joint! O, cursed spite, that I was ever born to set it right." So it went. These two lines, though their meaning became abundantly meaningful to him only at much later date, salvaged some of Hamlet for him.

In September the royal junketeers moved on to the famous University of Oxford, where an honorary doctorate was conferred on Struensee. Conscious of its own importance, Oxford received foreign scholars and celebrities with scant show of cordiality. Struensee's head was not turned by his new doctor's cap and gown. He knew very well that they commemorated his being part of the entourage of the English King's brother-in-law, not his medical achievements.

Shortly after this ceremony the party sailed from Southampton. The flat English coast, the last prominence of the Isle of Wight, sank beneath the horizon. The Channel's choppy seas imparted a sickly agitation to the vessel. Christian lay on a broad couch in his luxuriously appointed cabin, the coats-of-arms of Denmark and England paired overhead. His arms and legs hung lax, like a dying beast's, the cold sweat rained down his pale forehead. Repeatedly the King vomited. "I'm going to die," he groaned. "I know I'm going to die." Before leaving Southampton, overriding Struensee's express advice, he had drunk port wine with Holck, who also lay prostrate on the deck above.

Struensee, himself rather queasy, stood by Christian's couch while a servant held water to his lips. "It will soon be over," he comforted the King. He talked to him as if he were a child, and arranged the cushions so he could lie with his head partly raised. "Try it like this for a while," he said. Christian looked straight into his physician's eyes, and felt the impact of Struensee's warming and strengthening glance. The vitality in the dark blue eyes flowed through the King's weakling body, a phenomenon so often experienced by the Doctor's female patients. Christian even tried to smile, but the effort was too much. His lids closed and he murmured: "Don't ever leave me, Struensee." The Doctor looked closely at his seasick sovereign, lying propped up before him like a corpse on display in a coffin. The King's eyelids were bluish, the cheeks and temples hollowed. The birdlike nose seemed to have grown much longer in distress, and there was peevishness and malice in the tiny mouth.

It was really the first time that Struensee had ever examined the royal features in repose. Others, for reasons of discretion, would have turned away, but Struensee took full advantage of his medical prerogatives. Greedily he analyzed the pallid face on the pillows. It revealed beyond any mistaking the weary decadence of the stock from which Christian had sprung. It showed weakness and at the same time an impersonal sort of toughness and lust for life. Racial traits existed at odds with weakly individual ones. The contrast between carnality and impotence was almost touching. The King resembled a downy young bird of prey fallen from the nest and lying defenseless on the ground.

Mingled with the King's youthfulness already there were alarming signs of age, of quarrelsomeness and cynicism in the sucked-in corners of the mouth, in the narrow, boneless chin. Over the whole visage, spread like a delicate veil, was a quality that isolated the sleeper from the rest of mankind, a veil of chronic anxiety.

Struensee turned away and nodded to the servant to leave his post by the cabin door. Then he climbed up on deck, where the wind was blowing in strong gusts, forcing him against the rail. He breathed deeply, ridding his lungs of the sickly stuffiness of the cabin. As he stood there braced and looking out over the gray chop of the Channel, whether suggested by the whistle of wind in his ears, or by the crying of the gulls, the words of the play once again ran through his mind, as clearly as if someone had spoken them to him. "That I was ever born to set it right!" Swaying in keeping with the vessel's violent corkscrew motion, Struensee walked past Holck, who still lay groaning on the bare deck. He did not even glance down at him. Overhead the sails snapped and cracked in the wind with the sound of musket shots. He made his way to the bow. Far off in the distance he could see faint outlines in the blue-gray of the hilly shore. It was Normandy. The birthplace of conquerors, so they said.

★ VIII ★

FEW VOYAGERS, APPROACHING France by sea from the west, fail to be keenly disappointed. There are little towns with very dirty streets, houses that are neither white nor gray but some indeterminate soiled color in between, shutters hanging so precariously that it seems the first wind storm will surely tear them away. Nor is the land itself very attractive. There are row on row of hedges enclosing tiny fields, scanty stands of trees and low peasant houses. An occasional manor house or chateau looms white against the skyline. Some of the larger farms, squatting behind fieldstone walls, look like forts carried down from primitive times.

Struensee in his day expected great things of France, and was bitterly let down at first view. He had pictured the country romantically and materially, in terms of Versailles and the exciting boulevards of Paris. He had looked forward to elegant forms, sparkling wit, splendid buildings, pretty women and none of these things was to be seen in grim Le Havre. There was little to choose between Norman and Holstein peasants. The women were blonde and unpromising, anything but adapted for gallant adventures. French wine, however, was cheap and strong. In this regard, at least, Struensee was not disappointed. But to his amazement he soon found out that the people of the immediate countryside did not drink wine at all, but a sour, retchy fluid called cider.

If Le Havre and environs were a disappointment, the country between the port and the capital was a nightmare, not so much the landscape itself as the people who moved about on it. They looked like wild beasts, these French peasants. They were clothed in rags,

blackly unwashed, shaggy brutes. They lived in sod houses that a
Flathead Indian would have scorned. Their speech was rough and
marred by heavy gutturals. Their peculiar dialect seemed to have as
little connection with La Fontaine as Sicilian gibberish with Horace.
Indeed, it was a sort of ur-tongue, the universal dialect of destitution
and misery. The poor were at once inhumanly abject and inhumanly
bold. Women stretched out earth-colored hands to the coaches, begging alms. Children bit each other like dogs and rolled on the
ground to be rid of their fleas. The men stood off to one side, mute
and sinister, their naked feet and shanks crusted with earth like so
many children of Cadmus. If someone in the royal party tossed them
a few coins the women fought for them madly and, having got
them, pressed clenched fists to their breasts. During the performance
the men looked hangdog at the ground. But as soon as the carriages
were again in motion, they shouted imprecations at the retreating
wheels. They directed their anger especially at the coachmen and the
lackeys. Struensee found himself being looked at with eyes glittering
with hate and curiosity. He was heartily glad when this leg of the
journey was done and he was safe in Paris.

There, at last, he saw the towers of Notre Dame looking down
on the ancient Ile de la Cité, the great mass of the cathedral hulking
like a huge animal ready to spring. At last he saw the famous bridges
over the Seine, and the Louvre, the markets, the thickly settled
height of Montmartre. Everything was much like what Struensee had
always imagined, though not quite the same. The suburbs pressed
suffocatingly on the inner city. He was particularly struck by populous Saint-Antoine, in the midst of which rose up the Bastille, a
formidable bulk of gray stone menacing the whole city. The Parisian
bourgeois impressed the Doctor as uncommonly ill-tempered and
unwilling in the performance of their daily duties. No more in Paris
than in Le Havre, so far as he could see, were there any signs of that
lively spirit and elegance of manner he had heard so much about.
Indeed, an angry, uneasy watchfulness and rage suppressed marked
Frenchmen as a whole.

What Struensee felt so ominously was the life-rhythm of the
metropolis, the tremor in the mighty heartbeat symptomatic of catastrophe. As a foreigner with nerve-ends as yet not blunted by habitua-
tion he was much more conscious of the unrest of the times and
coming revolution than any Parisian native. He may even have
exaggerated the atmosphere of crisis. His own prejudices tricked him
into half-believing that any day, even while he was there, the people
would rise up, brandish their pikes and attack in freedom's name.

In this respect he was grossly mistaken. Elegance still had a
strong hold on the city; wit and cleverness still flourished in certain
quarters and *effeté* forms of love were still very much at a premium

where they could be afforded. In the garden of the Palais Royal could be found a thousand replicas of Rameau's famous nephew. Paris still harbored many exemplars of the amoral, cynical types described by Diderot in his cabinet of curiosities. Beaumarchais' lively characters still smirked and giggled on the stage at their counterparts in the audience. In the salons, under the soft, gold-framed etchings, Parisian high society discussed Helvetius' interpretation of the intellect, Buffon's writings on the animal kingdom, the doings of Manon Lescaut. And as always the talkers strove to attain smooth diction, scintillation, paradox. There was no apparent desire to get at the roots of things, excepting in the case of the Sorbonne pedants. A *bon mot* by Gallieni, a sharp aside by Chamfort was more significant in these upper circles than La Bruyère's observations on character or Rousseau's ideas on the origin of the state. And yet, in a roundabout, debased fashion, at least, the savant of Genf was given recognition in the Bois and the gardens of Versailles. His bucolic idyll was imitated in pageants distinguished by such props as beribboned shepherd's crooks and floppy straw hats for the girls.

The austerity of the days of La Fronde and Port-Royal had vanished in favor of idle play. Great thoughts had degenerated into pretty soap bubbles of fantasy, feeling into dalliance. The Parisian world was shot through with debacle. Many were aware of the coming storm, but they were either too weak to do anything about it— a weakness expressed in cynicism—or were so stupid as to imagine that impending catastrophe would be an exhilarating change, forgetting that the end of their society would also mean the end of their mortal selves.

In Paris Christian used his incognito much more intensively than in London, for here he planned to relax methodically and no critical brother-in-law shadowed him. His party took rooms in the Hotel York. The manager, knowing perfectly who Christian really was, received his visitor and entourage with the involved bowing and scraping reserved for royal guests. Christian ignored him and was annoyed when he insisted on asking whether the Count von Gottorp was satisfied with his rooms. They were the very best in the house, he kept on saying, the very best in Paris. Holck did all the talking. "Well, they're no worse than the ones we had in London," he said loutishly. "But the London ones were a hog-pen." Then he gave the manager a smart clout on the back. The man was radiant with delight at such a violent display of aristocratic good fellowship.

Hardly were they installed in the Hotel York when a commotion arose in the vestibule. Doors were flung open. In filed a whole company of lackeys led by a man ceremoniously holding a sealed letter in his hand. Smiling a honeyed professional smile the messenger presented himself to Christian, who had withdrawn in confusion behind the protective mass of Holck. "To the Count von Gottorp," said the messenger, his smile playing like a sun. "To the Count von Gottorp from His Majesty the King. His Majesty desires the pleasure and honor of the Count von Gottorp's company this evening at Versailles." The court lackeys had formed two long lines. At the head of each stood a chief flunkey wearing a firecracker-red coat and on his head an enormous wig. In his hand he bore a gilded staff, symbol of the royal dignity. The flunkeys all seemed to have fat white faces which they could compose in thoughtful folds of deference. Hotel guests gathered in the mezzanine to watch the show. Agog with curiosity they leaned over the balustrades.

Holck read the King's message aloud. The whole vestibule was densely pervaded with the odor of a sweet perfume. On the ceiling above cherubs fondled and kissed each other. The women in the mezzanine showed a great deal of white breast. Their hair fell softly on powdered shoulders. It was a curious tableau.

Christian scratched his buzzing head. "Well, I'll go," he said to Holck, then quickly added: "Oh, Holck, ask the fellow if it's true they hunt naked women in the Versailles park instead of deer. Ask him if we'll do that, will you?" The onlookers in the mezzanine tittered at this piece of Scandinavian gaucherie. The lackeys' faces did not move a muscle. Instead Holck told the messenger that the Count von Gottorp welcomed the invitation as a signal honor. He was looking forward impatiently to making His Majesty's exalted acquaintance. Christian would have liked to get in a word but Holck, having bowed out the French King's emissary, pushed Christian ahead of him out of sight into the interior of the suite, Struensee and Baron von Schimmelmann following dutifully behind. The crowd lingered in the mezzanine. The albino Dane, they told each other, was a curious animal.

That evening at Versailles for the first time in his life Struensee was actually overawed. He hardly dared to move, his throat was choked with awe. He kicked himself for it, but the feeling of intimidation would not pass. The great room shimmering with candlelight, the innumerable mirrors multiplying the salon into an infinity of salons, may have largely evoked his awe. The play of the famous fountains, for these had been turned on in honor of the royal guest and now filled the place with their monotonous, soft rushing, also may have contributed to Struensee's response of fearful wonderment. The guests themselves, their chilly smilingness, their studied movements, neatly chosen words, the knife-edge precision and speed of the French language which fell from their tongues were hardly calculated to put the provincial physician at his ease. The ladies, he thought, were unbelievably arrogant and forward. They wore black beauty spots on their enameled cheeks, their eyes were cool, their mouths cruel and disillusioned. The men had raddled features, from which any original capacity for expressing real human feeling had long since been eradicated by intrigue, financial chicanery and a relentless struggle for advantage. Nothing was left but a mask of false amiability, hiding emptiness and chronic discontent. Sodom and Gomorrah in silks and satins, thought Struensee, the still prosy pastor's son. He fought back his rebel sentiments, and blushed to think that some keen glance might have read his mind. This certainly is not the sort of world I'd like to see in Denmark, he told himself very secretly, and with that let the tide of the evening carry him along.

The Doctor was presented to the French King with the rest. Louis drawled a perfunctory greeting without even looking at his guest. Old, almost toothless and hardly able to walk without the support of a cane, the King still played at being a young man. His cheeks were rouged, his wig was immaculate atop his bald head. So powerful was tradition, so charismatic the French crown, that Struensee scarcely noticed the fatuity of the whole exhibition. In genuine humility like everyone else he bowed deep before the demi-god.

Christian was in high spirits and appeared to be conducting himself impeccably. It was not, however, the evening at Versailles which had buoyed him up, but the prospect of an inspection of Parisian night-life under the guidance of Holck. In keen anticipation of unforgettable revelations he put on his best manners for a few hours and actually behaved something like a king.

Louis indicated a lady with powdered hair, flushed cheeks and unnaturally bright eyes, talking some distance away to a group of men. He asked Christian how old he thought the lady might be. "That's the Marquise de Tinville," the monarch said. "What should you guess her age to be, my brother?"

Christian stared his blue-eyed stare. The lady in question had fine thighs and rounded knees. Her little feet were shod in high-heeled golden shoes. "I should say she was about thirty or so, Your Majesty," said Christian. "Perhaps not quite thirty."

"Well, you're wrong, sir," the King assured him triumphantly. He was delighted. "I must disappoint you, my dear brother," he continued. "The Marquise is fifty years old. Indeed, she has grandchildren, though I can't say she cherishes the brats, if what I'm told is true."

"That seems to prove, Your Majesty, that no one ever ages at your court," said Christian.

"Thank you for the compliment, brother," said Louis. "But let me tell you it's no easy matter keeping a youthful air. Do everything to preserve your youth, my son. You'll never regret it. Between ourselves, the Marquise has the whitest body in Versailles. She's unquestionably the most accomplished lover in Paris. If there is any refinement she does not know, I am not Louis. Yes, it just shows what can be done." And seeing Christian's greedy, vague smile, he said: "You think I'm jealous? Not this time, brother, not this time."

"Your Majesty is very kind," said Christian. "I shall try to follow your excellent suggestions. I've always taken Your Majesty as a model, if you will forgive the impertinence."

"Very good," said Louis. He took a good look at Christian. His old, wicked, wise French eyes were narrowed slits. "Very interesting," he murmured.

Shortly after this royal exchange Struensee caught sight of Christian bent over the durable Marquise. He was carrying on an animated conversation. The Marquise was leaned back in her chair, looking at the Danish King with obvious invitation in her saucery eyes. The pupils had been mydriatically dilated with belladonna, Struensee saw.

Watching this curious travesty of flirtation it suddenly seemed to Struensee that the candles were not burning so brightly as they had. The fountains seemed to be splashing more loudly, portentously, for some reason or other. The monotonous repetition of the mirrors, the artificially extended space, all at once impressed Struensee as a stupid, gratuitous lie. Strongly he felt the brittleness of the Versailles world, ruled by a decayed king who rouged his cheeks like a three-franc whore, where grandmothers plotted carnal adventure with a boy. Outdoors, all about Versailles, among the clipped hedges, the statues and the fountains lurked in the great night. Slowly it crept into the room, slowly it seeped into the very flesh of the King's falsely animated guests. It was the same night that blanketed all France. It lay dark on the Faubourg St. Antoine, on the corridored Bastille, on lonely farms and villages from Normandy to Provence. It hid from sight the earthen huts in which huddled half-naked peasants, turning and tossing with hunger pangs and the incessant nip of fleas. The French night was threatening, alive with hate. It flowed into the bright rooms of Versailles like some black miasma from Hades.

Struensee was greatly relieved when the soirée came to an abrupt end after the King felt himself too weary to go on with the show. As the hours passed the King's smile had become more forced. The mask was disfigured by countless small cracks. Carriages waited outside for the departing guests, the drivers sitting stiff as ramrods on their perches, flunkeys at attention at the running boards. With unseemly haste Christian clambered into the Marquise de Tinville's carriage, slamming the door to behind him before Holck could get in. "I wonder how they'll make out," Holck muttered to himself. "I'd like to watch them, I'd give ten thalers." He shrugged his big shoulders, laughed to himself and ambled back to his own conveyance. The little procession soon arrived at the Hotel York.

Struensee undressed, terribly low in spirit and glad to be alone. Not until he was safely under the covers, reading in a book, did he regain his usual equanimity. After reading for a time he let his book slip and fell asleep with the candles still lit. He awoke with a start. Holck was shaking him by the shoulder. "Doctor, Doctor!" he was saying excitedly. "For God's sake, wake up. We can't do anything with him."

Struensee looked up, drunk with sleep.

"The King," stammered Holck. "He's threatening us with his dagger. He won't let anybody into the room. The man's mad, I tell you."

Struensee slipped on his shoes, threw a dressing gown about his shoulders and ran with Holck along the corridor to the King's suite. Holck drummed on the door with balled fist. "It's me," he said loudly. "It's me, Holck. Be a good fellow, Christian, and open the door."

"Keep out, Holck," came the answer from within. "I'll stick you with this dagger. I know what you want." Then there was a groan. "You're the devil," said Christian thickly. "You keep away from me, do you hear?"

Struensee led Holck away. "Just let him alone for a time," he advised. "Don't get him more excited than he is. Let him simmer for a while."

For five minutes or so they both stood by in silence, Holck downcast, Struensee alert but calm. Presently came a protracted mumbling sound, then a fit of weeping.

"Now, you had better go, Count Holck," said Struensee in his medical voice. "I think it better for me to deal with him alone. I'll handle him, never fear. I'm used to this sort of thing."

Holck left without protest. He was obviously fed up with Christian's psychic peculiarities. Softly the Doctor knocked on the door. No answer came, and he tried again. Finally the King stertorously whispered: "Who's there?"

"Your doctor, Sire, Dr. Struensee," the other said as evenly as he could.

There was more silence, then: "What do you want with me?"

"I can hear you're not well, Sire," Struensee said. "I'd like to help you. Please let me in."

More silence. And presently: "That's right, I'm not well. I feel terribly sick."

"Perhaps I can help you."

"No, you can't," said Christian through the door panel.

"I would like to try," Struensee insisted. "Give me a chance."

"Who's with you?"

"Nobody, I'm alone."

"Wait a minute, then. I'll let you in. But nobody else."

Looking down at his own feet, listening all ears, Struensee smiled quietly to himself. Finally the door swung open and he walked in. Christian let him pass, looked up and down the empty corridor, closed the door and locked it. He was in his shirtsleeves and had his ornamental dagger in his hand ready for use. His blond hair hung disheveled about his face. At the moment he had a strong hermaphroditic look. His blue eyes were bulging with some inner tension.

"Would Your Majesty put aside the dagger?" Struensee asked. Hesitantly Christian laid the dagger on a settle. Then he fell heavily on the bed, put up his hands to his face and sobbed bitterly. Struensee let him weep. Suddenly Christian jumped up and said to Struensee: "Do you think I'm crazy? What do you think?"

"No, I do not think you're crazy," Struensee told him.

The King looked hard at the Doctor, laughed mirthlessly and said: "Yes, but what would you say if I told you that I've seen the devil? Wouldn't that make me crazy?"

"The devil?" said Struensee. "What do you mean? Tell me."

Christian became very agitated, fingered his mouth and began to pace the room. "I saw him here, right in this room," he told Struensee. "Yes, less than an hour ago. I actually saw him, I tell you. As surely as you're sitting there. Especially his eyes. I saw them, I tell you. Don't try to tell me that he wasn't there, either."

"And what did he say, this devil of yours?" asked Struensee.

"He didn't say anything," said Christian sullenly.

"Then how did he look?"

"He was dressed like a servant. In gold braid and all the rest of it, you know. And his face was terribly sly and smeary. Yes, he had a fawning sort of face. He kept on bowing to me until I thought I'd have to scream. He was like a drake in the spring, bowing and bobbing."

"Perhaps it was only a servant that you saw," said Struensee very quietly. "Could it have been, do you think?"

"No, no, no! It was not, I tell you it was not," screamed the King. "It was the devil, all right. Understand!"

"What makes you so sure it was?"

"I saw it in his eyes," said Christian. "The devil, I tell you."

"In his eyes?" asked Struensee. He was interested in this. "Tell me more about the eyes?"

"I can't describe them," Christian said. "They're terrible, though. They follow me all around. They want me to die. They look just like pieces of ice. That awful hypocritical face. It's terrible, Struensee. I can't stand it, that's all."

"Do these eyes by any chance remind you of some particular person?" Struensee asked gently.

This question made the King groan as if he were having a tooth drawn. He again got up, so genuine was his agony, and stumbled about the room before he came to rest slumped in a chair. "My God, how did you ever think of that!" he whispered exhaustedly. "It's true, they do remind me of somebody. But how did you know? Do you see them, too?"

"No," said Struensee. "Whom do they remind you of?"

"I can't talk about that. It's too horrible." Christian's face was pinched and blurred by fear. Sweat gathered on his forehead.

"But you must talk about it, Sire," said Struensee. "Otherwise I cannot drive away the ghost. You have to trust me. You must."

"I do trust you," said Christian. "I remember how you helped me on the ship. Even now, since we've been talking, I feel better. Don't laugh at me, will you. Nobody ought to laugh at me. Or despise me. But they do, they always do."

"Well, then, tell me," said Struensee, his eyes searching the King's gravely. "Speak up."

"They were my mother's eyes," Christian burst out. His hands fluttered and flittered like dead leaves in the wind.

"Your mother's?" said the Doctor. "So it is. Now, tell me more about them."

"My step-mother's, I mean," said the King. "Listen to me, Struensee. I'll tell the whole story. Everything. You're a magician. You can get rid of the devil, if you want to. I know you can . . . Do you know Frederiksborg? The castle?"

"No, I don't," said Struensee. "But you can tell me."

"Frederiksborg is built on a lake," said Christian. "The lake is so beautiful. In the summer it's full of pond lilies. Don't you like pond lilies, Struensee? They're so white. And cool. When I was a boy that's what I liked to do best, go out on the lake and pick pond lilies."

"Continue," said Struensee. "I won't interrupt you."

"Of course my own mother never took me out to get pond lilies," Christian explained. "But the woman my father married, Juliana, was like a real mother to me. I forgot the other one, the real one. How I loved Juliana's dark eyes. She used to take me on walks to Klampenborg and Fredensborg. I used to sit at her feet on a little stool when she was reading to me. Sometimes she did crocheting. How happy I used to be, just looking at her and imagining she was my mother."

"Why don't you go on?" urged Struensee. "Is that all there is to it?"

"I will, I will," said Christian. "Well, she had a son, her own son, my step-brother, Frederik. I hated the baby, I hated him. I hated his fat hands and his bare head and his awful screeching and crying when he wanted something to eat. I used to think how wonderful it would be to smother him in the pillows.

"I tried to make believe that nothing had changed, but in my heart I always had a terrible feeling. Nothing was really the same again when Frederik came along. I had an awful pain in my heart. Anyone could see my step-mother was different after she had had the baby. She still patted me on the head and kissed me, but never the way she did before.

"One day we went out on the lake. The baby was with us in the boat, lying up in the bow in a cradle they had made for him. Juliana and another woman were sitting side by side in the stern of the boat and a servant was rowing us along. I crouched down in the bottom of the boat. I wanted my step-mother to look at me, so I tried to pick her some pond lilies. As we moved along I bent over the gunwale and reached for them. They were so cool and they smelled so sweet it made me laugh. I tipped the boat and the chamberlain who was rowing told me that if I didn't sit still he would throw me in the water. I made a face at him and in a temper he gave me a little shove. I lost my balance and fell overboard.

"I sank like a stone, I remember, and everything was green. I tried to breathe and my lungs filled up with water. I tried to cough out the water. I tried to shout and pretty soon there I was, on the top. How strange everything looked. Everything looked . . . how shall I say . . . hateful and angry. Before, just a second before, everything had been so pleasant. Everything seemed to want to kill me. It was so strange. Imagine the blue summer sky looking like that, the smooth water and the flat pond lily leaves. You understand, Struensee? I saw it all with wonderful clarity. It didn't take me a second to see it, even though I was flailing about in the water.

"Then I happened to look up into my step-mother's eyes. Naturally I thought she would want to help me, to save me. Naturally! Why not? I began to scream and choke. Mama, mama, I cried out. Then I read the look in her eyes. She was leaning out over the edge of the boat looking right at me. I could see she wanted me to sink and drown and be dead. Then the way would be free for her own son to have the crown. That second I lost everything. I wanted to die. I wanted to drown right in front of her eyes. Indeed, I went so weak that I slid under the water again. I wanted to drown. I tell you, Struensee, at a moment like that nothing is sweeter than drowning. But the man at the oars got hold of my collar and hauled me back into the boat.

"Now she said kind things to me. She brushed my hair back from my eyes. I was sick as a dog from swallowing so much water. I vomited a great many times. Not only on account of the water, either. Because I had been so badly used by her. Yes, that was it, Struensee. Because of something I simply can't put into words. What I had to live through. The fact that everything was a pack of lies. Nothing but pretense. Everywhere, all around me. Love, honor, candor . . . nothing but lies, lies, lies. Do you follow me, Struensee?

"From that day on I never picked any more lilies from the lake. I didn't care any more how white or pure or cool they might be. For me their long stems were like snakes, ready to coil around my legs and pull me down to the bottom. Damned hypocritical things. And my step-mother kept right on pretending to like me. She was friendly enough to see her. But she knew I had seen through her game. I avoided her all I could. I was glad when she went away to Fredensborg for good. She was dissatisfied with my father, she said. But he had seen through her, too. I understood the poor man. He broke on that Juliana like an egg on a rock. He simply never understood that Juliana was just like all women. He should have taught her some manners, the snapping bitch. He should have locked her up, he should have thrashed her until she fell to the floor. My grandfather Christian would have fixed her properly. He'd have softened her up. Yes, he'd have handled her like a peasant drab. But we? We're weak, we're lost, Struensee. Even women do as they please with us."

"Well," murmured Struensee. "So that's how it was."

"I hate all women," said Christian, spittles at each corner of his little mouth. "I hate their innocence, their love, love, love. And their silly talk. A misbegotten race of liars and cheats, that's what they are. When I told you that in Celle, you despised me, I noticed. Did you know whom I was referring to?"

"Yes, I did," Struensee said.

"Oh, you'll get to know her. Don't be taken in, my friend. Don't let those big eyes fool you. Don't lose your head over that smooth forehead and those pretty legs. If you only knew what goes on in that head, Struensee, if you only knew. Remember the pond lilies. I don't mind if you amuse yourself with her, not even that. Do it, if you want to. But for God's sake, don't fall in love with her. Love me, not her, for I'm your friend."

Struensee stammered politely outraged protest, but the King waved it off. "Don't be so stodgy," he said rapidly. "You've done me a service, haven't you? But now I want to know how it is I see the devil? Is it because of the strumpets I'm always playing around with? The Marquise de Tinville, for instance?"

"The devil," Struensee began carefully, "is only an illusion that you create yourself, Your Majesty."

"But I assure you that he was real enough," said Christian.

"He is real only so far as the feeling which created him is real," the Doctor corrected him. "But that does not mean that what your eyes thought they saw is real. There is the illusion and the reality of what brought about the illusion."

"And what is this reality?" asked the King.

"Fear," said Struensee. "You are afraid."

"I admit it," said Christian, almost gladly. "I admit I have been afraid. But what am I afraid of? Am I not the King? Nobody threatens me. And if they did, I have soldiers to protect me. I have nothing to be afraid of."

For a time both were silent. Then Struensee said slowly: "I will talk openly with you, Sire, even though I'm going to run the risk of injuring your self-esteem."

"Do that," said Christian. "Don't hold back on my account."

"Your fear, Sire, is nothing more than fear for your own mind's health. And fear that you will fail your destiny. So far you have not succeeded in fulfilling what lies within you. The will to bear great responsibilities is in your makeup, yet nothing has come of it. You castigate yourself for this. You punish yourself by inventing a devil. You threaten yourself with mental death to bring the errant part of your being into line."

"Perhaps you're right," said Christian feebly. "It sounds likely enough. I feel right now the way I did the other time. It would be better for me to drown." He again put his hands up to his face and commenced to sob.

Struensee watched him for a moment and then said softly: "But the other time the servant pulled you into the boat, or whoever it was. Today I am on hand. I can be the one to help you this time, if you'll trust me and follow my advice."

Slowly Christian took his hands away from his stricken face and stared at the Doctor. It was the same as on the ship. A magic power and will streamed out of the Doctor's eyes, restoring and supporting him. On an impulse he fell to his knees before Struensee, seized his hands and would have pressed kisses on them had Struensee not pulled away. "No, not that way," he said to Christian. "Never forget that you are the King, and that I am your servant." Then he persuaded him to try to sleep. Willingly Christian removed his clothes, following Struensee's instructions like a child. He stretched out in bed. Presently his eyes closed and the sound of gentle, deep breathing filled the room. A new day was lighting up the windows. Heavy wagons were rumbling over the cobbles, broken fragments of pedestrians' conversation came into the room. Paris was waking to another day.

Struensee extinguished the candles and shut the door softly behind him after a last glance at the sleeping King. In the corridor he ran into Holck, who looked very worried. "Has he calmed down yet?" Holck asked eagerly. "He's sleeping," said Struensee.

"What was wrong with him? Did he have a fit?"

"Nothing like that," said Struensee evasively. "It was a crisis. I've been expecting it since we were in Celle, Holck."

"So?" said Holck. He did not understand. "Is that dangerous?"

"On the contrary," said Struensee. "Altogether a good thing." Then he smiled sardonically at Holck, wrapped his dressing gown more tightly about him, and said: "In a sense, I suppose, it may prove dangerous. But we shall have to wait and see. Shall we not?" He waved his hand and went down the corridor and into his room, Holck looking after.

"Is that fellow pulling my leg?" Holck said to himself. Contemptuously he snorted derision through his large nose and went his way.

⋆ *IX* ⋆

COUNT HOLCK SOON discovered to his dismay what the crisis in the King's life meant, at least so far as his services were concerned. Very rapidly he was demoted to second fiddle position. Now it was the Doctor from Altona who was constantly in Christian's company, from the morning *levée* until bedtime. It was no longer Holck's counsel that the King followed, but Struensee's, though he was very cautious at this point about sticking in an oar. He knew perfectly well that his ascendancy would arouse jealousies and hatreds, and so curbed his impetuous temperament with an iron hand. This was not an easy thing to do. An itch to rule infected him. He saw his suddenly increased importance reflected in Holck's injured, suspicious glance, in Schimmelmann's ever more conservative admonitions, in Christian's readiness to yield. This sensation of power was all the more intoxicating in that Struensee had won his position thanks only to his own energy, insight and tact. The fact that he was a commoner without a trace of rank or privilege strengthened his own warm opinion of himself.

The effects of Struensee's influence on Christian, for an interval, at least, were amazing. It seemed as if the King were acquiring new features, an entirely different facial expression. The superficiality and birdlike emptiness retreated from sight. His laughter became less sarcastic, his gait more manly and confident.

Schimmelmann could hardly believe his ears when Christian suddenly commenced asking questions about Danish finances. Many times Schimmelmann had discussed budgetary matters with the Doctor, for the theme was close to his heart, and now he heard Christian repeating the Doctor's ideas. And yet for once Christian was not merely parroting ideas vaguely understood and imperfectly mimicked.

He actually spoke, it appeared, out of inner conviction, using his own language, which was much more elegant than the language typical of Struensee. He talked about reducing the costs of maintaining the court and of cutting down the bureaucracy, which was multiplying like a patch of weeds. Schimmelmann involuntarily looked around the room for Struensee when he heard these things. Where was he! It turned out that he had been away somewhere since morning. The Doctor's magic must work from afar, Schimmelmann thought ironically.

Christian informed his financial adviser that he had decided to cut short his grand tour, not only to spare the already depleted national treasury further strain, but also because he wanted to come to grips with the question of freeing the Danish serfs. Moreover, he said, there were a dozen other matters that needed his immediate attention.

"What would there be in Rome, or Vienna or Dresden?" Christian said, nearly taking Schimmelmann's breath away. "After all, they have nothing to offer that's not an imitation of Versailles. And the whole point is, I must rise above the Versailles level."

Holck was stricken dumb when he learned of the change in the King's plans. He had promised himself a taste of Italian opera, he had looked forward to the neat sights of Dresden, all manner of gay adventures, escapades with theater women, new friends to exploit. He ran directly to the King, scolded him and said that he was very much against so radical a maneuver.

"Well, then, Holck," Christian told him, "why don't you go on alone. I'll stand back of you, my dear fellow. Your expense, I mean."

This reply hurt the Count. Plainly the King was tiring of his company. He protested, saying the trip without Christian would be no trip at all. I'm bound by eternal friendship, he told the King.

The evening before his return home to Denmark Christian gave a dinner honoring the literary lights of Paris. D'Alembert, Helvetius, Maupertuis and many others attended, the whole encyclopedist group who proposed to create a new kind of society based on reason rather than on tradition. In spite of their professed revolutionary aims the men of letters looked like anybody else. They wore silk coats exactly like other people of substance, they had wavy wigs on their heads, their hands were white and soft, they behaved decorously; in conversation they sacrificed profundity for the phrase. The revolution they had in mind was not to be realized by physical rebellion, they claimed, but by the influence of enlightened minds operating from the top down.

Christian actually charmed his guests. His facility pleased them greatly, even impressed them. The faintly Swiss accent of his French quite enchanted these critical Gallic savants. Reverdil, the sober

Swiss, had wrought better than he knew. Besides, Christian was young, and they were old. It flattered them to hear their own ideas coming from the mouth of a youthful king. Their attitude was quite paternal. Whenever Christian, as happened occasionally, stumbled over an idea or became entangled in complexities beyond his scope, they quickly rushed to his rescue, yet so adroitly that no one could accuse them of being patronizing. Struensee kept strictly in the background, and spoke only when he had a chance to clarify or reinforce Christian's ideas. Count Holck chafed in a fog of perplexity. The word-play made him dizzy.

On the way back to Denmark the King's party stopped over for several days in the little capital city of Cassel, where Christian's sister and brother-in-law made their home. They lived on the outskirts of the town in Wilhelmshoehe Castle, a sort of vertical distortion of Versailles. Behind the main castle building rose up a steep height, the slope of which had been carved out into terraced pleasure gardens equipped with the usual balustrades, statuary and fountains in the French mode. This laborious declivity was crowned by a many-columned temple of love.

The dukes of Hessen-Cassel lived on a generous scale. Though they seldom took time out to look at them, their picture galleries were well stocked with Rembrandts. Their zoo was plentifully supplied with odd animals, their bedrooms staffed with the prettiest girls of the countryside and, in lush times, with choice trulls imported from foreign parts. Their display of status cost money, a great deal of money. Since the ducal lands were not rich, indeed, nothing but a scrawny territory without hand industries of any sort and the most improvident sort of agriculture, they had hit on all manner of curious projects to keep their heads above water. They sold their own subjects at a good price and packed them off to serve as soldiers for more ambitious nations. Not a wink of sleep did they lose when these poor wretches were shipped wholesale across the sea. At this very period they were dickering about the sale of more regiments to Great Britain, for use in the North American colonies.

Not unnaturally the Hessian peasants themselves were anything but enthusiastic about the migratory plans of their masters, as little as the colonists on the receiving end. But their sentiments aroused no response in the lusty dukes. They thought in large terms, they refused absolutely to fritter away time on sentimental trifles. Their only regret was that the sale of subjects had definite limitations. The population was woefully small to begin with. Further inroads on the ducal manpower would only dilute Hessia's already feeble international reputation.

Apart from the sale of human souls, the dukes had many other irons in the fire. They had set up a lottery, with the receipts immense, the winnings small, as a lottery should be. Every loyal Hessian had to take a chance or run the risk of gravely displeasing their Serenissimi. The tax collectors, too, were busy as bees. Life in Hessia in good measure consisted either of paying taxes or sitting in jail. Wits noted that Hessians breathed with caution, thinking air was taxed. Some dukes dreamed of manufacturing gold by alchemic process, for instance the Elector of Saxony, though his man of brains, the alchemist Boettcher, to date had succeeded only in inventing porcelain. They were also intensely interested in the business of discovering hidden treasure, though thoughtful observers asked themselves where the dukes imagined treasure could be found in such niggardly climes.

The speculators, day-dreamers and swindlers of all Europe passed through the court at Cassel, leaving wild plans behind. Invariably they were welcomed and entertained. The Duke at Cassel never quite abandoned the hope that one day he would hit on a financial genius who would recoup his fortunes.

Among these dubious wanderers there arrived at Cassel a certain Count Alessandro Cagliostro, accompanied by a fascinating lady who went by the name of Countess Lorenza Feliciani. This couple aroused great interest wherever they went, the Countess because she was dark-eyed, southern in look and not chary about bestowing her favors, the Count because everyone felt that deep mysteries lay within his ken. Of course, as always there were hardheaded doubters who said that the Countess was nothing but a lowborn Italian who once had been employed in a London brothel. The Count, they declared, was no count at all, but the lady's former pimp.

For his part the Count ignored all libels. He looked majestically out into space, he turned graciously to those prepared to honor him for his rare gifts. His followers, among whom were numbered the ruling houses of Europe, were amazed by the astounding revelations that he whispered very privily into their ears. How disarmingly matter of fact he could be! It was something to watch.

He told them, among many other things, that he was over two thousand years old. He said he had attended the Wedding at Cana. He actually described the wine vessels, the bride, the guests and every other detail. This was a most amazing performance, since the event, according to best reckoning, had happened seventeen hundred years before. He was especially attentive to the ladies, though he was by no means a good-looking man, rather small, in fact, a thickishly built sort with a dark olive skin. His words could never pass as well-chosen, his manners suggested the servant in a home of modest pretensions. His eyes protruded, his gestures were large, his look lofty, however, when he related some incredible memoir from his two thousand years of existence. He drew the ladies to him as honey draws flies.

Who, indeed, would not enjoy the company of a man who had seen Our Lord, Jesus Christ, face to face, who had munched dates with St. Paul, who had conversed intimately with Marcus Aurelius? He had also met interesting people in what one might call his mature years. Count Alessandro had an affinity for spiritual greatness, he let it be known, for the mystic things of life. Alchemists interested him retrospectively far more than kings or generals. He was especially attracted to the mysteries of ancient Egypt, though unfortunately he had only known them second-hand, since they had happened long before his time. Nevertheless he claimed more than average in this esoteric field, for both Philo and Plotinus had confided a great many choice facts which they did not think wise to include in their published writings.

He proposed, so he said, to reorganize Freemasonry in Cassel according to the ancient prescripts of the Egyptians. Oddly enough he did not exhaust his talents in mighty reminiscence, but was ready to perform positive works. Women verging on old age he would present with a pomade absolutely guaranteed to remove all wrinkles. Some he gave his "Egyptian wine," which brought back the fire of youth and made its users quite irresistible. Men who doubted their virility were given a "refreshing powder" making them more active than August the Strong who, so Cagliostro pointed out, in his time sired three hundred children. To those who whispered complaints about the coldness of their wives, he gave an "extract of Saturn," warranted to make frigid women as warm as little kitties in rut.

But these gifts were small coins that Cagliostro threw to the crowd as come-ons. His real pitch was reserved for the select, the initiated. His choicest gifts derived from the fact that he could communicate with and command the spirits. To get him to perform magic feats, however, he asked belief in himself. Nothing is more humiliating to a spirit, he would point out, than to have his existence doubted, even by proxy. Then he would sigh and say: *"Pour soulager l'humanité, je travaille comme un boeuf."*

Cagliostro had a very wide acquaintance in the spirit world, but was especially close to the Great Kophta. On certain ritualistic occasions, indeed, he seemed so close that the spirit worked and spoke through him as if he were another Balaam's ass. Cagliostro admitted that he had the Great Kophta to thank for practically all his wisdom. Kophta had given him mysterious weapons, in the form of a snake coiled about an apple, and a motto reading, "I am what I am." From Kophta, too, came his magic triangle with Gamaliel, Raphael and Uriel posed on various sides. This last gift from the spirits could be used for any number of talismanic purposes, from the adjuration of angels to the discovery of hidden treasure.

When the King's party arrived at Wilhelmshoehe there was great excitement at the court. Cagliostro had promised not only to have the Great Kophta appear a few evenings hence, actually make him visible to the dullest eyes, but also to talk over with him a new mathematical method, the "reduction of astrological calculus," by means of which Cagliostro proposed to foretell the winning numbers in the next drawing of the Hessian lottery. This last was the Duke's idea. He was of a mind to buy the winning tickets for himself.

In the natural course of events Christian and his party were invited to the séance. The evening before Struensee met the incomparable charlatan. The Doctor saw nothing particularly interesting about the man, aside from his white shoes with red heels. His appearance was passably good. There was nothing to find fault with, nothing to praise.

"How is it, pray tell me," Struensee asked the bogus Count, "that a simple triangle can have a spiritual effect?"

"That lies in the deeps of nature," Cagliostro replied and looked into Struensee's eyes with oddly disconcerting intensity.

The Doctor, suppressing a smile, said to this: "All philosophers agree that the corporeal works on the corporeal, the spiritual on the spiritual, and not otherwise. Yet your triangle is corporeal and has spiritual effect. How do you explain that?"

"No, not at all," said Cagliostro swiftly. "The triangle is only a symbol. Its purely component nature gives rise to something spiritual, namely, a certain constellation of spirits, who are not in the paper, but in my head. This constellation is favorable for the appearance of the Great Kophta, for he is also an essence of six angels."

"I don't understand that at all," said Struensee. "What do you mean by 'purely component'?"

Again Cagliostro looked long and carefully at the Doctor. "It's just the same as starry constellations," he explained. "When the sun is in the sign of the Ram, spring appears."

"That's not true," Struensee objected. "It is the angle of the sun as it strikes the earth that causes springtime. The fact that the sun is then in conjunction with a certain group of stars is purely coincidental."

"Everything is bound together, everything has a certain order," said Cagliostro grandly. "Moreover, Doctor, I suggest that you find out the why of the why before you commit yourself."

The next evening according to schedule some twenty persons gathered in a small round room. The windows had been covered over with silvery-gray hangings. The spectators were in an uncomfortable mood, half scared, half curious. The men and women whispered incessantly to each other, drawing reassurance from noise and propinquity. Eventually Cagliostro made his entrance. He glanced sharply at the audience and immediately a heavy silence reigned.

The magician wore a flowing black cloak thrown loosely over his shoulders. He bent forward and with black chalk drew the magical triangle on the floor, thereafter he began to murmur softly to himself. Presently he hoisted himself to his feet and asked that the candles be put out. It became very dark, almost pitch dark in the room. The audience breathed heavily as if the loss of light had also robbed them of air to breathe. A single thin shaft of moonlight found its way through the heavy drapes into the room. It struck exactly in the center of the triangle.

Nothing happened. Time seemed to have slowed down; seconds passed like minutes. Cagliostro sighed. "There is an unbeliever amongst us," he announced. "The spirit is unwilling to come."

Then there was silence again, and gradually a whispering and a rustling became audible. Something rose up from the middle of the triangle. It did not resemble a human form so much as a floating veil. Struensee, condemning himself even as it happened, felt the hair rise on the back of his neck. What damnable nonsense, he thought, but against his will was fascinated, horribly fascinated.

"Great Kophta," he heard Cagliostro say, "teach us your mysteries."

The answer came in a remarkably clear, well-modulated voice, apparently a woman's voice, and seemingly issuing faintly but clearly from some distant point. "What do you want to know?" the voice asked resonantly and the audience shuddered.

"The astrological numbers," said Cagliostro breathlessly.

The spirit seemed to be mediating this request. After a pause, however, the answer came. "The numbers are sacred," the voice said. "Numbers are everything. Furthermore, I am not free to do as I please about this. I cannot reveal to the many what must remain forever concealed from them. But you may seek in the hermetic books."

A sigh of disappointment rippled through the audience.

"Tell us more," Cagliostro ordered with a show of impatience.

The spirit seemed to have been waiting for this opportunity. Without hesitation the voice said: "There is a king amongst us. A king of midnight."

"We know that," said Cagliostro, pretending increased impatience, making it very clear that the audience was such that it needed no elementary instruction.

"I see them reaching for his crown," the spirit continued.

"See whom?" Cagliostro asked. "Speak more clearly, Great Kophta."

"One is young and handsome. The other has gray hair. They are reaching out their hands."

Christian, seated directly in front of Struensee, started to rise in his seat. He whispered disjointedly to himself. Struensee feared another nervous attack. Soothingly he put his hand on Christian's shoulder, and the King settled reluctantly in his chair.

"I see an unbeliever," said the fine spirit voice. "He is behind the King."

Why, the man's unashamed, Struensee thought in a panic, I've got to stop this before it gets out of hand.

"What is wrong with this man?" came Cagliostro's voice.

"Ambition," was the prompt answer. "He is an ambitious man."

"Well?" the magician urged.

"He will come to grief unless he conducts himself more modestly. Denounce what you have prayed for, ambitious one. Pray for what you have denounced. That is my word for him."

Struensee was both amused and alarmed by Cagliostro's boldness. The words left his mouth before he was really aware of what he was doing. "What am I praying for?" he asked the spirit loudly.

"Who is that? Who dares to interfere?" intoned the spirit voice.

"Answer him, Great Kophta," Cagliostro beseeched.

"Power, he is praying for power."

To his dismay Struensee felt a pang of fear and regret. He's not only bold, he thought quickly, he knows what he's talking about. He knows more about me than I'm ready to admit. But aloud he said: "And what have I denounced?"

"Obedience, you have repudiated obedience."

"In what respect?" Struensee called loudly, forgetful again of where he was.

"Obedience is that which is mightier than the mightiest."

"And what is that?" asked Struensee.

"Answer him, Great Kophta."

"That is godliness, before which all spirits bend."

Despite a great effort of will Struensee felt showers of horror course up his spinal column. His hand, resting on the back of the King's chair, began to tremble. What can be the matter with me, he thought, why am I so affected by this miserable, generalizing faker? It's all nonsense, sheer mummery. It's either himself ventriloquizing, or he has an accomplice, hidden off somewhere. But how does he see through me? he asked himself. He is surely a student of souls, the best I've ever come across. But what he means by godliness is really only superstition. He knows this quality is strong in these tired, brittle people. He is using them, playing with them. All they want is some miracle that will shield them from reality. Why, he knows them to the very roots of their twisted little souls, this fabulous Cagliostro. The man's a genius of a sort, Struensee told himself, and I had best watch my step.

The duel of wills seemed to continue soundlessly. The audience squirmed and let out nervous coughings and sighings. Then the voice came again: "You don't believe me, but you should." After this pronouncement all was perfectly still and relaxed. The vague form in the dark sank, the single shaft of light melted away and it was pitch dark.

"Candles, light the candles," said Cagliostro, talking as if he were exhausted. The door was thrown open, a servant entered and lighted the candles. Cagliostro, still enfolded in his voluminous mantle, was slumped on a chair. Sweat stood out on his forehead. A sigh of release went through the assembly. Everyone rose, with a swishing of skirts and the soft clinking of daggers. Presently the room was cleared. Going out the women looked over their shoulders at Struensee. He was nodding where he sat. Shortly he really did fall asleep. He could feel his sense leaving him. He seemed to be sliding rapidly down a steep black shaft into the earth.

Struensee struggled awake, thick with confusion. Cagliostro was sitting across from him, measuring him with his strange eyes. The Countess Feliciani was bending over her master, her hands on his shoulders. Having looked his fill Cagliostro arranged his cloak, stretched, yawned and lazily got to his feet. "I see the Great Kophta took quite an interest in you, Doctor," he said casually.

"Yes, he hit the nail on the head, Cagliostro," said Struensee. "And he did it though the room was black as ink." His tongue felt thick, he had to force a laugh.

"The spirits can do it every time," the charlatan told him slowly. "Peculiar, isn't it?"

"Very," said Struensee. "Where did you find out so much about me, sir? We've hardly talked together five minutes."

"I?" He deprecated the very idea of his knowing by spreading out his hands in the Italian style. Idly Struensee noticed that the fingers were liberally ornamented with jeweled rings. "Why," he heard the charlatan say, "I had absolutely nothing to do with it, not I. Indeed, it surprised me to hear that you are an ambitious man. You see, only a spirit can read minds."

"I admire you, Cagliostro," said Struensee. "You know what you're doing. You will always manage."

The charlatan was flattered by the Doctor's candor, a candor not without envy and fear. A shimmer of a smile passed over his ugly face. "The Great Kophta has his good side," he said gravely. "Now and then he is upset by flippancies, I should imagine. One has to be very careful, very discreet."

With this he offered the Countess his arm, bowed politely to Struensee and left, leaving the Doctor behind in the empty room, staring after him. Then Struensee noticed that while talking to him the charlatan had slipped off his cloak and forgotten to pick it up. There it lay over a chair back. Struensee went for it with a rush, shook it, searched every seam. But it proved to be only an ordinary cloak, revealing no sign of veil or cloth that might have served to produce the illusion of a human form in the darkness. Then, on second search, Struensee discovered a piece of folded paper tucked away in the corner of an inside pocket. Excitedly he opened it and read. "Dear Doctor," the note read, "you are much too simple for your own good. Watch out, sir. Not for me, but for yourself. Your most humble servant, Count Alessandro Cagliostro."

Waves of hot and cold ran through Struensee. He caught sight of his own reflection in a mirror and saw that his mouth was sagging. He shook his head. He felt terribly tired. Aloud he mumbled: "Damned extraordinary fellow. I would never have thought it, never."

The King's party moved on towards Denmark a few days later.

BOOK TWO

Politics and Love

ON A BEAUTIFUL, CRISP winter morning Christian and his entourage arrived in Roeskilde.

Roeskilde had once been the capital of Denmark. Now it was a somnolent little town of medieval aspect. It had a solid Romanesque cathedral in the crypts of which the former kings of the realm lay buried; a thickly walled structure with heavy doors flanked by bold towers of red brick. There were many old, old houses in Roeskilde, with steep, coppered roofs that caught the sun.

Here to Roeskilde came Caroline Matilda to meet her returning husband. Having seen her at last, Struensee was forced to revise his preconceptions of the Queen. On her combed-up hair she wore a little sable cap, which somehow gave her a ready, enterprising air. A mantle of the same kind of fur was loosely draped over her shoulders. The wind, whipping the folds aside, showed the carmine red silk of the lining. The Queen was slender and taller than her husband. Her most striking feature was the full, rich lips of her rather wide mouth, which stood out in marked contrast to the smooth oval of her cheeks.

"You are taller, Madame," said Christian reprovingly, looking his consort over from head to foot.

"One gets older, Sire," she told him.

He kissed her hand then both her cheeks.

"But I am not growing older," he said. "What did Walpole say about me, Holck?"

"He said you look like a fairy-king, Your Majesty," said Holck, grinning wickedly. "You'd just stepped out of your hazel-nut," he said.

Christian laughed and the Queen smiled politely at this bit of cleverness.

"I think it was brazen of him," another voice put in. It was a woman with a strong, hard face who had spoken, a woman in her forties of matronly build. Her hair was lightly grayed, her eyebrows a deep black and the eyes under them also jet black. The intelligence and energy of these dark eyes was marred by hard cunning. At her left stood a youth of sixteen, her son, who resembled her, in part, and in part Christian's strain. The mother, dressed in black, a very elegant figure of a woman, swallowed up the youthful presence at her side.

"Why, mother!" said Christian slowly. "So you came to Roeskilde, too."

"I come to Roeskilde quite often," she said drily. "Kiss me, my son. Here is your brother. You look very well, Christian."

"I have him to thank for it," said Christian, pointing behind him.

"Count Holck?" Caroline spoke the name with icy contempt, not even trying to conceal her dislike. Her light-blue eyes hardened and looked at and through Holck.

"No, no, not my Holck, though he's a fine fellow," said Christian maliciously, watching his wife's face. "I mean my physician. You've never met him, but I'm sure you will enjoy making his acquaintance. Come here, if you will, my dear Struensee."

Struensee bowed deeply to the Queen and the Queen-Dowager. Both women looked him over with intense curiosity.

"You have helped my son," said the Queen-Dowager. "We are very grateful to you, sir."

Again Struensee bowed low. "It was a simple matter," he mumbled. "My duty, Madame."

"Yes, it was very simple," said Christian. "Just think, my dear ladies, he took me back into the past and everything became as clear as crystal. No more confusion after that."

"The past?" said the Queen-Dowager. "What do you mean by that?"

"That's my secret," said Christian and tittered like a girl. "Or our little secret, I should say. Which the Doctor is not at liberty to divulge to a soul."

"Well, for one I don't know as I want to know your little secret, Sire," said Caroline Matilda tartly. "I hope your Doctor has more discretion than Holck. We all know how he keeps a secret, do we not?" Saying this she looked squarely at Struensee, seeing him, yet not seeing him in a most discomfiting gesture of hostility. Then she turned severely away, her pretty nose in the air.

It was obvious, Struensee saw, that she had him measured as another Holck, just another parasite. He was quite taken aback to be so casually misjudged. His feelings were keenly stung. He had found an enemy where he expected none. Only the devil can get along with women, he told himself sourly, especially when they are young and full of whimsies. And so, excusing himself, he went to his carriage, to find Annette von Gaehler waiting for him. She put her arms around him and kissed him heartily. The smell of her hair in the cold air made him faint with desire. "Come into my carriage," he said to her. "Will you do that?"

"We have to be careful," she whispered. "We're not in Hamburg now, you know."

"Your husband?"

"Husband! Of course not," she said. "He's not jealous." Then she commenced to talk very fast and out of joint, always peeking over her shoulder. She told Struensee how Brandt had left Copenhagen, having fallen out of favor. Count Rantzau, from whom Struensee had expected so much, was with his regiment in Glueckstadt. Struensee was mystified by Annette's agitation. A lock of her black hair fell out of place and the wind tossed it against her white cheek. Never had she looked more desirable to the hungry Struensee. He put his arm around her and whispered into her ear. "But you, my dear," he told her, "you're still here, aren't you?"

"I don't know," said Annette vaguely. She pulled away with a jerk. She was afraid.

At this moment, appearing like magic from out of the ground, it seemed to the engrossed Struensee, a man stood between him and Annette. He wore a long red coat, heavily trimmed with fur and decorated with a broad gold band across the breast. His thick black brows were pulled up into his forehead over little sly black eyes. His nose was wrinkled as if he were trying to test the smell of his own breath, a breath at the present heavily perfumed by gin. With him he carried a heavy stick with a gold knob on it as big as an apple.

"What do you want?" Struensee demanded.

"I am Filosov," the man said, and underscored this announcement by whacking the frozen earth with his stick. "And Filosov never jests. General Piotr Ivanovitch Filosov." Having said this much he stared angrily at the Doctor, who was taken off guard completely. Uncertainly he turned to Annette. She was red as a beet with embarrassment.

"What . . . what . . ." Struensee said. "What's going on?"

"So, *une bête*," said Filosov and added loudly: "Are you not aware, my good man, that the fate of Denmark, which includes your own, depends entirely on Russia and the generosity of the Russian Tsar? Come, don't you know that much?"

"No, I don't," said Struensee.

"Well, there's not much point in my wasting time on you, then," the big man said. "You're a physician, they tell me."

"I certainly am," said Struensee. "Do you object?"

"The best thing you can do, my dear fellow," said Filosov, "is hang close to your leeches and clysters and stop annoying the lady who happens to be my heart's choice. Now, kindly leave, sir."

"Did anyone ever tell you," Struensee asked, "that you have gall enough for a regiment?"

"I am an autocrat and I don't conceal the fact," said Filosov. "As for you, Doctor, you're making a mistake, sticking your nose into politics. And you'll never be able to do anything for this lady's husband, whereas I can blow him to the heights like a feather."

"What the devil are you raving about!" yelled Struensee, stung to fury. "Madame, has he the right to talk this way in front of you?"

Annette flushed darkly. It was obvious that Filosov did have the right. "He exaggerates a little," she said. "But he is my friend and my husband's friend, too. Please don't be angry. You see, he's an original. That's just the way he is."

"An original! How delicate you are, Madame!" Struensee was seething. "Au revoir."

He turned on his heel and bolted into his carriage. Black with frustration he looked out the window into space as the horses trotted off into the open country. The land was a level plain, relieved by long, low hills. The air was soft with the damps of the nearby sea. The outlines of the leafless tree crowns, the walls and the roofs of the houses were blurred, as the Dutch masters have depicted such scenes with soft chalk on gray paper. The hard little branches of the fruit trees were like rheumatic fingers against the pale winter sky. Dirty snow lay in the long furrows of the fields, wary crows waddled in search of forage on the half-frozen earth. As the carriage drew near they cawed wildly and swept away into the air.

Moving at a trot over this unrewarding landscape Struensee's carriage caught up with a small figure by the side of the road. It was a young girl, the Doctor saw, craning his neck out the window. She was dressed in a faded dress of wool and wore a bonnet over her blonde hair. At once he recognized the little girl of the fisherman's hut. Holding a bundle in her hand she patiently waited for the carriage to go by. Struensee had the coachman stop.

"You, there," he said. "Antje Maria, what are you doing so far from home?"

At first the child was going to run away across the fields, but seeing who the Doctor was, she smiled happily up into his face. "You're the doctor," she said. "Aren't you?"

"Come," he told her, "get into the carriage beside me."

"My shoes are awfully dirty," she objected, looking at the carpeted carriage floor. "I'll make the floor dirty."

"Never mind that," he said. "March. Get in." She did as she was told. Struensee drew her down beside him and the carriage moved away.

"Now, my friend," he said to her with many a side glance, "what adventures are you up to? Are you off to make your fortune."

"I don't know," she told him. "Last spring my father didn't come back from Finland. We haven't given up hope, of course. But mother thinks I should try to find some work in Copenhagen."

"You're too young for that, aren't you?" said Struensee.

"Oh no, I'm fourteen years old," the child assured him. She had settled back comfortably on the cushions. "Mother says it would be a a great help to her," she added.

Heavy with thought, Struensee contemplated his small passenger. "What do you have in your bundle?" he asked her.

"I've got a dress," she said. "I've got a shirt and a pair of shoes and some bread. And I've got a sausage and the Bible."

"The Bible?" he said. "That's a very heavy book, if I remember. There are Bibles everywhere, you know. You needn't have brought that one with you."

"Yes, but this one is my Bible," the child explained. "Mother gave it to me. I read it when I'm not happy."

"You do?" said Struensee. "What do you read in it mostly?"

"Oh, everything," the other said grandly. "I read about the Garden of Eden. And about Abraham's sacrifice and Jacob's ladder and Joseph's dreams. Sometimes I read all about the Tower of Babel and what Jonah said when he was inside the whale. And I read about Job. He used to scratch himself with a piece of broken pot he itched so much. And then I read all about Our Lord, how he went through the villages healing the sick and driving out the demons. Oh, I read everything!"

Struensee smiled at the child's pride in her knowledge. Seeing his pleasure, she smiled with him. "And do you understand all you read?" he asked her. "Tell me the truth, now."

She thought this over for a long time as the carriage drummed and swayed its way along. Finally she turned to Struensee and looked at him almost beseechingly. "No, I don't understand most of it," she admitted. "It's much too wonderful for that. And I don't really try to understand, you know. I know I don't learn much. But I dream, though. I do that a lot."

"You dream when you read?" said Struensee. "Is that what you mean?"

"Yes, I do, and then it's just the same as if I were really there," the girl said. "I see the animals in the Garden of Eden, just like cows out in the pasture. I see the four rivers and our two ancestors walking around. Then I'm very happy. I feel as if I were really there, you see. I can even feel a nice wind blowing through the leaves of the big trees. That part of it is awfully nice." She stared wide-eyed at Struensee. "Why, do you think doing that's a sin?" she asked.

"Sin?" She had caught him napping. "No, not at all." Then he said quickly: "I don't suppose you have any money, have you?"

"Yes, I have," she said. "Ten groschen."

Again he had to smile. "I don't know why it is, Antje Maria," he said, "but you always seem to put me in an excellent humor. Now, my child, let us be still for a time. You can look out the window if you like."

As the afternoon was drawing to a close the carriage entered Copenhagen through a city gate guarded on either side by sentries who presented arms, seeing the royal coat-of-arms. Pedestrians snatched their hats from their heads to do the vehicle obeisance. The women curtsied, children waved their hands. In the many-paned windows of the big houses the dying sun burned a cold red, and there was a red glare on the steep gable roofs toppling over the way. In some of the windows candles had been lighted to welcome home the King.

Struensee's carriage rumbled over a bridge, where there were more hugely mustached guards again presenting arms. Then they were in the courtyard of Christiansborg Palace. A door flew open and out hurried a brown-haired young man in a white silk coat to meet the Doctor. "Chamberlain Warnstaedt," he introduced himself. "Do I have the pleasure of speaking to Dr. Struensee?"

"Yes, I am Struensee," the other said, and took an immediate liking to the lively young man. Warnstaedt had black eyes and a mild squint which gave him a gamin air.

"The King would like to have you quartered near him, Dr. Struensee," the chamberlain said. "Your rooms will be on the second floor. May I take you there now?" His oblique glance fell on Antje Maria huddled spellbound in the far corner of the carriage. "Who's that, Doctor?" he said. *"Parbleu, elle est une gosse, n'est-ce pas?"*

"That's my friend, Antje Maria, a young lady I'm very fond of," Struensee said. "One of my patients is her mother. Do you suppose, sir, you could find a place for her in the palace. Something to do, I mean?"

"No doubt, quite sure of it," Warnstaedt said promptly. "Come out here, Antje Maria. Heda, now!" He beckoned to a servant. "Bring this young lady to the housekeeper," he said, "and tell her that she belongs to the appanage of His Majesty's physician-in-ordinary."

"Very well, sir," chanted the servant, and took Antje Maria's bundle, handling it with as much care as if it were a bomb. With his free hand he led the bewildered child away.

Struensee and Warnstaedt walked up the long inner staircase of the palace together. Little marble gods shimmered smoothly in the candlelight. Servants stood about everywhere, and soldiers of the *garde du corps,* in snow-white uniforms with high grenadier helmets, were posted at every other corridor door.

Warnstaedt took Struensee confidentially by the elbow and said in a low voice: "You can trust me, Doctor. I'm a friend of your friend, Brandt."

"What happened to him, anyway?" Struensee asked abruptly.

"It's a peculiar story," said Warnstaedt. He led Struensee into an empty room and carefully shut the door behind him. "Palaces have ears at every keyhole," he said, "as many ears as tongues, and double. Anyway, about this Brandt affair. In Amalienborg there was living a great-aunt of the King, an old lady, brought up very strictly in the old-fashioned way. She was a friend of Swedenborg's. You can imagine."

"Who might he be?" said Struensee.

"You've never heard of Swedenborg?" said Warnstaedt. "Why, the fellow communicates with spirits! He can describe heaven and hell as well as his own backyard. He has second sight, they say."

"Second sight?" said Struensee. "Again I'm ignorant."

Warnstaedt was enjoying the Doctor's mystification. "Yes, he can see things take place hundreds of miles away," he explained. "Once when he was in Stockholm he saw a great fire in Goeteborg and was able to describe it to the letter. Then he sees things that haven't even happened yet."

"And do you believe such folderol?" asked Struensee. "My word!"

"I don't really know," said Warnstaedt. "But he's a savant of great reputation, and certainly he himself believes in his powers. And you must give him credit for using his powers, real or imagined, for the common good."

"That may be, but I don't believe in them," said Struensee. "Not by a damned sight, I might say, and no second sight at all. I've seen too many charlatans already."

Warnstaedt shrugged his shoulders and would not commit himself. "You may be interested to know," he said, "what Swedenborg has prophesied about His Majesty. He says that the King will run around on all fours through Christiansborg, howling like a dog and eating his food like a dog from a trencher on the floor. This animality, he claims, will come from his debaucheries."

Though not to be moved from his skepticism, Struensee cocked an ear. "Yes," he murmured, "please tell me more."

"Well, the point is," Warnstaedt continued, "this prophecy made a great impression on the Aunt Amalie I've just mentioned. She couldn't wait until she'd told the King all about it. And naturally His Majesty flew into a temper. He began to think about revenge, of course. But what could he really do? Swedenborg had left for London. And Aunt Amalie was a stout, pious, white-haired old girl. Very well-liked in Copenhagen. No poor person, they used to say, ever knocked in vain on her door. So the King decided that the least he could do was to play a practical joke on her, to even matters. He had his friend Brandt dress up in a bearskin and run on all fours through the palace at night. The old lady saw this performance and was nearly frightened out of her wits. The bear rose up on his hind legs and pretended to attack her. She fainted away. Someone sprinkled her with eau de cologne, took off her clothes—which she didn't like, by the way—and hustled her off to bed. Eventually she discovered that it was her nephew who had engineered the trick. She died six months later and left a tremendous estate, which was all signed over to the poor and the city of Copenhagen. Naturally that was a nasty blow for us. When the King went away this last time he was so provoked that he shipped Brandt back to Holstein to cool his heels."

"He put himself in an impossible position," said Struensee bitterly. "It's going to be a difficult matter to reinstate him, I can see that."

"I'm not so sure," said Warnstaedt. "Time cures everything, I've heard on good authority."

"Well, what about Count Rantzau," said Struensee. "What has become of that fellow, if I may ask."

"That's something else again," said Warnstaedt and looked very cross-eyed at the Doctor. "That's a matter of inside politics. It all hinges on Russia."

"Had Filosov something to do with it?" asked Struensee grimly. "I can easily imagine it."

"He did indeed," said Warnstaedt. "Why, have you ever met Filosov?"

"I have had that dubious experience," said Struensee. "Five minutes of his company will last me the rest of my lifetime."

"I take it you know Count Rantzau's earlier history?"

"I do," said Struensee. "That is, I know he served in the Russian army."

Struensee's dry tone for some reason tickled Warnstaedt. "Well, perhaps you may not know," he said, "that during his Russian period Count Rantzau was, if anything, overzealous to serve his masters. In fact, he was mixed up in the affairs that cost the Tsar's life and made Catherine ruler of all the Russias. You know how it always goes in such matters. The deed is appreciated, not the doers. And then, rulers are notoriously ungrateful, especially if they're women. It may have been that Rantzau wanted too much out of it. Personal emoluments, let us say. The Tsarina, if you like the type, is an attractive woman and I suppose one good turn does deserve another. Anyway, Rantzau left Russia a disappointed man. He plotted reprisal, I'm told, all the time he was helling his way through Europe.

"Now, there was a certain question of inheritance—I'm not going to bore you with the details. It was nothing, really, but a dispute over a tiny piece of land, an enclave in Holstein. Several states claimed sovereignty over it. In my opinion the land itself was valued very much out of proportion. In any case, after years of tugging and hauling, our foreign minister, Count Bernstorff, finally convinced the Russians it would be just as well for them to let their claims drop.

And you know how stubborn the Russians are when they get an idea into their heads.

"At this time, when the situation was hanging by a hair, Count Rantzau won the favor of our minister of war. No sooner did he feel secure than his old desire for revenge began to boil. He struck at Russia with all the means in his power. Filosov ran to Bernstorff and assured him that unless he kicked Rantzau out of Copenhagen, Russia would withdraw her tentative promises in the Holstein affair. Naturally, seeing his life's work in danger, Bernstorff had Rantzau sent posthaste to his regiment in Glueckstadt."

"Then it seems as if Filosov wasn't far wrong when he warned me to keep out of his way," said Struensee. "I took him for a fool."

"He is a fool," said Warnstaedt. "And a dangerous one."

Later, when Struensee was alone in his new rooms, he meditated on his difficulties. From somewhere down below in the palace he heard the tread of marching feet and the muffled roll of drums as the guard changed.

On the fireplace mantel was a Dresden china clock. The face was very gay, showing left and right a pretty shepherd and shepherdess. On top of the clock was Chronos, with hour glass and scythe, bending earnestly forward.

The clock struck the quarter hours with an oddly clear and tremulous note.

★ *II* ★

THE KING'S NEW physician-in-ordinary went about his duties unobtrusively. They were by no means onerous. He had much free time on his hands to do as he pleased. Frequently he went out into the city and quickly conceived a deep liking for Copenhagen. The weather was warm, with much rain and overhanging clouds. The wind blew in off the sea, a standard feature of the city's damp climate.

Most of all he liked to visit the Fishmarket, to stand on the quays and look out into the gray channel, to watch the fishermen unload their catch in big baskets for sale ashore He liked to mingle with the crowd, to listen to people talking and haggling in a language foreign to his ears. Indeed, he altogether liked, for once, to be an outsider looking on in pleased detachment.

He also investigated the seafood restaurants, the best purveyors in the city. They were to be found in old buildings in the waterfront district and had long wooden tables, creaky, uneven floors and small-paned windows through which could be seen the commotion of the market. The tables groaned under a tremendous weight of oysters, fish, cheese, bread and wine. Struensee soon found that his appetite was not equal to the Danish scale. When he drew away too soon from the board the proprietor would rush up and inquire whether he thought the fish stale or the oysters leathery.

Evenings, if not engaged at Christiansborg, he would walk through the magnificent Kongens Nytorv, past the brightly lighted coffeehouses to the Bredegade. Up this thoroughfare he would stroll and inspect the city homes of the Danish aristocracy, white buildings with twisted garlands and rosy wreaths of sandstone over the window frames. The courtyards of these houses were separated from the street by ornamental fences of wrought iron into which ingenious smiths had worked the owner's coat-of-arms and monogram. At this evening hour of the day a considerable traffic of carriages moved through the Bredegade, in and out of the courtyards. The soft candle-light in the windows was muted by white tulle curtains. Struensee sometimes heard the sharp tinkle of a spinet and women's purling laughter. All this worked like wine on his eager senses. The whole neighborhood was permeated by an exciting smell of roasted coffee, tinctured by the smell of harbor water and fish drifting up from the dockside.

Inside the fine homes of the Bredegade easy life and love held sway. Court chamberlains and petty noblemen, pages, generals and colonels, court councillors and clerics, with their wives, sweethearts and mistresses, all wearing their most brilliant smiles, sat about the faro tables, played quinze, or listened to a new piece of music by the indefatigable Rameau, cleverly balancing cups made of the purest Meissen. But most of all they simply talked, for the period was extremely devoted to social conversation.

There were times, to be sure, when conversation degenerated into brute gossip. The guests liked to whisper thrilling indiscretions. They told each other about the amatory adventures of Lady So-and-So, and about the incredible *faux pas* that Chamberlain Such-and-Such had committed in the King's presence. Hiding behind their masks they probed into each other with insectivorous precision, seeking out small items that might increase their advantage. Women set the tone of the gatherings. They guided the talk, they played with small ideas like so many little balls stuffed with down, catching and tossing them back and forth ever so daintily. Never did they weary of verbal distractions. The charming possibility of making romantic connection, the certainty that they were desired, flushed their faces prettily in the candlelight, lent their light voices a confident ring, made their movements lithe and alluring. They felt themselves to be exactly what they were, the only meaningful factor in their de-cadent world, whose function it was to make life as sweet, mysterious and important for their male opposites as lay within their power.

At the same time these women were not wholly satisfied with their passive role of being wooed and won. They actively campaigned for desirable males, not so much for the physical requitements the stalwarts might offer them, as for the pleasure of the hunt and its material rewards. With typically feminine lack of shame they used their yielding bodies and practical wit to gain social position, political influence, money and land. Looking at them no one could possibly know that the heart beneath the tender white bosom fluttered with joy at the thought of having a new equipage in which to lord it about, that those dark, passionate eyes were dreaming of the sale of a cargo of coffee still on the high seas, that the mind behind that splendid forehead was not nobly cogitating Klopstock's lofty homilies, but scheming to dance with the King at the next court masquerade.

The males of this society were anything but sentimental. They saw through the female game with ease. One of their prime amusements was to guess the ulterior meaning of suddenly tender hand pressings, of kisses blown from rosy fingertips, of the voice's stirring tremor. It amused them, too, to play the women's own game, to ensnare with false pretensions. Their vanity was flattered to have so much attention from the other sex, even though it might be spurious. Into this *effeté* situation Struensee swam as boldly as a pike into a carp pond. Whatever they might have, these people certainly lacked purpose and energy, qualities which the Doctor had in abundance. The women were used to endless theatricalities in their courtships. Now someone came along who was good to look at and who told them as simply as closing his hand that he would very much like to sleep with them, if possible that very night. On the following night, as a matter of fact, he was engaged. His frontal attack nonplussed the women. They gave readily to a man able to introduce novelty into their sexual routine.

Struensee became something of a sensation in the Bredegade. He was invited out morning, noon and night. Annette von Gaehler was astonished to see her provincial beau develop into the lion of the hour. Quickly altering her tactics she strained every nerve to hold him, using her lush physical charm freely. This provoked Filosov severely. Annette he considered his very own, his hard won property. Now he was forced to share and share alike. He drew closer to the lady's husband, Colonel Gaehler, when he played host of an evening to promote his glittering wife's cause. Covertly he admired her from a far corner while she paraded her tinsel. At bottom, Colonel Gaehler, too, was infatuated by his wife and could never forget that up hill and down dale she had backed his military ambitions.

For some time Filosov played with the idea of tipping the Colonel off about his wife's new affair, until he noted, very shortly, that the Colonel was quite aware of the way the wind was blowing, and accepting the new intruder with as much equanimity as he had previously accepted Filosov.

The Russian was at his wit's end. He could not very well threaten Count Bernstorff, the foreign minister, simply because his beloved Annette had deserted a Muscovite for a provincial German allegiance. But his jealousy became so acute that the veneer of civilized behavior wore through. One evening in the Royal Theater—Voltaire's *Zaire* with King Christian in the cast was being given—Filosov's volcanic temper got out of hand. Indeed, he so far forgot himself as to spit in Struensee's face. Struensee wiped away the spittle, unable to believe what was happening to him. Filosov let fly with a second pellet that caught the Doctor on the cheek. Now Struensee was nettled. He took Filosov by the collar and ripped him headlong out of the stall into the theater corridor. Having got him safely out of public view, in the fashion of an Altona rough, he planted a solid kick just below the Russian's kneecap. This chilled the Muscovite magically. "Your conduct, sir, is an abomination," Struensee said, breathing like a porpoise cast up on the beach. "I demand an apology."

"I'm insulted," screamed the Russian, nursing his leg. "I can't apologize to you. Should I apologize to someone beneath my station."

"You will apologize," Struensee said between his teeth, "or I'll tear your thick head from your shoulders." And with that he drew back, letting Filosov scramble to a sitting posture.

"Remember that when you lay a hand on me, you are attacking all Russia," said Filosov. "I am inviolable . . ."

"You think so?" said Struensee.

". . . I am inviolable and everyone knows it. When you touch me, you are insulting the Tsarina of all the Russias."

"Don't be a fool," said Struensee heavily, his temper ebbing. "You underestimate your Empress. She'll know how to handle an animal like you."

Filosov was suddenly impressed. "But you dare not have relations between Russia and Denmark deteriorate on your account, do you?" he said stubbornly.

Struensee burst out laughing at this *non sequitur*. He looked down into Filosov's glittering eyes. "Perhaps not," he said quietly. He felt as cold as ice. "Get up off the floor."

Filosov did this, brushed himself off, grinned and took hold of Struensee's sleeve. "Let us take the middle road," he whispered. "The middle road is best. What do you say? We shall divide the apple of discord, pips and all. You have Gaehler the first three days of the week and every other Sunday, and I have her the rest of the time. How about that?"

"And how about Gaehler herself?" said Struensee.

"Never mind about her," said the Russian. "What has she got

to do with it. You're the strangest fellow I've ever met. No wonder they talk about you."

"I don't follow you," said Struensee.

"Don't you realize that women don't arrange a liaison," the Russian said. "We do it for them. Shall we treat them like equals?"

"That's all new to me," said Struensee. "I'm surprised to find you in the employ of a woman. How do you account for it?"

"That's different, completely different," said Filosov. "The Tsarina is an exception. She is Russia. She is more than herself. Well, how about the other thing?"

"I bow to the irresistible," said Struensee. Again he burst into mirthless laughter.

Annette was surprised to see how amicable were Struensee and Filosov when they returned to their box. After a moment of doubt, she smiled and nodded encouragingly in their direction. Her husband was sitting in the box directly behind her. "The gentlemen have made up, I see," he commented. "The best thing they could do. Aren't you happy, my dear?" So saying he bent forward and breathed a small husbandly kiss into her ear.

"Yes, I'm glad, so glad," she sighed. "It's so wonderful to have three understanding men to depend on."

After this incident Annette saw much less, in fact very little, of Struensee. He visited other houses, always seeking out women. Others now enjoyed the virility hitherto reserved for Frau von Gaehler. For example, there was Frau von Holstein, billowy and blonde and always merry. She was one of Brandt's friends. Each week he sent her letters telling her how much he longed for her and the diversions of Copenhagen. She would read his letters and let them flutter away, saying pensively: "I long for him, too, poor thing. Holstein says he's the nicest one I've ever had. Isn't there anything, anything at all you can do for him, dear Struensee?"

"Not yet, Madame," Struensee would assure her. "But I won't forget him."

Then there was Fraulein von Eyben, the Queen's lady-in-waiting. Apart from the fact that she was good-looking, slim and tall, Fraulein von Eyben was a goldmine of useful information. The Queen trusted her and talked to her freely about her childhood and youth in Carlton House, about her impressions of Germany and Denmark and her concern about Christian, who, in defiance of Struensee's advice, had drifted back to his former hellrake habits. Fraulein von Eyben was a physical type who looked much better in negligee than when fully clothed. The styles of the period failed to do justice to her long-limbed attractions. She had red hair and violet eyes. Struensee thought it sinful to comb up such lovely hair and powder it. He would have liked to see it falling down over her white shoulders in shining waves, but she would not be convinced. For her Struensee had a pet name, "Gudrun," after the heroine of the old saga. In actual fact the name applied so far as beauty and heroic looks went, but there it stopped. Fraulein von Eyben had no character. At first meeting Struensee had great hopes, for he was deeply attracted, but his paramour rapidly disillusioned him and he soon tired of her society as a steady thing.

It was amazing how much alike they all were, these women of the little northern metropolis. Struensee soon realized that their gestures and small amiabilities were highly artificial. Their train of thought, the very timbre of their voices were elaborately cultivated. Even in bed they showed no signs of individuality, so thoroughly stylized was their makeup. Their love-making was tempered and discreet, they gave their bodies for a little, but never their feelings. The sighs and little cries that at first Struensee had understood to be signs of ecstasy proved to be nothing more than a mechanical reaction deemed proper to the cohabitation experience.

In fact, Copenhagen high society as a whole had something of the jerkiness and forcedness of a mechanical toy, something of the clock-like motion of the *harmonia prestabilitata* invented by Leibniz. Struensee's "Gudrun" was a typical disappointment. The helmet of pagan red gold was a lie and a sham. She was really much more like herself when she wore her hair powdered a deathly white. Struensee complimented her on her long, fine legs. She was unconvinced. "You should see the Queen," she said. "She's a thousand times nicer with her clothes off than with them on. If I were a physician . . ."

"That would be a fine scandal," said Struensee. "Strange ideas run through your head, my sweet."

There were times when Struensee thought back regretfully on the women of the Holstein petty nobility who had opened the way for him out of obscurity. In retrospect they seemed far more sincere and truly feminine than the ladies of the capital. A man at least could actually talk to them. With them it was not always necessary to chatter nonsense. When they took a man into their confidence, at least there was an off chance that they actually liked him. Love to them conceivably might be more than an accepted means of topping off a gossipy evening.

Struensee persisted romantically in his search for a "woman with a soul." Finally he believed he had found her in a certain Frau von Gabel. In the first place she curtly refused his offer of a liaison. This young matron was small, dark-haired and had large black eyes that almost swallowed up her delicate face. She was married to a privy-councillor who governed the Danish province of Jutland. She was in Copenhagen only for the winter months to escape the raw weather of the peninsula. Struensee, with an observing medical eye, saw that she was tubercular, and advised her to travel south. She smiled wearily and told him that leaving her beloved Denmark would be the death of her. No, she would stay if she forfeited her life, which Struensee privately commented she certainly would.

Frau von Gabel told him about Jutland, about the broad, rough moors where, on the heights, there lay granite blocks marking the graves of extinct peoples, perhaps of the Cimbri, so she said, who had once fared south to be hacked to death by the short swords of the Romans. She talked about the deep fir forests and the duny wastelands covered with wiry grasses, about the western coast of her homeland, and the estates of the region, these surrounded by heavy stone walls.

She dreamed about her youth, talking softly and trustingly as if she had known Struensee all her life. She told him how they had all used to gather about a great fire in the fireplace, the whole family, parents and children, to listen to folk tales spun out by an old shepherd, tales about the iron-encased riders of King Christian, about witches riding over the misty moors, about spooks at midnight and green-haired water-women with bulgy eyes who lured young men down to rob them of their souls.

Struensee did not particularly like to have the pretty young woman dreamily talk away the hours. He considered it an unhealthy and silly practice. Stories about the misty primeval world made him uneasy. He darkly sensed that they might be something more than mere fairy tales, maybe the echo of the actual experiences of intuitively superior people long since forgotten and vanished into dust. Hearing about these magical curiosities always evoked in him the same creepy sensation as when Brandt hummed the lines written by Claudius, the German poet:

> "Black the wood and stilly deep,
> While upward from the meadows creep
> Gray mists mysterious."

How strange it is, Struensee would think, that so delicate a creature should be so morbidly preoccupied.

Yet Frau von Gabel, he found out, could be gay as well. She could tell about the long skating trips of her youth, the fish-spearing expeditions, the apple harvests, the slaughtering feasts, the summer dances in the grass, with St. John's fire lighted on the hill and the countryside glowing redly. But even in her brightest reminiscences there was an underlying strain of melancholy, the somberness of the North. And this displeased Struensee, for it was his nature to crave the luminous, the sharply defined, the understandable, the rational. At the same time, according to the principle that opposites attract, he was drawn to the fey creature from Jutland, not erotically, but in a mood of brotherly warmth and respect. Indeed, Frau von Gabel was the first woman he had ever treated otherwise than as an object of conquest. He realized that she was pretty and that not a soul in the Bredegade thought of their relationship as limited to mere amity. Nevertheless, after a more or less half-hearted attempt to have her, this as much a concession to polite behavior as genuine desire, he contented himself with the gifts of her spirit.

This young woman knew the common people. She had grown up among peasants, shepherds, woodcutters and fishermen. The master of the aristocratic country estate in lonely Jutland where she had spent her childhood had been more like a *pater familias* in his dealings with his dependents than a feudal lord. Often she gave Struensee her opinions on what should be done to further the people's welfare. And when she talked in this vein he was genuinely interested. He sensed that she was really willing to sacrifice herself to an idea, should opportunity arise. She had a talent for self-sacrifice, even for self-annihilation. Struensee thought it might have something to do with her consumptive yearning for peace and her intimacy with death.

Many sunny winter afternoons Struensee sat in Frau von Gabel's comfortable living room. The silhouettes of her parents and her sisters hung in black frames on the wall. Under glass on her sewing table was a sprig of Jutland heather.

★ *III* ★

*S*TRUENSEE HAD A conference with old Councillor Berger, the King's old medical adviser. The new favorite had expected Berger to be anything but cordial, and was surprised when the old man greeted him beaming with pleasure.

For a time they talked shop. They discussed universities, famous colleagues and baffling diseases. They ventured opinions on the homeopathic school of thought championed by the unfortunate Hahnemann, on Mesmer's psychiatric theories and Gall's phrenology. They both agreed that none of these hypotheses was worth serious consideration by practical men. Then, having smelled each other out, Berger broached the subject that had been in the back of his mind all along, the King's health.

Berger, a stout, gray-haired man with ruddy cheeks, politely suggested that the King's sickness was not organic. It was, he believed, so-called "heart-sickness," or *folie de coeur*. Struensee countered by saying cautiously that he had heard of this curious malady, but had never come across it in his provincial practice. It was up to the old councillor to explain himself. He thought for some time before he spoke.

"It's not easy to give a clear picture of this defect," he said finally. "Medical terminology is really limited to anatomy, physiology and pathology. If we apply it to disturbances of the soul at once it loses validity and may even be misleading. To talk scientifically about the condition we should have some idea of the anatomy and physiology of the soul. But these sciences have not yet been invented."

"I agree," said Struensee. "Can you suggest any substitute measures, Councillor?"

"Nothing satisfactory," said Berger decisively. "We must simply wander in the dark. We will have to use the concepts of metaphysics, moral philosophy, yes, even theology, as best we can. A simple physician like myself feels very ill at ease groping his way along on such terms. We are almost sure to stray off the path into swamps of conjecture and sink in up to our necks. But in this case, since the welfare and health of the patient is bound up with the well-being of a whole people, I'm going to lay my cards on the table, even at the risk of making a fool of myself."

By deprecatory noddings and polite grimaces Struensee let old Berger know that never in the world would he judge his views ridiculous. The old man cleared his throat and tugged learnedly at his nose.

"*Folie de coeur,* as I see it, comes when a person loses faith in himself," he began. "If I were a pious man, and I suppose I am at times, I should identify the condition with the soul's doubt of its own destiny. It arises from the fact that the soul, so to speak, has no vocation. A soul without dedication results in *folie de coeur.*"

"Very reasonable," said Struensee. "Pray continue, Doctor."

"Exactly why is this disease called *folie de coeur,*" Berger said carefully, warming to his subject. "It is so called because the subject's feelings are primarily affected. They become confused, they work at odds. The understanding and the capacity for rational thought are only secondarily affected. They are eventually, but not initially, drawn down, as it were, into the maelstrom. Now, I believe that a person showing these symptoms has suffered a severe shock at some time or other, probably in youth. He has never recovered from the blow. The situation is analogous to one involving a physical heart ailment, which can be brought on, as we know, by a severe strain. Or even by fright.

"The most unfortunate aspect of the ailment is that the patient stubbornly refuses to reveal the source of his injury. And this not only to others, but even to himself. He believes that his heart could never endure revealing the injury. This reticence, which even extends to the self, in my belief is a cunning trick of nature calculated to hold the person together as a personality. At the same time, running counter to this trickery, is the heart's inborn tendency to be garrulous, to strut before the world telling everything. Now, observe, the heart cannot speak out directly about itself, for it must keep its secret. And so, unable to chatter freely, it chatters indirectly, inventing an infinity of guises. When the heart would weep, it cavorts like a clown. When it would pray, it utters blasphemies. When inclined to foolishness, it drones like a pedant.

"Now, think, when these fancy-dress pranks, these deceptions and theatricalities have continued long enough the heart no longer recognizes its own falseness as such. In sum, it loses its identity. Behold the sick man. He has a face of his own like everybody else, he has certain attitudes towards life. Outwardly he looks like a healthy man, with all the organs and faculties of a healthy man. But in reality he is as hollow as a porcelain figure. He has no self, Dr. Struensee. That is, he may still have a self, but this true self is so thoroughly hidden and buried and tucked away that even he himself cannot find it. He has crawled into a fear-ridden corner, he has ducked out of sight, cramped himself into as small a space as possible. In this posture he doubts the very existence of himself. He simply doubts. He doubts everything, himself and everything in the world.

"This, mind you, is hard to endure. It is doubly hard, as you can imagine, if the sick person chances to be a king. In this case the patient has more to do than merely relate himself soundly to the world. He also is a symbol of a whole people, and as a symbol must also relate himself effectively with the world. Imagine, then, Dr. Struensee, the horror of not feeling oneself a fixed person, a dependable person. In fact, of feeling oneself inferior to any peasant boy in this respect. Obviously it would be enough to drive anyone mad.

"But woe to him who sees through this dilemma of the King's! The man who really understands his sufferings and explains them to him will surely pay for it. For an hour he might be the King's favorite, but no more than an hour. A king cannot be a king on anyone's sufferance."

Struensee nodded his head and in the midst of the nodding shuddered as a little chill involuntarily passed over him. Berger, fortunately, did not notice. He rubbed his chin, engrossed in his own line of thought. "A couple of days ago I was in the city early in the morning," he said. "People were on their way to work. The streets were alive with children all scrubbed and off for school. Why, it was a picture of freshness and industry! It did my heart good, sir.

"Now, as I got near Christiansborg, I saw a crowd gathering. I heard howls and whistles. I hurried up to see what was up. It was the King. His Majesty was drunk as a fiddler's bitch. He was staggering home to the Palace. He was pale and sick and his hair hung about his face. His clothes were filthy, his hat hung over his ear. A pretty, pretty sight, my dear Struensee, so bright and early in the morning.

"I tell you, the crowd came near to stoning the man. Imagine, their own King. I said nothing, for of course there was nothing to say. The people were right, according to their lights. They know nothing about the King's sickness. Anyway, come right down to it, any scoundrel might plead sickness, and where would we be then? No, the people were right, absolutely right. Anyone who acts like that, no matter what the grounds, certainly forfeits his right to kingship and the respect accorded the crown."

"I know, I know, Councillor Berger," said Struensee nervously. "My sympathies in good measure lie with the people. But what shall be done, may I ask? We hardly want revolution or civil war. Not I, at least. And so we must restore him to the level of kingship. We must, in short, make him a healthy man."

"But is that possible?" objected Berger. "Doesn't this case concern the ministers of the gospel and the statesmen more than us physicians? Isn't this sickness a moral thing?"

"No doubt of it," said Struensee. "But where is the cleric or statesman with the insight to understand the disease, let alone cure it? Dogma and political platitudes do no good here. The confessional might be of value, I suppose. The patient, I'm sure, would like to confess, if he dared. But if he did, the confessor would immediately begin to belabor him with admonitions to believe in God, to trust the Lord and so on. What good do you imagine that would do a sick man? He simply has no capacity for belief at this stage. He is incapable of love, of reaching out beyond himself. It would be like asking a man with two broken legs to run a race."

"How do you know all this?" Berger asked. "We seem to think much alike."

"Well, I talked with him in Paris," said Struensee evasively. "He let me have a glimpse of what was going on inside his head. I thought perhaps he would do it again, having done it once. At first, indeed, I was sure I had his confidence. Then suddenly he began to avoid me. My presence gradually became oppressive to him. But I'm rather stubborn. I don't give up at all easily, especially in a life and death matter like this. But the formalities of the court, state business, all these court balls and receptions give him endless opportunity to keep out of my way.

"In any event, one evening I did succeed in cornering him. He stood with his back to a window, I remember, while I was asking him how he felt. He looked down at the floor, he gave incoherent replies and tried to turn the subject. Then, when I would not be dissuaded, he became surly and acted mum. He drew his brows together . . .

like this. Really his face looked like a mask. His eyes were not properly focussed. They had a blurred look. Then he let himself go. He was as full of hate as a tick of blood. I know what you want, all right, he said. I know what you're sneaking around me for. It made my hackles rise to hear him. Yes, you want to make me well, don't you, he said.

"What a curious thing to say, Councillor Berger. In all my experience as a physician I had never heard the like. The chills ran up my back. You might easily imagine that it wasn't he himself who was saying it, but the demon of his sickness, if there is such a thing. I answered him as calmly as I could. Making you better is, indeed, what I propose to do, Your Majesty, I told him. He looked at me in amazement, as if he couldn't understand what I was saying. Then he excused himself, pleading an engagement."

Berger wagged his head dolefully and sighed. "Yes, I've had the same experience with him a dozen times," he said.

"But I'm not giving up," said Struensee. "I'd rather go back to Altona than play the silk-stocking parasite at the court. Since he is determined to avoid me, I'm going to influence him through somebody else. Through Frau von Gabel, to be exact."

"Frau von Gabel!" said Berger. "Why, the woman is sick herself!"

"I realize that," said Struensee. "Nevertheless, she's sound enough of spirit. She's also extremely intelligent. And she has a keen sense of responsibility. Finally, she's attractive enough to attract his interest."

"Perhaps, perhaps," muttered Berger, looking squarely at the other. "Don't think it presumptuous of me, my dear colleague, to question your therapy. Yet isn't it rather outside the usual medical procedure? Don't you consider it . . . well . . . a trifle immoral?"

"I'm not so sure," said Struensee. "Don't you think it would be less immoral, if a choice must be made, than letting a man destroy himself and destroy the state with him without lifting a finger to stop it?"

"You're taking a terrible responsibility," said Berger. "Assume that everything works well and that he takes to Frau von Gabel. Would she be able to stand it? I'm sure I can't imagine it."

"I will support her," said Struensee. "She can lean on me."

"And the Queen?"

"What has she got to do with it?"

"She's his wife, after all," said Berger. "If your plan works, it's bound to humiliate and injure her. Would it not be better to enlist the Queen in your plan?"

"I hardly know the Queen," said Struensee. "She keeps by herself. But a great deal has happened, I know, between her and the King. Of one thing I am sure . . . they no longer trust each other. If the Queen were involved in my project I feel sure that once the

King found it out his malady would grow worse. Furthermore . . ."

"Yes," said Berger. "Please go on."

"I consider the Queen to be the last person who might have a salutary influence on the King," Struensee finished. "She is far too flighty, too isolated. She has no worldly experience. She's incredibly naïve. Indeed, sir, she knows nothing."

"You consider her stupid?" Berger asked quietly.

"I do," said Struensee. "Stupid and conceited. A beauty, of course. But no brains."

"And yet you don't know her," objected Berger. "Do you?"

"Her conduct speaks for itself," Struensee said curtly.

"Well, my dear sir, I think you're dreadfully mistaken," said Berger incisively. "In my humble opinion, you could not be more wrong had you planned it. The Queen is anxious to do her very best. But what can she do at this court? She simply has to pretend hauteur and hide behind her station. Otherwise her sufferings would be intolerable."

"You're an excellent, kind fellow, my good Berger," said Struensee. "Yet allow me to assure you that I am seldom wrong in my judgments of people."

"So?" said Berger uncomfortably. "That may be. Still, I must beg you to give up your project. Or at least delay it."

"No, I have my mind made up," said Struensee coldly. Then suddenly he smiled, impulsively reached for Berger's hand and shook it. "Please don't take my frankness amiss," he said warmly. "After all, we both want the same thing."

"True enough," said Berger and shook Struensee's hand. "Yet I cannot support your therapy. I can only wish you luck, sir."

Here they parted. Berger stood for a long time leaning against a chairback, thoughtfully shaking his head.

Struensee took Frau von Gabel into his confidence, according to plan. Cautiously at first, then more openly he talked about the King's health. In glowing colors he painted how a wise and selfless woman might rehabilitate the King. It did not take the young matron from Jutland long to catch Struensee's drift. She was not enthusiastic, but by no means insulted on hearing his indirections. The moral aspect of the scheme bothered her not at all, that is, so long as she believed the object to be moral. She was greatly drawn, however, by the idea of utter self-sacrifice. And, at the bottom, the idea of being the indispensable intimate of a king, of living within the innermost orbit of his power, was not unsympathetic to her.

A curious mixture of noble womanly feeling and niggardly womanly reckoning finally brought her to a point where she imagined that Struensee's plan was practically her own, although in cold truth she was neither unmoral nor energetic enough to have conceived any such plot on her own. Beguiled by Struensee she came to believe the problem was relatively simple. Participation in a scheme for kingly salvation so excited her that she bloomed. She even seemed to grow taller. Her dark eyes were more soulful than ever, larger than ever under the powdered, swept-up frame of hair, a heavy crown contrasting dramatically with her exquisite, small-boned features. She took a renewed interest in her dress. Her gowns became increasingly decolleté, her crinolines more billowy. The little provincial belle emerged from the chrysalis as a *morceau de roi*. There were many occasions when Struensee regretted having groomed her for another's use, rather than for his own.

May had come and the court had moved to summer quarters at Frederiksborg. Here, in idyllic, garden surroundings, it was easy enough for Struensee to have Frau von Gabel introduced to the King. Presently, to the conspirator's gratification, the two showed a marked tendency to draw apart from the rest of the company. Together they took rides in a gondola on the lake. Afternoons, when others went rowing, they explored the garden terraces. Led on by the barking of Christian's busy poodles, they lost themselves in the beach woods. They made a trip to the church ruins and found them dappled with the warm afternoon sun filtering through the beech leaves.

Struensee read his plan's success in the King's sickly preoccupation and in Holck's chronic air of annoyance. The whisper and buzz of the courtiers, and the abrupt way which the gossiping came to a stop when the King entered the room, indicated that all was moving according to schedule.

During this period Christian brightened up and often engaged Struensee in long conversations. Struensee also got in the habit of chatting decorously with Count Bernstorff, minister of foreign affairs, who could not conceal his pleasure in the King's changed appearance. The King's physician-in-ordinary began to feel that he could afford to relax a little. He enjoyed the pleasures of the table, particularly the wines, which were so very much better than those available in Altona. He began to pay some attention to Annette von Gaehler and to Fraulein von Eyben of the long, slim legs.

Of a sudden it seemed to him, now that his mood had lightened, that all women were more lovely, desirable and gracious than before. He swam along through space behind his happiness, like the tail behind a comet. As a matter of fact, with the coming of spring and removal to country scenes the women had changed for the better. Laying aside their heavy winter clothing, their furs and warm hats, they likewise laid aside some of their arrogance and fancy manners. They put on light summer garments of silk and taffeta. Over their sweetly swelling breasts they wore lacy trim. They let their hair fall down over their shoulders, as became aristocratic versions of the shepherdess. It was Struensee's first experience of female metamorphosis, and it tickled him strongly.

He enjoyed the friendly tête-à-tête in the evening, the improvised dances, the musicales and the amateur theatricals in which the King himself took leading parts. The only real fly in the ointment was the Queen Mother, who occasionally visited Frederiksborg with her son. At the theatricals she would sit rigidly in her chair, not permitting the faintest smile to cross her royal features no matter how comic the lines. If her son laughed out loud, she would glare at him in anger, causing him to bite his lips. Then he would bend towards his mother and adjust the shawl about her shoulders with tender solicitude, like a lover.

The Queen-Dowager appeared not at all hostile towards Struensee. Several times she had him summoned so that she might inquire about the King's health. But there was something in the woman that bade the Doctor beware. The black eyes under thick brows, still beautiful and luminous at times, could alter their glance without warning and thrust like daggers when they encountered an object of dislike. Apparently the Queen-Dowager entertained warm feelings only for a small minority, and for the many knew only revulsion. Count Holck, the chamberlain, Warnstaedt, Fraulein von Eyben, Count Bernstorff were all numbered among her enemies. On the other hand she was fond of Filosov, who groveled before her like a worm. There were many signs that notwithstanding her withdrawal from society she had not completely abandoned hope of playing a grand political role.

As for Struensee he had never dealt with this large type of woman before. He always felt a little helpless when she talked to him with cultivated bluntness, as if he were a stable-hand. The gradually developing relationship between Christian and Frau von Gabel evoked wry amusement in Juliana. "Apropos," she once said to Struensee, as they were both looking at the retreating pair, "the little one is certainly going to burn her fingers, sweet dear."

Struensee looked down uneasily at his shoes. The Queen-Dowager smiled inscrutably into the distance, fanning herself with a decorative fan set off with scenes after Boucher. "Apropos," she repeated, for it was her unpleasant custom to introduce her observations with this patronizing phrase. "Do you think that the King's sickness is something mental, Dr. Struensee?"

"He has certain difficulties of that nature, Your Highness," said Struensee.

"Has he ever talked with you?" she asked quickly, so interested that she forgot to fan herself.

"The King is very reticent," said Struensee.

"Do you think so?" said the Queen-Dowager. "In my opinion he talks far too much. Like a child."

"Perhaps he talks to hide his troubles," Struensee suggested.

"I see," said the Queen-Dowager. "And do you think you can cure him of that?"

"I can try," said Struensee.

The Queen-Dowager fanned herself with much decision and turned half away. The Doctor examined her profile. Her throat was still handsome, her chin firm. She turned back to the Doctor and looked at him with great irony, irony verging on derision. "*À propos, mon bon médicin,*" she said, "if you can cure that fellow, you'll be a greater magician than Cagliostro."

Struensee's vanity was piqued, though he realized that she was deliberately baiting him. "Madame, a great many things are possible to the scientist," he told her, "that a charlatan can only pretend."

"Oh, scientists are too stuffy," she said, smiling finely. "They always come a cropper with their laws and their formulas. But you, my dear Doctor, seem to be the happy exception. You have the scientific spirit without cramming it down our throats."

Struensee rose and bowed. "May I thank Your Highness," he intoned, "for an undeserved compliment."

And so the battle of wits passed without untoward result. It was a sham battle, no more. Nevertheless, this innocent alert let Struensee know that once he really came to grips with the Queen-Dowager, it would be a fight to the death.

Then came the June evening when Frau von Gabel rushed into Struensee's rooms without knocking. She was sobbing so loudly that he hastened to shut the door fast behind her. He was in his dressing gown, ready for retiring, and had just risen from his dressing table, where the candles on either side of the mirror were still brightly burning.

Frau von Gabel threw herself on Struensee's bed, buried her head in the cushions, not bothering about irreparable damage to her coiffure. Her shoulders shook from racking sobs. The Doctor, after some hesitation, took her hand and it rested lifelessly in his own.

"I can't keep it up," she said through her tears and chokings. "I can't do it, I can't."

"What happened?" he asked, fearing the worst.

But she would give no answer, and continued to weep torrents into the bedcovers. Struensee shrugged his shoulders and waited for the storm to relax a little. As he watched her narrowly with his physician's eyes she suddenly twisted herself about on the bed and threatened him with clenched fists. The helpless gesture was both pathetic and comic, and Struensee nearly smiled. This she saw and at once sprang to her feet, wiped away the tears and began to adjust her clothing, woman-fashion. Her cheeks glowed feverishly, her eyes had the excited, vague look of one coming down with pneumonia. "You have humiliated me!" she hissed at him breathlessly. "You're a scoundrel, you're no good."

"Is that so?" he said without feeling any emotion. "Why?"

"I cannot go on living this way," she said. "I am only half alive."

There now arose in Struensee an overpowering hatred of all femininity. Fumes came up from sulphurous depths, where the ancient hatred of the sexes glows implacably. The total existence of obdurate womankind revolted him at this moment. With great effort he held his raging contempt in check and said evenly: "Madame, you complain about me. But you are no longer a child. You entered into this compact freely." But hardly were the words out of his mouth than he realized he had erred. Now she will remind me that she is a woman, he thought, and so different from me and not liable to masculine obligations. He was not mistaken.

"You're clever, aren't you," she said, sighing. "You knew what you wanted, all right. You used me in your miserable little chess game. Like a pawn. No more important than that. What does it matter about throwing away a pawn to keep the King out of check. That's your brilliant idea, isn't it?"

"Of course it is," he said. "Didn't you know? I thought I had made it clear to you. But you exaggerate, in any case." After all, he thought remorsefully, there is something to her argument.

She moved closer to him, and pointed dramatically to her breast, all but uncovered and tender under the gauzy batiste. With more tears welling into her eyes she said: "Haven't you ever realized that I'm a woman, Struensee?"

"Whatever has come over you?" said Struensee, and immediately wished he had not inquired.

Now she fumbled for her handkerchief, found it, and cried into it, her nose pressed into its folds, her neck bowed enticingly. She raised her eyes and looked at Struensee in anguish. "Can you allow that animal of a man to use me like a thing!" she said. "First he dirtied my body, then my soul. Can you stand it? How he tittered at me, the foul maniac." She laughed bitterly, quaking all over. "How could I ever have imagined it, how could I!" she said. Then she looked stonily away.

This performance jolted Struensee and he could think of nothing to say. They looked at each other. And then, without warning, Frau von Gabel threw herself into his arms, embraced him tightly and covered his face with damp, hot kisses. "Struensee, beloved," she whispered frantically, "don't you know that I dream of you day and night since you first . . . since you first wanted me?"

[153]

"Dream about me?" he said stupidly. "You do?"

"Oh, dear, dear," she moaned like a child. Warm tears rolled down her cheeks and wet Struensee's chin. "You don't love me," she groaned. "I know it. I'm not reproaching you for it. It was all my fault. It's time I grew up, I know. It's true I knew what I was doing. But no matter what I did, I thought all along that you must love me. I did it for you."

"But I do love you," said Struensee woodenly.

"No, not that way," she whispered and pulled away from him. "I don't really know why I ever came here to you. Perhaps I wanted revenge." She took another step away from him. Her eyes seemed to squint, as if the muscles had lost control of the eye-balls. "Yes, yes," she said sarcastically, "now you can laugh at me with your friends, with Warnstaedt and all the rest of them. Why don't you throw me on the bed, Struensee? Why don't you strip off my clothes and do anything you want with me? Other people have. Go ahead. You do it, too. Isn't that the way to handle a common whore, Doctor?"

Struensee was confounded by so much feeling. He felt a little sick. "Be reasonable, my dear," he said. "Try to be reasonable about it." His own words rang hollow. "For God's sake," he implored, "try to keep a cool head, will you?"

"Reasonable!" she shrieked. "Are you afraid of a scandal? Don't worry about that. Come now, how about giving me a louis d'or for my work. He did, you know, and I'd like another. You're very sweet, he said, so here's a little something. I don't think I'll want you again, he said, for you're really much too complicated for my vulgar taste. And you mustn't think I owe you all Denmark just because we tiddled away a night in bed, my dear. A louis d'or is one thing, Denmark another. Look, he said, it's got Louis' picture on it. There's Louis, with laurel around his head. It will make you think about your own little king, Christian the Small. Count your earnings and say a little prayer for Christian, like a good little girl."

Struensee swallowed hard, hearing these peculiar revelations. He was enormously relieved to see that, having confessed all, Frau von Gabel was getting herself in hand. "You and your eternal reasoning are all right, Struensee," she told him in a different, calmer voice. "What did happen, when it's all summed up? Nothing worth mentioning. Why, I can't say I even lost my maidenhead. I simply went to bed with the King. And I was mortally disappointed, let me tell you that, sir. But what of that? Women don't need to sleep with a king to be disappointed. It's stupid of me to make such a fuss. *Tant de bruit pour une omelette.* Now I'll get out, my reasonable friend."

"Already?" he said. "Do you . . ."

"Yes, I have to go," she said. "My carriage is waiting outside. I didn't last long in the business, did I!"

"I'll go along with you," he told her quickly. "Please allow me to do that."

"I think not," she said. "I want to be by myself, I want to get certain matters straightened out in my mind. But . . ."

"Yes," he said, eager to please.

"You may kiss me goodbye if you like."

He kissed her tentatively on the mouth, and felt her lips quiver under his. She kissed him back lightly a last time. In confusion he opened the door for her. In the corridor she turned and said: "We'll not see each other again, Struensee. I'm going back to Jutland very soon."

He bowed silently to her, his face drawn with concern. He felt momentarily that he really did love this sensitive, dark-eyed woman. Her leaving left him empty as a dry gourd.

"And from now on, Struensee," she said, "don't play with women, I beg you. You have no idea how painful it is to them." Then she pulled down her mouth sardonically. "But you'll always play with women, won't you," she said. "I'm almost jealous, I really am." Then she glided away, holding up her billowing dress above her ankles. He stared hard after the small figure, head held high, until it had disappeared around a corner.

Alone in his room he put out the candles and sat down near a window giving out on the lake. The water was a black platter in the night, barely outlined in the weak light of a waning moon. White swans were drifting like ghosts through the murk, the wind was stirring uneasily in the beeches. He sat this way a long time, sunk deeply in himself, quite unable to gather his thoughts. He felt the young woman's pain flowing into his own heart, soaking it through with an agony of longing. Now he was himself infected with love, now he believed that he loved none but her. He imagined life with her. How she would cling to him, her eyes wide, seeing everything, but mostly him. He could not bear the thought of not seeing her again. The thought of it was so painful that he jumped to his feet and pressed his burning head against the cool panes of glass in the tall windows. When the morning twilight began to creep into the room and the throstles were singing he lay on the bed and kissed the pillows where Frau von Gabel had shed copious tears.

The very next day Struensee left for Copenhagen in pursuit of Frau von Gabel, but was refused admission to her home. Madame was not in, the maid told him, staring at him with undisguised curiosity. He came again and again, and was consistently turned down. Often he wandered through the Bredegade, hoping to catch a glimpse of her, to see her through the windows at night. He would stand in front of her house, trying to peer through the drapes, which hung so sadly and matly in the dark. It was like standing before the altar of a temple, he felt. Not until the faint flow of candlelight somewhere in the interior of the house went out for good would he give up his vigil and walk off up the street, murmuring a prayerful wish for her safety and well-being.

But his mood was not all romantic sadness and longing. He was conscious of the brilliance of early summer all about. It gave his mood a fine gloss. He secretly liked the people's vigorous response to the long sunny days, he liked the pleasing crowdedness of the city. Everything seemed livelier, more real and more poignant than ever before. The towers of the city, pressed smooth by brisk winds from the sea, the neat houses rising up story after story from the street, all seemed to partake of some keener, heightened reality. Behind all the glittering windows and the white curtains and geranium pots were there not women and more women? Were they not watching over the life of the city from within their still rooms? Struensee conceived a deep affection this summer for Copenhagen.

The day finally came when Struensee's beloved left, as she had promised, for Jutland. He watched the black coach leave, piled high with coffers and drawn by chestnut horses of the heavy Oldenburg strain. Then she was gone for good from the Bredegade. Now the house was quite empty, a temple unadorned. The drapes at her windows shimmered no more. No more could he act out the hope of seeing her small silhouette behind the window. Accordingly he journeyed back to Frederiksborg. There his friends assured him that he had become very absentminded. For a time he inclined to be aloof, but eventually was drawn back into the swirl of court life. Once more he took up the endless chain of contrived pleasures, of small jealousies, of miniscular struggles for kingly favor, of small-minded gossip which, in sum, made up the life of the court. Frau von Gabel's dark-eyed, accusing image dimmed from day to day.

Once more concern for Christian's health occupied the Doctor. There were good days when Christian behaved fairly normally, alternating with days when he smashed the mirrors into splinters and hurled expensive pieces of porcelain against the wall. He sliced tapestries into ribbons, he tore off the coverings from the furniture. Often he would cry out wildly for Holck, and offer to fight him. Holck invariably consented and let the King pummel him as much as he liked, for he did no more damage than a feather pillow. Evenings Holck would take the King off to debauchery in the Blaagard, and the people of Frederiksborg breathed easier for a few hours to be rid of them both.

Shortly after the King's turn for the worse, news came that Frau von Gabel had died. In fact, her husband, the privy-councillor, was the one who brought this depressing information. Tears filled his eyes when he told Struensee about the circumstances of his wife's decease. The husband was a large, awkward man with big shoulders and long apish arms that he habitually kept hanging pendulously at his sides. His hands were fashioned not for the quill but for plow-handles. Standing in abysmal dejection before Struensee he told his story, and was moved to see how deeply the Doctor was affected. Indeed, he was so moved that he embraced his wife's onetime friend.

Frau von Gabel, of course, had died of consumption. Her disease had suddenly flared up into an acute phase. Her husband, however, blamed himself. He told Struensee that he should have taken her, like it or no, to Pyrmont, or perhaps to Lucca. During her last days, he said, the deceased had often mentioned His Excellency, the Doctor. The Doctor must have been a true and honorable friend. Gabel fumbled in his pocket at this excruciatingly painful juncture and drew out a package which he untied with his great sausage fingers. This little thing, he said, snuffing up his hairy nose, this little thing his wife had planned that the Doctor should have as a keepsake. It was a medallion in the shape of a heart. After several attempts Gabel managed to unsnap the cover. Inside was the miniature of a young girl carefully painted on porcelain, a pretty young thing with rosy cheeks, heavy hair and laughing eyes. She had looked just like that, Gabel explained, when they were first betrothed. He then handed over the memento to Struensee, who bowed his head and dropped it tenderly into his pocket. He was much too moved to speak.

The following day Struensee cleared out. He left for Copenhagen, unable to endure the artificialities of Frederiksborg another day. The huge Christiansborg Palace was empty. His steps echoed in the deserted corridors of the place. His quarters were painfully clean, to such degree that they struck him as inhospitable. By the merest chance he wandered into the Palace chapel, which he belatedly discovered was located only a few doors away from his own apartment. A large, gilded crucifix hung over the alter. The glass lusters dappled the marble floors with flecks of light. Looking up between the columns of the chapel, which fanned out into mussel-shell shapes at the top, Struensee could see the murals on the lunettes at the upper edge of the wall. The colors were deep, saturated reds, bright banner blues, smaragd greens, all in the Italian style, but undoubtedly from the brush of some conscientious Danish imitator.

Struensee was repelled by the showiness of the chapel and the garishness of the murals above all. There was Mary Magdalene, a full-bosomed lady with long, golden hair hanging down to her hips, holding in soft, round hands the vessel containing the precious balm. Godless though he was, Struensee was particularly offended by the gold Christ, a delicate young man who seemed to be hanging quite painlessly on his cross, smiling a sweet and self-pleased smile as if crucifixion meant no more to him than having his hair trimmed. In Struensee's mood of loss and self-condemnation this elegant, bonbon sort of Christ affected his senses most unpleasantly. In concealed depths of his soul the godless one rebelled at the frightful blasphemy of the effeminate, languishing pseudo-Savior. He was somehow ashamed by the mere fact that anyone should be so ill-advised to portray the most moving of all deaths as a sentimental event. Why? Why had it been done at all? It had been done this way, Struensee realized, to please the fops and strumpets of the court, to assure them that their pointless lives would be extended into an equally pointless eternity, with the golden youth on the golden cross bearing witness to this sickly sweet prospect.

Struensee felt thoroughly gutted of spirit. He looked around vacantly for a few moments more, and left with his head hanging on his chest. Outside in the corridor he was moved to think of Antje Maria. She had scarcely crossed his mind since he had delivered her over to one of Warnstaedt's servants. Incredible, he told himself, that I should have neglected her this way. Seeking information from a passing palace flunkey, he was told that she was working as a probationer in the kitchen. Struensee descended winding flights of steps and arrived at the vaulted cellar, where Christian had once taken refuge under the bed of his manservant, Kirchhof, to escape Reventlau. Mattresses, broken chairs, dusty chests and unwanted pictures were stored in this lower region of the palace. Baskets of vegetables were piled under the arches, and an incredibly numerous collection of brooms, brushes and pails. Struensee had the curious sensation of having wandered into the bowels of the palace organism, the soiled insides of the outwardly resplendent beast. Everything in the cellar was real, only too real. A suffocating smell of onions, beer, strong soap and cabbage on the boil permeated the air.

In the palace kitchen proper—Struensee could see them from afar through the arches—stood several huge copper kettles, polished to great brilliance and all ready for use. The tiles on the floor were scoured clean, the big wooden table was spotless. The ovens were not in use, but all shiny black and waiting, with the exception of one. From this heated oven issued the pleasing odor of freshly baked bread, reminding Struensee that he had neglected to eat since the morning. A mild twilight, greenish from the reflections coming from the canal water, shimmered in the space and dyed the whitewashed vaults and pillars.

Struensee found Antje Maria sitting on a stool, her back turned to him. She was busy peeling potatoes. He recognized her flaxen hair under the stiffly starched kitchen-maid's cap. With a gay plip-plop she let her freshly peeled potatoes fall into the water, the while she hummed a simple country song to herself. A warm wave of delight flooded through Struensee. "Antje Maria!" he called. "Look here. It's me!"

Squeaking with surprise, Antje Maria whirled about on her stool. "Why, Dr. Struensee!" she exclaimed. "It's you!" She had grown a good deal, and was now an adolescent young woman. She wiped her hands and fitted her cap squarely on her head. Her cheeks were ruddy with health. "Really, Dr. Struensee," she complained, "you oughtn't to come down here, not into the cellar!"

The Doctor hoisted one leg over a stool, smiled happily for no particular reason at all, and said: "But what else could I do? I'm perishing of hunger, Antje Maria. Can you feed me?"

"You are!" she said. "Isn't that awful!" Already she was casting around to see what could be done to remedy the situation.

"Wait, wait, now," he told her. "It's not as bad as all that."

She fetched him a wooden plate, a knife and fork. She sliced him off some thick slices of a smoked ham packed with many others on a wooden rack. She broke off a chunk of dark-grained bread for him and got a blue pot of fresh butter. Then she found some beer. He watched her quick movements, the swish of her short skirts, the flash of her strong white calves. Her wooden shoes made a great clatter as she hustled to do this and do that. He ate and enjoyed the meal, she sitting by, watching his every mouthful, giving him more and more ham.

"Enough, that's quite enough, Antje," he told the girl. "I don't want to eat King Christian out of house and home."

"He'll never know," she whispered to him. "So you needn't worry."

This made Struensee laugh aloud. Having read his face carefully, Antje Maria laughed rosily with him. He drank his beer, which was light, spicy and very refreshing. He wiped the foam from his mouth with the back of his hand. "Are you happy, down here among the potatoes?" he asked Antje Maria, seriously.

"Yes, I'm all right," she said, as serious as he. "They're all so nice to me, even the first cook. All the cooks and the butcher and the vegetable women are nice to me."

"Good, very good," he said. "At least I've done one decent thing in my lifetime."

"Why, Your Excellency always does good things," said Antje Maria reproachfully. "You shouldn't ever think different."

★ IV ★

S*TRUENSEE WAS SUMMONED* to an audience with the King, who lay abed. Impatiently Christian waved everybody out of the royal bedchamber. "Get out, all of you," he shouted at them. "It makes me dizzy to have you all moving around like fleas." Scraping and bowing they backed out the door, and Christian sealed their departure by tossing a teacup after them. Then he put his hands to his cheeks and pressed them together hard. "I have a terrible noise inside my head," he told the Doctor. "As if something were being sawed apart inside it. Everything seems muddled inside my head. There's no longer any pleasure in living. I'd kill myself if I knew a good way to do it. That's why I've had you brought here, Struensee."

For reply Struensee laid the flat of his hand on the King's forehead. "You have a fever, Sire," he said. "We must try to stop it."

"Your hand feels wonderfully cool, Struensee," Christian said. "I've made up my mind about the other, though, and that's all there is to it. What do you advise. I don't fancy jumping out the window. I suppose I could hammer my head against the wall, but that doesn't appeal to me, either, for obvious reasons. Tell me a better way. It's up to you." He looked eagerly at the Doctor. "Is it bad bleeding to death in a tub of warm water?" he asked very privily. "I've thought of that."

"Let us talk sensibly, Your Majesty," said Struensee.

"Yes, yes, I know you want to talk me out of it," said Christian. "You'd like to convince me that everything's my own fault. You're a great sophist, Struensee. If anybody listens to you long enough, he'll be convinced that black is white. Never mind that. What's the easiest way to slide out of this world?"

"I can't do that," said Struensee.

"Drowning might be a good way," said Christian, with comic intensity. "At least that would please my dear step-mother, even if it did come ten years too late. But when I think it over, I realize that someone would only pull me out before the work was done. How am I going to find release, Struensee? That's what I want to know."

"You know perfectly well," Struensee told him, "that you'd rather live than die."

"Under one condition."

"And what is that?"

"That I'm not a lunatic," said the King. The mere saying of the word made him shudder. He reached for Struensee's hand. "That is why I've called you in," he said. "I'm not talking to you now as king to subject. As friend to friend, I ask you, Struensee, to tell me the truth. Am I going insane? Wait a minute, now. Don't answer too quickly. Don't fob me off. And don't spare me, either. I won't have it, I tell you. You're different, I hope, from these dung-grubbers who hang around me. Struensee, I think I'm going mad. I know I am."

"First I'd like to know what makes you think that," said the Doctor. "Tell me."

"I'm not as stupid as you might think," said Christian. "Insanity runs in my family, I'm sure. Once we were really great people. But my grandfather was an indifferent sort, you know, and my father was obviously incompetent. Now I come along. What can I expect? Idiocy or lunacy. That's about all. Then I have these awful noises in my head. I tell you, Struensee, it's depressing beyond endurance. It's a soft roaring, if you can imagine it, a deep buzzing. It penetrated even to my dreams. Even when the noise stops everything seems empty and ugly and disgusting to me. I really don't know why I go on living. Why should I? Actually I'd be a lot better off dead, and you know it. What's the point of this world? Where is it heading? If I'm obsessed with thoughts like these, doesn't that prove I'm crazy?"

"I don't think so," said Struensee. "Not necessarily."

"Why don't you?" said Christian belligerently.

"Because everybody has the same thoughts and sensations at some time or other," the Doctor explained. "Though not many talk about them."

"Have you had the experience?" asked Christian.

"I've had my troubles," temporized Struensee. "Yes, there are times when I doubt life. I've had the feeling that the world is built on the rim of an abyss. Any moment it might collapse, I sometimes think, and disappear forever. But these fits of depression never last too long with me. I try deliberately to fight them off. Why should I accommodate myself to such a swindle? I got busy. I did something. I reminded myself that life comes to everyone like an empty jug. It's my job, I told myself, to fill up this jug with accomplishment. And let me tell you that every time I overcome a fit of weakness, I feel unusually well, very much on the *qui vive*. The effort is distinctly worthwhile."

Christian listened closely, his brow wrinkled with concentration. "It's hard for me to understand," he said slowly. "I believe I understand what you mean. But you're so different from me. It's in the cards that you should be a happy man on the whole. I'm different."

"What makes you think that?"

"In the first place, you're a doctor," said Christian. "You heal people, you lift them up, you help them. But I? I am only a king. If I want to do something positive, they fall on me and cry, you can't do that, you can't, you wouldn't dare. No. You have to stick fast, like a toad under a stone, they tell me, otherwise you'll jeopardize the precious crown of Denmark. Since I threw out Reventlau, they're rather careful about how they nag and suppress me. Yet they still do it. They resist me with a tenacity that you cannot possibly imagine. Do you think I enjoy always signing my name to papers that I don't understand? Christian Rex . . . the same old thing, time and time again. Sometimes I put a curl under the X to vary the proceeding. That's how low I have sunk, my good fellow."

"Well, then, don't do it," said Struensee. "Your Majesty must project his will. You, too, could get things done. And of course on a far greater scale than is possible for ordinary mortals. Believe me, Sire, we have to fight to win. We cannot sit down with hands folded and win the battle."

"What do you know about battles and obstacles?" said Christian. "Actually, what do you know?"

"I know a great deal, in my way," said Struensee and laughed drily: "I've had a thousand difficulties to overcome in my time. I've squabbled with professors, parents, colleagues, ministers, with my patients. There have been periods when I was sure the world was determined to crush a certain worm called Struensee. But the devil take it, I've always thought. I'll not be conquered by a mood. I am Struensee, and Struensee I shall be."

"But that's wonderful!" said Christian ingenuously.

"Why, just think, Your Majesty," said Struensee. "Think how I'm struggling with you this very moment!"

Christian looked up at him open-mouthed, understood and laughed. He shook with hysterical release. "You're a sly one, Struensee," he gurgled. "You do pick me up, I must say. When you're around I always feel as if that other miserable little Christian were crawling around my feet. But still, it makes me sick and dizzy to stand erect too long. Do you understand? It's too much for me."

"Come now," said Struensee. "I cannot believe that."

"I'm no Prometheus like you," said Christian.

"Ridiculous," said the Doctor.

"No, not at all," said Christian. "I mean it. It isn't so much what you say, as how you look. That high forehead of yours. The way you deal with people, the way you use your hands. You're not afraid. You are Struensee." He looked down wide-eyed at his toes sticking up Turkish-fashion under the covers. "The only time I have courage is when you're with me," he continued. "I have realized that since the terrible time we had in Paris. I'd like to do without you, for it's hardly flattering, you know. I've tried to. But here you are again, and so it is. Already I feel better. But there's one thing you must promise me."

Struensee raised his brows quizzically.

"Do not despise me, Struensee," he said. "Not that, for your sake as well as mine."

"But why should I?" murmured Struensee uncomfortably, and to himself that confessions too searching would never do. Then he was inspired to add: "I've accustomed myself to see my own and others' weaknesses objectively. I see them as forms of sickness. As such they are not to be despised. I am a physician. I must mitigate and heal them. That is my way."

"How extraordinary, I must say, that you have never asked me for money, or some sort of title," said Christian, sticking to his own line of thought. "Obviously you could have had what you wanted. I've been waiting for you to come begging like the rest. You're too proud, Struensee. Now there's no more need of your holding back. I am going to make you my secretary. That will keep you around me. Of course I won't expect you to perform any secretarial tasks. I will simply want your advice on matters of state."

"I thank Your Majesty," said Struensee and bowed.

"Think over my proposal," said Christian, studying the Doctor minutely. "Remember that in fact your post will be the highest in Denmark next to mine. You will be right at my side, giving me your counsel. If you really think that I can save myself only by being a king, then show me how it must be done."

Triumph swelled Struensee's heart. Abstractedly he walked up and down the room, his hands linked behind his back, the King following him with his eyes. He came to a halt by a window and looked down into the broad courtyard where sentries were posted all about. "Your Majesty," he said abruptly, "as a beginning I strongly advise you to grant full freedom to the press."

"To the press!" said Christian. "What would Bernstorff say? And the church people?"

"You are the king," said Struensee. "What do you care about Bernstorff and the clerics. If it so pleases you, it will be done."

"Yes, yes, it will be a fine joke to see their faces, won't it," he tittered. "How they will curse me! Terrible, it will be terrible. But what about this freedom. Do you think it will prove dangerous?"

"On the contrary," said Struensee. "It's the lack of freedom that's dangerous. So long as people talk and have their opinions printed, they won't shoot. And shooting is what ultimately concerns you, not verbal brickbats. But it's not that alone. It's not a purely negative move. A doctor must have his finger on his patient's pulse to get some idea of what's wrong. The Danish people is your patient, Sire. You shouldn't have to guess your way along. Let the people describe how they are feeling through the press."

"It's a daring thing to do," said Christian. "I'm not so sure. You don't understand these church people."

"Sire, do not forget that a generous act evokes the world's admiration," said Struensee.

"Tell me, Struensee," said Christian. "Do you think that making the press free would be as important, say, as winning a battle? Leuthen, for instance?"

"There is no comparison at all," said Struensee. "What does a battle amount to in the long run? A mere incident in a wrangle over who shall control this or that province. Who is interested in that? Do you care to read about the battles of the Romans? But making the press free will mark a step forward in the growth and progress of all humanity. History will naturally never forget the man who takes this step. His name will shine long after the greatest general is forgotten dust."

"Well, then, get everything ready," said Christian. "You can write up the decree and I'll sign it for you. Now I think I'll go hunting. I feel ever so much better, my dear man."

Smiling, Struensee bowed low to the King and left the bedchamber. "Many thanks, many thanks, Struensee," Christian called after him. He actually leapt from his bed, and pulled the cord to summon his valet.

The following afternoon the people of Copenhagen gathered to read the King's proclamation. Dragoons had posted the placards in public places all through the city. The edict was simple and to the point, as edicts go:

"Since control over the search for truth is injurious to that end, and since, moreover, the examination and rectification of old errors and indurated prejudices is endangered by the fact that honest patriots, solely on account of personal fears, or of official warnings, or of hitherto prevailing opinions, have been prevented from writing according to their own insights, conscience and conviction, it is hereby decreed that there shall be unlimited freedom of the press in all states and lands of the King, to such effect that in the future no one shall be required to submit his thoughts or his writings, as heretofore, to the royal censor.

Christian VII, Rex"

The people could not believe their eyes when they read this unprecedented announcement. When they finally grasped what had happened, many rejoiced, others were dubious. Excitement ran through the whole city. Even those who could neither read nor write, who, of course, made up a majority, discussed the decree with great heat. Many of them seemed to fear that now all curbs were gone the long silent voices of demons would rise in a great clamor. "Let us hope and pray that all goes well," one good dame said to her neighbor.

In the bookshops there was a lively reaction. Plans were feverishly improvised before the King had time to change his mind. The most zealous rushed to their desks, snatched their quills and began to scratch like mad. Consternation reigned among the clerical elements. Pastor Muenter of St. Peter's said to his colleagues when they flocked to his rectory for advice, using almost the same language as the King to Struensee: "A bold experiment. Now we shall find out whether the city is Christian, or of Babylonian persuasion. What I should like to know is this, who advised the King to take such a step. Certainly not Bernstorff."

The King's cabinet met in emergency session in Christiansborg. Bernstorff rose to speak his piece, a solid statesman with a solid head on his shoulders. "This fantasy is quite impossible," he cried aloud in tragic accent. "The whole foreign policy of Denmark will simply fall to pieces. And think how many years I've labored on it! A thousand fools will start attacking Russia. Filosov will carry the tale directly to the Tsarina. It will be a catastrophe. You must go to His Majesty at once and advise him to countermand the proclamation."

"Who must go?" said Reventlau. "Are you thinking of me, by any chance? No, no, not I! Do you want me to have another stroke, good sir? And this time he might really clap me into the Kronborg to rot. He's capable of anything, the curd-brain. But Moltke, my dear brother-in-law, might be able to handle him."

Now all eyes turned to Moltke, a tall, haggard man with cold eyes.

"Not I," he said. "As much as I should like to accommodate you gentlemen, I have my family to consider. Don't forget that I am responsible for twenty-four children."

He said this last so drily that everyone burst into laughter. When the uproar had died down, Bernstorff tried again. "You, Saint-Germain, are minister of war," he said. "Courage is your *métier,* is it not? How about your doing it?"

"You know perfectly well that the edict doesn't even remotely concern my department," said Saint-Germain. "Why doesn't Your Excellency go see the King himself?"

"I dare not jeopardize my foreign policy," Bernstorff pleaded, quite unabashed. "At this very moment the affair is hanging by a thread. I'd like to know who the scoundrel is who put the King up to it!"

"Holck, it could have been that great lout," suggested Reventlau, who never forgot or allowed anyone else to forget that the gigantic Count had ousted his nephew, Sperling, from the King's favor.

"Holck!" said Bernstorff. "Hardly him! All that cretin thinks of is women and money. He simply hasn't got the wit to think up such a cleverly written thing."

"Warnstaedt? Could it have been he?"

"He would never even think of it," said Bernstorff. "He's far too superficial."

"Well, then, the Queen."

"She has no influence one way or the other."

"I have it," said Bernstorff. "Why, it's that damnable doctor. He's always sniffing around like a hungry dog. He was with the King yesterday. Of course he was!"

"The doctor? Do you mean that old fellow, Berger?"

"Indeed I do not," said Bernstorff, bristling with annoyance. "Not that old windbag. I mean the new physician-in-ordinary, Struensee. Now it comes to me where I've heard that name before. The man's already been in hot water for his liberal opinions. It happened some years ago. Of course! He got into trouble with the church."

Saint-Germain laughed until his shoulders shook like jelly. "I'd like to know the man," he gasped, "who hasn't been in trouble with the church. Really, you couldn't hold that against the fellow!"

"This is no time for levity," said Bernstorff. "Gentlemen, Struensee is a dangerous man. He dominates the King. From now on we can expect one unpleasant surprise after the other. And we can do nothing about it. We'll have to bow our necks ever so meekly. Struensee has shoved the lot of us into a corner. Since the King cannot rule, Struensee very plainly is going to do it for him. Mark my word, mark my word."

"Struensee rule!" Reventlau bellowed so loudly that the servants in the corridor raised their hands to their mouths. His bladder of a head was gorged with blood. "Has Denmark reached a pitch where a dirty bourgeois pill-roller can call the tune?" he shouted. "Never, never, I say!"

They looked at each other, all of them men of noble birth with gold-trimmed silk coats and immaculately powdered wigs. Carefully they looked each other over. There was not one among them who did not smell the rank smell of danger. Not only were their official positions threatened, not only their social pre-eminence and financial security. More than that. They felt the coming flood. The spring tides were gathering. Already a little water was quietly washing about their feet. These tides, whipped into huge waves by the hurricane passions of the mob, would surely drown the lot of them, grind them to pulp on the gravelly beach, destroy their very identity.

A week or so later this same premonition came, while scanning a letter from the French Dane, Reverdil, to a man sitting alone in a remote chateau in France. His peruke was cocked awry on his steep forehead, framing a withered old face. His dressing gown was stained with ink and coffee. Indeed, he looked as if he had not properly washed himself for the past fifty years. But his little eyes glittered with reptilian vitality and the evil folds around his old mouth deepened into seams of purest malice. *"Diable, diable,"* he mumbled toothlessly, "who would have thought that a country of cows would have dared! Things are never what they seem!"

The old man, of course, was called Voltaire.

<h2 style="text-align:center">★ V ★</h2>

*T*HE QUEEN WAS indisposed, not at all her usual lively self. Some time previously her brother, the Duke of Gloucester, had paid her an official visit. Gloucester, a bull-necked, jolly young fellow, much resembled the brother who was king of England. The Duke had found his sister changed, inturned, quiet and rather inclined to be testy. This had quite surprised him, though not nearly so much as he had been taken aback by his novel brother-in-law, the King of Denmark. But not being of contemplative makeup and having no taste for psychological prying, Gloucester had simply chosen to look the other way. This was contrary to his mother's wishes. She, the widowed Princess of Wales, had expressly instructed him to have a heart to heart talk with Caroline about Christian and, if she needed it, give her his advice. It was obvious that Caroline Matilda's letters, though they contained no specific complaints, strongly suggested an unhappy marriage.

Princess Augusta of Wales was a very ambitious woman. Her long friendship with Lord Bute—gossip had it that she was his mistress—had evoked in her a warm interest and considerable skill in diplomacy. She insisted on using her talents in furthering the fortunes of her many children. And like so many well-meaning mothers of this interfering stripe, her long-winded admonitions and advisings got on her children's nerves, not to mention the nerves of her sons- and daughters-in-law. Christian, after being given a sound talking-to, had whispered to Count Holck: *"Cette chère maman m'embête au fond!"* When she hinted broadly that she definitely did not approve of this whoring and sousing, he had smiled and said: *"Vous savez, chère maman, chacun à son Bute!"* This thrust at her own private life, or at what scandalous people conceived her private life to be, had struck the Princess to the quick. Since that time she had looked on Christian as by all odds the least promising of her sons-in-law. Caroline Matilda, her youngest daughter, was doomed, she privately thought.

But this remarkable woman's son, the youthful Duke of Gloucester, had no intention of spoiling his stay in Denmark with family arguments. His brother-in-law Christian he considered to be anything but a gentleman. Gentlemen did not mince about the stage in amateur theatricals. Nor did they have seizures of rage and smash windows. Nor did they treat their wives with cool contempt. Still, no one at the Danish court seemed to mind, and it would have been tactless for an outsider to change local custom. Gloucester preferred smooth sailing. He loathed busybodies. What did the poet say?

> "Be sure when once the grass is grown
> Above a matter better hidden,
> Some sheep will stray, a bag of bone,
> And nibble bare the horrid midden."

Besides Gloucester had given himself without stint to the round of pleasures that had been arranged in his honor. Hunts, balls and glutton feasts that lasted until the early morning hours had blunted any initial desire to stick in an oar. The heavy Danish cuisine, with its countless hors d'oeuvres and desserts appealed so strongly to Gloucester that after a meal he often soaked his feet in a bucket of ice-cold water to ward off attacks of apoplexy. The ducal visitor enjoyed himself immensely. He simply never got around to a showdown talk with his moody sister.

When he left with many embraces and assurances of fraternal esteem, Caroline Matilda took to bed. She was sick at heart and sick of body. She was losing weight steadily, and though this was marvellous for her figure—the house of Hanover all inclined to stoutness—it made her feel very low. Dr. Berger declared himself absolutely puzzled by her ailment. He called in other physicians, and they mooted the lethal possibility of diabetes. Dr. Berger shook his head, unconvinced. He talked with the King. Christian would not be trifled with. He was in a frivolous Gallic mood. He shrugged his shoulders and said: *"Qu' importe, mon vieux?* The dear lady probably has the spleen, whatever that is. *Passons la-dessus."* Berger insisted, however, that the King do something positive in the matter of his wife's health. Finally, to get rid of him, Christian said: "Why don't you have Struensee look into the matter?"

Caroline Matilda was very reluctant to consult Struensee. His part in her husband's affair with the unfortunate Frau von Gabel was known to her through court informers. This incident seemed conclusively to prove her original suspicion that Struensee, her husband's favorite, was immoral in character. She imagined him, by extension, as encouraging her husband to adulterous excesses. He was as much her enemy, she firmly believed, as the odious Count Holck, and Holck she really hated with a venomous hatred. During her brother's visit he had openly called Gloucester an "English ox" and had got away with it.

Regardless, Fraulein von Eyben conducted Struensee into the Queen's bedchamber one splendid July day. The white windows were thrown wide open and from outdoors came a warm, soft wind, laden with the perfume of roses in full bloom. Mathiessen, the lady-in-waiting, a busty, short, gray-haired woman, was posted at the Queen's bedside, ready to do or die should the dread necessity arise. Two chambermaids, Horn and Bruun, whispered in a far corner of the room as the Doctor entered.

The Queen was sitting up in bed, her legs drawn up under the silk coverings. Her hair was swept up in the style of the day, but left unpowdered to show off the natural platinum blonde color. This lovely coiffure was set off by a fine gold chain wound round and round her neck. The Queen wore a thin summer nightgown, cut deeply so as not to smother her breasts. Her big blue eyes were alive with nervous excitement, her lips pouted. Next to her on the bed crouched a white poodle, whose woolly hide she scratched and tiddled without thinking. Struensee felt very much the interloper. The intensely feminine atmosphere upset him more than he had bargained for. Accustomed to talk without reservation to the King, he was keenly conscious, *en revanche,* of the distance that cut him off, a bourgeois and a pastor's son, from a queen. In vain he assured himself that she was merely another young woman, naive and ignorant. His eyes fell on her hand which, exactly as when he had first seen it in Altona, was wearing the too heavy diamond ring. Involuntarily he blushed, recalling the romantically dedicated thoughts that his first sight of this lovely appendage had elicited.

"Dr. Struensee," said Fraulein von Eyben, making a deep curtsey. Her bold eyes moved expectantly from Struensee to the Queen.

"Good morning, Doctor," said the Queen, smiling a peculiarly constrained smile. "I see that you have lost no time carrying out the King's order."

"Good morning, Your Majesty," he replied, and bowed almost to the floor. "It was concern for Your Majesty's health that made me so expeditious."

The Queen laughed nervously. "Yes, yes," she said. "And now that you're here, kindly tell me what's wrong."

"I can assure you that it's not diabetes," he told her, gradually drawing closer and closer to the bed.

"Your diagnoses are remarkably swift, Doctor," she said.

"I was once a district doctor in Altona," he explained. "I am well acquainted, believe me, with the diabetic picture." And even more evenly he added, as an after thought: "I feel confident that I need no instruction in the question of diabetes."

"Really?" said the Queen. "And what is a district doctor?"

"A physician who treats paupers, Madame," said Struensee. "The state pays him to perform these services in the interest of public health."

"For paupers!"

"Yes, Madame."

"I see," she said. She slipped her tongue out through her teeth and nipped it thoughtfully.

"What are your difficulties, Madame?" he asked. "Could you describe them to me?"

"None, really," she said.

"Do you think you have a fever?"

"I am sure I have none."

"Are you fatigued?"

"I am when I dance for three hours," she said. "Otherwise I am not."

The crowsfeet around Mathiessen's eyes deepened and the chambermaids Horn and Bruun giggled behind their hands.

"And yet you say that you are unwell, Madame?" said Struensee.

"I am bored," she said, and yawned to prove it. "I am especially bored right now. I am sick with boredom, sir."

The blood rushed to Struensee's cheeks and he felt a little dizzy with mortification. The Queen watched this happen with savage amusement. Struensee turned away from her, a flat breach of etiquette, and began to pace up and down the room, as was his habit when deeply stirred. Presently he returned under full sail to the Queen's bedside, looked down at her and saw that she was extremely pretty, and prettier than ever now that she was amused.

"Bring me a mirror, if you please, Frau Mathiessen," he said. He handed the mirror to the Queen. "Look at yourself, Madame," he said coolly.

"Why?" she demurred. "I know my own face." Nevertheless she looked, like any woman.

"It's a very attractive face, is it not?" Struensee said. "And so much more attractive, don't you think, now that Your Majesty is smiling. At my expense?"

"Oh," said the Queen and let the mirror fall.

"I think I can cure Madame's sickness," he went on. "But I should not like to offend by rushing into the matter. If Madame permits, I shall leave now." He bowed, glancing quickly into her eyes as he did so. As he had hoped, there was a glimmer of disappointment in them. "If Madame permits," he said as he straightened his back, "I shall return tomorrow."

"Your diagnosis will be very interesting, I'm sure," the Queen said grandly.

The next morning Fraulein von Eyben again led Struensee into the Queen's bedchamber. This time there were no maidservants to disturb the scene, and even the lady-in-waiting Mathiessen quickly absented herself. The Queen was propped up in bed as before. She wore a black lace negligee over her nightgown, and about her throat a band of dark silk that accented the silvery blondeness of her hair and the whiteness of her fair skin.

"How does Her Majesty feel this morning?" Struensee began.

"Much the same," said the Queen. "Have you come to any conclusions, Dr. Struensee?"

"I have, Madame," he said flatly.

"How is it possible?" she inquired. "You haven't tapped my chest or looked down my throat. You haven't even taken my pulse. How do you know that I haven't got heart trouble? Or maybe my lungs are unsound. Or maybe, God forbid, I ought to have some teeth pulled out." Slily the Queen glanced at Frau von Eyben to make sure that she was appreciating the coquetry.

Struensee pretended to examine the Queen's bared teeth, which were perfectly white and sound, if somewhat larger than ordinary. "I am forced to discount all the possibilities you suggest," he told the Queen. "Heart, lungs, teeth . . . they're all quite healthy."

"What is it, then? Diabetes?"

"No, not that."

"Come, speak out."

"Madame has already recognized the source of her trouble," he said. "Madame is suffering from acute boredom."

The Queen looked at him and began to frown. "Today it seems that I'm the one who's the butt," she said. "Boredom is no sickness."

"I must contradict Madame," Struensee said. "When a pretty young woman in good health gets bored, presently everything goes wrong. She feels useless, then unwanted, then sick. She finds no purpose in living. This chronic frustration gets to a point where it makes the otherwise healthy young lady sick."

The Queen hitched up higher among the pillows and hugged her shoulders closer together. "So you're a student of human nature," she said rather sharply. "If you fancy yourself so much in this direction perhaps you can be so kind as to tell me what I should live for."

"I can't do that," said Struensee. "That you must find out for yourself."

"In short, you can't help me," the Queen said and contemptuously jerked her pretty shoulders and looked away.

"You need activity, Madame," said Struensee. "You badly need to move around. It is utterly wrong for you to lie in bed and brood."

"Activity! Movement!" The Queen's eyes blazed. "Do you think I am merely pretending to be sick, sir? I am dead tired this very moment. Why, I can't stand on my legs for more than an hour at a time."

"Now you are really pitying yourself, Madame," said Struensee. "You are a remarkable expert in souls, I must say," she retorted acidly. "Don't you dare pry into me as if I were a nasty clock. Do you think I'm some sort of mechanical doll, I'd like to know? Nodding and blinking and poking one foot in front of the other? If you do, my dear Dr. Struensee, you're very much mistaken. As a matter of fact, my good man, the activity you prescribe disgusts me beyond measure. I'm tired of pirouetting around in empty circles. These court balls and fêtes and bazaars and trips to the lake revolt me, sir. I won't have any more of it. Now, what do you say to that, Dr. Struensee?"

"Very good," he told her. "Rebelliousness is a sign of returning health, as we know."

The Queen was taken off guard. Her eyes grew large and very blue. A smile twitched at the corners of her mouth. "Why, my good Dr. Struensee," she said, comically sighing, "you should be ashamed of yourself. A student of nature. A dialectician. Overcoming a poor, inexperienced woman. Do you think that fair?"

"Perhaps I am a little dialectical," said Struensee, pretending to be crushed. "I beg Madame's pardon most humbly."

They stared at each other, mutually nonplussed. Then Caroline Matilda began to laugh. At first the laughter bubbled in her throat and would not come out. Her eyes narrowed and sparkled and at last the amusement within her was irresistible. She laughed like any other vigorous young woman, loud and clear, and Struensee laughed with her. He held his hand on his hip, and looked down at his pretty patient in a decidedly unmedical fashion. Fraulein von Eyben, watching this dumb show, let her chin drop in sheer amazement. She could not for the life of her see what was so funny. At the same time she experienced an unaccountable pang of jealousy.

"What sort of comedy are we playing, I should like to know," the Queen said, still giggling and chortling. "But now I want to have some real, concrete medical advice, Dr. Struensee. And I do hope you won't prescribe any horrid little pills."

"I prescribe a horse, Madame," said the Doctor. "That is . . ."

"A horse?" the Queen echoed. "What do you mean by that?"

"I mean you must go out riding horseback," he told her. "Do you know the Danish countryside, Madame? Do you know the paths through the woods of Klampenborg? And the moors and villages and the ponds in the morning sun? Everything is waiting to be looked at, you know." He pointed out through the window. "A Queen should know her own country, surely. Madame, the world seen from horseback looks quite different than when seen from a window. I often go riding in the early morning. It's a splendid thing."

"I used to ride a great deal in England," the Queen said pensively. "In Hampton Court Park, with my brothers. I always used a regular saddle. I dislike hanging onto one of those side-saddles. It spoils everything, don't you think?"

"Ride as you see fit, Madame," he told her.

"I don't really think I could," she said. "It would cause comment."

"Madame, you are free to ride as you like," he said. "Let the Philistines shake their heads. They'll get used to it."

The Queen looked at Struensee hopefully. "My mother says," she began. Then, after cutting herself off, she added: "But no, Dr. Struensee, you're quite right. I simply cannot go on living with so many qualifications hedging me in. I'm going to ride. With one proviso."

"Yes?"

"That you share my notoriety. You must ride with me."

Struensee detected something new in the clear blue eyes, something which belied the mockery of her words, an invitation to be protected. "Naturally," he said very quietly. "That can be arranged, Madame. Your command does me great honor."

"It is not a command," she said. "It is a request."

"Your requests are commands," he said and bowed.

"Dr. Struensee, I beg you not to play the courtier," she said. "Come along with me freely, or not at all."

"I should like to, Your Majesty," he said simply.

"That is what I wanted to find out," the Queen said, and turned red as fire.

Showing him out Fraulein von Eyben said tartly: "Well, Doctor, you seem to do very nicely with her, don't you!"

"You think so?" said Struensee. "So it would seem." He laughed and confidently put his arm around von Eyben, found her lips and kissed them hotly.

"You! You'll make me say something I shouldn't," scolded von Eyben, and busily wiped her lips with her handkerchief. "You're a Don Juan, no more, no less. Women simply aren't safe with you."

"A man does what he can, long-legs," said Struensee. "Here, give me another kiss."

Still laughing he broke loose from Fraulein von Eyben and marched briskly out of sight down the long palace corridor.

★ VI ★

THE BRIEF SUMMER of the North had to come to Zealand. Day after day white clouds wandered across a high blue sky, making long shadows that raced over the bushy green landscape about Klampenborg, ancient hunting preserve of the Danish kings.

The beeches, resplendent and massy in full silvery green foliage, cast a pleasant shade. In the glassy green twilight that filtered through their leaves it was delightfully cool even at midday. Within the stands of beeches the earth smelled richly of humus and fungi, and gnats danced a mad and merry dance in shafts of light. Here and there were low damp places where a brook wound through the woods, very flatly and slowly. Tall rushes grew at the edge of the brook, buttercups of varnished yellow and pale forget-me-nots, these sometimes in thick clumps and sometimes, again, scattered over the quaggy ground.

In this same territory, where the island's original landscape had been jealously preserved, there were also places where the heather grew, coarse grasses, broom scrub and prickly juniper. Here, out in the open on high dry ground, the sunlight glowed and glittered and dragon flies came up from the sedges, their stiff veined wings shining and flashing. The earth shapes, long low hills and broad shallow valleys, showed with crystalline clarity against the horizon. On some low heights, growing mostly solitary, or occasionally in clumps of two or three, were oak trees, grim old fellows, with knotty, goutily knobbed limbs, but tenderly green of leaf, in contrast to the powerful musculature.

This green world of Klampenborg was at its best in the forenoon, after the night mists had evaporated, when the cuckoo sang his loudly resonant song, like water gulping forth from a bottle with a narrow neck, when the mourning doves were cooing from the woody close. On bright mornings it was a delight to be young and beautiful, to feel oneself borne up by the sheer spaciousness of the landscape, to breathe in sweet air spiced with a hundred essences of earth, swamp, wood, field and pond.

Each morning during the fine summer weather Struensee and the Queen went riding, away from the richly furnished apartments of Frederiksborg. Gaily they imagined themselves as venturesome conquerors, pressing forward into strange country. Their euphoria was great, their spirits winged.

It was all quite new to the Queen. At last she could escape her arid existence. At last it had happened. A new world had opened up before her thirsty senses. She noticed the change in herself immediately. The summer scent, the rush of the wind through the beeches, the movements of the horse beneath her, everything she experienced was beautiful and full of rapturous promise. The splendors of nature acted like a magic key releasing the rusted wards of her soul, letting the whole world stream in refreshingly. Behind her was resignation, humility and the intolerable thought that the rest of her days would have to be spent in a stuffy twilight populous with ladies-in-waiting, courtiers, and the usual fine ladies and gentlemen.

Struensee was no stranger in this new outdoors scene. Often he had ridden alone through the park, or with Annette, at least on the days when she was not claimed by Filosov. Every nuance of Klampenborg was familiar to him. At first, then, he hardly noticed, unlike the Queen, when the wind off the sea swept in a little squall and flurry through the beech crowns, twisting them white. When the wild doves gurgled and cooed with unbearable longing, enchanting the woods and heathland, it was commonplace to him, but not to her. But gradually he, too, was captured by the idyllic mood. The young Queen, he presently came to understand, did have something fresh and desirable to offer him after all. It began with small things, her intense pleasure at the sight of a fallow deer springing over a thicket to get out of harm's way, his wide, liquid eyes liquid with alarm, or her pleased laugh when a hare doubled on his tracks, or her willingness when he proposed a little gallop over the moor.

At first the Queen was accompanied by a groom, but both riders soon found this official third presence irksome. Thereafter they rode together alone. If they halted to rest the horses and give them water, it was natural that they should talk. They exchanged polite monosyllables on some neutral subject. They commented on their horses, on what they had seen that morning. In good time these stilted overtures lengthened into genuine conversation. If equestrian exercise had been the Queen's original motive in fleeing to Klampenborg, soon Struensee's company was her prime excuse.

Caroline Matilda's early youth had not passed unhappily, but she had never had a friend of her own sex, or any sort of confidante. Her father, the Prince of Wales, before her birth had died in the arms of his dancing-master, Denoyers, as the result of a hard-drinking life. As for her mother, she had always been too distant, too preoccupied with the long-range material welfare of her children, to waste any time on their private feelings. A marked difference in age had separated her from her brothers and sisters, kind and goodnatured though they always showed themselves towards her. Not a soul in Carlton House or Buckingham Palace had troubled his head about the funny little girl with the light hair. Occasionally her grandfather, the senile King of England, had remarked on Caroline's promise of good looks. But that was about all.

Hope of better things loomed when the King of Denmark put in a bid for Caroline's hand. Of course, available information on Christian was none too encouraging. There were undeniable rumors of scandal and personal eccentricities. But in any case Christian was very definitely a king. This fact, according to Caroline Matilda's mother, covered many a fault. One would hardly haggle over a few loose threads when buying a Gobelin, she pointed out. Caroline's mother had not hesitated a moment in sacrificing her daughter to a cloudy, if exalted, future. As part of her maternal duty she had initiated her betrothed daughter into the mysteries of sex. "Embarrassment," she said, "would be inexcusable."

These revelations were extremely painful at the time to the strict-minded Princess of Wales. She might have spared herself. Little Caroline, who had inherited a great deal of the ancestral sensuality, already enjoyed a working knowledge of sexual fundamentals gained by eavesdropping on the servants, whose conversation was rich in carnal reference. Discovering the facts of life, indeed, had been far more diverting for little Caroline than practising on the spinet, or receiving instruction in what her mother called "hortulan embellishments," that is, the art of ornamental gardening.

From the servants, for instance, she learned all about the lovely and quite incredible Miss Chudleigh, the *enfant terrible* of English society during these years. Caroline heard them whisper how one day at Lord Chesterfield's Miss Chudleigh had publicly admitted that she knew everyone was saying she was the mother of illegitimate twins. To which, quick as a flash, the clever Chesterfield had said: "Indeed? Well, personally I never believe more than half of what people say." And another interesting item about poor Miss Chudleigh concerned the time she appeared at a masked ball in the costume of Iphegenia about to be sacrificed at Aulis to redeem Agamemnon's becalmed fleet. Noticing the alarmingly décolleté cut of her antique gown, Lord Bute, being remarkable for his candor, said to her: "What are you thinking of, my dear lady? Is it your bowels that you want the Prince to see?"

Anecdotes of this genre were passed back and forth at the "Cocoa Tree" by the bloods. Sir Horace Walpole, Earl of Oxford, invented innumerable spicy comments that went the rounds and generated more in passage. Eventually the stories fell into the hands of the royal servants, and thereafter it was no time until they were in Caroline's possession. The sensuality of the times was extreme. License was rife in the streets and in the palaces, in dockside pub and elegant coffee-house. All London itched in Caroline's youth, and she was hardly the sort to escape an epidemic influence. In short, she knew enough about the delights of coupling to expect a good deal from marriage. Essentially she had been quite cheerful about setting off on the journey to Denmark, even though tears of contrition had flooded her eyes when her mother let her go with: *"Dieu vous ait dans sa sainte grace, ma petite."*

Her marriage, however, had proved to be a crashing failure. Her man had possessed her, of course, but as casually as a barnyard cockerel mounts a hen, without love or sweet duration. She had borne him a child, and afterwards wondered dumbly how it had ever happened. Marriage, it appeared, was a dreadful fraud. Afterwards she lived under Christian's roof, but miles away from him in spirit, without love, inclination and not an atom of trust. The King, sad to say, turned Caroline's stomach.

Now fate had thrown a real man in her way, a man who cut a far more imposing figure than any of the courtiers, a man of intelligence, experience and decent manners. In fact, Struensee was so perceptive, she found, that at times his insight was discomfiting. Like a flash he read what gleamed unspoken in her eye. But best of all Struensee was a man who actually listened to what she was saying. He actually urged her to elaborate and clarify her ideas. This was a vast relief after years of conversation with the merely polite, who yawned at her and tried to see her ankles over the backs of their hands.

It did not matter so much what they talked about. It might be her brothers and sisters, it might be trivial childhood experiences, or any such thing. She might describe her pet animals, her dresses, her birthday parties, sometimes letting him have a glimpse of the loneliness of her former surroundings. It was the speaker herself, Caroline could not help but see, who attracted Struensee, who drew him to her like a magnet. He could not have enough of her naive sensuality, her unspoiled pleasure in life, her youthful freshness. Each day out in the open made Caroline bloom more brightly. The lacquered surface of the worldly young lady of the court eventually disappeared.

There were times when Struensee observed in the Queen an astonishing resemblance to his protégée, little Antje Maria. True, the Queen spoke with a quite different accent, usually in smooth, quick French. Her movements were much more self-confident and graceful, perhaps. But those subjects which she intuitively deemed of importance were surprisingly often subjects to which Antje Maria would have reacted, though with less verve and assurance. What drew Struensee to the Queen was the young woman in her, her exceedingly feminine response to the world at large. It was a new experience for him, and he valued it greatly. Up to this point he had been a lady's man. He had dealt with experienced, ambitious, socially conscious types almost exclusively. As for Antje Maria, the exception, she was hardly more than a child. Even Frau von Gabel had not been entirely unknowledgeable, as her rash acceptance of his scheme of rehabilitation for the King had so sadly demonstrated.

It was inevitable that eventually they should talk about the Queen's marriage and so about the King himself. The King, certainly, was the personality on whom both their futures hinged. Using great tact, hesitantly, smilingly Caroline Matilda described her manifold disappointments. Sometimes she mocked her swollen expectations of marriage. Being a man of medicine Struensee was able to talk with considerable fluency about ordinarily delicate matters. He did not conceal from the Queen the fact that he was genuinely concerned about the King's mental health. He ventured the opinion that by rights the King long ago should have overcome the defects of an unhappy, loveless youth. He and privy councillor Berger had gradually come round to the idea that Christian's peculiarities might have a more serious background than mere resentment against the environmental pressures of his boyhood.

Struensee's serious diagnosis frightened the Queen. He painted the dangers which the King's malady might visit not only on her, but on the whole population of Denmark. At eighteen Caroline Matilda was a healthy egotist and had never thought at all about such grim possibilities. She realized to her dismay that her marriage was more than distasteful. At any time the very ground under her feet might give way. Struensee made her understand that in an absolute monarchy everything depended on the head of the state. With him disabled the whole social structure might rapidly deteriorate into chaos, at least for an interval.

Had Struensee been a seasoned statesman he might have thought a little differently. He might have qualified his case had he taken into account the vitality of the centuries-old tradition of personal rule, the tenacity of the petty landed aristocracy, the essential conservatism of the bourgeois urban elements. All these could confidently be expected to function as a bulwark against catastrophic change. But for Struensee, who was not a seasoned statesman, but an idealist, these mitigating factors were of minor importance. Though not unaware of them, in his mind they were as nothing compared with the obvious and refulgent power of the kingship itself. With that gone, he was convinced, anything might happen.

Struensee's innocently arrogant way of thinking—it was typical of one with an exaggerated consciousness of self—pleased Caroline. Discounting his too confident manner, he actually did have many worthwhile things to tell her. The Queen considered him wonderfully masculine as he declaimed his beliefs to her, she listening with childish attention and awe. He described how a new historical period was dawning, an epoch of fulfillment, in which mankind at last would come into its own, in which man would be master of his own fate. Glowing with conviction he assured her that at last man would walk upright, stiffened by his faith in reason. Man would throw aside the crutches of superstitious belief, he declared. He would free himself from the cramping effects of supernatural terrors, strip away the moral inhibitions deriving from these fears. How could anyone doubt, Struensee would tell the Queen, that mankind was facing the millennium with courage, reason and disregard of interim consequences. If this consummation did not exactly measure up to the promise of paradise, at least it would be a concrete advance in the right direction. It would be something to enjoy here and now, not in any woefully presumptive after-world.

Caroline Matilda, who beyond the *Princess of Cleves* and La Fontaine's *Fables* had never really read a book, believed every chiliastic word that Struensee uttered; believed without reservation. Struensee's flow of language by itself enchanted her. Never having heard anything of the like before, and never having herself thought a single thought about mankind's destiny, in Struensee she imagined she was dealing with a titan, a man, indeed, of Caesar's rank, one something like the Peter the Great she had vaguely heard spoken of.

Luck, good luck, had brought this rare creature to her, just at that critical moment when she—and, as he himself repeatedly reminded her, the times as well—was primed for change. Right at her side was the man to take charge, to lead the way to a better, keener life. It would come about that way, surely. She believed this not only as a queen, but more importantly as a woman. In this man's company she could laugh, she knew the brilliance of her own eyes, she could feel the sweetness of her own lips. There must be something to a man who could bring these desirable phenomena, she told herself according to womanly wisdom. All the ancient and ever renewed arts of womanhood she now discovered in herself. She turned eagerly, with burning anticipation and curiosity, to try herself out, to see what effect—surely a great one—they would have on the dull, dull world.

Suddenly her choice of clothes became an important problem. She became so fussy that Mathiessen often bitterly complained to the servants. The Queen, she said, was really becoming absurdly demanding. She began to take infinite pains with her hair and her hands. Whole evenings she would spend examining her features in the mirror, speculating on whether her lips were too full or just full enough, whether her shoulders were perfectly round or not. There were times when she despaired of her appearance, but in general self-examinations left her warm and pleased. When she finally got around to going to bed, she read herself to sleep with Montesquieu's *Lettres Persanes,* Voltaire's *Candide,* Rousseau's *Emile.* The words mingled strangely with her dreams. Caroline's whole day was now completely taken up. The last trace of her neurotic letdown had vanished.

Like all recent proselytes she tended to hold all she had learned from Struensee and from the books he had recommended as the very pinnacle of wisdom. Fraulein von Eyben was confounded when the Queen explained to her how she planned to bring up her little son, Frederik. He was to be raised, she said, as a child of nature, according to the model described by Rousseau. He would never wear shoes or stockings, even in winter, Fraulein von Eyben was interested to learn, and would eat a diet composed of rough, dark bread, vegetables, eggs and milk.

The basic attraction of Struensee's ideas for Caroline depended on the fact that they were not limited to theory, but actually demanded her active co-operation. His plans were not figments, but proposals which she personally might be very instrumental in bringing to fruition. These plans went far beyond her son's future education. Struensee confided to her his hope of freeing the Danish serfs, of curbing the privileges of the aristocracy, of liberalizing the legal code. He broached the idea of the people as an electorate choosing representatives for a legislature. He pictured for her a prospect in which the Danish royal family and the Danish people would forever be harmoniously related as parents and children, mutually bound, mutually dependent and mutually fulfilled. Denmark, he told her, would stand like a rock in the flood when on all sides the European monarchies were shattered by revolution and civil war.

These political flights of fancy quite carried away the tender Queen, and small wonder, since they had turned far better heads than her own. Working from the top down it was Struensee's hope, by means of royal directives to the counsellors and ministers, to undertake social revolution, to swing back the doors of a new epoch without unrest and bloodshed. The plan was both humane and ingenuous. If Struensee had thought the matter through he would have realized it. He would have seen that, in common with all political forms, an absolute monarchy, ridiculous as it may appear to alien view, has its devoted and tenacious adherents. In his day, indeed, any number of resourceful people depended entirely on royally grounded privilege. These people would defend their prestige and prerogatives with every means at their disposal. At the first sign of a move to knock the old props from under them they would strike back, not hesitating to use violence and murderous schemes of reprisal. It was stupid, had Struensee considered the matter, to blink the fact that the serfs' owners, that is, the landed nobles, together with the majority of the clerics and the richer merchants, would react vigorously to his proposed reforms. But so great was his contempt for these dull folk, these stubborn, superstitious, greedy reactionaries, that he did not take them seriously as a potential hindrance to his plans. The idealist was drunk with his ideals as surely as the reactionaries were fuddled by their own meanness. Even Caroline Matilda was somewhat flabbergasted when, waving his hand carelessly, he consigned a whole class of people, the church dignitaries, to the dustbin. We'll get rid of them, he told her, for they're a frightful nuisance.

Struensee, on his side, was aware of the Queen's admiration. Her close attention flattered him to the core, generated bolder plans, more exquisite eloquence. He loved to look into her blue eyes, shining with belief and enthusiasm. He loved to watch her sweet puffs of lips working arduously as she manufactured warm words to match his own. He was moved to the very quick by the sight of her platinum hair, welling out from under her three-cornered hat with the heron feather on it. How beautifully it fell down over her brave, round shoulders. His exalted sensations were heightened by the fact that the trusting creature looking into his eyes was the daughter, wife, sister and mother of kings. A charming, unsuspicious, feminine of great and fateful generations lay like a warm bird in the hollow of his hand.

Yet at this stage of the game he did not believe himself in love with Caroline, however much he might admire the radiance of her youth and the charm of her innocence. There were times, indeed, when he was a little annoyed by this superlative innocence of hers. Somehow it was a silent reproof. Her matter-of-factness, too, in accepting his small services, when he held her stirrup, when he handed her the reins or relieved her of her riding whip, faintly irritated him, though he was immediately ashamed of himself for being so small of heart. Sometimes he could not resist the temptation to air this ingrained hostility. "You're sitting askew in the saddle, Madame," he would say. Or when she held her tongue and gave herself up completely to the exhilaration of riding, he might say: "You seem to be in poor humor, Madame." Then she would look at him in surprise and characteristically stick out the tip of her tongue, close her front teeth on it and blush. Having conquered he would feel infamously mean of spirit, and would have liked to fall on his knees in the dust to beg forgiveness. Once, out of a clear sky, he did stutter something about forgiveness. But the Queen only stared at him in amazement and inquired what could it be that was troubling him. He turned beet red and murmured something about being afraid that the cinches of her saddle were slipping loose. Pretending a vital interest he reached under the horse's belly and drew the cinch strap a little tighter. But Caroline Matilda saw through his stratagem and that morning was gayer than ever.

Struensee could not suppress his lust for political action. Hardly had he assured himself that Caroline was not unsympathetic, hardly had he seen that his ideas carried her away, than he began to cast about for a role which she might fill in his grand scheme. Night after night he tossed in bed thinking about it. Finally, like a revelation it occurred to him that the Queen was really the woman to do what Frau von Gabel had tried to do and failed. If he were able to reconcile the royal couple surely nobody could accuse him of immoral intent in snuggling so close to the throne. He asked himself why this obvious maneuver had not occurred to him before, then excused himself with the thought that only recently had he discovered what a vital creature the Queen really was. The play was becoming strenuous, he told himself. First the King, and now the Queen. Of course, as yet he had no knights, rooks or pawns. But they would appear in good time. He thought about Count Rantzau and his friend, Brandt, both of whom were writing him melancholy letters from the wilds of Holstein, begging him to do what he could to restore them to royal favor in Copenhagen. He had not forgotten them.

Experimenting with Caroline he told her that it was her duty to love the King, to support him in his weakness. He was moved and anxious when he told her about the dangers threatening Christian, about how disastrously he swung back and forth between good and evil. His words were fiery, hard imperatives when he outlined Caroline's queenly duties.

Caroline Matilda, almost humble in her love for Struensee, believed her oracle's every word. It was not too hard for her to believe him, in any case, for the position that he accorded her in his expositions was much more important than the King's role. Having hitherto imagined her queenliness as a passive feminine attribute, a reflection of the pomp and circumstance of the monarchy, at first Caroline was rather shocked when Struensee urged her to quit playing queen, and really be queen. Yet she was flattered by Struensee's high opinion of her. He cited the impressive example of the Tsarina Catherine of Russia. He told her about the Empress Maria Theresa of Austria. Why should she not stand beside these other two, the most glamorous women of their time? Of course, as Struensee admitted with a smile, her competitors might outdo her in certain respects. But none would be younger or more attractive or of finer nature than she. Being younger, he assured her, she would be so much the more liberal, more like Joseph, son of the Austrian Empress.

Carried away by his own image, Struensee described a wonderful future—Caroline Matilda, one of humanity's greatest benefactors, womanhood enthroned. Was it not the people's most grievous need to be governed by the feminine principle, the natural way instead of the hard, dry masculine way, with all its boresome and inept cabinet strife and dogmatic concepts of the law? Was it not a wonderful dream, a glittering, breathtaking possibility, to have absolutism overcome by womanhood acting, for the last time, with absolute power? Yes, Caroline would make new laws. They would lift the weary peoples of Europe from the dust.

How Struensee could talk! His tongue turned on a greased swivel. How dark his eyes were, how imperious the motions of his hands. How tall he loomed before her, a pillar of a man made for embrace. It was Struensee the man, the epitome of masculinity as women understand it who cast the die. The Queen let herself fall in line with his thoughts and his plans not so much out of private

[182]

conviction as on account of her being sucked within the orbit of his stronger personality. The quality of ambition that she had inherited from her mother, previously dormant, now rose to the fore, but the decisive factor was her physical love and need for Struensee. Love was the thing. She, the little person, the gentle, smooth one, became giddy when Struensee named her in the same breath with the Tsarina of Russia. Fundamentally she had enough clairvoyance to realize her limits. She sensed that one had to be made of different, harder, rougher, more durable stuff than herself to wield power, like Catherine, over millions of subjects, to make them dance to her tune. But what woman would not be pleased, against her better sense, at least to toy with the notion of being another Catherine? What woman would not like to be thought, at least hypothetically, a person capable of supreme will and intelligence, even though the same median sort of woman might not want to live through the experience in hard reality? At least it was profoundly flattering to think that she had potential capacity for development in the eyes of a man whom she considered a genius.

Caroline Matilda dreamed of the future like Struensee, but her dreams were quite different from his. They were haunted by no visions of power, or fame, or the hope of freeing the people. Rather by hot visions of physical love, happening over and over again. Struensee created this mythical future for her, for her who had been so cruelly neglected amidst luxury and ease. He had formed the prismatic world of love for her. There were moments, when, to the infatuated Queen, it seemed as if this demi-god of a man, having waited on her coming since childhood days, had actually created the enchanted world of Klampenborg for her private delectation, as a sort of salute to the unspeakably desired release into activity of her womanhood.

When they rode mornings along the beach and the tongues of spent surf licked about the fetlocks of their horses, when the salt wind tilted her hat over her ear absurdly and ruffled her hair, she did not think about sea or wave or noble things, but always about Struensee, as if he, personally, had arranged this delightful buffeting. Quite lifted out of herself by devotion she would listen taut as a harp string to the hollow thundering of the sea and imagine just then that she felt the earth give.

She became wonderfully conscious of the mystery of the natural world. Heart in her throat, she listened to the storm's thundering, to the sob of rain and the wind's rush through the trees. The blue lightning flashes lit up her bed, revealing for a second the curved cherubs on the mirror frame, making the mirror itself into a silvery pool and blanching her own hand lying limp on the covers. How the outdoors flooded in on her from all sides. How it filled her heart with intolerably poetic feeling. The narrow forms hitherto governing her life cracked apart. The seed of self was free to grow. The ancient revelation that only when one is in love is one truly alive came to her.

A feeling of great sweetness was in her, carrying over from day to day. There came a morning when suddenly her knees felt so weak that she hardly had the strength to grip fast the ribs of her horse. She would have liked to slip out of the saddle and fall slowly and softly on the damp beach sand, there to lie eyes closed. But she pulled herself together and spurred her animal forward. She cantered, then galloped, as if by more rapid motion she could escape her own billowy feelings.

The flying hooves kicked up salt spray and sand. She could taste salt on her lips. The wind was in her hair, touseling it wantonly. So she sat, lightly bent forward in the saddle, her breasts lifting and falling in delicious rhythm under her blue dress with the heavy silver trim. The seascape itself was in her, so it seemed, the singing of the wind through the tough dune grasses, the shimmer of the woods towards which her mount was carrying her. She felt the splendid living pulse, the massive harmony in the passage of towering clouds over the sea. She was attuned to the bending grass, the ceaseless flood and retreat of the waves.

But most desirably of all she felt herself, her own body, young, strong and alive with vivid motion. Like the horse under her she flexed her muscles. As he surged ahead, she seemed to bring her whole being into a more powerful and yet feather-light harmony. The horse's big body carried her up and let her fall, in a great rocking motion which was ravishingly sweet between her thighs.

The sensation of extraordinary well-being, of fitting into the world, of pride in her young body possessed her, tightened her sinews. It flooded through her pelvic muscles with a great tickling as warm as blood. She opened her mouth wide and shouted at the sea. Her own shout rang in her ears as a strange descant. It shrilled out of tune, like the cry of the gulls dipping over the waters, so low their wing-tips brushed the curling chop.

Struensee watched this ruttish performance uneasily. He spurred his horse into a fast trot that he might not fall too far behind. Up the beach, also watching, were two fishermen mending their nets in the lee of an old hulk.

"Hey, you, Niels," said the graybeard of the pair. "That was the Queen, wasn't it?"

"She rides like the devil," said the young man, straining to look.

The old fellow scratched his head and sighed a deep sigh. "You're right," he said softly. "She's got the devil in her, that one."

THE SUN HAD passed the equinox, the warm weather was drifting to an end. The woods had been robbed of all their bilberries and country folk had started their annual search for hazelnuts. In the early morning the mist floated under the trees and everywhere spider webs glistened with pearls of dew. St. Martin's summer had come. Although it was still warm at noon, warmer almost than during high summer days, great flocks of starlings collected in the stubble, preparing as always to fly southward towards bright blue skies.

In these golden days beer was brewed for the winter, pigs slaughtered for the winter meat, apples and pears were put away in the cellar. According to old custom, a folk festival famous throughout all Zealand was held in the neighborhood of Klampenborg. Even the well-to-do people of Copenhagen were not above taking a carriage-ride out into the country to attend the fair, and there buy brown tarts, smoked eels and sprats, coarse, fat-specked sausages and other such kermis edibles. There were curious people to look at, Laplanders, fire-eaters, Indians and mermaids, who lay adorned with fish-tails in large, wooden tubs. The old sport of riding and tilting at a ring attracted many, so, too, the fortune-tellers. But the greatest feature was dancing on the green with peasant girls whose white calves were firm and smooth as beech blocks.

Her servants told Caroline all about this Danish festival. She loved to dance and the idea of moving incognito among the young people of her realm and finding out whether she could make an artless conquest or two was a great temptation. In vain Struensee, who, she said, must be her escort, tried to discourage the romantic expedition.

And so her maids got her a white peasant blouse embroidered in red, a sort of vest with big silver buttons to wear over it, four petticoats, a skirt of firecracker-red that gave her an hourglass shape, knitted white stockings and red shoes. To put the finishing touch on this costume she wore teardrop earrings. Her hair she braided and wound round her head and over it put on a red woolen cap. Then she was a peasant queen.

Struensee could hardly believe his eyes when he saw her. Her beauty was more striking in country trappings than in her rich court dress. With her little white ears showing and the curve of her cheeks revealed by her coiffure, with her eyes merry over the escapade, she looked remarkably younger, hardly more than sixteen at the most. Struensee's critically admiring eyes saw that one thing was lacking to complete the picture, a brooch to wear at her breast. He gave her, accordingly, an old-fashioned cross set with garnets. This simple bit of jewelry his mother had given him originally as a keepsake. She had handed it over to him very solemnly when he was leaving his parental home to seek his fortune as a physician. "God protect you, son, and show you the way," she had said, brushing away her mother's tears. "If you ever find a girl to love, you can give it to her." Now the Queen had the garnet cross. She blushed as she took it from his hand, and looked at it again and again as if it were an object of rare beauty.

"It's only a simple cross," he said apologetically. "It was in my family for a long time. My great-grandfather on my mother's side wore it in the battle of Luetzen. His body was found the morning after the battle on the edge of a wood, not far from the body of the Swedish king, they say, among a heap of dead cuirassiers and their horses. He had the cross clutched in his right hand. It's so old that the stones don't shine any more to speak of."

"I don't know," she said. "I think the garnets still shine, but not very much. They seem to be full of blood inside, don't they? Do you really want me to have it? You must value it a lot."

"I don't know anyone who has a better right to wear it," he said with great punctilio.

"It's a lovely thing, it really is," she whispered. Then she opened a secretary drawer and took out a round silver box set with a great many diamond chips. "You'll have to take this from me in return," she said.

"It's far too expensive," he objected. "I couldn't, Madame, if you please."

"It's just an old box," she said. "The diamonds have no particular value. But open it up."

He flicked open the cover with his nail. Within, blurred with age and woodenly drawn, was a man's portrait. The face was grim, framed in coarse hair growing very long.

"Do you know what that is?" she asked.

"I haven't any idea," said Struensee. "He looks like a strong man. And intelligent. But really, he badly needs his hair cutting!"

"That's Oliver Cromwell," she said triumphantly.

"The regicide!" he said. "But Madame!"

The Queen smiled him down. "In my country he is called the Lord Protector. He wasn't a murderer, not actually. An emancipator, don't you think?"

Struensee looked quizzically at Caroline. The little girl standing before him in peasant costume breathed pride and dignity. "You know, I used to keep a clock in this box," she went on to tell him. "But the box was a little too heavy. Then it seemed hardly respectable, I thought, to have the Lord Protector's ears always ringing with the tick of a lady's timepiece."

She laughed a tinkling laugh at her fancy and Struensee found himself smiling eagerly with her. "So I took out the clock," she said, "and there's no one I'd rather give the box to than my dear friend Struensee, who has taught me so much about Denmark."

"I thank you, Madame," said Struensee, stiff with conflicting emotions.

The maids Horn and Bruun hovered in the background curiously watching the exchange of presents. The Queen and Struensee were talking in French and so they understood only scraps of the conversation, but the sentiment of the occasion was obvious enough.

The evening at the fair was a great success. Warnstaedt and Fraulein von Eyben, together with Struensee and the Queen, made up the party. They ate hot sausages and brown pastries. The ladies let themselves be pushed high on the swings. Gay lanterns hung from the trees and a considerable crowd milled about the booths. They even visited the fortune-teller. She was an old Lapland crone. They found her sitting in her tent beside the coals of a small fire. Two wicked eyes glittered in the dirty gray of her face, which appeared to be made of worn leather. Her nose was broad and concavely sunken, her cheekbones stuck out in knobs, a pet daw perched improbably on her left shoulder.

"Pretty girl, pretty girl," the old woman croaked at Caroline. "Come right here to little mother and she'll tell you your fortune. Who doesn't want to know her fortune, pretty girl! Maybe you'll have love and luck. And maybe you won't. Come and find out, dearie."

Fearful, but too curious to resist, the Queen entered the tent. The old Laplander seized her hand and stroked it greedily. "What a lovely, lovely hand," she said. "You have many servants and are not what you appear to be, my treasure." She studied the Queen's face. "You have a rich man, my dove," she said, "but you love a poor one. Give me some money, now."

Struensee flung the fortune-teller some copper coins. Her claws reached for them swiftly. The daw hopped excitedly on her shoulder and laid his bill against her dirty gray hair. "My wise bird," she said, grinning broadly, "you aren't trying to tell me what even a blind man could see, I hope. Your excellency must take care, however. Yes, my fine sir, take care. And you, too, sweet dove. Watch what you do. There are many eyes, many ears keeping watch over you."

Struensee snorted in contempt and chagrin. "She's talking the usual nonsense," he said. But Caroline was depressed and glad to get out of the tent. Everything inside smelled strongly of oil and fish and scuffed earth. Once again safely outside in the cool autumn evening they all looked at each other and laughed, as if by so doing to exorcise the old crone's sardonic warnings. It was not too hard for them to forget how easily the old faker had penetrated their deception.

Not far from the fortune-teller's tent was the dance floor, a wooden platform lighted by pretty lanterns. The musicians sat in a huddle, faces red with brandy and already more than a little drunk. The fiddlers scratched, paying no attention to time. The bass viol rumbled solemnly. The man playing the Jew's harp introduced crude trills and variations into the melody. But notwithstanding its tunelessness, the music at least had a mighty pump-handle beat, and this quite sufficed for the dancers.

Girls were much in the majority, almost all of them simple-faced albino blondes. All wore frocks of the same cut, these commonly of some solid color, bright red, light blue or leaf green. On and on they whirled about in a writhing circle, showing a delightful deal of white stockinged leg and decorative garter. The liveliest among them, in fact, sometimes twirled with such abandon that their white thighs were revealed, to the great delight of the male spectators. Seeing white flesh they would clap like mad, hurl their caps to the ground and bellow raucous approval. The peasant men stamped out the time with clodhopper feet, and whacked their palms together. They behaved like grouse in the spring of the year, showing off and dancing before the chosen one. Often, carried away, they grabbed the girls' hands, or threw their arms about their waists and whisked them off their feet. In such case the girls would draw the interloper into their whirling midst and carry him round and round the platform until his brain was addled. Presently, after a few forays of this sort, the men and women paired off.

Struensee was horrified at the idea of hopping about in a folk dance. But there was no holding back the Queen. Though awkward at first, Struensee quickly adjusted himself to the pounding rhythm and soon was turning and bobbing with the best of them. The women's gestures, inviting and spurning at once, excited him immensely. The smell of their warm hair and excited bodies set him on fire. He soon found himself trying modest variations on the standard steps, sign enough that he had mastered the situation.

The Queen revolved tirelessly and when Struensee, spanning her hips with his hands, lightly lifted her off her feet, she smiled into his face and pressed her hand eagerly on his shoulder. Suddenly the chill thought struck him that he was definitely overdoing his medical responsibilities. He was so shocked at himself that he came very close to letting the Queen tumble to the floor. Just then everyone changed partners. Afterwards Struensee danced mechanically. He hoisted all sorts and shapes of girls into the air and spun them about.

blondes and redheads, midgets and giants, slender and stout ones. He peered into a kaleidoscope of female faces, some pretty, some coarse, some shiny with lust, some reserved, some ecstatic, some quite unmoved by the dance. But Eros rampant no longer riveted his attention. Only one thought turned in his brain. Have I fallen in love with her? Have I?

He had just taken hold of a girl's hand—she seemed especially light on her feet and terribly young—when he heard her say to him: "Dr. Struensee!" He lost step and looked closely into the girl's face. No mistake, it was Antje Maria. "What are you doing here," he asked her, slowing down to half time. "Who let you come here, my child?"

"Why, I'm just dancing the same as you are," she said, and then they both burst into laughter.

"I mean," he said, trying to catch his wind, "it doesn't seem quite right for you to come here all alone."

"Oh, but I'm not alone," she said. "The whole kitchen crew from Christiansborg is here, all the maids and cooks."

"They are?" he said. "Well, how do you like it at the castle?"

"It's wonderful," she told him. "Though sometimes I'm sad."

"And why?"

"Because you never come and see me, Dr. Struensee."

He nodded his head, feeling very silly and owlish, and underneath wondering how much Antje Maria's cooks and maids had noticed. "In the winter I'll be living in Christiansborg," he said. "Then we can see each other more often."

"That will be nice, won't it!" Antje Maria said ecstatically.

"I'm sure," said Struensee. And then he added as an afterthought: "By the way, Antje Maria, do you have a sweetheart these days?"

"A sweetheart?" she hedged.

"Yes, someone who likes you," said Struensee.

She looked up into his face, bit her lips softly and blushed. "Oh no, no," she said very positively. "I could never love anyone else, you know."

Then she was pulled out of his hands and whirled away. She looked at him again through the crowd, triumphantly smiling. They grow up quickly, Struensee thought, prickly with embarrassment. He left the floor, mopping his brow, and fell into conversation with a peasant boy. "Brother, you have the prettiest one of the lot," the boy said to him. "It looks as if they'll pick her for queen."

"What do you mean?" asked Struensee.

"Don't you know!" the boy said. "They always crown the prettiest girl the queen of Klampenborg. She gets a crown of flowers and they give her a new dress. Everybody's saying that your girl is the prettiest."

At once Struensee went to Caroline and told her that the time had come for her to leave. "I could have danced for hours more," she complained, but otherwise did not resist.

Once safe in the carriage and rolling towards home, he told her about her lost opportunity. "How strange it is," she said, some time later. "Tonight, when I was dancing, for the first time I really felt like a queen."

★ *VIII* ★

*T*HOUGH IT WAS November the court still lingered in Frederiksborg. There was little pleasure in it for most of the guests. The ornate rooms and immense halls were cold and damp. Mists hung over the lake, the garden paths were carpeted with molding leaves. But the King and Queen, whose apartments were amply heated by large porcelain stoves, were warm enough. So much did they enjoy the uninhibited country life that they could not make up their minds to return to Christiansborg.

The deerhunting season was on. Early in the morning before sunup the hounds could be heard belling and yowling out in the castle yard. There was a great shuffling and stamping of horses' hooves as the party gathered, and afterwards, as they filed at a slow canter over the bridge, someone snored loud and long on a huntsman's horn, saluting the morning.

Christian was very fond of hunting and now, for the first time, his wife accompanied him. He could not properly accustom himself to having her ride expertly beside him. He laughed in wonderment when she sailed along at a gallop over the moors and raised herself in her stirrups to clear a hedge. This new queen interested him. He tried to impress her by enlightening her on the fine points of the chase. He did it this morning, at considerable length.

Remembering Struensee's admonitions, the Queen smilingly heard out all the King had to tell her. She looked very pretty in a dove-gray fur cap with heavy ribbons hanging down from the gold band. She had on besides a scarlet coat, suede trousers and high riding boots. The gentlemen marveled at her, so trim and young. Was this the same woman who had passed whole weeks brooding and locked away in her rooms? Something very plainly had happened to her. She laughed so loudly, she drank down the glass of Ruedesheimer served at breakfast with such unladylike dispatch, that eyebrows were lifted. Count Holck, who could not imagine a happy woman without a lover—preferably himself—lurking in the background, was positive he knew the source of the Queen's aboutface. He told the King so as he rode along beside him.

"So you think she's in love?" Christian said and laughed. "So much the better. It makes her bloom, at any rate. And I have sworn that I'll never stick my nose into her sentimental concerns. You know, when I have a woman myself, I hardly like to see her making long faces about it. But, my dear Holck, since you seem to know so much, who is it she's in love with?"

Holck meditated the question, so strenuously that three deep folds graved themselves in his forehead above his big nose. "In my opinion," he said finally, "she's in love with the Doctor."

"No!" said Christian.

"Yes, I think so," said Holck. "As incredible as it may sound, it's Struensee. He's always with her."

"But it doesn't seem incredible to me at all," said Christian. "He's intelligent and full of life. Furthermore, Struensee isn't a bad looking sort. And he's quite devoted to me, quite."

"Yes, but the man's a commoner!" said Holck. "As for his being devoted, I think that's an odd way of showing devotion."

"Well, he doesn't have to stay a commoner," said Christian and smiled coldly at his large friend. "How would you like it? Count Struensee. Not bad. And don't look so downcast, Holck. It makes you utterly ridiculous. As a matter of fact your news was quite a pleasant surprise, and right off you try to spoil everything. I was beginning to think that Madame la Reine had fallen in love with someone who simply wouldn't do. With me, for instance. Or even worse, with you."

"Really!" said Holck in great confusion. "With all due respect, Your Majesty, I don't know . . ."

"Of course you don't know, Holck," said the King relentlessly. "You don't know anything to speak of, not really. My dear man, you and I might as well toss this love folderol right out the window and be done with it. Think of it. Think of you and your whores diddling all night in Blaagard. Think of me, drunk in the gutter. Are such practices calculated to promote the affections? Obviously not. If anyone should know what a foul fellow I really am, it should be you."

"You have no right to condemn yourself like that," said Holck. "It . . . it just doesn't sound right!"

"You're priceless, Holck, absolutely priceless," said the King. "You should sleep more nights and get rid of the cobwebs. I'm not condemning myself. On the contrary, I'm only too glad not to be sighing for the moon. You don't suppose it would be any pleasure for men like us to have a woman in love with us, do you? Would you enjoy being catechized and nagged and pecked morning, noon and night? Like an ox with the warbles? For that's how love is, my stupid friend. A woman in love knows everything, everything, you understand, that goes on in her beloved's little mind. She can read the poor devil like a book. Why are you so serious, darling? Why are you making such a face, sweetheart? Do you love me always, even when you're alone, precious? That's the way it goes, a regular madhouse song and dance, Holck. Why, I'd tear my hair out by the roots after two days of it. Out by the roots, every single hair. I couldn't stand it. I'd rather lie on a bed of nails than sleep night after night with a woman who loved me. Sheer torment, I say. Indeed, it's bad enough to have this Struensee bothering me. He's next thing to a woman, the way he hangs on my neck. He's trying to reform me, to make me a great king. Very nicely and respectfully and gently, of course, but that's exactly what he's got up his sleeve."

"Why, that's treason!" said Holck. "What else? And you are a great king already, aren't you? Who is he to decide whether you're great or not!"

"Holck, for God's sake don't cloud the issue," said the King. "It's too utterly stupid and silly of you. Can't you and I ever talk seriously? I like to empty my spleen once in a while and you try to stop me. I might as well be talking to those tree trunks as to you."

Holck now put on his usual injured air, to be on the safe side. The damnably uncomfortable thing about Christian, he thought, is that you never know which way the wind's blowing. Sometimes he clowns, sometimes he talks with real sense. But aloud he said: "Christian, you must be in the dumps. How about a little visit to Blaagard this evening? What do you say?"

"The sad part of it is," said the King gloomily, "that when I get to Blaagard I don't feel any too spry." Malice cramped his face and he added: "I want to have my freedom. But what good is freedom unless I make some use of it? Well, an evening in Blaagard theoretically ought to be the answer, as you say. We might celebrate my final and absolute emancipation from the yoke of virtue." He tittered at himself and tapped his rather rabbity teeth.

Holck stared at him furtively, a thin smile of incomprehension on his slabby features. Being looked at made Christian titter more wildly than ever. He was so taken by laughter that he jerked back the reins, bringing his horse to a surprised stop. The echo of his laughter came back from a hillside.

"The devilish niceness of fate, Holck, I can't get over it," the King said shakily. "My little queen, my blue-eyed little blonde! It won't be long before she can't afford to look down her pretty little nose at Christian. Oh, that dirty fellow! Oh, such degradation. But never again. She won't be able to practise her English contempt on poor Christian. And the same goes for Struensee. Clever Struensee, who can take the King's soul apart like a watch. Take it apart, clean and oil it, put it together again. He'll do that no more. For he who loves must pay a forfeit, Holck."

"Your Majesty!" Desperately Holck tried to interpose. "Christian!"

"Holck, their guilt could be worse than they dream of," the King went on unheeding. "Perhaps, just perhaps, I say, for who really understands a lunatic like me, I staked my last copper of trust on them. I trusted my wife, I trusted my friend. In my peculiar way. But supposing—and I don't say it will happen—supposing, now, everything went to pot on account of the itch they feel for each other. Can you imagine it, Holck? I'd be a nothing, riding along between heaven and hell, neither here nor there. And don't look so frightened, Holck! I'm only discussing what might be. But the fact remains, that if you'd studied the difference between *possibilitas* and *actualitas* as I have done, you'd know that between them sometimes lies hardly enough room to fit in a red hair." The King snapped his fingers to show Holck what he meant, and suddenly his face darkened. "I'm afraid, Holck, afraid," he said. And then, in a dead tone, he added: "At the bottom I know very well I'm the guilty one. It's not they, with their silly love."

"I don't know what you're talking about, Christian," Holck protested desperately. "Will you be so very kind as to change the subject?"

For answer Christian ran his spurs into his horse's ribs and was carried away at a dead gallop. Holck looked after him in wonder, then trotted after, shaking his big head.

At the hunt picnic Christian was the perfect host. The conversation was very lively. Even the grooms and drivers, drinking their schnapps off to one side from the ladies and gentlemen, felt warmly towards the King. Approvingly they watched him as he forked delicacies onto the ladies' plates and made himself their chief cupbearer. When the time came for a toast he stepped into the middle of the throng, raised his goblet and said loudly: "To what we both love, Dr. Struensee!"

The Doctor bowed to the King, lifted his glass and replied: "To Denmark, Your Majesty."

The King drank, his eyes rolling, then wiped his lips with a lacy handkerchief. "Your toast was fine, Dr. Struensee," he said, "and can hardly be improved. But actually I had something else in mind." Again he raised his glass. "This time to the Queen's health, Struensee."

"To the Queen's health," the guests chanted in unison and looked significantly at each other. Caroline Matilda was pale under her little fur cap of dove-gray. She managed to smile, however, and said: "My husband is very gallant today. I propose another toast, exactly like his own—to what we love."

"To the King!" the company said dutifully. The drivers on the outskirts joined in with some genuine show of enthusiasm. Struensee kept a watchful eye on the King. He looked exceedingly amused and very much pleased with himself. Struensee wondered what would come next. But not a shadow of ill will was visible in the King's demeanor, and he did not develop his raillery.

That evening Struensee brooded over his own motives. Do I really love her, he asked himself. A sweetly painful longing grew in his breast as he imagined Caroline all his own, flying along, scarlet-coated and blonde, on her hunter, or sitting before her spinet in the evening in a crinoline frock, her eyes questioning and her lips apout.

But I do not love her, he told himself, not the way I loved Frau von Gabel.

He sprang up from his chair and stalked up and down the room. What is the point in fooling myself, he thought angrily. Why else should I have given her my mother's garnet cross. Was it just a passing impulse? Because she looked so young and pretty dressed as a peasant girl?

But does she love me?

He shook his head to escape the hornets of perplexity. He determined henceforth to avoid her whenever possible. He told himself that his feeling for the young Queen was only a passing infatuation, kindled by her adolescent charm, reinforced by a thousand small coincidences—her sickness, the inescapable intimacy of their excursions at Klampenborg, the morning freshness of their times together, the feeling of release evoked by woods and moors and beach.

He, the older one, would have to take the initiative and act reasonably. Yet even as he thought this, something in him laughed at his resolution. Something whispered, that's all very well and very moral, my dear fellow. But don't forget that she's very, very pretty and would be delicious all naked in bed. And don't forget that she loves you, and wants you and that she will be intensely unhappy if you don't return her love. Then, of course, you'll never have such an opportunity again, for you're no spring chicken as it is right now, my good fellow.

Struensee was another Hercules at the parting of the ways. He was enormously relieved when, after the first snowfall, the court moved back to Christiansborg. In Copenhagen the many little liberties and confidences that country life had generated came to an abrupt end. The detailed formality of traditional court life again took hold. The Queen was constantly surrounded by her ladies. As majestically as her years allowed she swept over the parquet floors, wearing a billowy crinoline, her hair powdered white, and so played the queen. Generals richly blazoned with gold braid bowed before her passage. The girl who, in excited moments, stuck out her tongue-tip, apparently had grown up. There was no coquettish Caroline of the beech woods.

And yet there were times, sitting at the long table with the candles burning evenly in big porcelain holders, when Struensee would hear a clear peal of laughter. His heart would swell with pain and regret. Looking up in his distress he would find two blue eyes staring into his, proudly questioning. Presently the eyes would turn away fretfully, and not seek his again that evening, no more than if he were one of the lackeys lined up in a row behind the guests' chairs. Despite his vow to be sensible, this would pique him. Then he was sorely tempted to find some way to be alone with the Queen, that he might accept her challenge. How delightful that would be, with Copenhagen gray and still beyond the thickly draped windows, with roofs snow-capped and icicles at the eaves.

Once Struensee walked by the Queen's apartment and heard her singing. Her voice was husky. She did not do very well with the little piece by Rameau. But the very impurity of the voice touched him. Within the huge palace, a structure of a thousand rooms and innumerable guarded corridors, the voice, mingled with the spinet's thin and hesitant tinkling, brought to mind a caged woodland bird.

Remarkable how penetrating the voice was, despite its seeming lightness, and how suddenly it made the heavy, fixed mass of the palace seem hideous and unreal. A violent compassion flooded through Struensee. His hand of its own accord went to the doorknob. But the voice fell silent and he did not go in after all.

The great building crouched in silence. Uncertainly Struensee listened at the door, rooted to the spot, quaking with anxiety and desire. He felt sure, though he could not possibly know, that on the other side of the door the Queen was standing, like himself, with her hand ready to turn the knob, yet paralyzed by the same fear. His fate was in balance. The scales might tip either way.

He went away and had Antje Maria brought to him, for he loved to listen to her bright prattle. Sometimes he took her with him into the city and this he did now, to get away from himself. Antje Maria hung on his arm like a daughter, or so he chose to imagine, and marveled at the crowd streaming by, all muffled in winter clothes. "How do they all earn a living?" she asked. "What in the world do they all do?"

"Why do you ask that?" Struensee said indulgently. "In a big city like this, a capital, there have to be all sorts of laborers and artisans and merchants and servants. What is strange about that?"

"Yes, I suppose so," she said, unconvinced. "I see why, but I still can't quite understand it. I don't understand how all these houses and churches and markets and things got here. It seems so funny, seeing everything crowded together like this, when what we really live on comes out of the ground or out of the sea."

"You're a good little girl," he said and drew her closer to his side. "But really, you aren't very clever. Now, are you? Surely there are more important occupations than farming or fishing."

Antje Maria accepted his rebuke in silence. But presently she spoke up and said: "Do you know what Copenhagen makes me think of, Dr. Struensee? The Tower of Babel. That's what I always think. When I see so many people in the streets I have a feeling that no one really understands anyone else, as if they all talked different languages."

This amused Struensee. "It's just because you read too much in the Bible," he said. "You take the old myths far too seriously. Pretty soon you'll be telling me that I remind you of the wicked Nebuchadnezzar."

"I will not!" she protested. "How could you even think that, Dr. Struensee! But in a way you do remind me of somebody in the Bible."

"Who could that be?" Struensee asked, curious. "Saul, perhaps? Who looked for an ass and found a kingdom."

"No, I don't mean Saul," she corrected him. "I mean Joseph, who became a prince of Egypt and helped the people when they were hungry."

"Oh, that one!" said Struensee, greatly pleased. "But still I don't have any fine dreams. And then, Potiphar's wife doesn't like me!" He could have bitten off his tongue. He looked down quickly to see if Antje Maria had caught the allusion. "Let's forget the Bible, shall we," he said, forcing a laugh. "Dr. Struensee will go right on being himself, and I'm quite sure that Copenhagen isn't the least bit like Egypt."

Then he steered Antje Maria directly to the Christmas stalls. She was ridiculously grateful when he bought her some sweets and a length of cloth for a dress. She wanted to kiss his hands, but he drew them away. "If you want to kiss me," he said sportively, "kiss me on the cheek, my dear."

She strained up on tiptoe and kissed him carefully. He saw she had tears in her eyes. "What are you bawling about, silly!" he said. "Isn't the sugar sweet enough for you!"

"No," she said through her pretty little snuffles, "I'm just happy."

"A fine, fine way to be happy," he said.

She shook her head and tried to smile away the tears.

On the first evening of the new year a masked ball was given in Christiansborg Palace. Count Holck, official *maitre de plaisir,* had arranged the affair particularly in Christian's interest, for of late the King had suffered repeated fits of depression. His Negro slave, Morari, ordinarily a prime favorite with the King, went about with a frightened, dumb look. Christian, made violent by frustration, had struck him savagely on the head with a hoop. The King wandered about the palace in an evil mood, insulting the court ladies with his erotic insinuations, challenging the court gentlemen to fisticuffs and denouncing them as filthy cowards when they declined.

The impending ball aroused great activity among the well-bred womenfolk of the Bredegade. Both Annette and Fraulein von Eyben came to Struensee for help in planning their costumes. For himself the Doctor chose a black and red domino with a simple mask.

The ball was given in the royal theater. The stage was provided with a backdrop representing a Chinese landscape, complete with pagodas, little carp ponds, drooping trees, bamboo huts and arched bridges. In the stalls tables were set up to provide refreshments for the dancers. Invited members of the Copenhagen bourgeoisie were permitted to occupy seats in the upper circles, from which vantage they could at least watch the revelry, if not actively participate on the dance floor.

Coming into the theater Struensee was enveloped by a blanket of heavily perfumed warmth. The music sounded clear and far away, coming from some distant, pillared corner. Candles were lit in the stalls. Struensee, having looked around, felt little desire to dance. But his tall figure and slitted mask had an attractively sinister look, which quickly attracted the women. Emboldened by disguise they flirted openly with him, and presently he was whirling about the floor with the rest.

Soon he was pleasantly excited by the spectacle of so many round white arms gleaming bluishly in the candlelight, of shoulders like chiseled marble, of half-naked creamy breasts. There was a promise of infinite lust in the carmined mouths, the powdered cheeks, the myriad of perfect little ears, in the unnatural brilliance of hundreds of pairs of large feminine eyes. It seemed to him that all the costumed women, all the swaying, sensually pullulating creatures whose namelessness was tantalizing him, were in reality so many shifting personifications of a single creature, of woman herself, *femina,* kaleidoscopically blurring his senses, a diabola of endless variation.

The old imperious hunger for women waxed strong in him. He suddenly gave way to an unbridled desire to bury his face in welling, spicily perfumed hair. His heart began to pump like mad, sweat damped his palms and almost before he knew what was happening to him he was lost in the seventh wave of lust that bore up the masked gathering.

A demonic surge filled the theater space, so strong that even the prosy spectators in the balconies felt it seeping into their blood. Struensee, the domino, forgot Struensee, the doctor. Boldly he swung women about by their hips, boldly he whispered concupiscent words into their willing ears. He danced and the hours fled. At intervals he slaked his thirst at one of the refreshment tables. The tickling champagne and the cool, heavy Rhine wine added speed and scope to his drunken, whirligig mood, heightened the press of soft round knees against his own. Round bodies tumbled and squirmed in his lap. Heated mouths with frantic tongues clamped hard against his own in long kisses behind curtained places.

He found himself saying all sorts of foolish, meaningless things. Gladly he hearkened to female gibberish, as if each word were a costly pearl. And yet all the while he was conscious of waiting for a supreme moment, a desirable peak of tumescence. An almost intolerable descant of emotion tightened cords of expectation in him until the tension was beyond his power to endure.

The women of the ball were dressed like women of the Orient, like Turks, Caucasians, Indians, Japanese. Some were dressed in wide pantaloons, others in dresses of hourglass shape with tight-fitting vests to set them off, and still others were in white Grecian robes which encouraged fondling. Little figurines of Meissen and Sèvres porcelain danced about life-size. A majority of the women, it seemed, preferred smooth, simple stuffs of solid colors which suggested the mat, delicate sheen of porcelain. Where the faces showed outside the masks, they had an enameled look.

Lacking total requitement, after a time the fires died down in Struensee. He was now more able to enjoy and judge the different types of feminine beauty on display. Here he marveled at the delicacy of a throat, there at the rich fullness of a pair of shoulders, again at the pure curve of a neck, again at a wonderful pair of haunches. He leaned against a pillar and at his ease let his gaze wander over the fleshly particulars of the scene, noting a forehead's pensive quality, the wild tomboy air of another head, the hot look of a pair of dark eyes, the sweet innocent oval of another face.

It gave him pleasure to speculate on the identity of the different women, to decipher from fleeting signs not so much their names as their characters. He discovered the essential attraction of the masquerade, the paradox that the more masked, the more shown.

One figure especially caught Struensee's eye. The woman, or it might have been a girl, was dressed like a Georgian. Her slender white legs, otherwise bare, were covered up to the calves by boots of soft, brilliantly red Russian leather. A short, green skirt came only half way down her thighs. Over her shoulders she wore a short, armless, braided jacket of the same green color, and her mask, too, was of green silk. The costume was simple and striking. It was this simplicity that first drew Struensee's attention, that and the erect posture of the head. The girl wore her hair combed up and powdered white, leaving the ears free. Seen from behind pressed neatly against the delicate skull they suggested youthful daring and pliancy, and yet were at the same time poignant. No doubt the Caucasian girl was young. The texture of her skin, the dimpled knees, her tirelessness showed it. And the active gestures of her red-gloved hands were youthful—that anyone could see. She may be a Holstein girl from one of the big estates, Struensee thought to himself. She'll certainly have no trouble finding a lover. Hardly had he thought this than his heart began to race with excitement. He felt sure he had seen the girl somewhere before. The way she held her head, the way she moved about were familiar to him.

Then he saw that the Caucasian girl in green and red knew he was looking at her, and did not mind.

Nearer and nearer she danced to him, smiling at him through the slits in her mask. Once he thought she beckoned to him. Then he lost sight of her. Almost standing on tiptoe he looked hard all about the floor of the theater, trying to locate her. While he was still staring he felt a hand fall lightly on his shoulder. The Georgian girl stood by his side.

"You, domino," she said, "I'm terribly thirsty." Without preliminary she folded her arm in his and let him lead her to one of the stalls where there were things to eat and drink. His hand shook as he filled her glass with champagne and some of the wine spilled. She put her hand over his, after taking off a red glove and carelessly throwing it to one side.

"To you," he said, lifting his wine.

"To you, domino," she said. "To our love." This last she spoke in a whisper. She looked at him hard and long through the holes in her mask. Her eyes were a bright blue.

"Well, now you know me, domino," she said. "Were you waiting for me?"

"I never expected such luck," he told her. "I really didn't."

"My dear," she said, low and under her breath, "tell me quickly that you love me."

He put his arms about her and felt the fullness of her back under the thin silk. "I . . ." he stammered, "yes, I . . ."

"Let me say it for you," she said hotly. "Yes, I love you. I loved you the first time I saw you. But I tried not to. I got sick trying not to love you. Then you came and made me well. You didn't see then that I loved you. You kept me at a distance. Did you want me to perish of despair? Do you still?"

"No, no," he whispered back to her. "Please don't talk like that." Saying this, for the first time he kissed her full on the mouth.

"I love you," she said again, pressing her cheeks against his, this side and that. "Yes, I really love you, domino, my Struensee. I can't live without you, and that is the simple truth. Before, before you came, it was different. But was I really living then? Wasn't I dead before you came along? Haven't you opened up the whole world to me? How can you let me go now, now Struensee. How can you!"

He covered her shoulders, her neck, her ears with kisses. "Don't you see that I have to keep my place?" he told her passionately. "I can't do anything that might put you in an impossible situation."

"How coy you are, Struensee, how careful," she said. "Is it something terrible to be in love? Would you rather have me keep on playing the puppet among all the other puppets? How can you even think of such a thing?" She tore off her mask and violently shook her head in negation. Then, just as suddenly her mood changed. Now she was a wise child about to perform a clever trick. Sucking in her cheeks with delight she stripped Struensee's mask away, took his face between her hands and kissed him warmly, on mouth and cheeks. "I feel so sure of myself," she said, "when I'm with you and can love you. When you're not with me, it's like being alone on a desert. You must always stay with me, Struensee. Always stay with me, and then I'll be so happy, so very happy. All the time."

"Don't think me cold," he implored. "On the contrary . . ."

"Go on," she said.

"But I cannot help . . . that is . . . I'm so much older than you," he told her. "I've had so much more experience, Caroline. You can hardly understand what a difference it makes in a man."

"I hate you to talk in riddles," she said and stamped with her foot. "If I love someone, then I love, and that's all there is to it. What do I care what others think!" But at once she added: "Still, I'm not going to make trouble for you. I'll be discreet, I'll try to keep on playing the game. Providing that I'm sure I can see you at any hour of the day and come to life in your arms. That is what I want to have. It is my right."

"I'll always be near you," said Struensee dizzily. "I'll always be waiting for you to call me."

"Then I'm content," she said. "And will you always love me as you do now?"

"Always."

"Let us kiss the garnet cross," she said solemnly. She opened her blouse and took out the cross, which hung between her breasts on a thin silver chain. She kissed it first, then he did likewise. She looked into his eyes. His winy euphoria had vanished, and she was no longer coquettish in the least.

The violins played hopping music far away. The air in the theater had staled as the ball wore on. The masquerade paled before the deeper reality in their hearts. Caroline looked down at herself nervously. Her ballroom dress was not fitting any longer, she felt. Struensee took his cloak and draped it about her shoulders. Leaning against him, his arm about her, they slipped out of the theater together by a side door. Behind them they left far more than they knew.

★ IX ★

ALTHOUGH THE AIR was warm and roses were blooming again in the gardens of Rosenborg, panic held Copenhagen in its grip. An epidemic of smallpox had struck the city and was killing off the children by the hundreds.

Mothers tried to keep their offspring strictly indoors. The streets were strangely empty and lifeless without the shrill rumpus of children at play. Copenhagen, much more so than most cities of comparable size, had long been remarkable for its large population of young people. At twilight it had become a common sight to see small coffins being carried off for burial with the weeping parents following behind.

The people of the town, even the small minority who had no children themselves, found a dreadful fascination in this performance of early death. They looked and stared and afterwards walked away with lowered heads. Prayers of propitiation were offered in the churches. Indeed, Pastor Muenter of St. Peter's went so far as to prostrate himself full length on the floor before the crucifix, while the congregation knelt behind him on the hard flags, murmuring pleas for succor. The doctors could do little. They had the stricken put to bed, ordered the houses to be tightly closed and inuncted warm olive oil into the pustules. Many families who could afford it, people of the mercantile and aristocratic classes, simply fled the city altogether.

But the King's family dared not leave the city. During the crisis the King had no choice but make a show of standing by his extended family, the Danish people. Christian made no protest. He was barely in touch with reality in any case at this time. Mostly he whiled away the weeks playing games with his Negro slave, Morari. With Caroline Matilda it was a different matter. At the first sign of the epidemic she became acutely aware of the danger to her little son. She was passionately determined that he should not die.

She sat, this evening during the peak of the epidemic, at her child's bedside, sorely afraid that God would cause her boy to die as punishment for her illicit love. The thought possessed her as she looked down at him, sleeping peacefully, a blond cherub. The child's face was flushed from the warmth of the covers. She took him in her arms, sure of a sudden that the dreaded fever had infected him. Her imagination ran riot. She pictured how, shortly, he would toss and turn, how his blue eyes would glaze, how the pocks would spread over his rose-petal skin, how eventually he would stiffen in convulsions and his limbs chill and harden in death. Her fear was so intense that she pressed the infant suffocatingly to her breasts. He woke up and began to yell. His screaming convinced her. The boy had smallpox. God's revenge was imminent.

Pressing the screaming child to her, she rang for the maid and had her get Struensee at once. It was about midnight, but he came immediately. He took the child away from her, put it back in bed and took its temperature. The child went to sleep at once, smiling sweetly, cheeks still wet with tears. "The boy is perfectly all right," he told the Queen. "Don't worry about him."

Caroline sighed, profoundly relieved. She sank back in her chair and looked at Struensee with gratitude and love. "How stupid of me to disturb you at such a late hour," she said. "But really, I couldn't stop myself."

He looked closely at her and saw a pretty young blonde in negligee. He marveled at the smallness of her feet and hands and the feminine tenderness of her throat. Her concern for her child touched him to the roots of his heart. How different, Caroline the mother! Then he thought how he had not kissed her for months, indeed, since the first and only time at the masked ball. Suddenly, as deep and sure as a sword-cut, desire for her overtook him. He fought it down desperately and reddened with shame at the impropriety of desire at such a moment. Clearing the thickness from his throat, he said: "I'm afraid the child must be inoculated, Your Majesty."

Caroline Matilda had never heard of such a thing as inoculation. Struensee explained it to her, and assured her that only through inoculation could the child have any continuing protection against the disease. In any event, he told her, it would mitigate the disease, if it should strike, reduce it to a mild fever. The Queen was delighted, suddenly vivid with hope. Such a fine man, she thought, such a good man. Not only had he banished her current fears, but all her worry about the future. Her heart was full of love for him and for her child. Where one ended and the other began she could not have said. Her eyes shone. She took his hand and kissed it. Flushing with dismay he drew his hand back as if it had been bitten rather than kissed. He was glad to see that the nurse was still bent over the child and so could not have seen the Queen's rash gesture.

The privy council met the very next day. Cautiously the councillors told each other that it would not do to rush headlong into the matter of inoculating the heir-apparent. Struensee was a hothead, they said to each other. He was corrupted by a Gallic lust for innovation. He had certainly shown what stripe of rascal he was by getting the King to declare the press free of censorship. Was inoculation another instance of playing with fire?

[202]

And yet what could they offer in objection to Struensee's proposal? Their medical knowledge was limited to the practice of taking a seltzer powder mornings when they suffered from a hangover. They could do nothing against expert opposition. For the King's aging physician-in-ordinary, Berger, after some hesitation lined up on Struensee's side. The privy council dared not take the responsibility of letting the little crown prince die for lack of inoculation.

The privy council gave their permission and the child was innoculated. All Copenhagen, all Denmark, held its breath. In every street-corner, in every cellar pub Struensee's idea was hotly discussed, some favoring, others denouncing the principle of inoculation, without understanding the first thing about it, of course. Every fishwife considered herself an authority and hashed over incredibly irrelevant pros and cons. For one day the child had a light fever, then became happier and livelier than ever. Copenhagen rejoiced. A new weapon had been found to combat smallpox. The crown prince had lived through it, and now the children of all city burghers who could afford the treatment followed his lead. But strangely enough, as if death were now aware of the futility of his assaults, the epidemic slackened and disappeared.

Sickness was gone and the children played again in the streets. Lilacs bloomed in pale masses in the gardens of Rosenborg. On the island of Amager the horse chestnuts were in full flower, decked with white wedding candles. The nightingales sang at night in the undergrowth. Struensee now wore the Order of Dannebrog, heavy and silver, over his heart. He had been appointed secretary to the Queen. For the first time in his life he powdered his hair.

Caroline Matilda was vibrantly grateful. She wanted her new secretary with her all the time, on carriage-rides, out walking, during musicales, when new books were being read aloud, when letters were being written. When she played on the spinet, he bent over her, his cheek lightly touching her hair, and skillfully turned the pages of the music. When she stitched at her petitpoint, he held the ball of silk. In the morning, during the levée, he had to be there unconditionally while she sipped her chocolate. In the evening he was the last one to bow goodnight to her.

There was no doubt now that she was happy, but her happiness took an odd turn at times. She would flush, then turn pale, and showers of fever would run over her, after which ice-cold sensations would grip her neck. When he sat next to her at chess, she lost every game so abjectly that her partners could not possibly engineer an excuse for her.

On one occasion she caught Struensee joking with Fraulein von Eyben, complimenting her on her fine appearance. This harmless flirtation caused the Queen to break down in tears. Half the night she lay awake debating whether she should ask Christian to have the redhead banished to the Island of Moen from which region of cattle and wheat fields she had originally come. She heard that Struensee sometimes went into town with a girl from the kitchen. She was beside herself with rage. A terrible quarrel ensued, which ended with the Queen begging her secretary to forgive her for such feminine contrariety, and with her elevating the astounded Antje Maria to the post of personal maidservant.

Caroline and Struensee both felt that this tense state of affairs could not continue indefinitely. When the Queen's hand brushed Struensee's, when he touched her hair or her dress, she drew back as if she had come in contact with red hot iron. They both knew very well that they were poised on the edge of a chasm, with neither the strength to draw back nor the courage to spring forward into the depths.

One early afternoon in June, however, they were walking together wordlessly in the gardens of Rosenborg. All morning Caroline had felt depressed and had wandered restlessly from one room to another. Listlessly she had watched her child at play, listlessly she had let them fix her hair for the day. That morning she had scratched some words in a windowpane with her solitaire: "God keep me innocent, make others great." Underneath the etched letters she had added her initials, C.M. Thereupon she had had her carriage fetched, called Struensee and told him he was to escort her on a trip to Rosenborg.

Now she walked, bleak within, beside her beloved. According to habit they had been discussing the crown prince's education, though actually their thoughts were far from this neutral subject. Their talk had declined into incoherence and finally a painful silence. Their tongues were paralyzed, they were acutely conscious of each other. The weather contributed to their feeling of oppression. The air was humid and breathless. The birds had ceased their twittering, the swans rested immobile on the black mirror of the pool and the sun shone watery through a gray, muggy overcast.

The light of day yellowed as they walked distraitly among hedges and flower beds. An intolerable tension came over the green life about them, and menace crept like a serpent out of dark green leaf clumps. The humidity noticeably increased. Somewhere deep in the garden a lapwing began to call, presaging rain, and presently came the first crash of thunder. It struck their nerve-ends as if they were so many tuning-forks. Struensee, unable to contain himself any longer, took the Queen's warm, limp hand. He drew her to him and kissed her. Her mouth was half open and she received his kiss without responding. He drew her still closer to him, greedily smelled the perfume of her hair. Her breasts were hard against his chest. He could feel the thump of her heart. Heavy drops of rain began to fall, splashing on their hot skin. Caroline's blue eyes were big and starry.

The rain fell faster and faster. It clattered like hail on the thick foliage of the chestnut trees. The thirsty earth sucked in the wet and gave off a strong aromatic odor, a heady miasma of genesis that completely turned the lovers' heads. The swans in the pond lifted their heads erect. The water on which they floated took on a brighter, pewtery look and was heavily pitted by raindrops.

They ran together for the shelter of the castle. Caroline lifted her loose frock up over her knees to get leg room. As he loped along behind, Struensee watched the motion of her calf-muscles. She runs like a fine Arab horse, he thought to himself.

She was breathing heavily and had become drenched through by the time they reached the castle. Going in she turned and looked back at him, laughing richly. He opened the door for her. It was as heavy as a dungeon gate. It squealed and gave unwillingly and groaned like someone just waked from sleep.

Safely inside it was dark and stuffily warm. The honey odor of expensive burned-out candles was in the still air. There was a sweet fragrance of fine cabinet woods and furniture polish mingled with the delicate must of old Gobelin tapestry. All the appointments of the house were heavy and old-fashioned.

The room which they now entered was hung with the portraits of past kings and queens. Apparently preoccupied exclusively with themselves, they were posed against a variety of backgrounds. The men in the pictures wore heavy cuirasses made of overlapping iron scales, lace collars and ermine mantles lined with red silk. In some pictures white hands gracefully held a scepter, in others brown fists gripped sword hilts. Some faces were bearded, others smoothly shaven, depending on the prevailing mode. Some of the men were decorated with the Cross of Dannebrog, others with the Order of the Elephant. The women, too, young and old, good looking and plain, were so stiffly dressed that they might as well have been wearing armor.

Consciousness of their symbolic role, of status and royal dignity, hardened their faces. But behind this surface expression lingered the human quality, the individuality that through whole lifetimes had never found complete expression and which now, locked away in majesty, they appeared to be thinking back on with regret.

Struensee threw back the window hangings. After a struggle he managed to open one of the antique windows. The smell of warm rain and dank earth came into the room like a wave and overpowered the deathly stillness and must of the room.

Caroline stood in the middle of the room, looking up at the portraits ranged high on the walls. "How dead, how dead and doubly dead they are," she said and shuddered. "They all look like Christian.

Both men and women. They've all got a sort of foolish look. Haven't they!"

Struensee said nothing to this. His eyes never left the Queen.

"Some day they'll have me hanging on the wall, too," she added. "They'll make me look exactly like the rest of them. They'll give me a long, long nose. I know they will."

Still not saying a word he moved closer to her and put his arms around her. Her damp clothes stuck to her back. He could feel the heat of her body coming through the wet garments. She looked at him now as if she were suddenly seeing him again. "How I hate all those people," she murmured. Then she laid her face tightly against his. "But I'm not afraid of them," she said dreamily. "They're all ghosts, even those who think they are alive." And then she added: "Do you still love me, Struensee?"

"I love you, love you," he said hoarsely and kissed her on the lips and on her throat where it ran into her shoulder.

The Queen let out a little cry and went limp in his arms. She let her head rest against his shoulders and he lifted her up. He carried her to a long sofa and laid her down. For just a moment, when she first felt his hand on her hot flesh, she stiffened and drew back from his attack. Rapidly he undressed her, she trying to assist with pins and buckles. Then she gave way and was quickly lost in a blur of lust. Her eyes widened ecstatically, yet were blind, as if she were straining to see the invisible. She ran her fingers through his hair, her hand rapidly caressed the back of his neck. Great shudders shook her. She felt a sweetly shattering sensation spreading throughout her frame, penetrating its every nook and cranny, until she reacted with athletic enthusiasm. The exchange of feeling between her and Struensee was so profound that presently she could not ride up to him properly, and had to turn her head away to get air. She sobbed and heaved, half conscious.

In this fashion Caroline Matilda had her first real knowledge of love's requitement. Afterwards she was filled with a great, quiet wonder. When she lay back exhausted, and he was busy kissing her breasts in a dumb show of gratitude, she remembered bitterly how she had already given herself to someone else before Struensee, someone whom she did not and never could love.

How ashamed she was of her loveless marriage, lying naked with Struensee on the old sofa, the pile of the upholstery tickling her back. She had falsely sacrificed her body and her love. Her marriage was a farce. Then she recalled the obvious, that out of her marriage a child had issued. The thought confused her, for after all she did dearly love her child. Now, beside her, lay the man who had saved this child. She pressed her hands together and whispered something that barely caught Struensee's ear.

"What are you saying, my dearest," he asked.

She would not tell and instead looked into his face, saying: "I'm yours forever, as long as you want me." He nodded assent, smiling foolishly, looking and looking into the blue eyes.

"I'm going to leave him," she told Struensee. "I must tell him that I love you."

He pulled away as if nipped by a fox. "Oh, but that's out of the question, Caroline," he remonstrated. "Why, even if he were willing —and that might even be—he could never divorce you. You are the queen, Caroline. There's no getting away from it."

"But I want only you."

He stroked her hair to quiet her. "It's impossible," he declared. "A crown cannot be thrown away."

"Christine of Sweden did it," she reminded him.

"Yes, but on religious grounds," he told her.

"But you are my religion," she told him bravely. "Are you not?"

"So you say," he replied with an earnest kiss. "It's good of you to say it, at least. Don't you think I'd be a thousand times happier if I had you all for my own? On some country place in Holstein? In England?"

"You're telling the truth?" she asked.

"That's true, every word," he said. "How could you doubt it?"

"No, I don't doubt it," she said. "I merely wanted to hear you say it."

"Remember that so long as you are queen," he said, "you can do a great deal of good, and the people will bless you for it. You cannot and must not abandon the Danish people. It may seem unlikely to you, but a great deal depends on you. Would you not like to be a great queen, Caroline?"

"I'm not a great queen and nothing can be done about it," she told him. "Kiss me, Struensee, kiss me again."

"I beg you to listen to me, Caroline," he said. "Everyone loves you. Everyone respects and honors you. You can usher in the new world that the people long for."

"When you say it I can almost believe," she said. "But . . ."

"What?" he asked. "Tell me. What are you thinking about?"

She hesitated and then said: "I simply won't be anything more than your mistress."

"Yes," he said to her. "But we do love each other. Isn't that something?"

"No, it is not enough," she said and sat upright, propped up on the sofa with her arms behind her. She stared at the mask-like portraits on the walls. A look of bewilderment came over Struensee. "I know what I know," she said flatly. "We shall have a child, you and I."

"A child!" Struensee could not keep the shrill from his voice. "Poor Caroline! What a contrary thought." Mechanically he stroked her on the small of the back. "Don't you think you ought to put your clothes on, Caroline?" he suggested.

She laughed at his comical look and kissed him repeatedly. "Why, you look like a child yourself," she said happily.

"Yes, yes," he said shakily. "Of course, my dear."

"Don't you see," she explained in a gush. "If we have a child our love will be sacred, then. Nature will sanctify it. You believe in that, don't you? You've always told me about the goodness of nature."

"I see what you mean," he said lamely. He could not directly disclaim the powers of nature, since he himself had so strenuously advocated the natural way. How keenly, just then, did he realize that women have a dozen ways to prove a point to their own satisfaction, not the least of which is the artful disposition of their bodily attractions at the critical moment. "Yes, I shall be glad if we have a child," he told her, quite loudly, as if the louder he said it, the truer it would be. "And it will have to look like you. It simply will have to have your hair, sweet thing."

"Oh, no, no," she objected. "It will have to look just like you!" And she would have said more, but he pulled her down to him again.

Meanwhile the showers had passed and the sun had come out. Sunlight was slanting into the room. Throstles sang persistently in the garden. Rain-washed air came in cool gusts through the window. Love made Caroline Matilda very agile and full of energy. She wriggled off the sofa bouncily, hummed as she slipped into her clothes and fixed her hair before a cloudy old mirror. She folded her hands behind her head and stretched in sheer animal pleasure. "I feel so nice, so wonderful," she confided to Struensee.

He silently nodded assent and busied himself closing the window and barring it. He felt better when the drapes were drawn to once more. He refused to think that this performance gave him something to do, for which distraction he was secretly grateful. The situation was lightly, gently getting on his nerves.

"Can you come to me tonight," she asked. "I'd so much like to talk to you."

"Well, Caroline," he said. "I should like to. But . . ."

"When everything is quiet, I'll send Antje Maria to call you," she told him imperiously. "My doctor must come, you see, because I shall have a frightful headache. And my secretary will have to come, of course, because when my headache is better I'm sure to have some wonderful ideas to take down. You see?"

"Your doctor and your secretary will be there," he assured her with all the gallantry that he could muster. "And your friend will come calling, too. The one who loves you, you know."

"Oh, that one!" she said. "I don't know whether I'll let him in, not with the other two there."

"Then of course he'll break the door down," he warned.

"I'll call the guards," she said. "A hundred of them."

"Then he'll fall at your feet and beg for mercy," said Struensee.

"Then I'll forgive him and love him until his knees are wax," said Caroline. "Yes, I shall love him, love him to pieces." From somewhere in the old castle, somewhere up in the arched corridors, came a hollow, whispery echo . . . love, love him.

This was the same castle that Christian the Fourth, Denmark's greatest king, had preferred above all others. Here he had sat before his silver wine goblet in the company of the peasant girl, Wibecke, here had stretched out his long, booted legs to the fire burning bright on the hearth. Here the wet-nurses had handed him his children to have a look at them, legitimate and illegitimate, and all of them he had accepted with the same rough, warm love. Here his powerful voice had rung from wall to wall like a hunting horn, here the floors had shuddered under his solid tread. And so often he had laughed here, until the plaster nearly fell from the stones. He had been a rare, lusty fellow, this other Christian, and many had been the women he had gulled with talk of love. In this same castle he had died, simply turned his face to the wall and quietly perished without complaint like the man he was.

Had Struensee known something of these historical sentiments he would have been struck by the fact that the Queen, looking a last time at her husband's forebears on the walls, strongly resembled this other Christian.

"No, never like them," she said to the pictures. "I shall never look like them. For I have loved and they have not. I shall die without regret, at least. You will see, you up there!"

"What a grim thought!" Struensee said chidingly. He took her by the hand and trapped it in his own. Hand in hand they left Rosenborg.

BOOK THREE

Palace Revolution

*T*HE CHATEAU TRAVENTHAL is in Holstein, in the midst of an idyllic landscape of wide valley meadows and little hills, these often crowned with trees. The Chateau is anything but imposing. Shaped like a horseshoe and but one story high, it has many windows set in green-painted frames, and is half hidden by immense oak trees. It is a wonderful summer place, for the flag floors keep the rooms cool even on the hottest July days.

At this time the Chateau was in active use. The summer flooded in through wide open doors of the dining room wing with the cupola on it. People of the court sat about the round table, all dressed for country life and yet still stylish. In the middle of the table was a large vase filled with deep red roses. The women's laughter rang out light and clear, the men's deeper rumble was careless and confident. The Queen wore a simple country costume which showed off her white breasts to great advantage. She was the gayest of them all.

On Struensee's request Caroline Matilda had invited Count Rantzau and Brandt to Traventhal to be daily guests at the royal table. The two newcomers were more than ready to sing for their supper. They overflowed with anecdotes of all description. They basked joyously in the queenly favor, they sparkled like champagne.

Was there anything, really, that Count Rantzau had not experienced! He had lived among Russians, he had known soldiers, priests, courtesans, peasant wenches. In his blasé, snoring voice the graying Casanova gave his auditors generously from his store of spicy tales. From anyone else they would have been shocking, from Rantzau they were inimitable. He related how he had palmed himself off as the King of Greenland, in order to cheat a merchant who, so it turned out, was no merchant at all. He described innumerable amatory adventures. He pictured himself as being quite as much at home with serving girls who lived in garrets as with princesses from marbled terraces. According to his own admission he much preferred girls from the lower classes. They excited him more, he said, and of course in the lower classes even the youngest specimens were available for his aristocratic choice. He confessed that he had even pretended to be a monk that he might worm his way into the confidence of a pious, and yet unconsciously passionate, young lady. He told how he had been the drinking companion of the Marshal de Saxe. In

Paris he had written copy for newspapers, so he said, in Noyon he had posed as a physician, armed only with gall and a large syringe. This last adventure, like the bulk of the others, revolved about a woman. *"On sait, ces médicins!"* said Rantzau boldly, with a wink at Struensee. Indeed, the Count was a veritable cyclorama.

The Count's tone of *mechante bonhomie* as he depicted his picaresque adventures charmed the women. Their instincts were quite duped. Behind Rantzau's flamboyant selfishness and Mephistophelianisms, they wrongly imagined, there must be a hard, bright streak of masculine vitality. They believed they sensed naked power. But they were wrong, totally wrong. Count Rantzau was not the man he would have seemed. He was a faker, not a man of power and will.

If the Count fascinated the ladies by virtue of spurious masculine qualities, Brandt attracted them as a person cut out to tickle their sympathies. Brandt was a born player of second fiddle. He was the fellow who never quite came through, the fellow who should have been chosen and yet always, for some last-minute reason, missed out. His ugly-pretty face, a wicked boy's face, and his boyishly responsive feelings, revealed so eloquently in his oddly sad and reproachful eyes, drew the women to him unerringly. Tactlessly, foolishly Brandt had always plunged from one unlovely episode to the next, always discovering his mistakes just a little too late. From one scandal to the next he caromed, inevitably coming out on the short end of the stick. Struensee's rococo Parsifal was especially appealing to older women, women, say, verging on the climacteric. Blonde Frau von Holstein, among others, could hardly keep her hands off him. Listening to him recounting one of his misadventures she would laugh at him mockingly like the rest of the company, but in her heart would vow to console him at the first opportunity.

Rantzau and Brandt were natural complements, like pig meat and cabbage. In sterner times they would assuredly have dangled side by side on the gallows. But at the Queen's round table they occupied places of honor as interesting immoralists. They sat, indeed, at the Queen's right and left. At the end of the meal, to show her appreciation of their talents, Caroline would peel an apple for them, slice it in two and give each a half.

A few months before this highly specialized ribaldry would have offended Caroline Matilda. She would either have avoided such company as Rantzau's and Brandt's, or have banished them from her presence. Now it was different. Across from her sat the man she loved. If she cared to do so, and she did on occasion, she could reach out her toes and play with his foot. She could project loving glances in his direction just as she chose. He was no mere appearance, no sickly dream, no heated figment of imagination betwixt the bedcovers. He was a man in three dimensions who actually confronted her, who smiled and laughed at appropriate intervals. That made everything very different.

Caroline Matilda learned to like the two clowns because they were Struensee's friends and paladins. He liked them, therefore there must be something to them. That was how the Queen's mind ran. In long discussions Struensee explained to her that Rantzau and Brandt would eventually be indispensable both to him and to her. Brandt, having been appointed *maître de plaisir,* would keep the King amused, pickled in pleasure, so to speak. Rantzau, the man of experience and noble lineage, would bring the Danish landed aristocracy in line with reform.

And so Caroline had come to terms with the newcomers' alien tone. No longer was she offended by daring modes of address. Even when Brandt turned the conversation to religion, and remarked that he would gladly live up to the Decalogue, providing God took out the one word "not," she found the spirit to laugh at him. Even while she was giggling with the rest, the commandment "thou shalt not commit adultery" unfolded before her inner eye like so many huge letters hewn from stone. Resolutely she brushed her hand across her forehead. All that has nothing to do with me, she told herself. Circumstances are different in my case. My marriage is unhappy. And so on.

During meals Christian would sit head down over his plate and stuff himself like a pig. He would grab carelessly at plate or glass, pass it over his shoulder to the slave Morari and abruptly demand more roast or wine. As a rule the company paid little attention to him. But there were times when he became obstreperous and proved to be a grave nuisance. Frau von Gaehler, for example, on one occasion was unwise enough to observe that her coffee was too hot to drink. The King bent down over her cup and blew into it so hard that the liquid sprayed onto Gaehler's bare bosom, scalding her. The King shook with amusement, while tears of pain and rage welled into Gaehler's eyes. Only a sign from Struensee prevented her from causing an irreparable scene. Then there was the time that Christian took thick blue grapes and began to pepper the heads of the guests with them, commanding them to do likewise to him. "It's the Battle of Traventhal!" he told them wildly. "Everybody's got to play dead when he's hit. Except me, I mean. Look out! Here I come!" Whereupon he hurled a whole handful of grapes at Brandt.

Morari tried to spirit the King away from the table and into the garden. He was not to be budged. He struck the Negro with his clenched fist squarely in the face, so hard that Morari's nose leaked blood. Absorbedly Christian watched the blood run. "Why isn't your blood as black as your skin?" he said. "But in truth it's as red as mine, and I'm a king." A murderous look came into Morari's face, and at once Christian changed. "Don't be angry with me, Morari," he whined. "You're my only friend, Morari. I'll give you a nice ring. It's not your fault that I lost my temper. The damned traitors at this table are really to blame."

And yet such outbursts came relatively seldom. Usually Christian was either indifferent, or mildly interested in the court's goings-on, as if he saw them through a fine mist. He was highly amused by Brandt's clownery and self-directed sarcasms. Sometimes the King himself would interject a remark and it was astonishing how apt and witty it could be. When Brandt made his pointless comment on the Decalogue, Christian had muttered to himself: "Mmmm, let me see. Thou shalt kill." Then he had sprung from his seat, so abruptly his chair toppled over. "Well, now, supposing I take you at your word, Brandt," he had said, leaning over the table. "Supposing I kill you. How about it, Brandt? Denmark would merely lose one more scoundrel. Come now, what say you?"

Brandt was all confusion before the King's irrelevant assault. He did his best to parry Christian's fancy. "Not just now, Your Majesty," he pleaded. "Couldn't you wait until I've had my dessert? I'm so awfully fond of ices."

"No, at once!" shouted Christian. "On the spot, sir!"

"What have I done, Sire?" Brandt asked with mock tears.

"You've committed treason, that's what you've done," said Christian. "You refuse to obey your King's orders. Look what you're doing this very minute!"

"Then there's nothing I can do," said Brandt and kneeled down before Christian, bowed his head and pulled the lace collar aside to expose the back of his neck. Christian looked down on him uneasily, his eyes rolling and out of focus, a little fish knife in his hand.

"Well, well," he said at last, when the silence was becoming intolerable. "I see I can't cut his head off after all."

"Why can't you?" the others chorused.

"Look for yourself," said Christian quite seriously. "The fellow hasn't got a head to cut off! He was either born without one or he lost it somewhere along the way, poor devil."

Brandt scrambled to his feet with great alacrity. The play was over, the guests laughed heartily. In cold fact Christian rather liked Brandt, perhaps because they were alike in some respects, at least in being helpless drifters through life. Both covered their weakness with cynicism and buffoonery, though in Christian's case the actor was becoming the real person as his mentality deteriorated. Brandt, actually of sound mind, though outwardly as blasé and effete as the King, took pains to enlist Christian's sympathy for sycophantic gain. Like all insipid personalities he had a flair for the opportunistic move and from the start had fully realized it was now or never if he were to play a key role in Struensee's plans. His task was to entertain and distract the King.

Christian finally got rid of his longtime favorite, Holck, and did so without the slightest sign of compunction, as if he were dismissing a stable-hand. He did not even take the trouble to kick him out personally. Brandt relayed the message for him. Holck was pleased to accept a gift of money and henceforth consider himself exiled from the court. He was quite prepared to stand the shock. During his years of ascendancy he had carefully put away large sums coming to him in the form of presents and bribes and was by now a rich man. He had also married a rich woman, who was so kind as to die a year later, leaving a substantial legacy. At the time of his dismissal Holck was casting around for another younger lady of means to draw into his net. He also owned estates and plenty of land, all tax-free through royal dispensation. Moreover, he had been getting thoroughly fed up with Christian's bizarreries. Accordingly he slapped Christian's apprehensive go-between on the back with a hand as heavy as a hammer and called for a flask of port wine to be brought up from the cellar. This he emptied with Brandt, drinking two for one, and offering unasked-for advice as the wine eased his tongue.

Brandt quickly discovered that being Christian's right hand man was not all that it was cracked up to be, just as Holck had said. The King was in constant need of diversion, and the sort of entertainment that pleased him was not on an adult level. Childish games like hide-and-go-seek, tag, catch and wrestling, when repeated day after day, began to wear on Brandt. No matter. Christian could not be wearied. He had Brandt out of bed bright and early at seven, and was still romping with him in the garden at nightfall. Quite often Brandt had to creep around on the wet lawn looking for night-crawlers while the King held a lantern. The King was extremely fond of fishing and preferred worms as bait. In vain Brandt protested that the whole business of worming and fishing was unkingly and ridiculous. It was also a common sight to see Brandt racing like mad across the grass on Christian's order, hotfooting it after the fleet King, who loved to be chased and not caught. Sometimes the King, having outdistanced Brandt, would hide in the shrubbery and trip up his exasperated pursuer. If Brandt flew headlong, the King was enormously amused. At the table he would describe these heroic encounters in the finest detail, even while Brandt was sitting a few seats away with a bandage on his head, looking black with mortification. The guests, of course, dissolved into gales of laughter.

Brandt had imagined the post of *maître de plaisir* to be a very choice sinecure. He had always played the fool, now he was a fool in earnest. Struensee advised him to buy Christian two more Negro slaves to serve as royal playmates. For a considerable sum Brandt did purchase two Africans, a young man and a girl. These additions to his retinue deeply interested Christian for a while, especially the girl.

Count Rantzau invited the court to his nearby castle of Ascheberg, there to enjoy balls and feasts costing him, the chronic debtor, a small fortune. But Rantzau considered the money to be well spent so long as he was cementing his relationship with Struensee, from whom he expected great things now that he knew all about the physician's liaison with the Queen. In Glueckstadt Rantzau put his regiment through the paces to please the guests. Later he arranged a country weekend at Ascheberg, highlighted by a tourney in which Rantzau's peasants, some mounted on donkeys, others rowing boats, attacked each other with lances. The water tourney delighted the King. He laughed himself sick when one of the contestants was knocked into the water and shouted to the victor to break his lance over the vanquished's head. "Drown him!" he shouted. "Drown the brute!" The display wound up with fireworks. The Count's borrowed thalers disappeared in pinwheels and rockets, sizzling out splendidly against a black night sky. Sardonically Rantzau watched them go, his hands stuck squireishly in his pockets.

The next evening there was a ball, an event that the peasants of the locality talked about for many, many years to come. It was a dance in the country style. The Queen of Denmark, as the peasants told it afterwards, danced for ten Our Fathers with her Doctor, while Christian the Seventh by the grace of God hopped about like an idiot among his subjects and tweaked their peasant backsides.

These summery jollities went off without a flaw and everybody had a wonderful time. Yet heavy clouds were gathering over Denmark. Only one of the dancers, Struensee, gave them a moment's thought. Perhaps a few of the peasants, too, had some solemn notions the next morning as they departed at daybreak for their daily stint of fourteen hours in the fields. Perhaps some of the peasant mothers, their hands gnarled from too much work, their bellies sagged from too much childbearing, may also have mused a little on the morning after. But if they did, they still accepted their lot as inevitable, and blamed no one in particular for it. After all, the Count's schnapps had run down their throats like water. No one could say the Count was a piker, not their Count!

For his part, Struensee experienced some pangs of conscience the next day, thinking how he should have spent the wasted hours in his room, reckoning and planning. But the fact of the matter was, the more he dug into the problem of renovating Denmark, the more difficulties he disclosed. Fortunately he was not easily discouraged. Difficulties actually sharpened his zeal. He was more determined than ever to doctor the country back to health. As he saw it, the situation was all black and white. According to his nature he was unable to credit the idea that the Danish state, like any other, might conceivably continue half-sick for many decades without giving up the ghost.

The decree granting full freedom to the press on the surface, at least, had been a fruitful move. Struensee thought of it as a preliminary lancet-thrust probing the sickly consciousness of the people. In cold fact, however, freedom of the press had resulted to date only in a larger output of trash. Forward-looking ideas simply were not expressed. A positive enthusiasm for reform was lacking. There was no awakening of the Danish people. Everybody was far too busy with his own mean concerns. Influential court circles were obsessed by careers and pleasures, the bourgeoisie grubbed like fiends for thalers, and the peasants, as always, simply struggled to keep alive.

Struensee, waking during the night, would sometimes ask himself nervously whether what he had read really could be applied to the concrete situation. Was there anything to the fluent principles of the French philosophers that had so firmly captured his imagination when he was a doctor in Altona? Could it be, he would ask himself, that freedom, equality and a median life for all amid a bountiful nature were all so much moonshine? Was human reason as penetrating and resourceful as he had believed? Sometimes he felt like a man committed to the task of draining the ocean with a teacup. Presently, however, sleep would again overtake him. In the morning his doubts made him smile, and so the days went.

Struensee was very quiet and reticent these lovely summer days. The ladies and gentlemen of the court who hung on him and who would have liked to see him more talkative were no longer fully at ease with him. It was so important that they be ever ready to trim sail as the wind shifted. Jokingly they dubbed him "le silencieux." Actually Struensee was neither close-mouthed by nature, nor patient. He quite lacked the true statesman's ability to wait and wait for the opportune moment to strike. His natural desire was not to lead, but to command. His outlook was absolutist. He was an illiberal liberal, he would promote freedom by dictatorial means.

For the time being Struensee permitted himself no novelties beyond liberalizing the intent, on occasion, of this or that sentence in some order submitted by the cabinet for the King's signature. Some writs he caused to be permanently delayed, a few he had returned unsigned. In Copenhagen Bernstorff was well aware that it was not the King who was making game of his fancy state papers. He now realized that Struensee was the interloper, but for the time being played as best he could in a sour tune. The fact that the corrections and alterations were usually written in the Queen's steep, girlish handwriting also made for indulgence. To the poet Klopstock, who was Bernstorff's friend and who, indeed, lived in his house, the foreign minister said: "As you see, my friend, the wind is blowing from a new quarter. And it smells, if my nose doesn't lie, of perfume and powder." Klopstock, heavy with years and intellectual honors, was an extremely moral and dogmatic old man. He had long since forgotten his boat trips on the Lake of Geneva with bevies of pretty girls, the trips that Gessner had so scathingly deplored. Today, as suited an old bard, he shook his mane and complained about the "perverted gynarchy" that was ruining Denmark. He ordered his crony, Bernstorff, to "excise the horrid tumor from the body politic" before it was too late.

As Bernstorff himself pointed out, what could he do? Had the Queen no legal right to come to the aid of a helpless husband? Was it not, rather, her duty to help him? There was no gainsaying it. The true author of the marginalia of Danish state documents hovered safely in limbo behind the royal couple. To drag out into the light of day, to show him up for what he was, Bernstorff considered an unthinkable maneuver. The scandal that might very well result would be as bad as a revolution, and certainly would cost Bernstorff his office, perhaps his head.

The poet talked well, of course, Bernstorff thought to himself. In his political innocence—a rather endearing trait, as a matter of fact—he imagined that the world of politics moved like clockwork. How silly, Bernstorff reasoned, for intellectuals to meddle in politics. They should stick to moralizing, their true metier. Thinking these cynic thoughts the old warhorse would take a pinch of snuff from his gold snuff box, this a present from Christian's deceased papa, draw the brown powder up his nose and sneeze exquisitely. "Really, it's not so serious," he would say, all snuffles, to Klopstock. "So long as they keep their nose out of my Russian plans." Bernstorff always looped back in any discussion to his "Russian plans."

Struensee, as it happened, was thinking about other things than Russia, for example, about how to pay off the Danish public debt of some twenty million reichsthalers. This was the situation which he intended to exploit in levering his way into power. The bourgeois in him came to the surface in crisis. Thrown back on purely instinctual resources he thought and acted like any son of modest, sober parents. He had a totally different outlook on the getting and spending of money from the well-born folk who habitually managed the national budget. His money sense argued the necessity of balance and moderation in state expenditures, that first of all. The very first thought to come into burgher Struensee's mind was retrenchment. So he had always seen it done at home, when for instance the problem of paying for the winter's fuel had confronted his father.

And who was the greatest spendthrift in the state? Very plainly the King himself, and, by extension, the court satellites around him.

Conspicuously this would have to be drastically curtailed. There would have to be a stop put to royal gifts, to ten thousand thalers here, ten thousand there, as in the case of the parasite Holck. Such extravagances mounted up. The outlay on the theater, the opera and court balls was far too great. There were gentlemen of the bedchamber, ladies-in-waiting, maidservants and lackeys enough for three courts of comparable size. Twenty of them, in some instances, were assigned to a job that would not raise a bead of sweat on one person's brow. And the palace guards? Was it really necessary for a thousand young men, all in the pink of condition, to stand around in costly uniforms, cluttering up the stairs, doors and passage-ways of Christiansborg?

Not only the court proper, Struensee assured himself, but the state as a whole would have to limit its expenses. Foreign imports were much too high, particularly silk imports for luxury use. Conversely, the exchange of Danish grain and meat for Norwegian fish and wood would have to be notably increased. To do this it would be necessary to increase the agricultural production of Denmark. The petty aristocracy had turned large areas of their tax-free lands into useless parks, deer preserves and the like. Either taxes must be imposed on these non-producing lands, or they would have to be given over to the peasants for cultivation. Which in turn brought up the point that the peasants, so many of whom were still illiterate serfs, would have to be educated to proper land use.

A great wheel of ideas turned slowly and inexorably in Struensee's head. To teach the peasants there would have to be schools, and teachers for the schools. Where would they come from and who would pay for them? Moreover, more competent heads must be drawn into the government to assume the new responsibilities. Favoritism and nepotism would have to be obliterated. Positions would have to be filled by the most able, as determined by public intelligence and character tests. Then, after the Augean stables had been at least partially cleansed, the legal code would need revision. In the future, according to Struensee's grand scheme, the law must protect not merely the upper classes and the clergy, but all the people of Denmark, proprietor and pauper.

These were tremendous plans, and it was curious that Struensee, being neither fanatic nor stupid, should never have suspected that he would run headlong into dogged resistance. As a doctor he was accustomed to having his patients do as he prescribed, if not too exactly or too eagerly, at least with some degree of compliance. When he told his patients that refusal to follow his orders would entail serious consequences, almost invariably they knuckled under. Now all Denmark was his patient. He had taken the patient's pulse, measured the degree of fever, diagnosed the malady and was about to order the therapy. It seemed perfectly natural to him that the object of his ministrations should be grateful to the physician, who was actually improving the situation without inflicting any particular discomfort or pain.

He could not understand that in dealing with masses and classes he could not depend on his past personal experience. In this larger case success depended on an adequate degree of understanding spread out among large groups of people. This did not obtain in Denmark. Following the recipes of the French freethinkers, he took the condition for granted without even troubling to look for himself. He scarcely knew his own patient, beyond a few molar symptoms. He was quite ignorant of the essentially cautious and skeptical character of the Danish people. He completely underestimated their subservience to tradition. The fact that they might prefer a familiar evil to a foreign good was simply beyond Struensee's comprehension. He knew nothing of Danish history, and so lacked even a literary insight into the national personality. He did not even speak Danish! His relations with the country were strictly limited to court life, to a circle of highborn men and women as scantily versed in the specific traits of their humbler fellow nationals as Struensee himself. It was the custom of these upper class folk to converse among themselves either in French or in German. But never in Danish.

Nonetheless, he set about deploying his liberal French ideas among the Danes, without wasting time on overtures. He took the Queen into his confidence, and she marveled starrily at his projects. Women themselves may be the most hidebound realists, yet they gladly lend an ear to the idealist, especially if they chance to be in love with him. Moreover, the Queen knew even less about the people over whom she reigned than did her lover, Struensee.

He took Rantzau and Brandt into his confidence as well. At first both were taken aback by such grandiose proposals, but in good time accepted his plans, considering them to be so much humanitarian eyewash. He was building up a political front, they told themselves. They took it for granted that once words became deeds, the situation would develop in altogether unforeseen directions, so giving them a chance to profit. Their basic mistake was in attributing political genius to Struensee. His rapid rise to a position of influence blinded them. Besides, the sort of liberalism obligatory in all Parisian salons, and to which everyone in the swim pretended a certain amount of allegiance to avoid the social risk of being considered an old fogey, could not possibly result in any serious, practical changes, so far as Rantzau and Brandt could see. Liberalism was a fashion, a social phenomenon. They never dreamed that Struensee might think absolutely otherwise.

Rantzau and Brandt plotted for influence on their own account. It was the Count's express intention to pay off his debts and find himself a permanent government post that would yield affluence and power. Brandt, less ambitious, merely wanted to see Danish opera, theater and ballet as opulent as any in Europe. How Struensee would react or what might happen to Danish finances while the arts flourished did not concern Brandt.

It was about this time that Christian and Caroline Matilda went to Lueneburg, there to meet Caroline's mother. Princess Augusta of Wales, via the Marquis of Keith, English ambassador to Copenhagen, had been apprized of her daughter's affair with a certain Dr. Struensee. She had made up her mind to cut it off, root, stock and branch. Caroline suspected something of this sort, and had responded reluctantly to her mother's ever more importunate hints that she would like to pay Denmark a visit. Only when her mother offered flatly to come to Lueneberg, did Caroline give in with poor grace.

How great was this good dowager's astonishment when, directly behind Caroline herself, the infamous Doctor in person climbed out of the royal carriage to greet her. He was the last person she had wanted to see. And he was followed, to make matters more confusing, by an incredible ass of a man called Brandt. The meeting in Lueneburg proved to be a fiasco. The English Queen-Mother was unable to corner her daughter for a heart to heart talk. Either Struensee hovered in the background, or Brandt, spouting tactless witticisms. Meanwhile Christian, taking advantage of his incognito, got drunk night after night in the renowned Lueneburg ratskeller, and had to be lugged home in the early morning hours by servants.

At last, however, the Queen-Dowager of England did manage to have her daughter Caroline by herself for a few minutes during the levée. She wasted no time getting down to brass tacks. She had no effect on Caroline, who took her stand on such grounds as "the right to love." This point of view was quite new to the widowed Princess of Wales. There was one consolation. She found that her youngest child looked better than she ever had during her whole lifetime. She had grown taller and fuller, and in her eyes shone that fine glitter often seen in the gaze of happily pregnant women.

Parting from her favorite daughter the Queen-Dowager threw her arms about her, broke down in tears, kissed her excessively and whispered: *"Dieu vous ait dans sa sainte grace."* Then she left, bursting with concern over her child's waywardness. Pensively, shaking her head, compressing her lips she sat all alone in her carriage while it jogged over the monotonous moorland landscape. Poor thing, the Queen-Dowager mused, I do hope that everything turns out well. She's so inexperienced. He's quite a figure of a man, that Struensee. Better than Bute, if the truth be known. Such a pity he's only a physician.

Preparations were being made at Traventhal to move the court back to Copenhagen. These days reapers were at work in the fields, long rows of them swinging sickles and scythes. Behind them came the women, kerchiefs tied around their heads and long blue aprons protecting their clothes. They gathered the grain into sheaves which they bound together with straw, using their teeth to help make the knot. And behind them came the children, little blonde things, the youngest among them still unsteady on their feet. Their task was to pile the sheaves into stacks and to collect lost ears of grain.

Despite the laborious, sweaty work there was great good feeling in the harvest fields. It was bread, the very staff of life, that they were gathering in. The ring of the scythes in the morning was a merry sound. At evening tired laughter and song came from the homeward creaking wains. Peasant girls and boys sat in the straw, the dust tickling their naked arms and legs.

On such an evening, to escape the disruptions within Traventhal, Caroline and Struensee went out for a walk together. The reapers had cut their last row for the day. The horses, eager for home and fodder, were impatiently backing into place by the wagon tongues. Blue smoke from newly kindled fires floated straight up into the air, tinctured with the fragrance of frying bacon. The lovers climbed to the top of a hill where a single massive oak tree grew. From this elevation they had a splendid view of the whole countryside, out over endless wheat fields dotted with freshly cut stalks, over meadows where the kine were lowing to be milked.

Near the oak was a huge granite block, and here they sat down. The sun's warmth still lingered in the stone. They looked out beyond the Chateau Traventhal. Lights were just going on in the Chateau. They watched them twinkling through the heavy foliage surrounding the building. Far off, at the rim of a serene bowl of sky, stars were showing palely. The coming night rustled softly in the oak foliage. The wind was cool from its passage over the gray Baltic.

"Are you cold, Caroline?" Struensee asked the Queen.

"It's so strange, when the night is coming on," she whispered. "A little while ago everybody was so busy. The children and everyone were laughing and having a fine time. Now it's so quiet. There's nothing left but earth and sky."

He looked down at her, having caught a sad overtone in her words. He watched a look of mild suffering cloud her face. He kissed her and then for some while found nothing to say. At last, with some effort, she said to him: "I'm going to remind you of it again."

"What?" he said, alarmed. "Are you ill, Caroline?"

"I'm expecting a child," she said. "I thought I would have one, just as I told you in Rosenborg. Now I know I'm going to."

He understood slowly. "You're sure?" he said.

Her face was very pale and she began to cry. He kissed her and tasted the salt of her tears. "How long have you been sure about it?" he asked.

"Oh, long before Lueneburg," she told him, still weeping quietly. "My mother noticed it. I'm sure she did. Sometimes she'd look at me as if she expected me to say something. And I know she knows who the father is."

Struensee felt some extraordinary sensations. He shivered, he was growing larger and lighter, it seemed. "Take care of yourself from now on," he told her. "You've got to. Shall I give you my coat, Caroline? Let me put it over your shoulders."

"Never mind, it's such a warm night," she said. "You know, when the stars were coming out just now, I began to think how . . . well . . . how everything seems to happen to us. I was wondering just what will become of my child."

He put his arm more tightly about her and stroked her breasts and her cheeks.

"I'm glad," she said with decision. "Yes, I'm glad that we're going to have something that belongs to both of us."

★ *II* ★

*S*UDDENLY STRUENSEE EMERGED out into the open from behind the royal couple. Before his opponents could collect their wits he had dissolved the council of state. In place of it he organized a royal council, in which he took the leading role.

And Struensee soon found that in stormy times political power can be delegated, but not shared. Regarding himself as both captain and pilot, he could make use of hacks and creatures, but could draw no independent political personalities within his sphere. He became deaf to any proposal that might in the least modify his liberal program. He personally commanded. He watched every move with jealous eyes and ignored other intelligent liberals on whose support he might have counted. He filled all his posts with men chosen on the basis of personal loyalty. With the aid of this junta he proceeded to set in motion the plans worked out in Traventhal.

Since his ideas had been gestating for a long time, he spawned laws and edicts in astonishing numbers. Hardly had the Danish burghers recovered from their surprise at seeing court activities curtailed, activities from which many of them, of course, drew their livelihood, hardly had old army officers adjusted themselves to the shock of having their pensions cut, when along came more innovations. The silk mills were ordered closed, and in consequence the silk weavers were threatened with starvation. Then civil service examinations were announced.

A great number of Danish people considered themselves very badly dealt with in these reforms. Even the wiser minds, who saw the inherent desirability of Struensee's projects, were repelled by the author's haste and air of command. They also contained certain trivialities which provoked the ordinary Danish people far more than their broad intention. For example, Struensee had unearthed his old idea of legitimizing children born out of wedlock. He caused an orphanage to be founded, where unmarried mothers could leave their unwanted babes in a box provided for that purpose, after which they would be reared at the state's expense.

The clergy promptly interpreted this innovation as an official invitation to free love, and were confirmed in this horrid prospect when twenty children were collected the very first day. To a man the clergy said that henceforth Danish virgins would be as rare as hen's teeth. In fact, the majority of Danes, they predicted, in the future would be brought up in state orphanages. They damned Struensee's novelty, lock, stock and barrel. They implored their congregations to pray with them that God might enlighten the King. The immoral institutions must be destroyed at once.

A tremendous amount of gossip and rumor-mongering began to buzz in Copenhagen. Everyone whispered dire advices to everyone else. Sexual matters were within the scope of even the most stupid subjects. The majority might have no opinion worth the name so far as the larger features of reform were concerned, but in the issue of fornication and its by-products every man and woman qualified as expert. Honest fathers visualized their daughters living a life of sin and liking it. Why, the womenfolk thought, the girls will never get themselves married at this rate! Why, they argued, should men assume the burden of marriage and bringing up children when they can have all the fun they want for nothing. And with the sealed approval of King Christian to boot! Though of course it was really all that Dr. Struensee's doing.

It was the women, much more than the men, who raised a savage hue and cry. They thoroughly enjoyed the chance to feel virtuous and important at the same time. They vied with each other to see who could heap most invective on Struensee's state orphanage. Day and night they hissed female profundities into their husbands' ears. They believed, and would not be budged, that a girl who made a mistake richly deserved to be kicked around like an old stocking. They particularly disliked the discreet way the illegitimate children were spirited away under Struensee's system. If that went on, whom could they denounce? How would they know whether they were dealing with a virgin or a trull? What would it profit them hence-forth to toe the line? They might just as well take things easy. It was rank injustice, they declared, it cried to heaven for redress. Finally, wearied out, the menfolk admitted that the women were right. Any-thing to stop the whining and complaining and get to sleep. Repeti-tion won the day. Moreover, the women were not content merely to damn the deed. They analyzed the founder's motives. Why was this Struensee so concerned about the fate of illegitimate children? Speculation was colorful. The women's peculiar skill at spying and policing, their natural insight into vulgarities before which men would recoil, their inherent lack of generosity in moral issues, all led them to the conclusion that Struensee himself must be living with some woman out of wedlock. That was why he had such an interest in bastards. Busily they dug away at the egoistic roots of the situation, and found something that certainly seemed to square with fact. Actually, of course, Struensee's orphanage did not stem from any personal need, but from Rousseau, who incidentally had made ex-cellent use of similar institutions in housing his own unwanted children.

Well, the women argued, supposing the Doctor has a mistress, and there's no doubt he has, who is the woman? Most of Struensee's critics did not have even the remotest connection with the court. They all felt sure, however, that, unlike their own virtuous existence, court-life was a species of Gomorrah. And were not too far wrong. But who was the woman? Frau von Gaehler, Frau von Buelow, Frau von Holstein, Fraulein von Eyben? All were well-known beauties, all possible candidates.

Still, these possibilities were too easy, too obvious to satisfy the lady wiseacres of Copenhagen. Adulterous doings among the afore-named were too common, hardly worth a second thought. When Satan, the mighty one, set his mind on something, surely it must be something spectacular. And no liaison with anyone of the Copen-hagen demi-monde could ever be considered spectacular. Why, those Jezebels just could not keep their legs together, they said, and that was that.

Then light came to the inquisitors. The bread they were eating at the breakfast table stuck half way down their gullets. At first they hardly dared admit out loud what they were thinking. Even their dim brains saw the fateful possibilities of the situation. Should their tongues get out of hand they might be very unpleasantly implicated. They imagined themselves and their dear husbands being rounded up by the state police. So they kept mum for an interval, that is, more or less so, for it was too much to ask of human forbearance not to let slip tiny innuendoes, such as: "If you only knew!" or: "How I pity the King, poor little man!" The temptation for each to let her neighbor know that she, too, had guessed the worst proved too much for the good dames of Copenhagen.

What a joy it was, what a searching satisfaction, to be able to look down one's nose at somebody besides some poor servant girl trying to hide her bulge of sin beneath an apron. The Queen herself! One could ask no more. How delightful it was to realize in a great heart-swell that one was more virtuous than a queen, and so essentially superior to her. And think, how she lolled about in silks, with pearls at her throat and paint on her lips. Come to think of it, she did look like the daughters of Zion who angered the prophets. As for us, the critics thought magnificently, we wear linen and cotton, and though we may not look so hoity-toity from the outside, inside we are beautiful, which is more than she can say.

Unhappy Caroline, unhappy as any other woman whose reputation depends on the charity of her sisters. Besides being herself a supremely precious object of contumely, her lover was even more vulnerable than she, for he was a foreigner and an upstart. How dare he ride beside a queen of Denmark in Klampenborg, laughing and talking with her as big as billy-be-damned. Did he not air himself with her in the royal carriage, sitting next to her on the seat instead of taking his place up on the coachman's box where he rightly belonged? Yes, and they had walked alone together in the gardens of Rosenborg, pressed closer than two thieves. And was there not a story about the way she had danced with him at the fair dressed, if you please, as a peasant girl? This bit of public information, of course, derived from the servants Horn and Bruun. They liked to tell such tidbits as how, when Struensee was in the room, the Queen would send them off on useless missions. Yes, she would order them to find allegedly mislaid toilet articles. Later, you can be sure, they always turned up in the boudoir drawer where everyone knew they could have been found in the first place.

In all sorts of ways Struensee showed himself a genius in antagonizing the stubborn populace of Copenhagen. Hardly had the orphanage scandal died down than he gave out a new decree, this one designating the chapel of the Soellerod Hospital as a clinic for sexual diseases. That anyone should even dream of caring about such monsters as the venereally diseased was bad enough. Why should they not get what they deserved! But the virtuous were horrified to learn that the patients were to be named by name, publicly posted. Supposing that some worthy contracted the disease, by mistake, of course. Why, he would be marked for life!

In Copenhagen, as in any port city, venereal disease flourished. A little logic would have forced the conclusion that it was a good thing to isolate the sufferers and to help them to a cure by all means then available. Actually the only treatment was to apply quicksilver, which rapidly killed off the unfortunates if the disease did not. Among the medical profession there were intelligent men who recognized the soundness of Struensee's proposition. But even they wondered how anyone could be so unwise, in view of the denseness of the popular mind, as to pick out a hospital chapel for the experiment. It certainly suggested atheism, it was like a French joke.

Struensee himself remained blissfully ignorant of the furore. He had simply asked for a hospital site and a clerk had chanced to report that in the Soellerod infirmary there was an old, ramshackle section which for years had been used for the storage of potatoes. The difference between the venereally sick and neutral commodities like potatoes had never occurred to the clerk. The clergy, however, were far more sensitive to moral nuances. What is this Struensee going to do with the other churches in the city, they inquired indignantly? How many of them is he going to re-dedicate to the anti-Christ? They saw the Marble Church converted into an opera house, they saw St. Peter's serving as a public market. The Frelser Church, of course, would make a wonderfully spacious cat house for the better trade.

Now the clergy joined ranks with the womenfolk, their most willing followers in any case, and inveighed full blast against the new first minister of Denmark. They, too, invented a great many nasty innuendoes nicely studded with Biblical reference. The troubled faces of their female listeners, the head-noddings and head-shakings, were balm for the aroused guardians of Danish morality. An underground movement against Struensee, led by women and the clergy, spread like wildfire through Copenhagen.

From now on Struensee was condemned a priori. No matter what he tried to do, no matter if his proposals were well-intended, he was accused of chicane and inciting to moral turpitude under the pretense of public benefaction.

For example, Struensee was convinced that even poor people liked to enjoy the beauties of nature. There lay the broad, carefully tended gardens of Rosenborg Castle, right in the middle of the city, surrounded by a tall iron fence. Only on rare occasions did anyone ever use the park. Rosenborg Castle was old and damp, virtually unhabitable, in fact, and the King much preferred the gardens of Frederiksborg and Hoersholm. The upkeep of the older building was a senseless waste. And contiguous to Rosenborg lived the poor of the city, in crowded, lightless slums. Ragged slum children never saw flowers growing, never heard birdsong beyond sparrows' cheeping. It was these people, Struensee felt, who should use the park.

The gardens of Rosenborg were opened to the public. Sunday afternoon band concerts were arranged, and this, too, made the clerical elements mumble wrathfully. To them it appeared as if Struensee, by offering the indigent diversions, was secretly trying to make freethinkers and voluptuaries out of the mob. They were genuinely alarmed at the enthusiastic acceptance of Struensee's simple gifts.

Presently from all the pulpits of the town denunciations of lovers in the bushes began to thunder, of lovers squeezed close on darksome benches. Copenhagen was well on the road to hell, the pastors declared. Yes, the sacred institution of the family was rotten with decay. People began to hear rumors of certain evil characters, booksellers, writers and the like, who secretly met in the gardens secure from the eyes of the police to plot libertinage and discuss unholy subjects. It was said that a certain admirable married couple, strolling through the park, had overheard incredible blasphemies, namely, that Christ's resurrection was a myth. The apostles had just rigged up the story, the blasphemers had been heard to say, that they might save Christianity from bankruptcy. This project had proved successful, the heretics had said, only on account of the recalcitrance and stupidity of mankind.

The common people, who continued to frequent the gardens and enjoy the weekend concerts, oddly enough sided with the clergy. They were even glad that Struensee's wickedness had been exposed. Still, now they were safely posted on Denmark's first public enemy, there was no danger in going to Rosenborg and enjoying themselves. So argued the stockish louts of Copenhagen.

As with the gardens, so with all the other benefits which Struensee tried to give the people. The salt tax was suspended, and a substitute tax imposed on carriage and saddle horses. The common people owned no horses for luxury use. Regardless, in their confusion they considered the new tax unjust, a crime. They felt guilty and ill at ease without the salt tax. Had they not paid it since time immemorial? They missed it as they would have missed rain in April.

Then Struensee had many holidays done away with, holidays which had always been deemed a nuisance by merchants and manufacturers. Nevertheless the mercantile class now saw nothing but godlessness in the innovation, a crabbed scheme to deprive them of a few hours of well-earned leisure.

As the year wore on continued drought gave certain promise of a poor harvest. To prevent a rise in food prices and famine for the poor, Struensee bought up large quantities of wheat and rye at a fixed price, and rationed flour to the bakers, who could no longer pay for their staple on the open market. Although this transaction prevented a great deal of hunger and misery, the growers, the peasants who worked for the growers, the middlemen, the millers and the larger bakers all considered themselves done out of a nice bit of inflationary profit. And even the poor themselves, who gained everything and lost nothing by Struensee's intervention in the national economy, denounced the move. They said it was impious of him. If God wanted his children to starve in the year 1770, then they should have starved. It was not right to interfere with God's workings, they claimed.

In all these edicts, laws and directives at the very root it was not so much their actual content, or even their actual effect, that rubbed the Danish people the wrong way. Nor was it really what they conceived to be their immoral trend. At the bottom it was simply because the Danish people hated to wake up after slumbering for centuries in a comfortable stupor. Suddenly the people found themselves confronted with the loathsome necessity of thinking, of taking sides, of committing themselves to definite decisions. And of all things hateful, thinking was easily the most hateful of all. It was, plainly said, a scourge.

It was the most ineradicable and most nearly ubiquitous trait of humankind that Struensee had offended—mental laziness. Instead of gently rousing the Danes from their delicious torpors, he tore off the bedclothes and methodically poured jug after jug of icewater on their shrinking hides. And yet he could scarcely have acted other than precipitately. One decree evoked and conditioned the next in natural course. For what Struensee had in mind was not merely a series of reforms, but a total revolution, albeit a revolution minus bloodshed. It was his ultimate aim to transform an absolute into a liberal state, and this dynamic intent, once loosed, could not be stopped.

But was it possible to accomplish revolution by peaceful means, through decrees and new laws? It seemed not. The realignment of social forces in actual fact could not be accomplished without fanatic exploitation of human passions and deliberate use of criminal tactics. Was Denmark, in any case, ripe for change, mentally up to it? Were the serfs miserable enough to guarantee their support of a new regime? Had the Danish absolute monarchy adequately demonstrated its immanent shortcomings? None of these questions bothered Struensee.

One of his fatal weaknesses was his softheartedness. He was too easy with himself, too easy with others. Denmark might have followed him had he ruled the people with a heavy hand. If he had thrown some of his clerical detractors into the dungeons of Kronborg, and there allowed them to rot for a month or two with lice and rats for company, they might have learned to appreciate the difference between preaching and persecution. Similarly, had he arrested a few of his slanderers and had them publicly whipped in the Nytorv, the popular climate might have experienced a sea-change. Yet had he done these things, he would not have been Struensee, the idealist who believed that the idea, if it is manifestly good, cannot help but prevail. And his idea was good—the capacity of men for self-determination and a free life. At the same time he behaved contrary to his own idea of freedom. He forced reform dictatorially, he made full use of the absolute power of the monarchy.

This last paradox was evidence enough for the Danes that Struensee was a dishonest, wicked man. They made no allowance for the inevitable discrepancy between idea and reality. Then they disliked Struensee, in this same regard, as neither a native of Denmark nor member of an old family. A burgher from a foreign land—should they bow their necks to the likes of him!

★ III ★

LIVING AS HE was, strictly withdrawn from the currents of popular life within the King's castle, Struensee had no real notion of the trouble brewing in Copenhagen. He was also too busy and too happy with his plans, too pleased with his glimpses of the millennium to pay attention to whatever polite intimations reached his ears from his associates that all was not well. "To do right by everybody is quite impossible," was one of his favorite expressions. Criticisms he simply waved away.

With the fine autumn days the court was in Hoersholm. This castle, like Frederiksborg, was situated on a lake. Here the royal entourage ate in the Rose Room, so called because of its tapestries covered with blood-red roses. The situation in Hoersholm was not nearly so intimate as it had been at Traventhal. Ordinarily more than eighty guests sat down at the long table. The conversation was not altogether frivolous. Quite often, indeed, serious matters of state were discussed between courses. Rantzau and Brandt, men of influence in the new regime, behaved more circumspectly. Frau von Gaehler, whose husband had been made minister of war, ceased to flirt so conspicuously.

Among the newcomers to the royal board was a certain von Osten, a man with unusually bushy eyebrows, these originally red, but now dyed black. He was the new foreign secretary, having displaced Bernstorff. The initiated knew that at one time he had been the lover of Catherine of Russia, that is, when she was a slim young woman and not the gross, big-breasted hulk of the present epoch. Those in the know also said that Osten, after Tsar Peter's untimely death, had fallen out of the Tsarina's favor. Perhaps she had simply become fed up with his hairy presence, or there may have been other reasons. The Russian ambassador, Filosov, avoided his company, in fact, never appeared at the table when Osten was there. The fact that Annette von Gaehler had turned her attention to Osten, of course, accounted in part for the ambassador's coolness. Besides, he had no use for the liberal swing in Danish affairs. And in contrast to Bernstorff, now in eclipse, Osten and Rantzau, both of whom had had unpleasant reversals in Russia, were trying to improve relations with Sweden and France, and by so doing tip the balance of power against Moscow. Even in a liberal regime, it appeared, personal rancor and personal ambitions continued to have their usual jangling effect.

Since his political successes Struensee had put on weight. His features habitually wore a satisfied, rather benign expression. He kept his hair powdered, and instead of a physician's black coat, wore a red velvet one with facings in bright gold. Not only his appearance, but his nature had changed as well. He no longer bothered to listen attentively to others, he took it for granted that everyone should stop talking when he opened his mouth. It had become his officious practice to have dispatches and memos brought directly to the table as he ate. After scanning the paper he would give whispered directions to the secretary bent obsequiously over his shoulder. There were times when his thoughts drifted away so that he became lost in contemplation, in which event he would look up with a startled, annoyed expression if someone laughed, or if a servant pushed a new course in front of him.

In spite of his increasing girth, inwardly he was more restless than ever, and suffered from a chronic nervous tension that occasionally betrayed itself in a facial tic. The unending social obligations of his exalted position weighed heavily on him. Court life had become a wearisome routine. He constantly complained about sacrificing precious time on trivialities. He would have preferred to spend the whole day working with his secretary. The more he studied his grand project for Denmark, the more onerous and complicated it loomed. As time wore on he had no choice but to acquaint himself with the thorny particulars of legislation, public finance, commerce and the nation's social structure. Again and again he was embarrassed by his limited knowledge of facts. Often he longed for trained, responsible assistants to relieve him at least in part of his daily load of detail. In this connection he thought of his older brother, counsellor of justice in the service of Frederick the Great, and invited him to take charge of Danish public revenues and outlays.

It became his custom to appear very late at evening functions. Since Caroline Matilda never gave the sign to begin the festivities until he arrived on the scene, the whole company would often be forced to wait. Finally he convinced her that she must put a stop to so heedless a practice. Thereafter if he arrived late, Caroline would content herself with looking long and tenderly and reproachfully in his direction. Like so many women whose men are deeply interested in their work, she began to imagine a rival.

So meticulous was the Queen's jealousy that she did not even like Struensee to dance with the young women of the court. She ferreted out particulars of his once intimate relations with Frau von Gaehler and Fraulein von Eyben. Her love for Struensee kept her on the hop from morning till night. Evenings, when alone with her maidservants, she would inquire about their lovers in order to bring mention of her own into play.

"Love is all I live for," she once said recklessly to her maids. "If I had to, I'd follow my man to the gallows willingly, I'd stretch out with him on the wheel. Yes, I'd even go to hell with him, if I had to."

The maids were much interested in this admission. Cautiously they asked which man it was she was talking about. Caroline was already in bed, her nightcap on. Laughingly she squeezed her eyes together and boldly said: "Why, the King, who else!" Then as suddenly she became serious and added: "How lucky you girls are! How I envy you. You can pick out the one you want to love. That's wonderful."

Maidservant Bruun, who knew perfectly well that Struensee was the Queen's lover, said warningly: "But it's not good to gamble everything on one man, Madame, especially if you let him know he's got you. They're all fickle, the best of them. Sooner or later they change their minds and look around for someone else. They turn cold, all of them, if you just give them time."

This shot hit home far more than Bruun had expected. Caroline shivered, sat bolt upright in bed and cried out: "If the man I love were untrue to me, I'd go crazy. Yes, I would. I'd kill myself, that's what I'd do."

The maids were properly shocked by so much emotion in a queen. Having pulled together the bed hangings, they exchanged some knowing glances and felt very important. Sometimes the Queen's lover himself found her demands rather wearing, though by and large he was flattered and warmly reciprocated her display of affection. Still, her constant need of his presence and caresses irritated him. Struensee's feeling for Caroline had never been so pure and natural as hers for him, and could not be, considering the difference in age and experience. Now that she was bearing his child, his inclination was to behave towards her like any honorable married burgher after the heat of the honeymoon had slackened. He now much preferred amity and understanding to incessant ardors. Love, whatever else, was hard work.

In sum, the Philistine came out in Struensee. His worldly affairs were more important to him by far than his love. He did not fully see how much Caroline needed excitement in order to blunt the pangs of conscience. She was much more morally sensitive than he. She lived constantly under a cloud of guilt. The exact nature of her guilt was not really clear to her. She had never thought it through.

But she knew she was a serious transgressor, and knew it particularly when she woke up with a start, her hands folded across the little hill of her belly to stare blankly into the early morning grayness seeping into her room. At such times, bedevilled as she was by fear, she wished passionately for a return to sobriety and humdrum virtue. In the depressed moments even her great love seemed empty and futile, and her whole life a puppet show. Even Struensee seemed like a little marionette jiggling about among the miniature stage props. Thinking these desolate thoughts she would pray that God might fill her life with true meaning, tranquillity and happiness. Her orisons, however, fell flat. God remained mute as an idol of stone and she stewed away in her disgrace. Frustration becoming unbearable, she would jump out of bed, tear back the bed hangings, wrap her dressing gown about her and run down the corridor to her lover's chamber.

The fury of her kisses, the groans of her surrendering disturbed Struensee. He would stroke her bright hair where it had fallen in waves over her cheeks. In the end she would fall asleep with her head cushioned on his shoulder. That was her only way out.

Struensee would examine the lovely spent face. Close by it had a marble quality, a Medusa look. There was a bluish sheen beneath the surface of the flesh, the sheen peculiar to pregnant women. The lashes were long and light, the forehead doubly pensive in repose, the mouth marred sweetly by a quirk of sadness. At such moments love would overpower Struensee. He would experience the ancient masculine wonder at the opposite sex, a quite unerotic thing, such as Adam might have felt when he first looked down on his beloved, the reputed mother of mankind.

Yet Struensee saw only the physical poignancy of his little silver plaything. He failed quite to see her spiritual qualities. He was blind to the fact that her sensual extravagance was only an unconscious means of flight, a barrier raised against misgiving which flourished within her deeper self like weeds.

The Queen herself had no inkling of what was going on inside her. In her ignorance she fought despairingly against despair, against her feeling of crushing guilt, not knowing that at these very moments when most bereft the God on whom she was calling for help was near her. And yet she was much farther along the road to revelation than her lover. Her being with child might have been the source of her intuitive advantage over Struensee. Her excellent body was already tightening like a ripening fruit. The body's dark concern for the infant bedded in the womb sharpened the upper consciousness, gave the eyes a deeper look. This grave look, a mysterious contemplation of the self, was particularly marked in Caroline. It seemed as if she were watching her body slowly reproduce. Her intense interest in the physical change occurring inside her body led her to the very threshold of an actual change in her personality, and so in the general direction, at least, of a more mature reaction to moral and spiritual problems.

Struensee lived far removed from these sentimental phenomena. A certain coarseness in his nature, which expressed itself originally as complacency, hindered any progress he might otherwise have made towards moral understanding. His power-seeking also blunted his sensibilities. Preoccupation with great affairs, indeed, is an excellent device for escaping the essentials of life. Struensee had no idea at that time that his planning itself might be a flight from reality. Yet sometimes he did dimly realize that his mistress, though she was fifteen years his junior, had about her a sheen of spirituality that he lacked. He argued against this feeling and he would not admit its validity. He even became jealous of it. Should the Queen, so obviously his social superior, also become his superior as a person? There were times when he revenged himself on her for his feeling of inferiority.

One evening by mere chance he went up to the card table where Caroline was sitting. Feeling him behind her chair, automatically she reached back and put her hand over his. A sweet emotion held her suspended, her one hand pressed over his, the other idly held her fan of cards. Here Struensee wrenched his hand roughly from under hers. "Madame, are you not playing cards?" he said acidly. "They are all waiting on you." Caroline flushed and did as she was told. The others lowered their eyes. Struensee watched the red creep up the back of Caroline's neck and bit his lips in mortification. It was a painful gaffe. He looked across the table at Count Rantzau, who returned his glance coldly and ironically, sitting perfectly still, unmoved, haggard, perfectly tailored and perfectly contemptuous. "Please excuse me, Madame," he said at last. "I must go. The King is waiting for me." He turned on his heel and went away in a deadly silence.

Incidents like this multiplied. On another occasion he caught himself mocking Caroline because she did not know the name of a flower someone had offered her. At badminton he complained about her awkwardness. When she put a string of small pearls about her coiffure, he criticized her for being so showy, and made a point of not talking to her the rest of the evening, instead flirting with Frau von Gaehler. Presently he noticed her reproachful look, a look verging on despair. This gave him morbid satisfaction. When they were alone again he kneeled down, kissed her bare kneecaps and asked for forgiveness, which she readily granted. She drew his head into her lap and whispered: "It was nothing, nothing at all, my love."

All men have a little of the Marquis de Sade in their makeup, and are virtually compelled to take some sort of revenge on the woman who binds them down with love. Jealous imaginings, mostly deliberately invented, pretended indifference, sulky silences, unjustified rebukes, hints of love for someone else evolve as a natural consequence of this condition. Their ulterior purpose is to exacerbate the pain and passion of the loved one, the better to feel power over him or her, to enjoy the beloved's helpless dependence on the lover's mood. Struensee's experimentation with this seedy side of love was contemptible in direct proportion to Caroline's marvellous innocence and vulnerability. He could not stop himself from trying his hand again and again, though oftentimes he felt later like sinking into the ground, so strong was his shame. He knew perfectly well the reason for his theatrical whimsies.

Actually, of course, Struensee's greatest distraction had nothing to do with his love affair. It was his friends, Rantzau and Brandt, who bothered him most. They had expected great things of the new government. Both considered the government to be a source of booty. Offices and revenues, as they understood it, belonged by natural right to those wielding political power. They realized, moreover, that anything to be had must be grabbed while the grabbing was good.

Among many other items, Count Rantzau had expected that his debts would be paid. He was rudely disappointed. He drew a good salary, of course, but that did him little good. As a matter of fact it barely sufficed to pay the interest on his debts, let alone diminish the principal. He had to mortgage his lands a second time to placate his more unreasonable creditors, those who refused to take interest alone. Why Struensee, the *arriviste,* did not simply advance him a flat hundred thousand thalers in gold and let him again feel solid ground under his feet Rantzau could not for the life of him understand.

Rantzau hinted, argued and petitioned in vain. Struensee put him off with sermons on the public debt. Economy was meaningless to a man of Rantzau's wastrel kidney. So searching was his disappointment that his aristocratic features became longer than ever and, if possible, gloomier. He began to believe that Struensee's explanations were nothing but lies. He considered himself betrayed, he, the willing friend. He imagined that Struensee was keeping all the bribes and all he milked from legitimate sources for himself. It was shameful that he, Rantzau the noble, scion of an ancient family, should take the skimmed milk, whereas his erstwhile protégé, an upstart, a mere pill-roller, mind you, lapped up the cream.

Even more bitter than his disappointment at not enriching himself through Struensee was his chagrin at finding himself subordinate in prestige. All along he had thought that a Struensee ministry would really be a Rantzau affair. Now he was faced by the harsh fact that the Doctor acted and thought exactly the opposite from sensible expectation. Struensee was the first name in Denmark, not Rantzau. The way Struensee cavalierly passed out decrees without even asking

Rantzau's opinion made the Count fume with rage. Not that he was interested in the content of the decrees. It was his vanity that suffered torments.

Rantzau finally realized that Struensee had no intention of relinquishing power, nor yet of sharing it. He could not even expect the post of minister of war, from which position he could have launched any of several plans of aggrandizement. General von Gaehler, husband of the dark-eyed Annette, had fallen into this important and lucrative post. Rantzau was appointed viceroy to Norway, which took him far from the court and the center of graft. It was a position without influence, hardly better than his previous one as commander of the Glueckstadt garrison. So far as Rantzau went, the whole reformist scheme was barren of tangible results. Smarting under neglect, harassed by his creditors, Rantzau began to look around for new connections through which he might recoup his fortunes. Personal loyalty was as foreign to his nature as concern for the welfare of the state. An egotist to the core, a sneaky fellow without conscience, seething with resentment, he was primed to undertake absolutely anything that might yield him the opportunity to shine and slake his appetites.

At the same time Struensee underestimated the Count's strength and potential menace. He saw him as a rather comic figure, with his silly debts, his nervousness forever prompting him to tell shady stories that shocked the ladies. What he failed to see was that the Count's buffoonery was a false front hiding considerable energy and determination to have power at any cost short of personal suffering.

However, Struensee did concern himself about Brandt, who was essentially so much more important to his cause than Rantzau. He handled Brandt much as he might have handled a woman whose weaknesses are well known and indulgently forgiven. There was indeed much to like about Brandt—his ugly-pretty looks, his astounding helplessness, his tomfoolery. Unlike Rantzau, no matter how much he acted, his acting never degenerated into mockery.

Yet it was more than Brandt's amiable personality that moved Struensee to lend him an ear where he was deaf to Rantzau. For one thing he was always around, always under foot, and simply could not be ignored. Beyond propinquity, he also had a key place in Struensee's overall strategy, for it was his task to keep the King happy. As always, this was a ticklish, thankless affair. Though by no means overburdened with brains, Brandt was not stupid. He knew very well how valuable he was to Struensee. The King, in fact, never let him forget that. As Christian's illness worsened, his conversation was rapidly becoming a gibberish of stereotyped phrases, these regularly interrupted by senseless outbursts of laughter or of rage. The King's company would have been a miserable burden even for a thick-skinned man, which Brandt was not. Nevertheless, he stuck it out, and Struensee was perforce grateful to him.

Exactly like a spoiled child, Christian wanted to be amused every single minute of the day. The only kind of entertainment that he liked involved a display of malice. He liked to play at anything sure to cause pain to his playmates, whether Brandt or the Negro slaves. He liked to commit small vandalisms in the palaces, to tear down expensive tapestries, cut chunks of upholstery from the furniture, smash mirrors, knock the heads off sandstone statues in the gardens of Hoersholm.

Senseless chattering and seizures alternated with periods when he sat for whole days on end, not moving a muscle, staring into space like a sick animal. There were other times, though these came more and more infrequently, when he at least foggily realized his own parlous condition. At such times he would weep for hours, his head down on his arms. Occasionally he would suddenly come to himself and in amazingly acute dialectic argue the pros and cons of suicide.

The vagaries of Christian's ailment exhausted poor Brandt. He had more than his fill of the senseless vacillations of the manic type, the nasty tricks, the wild rages, the idiocies succeeded by too elaborate arguments. It was all he could do to face the mind's underworld day after day. Yet Brandt did his duty, which was to hold the sick man in check. Sometimes he was so tired when night came that he slept on the bed without removing his clothes.

Aside from the rigors of his stewardship, Brandt feared that the King's malady was catching. He might lose his reason, too, he sometimes felt. More than once he caught himself uttering the same inanities as Christian, making the same apish grimaces, giving way to similarly engulfing bouts of melancholy. Once, after an especially bad day, he actually picked up a vase and threw it against the wall, as the King had done so many times. Immediately he ran to Struensee and begged to be relieved. But Struensee reasoned with him, showed him how everything depended on the King's being kept quiet. At the moment it was too early, but shortly he would see that Caroline Matilda would take over as regent, whereupon Brandt would be relieved from his horrid keeper's occupation.

Brandt would get away when he could and sit by the window, playing his flute. He longed desperately to be back in Holstein, back in his empty, ragged home. Pathos nearly overwhelmed him when he thought about his weedy garden where the nightingales sang. He could see his reedy pond dreaming in the moonlight. He was very often tempted to bolt and the devil with Struensee. What really held him as much as anything was his love affair with the blonde Frau von Holstein. At night he was often seen sneaking off to her apartment, a romantic white cloak over his back.

Frau von Holstein, at least, listened to Brandt's woes with deep sympathy. She was one of those women who are maternal with their lovers. Cozily snuggled on Frau von Holstein's large bosom, Brandt could relax and breathe a nice deep breath. Though she was kind to a fault, Frau von Holstein was not very bright. She had great trouble understanding exactly what it was Brandt was up to. She tended to be righteously indignant about Struensee, whom she condemned as the cause of her beloved's suffering and humiliation.

There were other matters, too, that cooled Brandt's affections for Struensee. He had thought of making a great thing out of his post as court *maitre de plaisir*. He had visions of the arts rising to new heights under his aegis, becoming the best in all Europe. But what had happened? Struensee would not even let him hire a couple of Italian singers, even though all they asked was thirty thousand thalers for the engagement. How miserly this Struensee! A penny-pincher. Did he know nothing of *panem et circenses?* How was he going to keep the people satisfied, Brandt wanted to know. If you make so much fuss about bread and herring, he told Struensee, why not a little fuss about the theater?

Thanks to Struensee Brandt's stage sets were shabby, his ballet girls crones, his music second class, hardly better than the sort of stuff squeaked out at the court of some miserable German princelet. Old Sarti, the conductor, stuck mulishly to his own ideas. He was a good enough musician, so far as he went, but he did not go far enough. He played Italian music exclusively; he had never heard of Haydn, Gluck or Mozart. And the audiences were getting thoroughly sick of watching the silly antics of Maestro Brambilla, who combined the arts of singing, sword-swallowing, tightrope-dancing and pantomime without being master of any one. When the audience was bored, Brandt explained to Struensee, it was not the performers they blamed, but the *maitre de plaisir*. Already, so Brandt had heard, people were calling him "the other Morari" and "Christian's white nigger."

Brandt got so down in the mouth that he stopped speaking to his friend Struensee. Instead he sent him letters packed with complaints and long descriptions of his grievances. He also inserted melancholy intimations about the future of Denmark. Struensee did not like these précis. Injured, yet commiserative, he wrote Brandt long letters in return, explaining everything reasonably, pointing out what was plain as the nose on Brandt's face. He begged Brandt to be patient, he reminded him how faithfully he had stood by him in the old days. Finally, against his better judgment, he had the King make Brandt a present of six thousand thalers.

Having got his six thousand thalers, Brandt was convinced that Struensee had felt himself in the wrong right along. It was just as

Frau von Holstein said. Struensee was trying to gag him with a miserable tip. Brandt was more self-righteous than ever. When at last Struensee lost patience and curtly accused him of ingratitude and disloyalty, Brandt was outraged. Thereafter he complained in the salons of the Bredegade about the "tyrant" and "the traitor to friendship" who lorded it about Christiansborg.

The unbelievable happened. Egged on by Frau von Holstein, Brandt actually plotted Struensee's downfall. Among his mistress' friends he hatched the idea that Struensee should be deported over the Oeresund by fishing boat. It was a weak, simple-minded plan. Tyrants, even idealistic ones, are not so easily dislodged. Testimony of Brandt's fundamental kindness and liking for Struensee, however, was his stipulation that the exile should be given fifty thousand thalers to live on.

Meanwhile in Norway Count Rantzau brooded like a thunder cloud. He had much more resourceful schemes for deposing tyrants in the back of his head. Until the time was ripe, nonetheless, Rantzau chose to bide his chance in grim silence.

Finally, there was Struensee, third member of the ill-assorted trio. He mulled over perfection, he looked far over and beyond the troubled mass of the Danish people. His friends had forsaken him one by one. For props he had only a mad king and a young mistress, she as doctrinaire in love as he in politics, and as blind to the impending flood.

★ *IV* ★

*D*URING COUNT HOLCK'S epoch it had been the King's insane practice to challenge his huge favorite to bouts of fisticuffs. Prior to Holck's arrival, he had done the same to Sperling. Both had readily fallen in with his humor, and had always been wise enough to let Christian have the best of it.

It had become a sign of favor in Danish court circles to have Christian do battle. His opponents took care to praise his skill, to make sure that he got in some solid blows. This was true of General von Gaehler, Lieutenant von Eyben, Hjorth, the running footman, the Negro slave, Morari, and many others. Christian, as a matter of fact, was not choosy about whom he fought. If he were out for a walk in the vicinity of Frederiksborg and came on a well-built peasant youth, or if he happened to see some solid burgher boy in the streets of Copenhagen, his fists itched to let fly. Coachmen and lackeys assigned to tend him had all they could do to keep him from random swipes at his subjects whenever the spirit moved. It was not out of consideration for the proprieties that they restrained him. They were afraid that eventually some hot-tempered young buck would turn on Christian and thrash him to a pulp, perhaps even kill him.

Gradually the eccentricity developed to a point where Christian simply could not get along without his boxing triumphs. They made him feel like a man, a conqueror. They brought him back temporarily into reality. As for the losers, they had no need to grumble about a black eye or a lump on the chin. Afterwards Christian was always more than solicitous. He poured out his royal magnanimity on the conquered, he did everything imaginable for them. When the victim had been properly beaten Christian regarded him as an unimpeachably loyal and deserving subject. Many a village bailiff, many a royal forester had his tact in enduring the kingly assault to thank for a comfortable, lifetime sinecure.

Ever since the summer at Traventhal Christian had had his pugilistic eye on Brandt. Repeatedly he challenged him to fight. Brandt, the *maitre de plaisir,* considered fist-fighting the lowest form of boorishness, quite out of the question for a man of good breeding reared in the French spirit. Consistently, emphatically, he declined invitations to do battle.

This hurt the King's feelings. He lost no opportunity to use his rank in baiting the unhappy Brandt about his squeamishness. Across the table he would say loudly: "Just take a look at him, the coward Brandt, the biggest sissy in all Europe!" Or when there were many ladies present he would punch Brandt unawares in the middle of the back, so hard that it would make him pitch forward ignominiously. Then the King would say, laughing like a hyena: "That's how a Danish king handles milksops and fairies!" Once, during a musicale on which Brandt had expended tremendous effort, one of the King's white poodles came running into the room and disrupted the music with his yelping. Christian shooed him away with his stick and said: "Why, I ought to make that little fellow my *maitre de plaisir.* He runs with his tail between his legs just like our friend Brandt!"

Not unnaturally these continuous humiliations annoyed Brandt, indeed, obsessed him with ideas of revenge. It nearly choked him to be humbled right in front of Frau von Holstein. He went with tears of rage in his eyes to complain to Struensee, who at the moment was drinking coffee with the Queen before an open fire. Struensee listened to him patiently. "Why not let him have his way, Brandt?" he suggested. "Why not fight him if he challenges you again?"

"I cannot fight," Brandt objected. "A gentleman does not fight with his fists, he fights with a sword."

"Yes," said Struensee. "but you know as well as I do it's only part of his sickness. Am I not right, Madame? Should he not give him what he wants?"

"Certainly," the Queen agreed, laying down her cup and smiling a soothing smile at the *maitre de plaisir.* "Do as he wants. He'll be all right when he's satisfied."

Brandt looked uncertainly, first at Struensee, then at the Queen. "I'll follow your advice, Madame," he said evenly, "though every bone in me argues against it. *Mon dieu,* what would my dead mother say if she saw me brawling with my fists like a drunken carter!"

At once Brandt presented himself at the King's apartment. "I'm quite ready, Sire," he said coolly, "I should be delighted to have a boxing match with you."

"You!" said Christian suspiciously. "Well, I knew you'd come around to it. I'm not really in the mood, but anyway, take my coat and hang it over the back of that chair." Brandt did this and then went to the door and locked it.

"What's the idea of that?" the King asked nervously. "Why are you locking the door?"

"So no one will disturb us," said Brandt. "This may take some time, Sire."

They squared off and danced about. It was a ludicrous affair. Christian saw an opening and slugged Brandt with a right on the ear. Brandt shook his head in a daze. The force of the blow had nearly finished him. Christian let him have a left under the chin for good luck, causing Brandt to bite through his tongue. The blood ran. Brandt's mouth was flooded with salty blood.

This was the point where Brandt should have confessed himself beaten. Christian expected it. Indeed, he let his hands fall to his sides and was smiling at his adversary with confident derision. But hot pain and the taste of blood released Brandt's anger. He was overcome by a consuming hatred for this useless, idiotic man who had pestered and nagged him for months, who had forced him into a disgraceful scene utterly against his normal inclination. His very conscience, his deepest intuition had warned him not to lower himself. Now rage was in him, not only the kind of anger evoked by pain, but anger at being compelled to flout his conscience and his code. No longer was the affair a joke, a trifle that a Holck would have shrugged off with a sneer.

Brandt's eyes widened, his teeth bared, his body shook with passion. He lunged at Christian and caught him flush on the eye before he could get up his hands. The blow knocked the King back and at once Brandt followed up with a solid punch on the chest. This tumbled the King over a stool and he struck his head on the floor with a solid thud. At once he got to his feet and shrieked: "Hey, you're trying to kill me."

"Put up your hands then, you silly bastard," Brandt shrieked back at him and gave him two more heavy whacks on the face. Then he took the King by the collar and ripped him this way and that so that his head rocked like a cabbage on his skinny neck stalk. Again Brandt manhandled him, raining blows on his face and soft middle, cuffing him about mercilessly. The King's shirt was nearly torn from his back, his right cheek was laid open. He put bloody hands up to his face and wept defenselessly as the fists drummed on his head. Finally Brandt stood away, breathing like a winded horse. "You've had your fight, Sire," he said in thick gulps. "I hope you liked it. Did you? Or do you want some more?"

"Don't hit me," sobbed the King. "Open the door. Go away."

Brandt slipped back the bolt. On the way out—his knees were now quivering—he looked back at Christian. He was terrified to see what extensive damage he had wrought on the royal countenance. The bird-like qualities of Christian's face were startling. The long nose, the chinlessness, the glassy eyes—all were horrible, horrible. Suddenly Brandt was ashamed, and afraid. With a strange little bow he slunk away.

Below in the card room a party was in progress. The guests sat about little card tables, engrossed in play. Bystanders carried on a conversation in polite whispers. Servants moved back and forth on tiptoe, bringing ices, wafers and sweet Spanish wines in decorative goblets.

Without warning someone was fumbling wildly at the large folding door and the Negro, Morari, hastened to assist. The candles shivered in the rush of the draught, and Christian stood framed in the doorway. He had no coat on, his blond hair hung in strings about his shoulders, his right eye was a big purple patch and on his cheek was a deep weal. His shirt hung off his shoulders, exposing his skinny chest. In one hand he dangled a book. The guests stared at him unbelieving. At first, so dumbfounding was the apparition, that no one rightly recognized who it was. Servants with their trays came to a dead stop. Struensee jumped to his feet and stared with the rest at the King. At her table Caroline Matilda remained perfectly still, her face chalky.

The King tottered into the room, raised his left hand and commanded silence. "Silence, silence!" he said very clearly. Not a word was uttered by the company. Everybody was frozen in attitudes of amazement. It was like a curse in a fairy-tale. Some of the guests looked drawn with fear. Something strange and terrible had come into the room, something utterly out of tune with the powder and perfume and all the effete creatures trapped there unawares.

"Mesdames, messieurs," the King began ceremoniously, "you all know that sometimes I'm not quite right in the head. But just the same I'm not always crazy, not at all. I've just come through a terrible

experience. Awful. A murderer came after me and almost got me."
A deep murmur of amazement pulsed through the room at this
announcement.

"Silence, silence, I say," the King said. "I would like you all to
know that I didn't like it at all, having someone come at me like that.
I thought about my dead father, who was such a friend of peace. I
dug into the library, as a matter of fact, and found that poem the
poet wrote for him. I thought it might give me some consolation.
For I'm a pathetic dog, if you come right down to it, and I need all
the consolation I can get. I haven't any honor, any respect and no
brains. Anyway, messieurs et mesdames, here's the book with the
poem. Look at it, I have it right here. Even though I despise the
whole lot of you, there may be one or two who will understand. So
here it is. Listen to this:

"Never does he weep before the conqueror's image,
Wishing to emulate. Hardly had his tender heart
Begun to feel, when a rude martial stride
He found too taxing for its gentle beat.

But to weep for a fame that's nobler still,
And needs no courtiers; to shed tears for the love
Given freely by a happy people; this often waked
The noble youth at the midnight hour.

Long he pondered the subtle thought
That God's true way is to bring peace and joy
To many thousands. At one leap thus he reached
The heights, and framed himself in God's great image."

This peculiar declamation ended, Christian paused dramatically.
The guests held their breath in a veritable panic of embarrassment.
Then he took up his theme again, allowing them no chance to
interrupt.

"There you have it, mesdames et messieurs," he said. "There you
see what the poet expected of my father. To be like God, no less!
But the task was too great. My poor papa didn't feel in the least like
God, poor man. In fact, he gave up and died when I was still a boy.
And I? Yes, there have been times when I've played with the idea of
being like God and having the clouds rain blessings on Denmark.
But it didn't take me long to discover that I couldn't play God any
better than my father. I'd rather have some fun with my black people,
if you want to know the truth. I'd rather knock the heads off stone
statues. For a while I used to be terribly discouraged. With myself,
I mean. Yet is it really my fault if I'm afraid to stick my nose in
where I know it doesn't belong? Besides, a man arrived who was

ready to take over the job of being God in Denmark. Very well. As the serpent says, he knows both good and evil. Just the right sort for the job. I took the opportunity, mesdames et messieurs, to retire with good grace. Why, even more than that! I modeled myself on Amphitryon when Zeus popped on the scene. Remember? But it's all too personal to go into right now. As a matter of fact, the only ones concerned are Zeus, Alcmene and Amphitryon. I don't really know what else I ought to tell you, mesdames et messieurs. My head's going round. It's going to split, the way it feels. If he really knows evil, he ought to take the evil out of me. I'm his friend, I wish him well. Among all the maggots that burrow into him, I'm the only maggot with a heart. And yet he lets me suffer, suffer."

Saying this, Christian groaned aloud, let the book slide to the floor and brought his hands up to hide his bruised face. Everyone stared at him, mesmerized with horror. But here and there an officer, a courtier summoned the nerve to look significantly at his neighbor. Fraulein von Eyben, glancing swiftly at the Queen, found the courage to whisper to a certain Colonel von Koeller. "So that's how bad it is with the King," she said. "So that's how it is!"

The Colonel shrugged his shoulders. "It looks as if it's time, all right, to start doing something about it," he rumbled.

"What do you mean?" she whispered eagerly, throwing back her mop of auburn hair. And when he only shrugged his shoulders again and stared at her questioningly, she moved closer and said: "Speak with Guldberg, if you're interested. Tell him I sent you. He'll take you to Queen Juliana."

"I'll do that," he said, and folded his big hands carefully behind his back, a rock of a man.

Caroline Matilda had risen hesitantly. Encouraged by a glance from Struensee she went up to Christian, took his hands from his face and chafed them gently. "My friend, my poor friend," she said. "You're tired. Let me take you to your room."

He looked at her empty-faced, his eyes bulging with self-pity. "What's wrong?" he asked. "Have I done something? I wanted to read you something out of a book, my dear. No importance, of course, no importance."

"What happened to you, Sire?" Caroline asked. "Did you fall?"

"Happened?" Christian explored the cut on his cheek. "Nothing much. I just thrashed that Brandt fellow, that's all. But the coward hit me when I had my hands down."

Caroline put her arm through the King's. "The King does not feel well," she announced, flushing darkly. "I am sure that tomorrow will find him well again and in good spirits." She left with Christian in tow. Struensee watched them disappear through the wide folding door. He drummed nervously on the chair-back.

"That snake," said Fraulein von Eyben, meaning the Queen. "I wouldn't trust her with a butcher-boy."

"She's six months along," observed Colonel von Koeller. "At least that and maybe more."

"Yes, she's big as a pumpkin," said Fraulein von Eyben. "The question is, whose child is she making?"

The Colonel, who had recently arrived at the court from Jutland, looked at her open-mouthed.

The next day all Copenhagen had heard about Christian's débâcle. The burghers were quite grim about it, the serving girls whispered behind their hands at the hearth and were thrilled. In the Fishmarket a thick, fishy lady, with one fine slash, severed the head of a haddock, and declared: "That's the way to get rid of a king, folks!" Her audience laughed with her mirthlessly.

★ *V* ★

*C*AROLINE MATILDA BORE a daughter in the late spring of the year. Frau von Mathiessen bathed the child. It had blue eyes and light brown hair and squealed happily in the tub. Antje Maria was assisting Mathiessen. She was delighted with her duties. She had to stand by and hand the Queen's lady-in-waiting powder and oil and diapers as required.

"Poor, dear little worm," said Frau von Mathiessen when she had bedded the infant in its cradle. She stroked the hair away from its heated face. "You deserve a better fate," she said. "You certainly do."

"Why, what more could anyone ask than be a princess!" said Antje Maria.

The lady-in-waiting pressed her lips together and looked hard at Antje Maria. "There are some things you'll understand a great deal better," she said drily, "when you're properly grown up and have some sense."

In the afternoon Christian came to pay his respects. He kissed his wife on the forehead and examined the baby in the cradle. He twiggled its nose with the tip of his forefinger. "There, there, my little lady," he said. The child yelled and Christian was amused. "It seems to be a lively child, Madame," he said. "I've always wanted to have a pleasing little daughter." He took the small bundle out of the cradle, kissed the infant and then handed it over to Frau von Mathiessen, who was hovering anxiously by, watching the King's every move. "She'll be christened Luisa Augusta," he said. Then he looked around vaguely at Caroline Matilda lying inert in bed. "I wish you speedy recovery, Madame," he told her. "Now I have to go fishing with Morari." The Queen sighed, and her sigh was deeply echoed by Mathiessen.

Struensee arrived somewhat later. He, too, looked the child over. It was fast asleep. Meanwhile Antje Maria brought chocolate for the Queen, and pulled up a taboret to the bedside. Then the lady-in-waiting, the Queen having signaled with her eyes, left the room, taking Antje Maria with her.

"My dear, my dear," said Caroline, and reached out her arms for Struensee. "We're alone at last, aren't we."

Hesitantly he kissed her, but she drew him down roughly and hugged him. Her eyes burned with fever, her mouth shook. "Now we have a child," she sobbed. "I'm so glad, so glad."

"You mustn't get upset," he warned. "Now is the time for you to be very, very careful."

"I'm not really upset," she said, wiping away her tears and smiling. "Actually I'm happy. But sometimes, I'll admit, I'm afraid about the future. When I was really unhappy . . . before, I mean . . . I never worried at all that way. If our happiness should ever come to an end, I'd . . ."

"What sort of thoughts are you thinking!" he said firmly. "And just when we have so much to thank God for."

"I have tried to thank God," she said. "He simply wasn't there to hear me. It didn't work, somehow."

"So?"

"I'll tell you how I feel," she said nervously. "I feel as if you and I are standing on the top of a mountain. I can see how we climbed to the top, every detail of the way, mind you. But when I look in a forward direction I see nothing but cliffs and terrible chasms. I'm so terribly afraid of falling and breaking my neck."

"You're just weak," he said, though he could not hide his essential concern. "It's just a fit of melancholy. Women often have this sort of thing just after the delivery. You'll simply have to live it through. It will be done, of course."

"Give me my mirror, please," the Queen said and worked herself erect in bed. The mirror had a silver frame decorated with fruit, roses and cherubs at play. She looked at the image in the glass, very close to, then farther away. The face within the frame looked different to her; more serious, more important, so she fancied. She saw her own small ears, tempting, almost bold as they peeped out from the blonde hair. "Do you know how I look just now?" she said. "I look just like a picture in Carlton House at home. It's a Mary Magdalen. She has red hair and is kneeling down before a skull. The picture isn't very much, but I remember how I was always afraid of it when I was a little girl. I didn't understand it then."

He poured more chocolate into her cup and sat down rather

primly on the rim of the bed. The sun shone through the tulle curtains, the jagged, greenly tinted shadows of chestnut leaves played over the coverlet. The room smelled strong of chocolate and powder.

"If she is only as pretty as you!" Struensee said impulsively. "Do you think she'll take after you?"

"Oh, she'll be prettier, much, much prettier," said Caroline, brightening at once as Struensee brightened. "And wiser, much wiser than I am. She'll really be a great princess, I'm sure of it."

"I want only one thing," he told her.

"Tell me."

"I hope she'll be genuinely happy, truly happy."

He got the child from the cradle and laid it down at the Queen's side. Then he sat down again on the bed. Smiling, he said: "Now, there I have both my girls, and I love both of them dearly."

The servant Bruun came into the room without knocking. She saw Struensee sitting on the edge of the Queen's bed, her hand in his. Murmuring confused excuses, she tiptoed away.

Many visitors came to Hoersholm for the little princess' baptism. The Danish Queen-Dowager, Juliana, arrived from Fredensborg Palace. She walked supported by a cane, for during the past winter she had suffered bad attacks of gout. But she was otherwise just as energetic as ever, her glance just as keen, her eyebrows as black and bold as ever under the powdered, stylishly swept-up hair. Her son, a pleasant, rather innocuous young fellow, was constantly at her side.

Juliana was also frequently seen with a middle-aged man of forty or thereabouts, a plain, bourgeois sort of man. His brown frock-coat, buckled shoes and white woolen hose were very much out of place amid pretentious society. This newcomer was called Guldberg. He was Juliana's secretary and her son's tutor. He was a short, stocky man with broad shoulders. His head, big as a melon and virtually cubic in shape, provided the finishing touch in a caricature of peasant durability. However, on more thorough inspection, the slits of light-blue eyes set extraordinarily far apart, with innumerable tiny folds at the corners, revealed that Owe Guldberg, though a peasant and a bumpkin, was anything but a fool.

The Queen-Dowager's servant and confidant was fully as much of a driving force as Struensee himself. His strength was of a different category, the harsh strength of the cavalry sword. He paid no attention to large ideas, indeed, he had none. He might have been called an arch-conservative, devoted to the principle of serfdom and rule by the landed gentry. But if he held any convictions along these lines it was only because the petty nobles happened currently to be his masters, and there was no choice but for him to use them as a pry in furthering his privy cause. A Dane to the core, he understood his own people instinctively, particularly their shortcomings. He needed only to look within himself to know how the more prosperous peasants and the burghers in their countinghouses and the fishwives in the market would react. In his own peculiar way he loved the Danish people. And he wanted them to remain precisely as they were, that is, the way he understood them.

When Struensee first came into contact with Guldberg he was inclined to dismiss him as an insignificant, vulgar and rather comic oddity. Indeed, at this time he paid little notice to Guldberg, for he was at the peak of his career. Everyone was paying him homage, and somewhere in the castle was cradled the child, his child, into whose coverlets the royal coat-of-arms had been embroidered. Why, amid such resounding success, should he trouble his head about such an obscure nonentity as Guldberg. Look at him, sitting mute and mum at the very end of the table, listening obsequiously to every phrase that fell from highborn lips, now and then daring to laugh moderately at something clever. Among the entire company perhaps only one really appreciated the talents of Owe Guldberg. This was the Queen-Dowager, Juliana, and even she tended to underrate her right-hand man.

In these tentative days Guldberg was hardly more than an omnipresent ear, a listening post for Juliana. He absorbed everything, heard everything. Gossip, lies and facts, all passed into his thick peasant skull, and there were trapped like flies in treacle. Nights, in his own room, this located in a remote wing of the castle far from the apartments of the mighty, he slowly, carefully ruminated all that he had acquired throughout the day. He moved forward among intangibles with the plodding, rectilinear directness of a farmer plowing a field.

When this tireless reckoner had finally totted up the score, two laboriously discovered facts stood out irreducibly. The first was that the sick King was in immediate danger either of being deposed, or of being done away with entirely, liquidated. The second was that Struensee's position at the topmost rung of the ladder was insecure in direct proportion to its height, and a little push would surely send him crashing to the ground.

Owe Guldberg's specialty was farsightedness. Give the man enough rope, and he'll hang himself, he would mumble comfortably to himself. Then he would roll over on his side and fall asleep like a log. Soon his terrific snores, loud and deep as a bassoon, would vibrate out through the palace window, out into the moonlit gardens where Caroline and Struensee were happily wandering, arm in arm among the nightingales.

Count Rantzau had also come to some definite decisions in the kobold fastnesses of Norway. His debts were bothering him worse than any barber's itch. Things were so bad with him that at times he contemplated suicide. But the idea of an adventurer ending up in shabby suicide was too ridiculous. In his roistering lifetime he had run up against so many seemingly unsurmountable difficulties and yet survived that he felt he could gamble again and win.

At the Nordertor in Copenhagen a particularly obdurate creditor had nearly stripped him of his carriage and horses on his return to the court from Norway for a visit. Only the payment of an expensive diamond ring right on the spot, this gesture reinforced by the creditor's sneaking reverence for all things aristocratic, had saved the Count. Otherwise the Count would not have been able to roll up through the linden drive into the courtyard of Hoersholm, seated in a splendid equipage outfitted with outriders, bodyguard and lackeys and all ready to be met like the grand seigneur he was by the Queen and Struensee.

Nevertheless, however self-possessed he may have appeared within, his despair had not abated. The sparkling raconteur—a roman candle of a man—who could tell a thousand jokes and anecdotes to make the ladies blush and laugh, who had no equal when it came to being the life of the party, was at the end of his tether. If suicide would not do, only one way was left—murder.

Rantzau was in the dilemma of a patient suffering intense pain and about to undergo an operation that may or may not help to relieve him. He was determined to improve his circumstances, for better or worse. Murder had become the focal point of this general intention. When he sat chatting at the dinner table, when he played battledore and shuttlecock with the ladies, when he tried his hand at cards and bent forward with a gracious smile over the green cloth of the gaming table, it was always the same idea of murder that turned and turned in his head. Murder had become a shining goal for Rantzau, a veritable *raison d'être*.

One evening while drinking with Struensee and Brandt he used the opportunity to breach his murderous notions in a roundabout fashion. Since at this time Filosov was again making representations against Osten, the conversation had turned to Russia and the fabulous successes of the Tsarina Catherine.

"No wonder Catherine doesn't like Osten," Rantzau said. "No wonder, in fact, that she doesn't care for the likes of me."

"They say that Osten was her very first lover," said Brandt.

"Many of her former lovers have made a good thing of it," said Rantzau. "Plenty of them are sitting pretty on their estates, enjoying a jolly income. But Osten and I, well, we're a couple of ghosts, you might say, a pair of ghouls. We remind the Tsarina of things she'd much prefer to forget. It must make her squirm when she thinks Osten and I are pretty sure to leave behind us certain interesting biographical notices for posterity. In French, of course—that elegant and very penetrating tongue. Not that they'd smirch her honor as a woman, of course, if honor she has left. No, they'd strike much deeper than that, I'm afraid."

"We're very curious, my dear Count," said Struensee.

Rantzau was a little drunk. He laughed recklessly. "The roots of political power, my good fellow, are always buried in muck, in dirty, sticky muck," he said. "And it pays to drag them out into the open only on one condition."

"And what is that, pray?" asked Struensee.

"That those who hear and see pay heed," said Rantzau. "They should be appreciated, my revelations; they deserve to be accepted as a guide for the future. Political situations may differ greatly in particulars. In general form they all fall into a few relatively simple categories."

"We're perishing of curiosity," said Struensee indulgently. "What are you driving at, Rantzau?"

Rantzau thought for a time and could not seem to make up his mind. Finally he said: "Osten and I . . . Never mind, I'll leave poor Osten out of it. I've no right to speak for him."

"Understood," said Brandt. "Please go on."

"Well, I was a servant of the Tsar's, in any case," said Rantzau. "As you know, Peter the Third, although he was grandson of Peter the Great, completely lacked the imperial touch. He was a beanpole of a fellow, with a simple look about him, a gawky way. Some people called him downright stupid. He had a wonderfully skinny neck and a big Adam's apple that worked up and down when he was excited, which was pretty much all the time. For the disorder inside the poor man's head kept him hopping . . ." he looked meaningfully at Struensee ". . . the way it does the heads of other people we might mention. He always liked to wear the blue Prussian uniform, this Peter. Frederick was his god. He'd made Peter an honorary Prussian general. When I heard about that, you know, I said: Why doesn't Your Majesty make the King of Prussia a Russian field marshal? Yes, Peter liked to play with toy soldiers. He had hundreds and hundreds of them. Many an afternoon I've spent in the Petershof with His Majesty mowing down the enemy with a pea-shooter. Out in the garden among the orange trees he liked to construct trenches and earthworks. Then he'd have us Holsteiners—I was one of them, of course—take his fortifications by storm. Oh, we'd yell our heads off! It was a big joke with the Holsteiners.

"At night we'd sit at long wooden tables. We'd drink terrific amounts of beer and smoke long clay pipes. We made so much smoke you couldn't see your hand in front of your face. Then we'd talk over the fortunes of war, that is, the war with tin soldiers. If the Tsar was drunk and of course he was, he'd make fun of the orthodox church. He was the titular head of it. He would address us as 'reverend apostle' or 'your holiness.' That was his idea of a joke.

"Sometimes he'd play for us on an expensive fiddle he had, one that Pieri made, they say. And he didn't play at all badly, let me tell you. He loved his fiddle tremendously. As a matter of fact he had quite a bit of insight into his own shortcomings. He called himself the 'honest dupe.' Since he was the Tsar he considered it his duty to have a mistress and so picked out a certain Countess Elisabeta Voronzova, who unquestionably was one of his most hideous subjects, and perhaps the least gifted in brains. Peter, you know, was a good-natured sort. Actually he ruled his country no worse than other tsars. He made his big mistake when he picked out the little . . . did I say little? . . . Princess von Anhalt-Zerbst to be his charming bride. I remember her as a good-looking young girl, full of spirit and strength, just bursting with ambition. On his side the marriage was happy enough. He respected her. He let her have her French books, her intriguing friends, her lovers. That was a mistake, such a terrible mistake. When he found out about her first adultery, he should have thrown her into the Fortress of Peter and Paul. If he'd done that he'd have lived happily and died in bed with everybody shedding tears by the gallon. But being not at all hungry for power himself, he simply couldn't comprehend power's attraction for others. He was almost idiotically harmless, poor devil.

"Now, it was the sister of this Countess Voronzova, Ekaterina Romanovna Dashkova, the Tsarina's namesake, you see, who originally got Catherine's dander up. For this Dashkova, who was an extremely desirable piece, by the way, was obsessed with the idea of freedom. As only a Russian can be obsessed. She dreamed about getting rid of Peter, then creating a Muscovite paradise. There would be an elected parliament, manumission of the serfs, the religion of reason. You know, the salad those Frenchmen . . . I always forget their names . . . threw together."

At this juncture Struensee opened his mouth, thought better of it, and said nothing. Rantzau watched him ironically through narrowed eyes. "This Dashkova . . . a handsome wench, let me tell you, and I'd have loved to play games with her myself . . . had no real idea of the Russian peasantry," Rantzau went on to say. "And she had still less accurate notions of her so-called friend, the Tsarina, who was a born realist in politics. Dashkova, accordingly, was given a part to play, namely, liberal reformer and humanitarian. And she had no idea that she was nothing but a front for the forces seeking a new arrangement of power.

"I, personally, although I was a man from Holstein, felt myself drawn more and more to the side of Catherine and Dashkova. Peter's nonsense really got to be too much of a good thing. He caused all sorts of trouble more out of pure stupidity than out of malice. He irritated the people, the church, the nobles and finally the guards regiments, and on these last his very life depended.

"And so in the end, as we all know, he was overthrown by Catherine, with the help of the Preobrashensky and Ismailovsky regiments. Some of the officers were Catherine's loves. These fellows stirred up the guards and prevailed on them to follow the Tsarina. She talked to them, you know. It was wonderful theater, wonderful acting. She rode up in front of the barracks mounted on a large, fiery horse. She had let her hair down and she wore a silver breastplate with the double eagle on it. Follow your little mother, she told the fools, follow your little mother and wipe out Peter's oppressive rule. Get rid of his Holsteiners and Prussians, those foreigners. Of course she might have pointed out that she, herself, was German, but she didn't. In any case, she looked like the mother of all the Russias, all right, when she came prancing up on her white horse.

"Now, when Peter had been deposed, and it required little effort to do it, the next problem was to get rid of him as a person as well as an emperor. He was taken to a lonely estate called Ropska, but that was only a temporary solution. For it's perfectly obvious . . ." Rantzau paused for more grimaces in Struensee's direction . . . "that a legitimate tsar, or a legitimate king, even if he is unsound, will always be a threat to his usurpers so long as he lives. You can imagine how easily the suspicious ones, the dissatisfied ones might crystallize about this tempting symbol. So long as the old ruler lives, the old tradition lives with him.

"The Tsarina might have had herself declared regent, acting in that capacity for her son Paul, a minor and the legitimate successor to the throne. Her lover, Gregory Gregorevitch Orlov, would have stuck by her. But this stratagem would not have eliminated the real danger. The person of the deposed Tsar would still have been on hand, sticking out like a sore thumb. Catherine and her clique arrived at the crossroads, the point where the political dilettante parts company with the true politician. There was only one way and everybody knew what that way was, though no one dared to open his mouth on the subject. Least of all the liberal humanitarian, Dashkova. It was the Tsarina herself who made the gambit. If he'd only catch a little cold, she sighed. Just a little chill, or something of the sort."

Rantzau emptied his glass in one gulp, filled it, emptied it again. Brandt wriggled about restlessly on his chair. Struensee had become as pale as milk. His lips were trembling. This was enough excuse for Rantzau to throw all caution to the winds.

"Don't misunderstand me, gentlemen," he said unctuously. "I wasn't there personally. All I know comes second-hand. Personally I don't like violence, even when it can't be avoided. That's the way the world goes. Shall I be hammer, shall I be anvil? Shall I strike? Or be struck? As for me, in a showdown I'm all for being a hammer. At the same time it's not nice to bathe one's hands in blood. And so I didn't. I let someone else do it, gentlemen.

"Catherine's Orlov was a giant. His hair was as long as Samson's before he met Delilah. He and his four brothers, all of them officers in the guards, were a formidable crew. They had no scruples whatsoever. And they did very nicely by the Tsarina.

"Peter was living in Ropska, as I've just said, confined in a room with all the curtains drawn. This was to keep the soldiers posted around the house from seeing him and perhaps feeling sympathetic. Orlov, in any case, came into this room with officer-candidate Baryatinsky and sergeant-major Engelhardt. The first things Peter asked for were his Bible, his fiddle and his Negro, Narcissus. He was horribly bored, he said, moping all day in a dark room.

They all agreed that it was a terrible pity and had wine brought in. Peter drank, and immediately thought the wine tasted very odd. Suddenly he was suspicious. He spat out a mouthful, and shrieked for milk, for anything that would do as an emetic. He kept stuttering something about what have I done to you, what have I done to you? In fact, he got so worked up that he vomited, and so threw up the poison. Now Orlov tossed him on the bed and the others held his head under the pillows until he had suffocated. But in his death agony he thrashed about so violently that he worked himself free. He managed to let out a cry that would have startled the dead. The guards heard his shrieks. They looked at each other, and didn't know which way to turn. Orlov then threw him on a chair so hard that he fell backwards. He smacked the floor with the back of his head and was stunned."

Brandt could hardly contain his nervousness. He ground sweaty hands together, horrified and yet fascinated by Rantzau's tale. Struensee's mouth shook tremulously. He did not interrupt.

"Orlov picked him up off the floor and set him back on the chair," Rantzau went on inexorably. "Baryatinsky began to look at that thin neck with the big Adam's apple. He ripped off a strip from the bedcover and moved in to garrote the Tsar. He tied a single knot, then Engelhardt took one end and he the other and they pulled with a will. Orlov watched this business and said, according to report: My God, how slowly the animal dies. Pull harder! Peter now struck out with arms and legs. His tongue shot out from between his teeth, his eyes popped out of their sockets. But gradually he could stand no more and his convulsions slowed down to a stop. Then it was very still, as you can imagine, in the darkened room. Baryatinsky started to cry, for he was only seventeen years old. Engelhardt took the Tsar's pocket watch. It was an expensive timepiece, I have heard, set with diamonds.

"When Catherine received Orlov that evening she went through the mummery of being told that her husband had just died from a most regrettable accident. She snuffed up her nose and dabbed with her handkerchief. Poor fellow, she said, poor, poor fellow. But at once she had her councillor Stroganov called and with him discussed the possibility of an immediate coronation. Later, after dinner, there was a musical entertainment which everyone enjoyed enormously. And in good time the Tsar was buried with the usual ceremonies. He lay as peaceful as you please in his coffin, for I saw him myself and can testify to it. They'd put a black cloth about his neck. I remember he was laid out in his Prussian uniform, the one he had always liked so much. The hat was too big for him and it kept falling down over his nose, which would make him look silly.

"Now, as you know, gentlemen, the Tsarina turned out to be a first-class ruler. However, the Princess Dashkova never got her opportunity to put those liberal ideas of hers into practice. As a matter of fact, after a quarrel with the Tsarina, some argument over the Tsar's death, Dashkova was exiled for life to her country estates."

In a heavy silence Rantzau drank deeply of his wine. "Well," he said reflectively, "that's how the Tsarina did the trick. Looking back on it, it was relatively simple."

"And criminal," said Brandt. He had got up and was standing leaned intently over the table.

Rantzau laughed belligerently. "I've told you that you have to make a choice," he said. "I hope you keep a tight mouth when the hammer blows fall. For you've asked for them, and they'll come, all right. Mark my words."

Struensee rubbed his forehead. There was a hunted look in his eyes. "I don't see the need of your alternatives," he complained. "In civilized times and civilized countries the transfer of power doesn't necessarily have to work out in that style."

"You really think so?" Rantzau snorted. "Why? Why, I ask you? Do you think you can civilize the lust for power out of existence any more than you can the hunger for food? If our bellies are full, how easy it is to be civilized. But when we're hungry, we'll do anything to eat. And so, too, with power. You must remember, my dear Doctor, that the struggle for power naturally leads to excesses. Beyond a certain point parleys and the exchange of ideals and the citation of laws all tend to develop either into small-scale or large-scale murder, that is, into war. And this point is arrived at so much the quicker if one of the parties concerned is weak and estranged from the realities of the situation. It's like a tug-of-war. The opponents may sway back and forth for a time. But if one side yields a few steps, the other side has won. The losers sprawl in a heap on the ground. Have you not noticed?"

"Yes, my good Rantzau, but you've forgotten something in your analogy," Struensee said. "In a tug-of-war there's the judge to take into account. He sees that the rules of the contest are preserved. And in the political tug-of-war this judge is the element of reason which is resident in each one of us."

"What a hopeless sermonizer you are," cried Rantzau. He was disgusted, exasperated. "Why you talk such nonsense I cannot for the life of me understand. Struensee, your preacher blood is coming out. You're as bad as old Muenter howling his head off in St. Peter's. What has morality got to do with politics, pray tell me! And why do you confine morality to public life? Why aren't you a moral man in private? You've got the cart before the horse, sir!"

Struensee flushed and stammered. "I don't see what political morality has to do with personal religion," he said hotly.

Rantzau doubled up with derisive laughter. "Struensee, for the love of God," he said, "why try to pull wool over my eyes. You know as well as I do that every moral idea is grounded in belief, and in nothing else. Reason doesn't preach morality. Do you really want me to believe that you feel sweet sentiments towards humankind? Don't make me burst laughing, Struensee. Love people? Oh yes, oh yes, how tenderly they rub their snouts against each other's hides, the hogs. Hogs, that's what people are, Struensee. They stink like hogs, they are hogs. People are disgusting, I tell you, they'll outsmell a regiment of polecats. No, no, Struensee, please don't play the fool. Lay your cards on the table, man. It's either God with unlimited power over us, or ourselves with unlimited power if we can get away with it. And in between there's nothing but chaos, mists, uncertainty, philosophical drivel, newspaper wisdom, a world by halves, the itchy dream-world of itchy little boys and girls. Do you understand me, Struensee?"

Struensee sighed heavily and thought and sighed again. "You can lash out all you like, Count Rantzau," he said slowly, "but I belong to the party of humanity and I'm going to stay there. Never, under any circumstances, will I become an accomplice in murder. I would never do it even if it made me king of the whole universe. My reason forbids it. And my conscience forbids it. I may be a fool, as you say. No matter. That is my stand. I will not commit murder."

"Well, that's good enough for me," said Rantzau savagely and reached for his cloak. "But one more thing before we part, Struensee. I advise you as an old friend, and I say it without trying to be clever, the best thing you can do is get out now while the getting's good. It will be better for Denmark and certainly better for you. Today you're more or less free to choose. Tomorrow very certainly you won't be. You're not the man to lead the country, Struensee. Believe me, you're not. Your humanitarianism will be the death of you. They'll garrote you with it, Struensee, the way Peter was strangled with a rag. Some Danish Baryatinsky will get you, my boy. I like you, I admit, even if you are in a muddle. I like you. But I can get along very nicely without you. Goodnight, then, Struensee."

"Goodnight, Rantzau," Struensee said mechanically.

"And you, Brandt?" Rantzau asked quizzically. "I suppose I shouldn't ask you. I can see you'll stick by your master. But don't you, for God's sake, try to instruct me in brotherly love. You haven't any preacher forebears, not as I understand it. Watch yourself, Brandt."

Rantzau swept out of the room, his cloak billowing about his legs, his tricorn hat held formally in the crook of his arm. His mood was dry and bitter, his face was alight with conviction. "It's the end, the end," he muttered to himself as he let a servant with a candlestick show him out. "For them, though, not for me."

Struensee and Brandt remained where they were at the table, staring at each other morosely. Both were sickly pale from lack of sleep and too much wine. Rantzau had left a frightful emptiness behind him. Struensee jerked involuntarily as if a cramp had seized him. "What kind of man does he think I am, this aristocrat of Denmark!" he blurted out. "How dare he propose that I murder his king!"

"It's base of him," said Brandt. "Everything is low and mean. Everything is rotten and poisoned. I wish I was in Holstein." He threw his silver cup into the corner, where it landed with a bright clatter.

Struensee looked thoughtfully at his friend. "No," he said, "you can't do that. It's much too late for that."

Out in the garden the thrushes were beginning to sing. It was a sad, sad song and the break of day was very slow and gray.

★ *VI* ★

*I*N HOERSHOLM THERE was a constant round of gaiety. Tuesdays and Fridays there were dramatic productions, Wednesdays Italian opera and on Thursday Brambilla put on a pantomime, or tried to hold his audience with an exhibition of skill "in the high art of balancing."

Mondays there was music. On the Monday occasions Martini and Paschini, the Italian pair of singers whom Brandt had finally rung from Struensee, were the principal attractions. Paschini sang mezzo-soprano, usually dressed in female clothing. He was a broad-hipped man. Rumor had it that he had lost his manhood in Algiers. It was known that for a long time he had sung in a papal choir. If anyone approached Paschini, that is, any man, to compliment him on his voice, or offer him a glass of wine, his partner Martini would turn fiery red with jealously. Afterwards they would be heard fighting in the ante-room like an old married couple.

And on Sunday evenings a ball was usually given in the Norway House, the walls of which were decorated with gold-bordered paintings of fjords, waterfalls and spruce woods.

On hot summer afternoons the guests would stroll in the gardens among the carefully trimmed hedges. The statues' heads, everyone remarked, had been laboriously restored. Gallantly the gentlemen relieved the ladies of their fans, to spare them the fatigue of fanning themselves. Among the company, from out of nowhere, a little boy would often appear, a half-naked little boy, very blond, with limbs as brown as a hazelnut. He would race over the lawns rolling his hoop, accompanied by other similarly half-naked youngsters. To the dismay of the guests, he would sometimes dash with his troupe into the miniature lake, frightening off the swans.

This small Pan was Frederik, heir to the throne. Jean Jacques, apostle of nature, would have laughed to see him, a small Émile, cavorting about in a Danish garden. But the courtiers, dull fellows, did not laugh. Rather they whispered angrily among themselves. They told each other how the poor, dear child—for that was what they called him—plowed through the snow barefoot in winter, and even slept out on an open porch in blizzards. Everyone took it for granted that sooner or later the boy would perish of lung trouble. Of course, the child looked anything but consumptive, though, as everyone said, it was just his kind that usually succumbed to the disease. How much happier, or at any rate nicer—that is, how much more like a respectable prince—the little man would have looked in shoes with buckles, in silk stockings, knee pants and a coat with gold facings. So everyone thought. And to top off the rig, they felt, he should have worn his hair in a tight little pigtail that would bob on his back as he ran.

The Queen, gossip had it, suckled her small daughter, Luisa Augusta, like any burgher goodwife. That, too, was scandalous. Weren't there enough wet-nurses in Denmark, with udders as massive as those hanging from the famous Holstein cows? Indeed, anyone with half an eye could see dugs by the dozen, eager for patriotic employment. Had the Queen of Denmark nothing more important to take up her mind than tucking nipples into an infant's maw?

Caroline Matilda was happiest, regardless, when her splendid little son, tired from play, lay on a carpet at her feet in the sunny pavilion, while the baby, cradled nearby, slept peacefully. She was completely happy then. Her laughter would ring out like a bell over the garden when the boy pestered the little baby and woke her up.

Christian seldom showed his face in public. Day in and day out he played with his Negro slave in a secluded part of the palace garden. Of late he had conceived a passion for taking long rides, on which he expected the company of his *maitre de plaisir*. Christian had hated Brandt since the day of the fight, but on the surface he behaved with a friendliness that approached devotion.

Brandt sat next to him in the carriage, his legs comfortably outstretched. The King would be squeezed over into a corner. If Brandt showed signs of ill nature and was inclined to sulk, Christian would take his hand and say: "Brandt, you'll have to be patient with me. I'm only a simple man."

"I know, I know," Brandt would say and yawn in a veritable convulsion of boredom. "You always say the same thing. Do you always have to fiddle in the same damnable key?"

Sometimes Christian's chatter had an overtone of real meaning. "Wasn't Rizzio, Mary Stuart's lover, murdered by Darnley?" he once asked out of a clear sky. "I mean her husband, Darnley, you know. And didn't she have Darnley killed afterwards?"

Brandt sat up in astonishment. "I don't know a thing about it," he told the King. "I've never dabbled in Scottish history."

"A pity you haven't," said Christian and for a time lapsed into silence. "But if Rizzio is killed," he said presently, "it will have to be done carefully. You know something, Brandt?"

"Yes?"

"Kings have a rotten time of it," said Christian. "Especially if they're weak and have pretty, easy wives. Like Darnley, I mean."

But Brandt was too busy with his own thoughts to catch the drift of the King's mumblings. Yet once again Christian made his point. "Is the King of Prussia still sleeping with the Queen?" he asked.

Brandt jerked to attention. "The King of Prussia!" he said.

"Struensee, that's who I refer to," said Christian heavily.

Brandt looked at him speechlessly. Christian meanwhile had taken out his watch and was playing with it, flipping it in his hand, peering at the design of the hands. "Isn't it odd," he said, "that time never stands still. Bless me, time's the very devil, isn't it!"

Brandt leaned back impatiently on the cushions. The man is utterly mad, he thought, he's hopeless.

And as they drove along, all varnish and gilt, pedestrians wondered at the way they sat together, Brandt lording it with his legs flung out, the King pressed small in a corner. Rumors spread that the King was being held prisoner by Struensee, and that the King's companion was no longer such, but a jailer.

Whenever he could, Struensee excused himself from the pleasures of Hoersholm and worked tirelessly at the business of reforming the state. He was intensely preoccupied with the great plan of liberalizing the Danish system of land tenure, that is, of dividing the land up into small freeholds. But the thousand and one distractions of current problems constantly generated by the machinery of the state kept him from tangible accomplishment.

Decrees, letters, circulars, *plaidoyers* mounted in a pile before Struensee. He had never imagined that ruling such a small country took so much time and effort. This was leaving aside such larger matters as freeing the serfs. With regret he pigeon-holed the plan.

A sickly compulsion constantly agitated Struensee. He was wound up, the victim of profound unrest. A dark feeling whipped him on, and the hours vanished, sacrificed irrevocably to his plan. In his feverish haste he made mistakes, especially gross errors of tact and judgment. Individual feeling, he told himself, had to be ruthlessly suppressed, should this be necessary, in favor of the common good. But the brewers and silk weavers, seeing themselves without a livelihood, the state pensioners and retired officers, seeing their pittances reduced, were not amenable to counsels of discipline and forbearance. Struensee's decrees, from their selfish point of view, were an outrage, a cynical repudiation of their rights, a deliberate attempt to ruin the old order.

Both Struensee and Brandt were given a baronetcy by royal command, that is, by their own command. The King's first minister saw to it that both he and Brandt received a gift of sixty thousand thalers to substantiate this rise in status. So that's the way the cat jumps, people said. No more titles, no more sinecures—except to the right parties!

The nobility laughed themselves sick when they say Struensee's coat-of-arms. It had a ship with a crown on it, symbolizing the ship of state, which sailed across a field of gold crossed by four blue rivers, this background symbolizing a paradise of plenty. There were palm leaves, meaning peace, on the escutcheon, and an owl, for wisdom. The owl held the keys of authority and power in its beak. Such a splendid affair! Grinning among themselves, the courtiers said that the ship really stood for the ship on which Struensee's grandfather had served as seaman. The crown, they declared, meant that he considered himself a king, whereas the owl stood for another predatory nightbird, who in the dark opened the strongboxes of the kingdom and rifled them.

In the pubs and dives of Copenhagen the common folk talked about the "coming Cromwell." It was well known that in a secretary drawer Struensee kept a gold snuff box ornamented with a likeness of the famous regicide.

About this time a hundred Norwegian sailors, having been dismissed from military service without the usual honorarium to squander, were hanging around Copenhagen making trouble. Without money, tobacco or beer to while away the hours, they hung around the docks, simply killing time while waiting a chance to ship home. These Norwegian seamen were husky fellows, browned by the wind and proud of the fact that they had smelled powder. They felt themselves to be the equal of any Dane, highborn or low. So spirited were they that they decided to make direct representations to the King, and with this in mind formed ranks and marched, singing, to Hoersholm.

When Struensee heard of their approach he inexplicably lost his power of decision and fled with the King and Queen to nearby Sophienberg. White as a corpse he sat next to Brandt in the carriage and talked incoherently about "bloody revolutions." The Queen, dandling her infant on her knee, tried to calm him, but he told her bluntly that after all she was not threatened by danger and could ill afford to talk. Christian's irrelevancies did nothing to improve the situation. "If only they don't kill Morari," he plained. "Slaves cost a frightful lot, and I'll never own another, I know that." The coolest head was Brandt. He took charge of the Crown Prince, and held him in his arms as they trotted off to safety.

The Norwegians duly arrived at Hoersholm and asked to see their "father," the King. When it was made clear to them that the King was not there, they broke into the palace, tiptoed through the rooms, admired the crystal chandeliers and the paintings in the Norway House. At last they all drifted to the kitchen, where they joked with the scullery girls and hustled some of them off for a bit of fun behind the potato sacks. The palace steward was wise enough to prepare a solid meal for them, with plenty of beer, wine and a little schnapps as well, to wash it down. Early that same evening the "revolutionaries" withdrew, in poor order but fine spirits, to Copenhagen and the docks. Afterwards Struensee ordered the usual parting donation to be given them, and they disappeared.

It was only a trivial incident, but Copenhagen carefully noted Struensee's frightened reaction. The townspeople laughed at the King's first minister, mocked him, raged at him. So the mighty Struensee was a coward! He had run like a rabbit before a handful of angry seamen. He must have a bad conscience, he must know at heart that he was an enemy of the people. The fact that Struensee had fled the field could not be controverted or glossed over. The burghers of Copenhagen kicked themselves for ever having believed that a man of straw like Struensee could be dangerous. How had they ever been bamboozled into obeying the commands of such a softy!

The people dropped all pretense of respect. Struensee was attacked openly in the newspapers. He was forced to withdraw his own decree, the very first one he had ever authored, making the press a free institution. But gagging the press did not help the situation. There were other ways to get at him. Once broken, the ban of silence could not be restored. A poster offering a reward of five thousand thalers to the man who killed Struensee was pasted to the walls of Christiansborg Palace and the principal churches of the city. This incitement to murder ended with these words: "Long live the King! Long live Denmark!"

The Queen's illicit relations with Struensee were openly discussed in the capital. Caroline Matilda was spoken of as "Madame Struensee" and, in scurrilous reference to the Doctor's former calling, "the barber's drab."

When Christian traveled to Copenhagen from the country the horses were changed at the Sorgenfrie Tavern. Great crowds gathered about the carriage. The people kept their distance, trouble darkening their faces. The men took off their hats, the women curtsied. But Christian merely looked right through them with his foolish, empty eyes and saw nothing. "Drive the fools away!" he ordered a lackey when he became irritated with the stares of the onlookers. Later they grew bolder and threw letters and notes into his carriage, containing complaints about Struensee, revelations of the Queen's adultery, protestations of eternal loyalty to the crown. "More of those damnable petitions," Christian absently commented and tore the missives to pieces without bothering to read them.

The Norwegians, everybody remembered, had protested without injury, even to their profit, and so more malcontents came to Frederiksborg, where, on Struensee's advice, the King and Queen had removed. The old castle was something of a fortress. It had moats and a drawbridge and inner courtyards. It offered much more protection against the mob than Christiansborg.

Delegations came and went without ever seeing the King. Each time the palace guards turned them back. Today it would be the silk weavers, petitioning to have their shops re-opened, tomorrow the dockworkers, a week later the men from the breweries.

Often at night when the guard was changing and the men were talking softly in the courtyard, Struensee would rise from his bed and look down from his upper window. Below the lanterns burned glumly. The guards, wearing a grenadier's uniform, paced back and forth with loaded muskets at shoulder arms. Was he really being protected, Struensee asked himself? Or was he a prisoner? Anxiety so searching that it took his breath away would overcome him. His hands dripped sweat. Shaking like a leaf he would throw on his robe and hurry to his beloved.

Then she would console him. She liked to do it, she liked to assure him that soon everything would turn out all right. "They'll all quiet down when they have work again," she would assure. But at the bottom she wondered about her man. He had altered so much.

He slept fitfully at her side, groaning in his sleep. When he was awake he spoke no more of his ambitious plans, but instead stared at the floor. "If it were only all over and done with," he would complain. "And the quicker, the better."

A committee of soldiers appeared at Frederiksborg, finding fault with the removal of their officers. Struensee chanced to run into them by mere luck while he was taking a walk in the park. They had no weapons when he spied them, in fact, were only discussing the matter quietly among themselves. They did not even see him. Nonetheless, he turned quickly off on a side path and rushed circuitously into the palace and the protection of his room. There, trembling like an aspen, he shouted for his secretary, who came on the run. "I want to resign," he said. "Make out my letter of resignation to the King. My God, if it only isn't too late. The soldiers are here."

"But under these circumstances you can hardly abandon Their Majesties, Your Excellency," said the secretary, paling as he stood at attention by Struensee's desk.

"They're not looking for the King or Queen," said Struensee. "They're looking for me." Then he was ashamed, terribly ashamed. "You're right, you're right, of course," he said. "I'll have to stay." He laid his head on his arms and sobbed.

In the meanwhile Brandt had come posthaste to see what was up. "Struensee!" he said. "What in the devil's wrong with you, man!"

"The murderers are in the palace," said Struensee, looking up at his friend. "They've come, they're here at last."

"Murderers?"

"The soldiers. I saw them."

"Those fellows!" said Brandt and laughed wildly. "My dear fellow, they left their petition with the officer of the day and marched off on his order." He looked very gravely at Struensee. "Don't you think it would be possible," he said, "for you to slow down the tempo of these reforms, Struensee? They're causing an awful lot of trouble."

Struensee was red in the face. He wiped his wet eyes with his cuffs, and got up to pace the room. Brandt and the secretary watched his peregrinations. "No, it cannot be done," he said finally. "My conscience is clear. I will not slow down things a jot. And I will not support any retroaction. Impossible."

Brandt raised his shoulders in helpless annoyance. Seeing this Struensee went up to him and said: "Brandt, my work is bigger than I am. But I have to get used to the fact, don't you see? Something in me gives way to panic when my precious carcass is threatened with harm. I feel split in two. One half of me would rather perish than admit defeat. The other half has the heart of a rabbit."

There was nothing for Brandt to say. He looked away and stammered something meaningless.

"I've behaved like a coward," Struensee continued. "It's hard to believe that a man like me, who has been chosen to do great works should so soon cease to count among the people. I only wish I had enough Roman courage to take the leap myself. I mean determine my own end, if this must be. But all the stoic maxims in the world don't help me. When I'm arguing with myself, and telling myself that life doesn't mean a thing, which it really doesn't of course, I feel a horrible pang. My life suddenly strikes me as something unique, absolutely irretrievable. It seems like a wonderful unfinished work. If I don't go on living, I feel, I shall have missed something of unimaginable importance. But for the life of me I couldn't name what it is. What could it be, Brandt? So many people have no use for life. Or at least life has no use for them. But I'm not like that. I have a task to perform. It's not so much what I want to do for Denmark. My task is really to fulfill myself, and that's that. But there's no knowing. Who imposes these tasks? And where is the final goal? How can I find and know it? Mysteries on all sides! I'm confused, my dear Brandt, hopelessly confused. It makes me afraid, it makes me into a coward, which I never was before. Brandt, believe me, I don't behave like this because I can't bear to lose my woman and all the rest of it. I could let the walks in the garden go, and the fresh summer air. It's this horrible feeling of responsibilities as yet unmet that eats at my heart and unmans me."

Brandt squinted more strongly than usual. "Struensee, my dear Struensee," he said wearily. "You're talking as if tomorrow you had to die. What are you thinking of!"

"Well, I may die," insisted Struensee hysterically. "How do I know? I have seen death come. Who can tell when it may strike? Should we not all live as if each day were our last?"

"That's too morbid for me altogether," said Brandt. "Personally I like to look forward to more summers. I want more roses, more sunshine, more pretty girls. Yes, more tomorrow is my motto. No matter if they never come to pass, I can still yearn for them."

Struensee smiled despite himself. "You're a lucky man, Brandt," he said. "You're what I'd like to be, brother. But Count Rantzau was quite right when he made sport of my preacher's blood. There's a long line of piety behind me. I'll never rise above it, Brandt. When I was younger I told myself I'd shed my skin if it choked me. But it can't be done. A man's heritage will have its way, whether he likes it or not."

After this conversation the two felt that their strained relations had been greatly eased. They felt much as of old, bound together for better or worse, as they had been in Holstein and in Hamburg.

At the end of September came a folk-festival famous throughout Denmark. In a little wood by a lake in the vicinity of Frederiksborg tents were erected. Six sheep and twelve pigs were broiled on spits over open fires. More than thirty barrels of beer were broached for the occasion, and practically every man was presented with a quart of rum. But there was no gaiety this year in the people's drunkenness. The holiday was clouded by a dark overcast of resentment. The mood showed itself in bold talk and brawling. The more the people drank, the crankier they became. At the dancing there were all sorts of fist-fights. The injured were bandaged and carried off to get their wind in the cellar of Frederiksborg.

When the early fall night settled down, torches were lighted and an enormous ox-carcase dragged out into the meadow. Everyone gathered about the fire to watch the great mass of flesh slowly revolve above the coals. The black carcase, the four legs stretched out still and stark, went round and round, licked by flames, and brought shudders to those susceptible to gruesome spectacles. The fire crackled when rivulets of molten fat from the seared body fell into it. A harsh odor of scorched flesh floated out over the gathering, whereupon a curious excitement stirred among the spectators. "The King, the King!" they shouted. "We want to see our King!"

Christian refused to come. Servants and gentlemen of the bed-chamber ran helterskelter through the corridors, frightened to pieces. Struensee sat at his desk as if nailed there. His hands shook, so bad was his funk. "This is the end," he told Brandt. "The revolution has come. It's the end for all of us."

Brandt sought out the Queen and prevailed on her to show her-self to the people in lieu of Christian. Holding the little Crown Prince by the hand—the child could hardly stand on his legs, so rudely had he been torn from sleep—Caroline Matilda hurried to the festival meadow, followed by Brandt and the ladies-in-waiting.

When the Queen appeared a dense quiet blanketed the crowd. What they saw was a young woman wearing a nightcap on her head. Her bright hair peeped out beneath the lace and glittered metallically in the smoky firelight. It was the little Prince that touched their hearts. A broad-shouldered, red-headed seaman, his shirt open at the throat to show off his mat of ruddy chest hair, thrust himself forward, rum flask in hand. Raising the flask aloft, he cried out: "Long live the Queen, and long live the Crown Prince!" Everybody shouted the words and hopped up and down in a fit of patriotic agitation. The people formed a thick circle about the Queen. The Crown Prince buried his head in his mother's skirts and peeked in terror at the huge figures hemming him in on all sides. "You needn't be afraid," his mother told him calmly. "They're all your friends, all these people." The little boy was not convinced. "I thank you all," said Caroline Matilda. "I regret that the King is indisposed and cannot greet you."

Brandt turned to the red-headed seaman and, in as comradely a tone as he could muster, said: "You have a fine ox there, my man."

The seaman looked with a long, critical, drunken look at the slowly twirling ox-corpse, and said, with a foolish laugh: "We'd rather have another kind of ox to roast, if you know what I mean."

"Another ox?"

"The enemy of the people," said the man brutally. "Struensee, you'd see how we'd roast that fellow over the fire."

Brandt took his dagger by the hilt, but decided wisely to let the slur pass unattended. His hand fell away. Caroline Matilda had heard. She stared silently at the black, flayed animal, wheeling ponderously through the yellow flames, at the bearded faces of the men tending the fire. She looked at the broad-bottomed women. Watching, she had raised her left arm across her bosom, and so held herself tightly, woman-fashion, while her other hand mechanically stroked her child's head. "Well, let us leave now," she said to Brandt, turned and silently moved away from the feast, head lowered.

Brandt and the Queen's attendants followed behind. No one cheered them as they left.

★ *VII* ★

NOBODY COULD EVER accomplish anything using the people alone. There it was, the hydra-headed crowd, the strongest single force in the state. Yet the crowd had no consciousness of its power. Even when aroused, it had no collective will, no clearness of outlook or purpose. And, above all, it had no courage.

Count Rantzau, more than ever disposed to get on in the world at any cost, told himself these truths a hundred times over, every day, in fact. Always in his private vision of revolution the people filled in the background. They were the scenery, the chorus. What was needed, very plainly, were some principals. To be sure, there was Rantzau himself. But he had reserved the post of director for himself, and wanted no part of acting. He knew how little gift he had when it came to taking the initiative in tyrannicide.

Having given the matter infinite thought, he decided to ally himself with the Queen-Dowager, Juliana. She was an ambitious woman. She had shown enough signs of that, surely, during her husband's lifetime. In late years she had been invited less and less frequently to the court. That and a dozen other small rebuffs must have rankled her. Like himself, she must have a consuming desire to get even, to improve her station, to be top dog. Like himself she must certainly consider Struensee to be the main obstacle between her and home. Did

Struensee not threaten her son's career? Would she not rise to the bait if she were assured that it might be possible for her son to replace the present first minister? And why not actually do this? The eighteen-year-old Prince would be pliable enough once installed in the job.

In pursuit of this argument Count Rantzau put in an appearance at sleepy old Fredensborg where Juliana lived. For the time being he contented himself with paying Juliana and her son the usual compliments, inquiring after their health, tentatively exploring the injustice of their lot and bemoaning the political situation in very general terms. Nothing too definite, nothing too serious. Moreover, Rantzau was quite taken with Juliana. The plump lady with the beautiful shoulders, gray hair and very lively dark eyes struck him as exquisitely aristocratic. Yes, she was the real thing. Compared to the Queen, Rantzau judged, Juliana was of far superior mold. When the Queen-Dowager reached him her hand as she bid him adieu, he kissed the long round fingers with considerable emotion. At that moment the idea popped into his head that this richly mature princess of the blood might even become his mistress. Why, who better could sweeten his declining years!

Thereafter he appeared much more often at Fredensborg and was delighted to observe that his comings were sincerely looked forward to. Juliana chided him gently when he remained away for a whole week, just to try her out. Rantzau, too, saw that Owe Guldberg was an important figure in Juliana's circle and made up his mind to try his scheme out on the man. That would leave him, the Count, in the clear and also spare Juliana any unpleasantness, if she could not in good conscience fall in with his plans, or dared not do so.

After dinner one evening at Fredensborg he went to Guldberg's second-story room to have coffee. Neat white curtains hung at the windows, and the window sills were decorated with pots of geranium and fuchsia. Guldberg himself tended these plants, carefully nipping off each withered leaf. In one corner stood a huge porcelain stove, with bright scenes from the Old Testament fired into the shining surface. A fine heat radiated from this delightful heat machine. It was now November. The park outside was bleak and sodden with rain and a cruel wind was stripping the last yellow leaves from black boughs. Carefully stacked in shelves were many books, all serious titles and all bound in pigskin. Countless silhouettes, framed in black, hung against the wallpaper. On a table were scattered sheets of a manuscript written in a fine, close hand. Guldberg was working on his "Confessions of a converted freethinker—by his own hand." This did not mean that Owe Guldberg had actually ever been a freethinker, but it amused him to palm himself off as such. It made his attacks on liberal sentiments so much the more dramatic, of course.

The converted freethinker aspect of Guldberg had no interest for

Rantzau, no more than the bourgeois appointments of the study. Even the excellent coffee that Guldberg poured his guest from a lovely white china pot covered with roses made no impression on the Count. His interest in the formidable peasant was strictly limited and he made no bones about it.

To his intense gratification Rantzau soon saw that his red-haired host not only had caught on to his veiled allusions, but was ready to offer a point or two on his own account. Accordingly Rantzau ceased entirely to jockey. "The time for decisive action has come, Guldberg," he said fluently. "There's a good chance of dealing with Struensee and his clique. Later on it might not be so easy."

"How do you propose to go about it, Your Excellency?" asked Guldberg, looking out of his sly little blue eyes over the rim of his coffee cup.

Rantzau did not hesitate. "Struensee and Brandt will have to be immobilized," he said harshly. "As for the rest of them—I refer to Gaehler, Osten and Struensee's brother—they are of no fundamental importance. They can either be imprisoned or exiled."

Deep wrinkles of doubt appeared on Guldberg's forehead. "You suggest that Struensee and Brandt be murdered?" he said quietly, keeping an eye on the door. "Or something of the sort?"

"I should like to avoid the use of the term 'murder' in this connection," said Rantzau, smiling foxily at Guldberg. "That is, since we understand each other."

"Well, well," said Guldberg, satisfied, and set his cup back on the table with elaborate care. "You can see yourself, my dear Count, that it couldn't possibly be a question of murder. My enlightened patron, the Queen-Dowager, and her son would never get mixed up in a murder. Struensee and Brandt must be brought before a court. They must be legally tried and judged. And executed, of course."

"Why all the trouble?" said the Count, disappointed. "Liberal ways of doing things are in style, my good man. We couldn't execute them for vice."

"I know, I know," cut in Guldberg, knitting his heavy brows. "But there are other considerations. I think it would be a grievous mistake to attack these gentlemen for their liberalism. You're an old military man, Count, and I hardly need tell you that a frontal attack is practically always a mistake. And the same holds true in politics. What we must strike at is Struensee's relationship with the Queen and Brandt's vicious treatment of the King. They must be tried, in short, on grounds of treason."

"How would you make treason out of it?" asked Rantzau reluctantly. "Where's your evidence. I never heard of any treason."

"That can be done," said Guldberg. "I've already got some evidence against Brandt. From Colonel Koeller, as a matter of fact."

Rantzau could hardly believe his ears. "Colonel Koeller!" he exclaimed.

"You can see I haven't been idle," said Guldberg, enjoying the Count's discomfiture. *"In Puncto* Struensee I also have managed to get hold of certain valuable information. As you may know, in Christiansborg a secret stairway runs from Struensee's apartment to the Queen's room. I had the Queen's maids sprinkle meal on the stairs and seal the lock of the back door with wax."

"Yes," said Rantzau. "What happened?"

"Well, I wouldn't have brought up the subject if the experiment had failed," said Guldberg coldly. "The next morning there were a man's footprints in the meal. The wax in the keyhole was broken."

"Why, you've got all the evidence you need right now," said the Count. His own idea of murdering Struensee suddenly struck him as exceedingly stupid.

"More than that," continued Guldberg. "I have also worked out the proper method of construing this evidence. You are undoubtedly aware of the fact, Excellency, that in political maneuvers it very often pays dividends if you can reveal the motive behind the criminal act. Whether or not the construction hits the mark is largely irrelevant. The people must have the crime imagined for them, so to speak."

"I understand that very well," the Count said, as if he had thought of it himself.

"Then you will appreciate the fact, or should I say the assumed fact, that Struensee and Brandt are persecuting the King and Queen," said Guldberg. "Very obviously that is what those scoundrels are up to."

"Is that so!" said the Count. "Aren't you stretching things a bit?"

"You are much too good-hearted, Excellency," said Guldberg. "The boldness of these criminals is simply beyond your conservative conception. What they are aiming at is to drive the King deeper and deeper into his sickness, then have him deposed and the Queen, who is a mere tool in their hands, declared regent."

"There you have it!" said Rantzau and struck the table so hard the pretty coffee pot bounced. "That's why the rascal didn't fall in with my plans that other time. He had a simpler way and I was stupid enough to believe in his damnable moral whining."

"Tell me about it," said Guldberg.

"Some other time," said Rantzau. "It happened a long time ago. I merely wanted the King to be . . . well, shall we say . . . disembarrassed of his cares."

"That's fine, fine," said Guldberg quickly. "As you say, the King must be relieved of his burdens. Unfortunately the revelation of the Queen's adultery and the revelation of the dangers which have been surrounding him for so long will almost certainly plunge him farther into confusion. In consequence I propose that the Prince Frederik, supported by his mother, the Queen-Dowager, be made regent."

"I agree to that without reservation," said Rantzau. "Or at least with only a few minor reservations."

"And what are they?" asked Guldberg sweetly.

The Count became visibly ill at ease. He cleared his throat at last and said: "I'm ready to offer my life and my services to further the fortunes of the Queen-Dowager. But I expect, not unnaturally, to derive some recognition, some concrete recognition, as matter of fact, of my devotion."

"Why, of course," said Guldberg. "Of course!"

"I expect," the Count went on, gathering speed, "that my debts shall be paid, and most regrettably they add up to a hundred thousand thalers or thereabouts. What do you say to that?"

A great weight lifted from Guldberg's spirit. He had expected that the Count would demand a ministerial post in return for his services, perhaps the post of first minister, which Guldberg had reserved for himself. He caught himself, just as he was about to clap the Count happily on the shoulder. "Why yes, naturally, Your Excellency," he said. "I shall speak at once with my noble patron. But I can already promise you, here and now, that your modest stipulations will be met to the letter. Yes, indeed, to the letter, sir."

Rantzau could have wept for joy. For the first time in his life he felt intimations of what it would be like to be a free man, rid of the horrid economic pressure that had always distorted his whole existence. He was thankful to Guldberg, he considered him more than sympathetic. Results went far beyond his fondest expectations. The Count's droopy, horsey features became quite sunny. Lines of chagrin melted away. He got to his feet, bursting with energy. "Well, what are we waiting for?" he said to Guldberg. "When do we get on with the business?"

"On with the business?" A chilly smile played about Guldberg's mouth. "Don't you see, Count," he said, "that the time to act is by no means in the offing?"

"Why all the pussyfooting?" the Count objected.

"You must appreciate that it's a very risky undertaking," said Guldberg. "Don't forget that it would be possible for Struensee to turn the tables on us very nicely, and have us indicted for treason. Don't forget that I must protect the Queen-Dowager and her son. Under any circumstances whatsoever. I cannot give the signal to move until I'm absolutely sure. Not only with regard to the plan of attack, but to its practical results."

"But in projects of this sort," said Rantzau, "there can't be absolute certainty. Only Boldness wins."

"But, my dear man," said Guldberg, "can you tell me who's going to help us do all this? Don't you understand that we two alone couldn't possibly bring this off successfully?"

"You're right again, Guldberg," admitted Rantzau. He mulled over the thought, then said: "I can bring my friend, Beringskjold, into it. He's an old friend of mine from the Russian days. He's terribly dissatisfied with the government, so I understand. He can't make his estate on Moen solvent on account of these new laws, whatever they are."

"I can count on Colonel Koeller," said Guldberg. "But we four are still by no means enough. We need twenty, thirty determined men. We need an exact plan of the Palace. And we must pick a time to move when Struensee, Brandt and the whole gang of them imagine themselves to be in perfect security. We must have surprise. Then we must win over the King, for it is he who must sign the order for arrest. Then, and not until then, can we count the play as won. Afterwards it will be easy to set the wheels of justice in motion against Struensee and company."

"*Mon dieu!*" said the Count. "You've thought of everything, you clever man!"

"One thing I cannot foresee," said Guldberg. "That's the opportune moment. Struensee himself will have to make that for us."

"What do you mean by that?"

"He must make one final glaring mistake," Guldberg said. "And I know that eventually he'll do exactly that, as sure as the sun will rise tomorrow. He's hopelessly entangled in his ideas. The man is simply unteachable. He works for the good of mankind, instead of seeing that Hans and Franz get a crust when they come abegging. Haven't you ever read about Don Quixote, Excellency? Struensee is a Don Quixote, a blue-eyed idealist of the north. But don't ask me to tell you precisely when or how he's going to dig his own grave. That's his affair. Our business is to be ready for the great moment when it arrives. We must have Struensee closely watched. People of his stripe, you realize, are unpredictable. At least I find them so, and I'm sure you do, too."

"I understand what you mean," said Rantzau. "But all this may drag things out for a long time."

"I hardly think so," said Guldberg and smiled. "You will be surprised, I think. He cannot sit still. Ideas plague him worse than bots in flytime."

After some further desultory conversation in this same vein, Rantzau promised to enlist more accomplices. The two men parted on the most amicable terms.

This year winter came early with heavy storms. The weather was so bad and darkness set in so early in the afternoon that deerhunting was out of the question. Life in the bone-chilling confines of Frederiksborg was hardly supportable. But Struensee had good reasons for keeping the court as far as possible from Copenhagen, at least as long as he could. He was mortally afraid of the people's discontent. Yet at last it became so very cold, and there was such an unprecedented succession of snowstorms that he could not longer reasonably delay giving the word to return to Christiansborg and face the music.

Struensee did not make this move, however, without taking certain precautions. He named General Gude the new commandant of the city. Gude was a man of sixty, white-haired, his breast habitually weighted with decorations. He had a big belly and was weak on his pins. Sometimes his voice broke and he squeaked like an old woman. To cover up this defect he roared all commands and substituted angry side glances for military prowess. Under the surface Gude was a decent sort and too unintelligent by far to be drawn into any intrigue. He was very fond of Aalborg aquavit, a strong brandy that he used even at breakfast to spike his coffee. The older he grew, the more aquavit and the less coffee suited his taste. One of his adjutants, having a little harmless fun at the general's expense, called straight liquor "café à la Gude." This worked back to the General, and in a tempest of wrath he ordered the company wit to be "confined to quarters for a week without wine or women." Such was good old Gude.

When Struensee imparted his fears about popular uprisings in Copenhagen, the General blew heavily through his mustaches, making the points quiver like the prongs of a tuning fork. For a moment he looked like an indignant walrus. Then, unable to respond in any other way, he thundered. "Nothing to it, simple as the alphabet," he bellowed. "I'll have thirty loaded cannon placed on the walls of Christiansborg and aimed at the city. I'll issue thirty-six rounds to each guard. If a sparrow as much as sings a bad note, I'll blast the city into rubble. By God, the bandits will find out what kind of man General Gude is, sir!" He blew a loud blast into his handkerchief. "Yes, Your Excellency," he added, "I'll blow their brains ten miles out to sea."

"Just a minute, General," said Struensee. "Don't you think that putting loaded cannon on the walls might cause more trouble? Of course, that would be just what we don't want."

"You don't know the mob, Excellency," said Gude in so many shouts. "The only time the mob respects anybody is when he has a club in his hand, ready to whack the first pair of knuckles that gets in the way. Do as I suggest. The military way is always the right way. Why, it has to be!"

Struensee was not convinced, but he gave in. Military men and ways had always been and still remained a complete mystery to him. Gude's plan was put into effect. The loaded cannon, their mouths gaping in all directions over Copenhagen, raised popular anger to fever pitch. Word spread through the city that Struensee was certainly holding the King prisoner now. The next step, obviously in preparation, was a *coup d'état* which would make Struensee absolute dictator of Denmark.

Rantzau rubbed his hands with glee. Sly old Guldberg had been right as rain on every count. And things would be better still. Much better. The Zealand dragoons commanded by General von Eickstedt had been brought into the city expressly to protect the King and Queen. Gude ordered the dragoons to patrol the town. The command nettled Eickstedt out of reason. Like military men of all ages and places, he was very touchy about his prestige and became jealous and soreheaded at the drop of a hat. He had expected that when his troops were ordered into Copenhagen he would be made commandant of the city. Instead he found himself taking orders from Gude. That absurd old cock shouted at him like a corporal, making mirrors quiver on the walls, while the clerks snickered behind his back. It was, as Eickstedt put it, a damnable insult.

No man of honor could put up with such nonsense. And it was that miserable *parvenu*, Struensee, who—undoubtedly with malice *prepense*—had forced him into an intolerable position. When Rantzau got round to sounding out Eickstedt, he found ready ears. The time was drawing near, Rantzau hinted, when interesting changes would be made. Things certainly could not continue as they were. Could they? Eickstedt strained to listen. He could not hear enough. Gradually, carefully, Rantzau lured him into the scheme of usurpation. He told Eickstedt, naming no names, that "an extremely highborn person, someone closely related to the King" was backing the enterprise, and would take over when Struensee was forced out of the picture. Eickstedt was all fire and flame, and Rantzau delighted with himself. Now he felt the comfortable sensation of having armed might at his rear. The Zealand dragoons were his.

The year was sliding along towards Christmas. Fresh disturbances broke out in Copenhagen. The guards traditionally assigned to Christiansborg were ordered deactivated, and were replaced by the Holstein infantry regiment. The "Pretorians," as Struensee called the haughty palace guards—they carried pikes in whitely gloved hands—took their dismissal very hard. For centuries they had been considered the cream of the Danish army. All their officers were drawn from the landed nobility and by custom were accorded unusual privileges. Even the common guardsman, who was picked for his superior physique and intelligence, considered himself superior to any line-sergeant. He could not be punished, like other troops, by flogging or running the gauntlet. His pay was three times that of the ordinary foot-soldier's. The girls of Copenhagen, even those from burgher homes, always said there was nothing in the whole wide world to compare with a guardsman. To be chosen for this regiment was almost as good as making a rich marriage, or coming into a legacy. It meant basking in the sun of royalty, sharing the charisma of the ruling house. And now there was to be no more palace guard regiment.

There were wild scenes on the Kongens Nytorv, where the guards were ordered for the ceremony of changing places with the line regiment. When the royal standard was brought out into the square, the guardsmen broke ranks, surrounded the flag and fell to their knees, hysterically kissing the fold of the precious emblem. "These are our colors," they shouted. "We have sworn to defend them to the death. We want no other. We will have no other." Their commander, a Colonel Sames, tried to calm them, but they hurled him into the gutter and reviled him as a traitor.

The townsfolk who had gathered to watch the sport sided with the guards. A band of dockworkers were especially vociferous and partisan, for reasons known only to themselves. "Bring on those infantry dogs!" they said. "We'll show them a thing or two." Women joined in the chorus. "You're the King's last protectors," they screamed. "He's a goner without you men. He'll be killed, that's what he will!" A gentleman of clerical bearing, a thin, dark fellow with eyes burning like coals, went from group to group and said his piece. "You see, my friends," he told everybody very confidentially, "you see what that barber Struensee has up his sleeve. He's taking the King's guards away so he can get rid of him at leisure." And to these observations the people replied enthusiastically: "Well, we'll see about that!" or "We'll never stand for that, not by a damned sight."

The women were more enraged than the men. They ignored the children clinging to their skirts, though the little ones were shivering from the cold and bawling wildly to go home. But eventually the crowd dispersed, the convulsion of excitement having run its course. It began to snow lightly. It was the twenty-fourth of December, Christmas Eve, and suddenly everyone longed to be home at his hearth, drinking punch and eating holiday food. About three o'clock darkness had covered Copenhagen. Somewhat later the churchbells, as usual, began to ring in the Christmastide. Through the dimly lighted streets and alleys of the city little knots of people wandered, singing carols.

Once the spectators calmed down the majority of the guardsmen were brought to order by promises of advancement in other regiments. The change with the line regiment was carried through after a fashion. Some guardsmen, however, asked for permanent release, and this was granted them. They were all in an ugly mood. The light from pine knot torches flickered ominously on their big faces and cast heavy shadows in the hollows of their cheeks. In their tall helmets, now being worn for the last time, they looked like huge giants from out of the forest. The snow, blowing hard through the streets, crusted their long mustachios. Up from the dockside blew the wind, moaning over the rooftops, driving before it fine showers of snow, sweeping grayly over the little huddle of men still holding fast in protest on the Kongens Nytorv.

In this peculiar fashion, then, the guards were dismissed. Henceforth infantrymen of the Holstein regiment were to stand in the sentry-boxes, the palace corridors and courtyards. They wore blue uniforms with silver braid and silver buttons. Everything was new and strange to them. Sometimes they presented arms to a lackey as he rushed by in his fancy livery.

The former commandant, Colonel Sames, taking leave of the guardhouse found time to exchange the amenities with his successor, Colonel Koeller. "You'll soon see some fundamental changes around this place," Koeller told Sames. "And it won't be long now, either."

"How so?" asked Colonel Sames wearily. The poor man was quite crushed without his guards.

Koeller measured him. "If you want to bear a hand," he said slowly, "come tonight to the rectory of the Holmen Church."

"You mean . . . ?" Sames wanted to believe, but did not dare. "That is, you feel there might be some chance of having injustice corrected, sir?"

"Come and see!" said Koeller. "Will you do that, Sames?"

"I'll be there," the other said. "I shall be there on the dot."

Afterwards Colonel Koeller took a good took at himself in the mirror. He was from Pomerania and had a broad peasant face, distinguished by a prominent, faintly curved nose and cheeks as full and red as apples. He was inordinately fond of himself, considered himself a model of masculine beauty. Well, he told himself, I certainly will cut a figure with general's epaulets and the Order of the Elephant! Indeed I will!

After the Christmas Eve services, shortly after midnight, one after another a file of men straggled into the rectory of the Holmen Church. It was still snowing, quite hard now. The men were heavily muffled up and their hats were pulled far down over their eyes. They were let into the house by the chaplain, Abildgaard, and taken directly to his study. Chaplain Abildgaard was the intense fellow who had circulated so busily among the crowd gathered to watch the guards disband.

The chaplain's guests sat around a circular table lit by a single candle. All the conspirators knew each other well—Count Rantzau, Beringskjold, General Eickstedt, Colonel Sames, Colonel Koeller and many of their trusted friends and subordinates. The curtains were closely drawn. Everybody wanted the other fellow to make the first break. Outside, muffled by the snow in the air, the sound of sleigh-bells was heard drawing closer. The company listened. "That will be Jessen from Fredensborg," the chaplain said and went to open the door.

They heard him whispering to someone out in the passageway. When he came back he had two men with him. One was an old gentleman, all bent over and wrinkled like parchment. This was Jessen, the Queen-Dowager's former servant, who now ran a small wine business. Jessen had accepted the assignment of go-between. Through his good offices messages passed regularly between the con-spirators in Copenhagen and the Queen-Dowager. The other new arrival, looking enormously wide in his winter clothes, was Owe Guldberg. He breathed asthmatically as he worked himself out of his wraps. At once he took charge of the meeting.

"Good evening, gentlemen," he said. "I come directly from my gracious mistress. She has asked me to greet all of you in her name, and to let you know that the time has come to act. At the same time, she wishes you to know that no blood must be shed if this can possibly be avoided."

"Everything is ready," said Rantzau. "All the troops in Copen-hagen—the Zealand cavalry, the Holstein infantry and what's left of the guards—are with us. Our own people are guarding the palace this very moment!"

"What did I tell you, Count!" Guldberg did not try to conceal his triumph. "Didn't I tell you that Struensee himself would clear the road for us? I know these liberals! I know their ignorant dislike of the military. If they had their way, every man who wore a sabre would be drummed out of town."

"The people are all on our side," a captain said.

"The people?" said Guldberg. "We must go easy with the people, gentlemen. We can't run any chances of their getting out of hand. What they don't know won't hurt them. After it's all over we can let them celebrate. They might even riot a bit if they like. But our revolution must be carried out without any people being dragged into it. Inside the palace, that's the place. *Entre nous,* as they say. Later we'll teach the people that it has been just as much their revo-lution as ours."

"Altogether an internal affair," said Colonel Koeller majestically. "Quite."

"But that we can do all this without shedding any blood," put in General Eickstedt, "I doubt very, very much. Really, that's expect-ing a lot of us, gentlemen."

"No bloodshed, no broken heads, nothing," said Guldberg. He raised a warning forefinger like a schoolteacher. "If we move ahead too precipitously there's some danger that the King may veer towards Struensee and protect him. And I need hardly tell you that in such event it would be very distinctly the end of us." He drew his finger across his throat to underscore the point.

The conspirators looked carefully at each other. Some of them were visibly worried. "It's an old, old story," said Koeller. "When there's any doubt, old soldiers always obey their superiors. There's no real danger, my good man. None at all."

"But supposing the King, who is the superior of all of us, personally orders the troops to protect Struensee?" asked Guldberg gently.

They had nothing to say to this. It was Rantzau who broke the impasse. "Guldberg is right," he said. "If the King should say the word, they'd follow his orders, not ours."

"They probably would," said Colonel Sames and General Eickstedt solemnly nodded approval.

Now everyone was gloomy, but Guldberg dispelled the mood with a hearty laugh. "Gentlemen, I don't want to sap your courage with all my pros and cons," he told them. "I merely want to impress on you that we must go into action when there's an absolute minimum of danger. There is a way to do this. Let me explain."

"Yes, do," said Koeller, rather huffily.

"Struensee, Brandt and the rest must be picked up during the night," said Guldberg. "The King must be surprised in bed and convinced then and there that it is to his advantage to sign the order for the arrests."

"Who is going to do the convincing?" asked Rantzau.

"His mother," said Guldberg smoothly. Amusement and triumph sparkled in his little blue shoe-button eyes. The officers' jaws sagged at this highly unorthodox proposal.

"Bravo, Guldberg," said Rantzau. "You've balanced the egg." An excited buzz of approval ran around the table.

"One more thing," continued Guldberg. "Surprise will be easiest when they imagine everything has quieted down after the guards affair. Just now, of course, they're on the alert, on account of what happened today in the Kongens Nytorv. But just give Struensee two weeks. By that time he'll have convinced himself that all is going well again. In about two weeks, if I recall correctly, a masked ball is being given in Christiansborg. When they're all abed and sleeping off their good time, we'll come knocking at the door."

"In two weeks?" said Koeller. "Why not right after Christmas?"

"Between Christmas and New Year," said Guldberg, "nobody does any washing. Or death will strike in the house. Have you heard the old saying? Or don't you people take any stock in what the peasants say?"

There was some dissent, but most of the company agreed that

Guldberg's proposal was the best possible. "Our friend Jessen," Guldberg told them, "will continue to keep me in touch with you at this end. We must all behave as if nothing were in the air. The evening of the masked ball we'll meet here again. I'll bring an important person with me."

"Agreed?" Rantzau looked around the table and there were many noddings. "Guldberg," Rantzau said boldly, "I shall expect Struensee to be done away with."

"Why, of course!" said Guldberg. "What would be the point in all this otherwise? With him still alive we could hardly claim success, very obviously."

"And you will not renege?" said the Count.

"Not I," said Guldberg, bowing deeply. "To make an omelette, so they say, a few eggs have to be broken. And now I have to go. There's a long trip ahead of me and it's snowing hard. I couldn't be seen here in Copenhagen. Good night and good luck, gentlemen."

"Luck!" the officers chanted in unison. Chaplain Abildgaard folded his hands, fluttered his lids and mumbled: "May God grant us success, for King and Denmark."

Presently the conspirators slipped out of the rectory, one by one, just as they had come. The snow was gradually letting up, and a full moon showed now and then through rolling, tattered clouds. When this happened snowy Copenhagen became an enchanted town out of some old legend.

Rantzau hurried along homeward to the Bredegade. He marched bent forward, his hands buried deep in his pockets. His steps were soundless in the soft new snow. He was anxious, for some inexplicable reason, almost downright afraid. Though there was nothing to be afraid of. Several times he stopped suspiciously and looked all around him, tensely inspecting shadowy places. Going through the Fishmarket—the empty stalls were thickly capped with snow—a large black dog sidled up to him, tail between his legs. He sniffed at the rim of Rantzau's coat, begging mutely for attention and something to eat. The Count, out of sheer nervousness, gave him a solid kick in the ribs. The animal grunted with pain and ran off howling.

On and on Rantzau trudged through the night, past still houses, over frozen canals, by crosses in drifty churchyards hemmed in by mildly shining iron fences. Some considerable distance behind him came the black dog. His ears were laid back, his long warm tongue hung out of his mouth.

★ *VIII* ★

*C*AROLINE MATILDA WAS very happy in her ignorance of impending disaster. She was buoyed up
remarkably by the feeling that her life was now ordered and spiritually
secure.

The weather was cold and sunny. Mornings Caroline sprang
eagerly out of bed, sometimes to stand naked before the mirror and
examine her body, all haloed with silver in the clear winter morning
light. She would fold her hands behind her neck, stretch luxuriantly
like a cat and strain upward on tiptoe so that her breasts stuck out
and the muscles showed in her thighs. I look like Eve, she would
think with a thrill of pleasure, and so thinking would posture
variously like a ballet dancer before the mirror. After this dumb show
the maids would come at her ring and help her dress. Then Antje
Maria would fetch in her little daughter to be given suck.

Later, after breakfast, she might go hunting with her falcons out
by the North Gate. She was not very good at it, but she loved the
birds. They sat lightly on her gloved fist, gripping and easing their
talons as they restlessly shifted. And when unhooded they would blink
their round, soulless eyes until equal to the glare, then lunge away
on blue-black pinions to climb steeply into the air.

Afternoons she liked to go sleigh-riding on the frozen sea, and
sometimes herself took over the reins. The horses responded with a
will, the sleigh flew almost soundlessly over the snowy ice, the wind
whistled softly in her ears. The seascape was wide, featureless, infinitely extensive, it seemed. Behind her lay Zealand, before her the
flat coast of Schonen. Off to the right in the glare of the sun was the
Baltic, where great flocks of hungry gulls hovered at the margin of
the ice. At the left the sound narrowed, and at its narrowest point
there was the small town of Helsingoer on the Danish side, a cluster
of snowy roofs with the square, abruptly truncated tower of the
cathedral springing up from them against the sky. In the foreground,
overlooking the ice-locked sea, was the Kronborg Fortress, a solid
mass of walls and towers.

Again and again Caroline's eye was drawn to Kronborg. In spite
of the almost carnival architecture of its main tower, and the sparkle
of its many windows in the sun, Kronborg was a sinister pile. It was
still the castle of Hamlet, a relic of a greater epoch brooding under
the low winter orb. Its black cannon mouths stood ready to fire and
splinter the plain of ice. Crows and daws flew in a cloud about the
main tower. Their raucous conversation came on the wind to Caroline,
a primitive sound indigenous to this world of sea, ice and flat shore.

How fearful it would be, Caroline would think, to be out alone and afoot on the ice, with night coming on, with the pale moonglade flickering on the water beyond the icy waste of the sound, dimly illuminating the far coast of Sweden.

But the young matron, all bundled up and warm in a fine coat with fur trim, her toes comfortable in soft leather boots, never worried her head too hard or too long over the fortress pile. She enjoyed watching the powerful musculature of her horses as they worked, she smiled when she heard laughter from the other sleighs, she felt the pleasant rhythms of her own warm blood. What was Kronborg in the face of such requitements! A ghost castle, inhabited only by daws and evil-doers.

Sometimes the sleighing party would stop and rest the horses out on the ice. The grooms would get to work at once and rub down the steamy animals with straw. The ladies and gentlemen would then drink hot wines spiced with clove. Afterwards there would be a snow battle, or they would dance together on a smooth place in the ice.

It was only in the evening that Caroline sometimes became depressed. Looking through her windows, eyes tired and smarting from too much glare and wind, she would see Copenhagen, blood-red under the sinking sun. The cupola of the Marble Church, the towers of the Frelser Church and of St. Peter's shot up into a sea of fire. There was an ominous quality in the spectacle. Caroline would feel wan looking at the intense glow. A little plaintive verse from childhood would come back to her:

> "Even though the sun shines bright,
> Still must it sink at night."

"Is something wrong, Madame?" Frau von Gaehler would inquire.

"I can't always be laughing, you know," Caroline would snap back, and instantly regret her show of malaise.

The mood would pass when dinner was ready on the long table, when the silver and the crystal glass were sparkling in the candlelight and the gaily painted porcelain ware was shimmering cleanly. There would be the rich odor of roasted meats and burgundy, and the sweet perfume of women's bodies, freshly washed and powdered.

Next came the decorous round of conversation, the men's *bon mots*, the whispered coquetries, enchanting, silvery peals of laughter. Then bed, soft and wide, the silken covers crackling, the sheets feeling just a little bit cool to the skin, just enough to make one shiver delightfully. Her toes would grope for the warming pan slipped between the covers at the foot. A last candle would be left on the nighttable. The porcelain stove would glow, exquisitely deep pink, in the corner. Outside the palace-watch made ringing steps as they paced back and forth in the courtyard, keeping safe the happiness within the palace. Then there was a copy of La Fontaine to read.

Presently a light footfall would be heard outside, then a tap on the door. The key would turn in the lock. La Fontaine would be thrown to one side. And so it was altogether a fairy world in which Caroline Matilda lived, a world thickly quilted with beauty, luxury and love. Within its limitations, this world was real enough. The nice aftertaste of the wine, the stove's warmth, the caresses of her lover were real and tangible. The fairy-story, so to speak, had become reality, a reality that could be seen and felt and touched. Caroline Matilda was not only Queen of Denmark; she was also Queen of Love.

There were at least two other people in Copenhagen, however— among a multitude, to be sure—who, unlike Caroline, were thoroughly unhappy. Although for a long time she had struggled against knowing too much, Antje Maria was unable completely to ignore the Queen's affair with Struensee. At first she had refused in horror to listen to the maids' gossiping, for though naïve, she was not simple enough to take palace gossip at face value. Ultimately Caroline herself, badly needing someone to trust and confide in, had herself introduced Antje Maria to the true situation, after which there could be no more room for doubt.

Antje Maria loved Struensee and the Queen as well. She was not jealous and did not begrudge the Queen her luck. But the Book! What did the Book say about such things? She opened her Bible and hurriedly examined its pages. The Book had a great deal to say. Moses and the prophets and even Jesus himself all had comments to offer regarding adultery. But at least Jesus had said: "He that is without a sin among you, let him first cast a stone at her."

In vain Antje Maria struggled against the magic of the Book. It was so much stronger, wiser and more experienced than she. She wept and prayed on her knees by her bed that God might forgive the lovers, even while little Luisa Augusta was sleeping nearby in her cradle. But God's word stood like a rock. The more she prayed, the more impenetrable seemed the rock.

Antje Maria was almost as fond of the King as she was of Caroline Matilda and Struensee, which made matters worse. Christian often visited the nursery, his hair, as usual, hanging in strings, his laces untied, his cheeks reddened from play with Morari. Though it was obvious to Antje Maria that the King was mad, he was still the King, the untouchable, anointed one in her eyes. She was sentimentally stirred when he bent over the child that was not his at all. Luisa Augusta always let out a squeal of delight when Christian appeared. She would reach up for the King's long hair to pull and yell in disappointment should he leave without having picked her up.

When he found the child asleep he would sit down very quietly, not speaking a word sometimes for a full hour. Having had his fill he would look about him in a daze, rise and slowly leave the room, his feet dragging.

On his first visit to the nursery he paid Antje Maria no attention, beyond looking at her sidewise in his foxy, squinty way. Indeed, at first he seemed to be afraid of her. Then the child had a spell of sickness. A monosyllabic dialogue ensued between nursemaid and King. After that he was more talkative. He inquired about Antje Maria's home, asked what her father did for a living, about her brothers and sisters. He saw her Bible and asked to look at it. He read some lines and then remarked: "It's a good book, all right. What a pity it ever got into the preachers' hands!"

Antje Maria, of course, was shocked by this peculiar sentiment. She considered it just another one of those crazy things the King was always saying. He was amused by the expression that came over her innocent face. "You don't understand that, do you," he said. "Of course you don't. But I'm by myself a lot, and I often think about such matters." He stared at her large-eyed, rather reproachfully, it seemed to Antje Maria, though she knew she had done nothing. "I'm depending on God, you see," he confided in a whisper, sending the chills up Antje Maria's spine. Then he turned abruptly, stalked out of the room and banged the door shut behind him. Antje Maria could not budge for a minute, so weak had her knees become. He knows everything, she thought to herself. She felt the King had provided an answer to the situation. Yes, God would take charge. How terrible that would be for the principals. Antje Maria was tied in a frightful knot of emotion. Her mind was all muddled, she had never been so unhappy in all her life. The sad part of it was that Christian had not been thinking of his marriage at all when he hinted a final appeal to God. It was his defeat at the hands of Brandt that had been troubling him.

And Count Rantzau, like the Queen's nursemaid, was anything but a happy man. Now that the plan had been worked out to the last dit and the consummation of his life's desire for security was in full prospect, a paradoxical uncertainty and discomfort had possessed the Count. He tried to shake off his mood of dejection, but could not. Day after day he sat at home in the Bredegade and let dismal thoughts devour his heart like a nest of worms. When Eickstedt or Koeller came to visit he feigned sickness and refused to receive them. He had the gout, he said, and it was killing him.

Ever since the conspiratorial evening at the rectory of the Holmen Church he had not been able to release the pressure inside his head. All sorts of fears bedeviled him. Supposing the plan misfired, supposing the King unexpectedly stood by Struensee and would not sign the order of arrest, supposing the King appealed directly to his soldiers over the heads of Eickstedt and Koeller. Then the plot would be condemned as treason. All of them would be locked up and face execution.

He walked to the window, and looked out into the twilight. It was a foggy afternoon, a grayness was steaming up from the melting snow. In the light cast by the lantern at the door Rantzau believed he saw the big black dog. He was lying in the gutter, or so it looked. Several times already Rantzau had had him chased away by the servants, but the ugly, stubborn beast always came back. This time the Count rushed off, cursing wildly, to his writing desk, ripped open a drawer and found a pistol. Carefully he opened the window, aimed and fired both barrels. The shots struck harmlessly into the snow. Slowly the big dog stood up, looking up at the window in the most chilling fashion. Then he laid his head back and howled towards an invisible sky.

The Count heard his servants coming on the run, his shots having attracted them. He put down the window, hurried to the stairwell, and shouted down to them. "Get that damned dog out of here at once," he roared. "You hear, you people!"

The servants came back presently, but the Count would not let them into his study. He talked to them through the door. "There isn't any dog out there, Your Excellency," a voice said.

Rantzau lost his temper. The veins on his temples swelled into thick strings. He rushed back to the window and looked out. There was no dog. Could he have imagined it before? "Well, he was there just now," he shouted through the door. "I just heard him howl." The servants said nothing to this. "Well, you did hear him howl, didn't you!" he added belligerently. "I say, didn't you?"

"No, Your Excellency," the voice answered respectfully. "We didn't hear a thing."

"Then get out of here," Rantzau screamed. "What am I paying you for, you stupid pigs!"

The servants did as he bade them. The Count listened to them clattering down the stairs. When they were safely out of hearing, of course, they would whisper about him. The Count was so sure of it that he bent down and put his ear to the keyhole. Presently he sighed, got himself in hand and began to walk back and forth, back and forth. Even if everything goes well, he thought, who's going to guarantee that Guldberg and Juliana will keep their promises? Suppose what they're really aiming at is to trap me somehow? Suppose Guldberg, Eickstedt and Koeller want to nab me for something and get rid of me?

The more he weighed these possibilities, the more likely it seemed that the whole conspiracy was intended to snare him as an enemy of the state. Why did Guldberg, for instance, squeeze those little eyes of his together the way he did? Why did Colonel Koeller laugh in that sarcastic, rough way? Would it not be better to rush to Struensee's side at once? Wouldn't Struensee be eternally thankful to him if he revealed the impending danger? But that, too, was a ticklish affair. Koeller and Eickstedt, being rude soldiers with no understanding of a grand seigneur's feelings, would think nothing of spitting him on their daggers if they ever got wind of his betrayal. And if things should go well for the conspirators despite his informing, would not this sly Guldberg monster have him prosecuted along with Struensee on charges of treason? Then, certainly, he would hang. It was a riddle with no solution, a mystery rooted in the Count's profound contempt for humanity. It was the demonism of betrayal betraying the betrayer.

On New Year's day, after the regular reception at court, shortly after the Count had formally congratulated the King and Queen according to the custom, he slipped into Struensee's rooms. "I want to tell you something, Struensee," he said without preliminaries. "You're in awful danger. I advise you to get yourself a sleigh and leave today for Malmö."

"What would I do there?" said Struensee. "To Malmö!"

"Well, then, go anywhere you like. Go to Hamburg, to Hanover, or to England, if you want to," said the Count. "It doesn't matter where so long as you get out of Denmark. The people are ready to revolt. Don't you realize it?" The Count was breathing heavily and beads of sweat ran down his temples.

"But my dear Count Rantzau!" Struensee said. "What's wrong with you? Don't you feel well?"

"Get away from Copenhagen, get out of Denmark," the Count groaned. "I beg you on my knees, leave at once."

"I simply couldn't do that," said Struensee. "Not even if I wanted to. I have to stay with the King. Furthermore, you're quite mistaken, Rantzau. The people have calmed down. The inflammatory talk has been stopped. The honest good will that I feel for Denmark is my best armor after all, Rantzau."

"My God, my God, Struensee," screamed the Count in despair. "What has good will got to do with it? What are you thinking of, talking such nonsense with your life at stake? It's a question of power. It's a question of who has the arms, the cannon, the men, horses, captains and what not. Don't you comprehend?"

"Good will and reason are the strongest powers," said Struensee. "You will see."

"How is it possible!" whispered the Count and actually wrung his hands in an extremity of frustration. "Don't you see I'm not here to philosophize with you. I'm serious, I'm here to warn you. Once again, Struensee, I'm telling you that your life hangs on a thread!"

"You're mistaken there, Count," said Struensee evenly. "Now that the palace guard has been changed, there can be nothing to worry about."

Rantzau struggled for words, and inwardly debated whether he should take the last step and reveal the conspirators by name and the plot in detail. He was about to open his mouth when Colonel Koeller came in. Rantzau shut up like a trap, and wondered dizzily whether Struensee would do the same. He saw Koeller was looking at him very coldly.

"What can I do for you, Colonel Koeller?" Struensee asked.

"His Majesty, the King, would like to see you, Count Struensee," Koeller said drily.

"Excuse me, gentlemen."

Koeller and Rantzau were left alone together. They stared at each other narrowly. At last Rantzau let out a little sigh and said: "The man doesn't know a thing, not a thing. He hasn't the least idea what's in the offing, Colonel. Take my word."

"Why," said the Colonel icily, "did you ask him?"

Rantzau laughed him off. "I was listening to him," he explained. "We have to weigh every angle, you know. Wasn't that Guldberg's advice?"

"He couldn't know anything," said the Colonel bluntly. "That is, he couldn't unless some dirty traitor has talked."

"Well, I feel sure there are no traitors among us," said Rantzau, a strange lightness in his tone. "There aren't any, I feel sure. Do you think differently, perhaps?"

"Let us hope so, sir," Koeller blustered. "For the traitor's sake, shall we say. For if anyone talked, he would have an end to remember. We'd crack his bones on the wheel. We'd impale him, sir."

"Come, come," said Rantzau. "Don't be so serious, Colonel. Let us talk of pleasanter things. Shall we?"

From this day on Rantzau was sure that he was being watched. He could have sworn that spies were following him through the streets of the city. When he turned to collar the men trailing him, always they had disappeared. During the night he would cautiously peek through the window hangings down into the street. He imagined that he saw a dark figure, hat drawn down over the eyes, leaning hard against the wall of the dwelling across the way. When he opened the window ever so gently, humming a song to himself, the figure vanished. In the slanting lantern-light he could make out nothing but the black flow of the gutter, gurgling down the street towards the drain.

Rantzau arrived at a pinnacle of unrest during the masked ball. It had been chilly all day long, but towards nightfall the wind suddenly shifted round to the west and a thaw set in. The warmish wind came in big gusts and spun the church vanes, shook house-beams and whipped tight the clothes of passersby, pinning their limbs.

Early that evening the plotters met in the Holmen Church rectory. Owe Guldberg was one of the last to arrive. With him came Prince Frederik, Christian's step-brother, hidden by a great deal of coat collar and scarf. The Prince took the seat of honor and at once registered a new complaint against Struensee. "Just think, gentlemen," he said in his humorless way, "just think what happened to me on New Year's Eve. I was just going to enter the royal box when that creature Brandt stopped me and told me with the most shameful lack of civility that the King did not care for my presence. He said that a special box had been reserved for me and my mother, off to one side. Naturally we didn't use it. I gave Brandt a nasty look, I can tell you. 'You'll rue this day, Count Brandt,' I said to him. That took the wind out of his sails. He bowed several times and mumbled something about it's not being his fault. The King had wanted it, he said. I looked right through the fellow. 'You've been a tool too long,' I said to him. 'And not of the King, either. The man you're working for is a traitor. I know who's trying to break up the royal family so he can control the King and the King's power.' That made him turn pale. And blush. Yes, he turned as red as a beet. He couldn't say a thing. He just kept on bowing and scraping like a mechanical toy."

"That was the way to talk, Your Highness," cried Colonel Koeller. "These dogs must be chained in their places."

"What intuition!" said Rantzau, *sotto voce*. "What a brain!"

"My mother and I, gentlemen, went right back to Fredensborg," the Prince continued oracularly. "Mama had tears in her eyes, gentlemen. She did, believe me. If we had ever entertained any serious doubts as to the necessity of this intervention—and, my dear sirs, I'll admit that even I have doubted—this incident erased them once and for all. I consider it an honor to be invited to meet with you people, to take my stand at the head of the movement to restore the ancient sovereignty of Denmark. I am yours, gentlemen, you can count on me. And as my mother has already told you, she is taking the responsibility of speaking tonight with the King, her son, to get him to sign the order for the arrest of Struensee and Brandt. Moreover, she tenders her royal gratitude, gentlemen, and commands you to be of good courage. You can move forward with complete confidence in her support. An undertaking so vital to the welfare of all Denmark cannot fail."

"So be it," said Chaplain Abildgaard and looked up ecstatically at the ceiling.

"May God preserve us!" cried General Eickstedt, apparently believing this the most appropriate response.

Guldberg, however, only cleared his throat. "Let us get down to particulars," he said. The officers hitched closer about the table and the chaplain left the room. In an hour everything had been thoroughly discussed and each move decided on. The conspirators left the rectory one at a time.

Rantzau waded along through wet snow. It was about nine o'clock. Melting snow gurgled in drainspouts and gutters, all Copenhagen was adrip. The streets were completely deserted. Here and there a dim light showed at a window. Oddly enough, though the night was dark as pitch, visibility was not bad at all. The icy melted snow soaked through the Count's boots. Walking along with much wiggling of his toes to squeeze the chill out of them, the Count tried to rise above the excruciating twinges of gout shooting through his bones. The Count felt rotten. He heard voices issuing from a house and something in the tone made him stop and listen. A rough female voice said: "If you get into trouble on account of it, don't come home crawling to me, you bastard." And then a male voice replied: "Not so loud, Mother, for the love of Christ! Supposing someone heard you!"

Thinking graveyard thoughts, Rantzau moved along. At every street corner, crossing every empty square, the wet wind caught at his cloak. Presently he found himself in an unfamiliar district of the city. He had lost his way in the dark. It was a section of poverty-stricken alleys, crowded with one-story houses with straw roofs. Somewhere along the way he must have taken a wrong turn. He saw a woman leaning against a doorway in shadow. Even in the darkness he was able to see that she wore a very short dress and high boots. "Where you going, stranger?" she lisped. "Come into my place. You'll find it nice and warm, stranger." And she laughed merrily to show him that this was really so.

The Count came to a full stop and asked where he was. For one crazy second he was tempted to drop the whole miserable business and bed up with the drab.

"You're in the Osterfeld, stranger," she told him and laughed foolishly.

Without a word he pushed on, slipping and sliding in the wet. Osterfeld was the district where criminals were taken for execution. Surely that was a bad sign. Suddenly everything seemed unreal to the Count, as if the scene in the rectory had happened in a dream. Everything was damp and dirty, the world was full of black and deadly bogles.

The Count tried desperately to get hold of his nervous system. He turned decisively in an opposite direction and moved towards the inner city. It simply can't happen, he told himself. Why, my life wouldn't be worth a thaler if the plot fell through. I'm going to tell Struensee. They are the traitors, not Struensee. I've got to tell him.

He went to Struensee's brother's home. The servant was shocked by the Count's theatrical expression. "The minister of justice is not at home, Your Excellency," he said. "I think he must have gone to the ball."

"But it's terribly important," Rantzau insisted, not taken in by this subterfuge. "I've simply got to see him. Would this help." And he actually slipped the astonished man a thaler.

"Perhaps I can reach him, after all," the servant said. "What shall I tell him, if he's still in?"

"Tell him that Count Rantzau wished to see him, and that he must at all costs come to my place in the Bredegade."

"Very well, Your Excellency," said the servant.

In actual fact the councillor of justice was very much at home, but had given orders not to be disturbed, for he was already behind time for the ball. When he heard that the supplicant was Count Rantzau, he said to his secretary: "I know this dreadful Count. With that fellow every hair in his nose is a state issue."

"Don't you think you ought to see what he has on his mind?" the secretary suggested. "One never knows."

"No, I don't think so," the justice said. "It can wait until morning, whatever it is." He smiled ironically at his secretary. "Come to think of it," he added, "what could it be but something to do with getting a stay on some of his debts."

Count Rantzau, having left the councillor's door, now began to experience an odd sensation. He felt as if any moment the world would physically collapse, like so much stage scenery. The world was becoming horribly insubstantial, it seemed. He pressed his hand against his throbbing temples and groaned aloud. What can I do, he thought, what can I do. He felt wonderfully potent pangs of gout, so strong they melted the stiffness right out of his backbone. I'm a sick man, he assured himself, I'm for the grave in no time. He hobbled homeward to the Bredegade, slipped as best he could out of his clothes and crawled into bed. He pulled the covers over his head and lay shivering and shaking in the darkness. Sleep would not come. He waited, without the least idea what he was waiting for.

General von Eickstedt went immediately to the barracks where the dragoons were quartered. These buildings were built onto the outside walls of Christiansborg Palace. He ran into Lieutenant Schleemann, officer of the day. Schleemann looked rather drunk. "Lieutenant," the General said, "I want you to have the horses saddled. The whole squadron. Have the troops alerted and properly dressed. I want them ready at a moment's notice."

"What's that, sir!" said the Lieutenant, clouded by wine and surprise. "Isn't everything quiet out in the city?"

"Never mind that," said the General. "I'm giving you an order."
"Very well, sir," the Lieutenant replied and came to attention.
Eickstedt hesitated a moment. "One thing, Schleemann," he
said, a fine wheedling note coming into his voice. "You'll have nothing
to regret, if you get what I mean. Now, get on with it."
"I hope not, sir," said the Lieutenant, still not comprehending. He
watched open-mouthed as the General wheeled off with a curt military goodnight.

The Lieutenant scratched his head foolishly, standing riveted
to the spot. What's the old fart thinking of, he thought. Is he striking
for a medal? Well, we all know what generals are, he said to himself
consolingly. Thank God they don't live forever. Then he felt duty
welling up within him, and went at once into the barracks.

"Attention, attention!" he roared like a herd of lions. "This is an
alert, men. Saddle your horses. Hup!" After his display of authority he
felt a trifle exhausted and twittery in the pit of the stomach. "Boy,"
he said to an orderly passing by, "fetch me a flask of cognac on the
double. This is a bloody damp night, if I ever saw one."

The guests were assembling in Christiansborg. A gentle humming
and thrumming of talk filled the ballroom. Everyone was standing
about attached to some small group, waiting for the royal couple to
put in their appearance.

It was about ten o'clock when the King and Queen entered the
spacious hall. Caroline Matilda wore an old-fashioned Spanish costume and a black veil over her platinum hair. She was prettier than
ever, so pretty that she evoked a general sigh of approval. She smiled
in all directions and seemed to be extraordinarily happy. The King,
dressed in a domino costume, gave the signal for the ball to com-
mence. The orchestra set to work and soon the floor was a great
swirl of dancers.

Christian went directly to his box and had a glass of champagne
brought to him. He talked slowly with Struensee. Very confidentially
he laid a ringed hand on Struensee's shoulder. "You're right, quite
right, Count Struensee," he said. "The upset in Copenhagen seems
to have died down. And I promise you that I'm going to sign the
decree freeing the serfs. But down there" . . . he indicated the dancers ". . . someone is waiting for you. Unless I'm mistaken, the
Queen keeps looking up here. We don't want her to fret, Struensee,
do we? One can't keep a Queen waiting, you know." Something
behind his own words made Christian smile pensively. He was still
smiling when Struensee left.

The Queen had her dance with Struensee and afterwards, as she
was standing beside her love, fanning herself, Prince Frederik arrived
late and came over to greet her.

"You got here awfully late, *mon cousin*," said Caroline.

"I had a very important piece of business to take care of, *ma cousine*," the young man retorted loftily.

"What more important business at your age," she objected, "than to dance and fall in love!"

"The younger generation is very serious, Madame," Struensee put in. "I fear they consider us, or at least myself, as terribly frivolous. Quite lost, I should imagine."

"Well, no matter," said Caroline. "For tonight, at least, I'm going to do as I please. May I have your arm, *mon cousin*? May I have the pleasure of a dance with a handsome young man?"

Struensee looked thoughtfully after them as they whirled away. Someone laid a hand on his arm, cutting off his quizzical thoughts. It was Brandt. "I'm afraid we're not going to have any champagne supper after the dance, Struensee," he said dolefully.

"Why not?"

"Frau von Holstein feels sick," Brandt told him. "And General Gaehler says he's indisposed, too."

"How odd," said Struensee, frowning. "Gaehler certainly appears to be in the best of health. Well, never mind. Let it go."

"We'll have our supper after the next ball," said Brandt.

"In any case, we'll have a good night's rest for a change," said Struensee. "To tell the truth, brother, these past few days I've been in wretched spirits. I feel terribly worried, for some reason or other."

"Is that so!" said Brandt. "Do you know, I've felt the same thing myself. What can it be? The unseasonable weather? When the southwest wind was blowing last night I felt as if I were coming down with inflammation of the lungs. I felt queer, that's all there is to it. Silly, of course. The bedclothes nearly stifled me. I even got out of bed and looked out the window. Nothing down below, of course. Just the same old black pit. The wind must have blown out the lanterns, the way it always does. I couldn't get to sleep again for the longest time. Rantzau's story kept buzzing around in my head."

"To tell the truth, I wish now I'd talked with him," said Struensee. "Tonight, you know, he wanted to get in to see my brother. Something must be up. But he didn't let him in. I have half an idea I ought to talk with Rantzau myself. It's only a few steps away, come to think of it."

"Oh, I wouldn't do that," said Brandt. "It wouldn't be worth all that trouble. Rantzau is such an old woman. He's always seeing signs and ghosties. He's jealous, too, Struensee. We know that. And what would the Queen say if you left now? Here comes Annette, too. She'll want to dance with you."

"I'll put it off till morning, then," said Struensee. "But tomorrow I'm certainly going to have a heart to heart talk with him."

"As you say."

After having danced with Annette and drunk several glasses of champagne, Struensee's misgivings faded away. The flattering jokes concocted for his benefit, the flirtatious eyes that looked his way all distracted his attention. He was trapped in a world of luxury, caught in a thicket of lush women and elegant men, in a caressing, pleasing tide of dancetime nonsense and candle gleam, a dreamy, lovely sphere lagging happily behind the fact. It flattered him tremendously to be an important part of it, it made his heart swell. It made him melt with tenderness to think that his mistress was highest in rank and most beautiful of all the lot. Time flew like magic. Each time he consulted his watch he was surprised to see that one hour, two hours had passed. As for himself, he felt as if time were standing still, as if he were dallying in eternity among a paradise of desirable women, with fine feeling and gaiety on all sides.

His glance fell on Colonel Koeller. The Colonel, for some reason or other, was staring at him with great intensity. Could the Colonel be drunk again, like the bag of wind he was? "Why aren't you dancing, Colonel Koeller?" Struensee inquired with studied offhandedness. How it tickled him to put the military, those essentially ignorant brutes, in their proper place.

"My dance begins later," said the Colonel mysteriously. His words were thick with wine.

"It must be a peculiar dance, indeed," said Struensee drily, "to wait so long for it."

"It is, sir," said Koeller. He grinned boldly through his ox-bow mustaches and showed yellow teeth.

The hours slipped away, the musicians wearied and could scarcely sit erect on their chairs. The candles, which nobody had trimmed for some time, threw less light than was proper and threatened to drown in their own drip. The couples on the floor danced ever more carelessly. Lovers by the score had sneaked off to the stalls to kiss and fondle. In many boxes the red hangings had been drawn tightly together.

Caroline left the ball at four. "I'll see you tomorrow morning," she said in passing to Struensee. "Good night, my dearest."

"Tomorrow morning," echoed her lover and bent over her hand. "Tomorrow and every day."

The ball broke up in a curious mood of hesitancy, as if something should have happened which had not. The musicians packed away their instruments, their faces the color of wet tripe. The servants began to clear away the dirty glasses and cups and set about snuffing out the hundreds and hundreds of candles.

Now the great ballroom was dark. From isolated corridors came women's laughter and snatches of homegoing conversation. A drunk sang all by himself, in singsong.

Then the whole palace was still. There was not even the sound of the watch. Indeed, that night there was no watch.

★ IX ★

*T*HE PALACE WAS all darkness and thick silence. Then, in the west wing, a shimmer of light moved along the row of windows giving out from the corridor. Leading the little procession of intruders was the wine merchant, Jessen, holding a candle. He was followed by the Queen-Dowager and her son. Juliana wore a fur cloak. Her fine, bold features, dominated by ominous brows, were set and grim. Sometimes her son glanced fearfully from one side to the other, but the mother looked straight ahead at Jessen's back.

At the critical moment Juliana had become the linchpin of the conspiracy. Her courage held the conspirators together. She alone among them would not have rushed home to bed now that the chips were down. This held even for Colonel Koeller, who was so drunk that he would not really have known the difference had he been ordered to storm the bastions of hell. General Eickstedt showed drastic signs of worry. He gnawed incessantly at his lower lip. Count Rantzau sat in a sedan chair borne by two dragoon lieutenants. At the last minute he had tried to beg off, saying that the gout was too much for him. But Koeller, who had looked him up in the Bredegade, would not be appeased. He had had to come along, even if it meant being carried. Now he lolled in the chair, gray-faced. His nose stuck out long and heavy, a pendulous thing, his gray eyes shifted with apprehension and his long, narrow hands shook as they gripped the arms of the conveyance.

Owe Guldberg and Chaplain Abildgaard brought up the rear. The chaplain was white as paper and kept his hands folded, the better to mumble prayers for his private advantage. Guldberg advanced on tiptoe. If any one of the conspirators looked like a murderer, it was he, a broad figure of a man with unruly red hair. Guldberg was armed with an enormous old-fashioned sabre which he gripped in small sweaty hands.

As they crept down the long corridor somewhere outside a cock crowed with shattering loudness. The clarion call brought them all to a halt. Rantzau groaned aloud as the bearers eased the sedan to the floor. "We'll have to hurry, gentlemen," Juliana said. "Soon it will be morning. Let us get on with our business." They hurried forward to the King's apartment.

"Don't you think it might pay to put it off for a little while," said Rantzau. No one paid him the slightest attention. After but a moment's hesitation, Juliana turned the knob, found the door open as had been planned and pressed on into the room. The others huddled along after her like sheep.

They found Christian asleep, buried in the pillows of his bed of state. His white poodle, Bellepheron, lay on the covers at his feet. The dog jumped up and crept whining over the bed. This waked Christian. He sat up, blinked, yawned and said heavily: "Is it time already, Morari?" Then he saw there was no Morari. He gave a stifled cry of fright and drew back hard against the back of the bed, holding his right arm across his breast to protect himself. "Murder!" he squeaked feebly. "Murder! Someone help me!"

"Calm yourself, my son," said Juliana. "You are all right. No one is going to harm you."

"Oh, the watch, the watch!" shouted the King. "Hey, come in here! Guards . . . here . . . help me!"

"There's no need of that," said Juliana calmly. "We've come here to save you, son, not to kill you. Now, stop that."

"I didn't ask you to come here," the King said tonelessly. "Who are all these other people. What do they want in here? Where's the guard?"

"At your service, Sire," said Colonel Koeller and moved forward in stiff officer fashion.

"Is that you Koeller?" said Christian, rather more calmly. "What's going on, pray? What are you doing in my bedroom?"

"We have discovered a plot against Your Majesty," said Juliana. "And now is the time to put an end to it. We can still cut off the traitors if you'll sign the order for their arrest, my boy."

The King looked at her with infinite mistrust. His hands folded and unfolded on the covers. "Get me a glass of water, Koeller," he said, and Koeller obsequiously filled a glass from the carafe on the night table. The King drank slowly and carefully in little sips, keeping his eyes on Juliana. "Who are they?" he asked suddenly. "Who are these plotters of yours?"

"Caroline Matilda is one of them," Juliana blurted out.

"That's a lie," said Christian. "The Queen is devoted to me."

"The Queen does not know what she is doing," Juliana said hastily. "She is only a tool for others."

"And who are they?"

"Brandt and Struensee and their whole clique, Your Majesty."

"Brandt!" said Christian. "He's a traitor, all right. He struck his king when he wasn't looking. But Struensee is my friend."

"But both of them are working together, my son," Juliana insisted. "Why didn't Struensee banish his friend Brandt from the court when he raised his hand against you? The answer is simple: they're in the thing together. Probably it was Struensee who got Brandt to strike you."

"I never looked at it that way," said the King uneasily. "No, it's impossible. Why should Struensee hate me?"

"He doesn't hate you," Juliana said smoothly. "It is merely his ambition that misleads him. He wants to depose you, Sire."

Christian looked at her incredulously, but impressed. "You seem wonderfully concerned about me all of a sudden, mother," he said. "How did you get to know all these things?"

"Don't forget that I'm your step-mother," Juliana said forcefully. "Don't forget that your father's dying wish was that I should watch out for you. And that even if you don't love me as a son should. I simply consider my life and my boy's life to be bound up inextricably with your own. Furthermore, all Europe knows about this shameful affair between your upstart barber and . . ."

"That has nothing to do with it," the King said. "That concerns me and nobody else. I have my reasons, you understand."

"Can't you see," Juliana said with rising heat, "that this adultery is at the root of the situation. Haven't you noticed how Struensee has tried to estrange you from us, your nearest relatives? Do you imagine that his ambition will ever rest content with a ministry position? Hasn't he brought about the disaffection of the whole nobility? And hasn't he turned the people against the government? And then he took away the *garde du corps,* your very last protection."

"Infantry and dragoons are just as loyal to me as the guards were," Christian objected. "Isn't that true, Colonel Koeller?"

"And because we are loyal to you," said Koeller, rapidly backing water, "both General Eickstedt and myself are here with the Queen-Dowager to offer our services in a time of dire need."

"Yes, but you people don't know Struensee," said Christian. "You can't possibly know him as well as I do."

Rantzau cleared his throat, feeling much stronger now that the showdown was actually on him. "I'm very sorry, Your Majesty," he said, "to contradict that last statement. I have heard it from his own lips and from Brandt's as well that the King must go. And even worse."

"How's that!" whispered the King. "Worse, you say?"

"They tried to get me on their side," Rantzau lied boldly. "They asked me all sorts of questions about Russia. Namely, about the accession of the Tsarina Catherine. And of course about the Tsar's demise. You know how it happened, Sire. He was strangled by the Tsarina's lover. With a napkin, I believe. Well, they wanted to know all about that affair."

"No," breathed Christian. "No, no, not that." The sweat stood out on his forehead, his lips hung slack and tremulous.

"Brandt and Struensee, as I was saying, sounded me out," lied Rantzau in his normal snoring voice. "I soon saw that their interest in Peter was anything but historical. They suggested that I make common cause with them. Brandt said" . . . and here Rantzau glanced impishly at Owe Guldberg . . . "that if you're going to make an omelette, you have to crack some eggs. The crime they were plotting against Your Majesty was only too evident. I was so afraid for Your Majesty's safety that I turned in panic to Her Highness, the Queen-Dowager. And to the Prince, her son, and such patriotic soldiers and men of affairs as you see here now in this room. I wanted to save my King. Here we are, Sire. Decide for yourself between the murderers and ourselves. The respite these criminals have allowed you is running out, Sire."

Suddenly Christian put his hands up to his face and wept, discomfiting the little group about him to the very core. The tears rolled down his face, his shoulders shook. His weakness stood out naked for all to see. Juliana stared at him with contempt and satisfaction. The candle shook in Jessen's hand. Indeed, the old man looked as if he, too, were about to cry, and Koeller, wiping the damps of agitation from his brow, looked scarcely better. Rantzau's eloquence had won the day only too handily. Christian finally removed his hands from his stricken face. His eyes glistened with wetness and were horribly out of focus and vague. He slid aimlessly out of the bed. "I'll sign that thing," he said. "Give it to me. Quick, give it to me."

Now Owe Guldberg stepped forward, dropped down on one knee and tendered the King a paper.

"Who are you?" asked the King, the paper hanging limp from his hand. Guldberg horrified him. "Who is this fellow?" he repeated hysterically. "Tell me, who is he?"

"My secretary, Guldberg," said Juliana. "A loyal subject and a Dane."

"Is he?" said Christian. "He looks like a bad egg to me. But I may be mistaken. There is no knowing about these things." He glanced at the order in his hand as if it were a live thing. "I don't know," he said, "I really don't know. I hate to do this. But every man has only one life, and he has to defend it. But where will the Queen be taken?"

"To Kronborg, Sire," said Owe Guldberg.

"She must be handled honorably," said Christian. "And what about the others?"

"They'll be put in the Citadel of Copenhagen."

"I've got nothing against that," said Christian. "Brandt will find out then what a rotten thing he did to me." He returned the paper signed, to Guldberg. "Have Morari called, you," he ordered the kneeling red-head. "His Majesty's sleep is ruined. Get to your feet, you fool."

Struensee was the first to be arrested. When they came to get him he was still lying in his ball costume, fast asleep on the bed. Colonel Koeller, accompanied by a lieutenant, burst into the room.

"You're going to regret this," Struensee said to Koeller. He was still half fogged by sleep. "You ought to know that the person of the King's first minister is inviolable."

"The King stands above the first minister," said Koeller. "He has signed an order for your arrest."

"Let me read it," said Struensee, drawing on a shoe.

"No, not at all," said Koeller, grinning widely. "It's made out to the commandant of the Citadel. Why should you read it!"

"What is the charge, sir," Struensee asked angrily.

"I don't know," said Koeller. "You're the one who should know best."

"Do you mind if I wear my fur cloak?" said Struensee.

"Do," said Koeller. "Why not."

By the time the carriage arrived at the Citadel the morning was gray. Getting out, Struensee remembered the driver. "Give that fellow up there a thaler," he said to the lieutenant.

"Thanks, old man," the coachman said flippantly, "but driving Your Excellency to this chicken coop was such a pleasure that I'd gladly do it for nothing."

General Eickstedt knocked so long and so loudly on the bedroom door that Brandt had time to get his dagger in hand prepared to defend himself. "Are you thinking of putting up a fight?" said Eickstedt with all the military menace he could muster when Brandt eventually let him in. "You'd better think twice, man. The King personally has ordered your arrest."

Brandt threw his dagger aside. "There wouldn't be much point in skewering an old gander like you," he said coolly. "What I'd like to know is what that slow-brain is up to now. Personally I fail to appreciate this little comedy."

"Come along," said Eickstedt.

"Just a minute," said Brandt. He took his flute from a drawer, took it apart and dropped the pieces into his pocket. "It appears that I'm going to sit for a while," he said, "and while I'm sitting I can tootle a tune or two, can I not, General?"

Eickstedt grinned at him. "Tootle all you want," he said. He rather thought Brandt a man of courage.

Struensee's brother, the councillor of justice, General Gaehler, privy councillor Berger and von Osten were all arrested and locked behind bars. Others were given strict orders to remain under house arrest.

By nine o'clock in the morning the *coup* was finished. Only the Queen remained in ignorance of what had happened. She was sitting in negligee, suckling her little daughter in the nursery with the lady-in-waiting Mathiessen, the maids and Antje Maria in attendance when Count Rantzau had himself announced. The Count had made a remarkable recovery from his gout. He was his old self.

"Count Rantzau? So early in the morning!" The Queen was dumbfounded. "Why, I can't see the man at this time of the day," she said.

"The Count insists on seeing Your Majesty," whispered Mathiessen.

"He insists!" said Caroline. She handed the child back to Antje Maria. "How long since Rantzau has insisted!"

"The Count says he comes on the King's command," the lady-in-waiting explained.

"So that's it," said Caroline Matilda. "Then I'm lost. They've done it. I know they have."

At this point Count Rantzau came in. He had been mortified when the others had insisted he take charge of this most objectionable phase of the project. Now it seemed it might be rather amusing after all. "Kindly put your clothes on, Madame," he said affably. "I regret to inform you that you're under arrest."

"How dare you talk like that to me!" screamed Caroline. "I want to see Count Struensee." She ran to the rear door of her apartment. It was locked. In fact, Rantzau had locked it himself, and had the key in his pocket.

"You cannot see Count Struensee, Madame," said Rantzau. "The Count has changed his address. He's living in the Citadel at present, Madame."

"I want to see the King," the Queen sobbed. "He will help me, I know he will."

"The King does not want to see you, Madame," said Rantzau. "Indeed, that is exactly why he sent me."

"Get away from me," said the Queen. "The sight of you disgusts me."

Rantzau's long inquiring face turned dark crimson with shame. He controlled himself, however, and said in protest: "I recall the time when your sensibilities were not quite so delicate, Madame."

Without warning Caroline now ran to the window, even as Rantzau's slur was still floating about the room, and tried to open it. But she could not jump out. She had trouble with the window and the maids held her by her clothing. She lacked the strength to fight them off.

"Be reasonable, Madame," Rantzau implored. He was alarmed. "Submit to the King's will and it will be much better for you."

"The King!" Caroline was beside herself. "Don't mention his name to me. I've always despised him. I'll never give way to him."

"That's hardly the way to talk about your husband, Madame," Rantzau said. "He might take exception to remarks like that, I should think. And please don't be so excited. As a gentleman I'm willing to overlook your extravagances."

"Gentleman! You're no gentleman," said Caroline recklessly. "You're a coward and a rascal and you know you are."

"Why does Your Majesty insist on discussing my shortcomings," said Rantzau. "There's really no point in it. It would be much better if Madame dressed. Or shall I order the maids to dress Madame forcibly. That I certainly do not want to do." Rantzau was looking with unfeigned interest at the Queen in undress. One of her breasts was definitely visible. How smooth her hair, how large her distracted eyes. A wonderful, prime piece, thought the Count, I'd give ten thalers for it, I'd risk my neck, by God.

The Queen caught Rantzau in the act of measuring her charms. "Get out of the room," she said viciously. "Get out of here, you coward."

"You've been placed in my charge, Madame," said Rantzau, "and if I weren't so zealous about your welfare, your attitude might very well irritate me, in which case I wouldn't think of getting out, or anything like it. But if Madame so wishes, I'll turn my back. Even though my eyes are as good as the next fellow's."

So saying Rantzau did turn his back and pretended to examine an etching, hanging all framed in golden scrollwork on the wall. The Queen finally allowed the maids to dress her. Her breasts rose and fell in spasms of unhappiness. Sobs caught in her throat, tears rolled down her cheeks profusely and her nose turned quite red. While the maids were tying her bodice, she stepped closer to the mirror and hastily powdered herself. She thought for a moment, then drew the heavy diamond ring from her finger and threw it on the table. She opened a small leather box and took out the old-fashioned garnet cross that Struensee had given her. This she put about her throat. "Well, I'm ready," she said, speaking to Mathiessen.

The Count tried to keep the greed from his eyes. She held her head proudly and had regained her ordinary queenly composure. "Would Madame like to take my arm?" he asked hopefully. For reply Caroline brushed past him, saying nothing, looking straight ahead. Her women followed behind, Antje Maria carrying the little princess.

Early in the afternoon of the same day a heavy black coach drew into Helsingoer, accompanied by a detachment of Zealand dragoons wearing the regiment's green uniform. The Queen occupied the rear seat of the coach, sitting next to Mathiessen. On the opposite seat was Antje Maria, holding the infant princess. And next to her was Lieutenant Schleemann, a naked sabre held between his knees. The young man looked miserable. Now and then he glanced, eyes full of wonder and sadness, at his beautiful queen.

She paid no heed either to him or to his sabre. He noticed that every time her fingers wandered up to her throat to play with the garnet cross a painfully tender smile would creep over her lips.

Lieutenant Schleemann, eighteen years of age, was very susceptible to pretty women. Just to look at Caroline made him swallow a lump as large as a pigeon's egg. Afterwards, having looked, he would stare out the window in order to collect his wits. It was snowing fitfully. The sound was gray as death and the Swedish coast hidden by overcast. The road turned sharply and Kronborg hove into view, rising up behind mighty walls, with a renaissance tower toppling high over gabled roofs. They were at the end of their journey.

BOOK FOUR

Fullness of Time

"Arise, Ethintus, tho' the earth-worm call,
Let him call in vain,
Till the night of holy shadows
And human solitude is past."
                          Blake

"The crowd, the mass, the mob, the world-historical
  conflict are left outside."
                          Kierkegaard

★

FOR THE FIRST TIME in his life, Struensee was really alone. In other years, of course, he had been physically alone, in his study in Altona, in his coach riding over the back roads of Holstein, at night in Frederiksborg. But in these situations, solitary though he might be, a thousand hopes and plans had buoyed him up. Now it was a different story. He sat in his dungeon like a frog in a well. Heavy damp walls constructed of huge stone blocks shut him off irrevocably from the outer world. Water was dropping somewhere all the time. The drops seemed to hesitate just before letting go. Each drop was separated from the next by a considerable interval, as if measured off by a slow pendulum geared to an intolerably slow flow of time. Struensee listened with every nerve to the drip of water. He felt that he was almost grasping the mystery of time itself, essential time. How heavily it dripped. How much more inexorable, pitiless, imperious it was than the ordinary minutes and hours, the kind spent in sunlight or candlelight and read off the dial of his watch.

Struensee stared at the bare walls. Horror was cramping his heart. For a moment the sickly notion came over him that already he was dead and gone. Johann Friedrich Struensee was no more. He was lost in a flood of nothingness, drowned in eternal nullity. He braced himself, threw back his shoulders. He looked around carefully to find his bearings. A dull half-light came through a round barred window high in the wall and was all but cut off by the heavy arches of the ceiling. The cell was very scantily furnished. They had given him a rickety wooden table, a three-legged stool on which he now sat and a bed of naked planks covered with straw. Even this much comforted him, however. At least the objects about him were put there for his personal use, and would buttress his personality. He was still something more than nothing at all.

Hollow steps drew near, a key rattled in the lock, the rusty wards squealed as the key turned and the heavy cell door swung back. An elderly man stood in the opening, a big key-ring dangling from his hand as if it grew there. His unshaven cheeks were deeply seamed and hollowed out. The eyes lay deep in the skull, and the face was pale as wax from many years spent amid lightless, airless spaces. He was a very tall fellow, all bent over and—this particularly attracted Struensee's attention—several buttons were missing from his shabby blue uniform.

"I'm called Juel," the newcomer said in a ridiculously deep voice. "I've brought you some water." He reached Struensee a clay jug and the prisoner drank deeply. The water was sweet and at once it refreshed him. His old energy seemed to come flowing back. "Thank you, Juel," Struensee told the warder.

"An order, an order from up there," said Juel softly in a basso rumble and pointed with his finger. "It's your water if you want it."

"They're treating me like a common criminal," said Struensee, suddenly remembering. "What's the idea of that?"

"Your Excellency has a very good cell," said Juel. "Norcroso was the last to use it before you came."

"I've never heard of him," said Struensee. "I am not an authority on criminals."

"He was the pirate," said Juel, scratching his old head ceremoniously. "He operated mostly in the West Indies and was captured by the navy. He'd plundered several vessels, they say, and killed a great many people. But take him by and large and he was a cultivated man. A man of the world, I'd say. It was always a pleasure to hear him tell a story, Your Excellency."

"What happened to him?" Struensee asked, wondering why he asked when of course he already knew, more or less.

"He stayed here three years," said Juel. "Then he was hanged. He was a good looking man, like yourself, if I may say so, Excellency. Quite different in appearance, however. He had black curls and rings in his ears. The girls in Copenhagen, they tell me, cried in the street when they were carrying him off to the scaffold. He decorated the cell with his coat-of-arms, as he called it." Juel pointed a skinny forefinger. "There you are," he said. "That's Norcroso." Someone had drawn the skull and crossbones in several different places by scratching the design into the stone.

"Well, I suppose he got what he deserved," said Struensee.

"He did," Juel admitted somberly. "In fact, Excellency, everybody that comes here as the King's guest gets about what he deserves. But . . ."

"But what?" said Struensee. His voice wobbled in his throat.

"Oh, it was just something that popped into my mind," said Juel. "I never could see why all the people running around free on the outside should never get a taste of it inside here once every so often. God knows they're mean enough to deserve it. A little peace, a little time to think things over would do them all a world of good. When you come right down to it, God didn't create them just to put things over on other people the way they do and make their wives big with child whenever they have a mind. You see, in here it's just like being in church. Yes, it would do everybody a lot of good to pay us a visit."

"You seem to be a philosopher of sorts," said Struensee, and was nettled, whether by himself or by the jailer—he could not decide.

"No, I'm not," rumbled Juel pontifically. "I'm just another spared monument of God's mercy, sir. But what I'm trying to say is that this place either breaks your spirit, or improves it. You either fall to pieces, or you're saved."

Struensee looked at his jailer, quite stupefied by his evangelical demeanor.

"But we really have to get a move on now, Your Excellency," Juel went on. "Otherwise I'm going to get into all kinds of trouble with the smiths. Those people have no more feeling than their hammers, if I do say so."

They left the cell and wandered through a labyrinth of passageways. They crossed stony courts, they trudged up and down stony flights of stairs. Eyes watched them as they passed the barred slits let into the cell-doors, curious eyes, malicious ones, sad ones, indifferent ones. In one cell was a very young woman who pressed her face hard against the barred slit. Her hair hung about her face and she was as pallid as hoptoad's belly. "Give me my child, give me back my child," she shrieked at Struensee. "Give him to me, please!"

Juel stopped in his tracks. "Now, Karen, don't be so insulting," he said. "Watch your tongue." Then to Struensee he said: "That one murdered her child. Now she accuses all the prisoners of having done it. That's human nature for you. She's just turned sixteen years old, too."

"Horrible, horrible," muttered Struensee. He felt very queasy. "What will they do to someone like that?"

"Tomorrow or the next day they'll take her out and drown her," he whispered into Struensee's ear. "You know, the same way she drowned the baby in the tub. An eye for an eye, a tooth for a tooth. That's how it is here with us, Excellency."

"And you call it a church of sorts?" Struensee joked. "A fine, fine church, indeed!"

"Yes, but it's more than a church, of course," Juel insisted. "It's a place of justice, too, is it not?"

The fellow's cracked, Struensee thought to himself. If I keep listening to him, I'll be as bad as he is.

Eventually they arrived at an open space, a square hole shut in by high walls, and open to the sky above, which showed as a little square of oyster gray. Three workmen were awaiting their arrival, three roughs in much-mended hose and thick shoes. Despite the cold their grimy calves and hairy chests were bravely exposed to the weather. A charcoal fire burned bright in the forge. One of them stepped up without delay to the bellows and blew up the fire. The other, looking at Juel, pointed to a great variety of chains hanging from pegs on the wall. "Fifty pounds?" the man inquired. "Fifty-five?"

"Fifty," said Juel. He pinched Struensee softly on the arm to get his attention. "Norcroso had a hundred," he said, "but he was much more strongly built than Your Excellency. Going to sea developed his body."

"Hands or feet?" the smith asked.

"Both," said Juel.

The man with the hammer selected a chain and let it slither like a heavy snake to the floor. Taking an end he passed it around Struensee's wrists and ankles, repeating the measurements to the man at the bellows. "Six inches, eight inches."

It was just like being measured for a suit. Presently a section of the chain was ready. They fixed it on Struensee, pulling him this way and that, slapping him on the shoulder to show him the way they wanted him to turn, as if he were a horse being shod. They handled him neutrally, with neither sympathy nor malice. They, too, were prisoners like himself. Wearily Struensee closed his eyes and let the smiths have their way with him. From a great distance a deep, powerful roar seemed to be coming to him, like the roar of a distant crowd. Horrified, he opened his eyes. For a moment he thought he was hearing a chorus, chanting an antiphony to his humiliation. But of course that was only a fancy.

The people had gathered in great numbers in the streets of Copenhagen when Struensee's arrest was made public. Rejoicing over the first minister's downfall good burghers and their wives celebrated what they sincerely believed was the end of their misery. Everybody put on holiday garb for the occasion. The crowd was straining to see into the King's coach, just then winding through the city in ceremonial procession.

Leading the way were dragoons of the Zealand cavalry regiment, preceded by their regimental standards and their musicians, drumming out a lively march tune on drums slung on either side of the saddle, blowing wildly on brass horns. Behind them came a large contingent of flunkies and running-lackeys. Then came the carriage of the King, a very impressive vehicle, excessively gilded, windows glittering, roof crowned with the Dannebrog. Eight white horses pulled this magnificent coach. Within King Christian and Prince Frederik sat on silk cushions. The crowd went mad with joy. Women were so moved by the royal spectacle that they wept.

The Prince bowed constantly to right and left, beaming graciously but with just the right note of *hauteur*. Christian crouched in the other corner, quite unimpressed by the commotion, mutely staring straight ahead. Now and then he reached down to feel for his poodle, Bellerophon, who lay buried under his knees. Sometimes he nervously stroked the broad, light-blue band of silk across his breast. Now he turned to his step-brother and said: "Have the coachmen use their whips. Clear away that crowd and let's move along. I'm getting sick of this nonsense."

The Prince, without interrupting his bowing, found time to throw a shocked look at the King.

"Why are you looking at me that way, you fool," said Christian. "I want to be alone, and the devil take you. I want to think. This shouting and screaming is getting on my nerves. Something must have made the people excited. I'll have to speak to Struensee."

"Sire," the Prince hissed softly into the King's ear, "I've told you twenty times that Struensee has been arrested. That is why the people are cheering."

"Mon dieu! I know you have," retorted Christian. "But the question is, why was he arrested in the first place?"

"What's wrong with you," the Prince said impatiently, and made a toothy grimace at the whole world to cover up. "You yourself signed the order for his arrest, Sire. He was threatening Your Majesty's person."

"Was he?" said Christian. "That was ungrateful of him, if it's really true. But I forgive him, anyway. So long as he comes to see me when I have one of my bad times. He's got to do that."

Why, he's really beyond understanding anything, the Prince thought, and grimaced some more to hide the thought. "The people have demanded that he be removed from office," he said aloud, "and this has been done."

Christian meditated this fact. "Well, I suppose it serves him right," he said. "He never stopped bothering me about the people. It was the people want this and the people want that. Rights, representation, freedom, land, equal opportunity, I never heard the like of it. Now he knows what they're like, those precious people of his." The King chuckled to himself. "You know, *mon cousin,*" he said in an aside, "as a matter of fact, I, personally, don't really like anybody except Bellerophon and Morari. Thank God Bellerophon is a poodle and Morari a nigger. Thank God, I say, for small favors."

"I am most grateful, Sire," said the Prince grandly, "for honoring me with your candor. You have an elegant way of expressing yourself, I'm sure."

Christian did not even hear this retort. He was lost in himself again. His fingers strayed mechanically over the poodle's woolly hide.

Behind the King's carriage marched the Copenhagen mob. They had made a garishly colored dragon out of wood and paper, a huge figure that opened its jaws and emitted clouds of steam. At either side were men carrying placards giving notice that the mock beast was: "Count Struensee, the dragon Apollyon, who would devour all Denmark." This dragon attracted more attention even than the King's coach. Everyone cried something about death to the monster, death to Struensee, or the like. The poorest folk and the most thoroughly disenfranchised easily gave out the loudest and most blood-curdling curses.

It was the roar of this crowd that had come on the wind to Struensee in the Citadel courtyard. Although he could not distinguish a single word, and though the sound came to him more like the roar of distant surf than a sound of human origin, he correctly intuited its meaning.

Now Juel led him back to his cell. He walked very slowly, weighted down by the unaccustomed chains. Once again the row of eyes stared at him as he passed by the gratings, but this time he paid no notice and the child-murderess did not scream at him.

He was glad, infinitely glad, to be back again in his own dungeon space. He tried to sit down on the three-legged stool but the chains toppled him over. So he lay down on the planks and stretched out. Juel showed him how best to arrange himself, skillfully distributing the weight of the iron. "Sleep at your ease, Excellency," he said in his mild, deep way.

And Struensee did try to sleep. It took a long time for sleep to come. He shifted his position again and again, attempting to discover the one comfortable position, but no matter, he could not forget the chafing drag of the chains. At last, however, he was able to doze fitfully. Almost at once he had a sickly dream, in which it seemed that a monstrous weight was bearing down on his heart, a weight that he understood to be the weight of the earth. Horribly confused, feeling it more than seeing it with his eyes, he realized that what was pressing him down was not only the earth but an immense cross. This astonished him.

He strained in his dream to be free of the load. But the weight increased and would not be budged. Then, still in his dream, he saw a child near his three-legged stool. At first he thought it must be the murdered child, but after an analysis costing him so much effort that it made him sweat, he realized that it could not be that child. For that one was a baby, and this one already four or five years old. Moreover, its hair was cut short and it was plainly a Jewish child.

Could it belong to Juel? In his nightmare Struensee decided that was impossible, again after laboriously racking his brains, virtually exploring the whole universe of pros and cons. It was a completely incomprehensible child, conjured out of nothing.

It was, indeed, much less a particular, individual child, than it was childhood itself.

And yet, Struensee thought, it was also an individual, a little being in its own right with a pale face and very large black eyes, a creature with a specific look and set of features. Struensee, as so often comes about in a dream, saw the child's face rapidly alter before his eyes. It had a great number of alternative appearances, it seemed.

Therefore it was impossible to say whether the child was looking at him or, like himself, dreaming. Whatever the child's intent, its eyes were looking right through Struensee, as if he offered no more obstruction than a pane of glass. Likewise it was quite impossible to tell whether the child was well or ill disposed towards him. Yes, it was impossible to say even whether the child knew properly that he was there.

This conclusion did not upset Struensee in his dream. Secretly he hoped that the mysterious child would disappear as soundlessly and suddenly as it had appeared. For he felt that the invasion of his cell by a child, even though the child behaved so quietly, was a damnable injustice. The intrusion made him as bitterly indignant as had his arrest, his imprisonment, his enchainment and the whole vista of betrayal. He noted very clearly, although he disliked admitting it to himself, that the external painfulness and danger seemed of far less importance, and of different dimension, than the mute, intimate presence of the child.

He debated whether he should not dismiss the child, using some stern and yet not essentially unkind expression of disapproval, and as he was thinking this over he suddenly realized, or so believed, that the child had said something to him. Who else could have spoken? It must have been the child.

Whatever else might have been said Struensee caught only a single word. His name and no more. Struensee, the child had said. Struensee. He heard the cry clearly now, not with his ears alone but also with his heart. It was horribly mysterious, eerie, this calling out of his name. It was a gentle, but very penetrating and resonant sound. Hearing it filled him with terror, although actually his name had not been uttered in a threatening or a complaining way. Rather, the sound suggested a warning, with a quiet undernote of menace.

This cry was so moving that it waked Struensee. His heart was thumping wildly. He heard the cry echo far off somewhere, either in himself or outside himself, he could not tell. His whole body was like a tuning fork, suddenly struck a smart blow, so perfectly and sharply that it would not stop vibrating for the longest time imaginable.

What was it, what made him feel so strange? Struensee asked

himself the same question again and again, lifting himself awkwardly from his pallet. It was dark in the cell, the light from the high round window had disappeared. Outdoors it must be night, though what time of the night he could not tell. He walked about the cell, clanking his chains. Then he fell over the stool, and struck the floor hard. The chains bit into the flesh of his ankles, grinding the very bone. For the first time now the utter hopelessness of his situation struck him full force. He wallowed in misery. Almost eagerly he thought of his certain death, of the tortures and martyrdom that his enemies would gradually prepare for him. Would it not be better to do away with himself now?

All manner of terrible experiences lay in wait for him. But the most terrible, he felt just then, was that the child should come again and call out his name. What then? What could he say in reply to this intolerable summons? The other thing, that is, his enemies and his chains and humiliation, the other thing was bad enough, but against them he could pose his pride, his knowledge that he was suffering for the sake of a good idea, an idea which, though proscribed and spat upon for the time being, tomorrow might very well be prized by all classes, from the lowest to the highest. But this did not satisfy him as it should have. It was not enough to be martyred for humanity's sake. He suspected the unreality of his construction. That dreadful calling out of his name had confused the whole issue. The world after death had communicated with him. That was it. The world beyond was not, as he had always believed, a nothingness. It was a fabulous reality; it was now revealing itself to him, flooding in on him. His ideas and sentiments paled before this ultimate reality, his belief in the primacy of reason and the perfectibility of men, his faith in progress and the viability of mundane happiness. His whole outlook on life now wavered, thanks to the child, lost contour, became a sort of mirage.

Fear of death filled Struensee, now that death had ceased to be a state of not-being, as he had previously fancied it. And because he was afraid of the reality of the new kind of death that the child of the dream had announced to him, desperately he sought to restore the old familiar reality of death, which had been the focal point of all his previous thinking, the indispensable construct. Unable to do this he cried out and raised up his chains, as a flirtatious woman lifts up her skirts. Even as he did this he thought to himself, I am going mad, I cannot stop it. With that he lowered his head and ran like a bull full tilt against the stone wall.

The wall bounced him back with tremendous painfulness. His head rang and boomed with pain. He collapsed and lay still for a half hour or more. There seemed to be a great hammer at work inside his head. But below this massive pulse of pain fear was still there, crouching, waiting, unmoved. The discrepancy was so frightful that again he cried out in agony. Still crying and raving he struggled to his feet, again gathered up his chains and tottered head on against the wall. Immediately he slid unconscious to the floor.

When he came to there was a light in his cell. It was Juel bending over him with a candle and fixing his chains in a more comfortable position. The jailer had dragged him onto his pallet. "Your Excellency, I'm ashamed of you," he told Struensee. "You can't keep up this sort of thing, you know. You can't run away from yourself no matter how you try. Haven't you got more self-trust? Norcroso never tried to do anything like that. Of course, he did try to kill himself, in a way. But not your way. He had both *savoir-vivre* and *savoir-mourir,* my friend."

"To hell with you and Norcroso," said Struensee weakly. "To hell with everything." His head was a ball of pain.

"Wait now, wait," said Juel, greatly concerned. "Think what you're saying, Count. Everything covers a lot of ground, my friend. Be more careful what you commit yourself on."

"Well, then, to hell with you and your idiotic gabble," said Struensee. "I want to be alone. I have a right to. Every prisoner has. I demand that you keep children out of my cell. I won't have them staring at me and shouting my name just as they please. You hear me, Juel? Take that child away from here."

"But what child are you talking about!" said Juel. His long, baggy face drooped with concern. "Anyway," he said confidentially, "if there is a child in here, he will do you no harm."

"I refuse to listen to your comments, I can get along without them very nicely," said Struensee deliriously. "It's not a question of having harm done me. I just don't want that child around, that's all. Don't stick your nose into my private affairs, either. Don't be so damnably condescending and instructive. Anyway, who's really talking about a child! It was only a dream. It had nothing to do with you. It's my business and nobody else's. And how is it that you speak French? You and your *savoir-mourir!* Where did you pick that one up? An ignoramus like you." Sheer weakness cut him off. But for it he would have babbled on and on and endlessly. Anything to get that thing out of his mind. How weak and sick he felt. Far, far better to die. Now Juel was talking again. The voice came from far away.

"Please, Count Struensee," he was saying, "don't worry about me." On and on the old man talked, on and on, from far away. "You're quite right," he went on to say, "I am an ignorant man and I don't mean a thing to anybody. I'm a jailer and that's all. But I do take a certain interest, a certain pride, you might say, in my prisoners. When they brought you here, I knew right off that you were something special, just like Norcroso. You can learn a lot from His Excellency, I told myself, something besides a few scraps of French. I handle the rest of them, the run of the mine thieves, murderers and what not, with care enough; but I squander my full attentions only on the very few, the lucky ones."

"You're a miserable bastard," said Struensee through teeth clenched to hold back the pain. "Don't you ever stop talking. Go away, go away."

Juel swallowed hard, making a peculiar and ridiculous sobbing sound. His Adam's apple ran up and down as if greased. "It's very unpleasant for me," he said foolishly, "to be so completely misunderstood. But I can appreciate it. I often consider myself repulsive."

"You are repulsive," said Struensee. "Defend yourself if you have a good conscience."

"Are you talking to me?" said Juel.

"To you," said Struensee.

"Yes, but who can really say that he has a good conscience," said Juel. "You ask too much."

"Don't get me mixed up with your preaching," said Struensee. "I hate superstition. I hate it, I hate it. And you stink with it. It's running out of your ears." He struck the wooden table with his fist, making the chains clank loudly. Suddenly, just for a moment, he felt wonderfully strong, wonderfully restored. "If you keep up this jibber-jabber," he told the jailer, "before you know it we'll be arguing the question of original sin and the immaculate conception."

"But Your Excellency brought up the subject," Juel reminded him.

"Beg pardon," said Struensee automatically carefully feeling his bruised skull and laughing all at the same time. "I suppose you are a decent enough fellow under the skin."

Juel's Adam's apple commenced to trolley up and down. "You can just leave me out of it, Count," he said. "There are more important things to think of."

"To say the least," said Struensee. And then he added, on curious impulse: "Are you still angry with me?"

"No, I should say not," Juel assured him.

"Then if you aren't tell me what you think about that child I saw," said Struensee urgently. "It seemed terribly important to me for some reason or other."

"It is," said Juel. "I'm not exaggerating when I say that the coming of the child is the most important thing that can happen in a man's whole lifetime. But personally I don't know anything about the child. He has never showed himself to me."

"I see," said Struensee. "And why do you suppose he picked me out to come to, then?"

"Oh, you're not the only one, Count Struensee," said Juel. "As a matter of fact, Norcroso saw him, too."

"He did!" said Struensee. "Why, and he was a murderer, you say."

"The child likes to come to murderers," said the jailer triumphantly. "He likes to visit the women, too, I've noticed. Now, there's nothing strange about that. Remember, Excellency, there was a time— I was very young then, of course—when men committed murder out of longing for the child. If I am a terrible sinner, they said to themselves, the child has got to come to me."

"Incredible," mumbled Struensee. "But tell me, Juel, does this child ever appear to anyone outside the prison?"

"Yes, he appears everywhere," said Juel. "There's no telling when it will happen. But he prefers to come to those who can see no way out of their troubles. And he always comes to people when they're alone."

"Then he doesn't make his appearance in churches?" said Struensee ironically.

"Well, he might come there. I wouldn't know about that. I suppose it's quite possible. But the people wouldn't see him then in any case. Because in church they consider themselves to be too good, too safe. They don't need him there."

"So you're trying to make me understand that the child comes only under the most pressing spiritual circumstances," insisted Struensee.

"That's what I'm trying to say," said Juel, pleased. "Now that you mention it, I see it clearly. Yes, you're quite right. I knew that I'd learn something important from Count Struensee."

"What are you driving at now?" asked Struensee.

Juel looked down at the floor. "The child called to you," he said thickly. "Is that not so?"

Struensee felt himself turning weak and pale. His head was throbbing, a surf was inside his head. He could get no more words off his tongue. He struggled and finally managed to laugh raucously. "Why," he said with sudden fluency, "it's nonsense, sheer nonsense. It all comes from being stuck here all alone in the darkness. It comes from the damp on the walls, by God. There really isn't any child, of course. I was only talking, you know, only talking. Just talking."

Juel, holding the candle immobile, still looked down at the floor. "Go away, now, get out of here," Struensee ordered in his old voice of command. "Keep your insanities to yourself, my good man. Let me think."

"What a pity," said Juel.

"A pity!"

"That our pride is so strong," said the jailer. "I thought the Count had stepped over the threshold."

"So you did, then," said Struensee. "I don't know what threshold

[313]

you're talking about. The only threshold that I'm ever going to cross is the one in this cell. And when I do, I won't be coming back. I'm going back to Christiansborg, Juel, old cock. You'll see!"

The jailer left without a goodbye and Struensee balanced precariously on his three-legged stool. "My God, my God," he said to himself, "I must be a weak character to fall to pieces the very first days. I've still got friends. There's Caroline Matilda. She'll help me. I'm not really lost until I give up. Christ, my head, my head."

Feverishly, trying hard to ignore the muffling effect of the pain, he began then and there to plan his defense. He imagined glowing words of self-justification, so eloquent that they brought tears to his eyes. He virtually convinced himself that his imprisonment had been an awful mistake. In a few days, or at the most in a week or two, he would again be a free man. The worst that could happen to him would be banishment from Denmark. He resolved to accept the future with good heart. Once free he would move to France. In France men of spirit abounded. It was there that he belonged, not in backward, mean-souled Denmark, where nobody understood or appreciated his ideas. Come right down to it, his imprisonment wasn't such a bad thing, after all. Why, it was really a piece of luck. It opened the way up to broader, more fruitful fields of endeavour.

Once again he stretched out on his planks. The chains annoyed him, but he carefully divided their tug to make them bearable. Through the haze of pain he thought in fragments about all the other men who, for championing freedom and enlightenment, had rotted in fortresses, dungeons, galleys and the like. He thought about Campanella, Galileo, Bruno and Huss. He thought about Voltaire.

No doubt about it, he was cast of the same fine metal. This thought filled him with pride and confidence. Only in the very recesses of his soul, hardly perceptible, and quite unaccountable, he was conscious of a remnant, a splinter of despair. But compared with his self-induced wave of exaltation, a wave that encompassed whole peoples and whole epochs, this small nag was too insignificant to mention.

Before he dropped off to sleep he heard the regular drip of water on stone. It no longer irritated him. It was comforting, even. He felt hidden in time, pleasantly bedded in it. So long as time remained all was not lost and all might be won.

What he had really feared, though now he no longer admitted it, what had really flickered for a moment at the threshold of his awareness, was the hard truth that release from his torments, release from the complications of his life, indeed, release from life itself, lay quite outside time.

★ II ★

A WHOLE MONTH passed before Struensee learned the alleged reasons for his being thrown into prison. It was hard for him to get used to the chains, the constant twilight of the cell, the bad air, but he did his best. Sometimes he gave way to fits of depression. Again, there were times when he was positive that any moment the cell door would open and he would be allowed to step forth a free man.

The first couple of weeks, particularly, the attacks of despair were acutely devastating. He tore a silver button from his clothes and tried to swallow it. Juel carefully snipped off the rest of the buttons. Knife and fork were taken away from him. For a time Juel cut up his meat and fed it to him as if he were a child. He tried a second time to do away with himself by smashing his head against the wall. For this he was forced to wear an iron helmet until he showed signs of cooling off, which he rapidly did.

Spring had come early. During his walks in the courtyard he watched the little white clouds sailing across the sky. A fresh breeze sometimes blew down over the walls, bringing with it the tantalizing smell of canal water and of the green stuff growing on the banks. Once he heard a bird singing madly, as if for him alone. The will to live waxed strong in him. He continued to plot his defense. He asked for paper and ink, and these were given him.

The worst part of it was that he had always to grope along in the dark. He had no exact idea of why he was in prison, of what the specific charges would be. He feared that his brother, the councillor of justice, as well as Brandt and Rantzau, must be suffering a fate similar to his own. And why was it that Caroline Matilda never wrote to him, never even sent a message? Why didn't she send someone, Antje Maria, for instance, to explain what was going on and ease his mind.

He tried to pump the jailer, Juel. But the Citadel and its unhappy population were the whole world for Juel. Even if he had dared to talk, he would not have been able to contribute much information, for he looked on everything that happened on the outside as meaningless. Men in a condition of freedom simply did not interest him. When Struensee listened, all sickly attention, to Juel's stories, he had the horrible sensation that Denmark was populated exclusively by a breed of criminals. This demonic race, in Juel's concept, came to the Citadel, as it were, to find peace and respite from their perverted occupation. They were still criminals while in prison, of course, but at least they had either been judged and sentenced, or were about to be.

And from Juel's point of view, punishment was the preliminary to release into a higher state of humanity, it was a literally expiatory institution. And the curious thing was that Juel's bizarre outlook began to affect Struensee, not so much because of the grain of wisdom in it, as because it seemed to the prisoner to stem from the jailer's essential kindness and sense of justice. Indeed, Juel was always doing Struensee some small favor.

Matters finally reached a pitch where Struensee, like Juel, became estranged from the outer world and inclined to find fault with what now appeared to be its fantastic, stubborn disorder. In the Citadel if there was nothing else, there was order, barren though it might be. Rising in the morning, eating, exercising, retiring—all were part of a fixed schedule. Punishments were meted out punctually at ten in the morning, and most usually consisted of ten strokes with the rod. In the outside world, Struensee would remind himself, one day the serf might get twenty-five strokes, the next fifty, the next none at all. There was no set rule. This chaos repelled Juel. And though Struensee saw the humorous side of the jailer's argument, he came to regret most bitterly the pandemic disruption of the outer world. This disorder, for example, accounted for the endless postponement of his trial.

The same chronic condition of muddle, he thought, explained why Caroline Matilda did not lift a hand to aid him. Caught up in the whirl, she had simply forgotten him. Court balls, masks, hunts and Brambilla's magic lantern shows were more important to her, it seemed, than her dearest friend's plight. How it hurt him, sickened him. Yet he could not completely satisfy himself with such a glib explanation. When he remembered the actual Caroline, when he saw in retrospect the tender eyes, the gentle hands, he was no longer sure.

A morning finally came when Juel arrived at the cell in a state of flutter and agitation. The hearing was going to begin, he said. Struensee received this piece of news with profound emotion. It made him weak as water. The hour of vindication had come. Sitting in the coach taking him to the examining magistrate, he chewed his nails until the fingertips bled. A thousand things boiled and seethed in his mind.

The chains were taken off his arms and legs. It was wonderful. He felt so featherly light that it seemed the merest breath of wind could carry him away. A bench was shoved forward and he was ordered to sit down. It was richly upholstered and it was all Struensee could do to stop himself from stretching out on it and going to sleep on the spot.

Examining magistrate General Hobe sat behind his table—a large affair covered with green cloth and provided liberally with law books, ink wells, legal documents, quills and the like. The magistrate was flanked by his assistants, Braem and Bolle.

For the grand occasion Hobe wore his general's uniform, this decorated with gigantic epaulets. He was a fleshy man, gray-haired, a network of blue veins on his face. His assistants Braem and Bolle were both thin, pedantic fellows and in the court room looked as much alike as two peas in a pod. Throughout the entire hearing Struensee never got it properly straight in his mind which one was Braem, which Bolle. They looked like caricatures of the two kinds of law, common and statutory. Boredom, utter boredom, was on their faces, a profound, penetrating disinterest in humanity.

"It would be much better, Count, if you made a detailed confession," the General began. "This would make it much easier for the court and certainly lighten your punishment."

"What crime am I charged with?" Struensee asked. "And why do you talk of punishment before I have been judged guilty?"

"You are accused of high treason," said Hobe quietly and wrinkled his forehead.

"Against the Danish King and the Danish people," said Bolle.

"Against the Crown Prince and the Queen," said Braem.

"Against the whole world, apparently," said Struensee.

"Against the nobles and the clergy," said Bolle.

"Against the Queen-Dowager and Prince Frederik," echoed Braem.

"A comprehensive list," said Struensee. He drew a deep breath.

"Do you not admit, Count Struensee, that you illegally dissolved the Bernstorff cabinet and replaced it with a so-called royal council with yourself at its head?" the magistrate asked. "And that you did this in order to make yourself dictator?"

"The King dissolved the Bernstorff cabinet," said Struensee. "It was not I who did it. You will find his signature at the bottom of the order."

"But you drew up the order, did you not, Count Struensee?"

"I did not," said Struensee quickly. "That was done by Count Rantzau."

"So?" The magistrate was taken aback. "But you offered it to the King for his signature, did you not?"

"I had to do that in my capacity as the King's secretary," said Struensee.

"How did it happen that the King named you his first minister," said the magistrate. "Did you not suggest it to His Majesty?"

"I had the King's confidence," said Struensee. "He himself offered me the post."

"Kings do not offer," Bolle reminded him. "Kings command."

"You are quite right," agreed Struensee. "All the more reason why it was out of the question for me to refuse."

This was a ticklish moment for the examining magistrate. The legality of Struensee's appointment was undeniable. And on that account the whole indictment on the grounds of high treason could easily misfire. Now a series of decrees were brought into the court and were all found to be signed by the King and, with the exception of a few insignificant cases, all countersigned by the head of the ministry to which they pertained. In vain Hobe rummaged through the mass of papers. Each time the King's signature stared him in the face. Hour after hour passed in unprofitable hairsplitting and wrangling. Since Hobe could not attack the content of the decrees without attacking the King's authority, he accordingly shifted his tactics, and tried to establish the subversive intent of the decrees. Yet it proved difficult to elicit an undeclared intent.

"So you must admit, Count Struensee," Hobe said, "that the dismissal of the palace guard cannot be legally explained away. You wanted to get rid of the men protecting the King the better to overthrow him."

"The guards were disbanded simply in order to save money," Struensee came back. "The tremendous public debt made it imperative that something of the sort be done. The King agreed to the idea, moreover. The Holstein infantry regiment that took over the guards' duties were just as loyal to the King, and far cheaper to maintain. I believe, General, no one could ever say that the head of this infantry regiment, Colonel Koeller, was so partial to me that I gave him a key position in any hypothetical plot against the King."

"We can leave Colonel Koeller out of this altogether," said Hobe quickly and wiped the perspiration from his brow. "You must admit that you would never choose him to be commandant of the palace if you had it to do today. But let us forget him. Dissolving the guards still looks suspicious to me."

"Extraordinarily suspicious," said Braem. "Especially in view of the fact that we have found a picture of Oliver Cromwell among your effects, Count Struensee."

"And all the more gravely suspicious," added Bolle, "in light of the fact that the picture in question formerly belonged to Her Majesty, the Queen, as the maids have sworn under oath."

"What of that?" said Struensee, bending forward belligerently. "Do not many people own portraits without identifying themselves with the originals? Does it mean that one cannot own a portrait of a man without subscribing to his political principles? Was Frederick the Fifth another Caligula because he bought a marble statue of this Roman and had it set up in this museum?"

"How did the Queen happen to give you the picture?" said Hobe. "Her Majesty gave it to me to memorialize my efforts to reconcile her with the King," said Struensee.

"Was that all?" insisted Braem.

[318]

"Did Her Majesty not have a deeper motive?" Bolle asked.

"I have no idea what you mean," said Struensee. "I stand on what I have told you."

Hobe stared hard at Struensee, and Braem looked behind the magistrate's back at Bolle. "We'll have more of that later," said Hobe. "And now, Count, is it not true that you kept your hat on in the King's presence and also opened His Majesty's personal letters?"

"That is true, General."

"Does it not occur to you, Count, that such behavior obviously indicates lack of respect . . . If not worse?"

"But I did both on the King's express wish. He wanted the people around him to conduct themselves informally, since that was the way he comported himself. The King commanded me to read his private correspondence. Someone had to separate important from unimportant letters."

"Do you have a written order to that effect?"

"No."

"Do you not consider this lack of a written order to be distinctly suspicious?" asked Hobe, and Braem and Bolle affirmed the magistrate's suggestion with somber nods.

"But the King's verbally expressed wish is just as much a command to me as a written order," said Struensee. "It would have showed a lack of respect for his authority, rather, if I had bothered him with trivialities that had nothing to do with the welfare of the state. You could not have expected me to ask for a written order every time I opened a letter."

The hearing continued in this indecisive manner. It was nine o'clock and pitch dark outside when General Hobe called it a day. Struensee's chains were put back and he was returned to the Citadel. He entered his cell in a good mood. As he saw it, he had countered every accusation, destroyed every trace of suspicion. He felt confident of victory and was able to eat his supper with appetite. He tried to joke with Juel, but the jailer was out of sorts and offered only monosyllables in reply to Struensee's witticisms.

The next forenoon the hearing continued. Struensee observed at once that the examiners tended to shy away from the broad intent of his laws and reforms and concentrated their attention on matters which, from a reasonable standpoint, were highly irrelevant to a charge of treason. He noted, in particular, that the questions, unlike those of the previous day, hinged less on the legality of his acts than on their moral drift.

There was the question of the present of money, for example, that he and Brandt had received, at Struensee's own instigation, from the King. He drew the court's attention at once to the fact that someone in the ministry of finance had made a gross bookkeeping error.

Someone, indeed, had put a zero after the six, making what had originally been six thousand thalers into sixty thousand.

That looked very much like deliberate tampering and should have redounded at once to Struensee's benefit. Braem and Bolle peered with intense interest at their fingernails. But General Hobe was not to be so casually dissuaded. "Let us assume, Count," he said, "that the registration of the larger sum was a bookkeeping mistake. Aren't you ashamed, nevertheless, at taking sixty thousand thalers? Do you not consider it to be a sizeable amount?"

"Why should I be ashamed!" exclaimed Struensee. "After all, it was a present from the King."

"That's right," said Hobe, slowly and menacingly. "But shortly before this, if you recall, on your own initiative you had a circular distributed, saying in effect that on account of the state's heavy indebtedness royal gifts should be kept to an absolute minimum, if not altogether done away with. The pensions of elderly officials and officers were drastically curtailed, and in some cases entirely stopped. The manufacture of luxury articles was forbidden, imports were cut down. Don't you see, sir, that between these counsels of economy, however good and desirable they may have been in themselves, and the fact that you have yourself given a sum of sixty thousand thalers there lies a glaring discrepancy? In other words, do you not admit that you readily accepted gratuities that you denied others? Does not your reputed concern for the financial well being of the state strike you as a barefaced hypocrisy? Were your reforms, morally considered, nothing more than egotistic projections? And were not the incessantly emphasized grounds for these reforms nothing but idealistic soap bubbles and foam, which you threw in the King's face and in the face of the community, merely to blind them and to cover up the unspoken, true and realistic intent of your maneuverings?"

"I swear that I intended the best for Denmark," said Struensee with great emotion, rising up from his inquisitorial bench.

"So you say," retorted the magistrate coldly. "But why did you accept the money, pray tell me? You knew better than anyone else the condition of the state's finances. Did you not? Why did you allow your friend Brandt to stuff his pockets?"

"I needed the money," cried out Struensee.

"We all need money," said Braem.

"Yes, but I had no fixed income," protested Struensee. "I have no property, no means of any sort. I was entirely dependent on the King's generosity. And the same holds true for Brandt. You know that Denmark would not expect me to serve the country without recompense, although I would have done it, had I had the means."

"That's what they all say," Hobe countered harshly. "The fact remains that you broke with your own publicly declared principles.

And it is up to the court to decide whether this breach was a deliberate crime or mere thoughtlessness. The issue cannot be ignored."

Struensee was confused, and Hobe capitalized on his confusion by bringing up the subject of the Crown Prince's education and care. He enumerated all the things that had shocked the courtiers, the frequent bathing of the child, his lack of conventional clothing, his going about barefoot, his sleeping in open rooms, his simple diet, his lack of servants, his peasant playmates.

"The physical welfare of the Prince was entrusted to me and Dr. Berger," Struensee admitted. "We did the best we could according to all we knew of medicine."

"You must admit, Count Struensee," the magistrate droned, "that your methods represent a very peculiar way to bring up a child, especially if this child is a prince."

"It is the modern way of doing things," said Struensee. "It is a method intended to further the child's resistance and health, and has nothing to do with what medically uninformed people may think. The great philosopher Rousseau himself, I might point out, has recommended this form of upbringing. It is designed to make the boy spiritually and physically sound. It will keep him uncorrupted and free from the evil effects of flattery. It will preserve him from the dangers of being with adults all the time, and never meeting the resistance of other children his own age."

"Rousseau's opinions, to the best of my knowledge, are as yet unproved," said Hobe icily. "Many people, indeed, condemn him as corrupt and an enemy of civilization. But however that may be, you had no right to make the Crown Prince into a subject of experiment. The heir to the throne is far too important a personage."

"I did not do this, of course, on my own responsibility alone," said Struensee. "The boy's mother agreed with me and encouraged these methods."

"And why did she encourage them, Count Struensee?" Braem put in.

"I assume she did so because she recognized their validity," said Struensee, taken off guard. "She was moved to believe in this sort of upbringing mainly because of her knowledge of the King's youth. The tradition in which her husband had been reared very obviously had disastrous results. The Queen wanted more than anything to avoid a repetition of his experience. She was perfectly justified in fearing the results of such barbarities."

"Do you really expect us to believe that that was why Her Majesty followed your advice?" Bolle asked.

"Why, what other grounds could a mother have?" shouted Struensee, touched to the quick by Bolle's insinuation. "Why, didn't she love her child like any other mother?"

"That's the question," said Bolle and glanced slyly at Braem. "The question is, did she love her son, or somebody else for whom she was prepared to sacrifice her child?"

Struensee half rose from his bench. But before he could frame a reply, Hobe intervened, and said: "We'll take up that matter later. Now let us consider the crimes of Count Brandt."

"Brandt!" Struensee was nonplussed. "Then he is accused, too."

"Certainly," said Hobe. "You might recall, Count Struensee, that your friend visited physical injuries on His Majesty, that he so far forgot himself that he actually struck him with his fists. Count Brandt has admitted it and regrets it deeply."

"Is he in prison, too?" said Struensee, almost in a whisper.

"Naturally, that's the place for him," said Hobe. "And he has also admitted that you, Count, advised him in the Queen's presence to strike the King."

"But gentlemen!" protested Struensee, anxiously searching the magistrates' faces. "You misconstrue Count Brandt's behavior. You have put the wrong construction entirely on his testimony. It was all nothing but a joke."

"Do you consider it a joke, Count Struensee," said Braem, "when a courtier humiliates and beats his King?"

"No, certainly not, if it were a question of a deliberate assault," said Struensee, gathering his scattered wits. "But in this case it was different, you see. It was the King's well-known habit to invite men in his entourage to box with him. He liked the sport of it, shall we say. Count Holck, Warnstaedt, Sperling—all fell in with his pleasure. Brandt, as a matter of fact, refused him for a long time."

"Wasn't it his duty as a nobleman to avoid such unseemliness at any cost?" asked Bolle.

"That was precisely how Brandt felt about it," said Struensee. "But the King was insulted when Brandt refused him his pleasure. He called Brandt a coward. One evening, I remember, he threw a lemon at Brandt, hit him on the head with it. 'You're as yellow as this sour fruit, Brandt,' he said to him. The King, in other words, repeatedly humiliated the man in the presence of ladies. Finally Brandt came to me and asked me for advice. I advised him to let the King have his way and bring the issue to a close."

"Then you admit it," said Hobe, satisfied.

"I admit that I told Brandt to accede to the King's wish," said Struensee. "But it would hardly be right to infer from that, that either Brandt or I had any evil motive."

"It is the duty of the trial court to judge these happenings," said Hobe. "I cannot do it here. We are merely seeking facts. We are trying to find out what actually happened, and nothing beyond that."

"Yes, but the very fact that the Queen was there proves that we had no ulterior motive," insisted Struensee. "She would certainly never have permitted anything untoward to befall the King."

"Do you believe that?" said Braem.

"Do you really think so?" echoed Bolle.

"We'll take that up later," said Hobe. "Tomorrow morning. The hearing is over for today. It's getting dark again."

This time when Struensee again sat enchained in his cell he was in a very tense frame of mind. It was obvious to him that he had not come off so well as the day before. But what upset him most was the fact that the examining magistrates held a trump card up their sleeves. The real and unanswerable charge against him had yet to be made. All that had been discussed up to this point lacked a focal meaning to tie it together.

Juel came to the cell as usual and was livelier than the day before. The worse Struensee felt, the better Juel, for misery was his *métier*. He rattled his keys and beamed at Struensee like an old nag nibbling hay. "Yes, when you come right down to it," he told Struensee, "the main thing is for the prisoner to realize his own guilt. What they do to him on the outside, what the judges and the courts do to him, that's all beside the point. Whether they find him guilty or innocent is just a technicality. The real thing is here . . ." Saying this he pointed cabalistically to the left side of his breast.

"You get out of here," Struensee said viciously. "I'm fighting for my life, you damned fool, and you tell me it makes no difference. Where's your heart!"

"Yes, but it all depends on the judges," said Juel obstinately. "And what they think doesn't count, not really."

"Get to hell out of here," shouted Struensee and menaced the cadaverous jailer with his chained hands. "Rave somewhere else for a change, if you will."

Juel sighed and left the cell without offering reprisal.

All that night Struensee lay awake. In a fever of anticipation he tossed back and forth on his bed of planks. His bones ached horribly from the chafing of the chains. He grumbled bitterly to himself, he pitied himself intensely. Tomorrow morning he would have to face the examining magistrates again. Tomorrow? He saw the cell gradually lighting up. There was the stool. And the jug of water. Why, tomorrow had already come! How bare the place. The man of pleasure has become a monk, Struensee thought with a grimace of disgust. So here I am, he told himself, all rigged out like a medieval ascetic. All I have to do now is to ask for a whip with thongs to flagellate some spirit into myself, he thought as he struggled to his feet.

He was deadly pale from worry and lack of sleep when he arrived at the magistracy, so weary that the muscles at his mouth and eye corners twitched. He did not calm down until they had taken off his chains and he was once again installed on the comfortable settle before the table.

"Today we will move into *medias res*," Hobe announced with a thin smile. "We have been wasting a lot of time, I fear."

"In *medias res*," said Braem with relish.

"In *medias res*," said Bolle.

Struensee looked at them, pale, large-eyed with apprehension. He felt as if he might faint. Somehow he managed to hold himself up and even forced a little smile. But within he felt as full of guilt as an egg of yolk.

"To make a long story short," Hobe said, "what were your relations with the Queen? Was she your mistress?"

Now Struensee felt the floor rise and fall under him, so great was his anxiety. He staggered to his feet, supported himself by holding onto the back of the bench and shouted: "You'll pay for that, I tell you. You have insulted the Queen!"

"Sit down, sit down," said Hobe coldly. "Isn't it true that you seduced the Queen? That you spent hundreds of nights with her in her bedchamber, sharing the same bed? Isn't it true that in the most contemptible fashion you betrayed the King, who was your trusting friend? Isn't it true that you got your Queen with child and would even like to see this bastard issue seated on the Danish throne? Isn't it true that everywhere, in Christiansborg, Frederiksborg, Hoersholm, Traventhal, Rosenborg and other places you violated the sanctity of the royal establishment? Did you not, like a rabid animal, use the Queen, encouraging her to forget entirely her conjugal obligations, for purposes of sexual gratification? Was not the object of your sexual activity the King's wife, your friend's wife, the Queen of Denmark? I ask you, Count Struensee, can you deny any of these charges? Here . . ." he raised the crucifix on the table . . . "dare you swear that what I say is not true? Do you dare give the lie now to a thousand accusers?"

"How can you talk about such things," groaned Struensee. He was helpless before the onslaught, unmanned.

"It is my duty as a magistrate to bring up these matters, however distressing they may be," said Hobe. "I do not like to do it. For it involves the Queen, to whom we all owe respect, or most certainly should. But the evidence in our possession is irrefragable. We know the corridors that you used to get to the Queen's bedchamber in Christiansborg. We have footprints that have been measured and found to correspond exactly with your own. We have the depositions of servants who have come upon you alone with her in the most compromising situations. The interior guard of the palace, the ladies-in-waiting, the ladies of the court—all of them have seen you with her and with your hands on her. It is a public secret, Count Struensee. As you yourself know, neither you nor the Queen ever troubled to conceal your revolting turpitudes. On the contrary! You flaunted the fact that you were lovers. You seemed to take a perverse pride in it. So did the Queen. I could read something to you in this regard" . . . he pointed to a heap of papers . . . "from the written evidence, but I will spare all of us the infamous details. I will not, for example, go into the red weals observed on the Queen's breasts, and presumably caused by your bruising kisses. I won't dwell on the tumbled, stained bedclothes, nor the garters made of red and white silk which you gave to the Queen, and which she habitually wore. Yes, that present was indeed 'full of sentiment and tender memories,' as the Queen said to the maid Bruun. I consider it beneath the dignity of the magistracy to dig around in such filth. I assume your feelings are the same. Therefore I ask you simply, were you, or were you not the Queen's lover? Yes or no?"

"I refuse to answer," said Struensee feebly. "I will not discuss the Queen. I respect her too much for that. It's not the way you imagine at all." He ran his hands distractedly through his hair. "Don't you people think there can be anything pure at all in the world? Don't you?"

"Not in your case," said Hobe. "Not only the evidence, but the Queen's own conduct speaks for itself. When she was arrested, she said: 'I'm lost, I'm lost forever.' Does that indicate innocence?"

"The Queen arrested!" Struensee's voice cracked. "You're trying to trip me up. No one would dare arrest the Queen!"

"The law stands over queens," said Hobe, rummaged among his papers and threw a document to Struensee across the table. "Look for yourself. It's the *lettre de cachet*."

Struensee held the paper close to him and read. His lips shook with excitement. Indeed, it was an order for the Queen's arrest, signed by Christian and countersigned by Rantzau, who had appended a notation to the effect that the order had been carried out.

"Well, that finishes me," said Struensee. "Where is she?"

"I can tell you that, if you like," said Hobe. "Though what difference does it make to you? The Queen is in Kronborg Fortress."

"In the state prison," said Braem.

"In jail, like yourself," said Bolle.

Struensee put his hands up to his face and the tears came. "It's my fault, all my fault," he said thickly. Now the end seemed certain to him. All along his hopes had ultimately rested on the prospect of the Queen's intervention in his favor.

"Who else has been taken?" he asked weakly.

"All of them have been arrested," said Braem. "Your brother, the councillor of justice, for instance. Gaehler and his wife."

"Privy councillor Berger and von Osten," said Bolle.

"Old Berger!" said Struensee. "Why, you know perfectly well he did nothing. No one could be more innocent than he."

"Indeed," said Hobe and irritably pushed away the papers in front of him. "Nevertheless all these people and many others are under arrest, with their servants. On your account, Count Struensee. Don't you think it's about time you made a complete confession of guilt? That would at least make matters easier for your friends. And then even you might be able to anticipate the King's generosity."

"What is there for me to confess?" said Struensee wildly. "It is simply not true that I ever aspired to the crown, or contemplated treason in any form."

"But it is true that you were the Queen's lover," said Hobe.

"Undeniably true," said Braem.

"A fact beyond negating," said Bolle.

Struensee fell silent and tried to think over the court's proposition. But he could not. His mind buzzed, his mouth was dry with fear, his temples throbbed. For a moment inwardly he saw Caroline Matilda, pretty, pampered, delightful Caroline. What could happen to her, the daughter of a king? Nothing, of course, not really. The hangman would never dare slip a noose about her throat, for behind her stood England. Behind her loomed great rows of cannon poking their snouts through the wall sides of innumerable frigates. Behind her stood many red-coated regiments and an empire that stretched from India to America. But who stood behind Struensee? Nobody. Poor Struensee was alone.

The magistrates let the yeast of doubt do its work. Hobe looked intently up at the ceiling, fingertips together beneath his pursed lips.

Perhaps they will torture me to force a confession, Struensee suddenly thought. And this after he himself had banned the use of force in the process of indictment. Why, the mere fact that it had been he who instituted this advance might give them the idea of throwing his good works back in his face. Still, they had made no threats, there had been no signs of physical intimidation. Well, that meant they simply took torture for granted. Thinking these dismal thoughts, Struensee's fear became rage. Anger towards Caroline for her love flared in the prisoner, hatred of her for her yielding, profound dislike for having lured him into such a mess.

He was reeling from lack of sleep, tormented by weakness after a night of intense and aimless thought, sapped by the weeks he had been left in a cell to soften up. Then he had never really gotten over the concussion from banging his head against the wall. Struensee was at low ebb. He was obsessed by a guilty image of his friend Brandt, his brother, Annette, good old Berger, all sitting unhappily in prison cells like himself.

His confusion was so great that he failed to see he was feeling only an imagined concern for his friends. He failed to realize that his anger with the Queen was essentially anger with himself, resentment of the innate incapacities of his own character. He had done very nicely so long as his principles were succeeding. Now, when they had soured and he might die on account of them, his cowardice stood revealed. And he hated himself for it.

Hobe looked on the ceiling. Could he be reading the answer to his questions from the cracks in the plaster?

"Supposing I confess," said Struensee. "What then?"

"That would make things easier for you," Braem said softly.

"Truth can always hope for clemency," said Bolle, more softly still.

"Well, I confess, then," screamed Struensee. "Does that satisfy you? I confess!"

Hobe came down to earth with a crash. "At last," he said warmly. "Now we're getting somewhere. Sit down, Count Struensee, pray sit down. Give him a glass of water, Councillor Bolle. Don't you feel better already, sir, with such a load off your mind? Don't you?"

"I don't know," said Struensee abjectly. "I don't know whether I feel better or worse." He slumped down on the bench like an old sack.

"You must understand, Count Struensee," said Hobe rapidly, "that a simple verbal confession is not enough for us. We need details. Tell us everything. In consideration of the extremely delicate nature of your confession I won't use a scribe. Magistrate Braem will take down what you have to say."

Eagerly Braem pared a quill and dipped it into the inkpot. Struensee proceeded immediately to tell the story of his love affair, hesitantly at first, then more quickly, ever more quickly, in such spate that Braem had trouble keeping up with him. He tried to avoid all mention of intimacies, but Hobe would not let this pass.

"When did you first have intercourse with the Queen?" he asked. "That's what we'd like to know."

"In the spring of 1770," said Struensee.

"You don't know the exact date?"

"I've forgotten," said Struensee. "Maybe it was the early summer."

"Well, that's not too important," said Hobe genially. "Where did the act occur?"

"In Rosenborg."

"In which room?"

"In the salon of Christian the Fourth."

"Write that down, Braem. At about what time of the day, Count Struensee?"

"In the afternoon," said the prisoner. "Yes, in the afternoon."

"Afternoon," said Hobe. "Get that down, Braem."

It was a fearful experience, exposing the minutest particulars of his love, but Hobe drew them forth mercilessly, as a dentist draws teeth, bleeding roots and all. Down they went on the paper, couched in a dry factual language admitting no qualification. Struensee complained at this. "But really it wasn't at all like that, General," he objected, when something was read back to him. "How shall I express myself? It was much purer than it seems. It was by no means displeasing or lacking in taste."

"I am aware of that," said Hobe. "But we cannot dwell too long on imponderables. The facts are enough for our purposes. That's what we want, facts minus the tinsel, sir."

Struensee's confession took a good deal more than an hour. Braem laid the paper before him. Struensee signed without even reading it. He had an enormous desire to be done, to be out of the room, away from the stale air of the courtroom, away from the sight of legal documents and legal faces. He wanted more than anything to be away from Braem and Bolle, away from the casuistries they spat at him in little wet balls, leaning forward, meanly peering out of narrow, gray faces to gauge the damaging effect. He was afraid that he would collapse if he stayed there another five minutes. His relief was profound when Juel arrived to take him away.

When the magistrates were alone, Hobe said to his assistants: "Well, gentlemen, we certainly had a most unexpected success today. I was prepared for a much longer hearing. Very much longer, as a matter of fact."

"So was I," said Braem. "His position was legally sound all along, if he had only had the sense to hang on. I noticed that all of a sudden something gave way in him. I saw it when it happened. The main beams seemed to give way and the whole house crashed down."

"I've often seen the same thing happen," said Bolle. "It was weakness of character."

"Maybe it was more than that," said Hobe. "Don't forget that his father was a minister of the gospel, and that he grew up in a very pietistic household."

"What do you imply there exactly," said Bolle.

"It might have been his consciousness of guilt," said Hobe. "His conscience began to pain him. It blinded him to his own advantages."

"That's what I meant by weakness of character," said Bolle. "And besides, you know, he was always a man of the world. A crass materialist, I'd call him. How he fancied himself! Now he discovers that he has a conscience like anyone else. He is amazed. He asks himself, what am I, really? Am I a materialist, or am I a Christian? I cannot be both at the same time. Imagine the strain."

"However that may be," said Braem, "I don't think it very gallant of him to tell on the Queen. It shows he must have been badly brought up. It certainly argues a lack of courage."

"But thank God that he told us what we wanted to hear," said Hobe. "You know perfectly well, gentlemen, that we really don't have any solid evidence on the question of the Queen's adultery. We have rumors, servants' gossip, court talk, the bed, the marks of the kisses and so on. But that's not substantial evidence. No one ever saw them in bed together, not actually. And we all know it. Any defense counsel could have knocked it all into a cocked hat in two shakes. But he'll have a time on his hands, believe me, trying to explain away this little sheet of paper." Hobe flicked the confession with his forefinger. "But even now," he continued, "this isn't going to suffice. The Queen's word will count far more than Struensee's, naturally. What we need is a confession from the other person involved. We need the Queen's signature. Then the last loophole would be sealed off."

Braem and Bolle nodded earnest assent. "She will make trouble for us," said Braem gloomily.

"Ah yes, no doubt, no doubt," said Hobe and smiled. "But consider, gentlemen, isn't it rather charming when a pretty young lady makes trouble for us?"

Braem and Bolle nickered like goats.

★ *III* ★

CAROLINE MATILDA WAS held in custody in the tower of Kronborg. The room was like a bird cage. She could look out of it far over land and sea. It was a simple room, whitewashed, with four closely grated windows letting in an amplitude of light. The furnishings consisted of a simple bed, two chairs and a bureau with a badly blurred mirror.

They had laid a Bible on the table, Gellert's poems and some books on religious subjects. During the first days of her imprisonment Caroline had refused to eat anything. She had passed a great deal of the time quietly weeping face down on the bed.

But slowly she got used to her rude surroundings. She was much consoled when they allowed her to continue suckling her infant daughter, Luisa Augusta. Each morning she impatiently waited for Antje Maria to arrive with the child. The infant appeared to feel quite as much at home in the prison-fortress of Kronborg as in luxurious Christiansborg, and this, too, comforted the mother. She laughed as she saw the baby smile and reach out her arms to be picked up. When she had her child, Caroline Matilda forgot entirely that she was a prisoner. The guards, during these visits, often heard her bright purl of laughter.

Later, when Antje Maria had taken away the sated, sleeping child, Caroline's misery would creep back over her. Hours on end she sat woodenly on the bed, thinking dull, fruitless thoughts. What she feared most was her mother's distress and the unpleasantness she was bound to cause her brothers and sisters. How would the English people take the news of her imprisonment? She knew that her family would stand back of her. But how would Parliament act?

She asked to see the English ambassador. Lieutenant Schleemann told her politely that such a meeting could not be arranged at this early date. She inquired after her friends. All that Schleemann could tell her was that Struensee and Brandt were still imprisoned in the Citadel of Copenhagen.

The days dragged along. She spent hours at the windows looking out over the sea, which was frequently whipped by storms at this season. The water would writhe strangely against the horizon, making weird shapes. Sometimes she saw ships crawl slowly by, ships from Luebeck, from Russia and once an English vessel, as she could tell from the ensign. A cannon boomed, the ship dropped sail and a boat put out from Kronborg carrying officials arranging for the passage through the straits. Presently sails were hoisted into place and the ship tacked slowly to the southward.

Nights were the worst of all. She lay awake listening to wind moaning and groaning about the tower. It was forever rattling the window-frames. It sighed in the corridors like a ghost, it rushed and roared, tearing tiles loose from the steep roof. During a lull she could hear the crackling plaints of the daws taking refuge under the roof beams. On such windy nights it was easy to fancy that a curse was on the fortress of Kronborg. Her heart beating madly, Caroline would jump out of bed and press her face against the window. Outside there was nothing to see but troubled darkness. At the very most she could make out a pale streak of moonlight as the clouds broke for a moment, just long enough to give her a glimpse of the riven surface of the sea.

Looking from her height into this primeval scene it seemed to Caroline that the darkness, the wind, the wild sea, the driven birds, her own life and all being were somehow intermingled and displayed in all brutal nakedness and truth. Wearily she would light her candle. It would not burn properly, of course. The tiny flame made uncannily mobile shadows on the whitewashed walls. Caroline Matilda would open the Bible and leaf through it aimlessly. Once her eyes fell on the words of Isaiah: "Enter into the rock, and hide thee in the dust, for fear of the Lord, and for the glory of His majesty. The lofty looks of man shall be humbled, and the haughtiness of men shall be bowed down." Listlessly she closed the book. In her tower room she felt trapped between worlds, and repudiated by both. One was the elemental world of nature, a world of storms and waves. And the other, speaking to her out of the book, was equally strange to her frightened heart. It seemed even more terrible and pitiless, because it was planned —all determined beforehand.

The next morning she would dismiss her gloomy introspections as morbidities of the night. She was only twenty years old, after all. Her vitality held the upper hand. She nursed her child, caressed her, wondered at her round limbs and smiling eyes. God has given her to me, she would think. Then the prophets' words meant nothing to her.

Suddenly the child fell sick with the measles. They wanted to keep the child away from her so that she, too, would not be infected. But she insisted on having the child with her every day, to look at it and take care of it. A sick anxiety was with her all the time the child was sick. Was this God's punishment? Was that the way He humbled queens, by taking away their innocent children? She prayed, she begged God to be kind to her child. But, as in Frederiksborg, she felt no answer to her prayers. God remained aloof and silent in his nowhere. Her passionate pleadings for mercy were in vain. And this time there was no lover to run to, no one to console her in his arms.

She stopped eating. She begged Lieutenant Schleemann, as a token of contrition, to give her food to the other prisoners, for there were many others beside herself sitting in Kronborg on account of political misdemeanors. Lieutenant Schleemann was always ill at ease in Caroline's opulent presence. He never left off tugging at his collar to ease his embarrassment and bumptiousness. Reluctantly he gave in to her wish, running grave risks by so doing, for it was strictly forbidden to feed prisoners more than their regular ration.

Among the prisoners working on the masonry of Kronborg Caroline had noticed an old man with long white hair. He seemed definitely more miserable and decrepit, if possible, than his companions, and as if for this very reason kept apart from them as much as his work allowed. The Queen pointed out the old man to her jailer. "See to it, Lieutenant," she said, "that he at least gets some of my food."

"But he's the worst criminal in the prison," said the Lieutenant.

"What did he do?"

"He was a spy, Madame," said Schleemann. "And now he's serving a life term. He can thank the clemency of the former King for his life. He was originally condemned to death."

"All that I care about is the fact that he is a human being," said the Queen. "I can't be staring all day at anyone as unhappy as that. I simply won't stand it, Lieutenant."

"I shall do as Your Majesty wishes," the Lieutenant replied quiveringly.

From this day on Caroline Matilda saw that the old man worked nearer the rest of the gang. Sometimes he even talked with the others. This she took as a good sign.

The question of whether there was any relationship between her baby's illness and her illicit love affair fed the maggots of doubt that infested Caroline's loneliness.

One day, out of a clear sky, she remembered a small experience from childhood. It all came back to her with wonderful clarity and at once took on a new dimension. Out of greed and daring she had stolen a pear from her grandfather's espaliered fruit trees. The old King liked immensely to pick the fruit himself, particularly the big ones, and afterwards give them to some favorite or court lady. And this pear had been especially large and flawless. Out for his morning stroll, the King had looked for his pear, and missed it. He had been very angry with the gardener, indeed, the incident had clouded the whole day for him. The gardener, he had threatened, would have to go.

That night Caroline had been unable to sleep. "You know, I couldn't pray tonight," she had complained to her lady-in-waiting, who was sitting beside the bed, her sewing in her lap, until her charge settled down.

"If you can't pray, my child," the lady-in-waiting had said, "you must have a lie in your heart. If we are hiding a lie, God can neither hear nor see us, for He is given over to truth alone."

The next morning, remembering this admonition, she had run into the garden and burst out with the truth. "I stole the pear," she had said. "I did it, Grandpa."

But the King had already forgotten the incident. "What pear are you prattling about, you pretty thing!" he had said.

"The one you missed yesterday," she had said, and dissolved into tears.

"That was dreadfully naughty of you," the King had chided her. "You simply could have come and asked me for the pear."

There had been more sobs and snivels and nose-wipings.

"Now, now," the King had said, patting her head. "I would only have given it to someone. It belongs to you . . . after the fact. Quite all right, my sweet."

And then he had laughed and gone on with his walk. The courtiers who were with him had laughed, too. She had watched him go, her mouth gaped open in puzzlement, but feeling so very much better than she had. She had prayed perfectly well that evening and sleep had come with no trouble.

Remembering this incident, Caroline resolved within her heart to admit, when proper opportunity offered, the leaden untruths now weighing her down. But having resolved to confess at large, presently she would hesitate inwardly, realizing how bad her admissions would be for her lover.

In the meanwhile her child recovered from her attack of measles, and she put aside her moral cogitations.

She was still wavering, torn between truth and deceit, when called before the examining magistrates. General Hobe stood at attention when she came in, and bowed deeply and humbly to her. All the time he was cursing himself for undertaking what now appeared to be an impossible task. If England interfered, or if the Struensee clique, through a whim of the King, should again stride the saddle, he would assuredly forfeit his head. Assistants Braem and Bolle made themselves as small as possible behind the magistrate's broad back. They kept their mouths shut and repeatedly looked away over their shoulders, only to snap their gray, expressionless faces forward the next moment like two owls on a branch.

General Hobe proceeded with the examination as if walking on eggs, always using parables and peeking around corners.

"You want to know, General," said Caroline sarcastically, "whether Count Struensee" . . . she blushed to her hair-roots . . . "whether there were certain intimacies between him and me?"

"With full respect for Madame," replied Hobe, "that is what this examining court would like to know."

"Then why don't you ask me, Hobe, instead of beating around the bush!"

"I earnestly desire not to be offensive towards Your Majesty."

"It's your duty to offend, if the situation requires it, Hobe," the Queen said. "You're an old soldier and an honorable one, supposedly. You needn't have applied for this dirty work. But now you've got it, don't shirk."

"But it's very painful, very distressing, Your Majesty," stammered Hobe. "The King commanded me. What . . ."

"Please spare me such nonsense," said Caroline. "I know my husband. All this business is a plot engineered by my mother-in-law. Why, the whole world knows it. And you know perfectly well the King would sign his own death warrant if you put it in front of him persuasively." Then she bethought herself. She might have chosen a less striking image. "However," she went on rapidly, "to cut it short, I may say that I do have a very high regard for Count Struensee, more than for any man in the world. As for the other . . . no . . . I admit nothing."

Now Hobe accepted a document that Braem gently poked in his direction and pretended to examine it. "I see, I see, Madame," he said to the Queen. "In that case Count Struensee has grossly perjured himself. He must be in contempt of court in the most memorable fashion. Should this be the case, we shall see to it that he gets his desserts. He will be broken on the wheel, Madame. For what he has done, he deserves to be drawn and quartered."

Caroline Matilda lost color at the mere mention of these cruel possibilities. "Let me read the paper, Hobe," she whispered. "If you please."

She moved away a few steps to the window and read. Her eyes widened at what they saw, her face became a pale mask. She felt her heart thumping hard against her bodice, so hard that she felt she would have to loose the fastenings then and there in order not to suffocate.

Caroline was not so much horrified by the fact that Struensee had publicly implicated her in adultery, as by the manner of his confession. In sober, unmistakable handwriting the whole course of their affair lay before her, recorded step by step meticulously. Each kiss, each embrace, each rendezvous was duly accounted for. Not a single circumstance had been overlooked. The secret stairs. The creaking door opening into her bedroom. The rumpled bed. The kiss marks on her breasts. The present of the gaily-colored garters. Fact followed fact. Everything was down on paper except the emotion that had given rise to the facts. Nothing about his love, nothing about her love had been recorded.

Like Struensee himself, the Queen was nonplussed by the great difference between the living, sensual experience and the literal enumeration of its particulars. It's not true, she thought to herself, I simply never could have done things like that. She looked out the window, down onto the heavy paving stones of the palace courtyard. Farther beyond were the heaving waters of the sound, gray under a gray sky. The cold crept up her legs. She felt a chill enfold her, wrap her round like a great cold snake. At the moment, had not the windows of the room been barred, she would have leapt through them to her death on the paving stones below. Glistening with cold and damp, they beckoned to her imperiously.

This way or that her life was ended. Her womanly existence had been hacked off at the root. But she never thought to complain about her chicken-hearted lover. She felt no hate for him who had betrayed her most delicate secrets. She did not even ask herself what had led him to confess.

She felt the whole course of events had been prompted by some ineluctable fatality. She had been carried along on a dark stream, impelled by a flow more irresistible than the tides of the sea. Everything showed the mark of immutable logic. Her lonely youth, her unhappy, ill-advised marriage, the sudden appearance of a man who physically appealed to her, then disaster. Even Struensee's confession seemed to have come as a matter of course. He was not to blame for his given nature. Destiny permitted no recriminations, for destiny was blind and dumb.

Staring out the window a sudden and mighty revulsion against being the tool of blind necessity possessed her. Something in her shrieked out in agony for freedom and self-subsistence. Her heart yearned profoundly for tranquillity.

In her extreme need there came a most shattering experience. It was a pang of revelation and release, a fleeting contact with the spiritual source, that came to her. She felt a searching weakness and had to clamp her hands on the window sill. She swayed and bit her lips to prevent herself from crying out.

Still mutely fighting to master herself, she wheeled about and faced the three magistrates. They were all watching her, three pairs of eyes devouring her misery. She tossed the paper to Hobe across the desk. A vast sickness was in the pit of her stomach.

"*Eh bien,*" she said thinly, almost frivolously, "*je signerai, messieurs.*"

Hobe started and cocked his head. "What was that you said, Madame?" he asked.

"I said that I am ready to sign."

"The paper?"

"No. I'll dictate my own paper, if you please, sir."

"As you will, Madame," said Hobe and bowed across his desk. "Braem, get a quill. And some paper. Get on with it now and write down what Madame dictates to you. Come, hurry!"

"Never mind that," said the Queen. "I've decided to write it myself."

"So much the better, Madame, if it is no inconvenience," said Hobe. He could hardly contain his elation.

Caroline sat down and resolutely commenced to scratch with the quill. "I, Caroline Matilda," she wrote, "swear by Almighty God that I love Count Struensee and that I have considered himself to be my husband and I his wife before God, and have given myself to him as he to me. I beg my unhappy friend Christian, King of Denmark and Norway, to forgive me for the injustices I have done him. It is my hope that he will be happier without me."

She gave the paper to Hobe, who read it through at a glance, his mouth working. He stared across his table into Caroline's eyes. The roundness and childlike quality of the face, it seemed to him, had disappeared within these past few minutes.

"Is that good enough for your purposes?" she asked the chief examiner in the same thin, disturbing tone.

"That will do perfectly," he said and bowed. "But is Your Majesty sure she knows exactly what has been written?"

"I am sure of it," she said. "I have simply abrogated an unhappy relationship that never was a marriage. I divorce myself from Christian."

"That is what the document will imply in any court," he murmured apologetically.

"Very well," she said. "That is what I want."

General Hobe was exceedingly uncomfortable. His inquisition had been successful beyond expectation, but still it had not proceeded according to emotional schedule. He suffered now from an odd feeling that he was the indicted, she the judge. It was quite different from what he had felt towards Struensee, who had so laboriously defended himself for a time. "You have all my sympathy, Madame," he found himself saying. "I have only been doing my duty."

"All right," the Queen said.

"Permit us to withdraw, Madame," Hobe said, inclining his head. She nodded her head once in assent.

The heavy door closed behind them. She walked over to the window to look out. In one place in the sky, she saw, the low-hanging rain clouds had parted, allowing the passage of a shaft of light. It struck the sea slantingly, making a coldly luminous area lighter than the rest. As she watched a gull sailed through the shaft of light. Its wings were so silvery and carven that it did not look quite real. It might, itself, have been made of the same luminous substance.

★ *IV* ★

WHEN STRUENSEE RETURNED to his cell after his confession, he sank down crushed and exhausted on his stool. Juel was very sympathetic, as usual. He studied the prisoner's face intently, almost marveling at his dejection, it seemed. When he left, he went on tiptoe.

Struensee's thoughts wandered feebly, all out of control. He sank deeper and deeper into a morass of despair, and could not stop himself. He came to with a jerk and stared all around the cell, his nerves screwed tight. Something in the cell had changed. Or had it. It was the same cell, the same bed, the same table. Then he saw what subconsciously had caught his attention. Someone had put a thick, old-fashioned book on the table. Without bothering to rise he hitched his stool closer and examined the book. The title on the title-page was printed in large, dull red letters, and had the rusty look of faded blood. *THE ROOM OF DEEP MOURNING, or The Rise and Fall of Great Gentlemen,* the title read. Beneath, in smaller black letters, it said: *For the instruction, edification, example and admonition of the world, by Erasmus Francisci, magistro artium, in the good city of Leipzig, anno domini 1665.*

The book was full of primitive woodcuts, their rude lines often broken off casually in the midst of a baroque sweep. The figures typically showed naïvely astonished faces as if they were wondering how they ever landed in such a peculiar book, clothed as they were in short tunics. Scattered through the text and emphasized by the use of red lettering, were many Christian homilies, quotations from the evangelists, Thomas a Kempis, Augustine and Luther.

Struensee only too readily understood what his unknown tutor was driving at. Instantly the book reminded him of his childhood, for he had seen many similar ones on the shelves of his father's library. Since there was nothing else to divert him, and since the large type allowed him to follow the script even in the cell's bad light, he began to read.

His hands propping his head, elbows on the table the better to hold up the weight of the wrist chains, he lost himself in the stories of Egmont, Demetrius, Maria Stuart and Monaldeschi. He often looked up, smiled to himself and shook his head. But presently the book really caught him up. After weeks of being intensely absorbed in his own troubles, he suddenly realized that they were anything but unique. There they were, repeated again and again in various guises, right under his very nose.

What had Egmont done to deserve his end? What had Mary, Queen of Scots, done to merit decapitation? The state was portrayed as inhuman, a brick oven in which human sacrifices were roasted to a crisp, a leviathan that gulped people whole. And yet, looking at it another way, the people of the book, at least some of them, could not be given a clean slate. Their guilt was extremely personal. Egmont had been too magnificent, too loud of manner, too careless and credulous. Mary, Queen of Scots, had been too good looking for her own good, too blasé, too sensual and ready to love. Struensee was interested.

There was something in the very aspect of the book, in its oldness and fatness and in the shape of its type. As the title suggested, the book did evoke an image of a mourning hall, a place hung in black and equipped with a block and axe for the despatch of the condemned. Yet running through the gloom of the book there was a curious streak of light and joy. These great gentlemen and ladies had fallen hard. But they had not allowed themselves to be crushed by foul circumstance. Death had lent them an added dimension. Erasmus himself pointed out this paradox. Remarking on it, he quoted Luther, to the effect that we find life in the midst of death. That is, we draw strength from our proximity to life immortal.

Immortality! Struensee glanced up absently at the window in the wall. It was getting so dark that he could no longer see to read. Ever since losing his childhood beliefs, he thought, immortality had been only a phrase to him, something other people talked about for what that was worth. He had always felt that the immortality of conventional people was a dubious thing. Now it seemed actually repellent. To care whether the dead were thought of by the living as worthy or unworthy, or perhaps not worth the bother either way, surely was the very acme of stupidity. To care about the immortality of one's works, too, was ridiculous, or to worry about perpetuating oneself through one's children. Struensee thought of his own daughter, and was not in the least consoled. Even this knowable form of immortality was too impersonal to do him any good. Struensee clung hard to his own personality.

But how had the others faced death, the people of the book? They had accepted the end, they had received death graciously, they had willingly laid their necks on the block to receive the bite of the axe. Moreover, they had often forgiven their accusers, the judges, the executioners. Out of the least volitional of all experiences, out of death itself, they had created an act of freedom. And for that reason, according to the book, they were not common mortals, but souls of stature.

Meditating this phenomenon, Struensee realized that something very personal, a deep feeling of trust in something, had prepared them for the final exaltation. Something had steeled them to walk forward boldly into the abyss without a backward glance. Having said a short prayer, laughed an amused laugh, having made a little joke, they were gone, like anyone leaving one room to go into another. For they believed in something. Something made them different from the rest at the supreme moment.

This thought, if nothing else, lightened Struensee's mood. At least the seemingly impossible had been done, and presumably could be done again. Forgetting his chains he paced the now dark cell, back and forth, making a steady clanking. He felt that he had a new task to accomplish. His heart yearned to achieve greater scope. It was an experience that he had had many times before, an intense desire to know himself as elect. An old maxim came to him—*multi multa sciunt, se ipsos nesciunt*. Many know much, but few know themselves. He flushed brick red with shame in the dark.

Looking back on his life it was a worthless bauble. What else but tinsel his easy talk about freedom, derived second-hand from second-hand philosophers? There lay his fine ideas, all strewn about like so many birds with broken wings. There sprawled his good will, broken to bits. There, too, lay his love, a muddied thing, a thing betrayed and smashed.

All the people of his circle who had trusted him he had betrayed. He had let down the sick King, for it had obviously been his duty to help and perhaps cure him, certainly not to take his wife in adultery, however great the allure. Brandt, too, had needed guidance, almost as much as Christian. And what of Frau von Gabel, who had come to him with questioning eyes? What had he done to her? And even Annette von Gaehler, frivolous as she was, should not have been shared like an animal with Filosov. And the people, what of them? What of all Denmark? Had he ever tried to feel the people's pulse, to ferret out their needs and weigh their capacities? No, very plainly he had not. He had handled them from above looking down, wrapped in his own pedantic conceit. Instead of plunging into the mob, he had skirted them. In arrogance he had decreed and ordered, not genuinely caring at all about the people. He had chosen to ignore the long, hard road to millennium in favor of alluring short-cuts.

Was that all that he had been? This splendid, gallant, charming Count Struensee, first minister by the grace of God and the wish of Denmark's king? Was he the same man who had come to a bad end after a confusion of sensuality and experiment with command? Well, here he was, in any case, in a cell, chained, a most serious fellow indeed.

One thing he saw plainly in this bout of self-searching. His downfall had not been generated altogether by his enemies. Rantzau was a scoundrel, of course, Guldberg a creature of remorseless ambition, Juliana a supercilious, coldhearted animal, and yet their various forms of self-seeking were no more to be condemned than his own. The very soul of mankind was at fault, corrupt.

As a blind man feels a smooth, high wall, he felt the enormous irony of fate. He had been judged by his own kind, the false by the false. His case required no such props to carry it off as an avenging angel of justice, dangling scales and sword and sonorously ordering him to account. His crimes had not been that important. The decadent, seamy Rantzau, ox-witted Koeller, mean-minded Guldberg had served quite as well. Yet behind the comedy of retribution he felt a great seriousness, a seriousness, indeed, which presently concerned only himself, but which, it was possible to imagine, or if not tomorrow at least eventually, might very well affect the whole world.

Early the next day when Struensee was still stretched out on his straw-covered planks the cell door opened and a stranger walked in. He was a rather odd-looking fellow, very bulky for his height, with a thin wreath of gray hair encircling a large, smooth skull. This large head, where small bits of eyes lay buried deep behind prominent cheekbones, was disproportionate even for such heavy shoulders. He looked, on account of the large head, like a puppet caricature. He wore a clergyman's gown of heavy black stuff and a narrow, snowy white collar.

Still dazed from sleep, at first Struensee did not recognize the man's calling, but gradually it dawned on him that the man was a minister of the gospel. This was indeed so, for the man introduced himself as Pastor Muenter of St. Peter's. "Yes," he said snuffling rapidly, "since you're of Lutheran persuasion, Count Struensee, or at least I suppose you were baptized in the Lutheran church, I considered it my duty to come to you."

"So it was you who left the book for me," said Struensee.

Pastor Muenter acknowledged it with a smile.

"Please sit down, sir," said Struensee. "Take the stool. I'll stay where I am, if you don't object. The chains bother me."

"Don't trouble on my account," said the Pastor. He sat down cautiously, as if fearful that the stool might explode beneath him like a mine, and let his eyes come to rest on Struensee. It was very disconcerting, his ceremoniousness. "Forgive me for staring at you, Count Struensee," he said quite unexpectedly. "What I've come to say isn't easy to express."

"Say what you like," said Struensee. "I suppose your aim is to prepare me for dying. That's your profession, isn't it?"

"I want to prepare you for eternity," Muenter corrected him.

"Come, what's the difference," said Struensee irritably. "Don't split hairs. If you have anything to say, speak it out clearly."

"Well, there's one thing I'd like to ask you about," said Muenter. "Is it an unpleasant prospect for you? I mean the likelihood that some day you may no longer exist? Think over this question, and give me an honest answer. I have plenty of time."

For the sake of politeness Struensee pretended to meditate the idea, though he knew beforehand what he would say. Indeed, all during his imprisonment the same question had been active in the back of his mind, though he had never squarely faced it. The truth of the matter was that he could not imagine post-mortem existence. Life after death had no meaning, no contour at all for him.

"Thought of being done for good, as you might know, is very painful to me," he said at last. "But all that I have learned, and all my experience as a doctor tell me that no panacea has or ever will be invented for mortality. Some day my time must come. It so happens that this ultimate experience is going to happen rather more quickly than I had anticipated. Even so, it is of no importance, and must be borne. I might easily have died as a boy, of consumption, say. And so, if you come down to it, I have had it pretty easy so far, and I cannot raise a clamor about what happens now. The only way, as I see it, is to take what must come with all the equanimity I can muster, and hope that the quicker it is over with, the better. That is what my reason tells me."

"And you are right," said Muenter.

"Really!" said Struensee. "I am surprised."

"However, in part I am forced to contradict you," Muenter went on to say cautiously, tugging at his snowy collar, smoothing his robes.

"You're correct enough when you say that reason can teach us nothing about life after death. On scientific grounds—or on what I prefer to call pseudo-scientific grounds—nothing is figurable beyond the finality of death. But—and you see how quickly I introduce this 'but'—reason is only a fraction of our total being. Our heart pumps without reason's aid. We breathe without analytical effort. We love without reason, as you must know." Muenter cleared his throat nervously, letting his last sentence sink in.

"The philosophers, not unnaturally, are proud of their superior faculties," he said. "In consequence, they have always tended to over-estimate the value of reason. Descartes, I believe, it was who uttered the monstrous idea of 'I think, therefore I am.' No, that is not true. One might think and think for whole eons without this thinking ever evolving into personal, substantial existence. Descartes would have been more nearly right, in my opinion, if he had put it this way: I think and among other things I think that I am. But that would be a platitude. Do you see my point, Count Struensee?"

"Of course I see," said Struensee, smiling against his will, for his visitor was now staring at him bulge-eyed with a remarkable show of menace.

"Allow me, sir," said Muenter, poking into his white collar, "to leave the sphere of reason and talk for a little in my own language. I say: *cogitor, ergo sum.* That is, I was thought, therefore I am. But this, too, would be mere sophistry were there no one to do the thinking, someone whose thinking is identical with being. And so this idea develops: God thinks, therefore I am."

"Your logic is excellent," said Struensee. "I cannot gainsay it."

"Except for the fact that it is not logic," said Muenter sharply. "It's not a question of reason any more, my friend. I have here abandoned reason for faith. Under no circumstances could I ever *know* that God had thought me and therefore given me being. I *want* it to be like that. I prefer to believe that Christ is the truth. And the more inwardly I believe, the longer I believe and the more fervently, the more clearly an inner voice tells me that I do not believe in vain, and that my belief shall be verified."

"I have heard of these 'inner voices'," said Struensee wryly. "Such a pity that they do not speak to me."

"But they can, and they will," said Muenter loudly. "It's not necessary for you to listen to me to be able to do it. As a matter of fact, it's something that each man must do for himself, even the humblest . . . if there is such a being as the humblest, which I doubt strenuously. Each must believe of his own accord, just as each must do his own dying. It is an act immanent within us, an act expected of us by God, by Him who is Himself the source of all true action."

"Yes, yes," said Struensee mechanically.

"What sort of God," Muenter went on without feeling the interruption, "would he be who could be arrived at by reason, by some sort of Euclidean method! What sort of God would he be, if man could imagine him. I won't even try to tell you, my friend, what God would be like on such niggardly terms. He would be a miserable, meaningless, idol. A Baal, no less, a fabrication, an abortion of the imagination." Here Muenter blew his nose with violence to relieve his interior conviction, took a deep breath, and tried again.

"But the hidden, living God," he intoned, "the *deus absconditus,* forever escapes our conceptual toils. To approach him, my friend, is the greatest of all risks.

"Supposing that the Messiah should appear from the clouds surrounded by legions of angels, accompanied by the blare of trumpets and the flashing of lightnings, his head crowned with a golden crown. Then anybody would be convinced of God's existence. It would require no effort to believe what could be so spectacularly seen. But no. The Messiah did not appear in this resounding fashion. He came as a poor man, a simple carpenter, a beggar, a vagabond. Why did he not show himself at least as a Roman governor, you might ask? Why was he not at least dressed in fine armor, why did he not ride on a warhorse? Not he. He rode on a silly, foolish ass, with an absurd foal trotting along behind. And think of the company he picked to be with! Were there no men of substance in Palestine he might have better consorted with? Were there no learned people, officials, well-to-do merchants, no men of the cloth? Yes. There was any number of them, and he might have drawn them all into his train. Instead he preferred the company of tax-collectors, traitors, do-nothings, whores, beggars. So it went, again and again.

"Is it reasonable that heaven should rejoice more over one remorseful sinner than over a thousand righteous ones? Is it moral, according to ordinary human concept, to hate mother and brothers if need be? Is it sensible to believe that the rich, among whom there are many good people, should be barred *eo ipso* from the kingdom of heaven?"

"I fail to see the point in all this," said Struensee. "You are piling up my difficulties instead of taking them away."

Muenter got up from the stool where he was balancing and paced the cell. "A God who can be completely understood by the exercise of reason alone is no God at all," he said. "At least he is not the Christian God. What does Luther say? 'To make us live, he first destroys us; to vindicate us, he visits guilt upon us; to bring us to heaven, he leads us through hell.' No, Count, I have no intention of relieving you of your difficulties. I know there are people who say that God is justice and that God is love. Why, that's heathen nonsense! Then there are people, I know, who would prove God by arguing that he is the first cause, the prime mover. Others say that his works are sufficient evidence of his existence. But having said so much it is only another step and we have God as Nature, or at least as that portion of Nature which happens currently to be known by us. God as such is not God at all. On such terms he is merely a fifth wheel. Even as first cause he would be superfluous. Inferences drawn from this concept are as misleading and arbitrary as Descartes' derivation of being from thought. Our understanding, in cold fact, can get along very well without God. But man is not reason alone, I insist. Man cannot live properly without the certainty of something which endures beyond the limited span of his individual personality. There must be something within him that resists destruction. Of course, he may know nothing about this interior certainty and indestructibility. It is possible that he may even deny their existence. In fact, this often happens in crisis, when revelation is near."

"Well, if crisis will do it, I am certainly in that condition," said Struensee. "Everything I used to value has turned stale. I don't care any more for the good of mankind."

"And why should you trouble your head about mankind at this juncture, my friend?" said Muenter. "Your problem right now is how to find yourself. As a matter of fact, it has been right along. The well-being of mankind is all very well. But not when used as an excuse by those who lack the courage to seek out themselves. Getting things done is fine, fine indeed. But first know yourself, I say, know why you are getting things done, and to what end."

"Yes, yes, but every decent person must think about the common good," exclaimed Struensee. "Don't you appreciate that?"

"The good of the whole comes about only when the constituent parts of the whole are guaranteed," said Muenter. "It is the individual, the single person who must face God, not the village, the city or any other collection of mankind. God does not ask what you may have done to further the good of mankind. He asks whether you are a true self, a whole person. He asks whether you believe in Him. That is no theory. Examine your own conscience, and you will find that God's eternal questions are ringing in your ears, if you will only hearken to them."

"That is precisely what I fail to understand," said Struensee wearily. "The world is a hopeless mystery. Everything seems so simple on the surface, and yet everything is a riddle, as it proves. Sometimes I think I am going mad, especially when Juel belabors me with his parables. Here in the cell, even, things feel different to my touch. I don't have the same tactual relation with concrete objects that I used to have. That water pitcher, for instance, or the bed I'm lying on. The light coming through the window doesn't seem the same to me. These chains seem strange. Everything strikes my nerves as different in some inexplicable way. I seem forced out of myself, unduly naked. And what I used to break my neck to accomplish now appears unreal to me, utterly fantastic. Perhaps I'm discovering reality. Or are there many realities? Do all prisoners feel like this? Is it confinement that's upsetting me? Is my will cracking? Am I sick?" Struensee put his hands up to his face, unable to express himself any more completely, choked with confusion.

"You are not sick," said Muenter calmly, and knelt by Struensee on the floor. "Yet I would not say that you are well. For the first time in your life you are experiencing the deadly weight of man's world. You are experiencing, too, what the apostle meant when he said that man is created for great things. These great things may look and feel quite different from what you may have imagined. They are not facile, they cannot be forethought. They require the dedication of your whole being. They become real and knowable only when you have given yourself up.

"And just now you are standing on the brink. Not on the brink of madness, but of salvation. You are still afraid of what people will say. The world's judgment gives you pause." Here Muenter drew back, let his words do their work and meanwhile plucked convulsively at his collar, as if drawing reassurance from this occupational gesture.

"I know how hard it is," he told Struensee in a milder tone. "I can appreciate how you must be sure of yourself if you're about to take a step that the crowd is sure to condemn. It's not easy to run the gauntlet of their vilification. For you will certainly be castigated for your seeming weakness. They will say that not only did you betray the state, but yourself as well. And not only this present crowd will condemn you, but all posterity as well. Never will you be celebrated as a hero, never till the end of time. That was Struensee, they will say, the man who repudiated his liberalism, who betrayed his ideals, and did it out of fear of death. For belief in Christ is always, as its author says, an insult to the pious, an absurdity to the clever. And so it will remain until the end of time. It will always be so, so long as the Christian belief is not watered down, popularized, made conciliatory. That is, so long as it is not made into another worldly device."

Struensee slowly took his hands away from his face. "You're right," he said slowly, looking into Muenter's face. "I am on the verge of a new life. You are right. But you must understand that this experience of standing at the crossroads is nothing new to me. For I belong to those who are neither good nor bad. The ignoble ones, as the poet says. God will spit us out of His mouth, the scriptures say. In other words, I belong among the majority of mankind. In the middle of the road. If this had never happened to me, if I'd never stumbled into this trap, I assure you that I'd have walked the fence all my life. Now I see that I cannot die so suspended. Being, real being, does not permit it. Yes, it is more serious, as you say, much greater, much more tragic and rending than anything I had ever imagined.

"When I was out of prison, a free man, I took my stand on the idea of good will. I was caught in a pretty net of fancy. I never really denied God. I merely looked the other way. I was so busy, you see. I rushed from one piece of business to the next. In order not to stop and see Him, if you will, though I did not recognize my dereliction as such. I thought it was the safe and proper way. Now that I smell death all around me, I realize I was wrong. It was a consistent refusal to face the issue and face myself. I made up my mind about many things, but never about myself."

"Well then, until I see you again, my friend," said Muenter and suddenly reached Struensee his hand.

"You're leaving so soon!" said Struensee. "Why must you go?"

"There's nothing more for me to do," said Muenter. "You know the decision you must make as well as I. Much better, in fact, than I possibly can know. If I should load you with remonstrances and admonitions and promises, it would only revolt you. Your decision must be the most personal one imaginable. It is so private that even the presence of another person, even should the other person remain perfectly silent and effaced, would be painful to you. Don't think that I wouldn't gladly accept the responsibility of your displeasure. Or even your anger, if I thought it necessary. But the danger is that out of defiance of me, or out of weakness, or perhaps even out of friendship" . . . Muenter rubbed his wreath of hair in embarrassment at such an unlikely thought . . . "you might be influenced one way or the other. Should this come about, then of course your decision would be worthless. Anyway, I find it unseemly to force myself on you. Even if you agreed with me today, even if you rejoiced with me and threw yourself in my arms, there would still be the danger that tomorrow you might cast me from you in hatred. And with a justified hatred, since it might derive from your desire to win back your own power of decision."

Struensee smiled and pressed the pastor's hand. "I can understand," he said. "You have a great respect for freedom."

"The very greatest respect," said Muenter. "Freedom of the spirit is what differentiates man from the rest of God's beasts."

"You are never done surprising me," said Struensee. "I know that you're no friend of reform."

"You are right, so far as I am not a friend of your reforms," said Muenter. "Yet don't think that I would not like to have the people universal and free. I pray for these things, every day I pray for them. Nor do I despise your good will, especially now that I am closer to you. But freedom that comes to us from the outside is no freedom at all in my creed. It's merely another form of slavery. It is merely a worldly device blinding us to true freedom. Freedom lies in positive action. It lies in a personal act of union with God which each must fulfill in his own fashion. No one is free merely because someone has manumitted him. Freedom must evolve of its own accord, as the shoot breaks forth from the seed. And in this regard it makes no difference whether I address a serf or a prisoner in chains. Not, understand, that I justify the institution of serfdom.

"Observe, however, the danger that the crowd, once casually unshackled, living riotously according to their pseudo-freedom, will in good time turn against the individual and attempt to smash the individual conscience and the individual choice. I fear and abhor the tyranny of the mob. For the truly free man is naturally a constant source of reproach to those who live in false freedom. What might come were the mob superficially free? Can you not imagine that eventually the crowd would begin to deify itself, to pray to itself, instead of living in God and in God's quiet freedom? And how very likely that the crowd, being superficially liberated, will seek to impose their own false concepts of freedom on others, and by so doing eradicate true freedom, which must forever remain a personal thing."

"One more matter before you go, Pastor Muenter," said Struensee hesitantly. "Why haven't you talked to me about sin. Why haven't you catechized me on such questions as Christ's sacrifice, the trinity and so on. Frankly, that's what I was expecting of you. Instead you talk about vindication through an act of belief. You tell me nothing about what I am to believe."

"You are right in that," said Muenter. "I might have gone into all these matters. They are certainly within my province." He stopped for a moment, not knowing properly what to say. "The foundations of our belief," he went on at last, "the small and the great catechism and all that has been carefully thought out and written down in fixed language, might only have impressed you as another scheme, no better than your own. But you must seize onto what seem to be the dry words of the catechism with passion, and passion comes only in good time. Without passion the words do not live within you. Once again we have recapitulated your task. With a man like you I need not worry about your never having heard of the Lutheran dogma. You were brought up in a minister's home. You may have forgotten some of the detail of your religion. But dig into your memory. Best of all, recall your childhood."

"Ah yes, my childhood," said Struensee. He forced himself up from his wooden bed with a rattle and clink of the chains.

"Go back to the very wellspring of your adult life," said Muenter. "There you will find your true self."

Struensee sobbed quietly. He felt miserable and yet feverishly happy all at once. He hardly raised his head when Muenter knocked on the cell door to summon Juel to let him out. Just as the Pastor was leaving Struensee hitched himself about and said: "When are you coming again?"

"In three days, I believe," said Muenter. "If you want to see me before that time, let me know." And with that he walked off down the long prison corridor.

★ *V* ★

WHEN STRUENSEE THOUGHT back on his childhood, an image of the main aisle of St. Maurice's Church in Halle took shape before his eyes. He saw the neat white interior of the church, with the big Bible laid open on the altar between old-fashioned silver candelabra, and behind this arrangement the picture of Christ crucified. In the picture it was night. Only the pale body of the dying Christ, a beardless, severe, thorn-crowned figure with a lolling head, the eyes tightly closed, lit up the composition. The arm muscles stood out taut, sinews drawn tight as piano wires, the bloody palms pierced by enormous nails, the slack rump, the bony knees and the long, limp feet all looked incomparably dead.

During evening services, Struensee now remembered, when candles were burning at the altarside, the eerie light emanating from Christ's stricken body seemed to glow more brightly with spectacular effect. Struensee saw himself again, looking intently at the picture. A little grayish snake hung down soft and dead at the feet of Christ. The snake interested the boy tremendously. He sensed that it was the snake which had enticed the ur-mother of mankind to commit mortal sin in Eden. This intuition he had never been able to put into coherent language and out of shame he had never dared ask his father to explain it to him.

Another detail of the picture which stood out in the candlelight was the inscription AD, the two letters cramped close together. The painter had put the inscription in a corner of the canvas. Struensee knew now that the letters were the initials of the master who had painted the picture in Luther's time. But as a boy the initials had been as much a mystery to him as the snake. He had an idea for a time that somehow the letters were directed at him personally. Shortly after his first Latin lessons—his father had given them to him—he thought he had deciphered the meaning. The initials stood for "anno domini," year of Our Lord.

Sitting on his three-legged stool remembering these things, Struensee smiled ruefully to himself. When was my year of Our Lord, he asked himself? Faintly he heard the echo of the light voices of the choir of orphan children singing the old hymn:

"Oh head, so dire molested,
By mankind shamed and torn,
Oh head, for mock invested
With a cruel crown of thorn."

Dimly in retrospect he saw his father, the broad back as he gravely climbed the pulpit steps, the boards creaking under his heavy step. Facing the audience his father folded his hands, bowed his head to the balustrade of the pulpit and prayed. It had always embarrassed him to see his father make so humble a gesture before so many people. It seemed overdone, theatrical. Now, alone in his cell, Struensee keenly regretted his boyish lack of understanding.

The year of Our Lord! Were they all years of Our Lord: the school years, the years spent in the dissecting room, the years as physician among the poor of Altona and the landed gentry of Holstein. Even the years of power, love and debacle had been years of Our Lord.

He tried to see himself in the distant past, tried to remember how he must have looked to others. At first everything was misty and splintered. He remembered the corner of the room where his bed had stood. He saw his mother, her head bowed as she sewed busily, a basketful of small clothes beside her on the floor, the candlelight making shadows on her face. He saw his father, quill in hand, this held like a weapon, so excited by his thoughts that he could not sit still. That had always happened on a Friday, for on that day the Sunday sermon had been composed. And on Fridays no meat was eaten in the rectory, nothing but plums and noodles. That was what the children had liked best, Friday plums and noodles.

Struensee saw himself standing at the window in his nightshirt looking out into the winter night. Outside snow was falling. The gables of the neighboring houses were lost in the swirl. Huge drays were moving through the street. Men with lanterns guided the animals pulling the vehicles. They were loaded high with household goods, the wheels squealed and groaned as they turned drily on their axles. His father, standing behind him, had said: "They are being driven out on account of their faith."

This picture faded and was succeeded by another. Now he saw the fat woman next door, the one with the double chin, the mountainous bosom and the smoothly combed hair. The fat woman was a kindly female demon, and nonetheless a demon because a woman. There was something dangerous about her. She pasted, stuffed, knit and sewed when the parishioners were making dolls in the rectory to be distributed among the poor children of the city at Christmas time.

The fat woman was restlessly busy, so busy that in her absorption the spittle ran out the corners of her mouth. It was impossible to keep track of her sleight-of-hand movements. She sewed with unbelievable speed. The fever of creation was in her and she made little burghers' wives, servant girls, queens, peasants and what not with indifferent rapidity. Sometimes to vary her theme she would make a male doll, usually a soldier. All her dolls were meticulously dressed. When she finished one she grinned momentarily at her handiwork, then almost at once lost interest in it and threw it into the big basket. The basket was full of doll-bodies, like the pesthouse during a year of plague.

The dolls had fascinated the three-year-old boy. The woman from next door knew how to give the doll faces a characteristic expression with a few strokes of a brush. She would dip the brush into the paint and miraculously produce a broad smile, or expressions of sarcasm, pride, sadness or perhaps of stupidity. This last was her favorite expression.

Struensee penetrated deeper and deeper into the landscape of his childhood. He felt vaguely that he was drawing closer to some essential, critical event. Half-forgotten impressions came to light in quick succession. Struensee let his memory empty itself in a flood of small scenes remembered, of faces and minor happenings. Then something caught his attention.

He remembered being in woods at twilight. The underbrush was heavy, pathless and grew high over his head. Everywhere blue showed through the dark green of the foliage. Struensee suddenly recalled where he was.

It had happened when he was about ten or eleven years old. In the spring he had had measles and so thin and sickly had this made him that his parents had sent him to live for a while with his aunt in the country. Again he saw the country rectory, the garden with sunflowers and beehives amid the fruit trees, the white church, the peasant houses with straw roofs, the rye fields and the meadows populous with grazing cattle. From the church tower he had been able to see the woods on all sides of the hamlet. The place was like a little island in the dark forest.

The forest was friendly enough during the daylight hours, but towards evening it became threatening. His aunt had warned him not to go into the woods after sundown. She talked about wolves, the remnants of a great pack, so she said, that had come into the countryside a hundred years before, from the east, at the time of the Thirty Years' War.

It was mid-summer now and berries were ripe in the woods. All the young people of the village took baskets and went picking berries. The girls he remembered all seemed to wear their hair in thick braids that hung down below kerchiefs. The boys went barefoot, and talked very boldly and bravely, though they were frightened enough of the unknown behind this false front. So there he was, the boy Struensee, picking berries in the woods with the village children.

Voices sounded different among the trees. When he laughed his voice sounded hollow and unreal. In some spots his companions' laughter made mysterious echoes and when this happened the littlest ones grabbed for the bigger girls' hands in lieu of their mothers'. How still it was in the woods. And yet how much rustling, once their ears had become adjusted to the comparative silence, a rustling compounded of thousands of unidentifiable stirrings, insectean chirpings, buzzings of beetle wings, branches chafing against each other, animals moving furtively through the undergrowth, the faint bubbling of spring water.

The boy gradually forgot his aunt's warning about the wolves. Farther and farther he wandered into the green forest depths. It was delightful to come upon a stand of beech, where the ground was covered with curled tawny leaves and fine green moss. He loved the spruce thickets, humming with gnats, airless and hot and strong with rough odor of resin. But most of all the boy liked the slopes covered with fan-shaped fern growth, covering a rocky detritus. Here there were blueberry bushes in great profusion.

The berries lured him on, masses of small round berries of lapis lazuli color set against a background of smaragd green. From one bush to the next he wandered, getting deeper into the bushy, ferny tangle. On some bushes the berries grew so thickly that all he had to do was reach up and strip them off, getting whole handsful of fruit at a time. The palms of his hands were red from crushed berries. Here the wilderness was a primeval wood. The ferns were very large, the bushes closed in over his head. Furiously, greedily he stripped off the blueberries. He imagined himself as a fairy prince bravely venturing into a dragon's thicket haunt to rescue the fairy beauty. It was not so much the berries themselves that lured him on as something unseen lurking among the bushes. He was caught up by a spirit of adventure, by the will to try himself out and capture the genius of the wood. He felt he must conquer the woods. Sweat streamed down face, his skin was prickly with gnat bites, his shirt torn by twigs, but still he lunged forward, making dead limbs crackle, tripping over them. The woods swallowed him up.

Hours passed unnoticed. Time was standing still. Suddenly a wild dove called from some hidden place. The call came to his ears as a sweet, sad monotone, vibrant with sentiment and enticement and sadness, yet colored by a gentle menace. There was one long cooing and then all was deathly still.

The boy listened intently, every nerve at attention. Presently the hidden bird cooed again, a shorter call than before. Now the boy looked all around. Somehow the woods had changed. The shadows, for one thing, had grown much longer. Golden flecks of light were dappling the leafy earth. The boy shouted for his companions. There was no answer. All about him, also listening, were stiff, sentinel tree trunks. Behind each one something or someone was hiding. He distinctly felt this.

Suddenly fear came over him and he ran with all his strength. He perspired freely, he tipped over his berry basket and all the blue treasure was gone. Yet, however hard he ran, he could not catch up his companions. However often he stopped to listen, cocking his ears, he could not hear the friendly buzz of their voices. Woods hemmed him in on all sides, an endless procession of tree trunks. Shafts of light shot down endlessly through the tree crowns. There were ever new rocky, ferny places. In the slanting light of late afternoon they looked amazingly sinister and even bewitched. The boy felt himself trapped in a region of witches, giants and cruel dwarfs who lived underground. The very stones seemed to have faces. These faces dogged this way and that, following him as he rushed along, sneaking after him. The demonic world had broken loose in him, and he ran pell-mell and vainly to escape it. But no use. The woods would not give him up. He was caught in a labyrinth. Even now, sitting in the cell, Struensee could vividly recall his childish terror. Even remembering it took his breath away. In vain he tried to smile off the foolish pangs of anxiety reverberating in his memory.

But even now when he was a man in full possession of his powers the world was hardly less fraught with hidden terrors. Like the boy with his berries, he had rushed about furthering his material plans and ambitions, fancying himself a great figure of a man. For a time, carried away by his heroic projection of self, he had managed to overlook the demonic elements of the world. And now, just as with the little boy out berrying, night had overtaken him. Now, as then, he found himself alone. There were no friends to talk to. The violins were mute, the dreams faded, Caroline's sweet flesh gone and he alone in the whole world. And this world was, if anything, more sinister and less incomprehensible than any childhood counterpart.

The boy Struensee had thrown himself on the ground in despair and wept bitterly. That had not held back the night. The doves were still and the owls commenced to whoo-hoo. The shadows fused together into solid darkness. Somehow darkness seemed to rise up out of the ground.

The boy made a bed of sorts under a beech tree growing at the edge of a glade. The earth under the beech tree was soft with moss. Carefully he wrapped his coat about him, closed his eyes and prayed. He prayed that God might guide him back home when it came light again, and protect him while he slept.

Even today he remembered how a wonderful feeling of relief had come over him, how the fear had ebbed away, how he presently began to experience a floating, swimming sensation, as if borne on deep waters. The night settled down, cool and by no means unpleasant.

He woke up out of a very deep sleep. Something had tickled his cheek, perhaps a swaying stalk of grass. What he saw made him weak with wonder. The woods looked enchanted. An unreal light filtered down through the tree tops and flooded the glade. The beech branches shone like pale silver. The grass, all hung with spider webs, was glistening. Dizzily he raised himself on one elbow and felt the coolness of the night and smelled the fragrance of the night air. He drew his jacket more tightly about himself. Slowly he realized that it was the full moon that had worked such a remarkable change. He got up and looked into the open glade. There a little herd of deer were browsing, their heads bent trustingly. A thrill of joy came over him at this sight of the deer in the moonlight. The world was so utterly peaceful, quite different from the daylight world. Was this the night that had so frightened him at home when he cowered in bed? It was just as beautiful as the day, though different, unutterably different and lovely in its own way.

Then again he was profoundly surprised, for over and beyond the glade where the deer were feeding the land fell away, and in the moonlight he saw his own village revealed in the moonlit valley below. There were the familiar scattered peasant homes, there the white church, the rectory and farther along, shimmering under the moon, the fields of rye, all ready and full, waiting for the scythe. Never before or since had he been so relieved. Never before or afterwards had he ever felt so completely sure that the world was God's world and that he, together with all things, rested in God's hands.

The boy dropped to his knees in the moonlight, a small figure at the edge of the forest opening, and thanked God as he had been taught to do. He thanked Him for the night, for the fields of rye, the wood, the village. In this moment of revelation he at least dimly sensed that without great fear he would never have been able to experience exquisite relief in more than ample compensation. What might superficially be called evil, as unpleasant as it had seemed at the time, Struensee now thought in his cell, really had been only goodness not yet fully revealed and understood as such.

Actually, of course, all this came to him clearly only in the tardy present, as he sat in chains. That other time, long ago in the forest, he had not thought things through at all, nor could he have done. In vain, too, he tried to recapture the physical exaltation of the child he once had been.

Now it was long after midnight. The enormous Citadel in which he was buried, all the twisting corridors, the cell rows filled with prisoners like himself, anxious like himself, despairing, indifferent, long since reconciled to permanent misery—all this huge complex was silent as death in the night. It seemed to him that the great structure, with its heavy walls and thick arches, was a world in its own right, stripped of all pretense and ornament, divested of chance. It was like a great brain with many convolutions; a labyrinth in the midst of which he struggled with the ox-headed god of death for the possession of that little skein of colored wool which was his childhood.

He remembered now how, the first night of his immurement, a strange and trusting child had appeared to him out of the darkness, a child who, so Juel had said, often appeared to inhabitants of the Citadel, robbers or murderers though they might be.

How could he do it, how work his way back to the full consciousness of childhood and there find the true Struensee? How perform the seemingly impossible task of not merely thinking as a child, but feeling as one? How was it possible for an adult man, burdened with much knowledge, hardened in cynical habits, to rediscover the simplicity of the child within himself, the simplicity which had led the six-year-old Struensee to fold his hands and peacefully sleep in a forest which he had fully believed was the lair of wolves and evil spirits, yet wake up safely in the bright moonlight and discover himself safely near to home?

Meditating this issue, Struensee realized that one thing and one thing only was prerequisite. It was the same thing that the charlatan Cagliostro had pointed out to him, the same thing that Magist Francisci had discovered in his heroes and heroines, the same thing, indeed, about which Pastor Muenter's conversation had revolved. And no matter how much he contemplated this crucial negation of self, no matter how fervently he tried to encompass it with his understanding, it would not come to him. For what was asked of him was not understanding, but a positive act of faith.

Trust in God was the factor that now seemed to Struensee to be the axis on which not only his own life, but all life, must turn in order to be fully realized. He admitted to himself that all attempts to live without God—his own attempt among countless others—of necessity had ended and would always end in fiasco. For living without God was like Baron Muenchhausen trying to lift himself and his horse out of the bog by pulling upwards on his own pigtail.

And yet he could not believe, he could not trust, though by this time his understanding was willing to be blotted out. Pride held him back, the pride of Lucifer.

Again he sank back into reminiscences of childhood. He remembered water being all about him, quick gay little waves. Willow trees drooped into the water, the warm summer air was shrill with the screams of boys at play.

Struensee knew where he was. That was the river of his childhood, the Saale River. How beautifully it ran in the warm summertime. The sky was filled with slowly drifting clouds, enormous, sculptured masses. And behind the river rose up the hill, on the top of which an ancient fortress lay in ruins. And the laughter of childhood, how sweet it was to think back on it!

Struensee saw himself going into the water on tiptoe and letting out a squeal of delight at the coldness of it. He saw himself wading in until the water reached nearly up to his hips. He heard the chaffing shouts of his friends as they sported about stark naked, making great splashes when they hit the water, playing tricks on each other with the avidity of small satyrs. Then, making up his mind, he dived underwater. The shock of the cold took his breath away. He came up spluttering, shook his head, blinked his eyes. Water was flowing through his hair. His body, a curious possession, glistened with wet in the sunlight.

A few strokes and he was out in the middle of the stream. How different the world looked from mid-river. Much larger, much more mysterious. The sky, for one thing, seemed higher. The hill was now an immense mountain height. Being in the water at river-level some-how brought all the features of the earth into sharper focus. In the water he felt released, a part of the river and of the earth. It was quite different from moving about through the thin airy element.

He turned over on his back. He felt the water buoying him up, softly, yieldingly and yet strongly. Now he had ceased to be a sep-arate person. He belonged to the stream, he was part of the stream's murmurous progress, its lively splashings, its undulant movements.

Struensee had closed his eyes to shut out the dim lineaments of his cell. His chains fell away. The river bore him along, the wonderful river of his youth. He saw pleasing landscapes, landscapes that he actually had never seen at all as a boy. Floating along imaginatively he saw Frederiksborg, and recognized it as such even in his deep reverie. There was the garden of Rosenborg and the blonde Queen. There was Christiansborg in marble splendor, beset with gardens in which walked the King. There was the Thames, and Versailles, crowded with women wearing their hair heavily powdered and piled up high on their heads. Farther and farther the stream carried him. He saw his study in Altona and the old man of bones, he saw the fisher hut on the shores of the Baltic where he had met Antje Maria. He was again in the anatomical theater of the University, and in his father's library. And yet all the while he was being carried onward by the river, on through all the deepest impressions of his life. Seen in retrospect from the river they seemed totally different from what they had been at the earlier time. Everything was on a grander scale, everything seemed higher, deeper, more meaningful, much more beautiful. And irrevocably beyond recapture.

Though this river passage was gratifying to the half somnolent Struensee in his cell, underlying the gratification was a presage of catastrophe. Suddenly the imagined waters began to move faster. Faster and faster the remembered images flowed past, as if time had fallen out of kilter, as if the years were piling up higgledy-piggledy, spewed out carelessly from some laboring machine.

He heard the water's roar and rush. Was it a spillway, or was it the sea? In any case, there was a smother of water ahead. His heart cramped with fear. The water now sped heavily, all roiled and torn, through narrow gateways and pressed against high white walls. Now he knew where he was. He was being carried through the Church of St. Maurice. The church was full of river water, but the silver candelabra on the altar-table were lit, even as the water flowed over them. His father stood braced in the pulpit, his hands folded over his head. His face was twisted in an expression of despair, his eyes were red from weeping.

The waves mounted higher, the candles went out. But still it was not completely dark in the church. The water was faintly lit up from within by a greenish-blue light. Like a corpse he let himself be carried along by the waves. Utter despair was in his heart.

At this moment the Christ of the painting stepped down from the cross. There he stood, Albrecht Duerer's Christ. With outspread arms and drooping hands still leaking blood from the wounds he mounted the altar and walked out onto the water.

"I'm sinking," Struensee heard himself call out from the water. "Save me, save me!"

The Christ from the painting bent down to him "What are you so afraid of?" he asked slowly. "Have you no faith at all!"

Struensee awoke from his reverie with a horrible start. His body was ice cold, as if he really had been immersed in water. His hands and feet were leaden and had no feeling. Yet deep inside him was a sensation of blessedness and comfort, as if there glowed within his being a source of warmth and light.

Slowly he folded his hands and thanked God on his knees.

★ *VI* ★

S TRUENSEE KNEW THAT his enemies would ask for his death. They had to get him out of the way. Not because he was a dangerous character in himself, or because there was any chance that he might be restored to his former position through the King's favor. Struensee had to die because the Queen-Dowager, Rantzau, Guldberg and the rest had to transform their palace revolution into a legal fiction. Nothing could provide a more durable aspect of legality than to have the principal object of their attack tried by a regular court and formally condemned to execution.

Moreover, only by the highly persuasive maneuver of killing off Struensee could they substantially forestall any potential countermoves which might in the future be hatched by liberal freethinking elements, or by the party largely dedicated to the freeing of the serfs, or lastly by the personal friends and admirers of the Queen. Struensee felt there was no chance that his enemies might relent even, say, to the extent of banishing him to some island off the coast of Norway, or of imprisoning him for life in some out of the way fortress. He was too well acquainted with the narrow and vindictive spirit of action on the statesman's level to harbor the slightest illusion about his fate.

The public prosecutor, Fiscal-General Wivet, was notorious for his bumbling stupidities, his coarseness of mind, his marvelous ignorance of the law and of legal forms. Like so many dull people he considered himself nonetheless to be the soul of wit, and since the employment of wit even in serious situations was a conceit of the times, the General let fly with his bombard sallies at every opportunity. The indictment was drawn up by his own hand, and he studded it with insults and heavily humorous references. The document read like an unhappy imitation of Rabelais. It was a caricature of justice. In some paragraphs the vocabulary drew heavily on the colloquialisms in use among Copenhagen fishwives. In other places were complicated quotations from the Latin, to show what a clever fellow the General was. Those who read the indictment mopped their brows and asked themselves whether Wivet could be serious. They whispered among themselves that the author of this stupendous hodgepodge, had he deliberately set his mind on demonstrating the essential illegality of the court process against Struensee, could not have done it more effectively. Even the Fiscal-General's personal friends, who by habit made broad allowance for his eccentricities, were alarmed.

However, whatever his shortcomings, the Fiscal-General had committed himself to no easy assignment. He was supposed to build up a case on the flimsiest of grounds. The only solid fact at his disposal was the Queen's adultery, and this fact, at the last, it was unanimously agreed to suppress. After some hesitation England had intervened. Lord North, busy as he was with a thousand other more important matters, had found time to speak a coldly warning word. The newspapers and Parliament had backed him up.

Having secured the Queen's confession the junta of conspirators had some idea of bringing her into court. The boldest among them, indeed, had proposed that she be executed, or at least annul her marriage to Christian and brand her children as illegitimate. But once England spoke up it was too late to carry out any such overweening project. The Queen-Dowager saw her hopes of putting her own son on the Danish throne go up in smoke. Storm clouds were gathering. From Lord Keith's thin lips, which opened and closed as he talked like a small pair of scissors, came the chilling information that an English squadron lay ready to sail from Plymouth, should it prove necessary to protect or revenge the sister of the English king. This was not quite true. The squadron was really outfitted for service along the shores of the North American colonies, where all manner of trouble was brewing. But in Copenhagen there was no way of safely calling Lord Keith's imperturbable bluff.

By this means the unfortunate Fiscal-General was deprived of the only sound argument for constructing his bill of particulars. He had no choice but grope his way along through a fog of conjecture. There was one other point, of no importance at first glance, which it appeared might be fruitfully developed. This was the fact that Brandt had fought with the King and thrashed him. Brandt's misdemeanor, if such it could be called, could be inflated all out of reason into a deliberate attempt to kill the King, this on Struensee's instigation, so as to clear his way to the throne. It was this argument which Wivet, in his grotesque fashion, set about constructing.

Brandt, like Struensee, occupied a cell in the Citadel. Sometimes he became thoroughly downhearted. Then he would play melancholy little airs from the operas on his flute. One he was especially fond of, *Mourir, c'est notre dernier ressort,* though actually he really had no confidence at all in any such doleful sentiment. He wrote a letter to the King and begged to be let off with banishment to a Holstein village. His letter was never delivered. Little did he realize at the time that it was not Struensee's affair with the Queen but his boxing match with Christian that had become the central theme of the indictment.

Considering how desperately Brandt had tried to avoid coming to blows with the King, using the incident as a leit-motif in ridding Denmark of the erstwhile usurpers had its humorous side. The irony of it did not escape Struensee. But he had by now accommodated himself moderately well to the thought that he was going to die a violent death, and was more or less indifferent as to the staging of the drama of condemnation. At the same time he was deeply troubled about his friend. He had got him into the mess, he had encouraged his frivolities in order to have a free hand in matters of state, and now it looked as if Brandt were to pay with his life, since the adultery issue had been shelved.

With his extravagances, his silly *maître de plaisir* ambitions, his contempt for the needs of ordinary working life, Brandt was not nearly so lacking in culpability as Struensee, letting friendship override cold sense, chose to think him. He had done as he pleased at the court so far as circumstances allowed. He had drunk gluttonously of pleasure and still thirsted for more. In so doing he had lost himself. The things Brandt had chased after were mean and pitiable. So much the more pathetic his downfall, from the viewpoint of the converted Struensee.

So far as he alone was concerned, Struensee felt that he stood before the bar of justice indicted on several counts. He merited condemnation as a creature of unbelief and idealistic pride. He had not erred in particular, but he had erred in general.

And he considered himself in no way responsible to the examining magistrate, Hobe, or in any way accountable in the matter of supposed crimes against the state as concocted by the Fiscal-General Wivet. During the actual trial the defendant replied only lamely, for mere form's sake, to arguments that he might easily have confounded, yet Struensee raised no objection to the travesty. Indeed, the whole convention of jurisprudence had come to mean nothing to him, since he felt himself indicted on a much higher plane of legality. The process of judgment had already taken place in his cell, within himself. The wordy, contrived play of worldly justice, he thought, was a painful farce.

In the real court he was not only the accused, but the judge, prosecutor, defending attorney and witness as well, however much he might have to strain to encompass these conflicting roles. He felt a great compulsion to go through the disagreeable business of self-examination, and this he did. The evidence dug up during months of self-inspection forced him to an irrevocable conclusion—that he was heavy with guilt. And death, as he now interpreted these things, was the natural consequence of this guilt. Had he not committed mortal sins? Yet, notwithstanding his state of contrition, Struensee's idealist's pride was still alive. He could not believe that Brandt might also have stood before a religious bar of justice like himself. Even in contrition he still considered himself to be a chosen man, forgetting that a man is unlike other men only if he thinks himself so. Still, prideful or not, he was filled with pity for his friend who, he believed, would have to die utterly against his inclination.

With these thoughts in mind Struensee had writing materials brought into the cell and there wrote an apology for his reforms and detailed answers to the accusations of the Fiscal-General. It was a laborious composition and took a full week to complete. His chains bothered him and the light was so bad that he could not see to write his usual neat hand. But the style was clear and simple. Fact marched after fact, always in step. Wanting nothing for himself now that he was no longer enslaved by egotism, wishing nothing but vindication for his ideas as such, able at last to speak out objectively, he spoke eloquently of the need for building up the state on a foundation of material justice. He openly admitted many mistakes made through inexperience, over-anxiety, haste. On the other hand he refused to alter his basic views, and would not curry favor with those who held his life in their hands.

Compliant in everything that concerned him personally, Struensee was inflexible in defending his ideology. He struck hard at his opponents. "It is much better," he wrote of the petty nobles of Denmark, "that the nobility live on their estates rather than at the court, should they wish to pass their lives in idling, for at the court they stand before the eyes of the world and set a bad example. If they wish, however, to be active in the government, they must begin at the bottom. Exceptions to this rule are justified only on real grounds, for example, in event of very unusual administrative gifts. Mere royal favor and a few years' residence at the court do not justify responsible participation in government."

From the question of barratry he went on to discuss the narrow-mindedness of the police state. "Morals cannot be improved," he wrote, "by police regulations and spying. The secret vices encouraged by the use of force are often the worst of all, compounded as they are by hypocrisy."

In his isolation, however, Struensee had ceased to be more than a formal protagonist of enlightenment and modernity. He had come to realize that the transiently new in time itself must pass into discard. His eyes were now fixed on eternal truths and goals, the norms that impress continuity on all periods, recent and long ago. He had come to see that the very fundamental difficulty of living up to these eternal factors justified mankind in God's eyes. Whereas these underlying imperatives were ever vital and ever new, the constantly changing externals of social behavior had no more meaning than changing modes of dress.

Struensee reread his apology slowly and carefully, meditated on what he had written, then wrote under the document: "Moral observations coming from a prison cell are rightly suspect. However, in this regard I wish to state categorically that I neither expect nor want moral exoneration, and that the foregoing remarks are in no sense intended to elicit clemency." He then signed the paper, folded it with precision, sealed it and gave it to Juel with instructions to have it forwarded to the court.

Pastor Muenter often repeated his visits. Struensee's new way of seeing things—his willingness to feel responsible to supernatural rather than to natural judges—rather disturbed the Lutheran divine. He had wrought more than he had expected. In many ways Struensee's attitude, he thought to himself, failed to square with orthodox Christianity. The Pastor listened. He saw clearly that in Struensee the world had missed an excellent preacher of the gospel.

One day Muenter arrived at the Citadel in dejection. With him he brought a document for Struensee, which he silently handed over. "Don't be so gloomy, my friend," said Struensee, without opening the paper. "I've already got the news from Juel. He said he didn't know which way the court had swung, only that they had come to a decision. But now I see that the end has come."

"Yes," said Muenter quietly, "it's a death sentence, all right."

Struensee did not reply for some time. "Well, it's a great relief," he told Muenter, when he finally spoke. "No more uncertainties now. But one thing still worries me. What's going to happen to Brandt?"

"His sentence is the same as yours."

"Why, that's imposible," said Struensee. The tears came into his eyes. "The poor fellow didn't do anything. The worst anyone could say of him is that he was ill-advised. Who would sentence a man to death for that!"

"The court simply chose to interpret his scuffle with the King as attempted murder," said Muenter. "You know how it is."

"But that's utter madness!" said Struensee. "Brandt couldn't kill a mouse. You know he couldn't. The King forced him into it. What a pity. How I regret ever advising Brandt to let Christian have his way. It's really my fault. Isn't it possible to ask the King for clemency in Brandt's case?"

"They say, though I cannot personally vouch for it, that when Guldberg signed his name to Brandt's death sentence he begged him to spare the prisoner's life," Muenter said. "But the King replied that he would pardon Brandt only if they pardoned you. The Queen-Dowager came in at this point. Guldberg implored her to lighten your sentence to life imprisonment, so that Brandt, at least, would not have to suffer an obvious miscarriage of justice. Yes, they say Guldberg talked as if he had not countersigned the death warrant at all! But the Queen-Dowager was deaf to his appeals. The more he talked, the more indignant she became. 'Where is justice in Denmark,' she is alleged to have said, 'if judges themselves plead the cause of regicides and adulterers. Brandt is just as deserving of the death sentence as Struensee. If he does not deserve to die for striking the King, then he certainly does for keeping my son out of the royal box.' Guldberg tried to catch the King's eye, hoping that he might intervene. But it was quite useless. The King was playing with his poodle and seemed to have forgotten everyone in the room."

"There's no hope from that source," said Struensee. "These are miserable times, believe me. It's no great loss to leave the world. Still, I wish most desperately that Brandt be allowed to live. If only long enough for him to find himself, as I have done." In his agitation he walked rapidly back and forth, dragging his chains heedlessly. "Let me read the sentence, friend," he said suddenly and slumped down on his stool. "Let us see what they have done."

He read down through a long list of fictitious crimes—criminal plotting, high treason, refusal to bow to the customary law of the land, attacks on religion, immorality. The liaison with the Queen was not mentioned specifically at all. The document was composed in the Fiscal-General's unique style. It was padded out with gratuitous insults, syntactical flourishes, hairsplittings, wandering lies. Struensee let the paper slip from his hands. "You know, my friend, the man who hatched this egg ought to be given a hundred lashes," he said. "If I'd written the court's opinion, you'd have had something to remember. Something severe and simple, I tell you. Still . . . what difference does it make, what difference, pray tell me!" Once again he reached for the paper and read. The final paragraph ran:

"According to article one, chapter four, book six of the legal code of the kingdom of Denmark, the Count Johann Friedrich Struensee, having merited this punishment, and in order that he may serve as a deterrent example for all others, shall be deprived of his honor, his life and his property. He shall, namely, be reduced from his rank of Count, and shall be stripped of all other titles and honors that have accrued to him through royal favor, and his coat of arms shall be destroyed by the executioner. His right hand, which he stretched out towards the crown, shall be hewn off while he is still alive, thereafter his head. His body shall be quartered by the executioner and then broken on the wheel. His head and his right hand thereafter shall be each impaled on a high stake, visible to all.

25 April, 1772 A.D., at Christiansborg by
Guldberg, Braem, etc., etc."

The warrant slid to the floor. Struensee's hands hung limp from his knees. Pastor Muenter laid his hand on the prisoner's shoulder. "How barbaric, the things people do to each other," Struensee said thickly, looking into Muenter's heavy face. "Still, I had counted on being broken alive on the wheel. I was wondering how I'd ever stand it. And so I suppose I ought to thank the judges for sparing me that much. As for the title of Count, taking that away is ridiculous. And as for what they do with my body once I'm dead, it cannot possibly make any difference."

The Pastor shook his head in agreement. Struensee carefully handed the warrant back to Muenter. "I'm no longer worrying about death," he said tensely to the minister, "but I can't get my friend Brandt out of my mind. How will he stand it. It's terrible."

"I think you can see him, if you like," said Muenter. "I'll see that you do."

"That would mean a great deal to me." said Struensee.

"Tomorrow evening, then," said Muenter. "I'll see what I can do."

Struensee threw his arms about Muenter. He wiped away more tears. "This place has finished my nerves," he said. "I cry now like a woman."

Muenter said nothing. He, too, was having trouble holding back the tears.

★ *VII* ★

LATE THE FOLLOWING afternoon Juel once more conducted Struensee to the little courtyard where the smiths worked at their forges. This time the hairy fellows did their work very quickly. The chains seemed to fall off of their own accord. Struensee flexed his muscles and felt inches taller.

On the way back to his cell he found he was still walking carefully as if crossing a bog, lifting one foot high ahead of the other. Chains were not so easily cast off. Struensee caught Juel looking at him shamefacedly and suddenly stopped, turned pale and was plunged in thought. Presently he went along without comment as if nothing had happened.

For a whole hour he walked up and down in his cell, restoring the circulation in arms and legs. When his movements had become more normal he sat down at his table and wrote. One letter he directed to Count Rantzau, thanking him for his kindness in days past and ignoring the days of treachery. He wrote another letter to his parents, thanking them for their love and begging forgiveness for the disorder he had introduced into their peaceful lives. He comforted them with the notice that he had found religious peace. These letters he sealed and handed over to Juel.

With this work accomplished, still sitting on his stool, he had the sensation of being posed on a high mountain top. Down below swarmed all mankind, with its pullulation of getting and spending and dying. He did not despise his fellows, nor gloat over their elaborate futilities. But he felt glad to think that no longer would he participate in their confusion and aimlessness.

And still there was one final worry that hung over him like a cloud in an otherwise limpid sky. It was the thought of Caroline. He had not been allowed to write to her in leavetaking. It was not her material lot that unsettled him, her imprisonment or the likely possibility of her being exiled. What he feared was that she would rebel against the fate that had caught her up. He visualized her as becoming estranged from her fellow-men, from life even and, finally, from God. She had every provocation. She might, he thought, become obdurate

[362]

in their common guilt, and hold guilt before her like a shield. He imagined her sticking fast to error, as he now conceived it, excusing herself with specious excuses, always blaming luck and the world and never herself.

In this sense he was drawn back from plateaus of exaltation onto the common plain of everyday and had to admit that never so long as he drew breath would he rid himself entirely of worldly tribulations. When his friend Brandt arrived, as Muenter had promised, they embraced warmly before saying a word. But all the while Struensee was thinking about Caroline Matilda. "Everything would be all right, Brandt," was the first thing he said, "if I were only sure that things were going reasonably well with Caroline."

"I've been thinking about her, too," said Brandt. "But I fail to see what they can do to her. We've all arrived at the same pitch, more or less, the three of us, and there's not much more they can do. We can only keep our minds open and have faith. That's all, so far as I can see."

"I never thought I'd hear you talk that way," said Struensee. "I'll tell you something frankly. When I think back on how I worried about myself these past three months, I'm ashamed. I had some reason, of course, but not that much. I'm ashamed that I forgot about Caroline and her troubles. It was egotism, pure egotism. She's a woman and she must need help."

"But how are you going to help her?" said Brandt. "How long do you think we've got!"

"I'll have to think about it," said Struensee. "I shall have to concentrate on it. Brandt, I'm a coward. Before I was a coward when it came to facing the world. I was afraid of that delegation of sailors, I was afraid of the military. Now I'm a coward before God. I'm afraid of a second death, having conquered the first kind of fear."

"But that's not true, Struensee," said Brandt. "Come, now. Think how we used to philosophize in the old days. We both used to think that Leibniz was more right than wrong. Remember? That we're monads, individual souls without windows, as the Baron says. Each one must mirror the world in his own way."

"What has that got to do with Caroline?"

"She, too, is an individual, like all of us. She has her own life to live out. You cannot change that."

"But she's so young, Brandt," said Struensee. "How will she stand it?"

"What has that got to do with it, being young or not young," said Brandt. "Young or old, queen or beggar, she must either be herself or nothing. I'm not pitying her on that account. Nor should you."

"I'm amazed, Brandt," said Struensee. "How sure you are! What's come over you! I don't recognize my old *maître de plaisir*."

"When there's no way out, why beat around the bush," said Brandt. "Don't you see, Struensee, that Caroline Matilda is finished? Her life is ruined. I don't doubt that she'll go on existing. But what a prospect for her! No, it's sheer conceit to think we can supervise women's lives for them, always coddling and protecting them. What is it we're going to protect them from, I'd like to know? Aren't they as well equipped to support life as we are? Do they not normally live longer than we? Why, they are better at living than we are, in my opinion. Are they not alone from the time they're born just as we are? Are they not alone when their children leave them. Do they not die alone? Why all these theatricals and pomposities about women? We can advise them, if they ask advice, but beyond that they must shift for themselves. The hardest nut of all to crack is oneself, one's own being. And that must be accomplished without help, whether it's man or woman. Each of us is alone responsible for his own life. And for his own way of dying as well."

"So that's how you see the thing," said Struensee. "And here I was prepared to beg your forgiveness for dragging you into this frightful mess, Brandt."

"You're the most stubborn man I've ever laid eyes on," said Brandt, shaking his friend by the shoulders. "Even in the last ditch you're conceited. More conceited than ever, in fact. You can't trust her to find her own way without your help. You don't trust my ability to go through with the execution without your help. So it goes. You have to do everything yourself, arrange everything, set everything to rights. Once your worries were confined to Denmark. Now, my dear fellow, they extend to heaven. But don't you think that's a bit thick? I know you mean well. But for God's sake let yourself go more. Let the God we hear so much about take charge for a change, will you!"

"I should only be too glad to do just that," said Struensee. "But what has come over you, Brandt, since you came to the Citadel? I don't know you any more."

"Well, I'll tell you what happened to me," said Brandt. "At the first of it I was floored. I didn't know what to think, where to turn. Not really. Then I began to hope. I played for days on end on my flute, so that I might live only in hope and not think too deeply and too much. I remembered my garden in Holstein, the pond and the temple of love with the straw roof that you liked so much. I thought about the thrushes singing towards evening and about the new moon. All that sort of thing. I couldn't bear the thought of leaving it all behind, all the nice things and, of course, my very precious body. So presently I was depressed, which you can imagine.

"But then, digging deeper into the matter, I saw that I had not loved all these other things on their own account, nor did I now.

[364]

It was merely the sensations they afforded me, the memories bound up with them, that were the attraction. It had always been that way since I was a small boy. Always the garden, the trees, the pond and behind them some strange, beckoning promise. I always thought of it as something musical. Without this other thing, this musical sort of thing as I understood it, they would have meant nothing much to me.

"And so I said to myself, and my intuition corroborated the idea, that as boy, youth or *maître de plaisir* I, myself, a bundle of sensations, had never been more than a sign for the other thing. I had been a note in a symphony. How shall I describe this unknown reality? It might be called Nature. Or the soul of the world. I don't know. What can a note in a symphony know of the whole? So long as it does not take itself too seriously, so long as it does not obtrude and lose its relationship with the whole, is that not enough?

"I realized this very clearly, Struensee, I saw that I could never step out of the symphony and subsist on my own. I saw that even death would never improve that fact. For I ask you, Struensee, is it possible to imagine anything or anyone leaving the universe completely, ceasing completely to exist? No. Everything is embedded in ceaseless change and everything is eternal. So I look at it.

"But this musical concept of the world did not altogether satisfy me. If there is such a thing as reincarnation I should like to be a young willow bent over the shore of a pond and dipping my branches in the shallows. A most desirable existence, don't you think? I should like to be a lark winging high in the sky, far above the meadow-land. Or a shadow in the night. Or something powerful. The sea thundering on the shore, the early morning wind, the consuming fire. But perhaps that would be too great, too inhuman, too terrible for a small soul like mine. Against the splendors of the sea, what am I? Nothing, hardly worth the mention." Brandt paused, stroked his forehead slowly, smiling ironically to himself. "In short," he went on, "I wasn't really satisfied with the world as symphony. Indeed, I took my little flute, and broke it over my knee. I discovered that I wanted my God to reside far beyond any universe of harmonies. He had to be more than the author of a symphony of the spheres that would maze my senses for eternity. I repudiated such a universe. I asked for a personal God. Not one with a human countenance, to be sure, but at least a God with personality. I felt it to be inherently right that personally, face to face, I should deliver him a reckoning. I wanted to be known by the one who had created me, and would eventually annihilate me. His severity appealed to me more than the musical droning of the world soul.

"With this change of mind, Struensee, my whole outlook on the situation changed. In most respects I was much less comfortable than

I had been, if that was possible. For the world soul is not interested, naturally, in whether man has lived like a swine, or whether he hasn't, whether he has betrayed his fellows or lived like a man of spirit. Saint or sinner, it makes no difference to the world soul. Being a counterpart of material nature, it is morally neutral.

"You see, moral goodness, love of humanity, sympathy, purity of soul, tolerance and all the other things that certain philosophers conceive to be derivative from nature are nothing but sentimentalities. Pantheism commemorates nothing but the shortsightedness of its supporters. Could the pantheist disprove me if I took a stand diametrically opposed to his? Supposing I claimed that the natural way is for everyone to hate his brother, to behave as cruelly as possible, to live only for survival? Is there not an abundance of evidence in Nature to prop this argument? And yet this theory, too, would be false. For Nature, as I say, knows neither good nor bad. Its main principle is survival. Morally it is neutral.

"But to cut the story short, in my need I longed for the God I had always made sport of in my ignorance. The world soul, the first cause, God as a manufacturer of universal watches and all the rest of that claptrap I threw right out the window. How hard it was to do that, Struensee! All the soft things of life, all the pleasures, the excuses, the familiar things—everything cast aside when you appear before the final judge as I now understand him. Nothing to lean on when he asks you: 'How was your life?' That is, he does not ask you; you ask yourself the question."

"But that's exactly it!" said Struensee. "You're describing what I've gone through myself. Yes. You must ask yourself the question. But it is His unseen presence that makes the question so terrible."

"Struensee, I always knew that you would come to this," said Brandt. He took his friend affectionately by the hand. "But I? How did it happen that He made himself known to me? To me, the clown? He was there before I thought about him or believed in him. He came to me when I was in despair like someone slipping in through a door left open by negligence. It was terrible. Like a flash I understood the futility of life, the talk, talk, talk that we all manufacture endlessly. I saw how hollow the philosopher's supposedly priceless wisdom. The entire clash and dispersion of humanity struck me as highly nonsensical, the way people live their lives in constant fear of each other. Always rushing to hide from the One who can save them, making a life's work of running away. I realized what an absurd waste my works of art had been. The shows I had staged, I mean. And what little permanent satisfaction I ever got from the women I have slept with.

"It was both cruel and laughable, Struensee. I trembled to think how without this thing happening to me I'd have gone right on living the same old way till I died. *Periissem nisi periisim!* Yes, I should have been damned for eternity if I hadn't had this piece of bad luck. I felt like a man who has been shipwrecked and finds himself washed safely up on the beach. I gave thanks for my redemption."

Struensee impulsively embraced his friend and kissed him on the cheeks as he had done once before on a spring morning long ago in the straw-roofed temple of love in Holstein.

"It all turned out so differently from what we expected," he said.

"It did, indeed," said Brandt, and shrugged his shoulders, making a wry grimace. And then he added, the old impishness creeping into his words: "In any case, it's not such a bad way to die. Out in the open before a crowd of people." Saying this a shadow darkened his face. "What about your work?" he asked. "I hadn't thought of that."

"My work?"

"These conservatives will turn the clock back wherever they can," said Brandt. "Out of hatred for you, if for no other reason. Being slaves themselves, they can think only in terms of slave and master."

"I know they will," said Struensee. "I know that, all right."

"You take it very calmly," said Brandt. "Have you lost faith in your reforms?"

"No, I'll never give them up," said Struensee. "Now less than ever. But, as you say, Brandt, I've always taken myself and my work too seriously. I wanted to do it all myself. Yet you, Brandt, found a way out of the thicket without my aid. Caroline will find her way. As for my reforms, they'll need time and many heads to make them work. Everything will come about in good time, even if I never live to see it."

"Perhaps you are right," said Brandt.

"I am in this," said Struensee. "That's the very nature of freedom. Each one of us must find himself, discover his own way out. Right now I understand why the Danish people rose up against me. The freedom that I was offering them was ordered from above. Really it was nothing but another, less onerous, form of slavery. But freedom is in no sense a commodity, Brandt, I have come to think. It is not something to be possessed, or bestowed. It is a condition of the spirit, a form of grace, as it were. How quickly those who profess to bring freedom can turn into tyrants! And one more thing I left out of reckoning—there can be no freedom without God. He is the spring from which freedom comes bubbling up. And He sees nothing but individuals, not masses of people.

"Gradually we come to the realization that people are not mechanisms, to be forced to do this or that. Regardless of how desirable the goal. Men stand free before God, and nowhere else but in the sight of God. Without practical goals, without being a member of society or of the state or of the church. We either serve God in freedom, or Moloch in slavery. Moloch has many names—state, church, business, money, family, happiness, piety, pleasure. But they all boil down to the same condition of servitude.

"Yet I never saw the truth of all this before. My work was a failure, full of loopholes. The will to do good was there, but that was no excuse for blindness. The greatest tyrants may have good intentions. Many of them on their deathbeds have excused their imperious conduct on the ground of good intentions, as we know. That attitude now repels me to the core. I'm not unhappy to have the work taken out of my hands. We're all forerunners of someone else, Brandt, even the best of us, and I certainly do not belong among these."

Juel opened the door, making it creak loudly. He stood in the doorway with his key-ring and a candle stuck in the neck of a bottle, which he set down on the table. "It's late, gentlemen," he said deferently.

"That's right," said Brandt. "Now we have to leave."

The two friends, feeling more warmly towards each other than ever before, embraced for the last time. Brandt tore himself loose and rushed out into the corridor and off without looking back. Juel followed after, shaking his head.

Struensee stayed where he was for a long time, staring at the lock in the cell door with a puzzled, foolish look. Then he took the Bible from where it lay on his wooden bed and read in the passion of Our Lord as described in the book of Matthew.

After reading the ancient words, he folded his hands on the book and rested his head on his hands. Before him the candle burned with a still, bright little flame. There he rested immobile, his head on his hands, until the candle guttered out, just about the time that the first shimmer of dawn came slanting down through the window high up in the wall.

★ *VIII* ★

IT WAS SEVEN in the morning when Juel came again. He found Struensee asleep, head down on the table and the candle burned out. He shook the prisoner awake and at once Struensee snapped erect.

"Time already, Juel?" he said.

"It's time," said Juel in his deep froggy voice and looked away in the direction of the cell bed.

Struensee washed with water from a basin that Juel had brought for that purpose and shortly the Citadel barber came and shaved him. Another jailer arrived with the prisoner's dress clothes over his arm and Struensee slipped out of his drab prison garb. He was putting on his blue velvet coat with silver buttons when Pastor Muenter arrived. Muenter was dressed ceremoniously in black gown and rigidly starched collar. The cell was so crowded that everybody was getting in the other person's way. Presently a lieutenant of the Zealand dragoons arrived and showed his impatience as he waited for the prisoner at the cell door.

"It's like all the commotion just before starting out on a long trip," said Struensee, and was nervously pleased with his own aptness.

Juel offered him a cup of hot coffee, but he declined it in favor of water drunk directly from his pitcher. For some reason Muenter looked even more official than usual and, if possible, behaved more formally. He looked exactly as Struensee's own father had looked Sundays in the pulpit.

"Are you ready, my son?" he asked Struensee, measuring him.

"Ready," said Struensee.

"Is there anything more you want?"

"Nothing."

"Perhaps you have something you would like to tell me."

"I thank you, Pastor Muenter," the prisoner said and shook Muenter's hand. For reply Muenter closed his eyes and moved his lips in prayer. After a moment of this Struensee pulled away, turned abruptly and said: "We'll go now and get this over with."

Juel led the way, his key-ring swinging and clinking busily, and directly behind him came the Lieutenant. Next in line was the prisoner, accompanied by Muenter. Then came the barber with his metal can of water and the other jailer, holding Struensee's old clothes over his arm.

Other times when Struensee had walked through the Citadel it had seemed like a maze, but this morning the corridors were marvellously simple and straight. In no time he was out in the warm morning sun, blinking in the light. Two coaches, each drawn by a pair of horses, stood in readiness, with a guard of dragoons for each. Struensee, from a little distance, silently watched Brandt clamber into the first coach. Like himself, Brandt was all dressed up in court uniform. He had a light fur cloak thrown over his shoulders. Juel produced a similar garment for Struensee. He stroked it tenderly after he had thrown it over the prisoner's shoulders, as if bidding goodbye to an old friend.

"Thank you, my good fellow," Struensee said to Juel. "Thank you for everything, friend."

"I'm proud of you, Excellency," whispered the curious jailer. "You're the kind of man I've always wanted to take care of. You've done much better than Norcroso the pirate, even. If there weren't men like you I'd lose all faith in my calling."

"God be with you, then," said Struensee.

"God be with you," echoed Juel. Almost at once, having stepped back, he struck up an animated conversation with the prison barber, who was manifestly not interested in what he was being told. "How I'm going to miss that fellow," Juel told the reluctant barber. "He was a great criminal. Not the ordinary kind, you understand, a really big one. You know, I hate to go back into the prison after leaving him. Why, there's nothing but windfalls in there, just a crowd of thieves and pimps. They don't mean a thing, alive or dead. Come right down to it . . . and I hate to admit it . . . they're about as bad as the people outside! You'll never learn anything from them, let me tell you. They're liars by trade and I'm sick of them. No better than greengrocers or kings. What a dismal world this is!"

The coaches swayed off down through the city. Struensee sat beside Muenter, but they did not exchange a word. Struensee watched the old gabled houses slide past the coach window. Two strokes of a bell came from St. Peter's Church. It was exactly half past eight. Like a dream, Struensee thought, remembering that by the time the same clock got round to striking the twelve strokes of noon he would be no more. The great adventure would be finished.

The thought left him with a curious, light, numb feeling which blurred his impressions of the streets, the houses along the way, pedestrians' faces. It was like a morning dream, dreamed just before waking. Infantrymen were stationed at intervals on both sides of the street, standing at present-arms, looking like big awkward dolls taken fresh from the box. The crowds milling about trying to catch a glimpse of the condemned had a hangdog look. Struensee saw a woman who was weeping, holding her apron up to dab her eyes, and this made him wonder. It was all quite different from his expectations. There were no wild outbreaks of hate or sadistic merriment.

Already, in fact, the people were disillusioned. The new regime, indeed, was far worse than its predecessor. With the death sentence ordered for Struensee and Brandt the people's sympathies had veered round to the opposite quarter. The prisoners had become objects of pity in the popular mind. The official wheelwrights had balked at having to construct a wheel on which to smash the dead bodies according to the directions of the court. The executioner had received a number of threatening letters, assuring him that he would be spirited away and himself hanged from the nearest bough unless he carried out his task as humanely and quickly as possible. The large detachments of soldiers and sailors guarding the streets were not there for reasons of ritual. Guldberg, like Struensee before him, feared the people.

The most astonishing feature of the ride to the block was the behavior of the children. In his cell Struensee had forgotten, or at least half-forgotten, what children looked like and how they acted.

There they were now, behind the line of soldiers, dozens of them, all looking goggle-eyed and grave at the passing coaches. Most of the boys were blonds and wore short white pants. And it seemed as if the girls' wondering faces were all sprinkled with freckles. Their hair was done up in braids and bound tightly to the head. They wore wide dresses and pressed hard against their mothers as the coaches passed before them.

Belatedly Struensee realized that he had not altogether lived in vain. At least he had done something that would improve the lives of the young people. He had been repudiated by his own generation, but not by a younger one. They would see the day of millennium, perhaps, that he had so fervently hoped and worked for, a day for which, in the popular view, he was now sacrificing his life. The people on this day, and on his account, were no longer subjects commanded to enjoy freedom. They actually were the embodiment of a coming revolution that, in the natural course, would wipe out the corrupt monarchic system. This much they had in common with all the children of Europe, Struensee thought.

In a moment of clairvoyance Struensee felt the coming change in the social order, felt the gathering presence of the gigantic wave, a wave like the steep side of a mountain become fluid. Ecstatically he imagined himself as the forerunner of this wave, and likened himself to the seabirds that presage storm. He felt himself quite lifted out of time, apart and above the flux of history.

But this was only for a moment. Almost immediately he sank back into his weary, bewildered self.

The coaches crossed the Kongens Nytorv and turned into the Bredegade. Now they were passing between the houses of Copenhagen's aristocracy, white in the sunlight, the green shutters shining. Between the houses were fine gates of wrought iron shutting off the neatly tended and swept drives into the mews behind. In a few of these houses the inhabitants had gathered at the windows to look, but in most cases the façades of the Bredegade were blank as the coaches passed by, seemingly not wishing to see the hated Struensee in his extremity, not wishing even to admit that such an unpleasant business was in progress.

The prisoner thought vaguely about the many evenings he had spent behind these very doors. Kaleidoscopically he remembered the whispered flirtations, the women's white shoulders, the candlelight and interesting shadows, the uniforms, the tinkling of the spinets. Now it was a dream, a puppet play. Puppets and dolls, that is what they are, he thought. The clever, ready women with highsounding names and white carved faces always frozen in pleased and meaningless smiles. The men, decked out in gold, smelling of lavender and eau-de-cologne, they, too, were puppets, hopelessly wooden, blasé and sterile. Even the young girls were like dolls, so, too, the maid-servants standing at the porcelain counter preparing hot chocolate for the guests. Even the houses themselves and the elaborate furnish-ings in them now seemed like so many props for doll-play—the furniture upholstered in silk, the Chinese tapestries, the crystal can-delabra. A pang of profound regret smote Struensee through and through as he recalled the hours wasted on this silly porcelain scene.

Now that he was riding along on his last ride with the brassy taste of death on his tongue he realized with intolerable clarity the truth that life is as earnest intended as death, that life cannot be lived in denial and evasion of death. Thinking this he felt the presence of death all about him, seeping through to his bones like a cutting gray wind off a winter sea.

The houses became less pretentious and the visible expanse of sky seemingly higher. The coaches were now bouncing along over the cobbles of the city's outskirts. Trees appeared along the way, clothed in fresh green. The stiff white bloom of the chestnuts was just be-ginning to open, the black earth smell of vegetable gardens floated in through the coach window. Already, Struensee noticed, the onions were sending up stiletto shoots of blue-green. Now and then a gust of salt wind from the harbor came to him, odorous with the pungent smell of tar, instantly evoking the image of wide, breezy spaces. He saw tulips nodding in the wayside flowerbeds. The shrubbery shook and rustled in the morning breeze, the trees nodded at him, like decorous gentlemen.

A cat sneaked out of a house, and he watched it as long as he could, craning his neck to do so. It crept belly down out of the house, carefully reconnoitering each move. Its back was covered with bits of straw. In this part of the town, Struensee assured himself, life is real, the way God intended it to be. Nets hung out drying in the gardens. Spades and rakes leaned against shed walls. The children's clothes were universally patched. The people of the district stood and moved heavily, as if the heaviness of the earth were in them. Their legs were inordinately muscular, no doubt from a lifetime of fighting the heave and fall of ships' decks. Even the omnipresent dogs and cats looked somehow more natural in this setting.

At one point Struensee's eye was attracted by a rectangle chalked up on a wall of plank. Wavering hands had divided the figure into squares and at each end attached two rude semi-circles. Inside one the word "heaven" was inscribed, "hell" in the other. This struck the prisoner as highly symbolic. He shuddered, twisted his head to get a last look at the childish scrawl, and continued to stare, neck twisted awry long after the coach had borne him out of view.

They were now heading directly to the open space of the Oster-feld where an immense crowd had collected to watch the spectacle.

Everyone was dressed in his Sunday best, overhead was a high, cloudless spring sky. A humming sound such as swarming bees might make arose from the gathering, but suddenly stopped as the coaches hove into sight. There came an intense silence, so complete that Struensee could hear every creak of the axles, every thud of hooves, and beneath, the stir of the wind off the sea.

Now the composite face of the crowd turned to the coaches and looked, horrified and set, as the vehicles were slowed down to a walking pace and slowly approached the scaffold over the soft earth of the open field. The scaffold, placed in the center of the open area, looked like an immense cube of black with its covering of black crêpe. It was an imposing structure, some twenty-five feet high and brought the execution into full view of the whole field. Indeed, it seemed tremendously high and toppling, a primeval object, standing as monument to all the world's groping and pain. It was a sort of altar, a ka'aba. About the scaffold were stationed some four thousand marines in dark-blue coats. In front of the scaffold the drummers took their places, directly by the stairs. Their drums dangled motionless at their sides, their sticks were held stiffly ready.

The coaches came to a stop finally at the rear of the scaffold, and backed up close to it. Struensee watched Brandt, white as a sheet, incongruously gay of dress, step down. He was supported by a Lutheran minister. Struensee put his hands up to his face and bent down to pray. Seeing him Muenter laid his arm about his shoulders.

There was a vibrant silence as Brandt mounted the scaffold. Struensee clearly heard the faltering scuff of his steps. A piece of black crêpe came loose and snapped in the breeze. There were broken voices up above, saying something official. Then came the roll of the drums, a challenging sound that raised the hair on Struensee's head. The roll of the drums was in his chest and guts. Then everything was still, except for the sound of a woman's weeping.

Cold as ice, his limbs weak as water, Struensee stumbled out of the coach and would have fallen off the footboard had not Muenter held him up. Without seeing anything or anybody, he pitched forward blindly to the scaffold, weaving through the ranks of the marines and by the drummers. Slowly and laboriously, sweating like a horse, he made his way up the scaffold stairs, inching his hand up the splintery railing.

Once on the scaffold height the wind ruffled the prisoner's hair and caressed his cheeks. He now looked all around. Below were the marines and the crowd, all looking up at him, their faces white as flowers. Beyond them was Copenhagen. He could see the cupola of the Marble Church, and the winding stairs about the tower of the Frelser Church. He saw a small sea of steep red roofs, he saw the tower of Christiansborg and the little peak of the Boerse. Off in another direction was flat country, broken by clumps of green trees. And still farther beyond was the great plain of sea, glittering like a buckler in the morning.

The floor under him seemed wobbly, his feet like stumps. The floor was made of newly sawn timbers. They were damp and a meaty, raw red. He could smell blood, Brandt's blood, of course. Struensee knelt down beside Muenter in great confusion and tried to pray. Then unaided he raised himself to his feet. A man in a black gown read off his sentence, but the wind carried away the sense, and this, too, struck Struensee as very symbolic, as if it were a higher justice that was contemptuously scattering mundane judgment like so much dust.

The executioner now stepped forward and the final act began. He was a heavy fellow, very blond and very tall. Even the traditional executioner's costume and the red and white cloak that fluttered about his shoulders could not make a personage out of his peasant being. His light hair was matted sweatily to his forehead and big drops of sweat ran down his cheeks, though it was far from warm up on the scaffold. Fear of the people's wrath was in his little blue eyes.

He bent his head forward, and said: "I now fulfill the King's command. The blood about to be shed does not stain me, for I am but carrying out my sworn duties, without hate, without pleasure, and with pity. As a sign of contrition, Count Struensee, I beg you to forgive me for what I am about to do to you. May God forgive all sinners. You and me."

"I forgive you," muttered Struensee, but his muffled voice was not heard.

The executioner bowed to the prisoner and handed his red and white cloak to an assistant. An official then handed him a wooden escutcheon on which Struensee's coat of arms had been painted. This he held up in the air and showed the people in all directions, after which he set it down on the planks and split it in two with a single blow of his axe. The halves he picked up and tossed over the side of the scaffold to the ground, where they landed with an audible thump. Then he pointed to the block and took a grip with both hands on his sword, swishing it and testing its swing. It was a double-edged weapon with a very large pommel. The blade glinted brilliantly when it caught the light. With one hand he directed the kneeling Struensee's neck over the narrow slot of the block and placed his right hand on a smaller one.

Looking out, deathly sick, from under his brows Struensee saw the world for the last time. He could just see the heads of the foremost line of marines. Beyond was a sea of faces, thousands of physiognomies dull with sadness, unilluminated by wit. He thought he saw a woman detach herself from the mass and lift up both hands in his direction, screaming something as she did so. Probably not a woman, but a girl, he thought, probably Antje Maria, as a matter of fact. He heard someone say very loudly and clearly: "He's a brave devil, you've got to give him credit for that!" Then the demonic ruffle of the drums commenced.

He felt the sword bite off his hand, and automatically let out a roar of pain, trying to rise from his knees even as he shrieked. It was not so much the pain that set off the reflex, it seemed to him, as a mighty impulse to say something, to speak out something terribly important for everybody, something in the nature of a testament that was now flooding his mouth to the brim. But before he could do this the sword was raised aloft again and promptly sliced through the back of his neck. Struensee was done.

The executioner finished his work with Struensee as he had with Brandt. He kicked back the headless corpse with his foot as if it were a slaughtered sheep. Next he took an axe with a long blade and cut freely into the middle of the cadaver. Aided by his assistant he succeeded in laying the viscera bare, which he drew forth—heart, lungs, liver, spleen and a long tangle of bowels. These he threw into a wooden bucket waiting to receive them, and the crowd emitted a deep sob as they heard the heavy wet plopping of the organs. The assistant was red with blood up to the elbows. His fingers dripped blood, his face was smeared with it.

At this point a young woman in the crowd who had been watching the formalities with bulging eyes was suddenly overcome by hysteria. Her shrieks set off, like a match so much tinder, a great explosion of hysterical shrieking. Madness broke loose among the spectators. One of the marines twisted sideways and fell in a faint to the ground. Children wept wildly and some of the men shook their fists at the scaffold, cursing crazily, screaming out their hatred of the executioner.

The executioner was sweating in streams. It came down his beet-red cheeks from the hair at his temples in rivulets. He took a quick look at the crowd and bent to his task in a frenzy. He split the corpse in two rough halves at the waist, not bothering to do a neat job. The upper half he split again, cutting into the sternum and face as if he were parting a log. Once his axe drove right through the body and stuck in the planks beneath, so that he had to fight and grunt to pry out the blade, the while holding down the mashed body with his heel. Splinters of wood and bone and bloody tatters of muscle flew when he ripped his instrument loose. The executioner was breathing like a foundered horse, gasping for air so great was his expenditure of energy. His work was done. Mechanically he brought a fat bloody hand to his face and wiped himself dry of sweat, even while he was nodding to his assistant to cover the now dismembered and unrecognizable Struensee with a length of black cloth. Together they rolled the pieces into a compact mass and carried their gruesome package down the stairs to the hearse, which already contained Brandt's remains. The head and hand were then lifted up for the people to see, then immediately put in a basket and brought below to the hearse.

The crowd quickly melted away. Faces were gray with horror and fear. The spectacle had been far less entertaining than anyone had imagined. Mothers could hardly carry their exhausted young ones. The majority rushed to the pubs, both men and women, and blunted the shock of the spectacle with schnapps. The execution was analyzed ten thousand times, acquiring new details by the minute.

"It was a dirty Swedish trick, a rotten piece of business," said a tall, grim fellow with the weather-browned face and light eyes of a Danish fisherman. "There are far worse men than those two, and nothing's ever done about it."

"I don't understand it," said a man with a bald spot that shone like grease. "What's the sense of cutting them up after they are dead? Why don't they just give the bodies to the medical students to practice on? Or why not give the worms a proper feed, I'd like to know!"

"I don't see why they don't just bury them and be done with it," croaked a fat old crone in a blue apron. "When I die, I want to be buried right and have some flowers over my grave. I want to lie there all in one piece while I wait for the resurrection."

"The only peace you'll ever find is floating in a bottle," said a drunk. "Drink up, folks, while you've still got a throat to do it with."

Everyone laughed at this. Executions, after all, did have their bright side. Before long the whole pubful was tipsy—men, women and children. Indeed, the entire proletariat of Copenhagen was drunk, drunk on top, sick at the bottom. When the four thousand marines marched through the town the rabble fell in behind, thousands of them, imitating the precision of the military, keeping step, swinging their arms in time. When the procession arrived in the Bredegade the people grabbed some drums and beat them like mad. Some of the marchers had trumpets and these they blew with shattering effect in the narrow cleft of street. The servants came to the windows and waved at the marines but their masters preferred not to see.

Two coaches followed behind this coiling flow of humanity. In the first sat Pastor Muenter with the younger colleague who had accompanied Brandt to the block.

"Well, I've lost a friend today," said Muenter. "I got to be very fond of the man. He was almost like my own son towards the end of it. But I'm not worrying about him. I'll be glad if I can die with as much resolution."

"It was horrible," said the younger pastor. "I thank the Lord we don't have executions every day of the week. I question whether I could stand it."

"Yet there are executions every day of the week," said Muenter severely, and his colleague stared at him in surprise.

The executioner and his assistant occupied the second coach. The executioner had stretched out his heavy legs comfortably and was sucking on his pipe. Slowly his spirit was coming back to him. Sometimes he shook his heavy head, made a puzzled face and spat a gob out through the coach window.

The hearse with the remains did not move from the scaffold until late afternoon when the city had quieted down somewhat. The conveyance was a rickety affair. The hind wheels squeaked and swayed in and out as they rolled along. The horses were nondescript beasts, fallow in hue, their joints gouty, their heads hanging with shame. One of them suffered from a disease which had caused most of his mane to drop out, the other was blind in one eye. The driver in charge of the hearse was a vague fellow who might have been any old age. He had let his whiskers sprout into a red stubble, his cheekbones stood out like knobs, his mouth was a cavern in which rotted stalactite teeth. On the back of his head hung a three-cornered hat, which he barely managed to keep from falling off as he shuffled along beside his horrid car, loosely holding the reins. The horses were so worn that from time to time they stopped of their own accord, to rest and think the situation over. The driver was uneasy and would allow them but little respite. "Hey, you spavined bastards, get a move on, or I'll murder you!" he would shout. "Har-rup, there!" And again the load of mutilated flesh crawled along under the afternoon sun.

On the way through the Bredegade blood began to drip out of the back of the cart onto the paving stones. "The buggers are leaking again," the driver muttered aloud, and was half moved to do something about it, but immediately thought better. Good enough for them, he thought, looking up at the fine façades on either side. I'd like to stink them all out, the high muckymucks, the blood-sucking bastards.

A great cloud of bottle-flies had collected about the hearse by the time the driver turned the horses into the Kongens Nytorv. Today the square was empty. The fish and vegetable stalls were closed tight. The few pedestrians avoided the very sight of the hearse, as if it were engaged in its occasional task of carrying corpses to the city pesthouse. Catching sight of it from afar, housewives drew tight their curtains and sought the rear of the house. This made the driver grin. His big black stumps showed as the warm pride pulsed through his veins.

At last the weary journey was done. The hearse arrived at the

Gallows Hill, which lay on the other side of the city from the Osterfeld. This was a thinly populated neighborhood, avoided by common consent. Two frayed bodies were already hanging from the gallows, their nakedness hidden only by tatters. Bones and skulls were scattered all about the area. It was like the great field of Ezekiel. The place might have been the scene of some horrendous giants' feasts, in the course of which gnawed bones had been scattered right and left.

Under the gallows were four wheels and nearby two high posts used for impalements. The sun was setting in a great flood of golden light which lit up the prospect in remarkable detail. Off in a wood the thrushes were singing their hearts out, the notes fluting higher and higher, then dying away to begin all over again. The driver put his hand up to his eyes and looked back at the city, all shimmering in a haze of gold. He sighed and began his work. The horses dozed, their old heads between their knees.

At midnight, as usual, the big bronze bell in St. Peter's gave twelve deep booms that went in great waves out over the city into the countryside adjacent, even as far as Galgenberg. There, on two tall posts, were stuck the heads of Struensee and Brandt. The hands were fastened atop two smaller stakes flanking the big ones, in such fashion that they pointed up at the heads. The dead faces were putty-colored masks. The corners of the lips were cramped, the lids were tightly shut. They seemed to be dreaming coldly. The hands, the fingers of which rigor mortis had curled up like claws, in the moonlight appeared to be made of wax.

That same evening Christiansborg Palace was brilliantly lighted. The violins sobbed prettily, the candlelight was kind to worn and worried faces. The ladies and gentlemen of the royal entourage were dressed, as always, in the finest silks, their faces were carefully prinked and powdered. Servants by the dozen filed in with ices, sweetmeats and champagnes of different vintage.

The Queen-Dowager sat between Prince Frederik and the King. She looked full, matronly, a fine figure of a woman in all respects. Her silvery hair was groomed perfectly, her big dark eyes had a lot of light and fire in them. "Now I have my two sons again," she said to the King.

But Christian said nothing in reply. As a matter of fact, he was busy making his poodle, Bellerophon, jump through his arms. "Hoopla!" he told the little dog. "Come, do it for papa!"

Count Rantzau was at the fireplace, for he thought it became him to lean on the mantel. Just now he folded his hands behind his back and looked up quizzically at the love gods sporting in plaster embrace on the ceiling.

The ladies and gentlemen of the court were amiable, exactly as they always had been. Still, for some reason the right mood, that is, the perfect mood, was lacking.

★ IX ★

OWE GULDBERG, THE King's new first minister, was intelligent enough to see that he had overplayed his hand by allowing so barbaric an execution. Indignation fulminated on all sides. Protests came even from distant Jutland. The small farmers and serfs were particularly incensed about Struensee's cruel demise. Many courtiers found it expedient to retire to their country estates.

Pastor Muenter's conversations with Struensee in the Citadel were recounted from Lutheran pulpits and soon became public property. Influential pietist circles also approved. These circles dominated an important section of the Danish bourgeoisie, including many provincial artisans on the lower economic level and some members of the patrician merchant class higher up. Owe Guldberg had the reputation of being a spokesman for this group, but his "conversion of a freethinker" could hardly be compared with the dramatic conversion of two such prominent figures as Struensee and Brandt against the background of the block, a conversion, incidentally, promoted by none other than Pastor Muenter, leading divine of the city. Nor had Guldberg anything to offer equal to the bizarre execution of his two erstwhile opponents. Death cast an aura about their names that nothing could erase. It began to look as if Struensee might rapidly develop into a folk hero. Indeed, Struensee dead threatened to be far more dangerous to Guldberg and his associates than Struensee alive.

Guldberg, in consequence, acted in haste to make the Danish public forget Struensee and everything connected with him. He could not, however, very well ban Pastor Muenter's discourses on the subject. Muenter even went to the trouble of describing the whole experience in a little book, which soon became popular reading among the church-going elements. But whatever could be done safely, the new first minister of the Danish state did to the best of his power. To the intense indignation of his fellow-conspirators, and particularly of Juliana, he pardoned all the dead men's relatives, friends and · followers. A few of them, like old Dr. Berger, he caused to be banished to provincial towns in Norway, where they would be soon forgotten.

His greatest problem by far was ridding himself of the Queen. She was young, pretty, charming. She had every quality needed to evoke popular support. Sympathy for her lover's harsh end quickly blanketed public disapprobation of adultery in high places. Many people, indeed, no longer believed that Struensee actually had been her lover, whereas others considered it only too likely, and openly regretted that they had not been in Struensee's shoes. The politician Guldberg saw plainly that the Queen was Struensee's natural political heir. With ease she would be able to muster an important following. She was a permanent threat to his regime, the potential focus of another palace revolution that, if successful, would doom all present incumbents.

The ticklish question of disposing of Caroline Matilda was hashed over at length with the English ambassador. During these discussions Guldberg tried his best to create the impression of pained solicitude, that is, an attitude becoming to one dealing with the august sister of England's King. Lord Keith, watching Guldberg's wrigglings with a cold and practiced eye, said flatly that Caroline Matilda must keep her queenly title. Providing that the scandalous lies about the Queen's former relationship with Struensee were suppressed, the ambassador added coolly, England was prepared to have Caroline Matilda move to the Hanoverian possessions of the English King, namely, to the town of Celle, where quarters awaited her occupation.

Guldberg weighed this proposition, which was really not a proposition at all, but a blunt command. He would have much preferred to see the Queen sail back to England, and good riddance to her. Celle was only a hundred miles or so south of the Danish frontier, much too close, in any event, for comfort. He saw the danger of her nearby presence with the King already sick, the Crown Prince underage and a large percentage of the Danish population chronically disaffected. But this solution seemed better, at least, than having the Queen stay on. Furthermore, when all cards were down, he had no choice.

"The main thing is that Her Majesty should leave Denmark quickly," he told the Englishman. "When will she be able to travel?"

"In two days," said Keith.

"How is that possible!" said Guldberg. "So soon!"

"I permitted myself the liberty of anticipating your assent," said Keith, smiling a thin, simpering smile. "With this in mind, as a matter of fact, I asked three men-o'-war to be deployed at the mouth of the Skagerak. They are waiting there right now to bear news on the Queen's situation back to England, my dear fellow."

"Is that so!" said Guldberg.

"Indeed it is," said Keith. "Furthermore, I must request permission to go freely in and out of Kronborg in order to make final arrangements with Her Majesty."

"Naturally, naturally," said Guldberg. "I'll have a secretary make you out a pass at once."

"And last of all, I must request an audience with the King," said Keith.

"That's hardly possible," objected Guldberg. "Your Lordship knows how difficult the King is these days."

"Ah, yes," said Keith, "but you have no notion how difficult my king is. He wants me to see his royal brother-in-law so that there will not be the slightest chance for misunderstanding with respect to the terms of the Queen's removal from Denmark. You see?"

"I won't stand in the way," said Guldberg. "But I don't understand what good you expect to come of this audience, Milord. I must ask you to limit your visit to a quarter hour. On account of the King's health, you know."

"That will be quite enough," said Keith, bowing stiffly from the waist and Guldberg hurriedly bowed in return. After Keith had left the room Guldberg remained where he was, scowling down at his writing table, for a long time.

Lord Keith found Caroline Matilda leaning over the parapet at the rear of Kronborg Fortress. This wall, according to the legend, was the same one where, centuries before, the ghost of the murdered King of Denmark had appeared to his son, Hamlet.

Caroline's fair skin was ashen against the dull black of her mourning garments. The only fleck of color in her costume was the garnet cross worn at her breast, and even this was no more than a dull sad spot of red. The wind came over the parapet in gusts off the sea. For May it was a very chill wind. It twisted Caroline's clothes in tight folds about her slender body. In her dark garb her figure had an antique, finely molded look. Tragedy had graved some faint, fine lines in her forehead. Her eyes were listless, her mouth clamped tight. It was plain that she had been tremendously affected by the tragedy without completely understanding its implications. Her expression was compounded of defiance and grief.

Lord Keith, who had known the Queen only in times of happiness, when she was bowing and smiling proudly at court functions, or gliding about the dance floor to pretty dance tunes, now scarcely recognized her. The change touched him. He was an old man with daughters and grand-daughters of his own. He thought of their carefree faces when he looked at Caroline Matilda.

"At last," was her greeting. "My good friend Keith!" In her emotion she put her arms around him and tears came to her eyes. The old diplomat, who was anything but accustomed to such demonstrations of affection, was thrown off his guard. He energetically rubbed the gold knob of his cane under his chin and swallowed rapidly.

"Well, I'm bringing Your Majesty some excellent news," he said at last.

"Is there any such thing as good news, Keith?" she asked.

"Yes, there is, Madame," he told her. "You are free to go."

"Free?" she said. "If I only really could be free!"

He explained to her how he had come to an agreement with Guldberg. Her lips worked as she listened closely to his story, but her eyes looked off into the distance over the parapet.

"It's going to be terribly hard to take up life again," she told him. "Everything's finished, quite finished. Everything that I ever had is lost. And by that I don't mean the throne, or any of the privileges of the throne. The old Caroline Matilda died right here in Kronborg. Now you want her to come to life again in Celle, a new Caroline, I mean. Why? It wouldn't be such a bad idea if they turned me over to the executioner."

"Madame is still young," Keith reminded her. "She may think that life is all over. But life goes on. In the end one always learns to live again."

"And what about my children?" the Queen asked suddenly.

"The Prince and Princess must stay behind in Denmark," Keith told her. "There is no way out of that."

The Queen put her hands up to her face and the ambassador did what he could to comfort her. "I realize how badly you feel about this, Madame," he said. "But the state will take good care of your children. And as often as I can, I will go and see that all is well with them, be assured of that."

"The state, the state!" she said tearfully. "Ever since I was a little girl I've had the state dinned at me. On account of the state I could never play like other children. I could never laugh as I wanted to, I could never dance. On account of the state I had to leave my home and family and get married to a cretin. The state brought me into this terrible situation. Now the state robs me of my children. Now I have to hand my children over to a woman who can't possibly give them as much love and care as I can. Is the state fitted to act as a father for my boy, too? Can it be a mother for my baby girl? Lord Keith! This monster is the ruination of everybody. And I am supposed to give over my children to such an evil thing."

"I've often shared your sentiments about the state, Madame," said Keith. "Believe me, I've often thought myself about the lies and brutalities that are perpetrated in the name of the state. I have often disliked myself intensely for being involved in such a dirty business. I've thought that surely I must be a cynical rascal to be so repulsively employed. But the fact remains, like it or not, that the state is a flourishing institution. The state must be dealt with as such. Someone must undertake to do this. There is no choice but try to bend the blind monster in the direction of civilized ends, Madame."

"You're right, of course, and there's nothing I can do," the Queen said, looking away again. "But during these past weeks I have often asked myself how it will be on judgment day when God, if there is a God, examines the resurrected. How will it be when he asks the soldiers and the judges and the king why they disobeyed his command not to kill. 'Oh, the state,' they will say, 'it wasn't really us, it was the state!' But God will say, I feel sure, that He never heard of such a thing. But if I know them, they will argue with Him. He will have to shut them up. 'You must have no other gods but me,' He will remind them. God will have the last word, or I'm very much mistaken." She stuttered to a stop, and blushed.

Lord Keith looked down at the floor of the parapet in acute discomfiture. He had great trouble trying to find any connection between God and politics. "I agree to everything," he heard the Queen say to him, and deferently looked up. "Thank you, thank you, Milord."

The next day the English ambassador presented himself at Christiansborg to have his promised audience with Christian. Guldberg led him to the King. "Lord Keith," he told Christian, "is here for his audience, Sire. I trust you are ready to talk with him."

"Lord Keith?" said Christian. "Oh, yes. My brother-in-law's man."

For several minutes Keith exchanged the usual polite compliments with the King, then suddenly introduced his point, which was a very sharp point, indeed. "I find it necessary to beg Your Majesty to show me the annulment of your marriage to the Queen," he said, "which I presume contains a paragraph to the effect that the Queen is free to leave Denmark without loss of her title."

Christian at once shied away from this frontal demand. "I love my wife," he whined. "Isn't it enough for me to agree to it verbally? Why do you people keep bothering me? It's downright cruel of you to expect me to sign a document giving away the woman I love."

Lord Keith raised his brows and looked over the King's shoulder at Guldberg, who at once made frantic signs for him to be patient.

"She's so blonde," mused Christian. He now took Keith by the lapel and drew him over to a window bay. "I want to see my wife," he whispered. "I want to see Struensee and Brandt, too. Why don't they come here any more? I want to see the fellows, you know, and talk to them the way I used to."

"They are dead, Sire," Keith told him mirthlessly.

"Dead! Really dead?"

"They are incontrovertibly dead," Keith assured him. "They have been executed in a most definitive fashion, Your Majesty. Your Majesty himself, if I may be so bold as to remind you, personally signed the order for their execution."

"That's right, I remember doing it," said Christian, still whispering. "I shouldn't have signed the paper, should I, Keith? They all fooled me. They told me I had to do it, when I hadn't. They said I had to have them executed to avoid trouble. But that trouble would never have come, would it?"

"The sentence has been carried out, Sire," said Keith wearily.

"Yes, yes, so it has," said the King stupidly.

"And considering the circumstances," said Keith, "Your Majesty will understand that the King of England has a certain intimate concern for the welfare of his sister, the Queen of Denmark. He thinks it best that she leave the country."

"My brother-in-law mistrusts me," said Christian slowly, muddled with sadness. "He thinks I am a murderer, doesn't he?"

"I have no idea what he thinks in that regard," said Keith, "but I feel obligated to tell you that he has certain suspicions in the instance of other circles. I refer to those people who have done so much to humiliate his sister, the Queen of Denmark. He is extremely annoyed with their behavior, if I may say so, Your Majesty."

"I see, I see," said Christian. "Nobody is looking out for me. Nobody gives a damn about my happiness. I might die for all anybody would care. Well, give my brother-in-law my regards and tell him how unwillingly I take this step. Tell him that I'll never marry again, though I'm still a young man. My life, tell him, is played out with a vengeance."

Lord Keith bowed. He could not keep a smile from puckering his lips.

"Bring the paper here, Guldberg," said Christian, suddenly raging. "There, put it down there on the table. I want to read it through. Do you think I cannot read? Or is everything in order, the way England wants it?"

"Everything is in order, Sire," said Guldberg unctuously and unfolded the paper that the King might read it. But he did not. Instead he scratched his name at the bottom.

"You're a filthy scoundrel, Guldberg," he said, looking up. "I dislike you, I dislike your impudent manner. I have seen other scoundrels. Rantzau and Eickstedt and Koeller, to name only a few. But you are the worst specimen of the lot. I should have the whole crew executed. Then at least my wife could remain in Denmark." Petulantly he swept the signed paper onto the floor. "There you are, you lackey," he said to Guldberg. "Pick it up. And when you've picked it up, get out of my sight and stay out." He stalked off to a door leading into another room of the apartment, tore it open, but remained uncertainly in the doorway. The white poodle, Bellerophon, pleaded to be picked up and when the King took the dog in his arms the little animal tried desperately to lick his face. This dissipated the King's anger like magic. "See, see how he loves me!" he said, laughing with pleasure. "Dear little beast, dear Bellerophon. Hope to see you again, Keith. Any time. Guldberg, do we have fireworks tonight?"

"We do, Sire," said Guldberg, not at all abashed. "They'll be given in the gardens of Rosenborg, Sire."

"That's fine, fine, my dear Guldberg," he said. "I'm going to take Bellerophon and Morari and hide behind the bushes. We'll frighten the girls to pieces. You'll see. Oh, you'll see!" Laughing to himself he gently closed the door and was gone.

Lord Keith bent down and picked up the document for Guldberg. "Allow me," he said very formally. His eyes looked right through Guldberg's broad face.

"Thank you, thank you," said Guldberg. He was frightfully ill at ease with Keith when he played milord. What went on behind those pale, expressionless eyes, he wondered, and why should a milord pick something up for me? Curious, curious fellow. "The King is odd today," he stammered apologetically. "Very odd."

"Yes," said Keith. "In fact . . ."

"What were you going to say?" said Guldberg.

"I was going to say that all the thrones of Europe are occupied either by idiots or whores," said Keith in his execrable Danish. "Do I make myself clear?"

"Yes, Milord," said Guldberg.

"In any event," Keith continued, "the Queen will leave Denmark tomorrow at noon sharp. Would it not be possible for her to see her little son before she goes? It is a parting for good, you realize."

"Impossible," said Guldberg, flushing darkly. "I can't do that for you."

"Have you ever noticed the existence of what is commonly called mother-love, Guldberg?" said Keith. "Or . . ."

"But it has nothing to do with me," said the first minister. "I'd take the children in my own arms to Kronborg, if it came to that. I'm no monster, after all."

"I see," said Keith.

"Would you risk more scenes?" asked Guldberg. "After all, I repeat, it has nothing to do with me."

"I believe you," said Keith. "I know who's pulling the strings. How peculiar that a mature woman, herself a mother, should deny another of her kind this favor. What harm could it do her?"

"Terrible, terrible," said Guldberg. "Since I became minister, I . . . well . . . I've often asked myself whether the game is worth the candle. All I do, it seems, is lend my name to cover up other people's dirty work."

"Well, all that glitters, you know," said Keith. "It's such an old story."

"Beatus ille, qui procul negotiis," said Guldberg. "When I was a family tutor in Fredensborg, sitting out in the garden with my books, I was a great deal better off."

"You paint a pretty picture," said Keith. "I suppose your predecessor was much better off, too, rolling his pills in Altona or wherever it was. Awfully hard to let go the bull's tail once you've grabbed it, isn't it, my dear Guldberg!"

Guldberg looked at the ambassador with suddenly widening eyes. What was he hinting at now! He smiled wryly as Keith rolled up the document, stuck it in his coat pocket and left. He was still smiling when Keith had left.

Captain McBride of the little English squadron lying in the sound off Kronborg was introduced to Caroline Matilda. Hastily she pressed the Captain's hand as he bowed to her, ill at ease and red of face, his nautical hat tucked under his arm. For the last time she then turned to Antje Maria and took her little daughter in her arms. Stormily she kissed the child and began to cry while doing it. The tears ran down the baby's cheeks and dampened its silky hairs. The tickling of the tears made the infant smile and reach with fat hands for its mother's face. Antje Maria began to sob in chorus. The Captain twiddled his hat and Keith looked away.

Suddenly making up her mind the Queen thrust the child back on Antje Maria. "Always stay with her now, Antje Maria," she said. "Now you're the baby's mother." She kissed Antje Maria and afterwards the child. Then she took Keith's arm. "Let's go away from here at once," she said. "There's nothing more here for me."

Quickly they walked across the courtyard and out the main gate of the fortress, the Captain following behind. Caroline did not look up at the big cannon, the mouths of which were pointing at the two English frigates and a cruiser dancing on a soft blue sea under the May sun. She saw nothing, so blinding was her grief. Blindly she stumbled along, supported by Lord Keith, down the stone steps of the quay, and let herself be helped over the gunwale of the longboat into the wide stern sheets, where she slouched with her head bowed. The seamen, twelve of them, bent to the oars.

She did not come to herself until she was standing on the quarter-deck of the Southampton. From the fortress tower the Dannebrog fluttered a brisk farewell to them. Presently came the deafening roar of a hundred-gun royal salute. The Southampton answered with a hundred and one, until the decks under her were quivering like jelly. She watched the seamen scramble up the rigging and out onto the spars, where they made sail. Overhead the union jack slatted and snapped in the breeze. The flag of Hanover, showing a rearing horse, flew underneath.

The ship heeled slightly and began to move with an irresistible, slow gliding, a fateful forward motion. The Queen was miserable beyond words. She thought how, at twenty-one, already she was banished from her children, forced to live in a small provincial city in Germany with nothing but her guilt to keep her company. Once again she looked at Kronborg, as she had so often done before while on sleighing parties out on the frozen sound. The many small panes of glass in the fortress windows were glittering like jewels. The steep tile roof of the main building shone like brass. She fancied that she saw someone, Antje Maria, of course, waving a white handkerchief to her from the battlements. Presently she sighed and turned away to look out forward over the bow of the vessel. The ship was headed due north.

EPILOGUE

From the Papers of
N. W. Wraxall, Esq.

AT LAST I am able to continue with my long interrupted tale. I am very much upset and tense. I have been wandering about the house like a caged tiger. My trunks are all packed. The day after tomorrow I am leaving and will see her again. To make the time pass quickly and profitably I have taken up my pen.

I returned to London in mid-November this year past, and the day after my arrival went directly to Downing Street, there to deliver the Queen's letter to Lord Suffolk and, if possible, to take advantage of the opportunity to speak personally with him. However he proved to be inaccessible on that day. Accordingly I kept my letter and went to Chidleigh Court in Pall Mall, the residence of Count Lichtenstein. The Count gave me a friendly reception. He was very much impressed when I handed him my letter. He read it through quickly and begged me to come back to talk with him in the evening.

The social set of Chidleigh Court consisted of people who spoke nothing but German among themselves and, so Count Lichtenstein assured me, understood hardly a word of English. Nevertheless I was reluctant to talk openly with him in their presence, since the lives of so many others depend on the absolute secrecy of the plan. The Count took me into the picture gallery and remarked humorously, as he pointed to the portraits on the wall, that he hoped I trusted their discretion.

The Count is a short, stocky man with heavy thighs and a broad, red face that betrays his Lucullan habits. He wears an old-fashioned periwig, a curly one, which tends to slip down crookedly over his forehead. He looks as if he might have stepped right out of a Rowland drawing. His sly, yet kind, eyes are all but hidden by rolls of fat, though they gleam with intelligence. This is the man of whom our George has such a high opinion, and correctly so, to my way of thinking. I, too, got the general impression that he would be a fine fellow to have around were the going rough.

He listened attentively to my story, sometimes shaking his head like a bull pestered by flies. Finally he said: "How is her health, my boy?"

"Quite good, I think," I told him.

"We have heard just the opposite," he said. "Quite."

"Her nerves are somewhat unstrung," I said. "But the prospect of seeing her children again has done a great deal to calm her."

"I'm very glad to hear that," he told me. "There would be no point in making long-range plans with an invalid for the principal. Don't you think that's true, my friend? For a venture of this sort you need endurance, strength and alertness. She would serve us all badly if she caved in the minute she landed back on the throne."

I was rather nettled to hear him talk so bluntly about so delicate a creature as the Queen, and did not hide my annoyance. However, this did not faze him. "I believe your assurances and will speak to the King," he said in a merry and positive voice. "At the same time you must be patient. You know, I suppose, about this awful business in the American colonies. It takes up practically all the King's time. His Majesty has scarcely a free moment for his family. I'll tell you something else, Mr. Wraxall. If I were the King, I'd go off to Hanover and leave these damned Englishmen to stew in their colonial troubles. As it is, the King's influence hardly amounts to a row of pins."

"If His Majesty is a family man," I said, refusing to be baited into hot rejoinder, "he should remember that his sister is badly in need of help. Surely she is a member of his family."

"He will, he undoubtedly will remember," said Lichtenstein. "But the whole Danish situation is rather hazy right now, you know. Many members of Parliament took Christian's side. By the way, I hear that he has completely collapsed into lunacy."

"He always was an idiot," I said angrily.

"More or less, more or less, I suppose," said Lichtenstein and laughed. "But he was also my King, young man."

"That is, more or less," I said, and we laughed together.

"One last thing," said the Count, quite seriously. "Don't try to see Lord Suffolk again."

"But I have this letter for him," I reminded the Count.

"Just keep your letter, Wraxall," he said. "It will be much better to handle the affair as a personal dealing between brother and sister. If the Cabinet and Parliament intervene, the delays and qualifications will be endless. Besides, if the King wishes, he can speak about the matter to Lord Suffolk himself."

I acceded to this advice. Several weeks passed. About Christmas I received the following letter from Count Lichtenstein.

"My dear young Friend:

"On your behalf I have spoken with His Majesty about the Celle matter. The King commands you, as I anticipated he would, under no circumstances to communicate with Lord Suffolk. He, the King, is very favorably inclined towards the plan and thanks you for your efforts in furthering it. However, it is very questionable as to just how far the King will be able to support your project, since it is unlikely that England can be officially involved at this point. Apparently Lord Suffolk will have to be sounded out. As soon as this conversation has taken place, you will hear from me, regardless of what the results may be. This will very like be towards the end of January.

"In the meantime, I remain, sir, your most humble and obedient servant, etc., etc."

At the end of January Lichtenstein sent for me. To my great joy the King had agreed to back up his sister's cause. He imposed certain conditions, however, to the effect that the Queen-Dowager, Juliana, the Queen-Dowager's son, Guldberg and all the others who had acted with hostility towards the Queen should notwithstanding be allowed to return unmolested to their estates and possessions. Moreover, the King would not recognize his sister's government until the coup had actually been accomplished and the new régime stabilized. He refused to assume any financial responsibilities.

A letter in the King's handwriting to the same effect had already left by courier for Celle. My duty was to follow the courier, and discuss the matter with the Queen, later inform Baron Buelow and his friends of the King's decision.

I left London at the beginning of February and arrived three days later at Helvutsluys. As far as the Westphalian border the journey was without incident. But at this point heavy rainstorms set in and flooded the Dinckel River separating Holland from Westphalia. The little Dinckel had become a lake. Here I caught up with the courier, who was much disinclined to risk his neck crossing the flood, and took over the Queen's letter from him. I made the crossing safely, losing nothing but a few expendable pieces of baggage enroute.

The roads were in a frightful condition. In every village I engaged peasants to help my coach along over the worst spots, having them work in relays from village to village. In spite of the fact that four horses were pulling the vehicle, it began to look as though eventually I would be stuck. Time after time my coach was mired up to the axles. Crossing the Weser in the vicinity of Osnabrueck the ferry came within an ace of capsizing with my coach aboard. The oarsmen, losing heart, fell down to pray, as did my asinine coachman, but I whipped them back to their posts and we managed to land on the other side a good mile downstream.

I was possessed by a veritable demon of impatience and spared neither horses nor men in my rush to get back to the Queen. I freely squandered money, flattery, curses and blows, as the situation required. In this fashion I succeeded in reaching Hanover in ten days. I arrived covered with mud, my hair matted to my head. I was half dead from hunger. The next day I got to Celle. Count Seckendorff advised me to continue immediately to Hamburg.

There I saw Baron Buelow, who was not expecting me. I ran into him by pure luck on the Jungfernstieg, the main promenade of the city, at that forenoon hour when a great many pedestrians were abroad. He was startled and gave me a sign to follow him. He led me behind the buttress of a high wall along the way. It was a lovely day in early spring. The many-towered city lay at our feet, and we had a fine view of the sunny basin of the Binnenalster and rows of tall houses crowding its rim. I felt extraordinarily well and alive, better than I had ever felt in my life. It seemed to me that I was surely within fair sight of my goal. The beautiful view of the big city, the crisp, sunny air heightened this mood of well-being.

Baron Buelow, however, was rather skeptical. "The English embassy in Copenhagen must recognize the Queen's government the moment the Queen-Dowager and her clique are taken into custody," he said. "We cannot wait until the new government has established its authority throughout all the provinces. Personally, I would risk a *coup d'état* without English support. But I doubt that my friends ever would. They have far, far too much to lose if the game fails, my dear boy."

I offered to go to Copenhagen and there try to induce his friends to fall in line with the current plan. He pressed my hand and said: "I thank you, my friend, for your willingness to give all you have for our cause. But I can take no responsibility for the others. Believe me, I know the personalities and the situation better than you do. If you go to Copenhagen, you'll only expose yourself to needless danger. Should you be arrested, there is always the chance that our plan will be exposed, which would cost many lives. What we need is the unequivocal backing of England, and England's positive help in bringing about the *coup*."

I saw there was no use trying to convince him otherwise. My face fell. "Then there's nothing I can do but travel back to England," I said dolefully, "and try my hand again."

"I see no other way out," he said.

It took me some time to make up my mind to this unpalatable decision, but finally I swallowed the pill. "I'll do it," I told him. "I've set my heart on seeing this thing through."

Accordingly I now returned to Celle and again talked with Seckendorff. He merely smiled at my disappointment and assured me that undertakings such as ours inevitably necessitated laborious preparation. He told me that I should come that evening to the castle drawbridge, from which point Mantel would conduct me to the Queen.

It was a rainy evening, I remember. At the agreed hour I was standing, heavily cloaked, at the drawbridge. It rained without a break. The water ran in rivers down my face and found its way inside my collar. Water poured from my hat brim as if it were a gutter. Mantel apparently had forgotten me. It was pitch dark. Inside the castle courtyard I could hear the watch changing, but could make nothing out.

Mantel finally did come, however, and told me in whispers that the Princess of Braunschweig had been visiting and the Queen could not have got rid of her any earlier without arousing suspicion. He led me through the cellar by a cobwebby staircase to the library. We made our way into this room by way of a book shelf that swung back as a door. Two candles were burning on a table where an open book lay. The lonely room—caryatids, I remember, were carved into the gleaming mahogany of the shelves—looked almost like a chapel. The table might have been an altar. I bent down over the book and saw that it was Rousseau's *Nouvelle Héloïse*.

The clock in the castle tower struck the hour with nine rattling strokes just as the Queen came in. She was wearing her carmine-red dress again, I distinctly remember. In the semi-darkness of the library the hollows under her eyes were dark with shadow. She looked more queenly than I had ever seen her. Her silvery light hair, brushed up high on her head, gleamed like a helmet. I dropped down on one knee before her and kissed her hand. I was so overpowered by her appearance and the surge of love within my breast that I could not speak. I had a mad impulse to cry out my passion. I felt that I should like to crumple my whole life together into a ball, my adventures, all the dangers I had lived through, the lonely travels and the lonely vigils and lay them all at the Queen's feet. What did I care just then for Denmark! What difference did it really make to me who ruled in Christiansborg! It was only on her account that my thoughts had been concentrated on Copenhagen for the past six months. And I did not revere the Queen nearly so much as I revered the woman. Not the Crown, but the Queen's smooth temples, her long hands, her lovely eyes, her gentle smile were my lodestone.

She did not sit down, though a chair had been made ready for her. She seemed to be pretty well acquainted with the situation and did not linger over my political advices. She thanked me warmly for all I had done. Then, as that other time in the park, she began to discuss people.

But now she had a different outlook on her life and the history of her man whose presence, so she said, she could still feel all about her. Not long ago she told how she had read a book by a certain Pastor Muenter describing Count Struensee's prison conversion. Now she, too, felt a desire to reconcile herself to the hereafter, both as a debt owed to her former lover and also to have a last slender, and yet unbreakable tie, so she said, binding her to him even in death.

I, however, found it quite impossible to feel my way into her religious mood. I had always considered myself to be a world-bound temperament, and although I have never denied the existence of a dark side of being, my mind has always been directed towards producing benefactions here and now on earth. Everything the Queen said now seemed to be affected by her current doubt of life. Her spirit was sadly changed, for the worse, in my opinion. She was like a bright bolt of cloth, one might say, after it has been soaked too long in a bath of black alkali. Listening to her one might think that life was a sickness, a distortion of an earlier and more desirable mode of existence.

Against my will, as I listened to her, I was reminded of Count Lichtenstein's warning words. Was the Queen in good health? Had she sufficient endurance and resilience to rule? Or could it be, as her manner certainly suggested, that she was much too other-worldly to perform her queenly duties properly. She would have me believe that only true Christians can be immune to the perversions of power, as the Greeks of old maintained similarly of philosophers.

I tried to turn the subject, and to this end recounted my little adventures in the flooded countryside of Westphalia. I had the satisfaction of seeing a gleam of interest come into the Queen's sad eyes. She laughed with me, hesitantly at first, then freely, and asked for more and more details. Again I saw the young girl come forth from behind the mask. At last we began to talk about childhood happenings and presently, on her request, I was telling her about my life at Oxford. She also wanted to know how London looked these days. She reminded me that she had not seen the city for seven years. We were both startled when the castle clock struck midnight. She took leave of me like an old friend, repeatedly expressing her regret that I had to endure the many discomforts and dangers of a long journey on her account.

She stopped for a last time at the half-opened door, the knob in her hand, and turned to face me. She smiled at me, I remember, and I thought she was going to say something. A sweet shower of expectation ran over me and I had to summon every bit of self-command to keep from crying out that I loved her. With her lovely head slightly bowed she was charming and desirable beyond compare. She nodded at me most intimately and closed the door behind her. What must she have been in other days!

I can never record all the difficulties that I encountered later in London while trying to carry out my mission. Such hours and days I spent cooling my heels in ante-chambers, such useless trips, such boresome, inconclusive discussions! I was burning with impatience and time was running out. Finally I had the satisfaction of receiving a letter sealed with the King's red seal by way of Count Lichtenstein. He told me that this time he had no idea as to the exact contents, but his kindly smile and the twinkle in his eye encouraged me to believe that all was well. With my own hands I have sewn the letter into the lining of my coat. Today is a lovely warm day. Happy children's voices are pealing up to me from the street. This time there will be no floods to reckon with. My God! How wonderful it is to be young, to have a charge to fill which will take me to a lovely woman whom I love.

May, 1775
Sandkrug, near Celle

I still cannot understand. A bird must feel as I do when, having a moment before been winging his way through the air, he suddenly finds himself lying helpless on the hard ground with a broken wing.

In Count Seckendorff's presence I have just burned the King of England's letter to his sister. I showed him the unbroken seal, then held a taper to the document at one corner. I threw it into the fireplace, where it slowly turned to black flakes of char. Nobody but the writer himself will ever know what the letter said. One more mystery to add to the world's great store. I took the precaution of scattering the ashes with the poker. Dust and ashes!

Yes, everything has crumbled into dust and ashes. The great enterprise, so sure to succeed according to all human reckoning, has come to naught. And come to naught, as well, is my love, a love so pure that I would have died for it.

At first I would not believe what they told me. I suspected betrayal. Then I saw the Queen myself, very quiet now, in the same library where I had conversed with her so long and intimately some two months before. Was this the mystery that I was sure she had wanted to reveal to me that time when she paused in the door, but did not speak?

There is no point in wallowing about in lost hopes. It will be a long time, however, before my thoughts cease to be focussed on my love. The image of her at the theater, in the blue room, in the French garden will always remain with me and guide my sensibilities for the rest of my days.

I will explain briefly. Her little blond page contracted scarlet fever and died. He was carried down to a coffin in the basement of the castle and there kept because of the contagious nature of the disease. They did not want the Queen to see him, or to say a prayer, as she urgently desired, at his bier. But eluding the watch she found her way to him, according to her heart's need.

The very next morning she showed signs of fever, though it is possible that the disease had lurked within her right along. Quickly she became delirious. The dead boy came to her all night in her dreams, beckoning to her. The doctor—he was called in from Hanover

—shook his head after completing his examination. During the night the Queen awoke and said to her old servant: "Mantel, I'm terribly sick. And I hope I die." To the pastor who remained at her bedside, she said: "Although I'm sick of body, actually I am well within. I don't feel any more sorrow. I forgive everybody and I hope that they will forgive me."

She died on the seventh day of her sickness, very easily, without any struggle at all, as if she were merely stepping out of a room, in her graceful way, to enter another.

She was laid out in the little library and there it was that I was permitted to see her. They had dressed her in her carmine dress and folded her waxily perfect hands over her breast. She looked younger than in life, I thought, perhaps because of the way they had fixed her hair. It was parted simply in the middle and combed down loosely on either side, so that her face was embedded in its silvery blondeness. Her cheeks, I noticed, had scarcely sunk in against the gums at all. Her lips were as full and bright, it seemed to me, as if she were still alive, and about them seemed to hover a faint smile.

About her throat they had left the garnet cross that once had been entrusted to me as a token of my allegiance. The garnets, glittering dimly, were like tiny newly opened flowers, as if the life that had once been in her somehow had become transmuted to the stones and now clung about the cross.

She was buried in the City Church of Celle, in the tomb of the dukes of Celle, a family long since extinct. A boy choir, as the coffin was being lowered into the hole, sang in German:

"Death is our father, and from him we go
To the grave, our cool mother, with her mingle below.
But when the Day cometh, come so sure as we die,
Our mother shall bear us into eternity."

September 1784
Trumps Street, London

I have just been collecting these old papers again. They are dreadfully yellowed and stained with age. My wife and my children have just come into the room as I write. My little daughter, whom I named Caroline, has just been bending, all eyes, over them, sniffing their moldy odor. "What are they, father?" she has just inquired. But my six-year-old boy, in his serious fashion, has just cautioned her not to bother me while I am in my study. "He's doing something important," he told his young sister.

Important, then! If we could only hold onto the promise of our youth! But man is a fickle beast. How strange my youthful effusions strike me now.

I have married and am happy enough, though my happiness is not the ecstatic sort I chased after as a young blood. It is a perfectly ordinary condition, rooted in a solid establishment, I am glad to say. There are cares that go with it, for instance, when the children fall sick with the croup, when bills arrive as bills will. But so it goes. When I asked my wife to marry me I did not wear the costume of the sorrowing young Werther. As a matter of fact I was dressed like any other conventional young Englishman, in a sturdy brown coat. My feelings, I should imagine, were adequately tender, but by no means of supernal delicacy.

Have I become a Philistine? Perhaps. I am much thicker around the middle, at any rate, and a member of Parliament to boot, an expert, so they say, in questions of foreign policy. And today, I might add, right out of a blue sky Lord North gave me a check drawn on the Bank of England to the tune of a thousand pounds. It is because of that that I am looking up my old papers. What a cloud of memories surrounds me!

There has been a revolution in Denmark and I fancy it is the same revolution, somewhat delayed, that I endeavored to bring about in my excursions across the little Dinckel and the Weser. Queen Caroline Matilda's son has been made regent. Towards the end of this change of régime a wild scene reportedly took place. Unhappy Christian, mouthing senseless, fearful nothings, was pulled this way and that, with his son on one side and his stepbrother on the other, each gripping an arm. Finally the son, who at sixteen is reputedly very muscular, struck a well-aimed blow on his uncle's chest, and knocked him off his feet. This made Christian, I am told, laugh like a hyena. He threw his arms about his son and without delay approved his regency over Denmark and Norway.

This palace revolution has been approved by England. The young man, of course, is our own King's nephew. Only a few Tories doubt our policy *vis-à-vis* Denmark. The Prince is a little too popular for their taste, and too plebeian. It is well known that he prefers to dance with peasant girls and has even been known to help them at haying time. In my considered opinion, these levities might be well excused in consideration of his youth. However, beyond this he often presents himself unannounced at holiday gatherings and proclaims himself the servant of his people. Admittedly I find this sort of thing rather over-done. I am reminded of the republican views of Messrs. Franklin, Jefferson and Washington, who so shamelessly detached our American colonies from us, at great cost to us in blood and money, and out of them constructed an independent federation of states. Still, it may be, so far as the Prince Regent is concerned, that his exaggerated friend-liness towards the people derives, like his other eccentricities, largely from his youth.

Somewhat later the same year Christiansborg burned to the ground. The burning tower of the Palace, from which height the Queen-Dowager once watched the execution of Struensee in the Osterfeld through a spy-glass, flamed like a great torch and lit up the whole city. With a strong west wind blowing the firemen were powerless to save the splendid structure. For a time it was feared that the flying embers would ignite all Copenhagen.

The next morning the ruins were a terrible sight. All manner of expensive furniture had been carelessly hurled out through the windows into the square before the Palace. The rooms were roofless, the immense crystal chandeliers had been smashed to smithereens. The marble palace chapel, where the fire allegedly started, was utterly destroyed. Only the cellars, with the big ovens, kitchen utensils and food stores, were saved. It looked, I was told, as if some sooty giant hand had reached down over the Palace, crushed it and swept it aside, so annihilating the gradually acquired splendors of centuries in a matter of hours. The London newspapers vied in describing the conflagration, and some of them had the temerity to announce that the fire was the symbol of an era's end.

About a month ago, to return closer to my thousand pounds, I was seated in Parliament behind Lord North. Only a few members were present that particular day. Someone was reading a very dry official report. Lord North turned to me and whispered behind his hand: "Mr. Wraxall, yesterday I was talking to the King. He told me that you once performed important services for his sister, the former Queen of Denmark. Is that correct? Or is it just another of the King's fantasies? I trust you know what I mean, sir."

I bent forward and in whispers told him how I had been implicated in the Danish plan to restore the Queen to the throne.

"I never heard of you in that connection," he said. "Why don't you come dine with me tomorrow in Bushy Park, Mr. Wraxall. We can discuss the matter at our leisure."

And so the following day I did dine with him. After the meal, over a glass of sherry I told him about the part I had played in the plot. He was very much interested and said: "Why didn't you mention this affair to me before, Mr. Wraxall?"

"I considered it a closed issue," I explained. "Moreover, it was not my secret to reveal. I could hardly reveal what the King himself kept secret up to the recent present."

"Didn't it ever occur to you, Mr. Wraxall," said North, "that a service of that sort deserves some sort of reward?"

"Well, Milord, I enlisted in the campaign of my own free will," I told him. "I had no political ambitions whatsoever. As a matter of fact, I did it . . . well . . . for purely personal reasons, you might say."

He raised his brows at this. "Yes," he said, "I understand that Caroline Matilda was a very attractive woman."

"And then," I continued hurriedly, blushing to the roots of my hair, for which I could have kicked myself heartily, "the plan came to nothing, you see. The Queen's death put a quietus on it."

He thought for some time, sipping at his glass, and finally said: "Would you be prepared, Mr. Wraxall, to accept a thousand pounds to compensate you for your very considerable expenditures of time and energy?"

I considered Lord North's proposal. On the face of it, it was a profanation of the Queen's dear memory. And yet a thousand pounds was a thousand pounds, seen upside down or sideways. I remembered vividly that the stables on my country place were badly in need of repairs and that the installation of a fountain on the front lawn would immeasurably improve the general prospect from the main windows of the living room. A hundred other things came to mind, really urgent needs, which a thousand pounds would enable me to fulfill. Then, my wife—I could imagine how her face would look should I refuse the offer of a thousand pounds on sentimental grounds. As a matter of fact the offer in no way affected my honor, rather put it, one might say, on a sound fiscal basis. "I should feel extremely grateful, Milord," I told the prime minister, "were you to compensate me so generously for my forgotten services."

And so here I am, a thousand pounds richer. I cannot, however, honestly share my wife's unconfined joy. A trace of chagrin spoils my mood. Even as I write these words, my doubts grow stronger. I almost envy the straightforward young man I was in those days, with all his ridiculous adventures, his lofty feelings, his precious mysteries. But enough. How seldom, indeed, does maturity realize youth's feverish hopes!

September, 1792
On board H.M.S. Seaford.

The sea is calm today although we are sailing through the treacherous Skagerak. I have moved the cabin lantern closer to my table and am trying to write in the wavering light.

I am returning from Copenhagen, which city I left the day before yesterday. About my political mission I am not permitted to write. I can only hint that to our ever increasing dissatisfaction Denmark is steadily moving closer to France, at a time when all the conservative, Christian governments of Europe look with horror and alarm on the revolutionary events that have shaken Paris, and by coalition are even now preparing to bring mob rule to a deservedly bloody end.

What a tempestuous world is ours, if I may say so. Scarcely had we recovered from the distressing events in our American colonies—

and I may say that I still doubt the viability of these so-called United States—when a similar storm broke out in France. It is still blowing at gale strength. All decent people are deeply concerned. They frequently ask themselves whether we may be at the end of civilized times.

I do not care to go into detail about this horror. I will not dwell on the National Convention in Paris, that assembly of murderers and thieves and tub-thumpers, or on the bloody guillotine in the Place de Louis Quinze, the armed mobs in the streets, the death of the Princess Lamballe and of so many other excellent people. The whole world already knows only too much about these hideous events.

Instead I wish to record something about Copenhagen. It is very curious, but everything that has come about in such a sanguinary fashion in Paris, in Copenhagen has been achieved without violence. I remember only too well that I, in retrospect, have had a hand in these profound changes, and am hard put to it to say whether I should regret it, or make up my mind to accept what apparently must be. I remember once assuring Count Seckendorff that I believed in freedom, and that I concurred in Baron Buelow's opinion that Denmark, like any other civilized country, should have a representative form of government. In truth, I was very young at the time and totally ignorant of political affairs. Yet even today, though I dislike admitting it, there is a certain dichotomy in my beliefs. Sometimes I am drawn this way, sometimes that. A most disgraceful confession, really, for one recently created a baronet by command of His Majesty.

I had only been in Copenhagen a few days when a monument to freedom was dedicated. The people called it the "Fridhedstötten." The monument is a plain, short obelisk, almost a gravestone, one might think. At the foot of the obelisk, on the four corner-pillars of the base, are female antique figures wreathed round with roses and myrtle. The inscription announces that the serfs are free and can henceforth move about as they will, no longer being bound to home and master.

Christian's son, Prince Frederik, attended the dedication of this obelisk to freedom, accompanied by his sister Luisa Augusta, the young Duchess of Augustenburg. When I looked at these two young people hemmed round by a shouting, happy throng I suddenly remembered that they were the children of the woman whom I had loved in my youth. I examined their features closely and saw that the future King looked like his mother. His hair was light, his lips full like hers and every now and then he stuck out the tip of his tongue, nipping it between his teeth, just as his beloved mother used to do. The small gesture almost brought the tears to my eyes. The Prince's sister is tall and rather darkly blond, with a round, candid forehead. She struck me as altogether an open-spirited sort, and I liked her modest costume. To me she looked like many another well-to-do burgher's daughter.

I heard later that the crazed King is especialy fond of her. When he suffers from his attacks and is overcome by insane rages, so threatening courtiers and servants with dire bodily harm, she is called in, for she knows at once how to calm him. He lives through her. She is a friend of the Danish poets and writers, and like her husband carries on a lively correspondence with European men of learning, many of whom she supports with gifts, not to mention with valuable criticisms and speculations of her own. All in all she is a most extraordinary, amiable and thoroughly delightful woman, distinguished by her modesty more than by any other attribute. Both she and her brother, and her husband as well, have labored steadily to free the serfs.

While I was watching the dedication ceremony, I heard someone mention the name Struensee. I turned around cautiously and saw that two sober Copenhagen burghers were discussing the man. "This is what he would have liked to see," one of them said to the other. "One could almost say that the monument is his."

"Right, right enough," the other agreed. "I remember him, only vaguely, of course. I was only a boy when I saw him. My mother often used to tell how he wanted to have me inoculated for smallpox."

After finishing my business in Copenhagen I tarried some few days to look at the palaces and gardens of the city. I went on this sentimental excursion in a bitter-sweet mood. I felt as if I were trespassing, if the truth be known, in the land of my youth. Every minute I expected to hear the stir of her silks on the parquet floor, to smell the perfume of her light hair, to hear the spinet she once played. How well I remember the songs of Gellert that she used to sing to her own accompaniment. Odd feelings, I grant, for a man getting on towards fifty.

At the beginning of September I was in Frederiksborg. How beautiful it is in Frederiksborg when the roses are in bloom even though the asters are already massed white and blue on the terraces. The enormous beech trees are held up by props and the entrance through the centuries-old drive is completely arched by their boughs. The castle itself, magnificently broad, dignified and quiet, is mirrored in the lake.

Walking up the ornamental staircase I arrived in a room where the walls were covered with pale yellow silk set off with a lilac flower design and framed in gold at baseboard and molding. The ceiling was shaped like a mussel shell and outfitted with a huge candelabrum. The thousand cunningly wrought glass crystals shook and tinkled softly when I entered. There were many chairs waiting to accommodate visitors, built with very delicate curved legs. Mirrors in gold frames hung on three of the walls and multiplied the room's space to infinity.

On the fourth wall, also framed heavily in gilt, was the portrait of a Danish king, Christian the Seventh. He had a retreating forehead, above which was perched a little white wig. His nose was long, his mouth small and red, his chin practically non-existent. The face reminded me of a bird, of a parrot, to be exact, or perhaps a puffin. This faintly comic and yet repellent countenance was emphasized by the tropic colors of the costume, the too splendid coat of scarlet with golden trim, the vest of rose silk and the broad light-blue silk ribbon slashing diagonally across the narrow breast.

The queerest thing about the picture was the eyes. They were large and watery blue and might even have been rather beautiful but for their vacuity. They looked neither out at the world, nor interiorly into the man himself. A look of faintly horrified surprise, of injured failure to understand was expressed by these curious eyes, and brought out even more by the set of the mean, red little mouth.

At this moment, as I was contemplating the portrait on the wall, a lady entered and interrupted my musings. It was the Duchess of Augustenburg. She carried a large bunch of dark-red roses. She was rather taken aback to find me in the room, for without special permission strangers were not allowed to inspect the castle whenever the royal family was in residence.

"My name is Wraxall," I said and bowed. "Sir Nathaniel Wraxall."

"Old Baron Buelow has spoken to me about you," she said graciously. "You were a friend of my mother's, were you not?"

"I have had the honor of knowing the Queen, Madame," I said.

"I know," she said, in the Queen's own husky voice. "Here they never talk about my mother, you know. But my brother remembers her a little, though he was very young when she went away. Was she as beautiful, really, as they say?"

"She was very beautiful and very good," I said, emotion taking hold of me.

She looked at me thoughtfully, then smiled, shrugged her shoulders and said, ironic and candid at the same time: "What a dreadful pity that beauty cannot be inherited, Sir Nathaniel!"

"But Madame!" I objected.

She looked now up at the portrait. "That's my father," she said, "though he no longer looks like that. He has aged prematurely. I'm going to see him this very moment. He's so very fond of roses." She looked down at the roses in the crook of her arm, carefully drew one out and gave it to me. "Not every lady finds a champion when things go badly with her, Sir Nathaniel," she said to me. "Please accept this in memory of my mother."

I thought, irrelevantly enough, of the thousand pounds and was so confused that I all but forgot to thank her.

Now the rose is nodding in a glass on my cabin table, gradually losing its petals. I feel that my old love at last is dying. Of course I shall collect the petals and preserve them in a paper. Perhaps, when I am a very old man, I shall show them to my grandchildren, God grant, and by that time they will be dried and rusty brown, quite unrecognizable, I suppose.

Indeed, all things pass. The present interlude, this night in the ship's cabin, in due course will be lost in memory. How pleasant it is to dream as the ship rolls and dips. My whole life and all my prospects, the young Duchess, my growing children, even the horrors of the Convention, all the events of the day, large and small, will become memories, little splinters of history, forever breeding new events forever the same.

But what is that? Why is the table reeling under my pen gently? Why do the ship's strakes groan? I hear sails gracking like musketfire. I can hear them through the deck over my head. Why is the lamp flickering so?

Of course I know. I felt it coming. The storm has arrived. We dream and are so sad about our past, but this only with a small part of our being. Mostly we struggle against fate and try to hold fast, as we have always done.

Yes, the storm is on us. I can feel it trying to swallow up my vessel. The waves are licking about us with a thousand tongues. Annihilation is roaring down on us across the North Sea, and would claim us but for the stout timbers of this ship and the stout hearts of the men who sail her. The sea will be a waste of combers. The wind seems to be blowing from the southwest, building up great walls of water.

A stormy night. And today I have been up on deck. The hull of our vessel is shuddering under the high seas. But at any rate it is morning and England is not too far away. It is morning everywhere, morning even in myself. Even in the mighty flow of history, roiled though it may be just now by catastrophes. A storm is buffeting the whole world, but still it is morning.

For this reason I welcome it. My ship is good. My heart is firm.